The Avatar…

God, Man, or the Antichrist?

a novel

by

TERRY RAY

THE RENEGADO PRESS

MYSTIC, CONNECTICUT

This is a work of fiction. Names, characters, places, and incidents are used fictitiously. Any resemblance to persons living or dead, or actual events, is coincidental. Certain extant places, organizations, and institutions are mentioned in this novel, but all the characters involved in them are wholly fictional.

Copyright © 2004 by Terry Ray
All rights reserved.

The Renegado Press
44 Whittle Street
Mystic, Connecticut 06355
Web site: theavatarthenovel.com

Printed in the United States of America
First Printing. June 2004

ISBN: 0-9754616-0-5

IN GRATITUDE

How does one begin to name – in order to express the necessary gratitude – all of the forces and persons that lead to a final result? As Leo Tolstoy observed in *War and Peace*, while one believes he is exercising free will in a given act, he is in reality, but a pawn for all that has come before him, that has made his act inevitable. Thus, bearing in mind the sagacity of Tolstoy's observation, I extend my general gratitude to all of the persons in my life – including Kismet, for her oft puzzling and more oft unappreciated gifts – that have made this novel inevitable. Unfortunately, your numbers are legion and defy human capacity to fully enumerate. I offer my specific gratitude to the following persons who have played a primary, contemporary role in the conception and birth of this novel:

Pam Fetterman, Deb McLaren, Mackelly Ray, Chris Miller, my wife – Cathleen Ray, Julie Dobish, Bill Trimarchi, Abby Morris, Fran Stineman, and Dee Klein. I must also express my great debt to Marty Chapman, whose frequent visits to my dreams, and daydreams, allowed me, through his eyes, ears, and heart, to write the story of *The Avatar*.

TTR

BOOK ONE

PAPA

CHAPTER ONE

May 15, 1993

Marty Chapman's hands began to slide down the steering wheel, lubricated by the nervous sweat beginning to seep from his palms. He hadn't seen a car in three hours and the road had narrowed from two lanes to one, from asphalt to gravel, from gravel to dirt. His fuel gauge had reached empty and had dipped so low the needle didn't move when he went over a bump. Marty anticipated, at any moment, his engine would choke and sputter on the final remaining drops of gas. When it did, his situation was hopeless.

Marty pounded his fists on the steering wheel.

"I can't believe this!!"

The trip had turned into a fiasco. He had been so convincing with his editor. It had all the promise of a block-buster piece. Their circulation demographics were perfect for it. Almost seventy percent of their readers were baby-boomers, for Christ's sake, he had exclaimed to his editor – and the sixties were their decade. They were the "turn-on and drop-out" generation. Those thousands of young anti-establishment rebels who went into the hills to get back to nature in their counter-culture communes were the folk icons of that tumultuous decade. What could have been a more natural piece for their readership than something on those commune hippies who didn't cop out – who stayed true – who didn't give up the faith? There had to be some of them who didn't sell out and trade in their love beads for a three-piece suit. Marty was sure of it. There just had to be.

That's how Marty sold it to Marla, anyway. And she bought it. She gave him two months' time… and a surprisingly comfortable expense budget. If it was really good, he might get the cover, she told him. It was his first big break. She wouldn't spring for a photographer – but Marty knew his way around a camera. Leaving L.A., it had all seemed so promising. For nearly six weeks he had hit nothing but deadends. He began to suspect that all those hippie sons of bitches really did cop out. Not a fucking true blue among them. He had found only one guy with promise... in Idaho – steered to his commune by a chance encounter at a 7-Eleven. He looked the part... long, but receded and substantially thinned, stringy gray hair – about the right age. He still had the beads, bell bottoms, and sandals. He said he had lived in Haight-Ashbury in the late sixties... had hung out with Timothy Leary for a time... was one of the original San Francisco love children. He described their cross-country trips in their psychedelic bus and their acid head-trips in compelling detail.

Marty wasted a whole roll of film and two audio cassettes on this mangy-looking middle-ager before some of the locals finally clued him in that this self-proclaimed hippie – who identified himself to Marty as "Zappo" – was, in fact, the son of a wealthy local banker in town and who had lived there – in Clanton, Idaho – all of his life and was a respectable lawyer, husband and father of three until about four years prior, when his drinking and drug use got the best of him, and he started doing this hippie thing. He apparently didn't do that full time either... a couple of weekends a month, he'd come back to town from his "commune" – several shacks out in the hills of which he was the sole occupant – get cleaned up and go out to dinner with his family. He'd stock up on food, booze, and drugs then go back out to the woods to resume his life as a neo-hippie. Apparently, the closest he had actually gotten to dropping out in his life – before he began this attempted replication of a life he had only read about – was his subscription to *Rolling Stone Magazine*.

Marty was on a last desperate attempt to salvage something from this journalistic disaster when he found himself on this dirt road in northwest Montana... at least seventy-five miles from nowhere... running out of gas. He had gotten a solid lead in Colorado Springs that near Bear Stump – a small town a couple hundred miles to the northwest of Great Falls – was a commune, still in existence. An anthropologist from the University of Colorado that Marty stumbled across in Colorado Springs told him that a few of his colleagues had come upon it about five years' back... said they'd talked to the people there... had even taken some pictures. The anthropologist phoned his friend, who had the pictures, while Marty was in his office. The friend said that he did have some pictures of the commune but wasn't sure where he'd put them. The anthropologist put Marty on the phone with Dr. Heindenthal. The good doctor assured Marty that this was an authentic hippie commune. They had old newspapers and photos of their community through the years. There was even a second and third generation living there. Dr. Heindenthal said, however – to correct the record – it was more like ten years – not five – since he had been there. He gave Marty directions.

Leaving the Springs, Marty had regained much of his initial enthusiasm for the story. He was sure there were communes still around, and at last he had a solid lead to find one. The description of this one was even better than he'd hoped. What a story it would be to interview three generations from a hippie commune! His mind raced at the possibilities. What, he thought, would someone be like who had been born and raised in such an environment! Wow! What would someone be like who had been exposed, exclusively, to the hippie culture and life philosophy? What a test of the sixties credo! And then a third generation! This could be prize-winning stuff... a significant work on cultural evolution in action. He got himself so worked up that he had to stop, more often than usual, to pee.

Following Dr. Heindenthal's directions, precisely, Marty had made every turn as directed... every goddamn turn. According to the professor's directions, he should have come across a big rock with "Freaksville" painted on it... said he couldn't miss it – the letters had to have been five feet tall, he said. After he got to Bear Stump, Marty did exactly as the good doctor directed... went north on Route 441 for about ten miles... then turned right onto a paved road – the only one Heindenthal said he'd come across. He said the road didn't have a sign... and it didn't. He was supposed to watch his odometer and, about forty or fifty miles back the road, he'd see the rock. Marty had already gone sixty miles and still hadn't seen any rock with "Freaksville" on it. Marty kept rereading the directions he'd written on the back of an envelope Dr. Strock – the anthropologist – had given him. He had done everything he was supposed to have done... Route 441... the right turn... forty miles. He had even seen some of the landmarks Dr. Heindenthal told him to look for... a small wooden bridge... a lake with a huge jagged rock jutting up from the middle of it. At forty miles he had seen some rocks... but there had been rocks everywhere along the road from the time he had started on it. There had been no rock with "Freaksville" painted on it... of that he was absolutely certain.

Marty began to second-guess himself. Maybe he had turned off on the wrong road... no... it was the only road he had seen coming out of Bear Stump – besides he had seen the little fucking wooden bridge and the lake with the rock. Maybe there were wooden bridges all over the place in this area... and maybe lots of lakes with sharp rocks, too. Who the hell knows? All Marty knew was that it was getting dark... the terrain was getting worse by the minute... he had no idea where he was... his car phone was showing he was out of calling range and, momentarily, he was destined to be out of gas.

Much of Marty's anger over his predicament was directed toward himself. He had always been the kind of person who jumped into things without paying enough attention to details. As for his present trip, he knew he should have done more desk research before he got into his car and headed east... but he didn't. As always, he was just too anxious to get on the road. Marty had filled up his tank in Billings, Montana but was so eager to get to the alleged extant hippie commune that the first time he looked at his gas gauge was when he had traveled so far back on the dirt road that it was too late to do anything about it. This wasn't the first time this fault of Marty's had gotten him into serious trouble and he hoped this time wouldn't turn out to be the error that was totally unforgiving. As the blackness of night fell upon him, his anxiety turned to raw fear.

Marty felt his heart jump and his lungs grab a sharp breath of air when the engine finally shuttered on its last gasp of gasoline vapors – then grow deafeningly silent. The cold grip of fear momentarily paralyzed him. He couldn't move or even think. As people in these circumstances often do… he started talking, out loud, to himself… calming himself by pretending to be two people – the scared man and the calm reassuring friend of the scared man.

"OK buddy… be cool. Just calm down."

The scared man listened to his friend and took a few long slow and deep breaths. His friend continued.

"Just think… c'mon just use your head."

The scared man started thinking. His lights were still on and he didn't want a dead battery. He rotated the light switch on the turn signal arm toward him and he was immediately submerged in absolute blackness. He literally couldn't see his hand in front of his face… he tried and he couldn't. He tried to remember if there was going to be a moon. How the hell did he know? He wasn't an astronomer… he was a city kid from L.A. Who worries about the phases of the moon? Well, did he remember a moon the previous night? Who remembers?

The scared guy finally found his voice and began to talk.

"All right. I'm out of gas. I can't walk back to Bear Stump… at least not at night… and I have no idea how far it is to any other town."

Marty's mind began to imagine the dangers that may be lurking about – wolves… bears… wild dogs… degenerates – like the people in *Deliverance*. With this last thought, he quickly locked the doors and tried to peer through the windows into the thick, impenetrable night. The darkness soon began to feel too close… as though it were pressing in on him. In a panic, he switched on the ceiling light. Like a diver coming up for a few breaths of air, he looked at his hands and around the inside of the car. It felt wonderful. It was as though he had been blind for years and had

had his sight miraculously restored. Suddenly he realized that the ignition must still be on for the ceiling light to work. He reached down to turn it off. He then remembered that the ceiling light works even when the ignition is off. Oh, well, he thought, probably shouldn't have the key on anyway. He wasn't exactly sure why... but it sounded right. He put his fingers around the ignition key and turned it to the left. He then began reaching up to turn off the ceiling light, but couldn't do it. He started looking around and breathing deeply at the same time... as though he could store up the light in his eyes and lungs before it was dark again. Several times he began to push the light switch – then lost his nerve – fearing the claustrophobic darkness more than a dead battery. It then struck him that the light from his car was probably shining like a beacon into that blackness around him and if some degenerate was out there, Marty was as good as asking to be attacked. With this last thought, his finger instantly shot upward to the switch and pushed it – immediately returning him to the thick darkness. He shuttered at the thought that some *Deliverance* people may have possibly already seen him. With this in mind, instead of provoking fear, the cloak of darkness now took on a comforting sense of protective concealment.

Marty realized he was beginning to get cold. It was late May... but in the mountains – in the thin air at this elevation – he knew it was going to get very cold as the night came on. He remembered that he had a sweater and blanket in the trunk. The T-shirt he had on just wouldn't do. He also knew he had a small flashlight in the trunk, as well... but didn't know if the batteries were any good or not. He also wasn't exactly sure where it was – it rolled around a lot. Obviously, to get into the trunk, he'd have to unlock the door and get out of the car. He shook his head... he didn't think he had the nerve. His other self finally spoke up.

"C'mon Marty... don't be a fucking pussy. It'll take you a couple of goddamn seconds to open the door... run back to the trunk and get the shit you need."

The demeaning insults of the brave Marty shamed the scared Marty into action. He thought his plan through in precise detail.

PAPA

First, he'd press the trunk release button... then he'd get all ready to jump out... hit the automatic lock for the doors – didn't want some degenerate jumping into the car while he was out – make sure he had the automatic door opener in his hand... run back to the trunk... wait... where was his sweater? Which bag did he put it in? Shit. When did he have it on last? Think. OK... the night he got to Colorado Springs, he had it on... put it on to go to get something to eat. What bag did he put it back into? Shit. The leather or the black nylon? Think. OK... when he was packing to drive to Bear Stump... this morning... the black one! Yes. That's right. He could picture it. All right. He'd run back... open the trunk... unzip the black bag... grab the sweater... grab the blanket on the... left side – yes – the left side of the trunk... forget about the flashlight... too hard to find... slam... no... don't slam... close the trunk quietly... run back... jump into the car... lock the door. Ten seconds at the most.

Marty took a deep breath then blew it out with a whoosh. He pressed the trunk button... he heard it pop open. Shit! He forgot! The fucking trunk light! He jerked his head around to look back. It was shining like a goddamn search light! Christ! Marty felt panic rising in his chest. Suddenly Marty felt his hand unlock the door and push it open. Before he realized what he was doing, he was out the door and into the trunk. In his panic, he simply grabbed the black bag and blanket, slammed the trunk shut and was back into the car with the door locked so fast that it felt as though time had stood still. He was so happy to be back in his safe, locked car that he felt almost giddy. He dug out the sweater and slipped it on. It immediately warmed both his body and heart. Like a warm meal can sometimes make a bad day seem not so bad, the comfort of that warm sweater adjusted Marty's perspective so that he began to feel almost silly about how he had been acting. Though he was all alone, he felt embarrassed. God, he thought, wait until he tells the people back at the office about this. The thought of it caused a small laugh to tickle in his chest and made his body relax. He climbed into the back seat and curled his body under the blanket. He assured himself – as he always did when he was worried about something and wanted to get to sleep – that in the morning he'd come up with a solution to his problem.

CHAPTER TWO

People were passing his desk... giggling at him. He suddenly realized he was naked. It made him feel small and made his penis feel as though it were all shriveled up. He felt like crying but then they'd only laugh harder at him. He had to pee really bad but, being naked, he didn't want to walk in front of everybody to the men's room. Marty opened his eyes. The windows were steamed up and his mind made one of those odd, waking connections with his evenings of adolescent passion at the drive-in movies. Through the translucent water droplets, he could see the gray of early morning. He felt a vague sense of agitation... then realized that, as in his dream, he had to pee like an Arabian racehorse. The slightest movement made his bladder ache. He raised himself up very slowly and wiped off the window. The fog was so thick he could barely make out the form of a pine tree, just a few feet from his car.

Marty unlocked the door and opened it. The cold, wet, fresh air rushed into the car... making him realize just how stale the inside atmosphere had been. The chilly, thick fog made his skin feel clammy and unwashed. He climbed out of the car and stepped over to the tree. As he was peeing, one of those fundamental questions that often materialize during early morning urinations, entered his mind. He pondered why guys like to pee on trees. It would have served just as well for him to have peed on the grass... but splashing his urine on that rough pine bark seemed to satisfy something primal inside him. After he finished his morning toilet with the universal male shudder – starting somewhere around the hips and ending in a final shake of the head, the significant question he had been pondering, returned, unanswered, to the unknown place from which these strange inquiries emanate.

After he had climbed into the front seat and had slid behind the steering wheel, Marty realized it strictly was out of force of habit... and for no logical purpose. Without gas, he obviously wasn't going anywhere. Marty was pleasantly surprised that he had slept so remarkably sound – considering the circumstances – and he felt an odd sense of pride for having done so. His mind felt refreshed and crystal clear. It was time to plan.

OK, he pondered, how far is it back to Bear Stump? Probably seventy miles or more, was his guess. He looked at his wristwatch. Six-thirty. How many miles can a person walk in an hour? He had no idea. He used to walk from his apartment down to the Santa Monica Pier – about a mile – in, oh, about fifteen minutes. That's around four miles an hour, he calculated. It would get dark that night at about seven. Twelve hours of daylight at four miles an hour – only forty-eight miles! Shit! He'd be out in the middle of nowhere at nightfall. That obviously wouldn't do. What a mess!

Marty's mind raced about for other options. His car phone. If he could get somewhere, where he could use his phone, he could call the police in Bear Stump and they could come get him. But what if he kept walking and still couldn't get into range? He'd be stuck again.

OK… he was out of gas. His car was going nowhere. It didn't look like anybody was going to be driving along this one-lane dirt road in the middle of nowhere, anytime soon. He couldn't just keep sitting in the car. What good would that do him? He'd eventually starve to death. He'd have to strike out in some direction. He had no idea – if he continued ahead – where this road led. There could be a town over the next ridge or it could go on like this for a hundred miles. At least going back the way he came, he'd be dealing with a known quantity. Well, he concluded, he really didn't have much choice. If he had to spend the coming night outside he guessed that's what he'd have to do.

Marty got out of the car and locked it. He pulled his two bags out of the trunk… sticking the blanket and the flashlight into the leather one, and began the long journey, back to Bear Stump. He decided that every fifteen minutes he'd check his car phone for service range. He didn't want to leave it on constantly, with the battery running low.

It was a few minutes before seven when he started out. For the first two hours the fog made walking difficult... being able to see only a few feet in front of him. Besides the fog problem, it was cold as hell. By nine o'clock, however, the cloudless sky was a shade of deep blue that Marty had never seen before, and the sun was searing brilliantly into his eyes. Even with his sun glasses on the glare was painful and it forced him to keep his eyes on the ground and avoid looking up. He surmised that, being from L.A., he was accustomed to having some smog between himself and the sun. The air was so clear in these mountains that he felt as though the sun and sky were reaching right down and touching him. Marty didn't like the feeling... he felt almost violated... as though it were an invasion of his privacy. He had the odd thought that it would be hard to tell a lie here. You couldn't hide the truth in such brilliant, penetrating light.

After a couple hours of walking, his shoulders began to ache from the bag straps. He decided to take a fifteen-minute break... resolving, as he did, that this would be his routine – a fifteen-minute break every two hours. Under the scant shade of some scraggly-looking pines, Marty sat down on a large, flat rock. It felt great to get the weight of the bags off of his shoulders... making them feel as though they were floating upward. Having pulled his car phone from his rear pocket as he sat down, he flipped it on and checked for service range. Still out of range. Christ!, he thought, aren't there any fucking towers anywhere in this God-forsaken area? He remembered seeing commercials for a mobile phone, where this guy is out fishing, somewhere in the middle of nowhere and gets a phone call. Sure as shit wasn't in this wilderness, apparently. Marty decided to raise hell with his mobile phone company when – if – he got back. What the hell good are they if you can't use them when you really need them? He decided there should be a system that covers the whole world... every square inch. There should be a satellite network or something. Marty began to wonder if maybe there already was such a system and his company just didn't use it. That would really piss him off.

The dryness in his throat ended Marty's critique of the mobile phone world. More details – water. Water hadn't been a part of his original trip planning. Realizing that he may not have water for many hours – or even days – made his thirst increase, exponentially. Marty tried to weigh the seriousness of his situation. How long, he wondered, could someone go without water, particularly if he's walking for twelve hours a day, carrying two heavy bags? Marty began to realize just how ill-equipped modern people are to cope with raw, unforgiving nature. He began to feel how unprotected and open to death ancient man must have been. It finally dawned on Marty – not in irrational panic, but in cool-headed deduction – that his situation was really very dangerous – perhaps even life threatening. He realized that if he didn't use his head, he could very well end up a dead man.

Suddenly feeling very small and very helpless, for a fleeting moment Marty felt an urge to cry... cry for someone big to help him – God... his mother... anybody big. Marty had always felt he was not a brave man. Actually, he believed that at the base of his being, he was, in fact, a coward. As a twenty-eight-year-old man, this realization made him feel ashamed. He had been afraid of just about everything when he was a little boy... from a dark room to the bullies in his neighborhood, who loved to chase and torment him. They liked to corner him, just to see him cry. They would call him "kike" and "Jew boy" to make him cry... then "crybaby" and "sissy" and "mama's boy" to make him cry harder. Marty hadn't become any braver as he grew into adulthood... just safer. There weren't any more childhood bullies around – and if there were, as an adult, he'd simply call the police.

As an adult, Marty began to realize just how vulnerable and unprotected children really are. A school-yard bully could drag you behind the fence during recess and pummel you... then threaten you with more if you told anyone. You'd want to ask someone to help you but were afraid. What hell children go through, he thought. Fathers tell their sons to toughen up and be brave – but as grown-ups, they're safe in their protected, adult, social cocoons. They forget – or intentionally put out of their minds – just how small and helpless and scared they used to be when they were little. Marty had decided that if he ever had a son, he'd never make fun of him for his fears. He'd remember his own childhood terrors and understand.

Given the circumstances of his childhood, Marty often reflected that a difficult life was a virtual inevitability for him. During the second world war, Marty's grandfather had moved his family from Brooklyn, New York, to – of all places – Wheeling, West Virginia. What Jew moves to West Virginia?... Marty had asked himself, time and again, growing up. He and his little sister were the only Jews in their school and they knew of only a few other families of their faith in the entire city. As it was explained to him by his parents, there were some Nazi sympathizers in the old Brooklyn neighborhood, who had painted some swastikas on the doors and windows of the family home – as well as having thrown bricks through the window of the family butcher shop. Myron Chapman, who had fled Germany in the thirties because of similar terrorism, feared the same was beginning in the new world. He wanted to get away from the big city, where there lived, he felt, the greatest concentration of dangerous, anti-Semitic extremists. In trying to avoid such people, Myron felt Wheeling was a good choice... having a very small Jewish population and thus not likely to attract the attention of his antagonists.

Brooklyn would have had its share of bullies too, Marty realized, but at least he would have some other kids around with names and noses like his, who might have had to wear a yarmulke... which his father insisted of him. To this day, Marty had never confessed to his dad that after several terrifying episodes... the last of which involving some of the school-yard cretins stealing his head cover and throwing it up into a tree, then making him climb up to get it – Marty being in mortal fear of falling to his death but more afraid of being beaten-up if he didn't do as they commanded – began, the very next day, stuffing his yarmulke in his pocket the moment he was out of sight of his house. This act of cowardice, and his guilty conscience about it, still plagued him to this day.

Now, here he was, again... faced with fear and feeling like he was back on the school yard again... afraid and ready to start crying. He was an adult now... but no cops were anywhere near to call for help. Out here, in a wilderness that was totally indifferent to his continued existence, he faced the terror of being absolutely on his own, to confront the terrible face of real danger. He would have to stand up and deal with the risks he faced, or he might very well die. This sobering realization shook a wave of courage through Marty – a rare and exceedingly pleasant experience for him. Feeling suddenly strong, Marty stood erect... his jaws tightened, his eyes narrowed, and his muscles felt ready to respond. He felt ready to fight – with no particular adversary in sight or mind. He spoke with command.

"All right, Goddamn it, I'm gonna get through this."

He critically assessed his situation. He had no water and it was at least a couple days walk, in the heat, to the nearest town, carrying a heavy load. Not good, he concluded, as an obvious given. First, he decided, he'd start by dumping all unnecessary weight. He unzipped his bags and inventoried the contents. Besides his clothes, the only other things he had were toiletry articles, camera, film, and journalistic supplies – tablets, pocket tape recorder, pens, and cassettes. He stood up and put the recorder in his back pocket... tied his sweater around his neck... then after rolling his blanket into a short, tight, oblong cylinder, he tied it with the shoe laces he pulled from his second pair of shoes. He took off his belt, slid it under the two shoe lace ties, buckled it, then slipped the belt over his head, across his chest, and under his shoulder... the blanket resting on his back. He zipped the bags shut and hid them behind the rock where he'd been sitting – resolving he would fetch them when he came back for his car.

Always the writer, it suddenly struck Marty that his present situation was actually a very good story in itself... "Reporter Stranded in the Rockies." It would be, at least, something to show for his time and effort. He pulled the recorder from his rear pocket, sat down again, turned it on – to record – and detailed his wilderness experience, up to the moment. As he was speaking, the morbid thought crossed his mind that if he didn't make it, somebody might find his recorder and have himself a terrific story. Marty mused that, if the writer were sufficiently beneficent, he might give him the posthumous byline.

Returning from his momentary, post-mortem fancy, Marty resumed the sober task of plotting his survival. Water was all he could think about at that moment. As he saw it, he had two choices – specifically set out to look for some water, or keep going and hope he might have the good fortune to find some before he died of thirst. Looking for water would take time. If he failed, he would have sentenced himself to just that many more hours of thirst. Of course, if he found some, his outlook would be dramatically improved. He decided that looking for some water, for a reasonable period of time, was worth the price.

Marty gave himself one hour to search... and decided he'd keep within constant sight of the road. All he'd need now was to get lost. He prepared to start up the rocky slope that rose steeply from behind rocks where he'd been sitting. He took off his sweater and blanket and pulled his recorder out of his back pocket and laid them on the rock, seeing no need to lug them with him on the imposing climb ahead. He decided to keep his car phone with him in the hope that he might get some reception on the hill.

Marty began making his way up the rugged terrain... winding around the huge boulders interspersed among the eccentrically contorted, rough-skinned pines. The red clay soil gave him good footing and he made steady progress. About a quarter of the way up the climb, as he passed a large flat rock, something black, lying on it, caught his eye. Curious, Marty walked cautiously toward it, to inspect. The black spot proved to be a very large snake... curled up and cozy in obvious enjoyment of his warming sunbath. The instant Marty's brain gave specific definition to the object, he recoiled in terror. Being the first snake Marty had ever seen outside of a zoo, the repugnance of encountering the shiny, slithering creature, a few feet from him, had such an effect on him that he began running blindly, back down the hill before his conscious mind caught up with his primordial terror and recognized what he was doing. As he jumped over a fallen tree, his feet tangled in some of the branches and he fell forward onto some jagged rocks – his right shin bone smashing into a sharp stone edge. The pain was excruciating. He grabbed his leg and lay on his back... rocking back and forth and moaning. It hurt so badly that Marty felt nauseated and tears of pain rolled from his eyes.

After about five minutes, Marty was able to regain sufficient composure to sit up and survey the damage. He leaned his back against the rock and looked down at his left leg. His jeans were ripped and blood was turning the light blue denim into a wet crimson. Seeing this, Marty felt his stomach churn and his head swim. He rolled to his left and vomited between his hands onto the red clay. After spitting away the foul aftertaste of his partially digested stomach contents, he enjoyed the temporary post-vomit calm for a few moments. He pushed some soil over his mess and moved several feet to his right away from it. Very cautiously, he put his right hand over his injury and lightly explored it with his fingers. The pain of even such a gentle touch was deep and revolting. His shin bone felt odd to him… realizing a moment later, to his shock, that the atypical sensation was the sharp protrusion of a broken bone. The pain and the enormity of the situation was more than Marty's pampered, city-bred constitution could endure. The world began spinning – then went black.

CHAPTER THREE

A late-model BMW pulled alongside the driver's door of Art Durbin's battered pickup truck. A late-teen male in the passenger seat lowered the power window. He waited until Art turned to look down at him then slowly raised a right-hand fist – the knuckles facing the owner. The middle finger rose, slowly and ceremoniously, then locked into a full, upright position, while the passenger spread his lips in a synchronized movement to form a wide, full-toothed sneer – just as the digit reached its apex. Having Art's undivided attention, the passenger dispatched a verbal message to accompany the symbolic communication.

"Fucking farmer!"

Apparently satisfied with his total expression, the passenger turned toward the driver, jerked his head in a command to proceed, and the BMW sped by Art's slow-moving vehicle. Art issued a disgusted snort. He looked at Ben – who was intently studying something in the woods on the passenger side – greatly enjoying the warm spring wind in his face and on his long, hanging and dripping tongue. Though it was obvious that Ben had missed the whole BMW incident, Art commented to him about it, anyway.

"Goddamn kids. I'll just bet they paid for that car themselves."

Ben continued his solitary reverie – adding to Art's agitation.

"Hey! Did you hear me?"

The increase in the volume and change in Art's tone of voice was enough to convince Ben that he had better display some concern over whatever was bothering his master. He turned his head toward Art, lowered his jaw even further and panted in Art's direction. Ben's interest in Art's problem had its intended effect. Art smiled.

"What are you so interested in? You see a rabbit, boy?"

Art reached over and mussed the fur on the top of Ben's head – then playfully pushed the large head away from him. Ben wiggled his lower body and stood up with his head toward Art. He started licking Art's face so vigorously that it pushed his head sideways.

"OK… all right… all right."

Art slid his hand along Ben's bulky frame to the base of his tail and pressed hard. Ben sat down immediately. Art turned off of Route 441 – onto the unmarked road. He pulled his leather pouch of tobacco from his rear pocket, unzipped it, and dug his well-worn pipe into the aromatic leaves. After he zipped the pouch shut and returned it to its pocket, he packed the bowl with his middle finger to just the right degree of compression, pulled his World War II vintage Zippo from his front pocket, and lit the tobacco with the enormous flame that issued there from. After several puffs, he tamped the blossoming coals with the same finger, then lit it again. The bluish smoke rose around his head and filled the truck cab before rushing out of his opened window. His body relaxed as the cavendish, black-cherry flavor of the smoke filled his mouth and encouraged his saliva glands. While he knew that smoking was probably taking time off his life, he figured the comfort and pleasure he was getting from it more than made up for the deficit.

Ben, having exhausted his canine capacity to remain attentive, carefully placed his body onto the truck's well-worn seat, then made minor adjustments to find the precise position of total comfort. Once discovered, he laid his head on Art's right leg and breathed a full-bodied, presleep sigh. Art mussed his fur again but Ben, having already adequately fulfilled his duty of consoling his master, did not feel compelled to respond. It was time for a nap and Ben took napping very seriously.

It was a good day. After the seemingly interminable mountain winter and a few days, now and then, that teased of its arrival, spring had finally decided to take root. The air was soft and warm to the touch. The earth had a smell again. Art turned the radio on…

to his country western station... and bobbed his head in rhythm to the mournful beat. The sixty miles back Old Log Road – a harrowing journey in the winter – was so pleasant on this trip that Art found himself wishing it were longer. Crossing the small wooden bridge, the loud thumping of the uneven boards under the tires caused Ben to momentarily look up. Visibly irritated by this discordant interruption of his canine reverie which he – being a dog – was compelled, by nature, to investigate, but finding it unworthy of his species – immediately resumed his blissful, afternoon dognap... returning his head to his customary spot on Art's leg.

Art brought his truck to a stop, behind the white car with California plates, blocking the narrow road. He got out of his truck to ferret out the cause and person responsible for such an ignominious act. Ben, feeling this situation *was* worthy of his attention, followed his master to assist in the inquiry. Art peered through the windows of the car and found it unoccupied. He tried opening the driver's door... thinking he might back it down the slight grade and over to the side, so he could get by. It was locked. He tried each of the other three doors... with the same result. As the car sat, with the trees and rocks so close to its sides, it was impossible for Art to get around it. Art shook his head in utter exasperation.

"Well now, shit."

Art started looking around for the driver. He shook his head again.

"What a stupid place ta park a car. Figures... from California."

Ben was sniffing the ground behind the truck – heading back the road in a quick step. Art hollered after him.

"Hey! Ben! Hey!! Get back here!!"

Ben continued on.

"Jesus... damn dog."

Art climbed in his truck and backed down the dusty road – until he found enough space between the trees to turn around, then began to follow Ben... yelling for him every few seconds. Ben totally ignored his master's page, moving at a slow, deliberate run – down the middle of the road – his nose close to the dirt. With Ben seeming to be on a mission, Art decided just to follow him.

About five miles back the road, Ben turned off directly to his right and headed into the trees. Art stopped the truck, got out, and followed him. Ben disappeared behind a large rock formation. Art caught up, and walked around it, seeing two bags lying on the ground. Ben, still sniffing, began to climb the hill. At this point, Art became a bit wary of the situation. It didn't look right. His eyes and ears sharpened – searching for anything out of the ordinary. Art felt adrenaline priming his muscles and senses for trouble. Though Art was nearly seventy-five, his rugged outdoor life had preserved a thin, tightly muscled body that many a forty-year-old would envy. Art was still a worthy match for anyone who had bad intentions toward him.

Several hundred feet up the hill, Ben disappeared behind another large rock formation. Moments later, Art heard him barking in an excited and somewhat agitated tone and he ran the ten yards that separated them. On the uphill side of the sharp rocks, he found a young man lying on the ground – motionless and on his left side with his eyes closed. The left pant leg of his jeans was soaked with blood below his knee. Art couldn't see any signs of breathing. He got down on his hands and knees and put his face close to the stranger's – still not discovering any indication of respiration. Art slid his left pointer finger below the man's nose and felt some warm air coming out. Art spoke to him.

"Hey... hey, young man. Hey."

No response. Art put his hand on the young man's upturned shoulder and gently shook him as he spoke again.

"Hey, buddy. You OK?"

Still nothing. Curiosity finally got the best of Ben. He'd stopped barking when Art arrived and stood guard – positioned a few inches from the man's tennis-shoed feet – ready to render assistance to his master if necessary. Seeing his master's willingness to touch the man, Ben took this as a sign that, apparently, he wasn't terribly dangerous. Excusing himself from guard duty, therefore, he joined Art at the other end of the man and stood beside him – shoulder-to-shoulder – with their faces only inches apart. Ben looked from the man to Art and back again – studying the situation, anxious to know where all this was leading. Deciding to get personally involved in this obviously serious situation, Ben set about to categorize this person according to a dog's primary frame of reference. He, thus, bent over the motionless body and began to sniff it with great intensity… searching for some odor, of which he could associate with one of his vast mental library of smells, collected over a lifetime of olfactory research. His vigorously wagging tail demonstrated his unbounded enthusiasm for this universal pastime of all dogs. A sudden jerk of the man's body startled Ben. He jumped back, bared his teeth, and issued a low, threatening growl.

"Quiet Ben. Sit!"

Ben reluctantly obeyed… trusting his instincts that indicated there was danger afoot. Art shook the young man's shoulder again.

"Hey fella. Hey."

The man opened his eyes, slightly… unable to focus on anything. After some blinking and some head shaking, both his vision and mind finally sharpened. He clumsily raised himself up on his left elbow and stared at Art. Art smiled warmly at him.

"What happened? Looks like you're hurt pretty bad, young fella."

This reference caused Marty to recall his bloody leg. He instinctively reached down for it.

"Let me take a look at that. Just relax, my friend."

Art gently touched the soaked trousers. He felt a bone protruding where it shouldn't.

"You got a broken leg, young man."

Marty found his own voice.

"How bad is it?"

"Well… you're gonna live – but we need ta get you to a doctor pretty quick. It's bleedin a bit. I'll tell ya what. I gotta pick up truck down there. Let's get you down the hill and into the back of it. We'll drive back ta Bear Stump. We have a little medical center there. They'll fix you up, right quick."

Much to Marty's amazement, this man, clearly advanced in years, nonchalantly slid his right arm under his upper back and his left arm under his knees and stood up with him in his arms, exhibiting little apparent effort. Marty looked at him with obvious skepticism.

"Are you sure you can do this?"

"Oh, it's not too far… we'll do er."

And they did. Art didn't even appear to be breathing hard as they descended the challenging terrain. When they got to the truck, Art laid Marty on the ground so he could undo the hook holding up the back gate… then picked him up again and sat him on the edge of the truck bed. He then climbed up into the bed and grabbed Marty under his arms and pulled him to the front of the bed – leaning his back against the truck cab, between a number of cardboard boxes filled with a wide assortment of grocery items.

"You just relax, young fella. We'll take er easy so we don't lose ya out the back."

Art closed the gate and hooked it. They began their trip back to Bear Stump – Art driving slowly… trying to avoid the bumps.

As the shock of his injury began to abate, the pain in Marty's leg dramatically intensified. Within minutes, it reached a point that he felt he could bear it no longer. He pounded on the cab window. Art slid it open.

"What's the matter?"

"The pain... it's so bad... I can't take it."

Art stopped the truck. He reached into his glove compartment and pulled a nearly full, half-pint of *J & B* scotch whiskey. He handed it through the window to Marty.

"This'll help. Drink it all."

Fortunately for Marty, he was a scotch drinker and *J & B* was, in fact, his brand. One hell of a coincidence, he thought. Marty began sipping the scotch, feeling like a cowboy in a movie who was about to have a bullet dug out of him. As thirsty as he was, the liquid felt like hot rain on parched earth and his thirst made him drink the booze much faster than he ordinarily would have. The speed of his drinking – combined with an empty stomach – did the trick, almost immediately. Marty's pain began to fade – along with the clarity of his circumstance, and his mood was quickly transmuted to that of a happy drunk. He leaned the back of his head against the truck cab and began singing. He would ask Art, from time to time, if he remembered a song... then would sing it. Art laughed, and lied, telling him that he sounded really good.

After nearly two hours on the road, the old pickup pulled into the small medical building parking lot. Art went inside for help and, almost immediately, two men returned with a gurney to transport Marty into the emergency room. The doctor on duty got the bleeding stopped, then had several X-rays taken of Marty's leg to assess the full extent of what was obviously a serious fracture. After studying the developed film, he informed Marty he had a very bad compound fracture and that they'd need to take him into surgery, immediately, to set his leg. Concerned that it may present a danger, Marty informed the doctor he had just consumed a half a pint of scotch. The doctor replied that from the smell of his breath, that was obvious, and besides, he said, his friend had told them about it... but they still needed to get his leg set... and he wouldn't want to be awake for what they'd have to do to him. Seeing that he was still concerned, the doctor assured Marty that the alcohol would not be a problem. When Marty awakened in the recovery room, he discovered a foot-to-hip cast on his left leg.

After watching him for several hours to ensure his safe recovery from the surgery, the nurses got Marty up and fitted him for crutches. They asked him if he felt well enough to leave the center. He didn't, but hating hospitals, he lied and said he was fine. He asked the nurses if the man who brought him to the center was still there. The younger of the two said he was.

Art was patiently sitting in the waiting room, sipping a cup of vending machine coffee, when Marty finally hobbled through the doors on his crutches – with the assistance of a nurse – and lowered himself onto one of the red vinyl seats beside Art. Though he was sober, now, Marty still smelled like an operating distillery. Art had explained the scotch story to the doctor when they arrived so he wouldn't get the wrong idea about Marty. The medical staff had put Marty's pants back on – splitting the left pant leg along the entire outer seam. Also splitting was Marty's head. The up-side of the scotch was history and he was now serving out the miserable penance that comes with the cruel return to sobriety. Despite his ubiquitous agony, Marty managed a sincere smile toward Art.

"Thanks... ah... ya know... I don't even know your name."

"Art... Art Durbin."

Marty extended his hand.

"I'm Marty Chapman."

Feeling the restrained strength in Art's grip, Marty recalled how Art had carried him.

"You know… you saved my life, Art. You really did. I would have died out there if you hadn't come along. This is like some TV rescue story. You never realize that these things really happen."

"Wasn't any big deal, Marty… glad ta help. What are ya gonna do, now? You can't be doin much travelin with a broken leg. I saw from your plate – you're from California. I'm guessin that was your white car out there."

"Yeah… that's mine. Like a dumb shit, I ran out of gas. I don't know what I'm going to do, Art… to tell you the truth. This is one screwed up situation… I'm telling you. You have no idea."

"You need ta get back to work right away?"

"Well… it's a long story, Art. I… ah… well, I'm a writer for a magazine and I've been looking for old hippie communes that still exist. I was going to do a story – except I couldn't find any hippies… kept running into dead ends. I was on my way to try to find a commune… back that road… whatever its name is…"

"Old Log Road. Used ta be a lumber mill back that way… long time ago."

"Oh yeah? Well, anyway, some professor in Colorado Springs told me there was a commune back that road… about forty miles back."

"There was… up until about three years ago. They got chased out. School officials got wind a the fact they had small kids back there who weren't goin to school. Police went out and found a hell of a mess. Kids were dirty… livin in filth… didn't look like anyone was takin care of them. Cops got the child welfare people involved. Ended up with the kids being taken from em… they ran the rest of em outa there. Was the big talk a the town back then. Apparently some a these people would come inta town, once in awhile, ta get some things… but nobody was exactly sure where they lived or how many of em there were. I guess one day they brought a couple of the kids inta town and that's how it all got started. I use ta see people, from time ta time, back Old Log Road… but I don't know if it was any of them or not. Some people go campin back there in the mountains. Hard ta tell who's who. It's big country. You could live out there your whole life and nobody would know it if you didn't want em to. Me… I been on the mountain some fifty years now. All by myself… cept for my dogs. Had Ben now for… oh, goin on eight years. Come out here after world war two. Believe it or not, I was born in New Jersey. Had enough of people during the war… didn't want nothin more ta do with em after that, and…"

"You mean to tell me that the commune's gone?"

"Yep… she's gone, Marty… sorry ta tell ya."

"Goddamn it. I can't get a fucking break here. What about the painted rock… the one with Freaksville on it? They told me I'd see it."

"You were told right, Marty. That rock's been there since the sixties. After the trouble with the commune, though, a lotta people from town went out ta see the place… after they'd all cleared out. Some a the do-gooder people cleaned it up… and scrubbed the name off the rock. Wasn't any big deal ta me but they said it was destroyin the natural beauty of the environment… or somethin along that line."

The two males, having exchanged all the pertinent information they felt was relevant at the moment, lapsed into a self-conscious silence. Art finally broke it.

"So now what, Marty?"

"Shit… I don't know. I don't know. What a mess. What a mess. My car is stuck out in the middle of nowhere… out of gas. I've been out on this assignment for over a month and have nothing to show for it except my own rescue story… which is not exactly national magazine material – not to take away from what you did for me, of course. I can't drive my car with a broken leg. Shit!

What a fucking mess. I wouldn't be at all surprised if I lost my job over this. How can I go out on any assignments with a broken leg?"

"You have any sick time comin?"

"Well… I got hurt on the job… technically, anyway. I suppose I might have workmen's comp coming. I'd have to check. Why do you ask?"

"I was gonna say that if you'd like, you can stay out at my place while you're on the mend. Got plenty a room… just me and Ben. You're welcome."

"I couldn't put you out like that, Art."

"Wouldn't be any problem. Might be nice ta have a visitor after all these years. In the fifty years I've been on my mountain, I never once hadda overnight guest – not a one. You just seem like a mighty nice young fella and good company. Might be good for you, too. You look like you could use a rest, my young friend."

"You know… as crazy as it sounds, it might not be too bad of an idea. I might even turn it into a story. How about it, Art… can I do your story?"

"Ya can if ya like… but there's not much of a story there."

"Tell ya what… Wait. Did I have my cellular phone when you brought me in?"

"One of those little pocket phones? I didn't see it."

"It was in my back pocket."

"Didn't see it, Marty."

"Do me a favor, Art… can you go ask the nurse if they have my phone?"

"Sure thing. Be right back."

Art disappeared through the swinging doors and reappeared, moments later, with a big smile and the phone in his hand.

"Said they forgot ta give it back to ya. Fell outta your back pocket when they took your pants off."

Marty dialed his editor. He explained to her what had happened… and asked about workmen's comp. Marla told him he was covered. He mentioned Art's offer and the possibility of a story. Marla was quite lukewarm about the story on Art but said it didn't much matter to her where he convalesced… here or there. He could do what he wanted. She said she'd see him in six weeks or so… then they'd talk. Marty didn't like the tone of her last sentence about their talking – sounding a bit foreboding. Marty folded up his phone and smiled at Art.

"Well… looks like you have a house guest, Art… or cabin… whatever you call your place."

CHAPTER FOUR

Art filled his gas can at the Bear Stump Sunoco and Marty's prescription for pain medication at the Bear Stump Grocery. Marty immediately downed a couple of pain pills with his service station Coke... his leg starting to throb – the *J & B* and anesthesia having lost their numbing effect. Marty resumed his station in the back of the truck – his straight plaster leg preventing him from sitting in the cab. They retraced their morning route. Marty told Art that he had some things hidden behind the rocks, below where he had fallen. Art revealed to Marty that he'd seen the stuff, and that he'd be sure to stop and pick them up on the way. After the stop for Marty's things, they drove on until they arrived at his car. Art got the gas can from the back and poured the heated, fuming fuel into the tank. He had Marty wait in the truck while he drove Marty's car the four miles to the turnoff for his cabin... said he'd have to walk back and it would be a bit. He let down the truck gate before he left – in case, he said, Marty had to take a leak. Art said he figured he'd be back in about an hour.

It took several tries before enough gas was pulled into the carburetor for adequate combustion. Art then drove Marty's car the four miles, turned right through an opening between some pines and parked the car behind a thick cluster of trees where, from the road, it was totally hidden from view. Art locked it up then started back the narrow road to rejoin Marty. When he got to the truck, Ben was sitting in the truck bed with Marty, getting acquainted with their new cabinguest. They seemed to be hitting it off, famously.

"You two look like a couple a old buddies."

"We had a long conversation while you were gone, Art. Seems we have a lot in common."

Art laughed... then climbed into the cab. He shouted through the open rear window of the cab.

"You comin up here, Ben?"

Ben stayed put beside Marty.

"You got a new friend, Marty."

Art laughed again, reached through the cab window to muss Ben's fur, then started down the road to the cabin. When he got to the turnoff, he followed the same route he had taken with Marty's car and parked his truck beside it. Art turned to give Marty assurances, through the cabin window.

"Ya can't see back here from the road… they're safe… don't worry, Marty. I been parking my trucks back here since Ben Franklin was a boy… and nobody ever touched em."

Marty nodded, acknowledging his belief in Art's assertions. Satisfied he had allayed Marty's worries, Art climbed out of the cab, leaned his arms on the side panel and smiled at Marty.

"We got a climb ahead of us, my friend. You go as far as ya can on those crutches… I'll carry you the rest."

"Whatever you say, Art."

Art and Marty made their way up the narrow rocky path, winding through the ever present rocks and pines. This being Marty's first time on crutches, progress was intolerably slow and Art eventually realized the folly in the arrangement.

"At this rate, Marty, your leg'll be healed by the time we get ta the cabin."

Art stepped in front of Marty, faced uphill with his back to Marty and bent his knees slightly… his arms hanging down at his sides.

"Climb up."

"How am I supposed to do that, Art?"

Art reached back with his right arm.

"Gimme your right leg first then wrap your arms around my neck."

Marty moved close to Art's back. He pulled his right crutch out from under his shoulder and let it fall to the dirt. Balancing on his left crutch, he bent his right leg forward – wrapping his right arm around Art's neck. Art encircled Marty's right leg with his same arm and lifted it slightly.

"OK... I'm gonna grab your left leg... don't go fallin, OK?"

"OK, Art."

Art reached back and found the plaster leg with his left hand. He was surprised how warm and unnaturally alive the inanimate surface felt. He wrapped his left arm around it.

"All right... hold on, Marty. As soon as I lift this leg, let the crutch drop and wrap your left arm around my neck."

Marty hesitated.

"You sure this is going to work, Art?"

"Don't worry... just do what I told ya. Ya ready?"

"Yeah... I guess."

"All right... on three, I'm gonna lift your leg. OK? Ready... one... two... three!"

Art lifted the plaster leg and Marty let his crutch fall. He lunged for Art's neck and flung his left arm around it... then squeezed with a death-like grip with both arms. Art struggled to get enough air up to speak.

"Easy… easy."

Realizing he was safe, Marty relaxed his grip.

"Damn! Hell of a grip you got there, boy!"

"Sorry, Art. Things felt a little shaky for a minute."

Art slowly plodded up the narrow path… avoiding, as best he could, running Marty's broken leg into any trees. Fifteen minutes later, they arrived at Art's cabin – situated not more than thirty feet from the edge of a sheer cliff that dropped, in a straight vertical descent, some three thousand feet, to a small lake in the valley below. In the distance, beyond the cliff, were a seemingly endless number of craggy mountains peaks – one behind the other – diminishing in perspective until they met, in blurred oblivion, with the distant horizon. Ben, having grown testy over the slow progress of the two noncanines, had run ahead and was sitting on the porch, impatiently awaiting their arrival. He stood and wagged his powerful tail as Art and Marty approached. When Art reached the front edge of the porch floor – that rose some three feet above the ground – he turned his back to it and kept moving to the rear until his legs made contact with the wood.

"OK buddy, I'm lettin ya down."

Marty instinctively reached down with his right hand and placed it on the splintery, unpainted floor boards as he descended. Art continued bending until Marty's right foot made contact with the ground. Marty balanced on his right leg until Art moved away from him – then bent his knee until his butt connected with the porch floor.

"You OK?"

"I'm fine, Art."

"OK… you just relax… I'll go back down for your crutches and the rest a the things. Won't be a minute."

Art disappeared around the side of the cabin to Marty's left. Ben greeted his cabinguest by thoroughly washing his right cheek with his long and dripping-wet tongue. As he waited, Marty surveyed the magnificent view. It was almost beyond comprehension... particularly for a man who had spent his entire life on concrete and whose horizons were constantly obstructed by man-made structures. It was so massively expansive that, after no more than a few seconds of exposure, it made Marty feel a bit woozy. He closed his eyes to allow his world to shrink to a tolerable dimension. It was actually almost too much to comprehend – as though there were some divine meaning in such expansiveness but was just too much existence, all at one time, for any human being to completely absorb and decipher. So, rather than try to take in all that was before his eyes, Marty studied certain specific sights, instead.

Although it was May... many of the distant peaks were still snow covered. Between some of the mountains, Marty could see mountain lakes – sparkling deep blue, reflecting the color of the perfect sky. Up to the tree line were the omnipresent scraggly pines, then, rising to the heavens, were immense steeples of sheer rock.

Art made it back in about ten minutes, carrying Marty's two bags, by their straps, in one hand, and a cardboard grocery box in his other arm. Marty watched him in awe as he stepped in long, spirited strides toward the cabin porch, humming some country-western tune, looking none the worse for the wear, after making the rough climb with his considerable load in hand. Here was a man, the age of Marty's grandfather, who had already performed several feats of strength and endurance that few men, half his age, could match... certainly more than Marty could do. Art's body was wrapped in tight, youthfully contoured muscles... and his mind seemed as quick as his body was sleek. Marty thought of his grandfather, back in West Virginia, a resident of the Sugar Creek Nursing Home – only a few years older than Art – shuffling along the halls with his walker – missing the majority of his teeth and not recognizing Marty ninety percent of the time. It's as though Art and his grandfather had worn two different wristwatches in life –

Art's running at a snail's pace – his granddad's spinning its hands in a blur. On Art's wrist, it said he was still a young man.

After Art had finished bringing up the rest of the grocery boxes, and Marty's crutches, he gave Marty a tour of the large, but sparsely furnished, cabin. It had a wide, stone fireplace where Art did all his cooking. To the right of the fireplace was a hot water shower – a bit of ingenuity that greatly impressed Marty. When Art had constructed the chimney, he had run a pipe from the nearby stream into the cabin's chimney, where it emptied into a stone chamber he had constructed. By pulling a little lever, extending through the cabin wall, spring water would flow into this rock container. When it was filled, a person would allow the lever to spring back to its original position – closing off the water flow. The heat of the chimney, when a fire was going, would warm the water in the chamber quite rapidly, Art told Marty. A pipe from the right side of the chamber, passed through the same side of the fireplace, and after a length of about three feet, it bent downward to a shower nozzle that had an on-off lever, controlled by a hanging chain. On the floor of the cabin – directly below the nozzle, were slits, cut between the boards, to allow the water to run out – draining onto the ground below. Art had suspended a large, round metal ring from the ceiling around the shower area, from which hung a plastic shower curtain… to keep the water from splashing into the rest of the cabin.

Art demonstrated to Marty how the shower worked.

"I only use this in the winter, a course. In the warm weather, I take a bar of soap and clean up in the pond.

"The one, way down in the valley?"

"Oh hell no, Marty. That'd take you a whole day ta get to. There's a little pond just a few hundred yards from here… straight behind the cabin. Course, you won't be takin showers for a while, with your cast. I can fill up a tub for ya. You can clean yourself up as best ya can til ya get that plaster off yer leg."

To the right of the shower, in the corner of the cabin, was the toilet. It had a round ring and plastic curtain arrangement – like the shower – for privacy. Marty puzzled over the need for privacy since Art lived alone but didn't pursue it. The toilet surprised Marty. Somehow he pictured mountain men using an outhouse. Of course, with running water into the cabin, there was no reason why you couldn't have an indoor commode. Marty figured that either movies or TV had given him the outhouse idea... Ma and Pa Kettle on AMC or the Clampets, before Beverly Hills. The question as to where and what the contents of the toilet ran out into, crossed Marty's mind... but, again, he didn't pursue it.

To the left of the fireplace was Art's kitchen. He had rigged up the same sort of contraption for sink water as he had for the shower – except the water pipe ran through the wall into a spigot. Above the sink was a crudely made cupboard with no doors on it. On the lowest shelf were a few plates and a couple of water glasses. To the right of the dishware, were several knives, spoons, and forks. On the left side of the cupboard was a wide variety of canned goods.

"Do you grow some things, Art?"

"Nah... soil's for shit up here... and it's too short a growin season, anyway. Get all my fruits and vegetables, cept for some berries, down in Bear Stump. I shoot my own meat and catch some fish, though... got a smokehouse out back. Wait'll ya try some a my venison. Tasty as hell."

Marty looked around the one-room cabin, and, seeing only one bed, wondered where he was going to sleep. Art picked up on his puzzlement.

"Don't worry, you ain't sleepin with me, Marty. I'll put a bed together for ya this afternoon. I got a extra mattress on my bed and plenty of blankets... even got a extra pillow. Matter a fact, Marty, you're lookin a little peaked right now. You need to lay down a bit?"

"Yeah, Art... I think I better."

"Okey doke. Tell ya what. You just go lay down on my bed there. I'll go an make a bed for you, then somethin fer us to eat. How's that sound?"

"Damn good Art... I'm starved."

Marty fell asleep almost as soon as his head plunged into the overstuffed feather pillow. Art went out and cut some three-to-four-inch-wide branches to make Marty a bed. He lashed the branch frame together with rope – then weaved a rope mesh between the sides of the frame, creating a surface upon which to lay the mattress. In a little over an hour, Art had it finished. To test its strength, he lay on the rope-weaved grid and wiggled around a bit. Satisfied, Art carried the bed inside and put it near his own bed, still bearing the sleeping Marty.

Art moved on to dinner preparation. He built a small fire in the fireplace then went out to the smoke house and sliced some cuts of venison from a carcass that hung from the ceiling – putting the slices into a pot he had carried along with him. Back inside the cabin, Art took the venison out of the pot and laid the smoke-blackened pieces of meat on a wooden cutting board and carved the sections of flesh into small square pieces with his foot-long hunting knife. Pulling several large potatoes from the twenty-pound sack on the floor, Art washed off the dirt, cut them into chunks and pushed them from the board into the pot. Art did the same with some carrots, onions, and celery. He added water to his mixture, shook in a variety of spices, put a lid on the pot, then hung it from an iron structure with an arm that extended over the fire. In about an hour, the saliva-piquing aroma of the bubbling stew filled the cabin – enticing enough to pull Marty back from his distant slumber. He sat up and saw Art stirring the pot.

"Damn, that smells good, Art."

Art smiled at him, then moved to the round, oak, dinner table and, with night falling on the mountain, he lit the kerosene lantern.

Marty struggled to get out of the bed.

"Need some help?"

"No… I've got to learn how to manage this for myself sometime."

Marty reached down and grabbed the set of crutches from the floor – placing one on the bed and grasping the other with his right hand. He put his right foot on the floor and pushed himself up with a crutch. Keeping the weight off of his left leg, he bent down and grabbed the other crutch. He stood for a while, balancing himself with both crutches. The deep sleep had left him a bit disoriented and feeling slightly dizzy. After the room stopped tilting, Marty made his way to the table.

Whether it was the many hours since he had last eaten, or Art's cooking, or maybe just the ambiance of having a meal in a cabin in the high mountain air, Marty believed that this may have been the best food he had ever eaten in his life. Having read about smoked meat in novels of the frontier, to be actually eating it made him feel as though he were tasting history. The stewing had made the meat quite tender and the tangy taste of the smoke was strong but surprisingly pleasant. Adding to the time-warp feeling of the scene, two bottles of home-brewed beer sat on the table – their white porcelain tops hanging on a wire apparatus from two holes on the bottle neck that allowed them to be re-sealed. Though they drank from the bottles directly, Art poured a bit of his beer into a glass to show Marty how clear his home brew was. He pointed out that not all home brew was this clear – in case Marty wasn't fully appreciating what he was seeing. The first half of his bottle tasted odd to Marty, having a very strong, malty flavor – not what a city-bred, tavern drinker, was used to. The last half, however – his taste buds adjusting and accepting the new stimulation – tasted great. Marty mused that he could get used to this life. Maybe Art wasn't so crazy after all, he thought, living up here all by himself. Maybe the rest of the stressed-out lunatics of the world were.

Marty ingested all solid and liquid nourishment in a matter of minutes without speaking a word. Art watched him with amusement.

"A little hungry, Marty?"

Suddenly aware of his lack of manners, Marty was embarrassed.

"I'm sorry, Art... I was starved."

Art laughed.

"No need for apology. I'll take it as a compliment on my cookin."

"I don't know if it's because I'm starved or your great cooking, Art... but this is about the best meal I ever remember eating."

"How bout some coffee?"

"Coffee sounds perfect."

"I'm gonna brew ya some mountain coffee, Marty. You'll just love it."

Art took a heavy, blackened-metal, coffee kettle with a wire handle from the fireplace mantle and filled it about half full with water. He hung it on the iron arm over the fire where the stew pot had been previously suspended. Art resumed his seat at the table and chewed the fat with Marty until the water boiled. In about five or so minutes, steam blew from the spout. Art took down a can of Maxwell House coffee from the pantry, pulled off its plastic cover and filled the measure that he kept inside the can. He lifted the kettle top and dumped the coffee directly into the water. He repeated this six times. Replacing the top, he sat down again.

"Give er about three or four minutes."

At the moment Art sensed was appropriate, he spun the iron arm out of the fire, with the kettle's spout pointing toward the table.

"We're just about there, Marty. It'll take a couple a minutes for the grounds to settle."

The settling process completed, Art took a very old-looking, ivory colored, thick-walled porcelain cup from the cupboard – the type Marty had seen used in forties movies, in working-class diner scenes – tipped the kettle forward and poured the blackish-brown brew. He handed the hot cup to Marty.

"Got any cream, Art?"

"Sorry."

Marty brought the cup to his mouth. He felt the heat rising and began to blow.

"A little hot."

Seeing the taste test was to be delayed, Art poured himself a cup. He immediately swallowed a large gulp of it – unaffected. Marty felt as though he were in a scene from a wild-west movie – he playing the pampered city-slicker greenhorn to Art's hard-as-nails leather-skinned cowboy. Embarrassed to blow again, Marty took a tiny sip. It burnt the hell out of everything from his lip, downward, but he was determined he would bear it without any display of suffering. Marty smiled – shaking his head approvingly.

"Great coffee, Art."

"Thought you'd like it."

Actually, after some feeling returned to Marty's tongue and the coffee cooled to a temperature that he could drink it normally, Marty made the same comment again – this time, sincerely. It was the best cup of coffee he ever remembered having. The fact that there were no grounds in it further impressed him. Several cups later, the men leaned back in their chairs to make significant observations about life, as men are prone to do after a good meal and coffee.

"Quite a life you've got here, Art."

"Has its ups and downs."
"Well it must have agreed with you pretty well… you're the picture of health. Hell, you're more than twice my age and you could outrun or outwork me any day. I've got a grandfather who's not much older than you, who looks like he could be your father. You've got the life here, Art… no neighbors, no boss, no noise… nothing but quiet and probably the best view anybody has, anywhere in the whole world. You'd pay three million in L.A. for a house with a view like this."

"I got a lot… and I got nothin, too. All I got is myself… and old Ben. Couple more years, Ben'll be gone… then it'll be just me til I find me another dog – if I get another one. It's hard losin a dog. I cried my eyes out, the last dog I lost. When I think a my life here, I think a that quote, 'It was the best of times and the worst of times.' I read in the paper about all the trouble in the world… the killin, rapin, bad water, bad air, people havin heart attacks over their jobs… hell of a lotta trouble right where you live, Marty… then I'm glad I'm here on my mountain. Sometimes, though, when I see pictures a families… the kids and grandkids – I know I have nothin… no trouble… no worries… too much of nothin. I started to leave this mountain a dozen times in my life… got part way'n come back. Couldn't think a anywhere to go. I got no family. I only had my old man when I got outta the service. Been dead for… shit, oh, lemme see… some forty years now – long time. Where would I go and what would I do if I left here? Quit school in the eighth grade. What could I do? Only thing I'm good at is livin on this mountain. I haven't seen any want ads lately for a mountain man… how bout you, Marty?"

Marty laughed.

"Not lately, Art. Are you saying you'd do it differently if you could? Would you have gotten married and had a family if you had another chance?"

"I never do that 'other chance' stuff. If there was another chance, it wouldn't a been my life… it a been somebody else's. I was dealt the hand I got. I never was good at makin friends… always pretty much kept to myself… like my old man did. I always wanted ta make friends but didn't know how ya did it. I'd hear all these people makin conversation about all kinds a things but I usually only had a few words ta say about anything. I guess you can tell the loneliness has loosened up my mouth a bit, huh? I never had a girlfriend in my life. I liked the girls but was petrified ta talk to em. Hadn't ever been around em. My mother died when I was just a little shit… no sister, aunts… no women in my life, period. I just never knew how ya talked to a girl – or boys either for that matter. The other boys liked me… I was good at sports and fightin. You know… that's all it takes with boys. They all liked me, but none of em was ever really my friend. I guess the biggest wish in my life was always ta have a good friend. Wouldn't a taken much, but I couldn't even get started. It's kinda like havin a handicap… like bein a cripple."

"You seem mighty friendly to me, Art. You're a good man… a very good man. You saved my life for Christ sake! You know what they would have done in L.A. if they saw me laying there? Crossed to the other side of the street. Hell, you're fun to talk to… a great host… you should have tons of friends, Art."

"Oh I've finally learned ta shoot the breeze. . . but you get inta habits. I just got inta the habit a bein alone. Don't really know what got inta me… invitin you here. Like I told ya… I never had a guest here before. Just one a those things… it just came out."

"Hope you're not starting to regret it, Art."

"Oh shit no… I'm enjoyin the hell out of it. If anything, it tells me what a fool I been to be alone for so many years. I haven't shared a meal with anyone since Malc MacDonald used ta come around – and that was years ago. That's a strange case. Still can't quite figure it out."

"What's the story?"

"I don't know if I should say or not. Probably shouldn't a brought it up."

"Why?"

"Well… I promised Malc I'd keep it to myself."

"Oh Christ, Art… are you trying to torture me? I'm a writer. You've hooked me. What's the story?"

"I'm not tryin to tease ya, Marty… it just popped up. Let me think about it, OK?"

"All right… but I'm going to keep buggin you about it… I promise."

"You do that… course it won't do ya any good. I'm real good at keepin quiet… had a lot a practice."

Art smiled. Marty returned it… then wiggled his eyebrows to indicate his intent to ask again sometime.

CHAPTER FIVE

It struck Marty as odd that mountain men seemed to have routines almost as rigid as his was in L.A. As the first week passed, Marty noticed that the days were spent according to a set schedule. Not having much else to do, he watched Art, closely, during their first full day together, out of curiosity, as to what mountain men do with themselves all day. Early in the morning, Marty was awakened by the sound of Art making coffee... water running – metal can hitting the sink top – porcelain clinking – kindling being broken – match being struck. Then the toilet flushed. Art let Ben out the door. He then drank his coffee and read a magazine. After he finished several cups of coffee, he put a plastic razor in his pocket, took a towel and a bar of soap and went out the door. Marty looked at his watch... six thirty. Art came back about seven thirty. He cooked them some breakfast – eggs, biscuits with butter and jelly, smoked meat, and coffee. Marty learned that Art cooked biscuits, once a week – on Sunday – in a Dutch oven that he hung over the fire. After breakfast, Art would go out to check his traps. He trapped a variety of small furry animals to sell their pelts in town. He was back at noon for lunch, usually consisting of meat, biscuits, cold tea, and an apple, to top it off.

After lunch, Art, Marty, and Ben would sit on the front porch for about an hour and shoot the breeze, and Art would smoke his first pipe full of tobacco for the day. After that, Art would leave to go fishing. There were several nearby fishing ponds with large populations of bass and pike... and a number of streams, swimming with trout. Art and Ben would usually get home at about four thirty or five o'clock, bearing the catch of the day for dinner, which Art would panfry with some onions. After dinner, they'd go back out on the porch with their coffee – talk and sit and look, until dark, while Art smoked several more pipe bowls. Art kept a checker board for his rare visitors, who were so inclined, and the two of them got into the immediate routine of playing until eleven o'clock, or so, under the light of a hanging lantern. Being the first he'd played since grade school, Marty lost nearly every game. He suspected that Art let him win the few games, that he did, so he wouldn't get too discouraged.

The days passed with little variation, and after the novelty of this new lifestyle wore off, Marty gradually began feeling more and more impatient and bored. With a cast on his leg, he couldn't join Art in his daily duties, and couldn't go very far on his own. He began to wonder if he could actually endure a couple of months of this life. Marty had always been the sort of person who was constantly on the go, for as long as he could remember. Never in his life had he stayed in one place for more than a few waking hours... let alone weeks or months. At certain moments, during that first week, Marty actually had thoughts that he might go insane if he didn't get away from that cabin and do something... go somewhere. After all, he was a busy writer from a sprawling, manic city. He was always talking to lots of people... driving around... on the Internet... looking for story leads. Here he was, now... alone on a mountain top with an old man and a dog, sixty miles from nowhere, with absolutely nothing to do. By the beginning of the second week, Marty had resolved to tell Art that he was sorry... but this just wasn't going to work. He was, somehow, going to get to the nearest airport and fly back to L.A.... back to civilization, people, noise, and activity. As noon approached and with it, Art's predictable and timely arrival, Marty was getting ready to break the news to Art, which he knew Art would take badly. It had become very apparent to Marty that Art was thoroughly enjoying his company. Marty felt bad about leaving, but knew he simply had to go. Awaiting Art's arrival and heavy with a guilty conscience, something very odd occurred.

Marty was suddenly overcome with a peculiar feeling of slowing down... as though a tightly wound rubber band inside him had just untwisted. It was one of the peculiar sensations he ever remembered experiencing, and he wasn't sure if he was frightened or happy. His breathing slowed down. His mind felt as though it had been thrown from a rapidly spinning merry-go-round to the profound stillness of the ground. Everything about him seemed to slow to a crawl... coming into a synchronization with the unnoticeable movement of the sun across the sky and the speed of growing grass. A peace descended upon Marty, such as he had never before experienced. His constant sense of urgency to be, always, somewhere other than where he was, dissipated, then vanished entirely. His muscles relaxed... his inner being lost its stiffness and became soft and elastic. He felt a never-before-experienced sense of contentedness. His face muscles melted into a pleasant, innate smile.

Marty had never felt like this in his entire life. It was totally new – but strangely familiar – as though he had once been like this, long before his most distant memories. He felt, inside, for the first time, the peace that he had seen in Art's eyes. He suddenly understood why Art was so healthy and so young. He knew, for the first time, what it was like to feel really well. He realized that he'd been sick for a long, long time... mentally and physically... without knowing it. He didn't know it because he had never known what it was like to be truly well. Suddenly, the thought of returning to his life in L.A. made him feel ill – like reliving a terrible sickness or a nightmare. He looked out at the distant mountain peaks... feeling as though he were seeing them for the first time. He found himself actually looking at them and thinking about them in the same moment – not looking with eyes, with his mind elsewhere, as he had always done before. He became aware of sounds and smells – the feel of his own fingertips – as if he had just discovered them. Marty felt as though he were waking up from a very long, frantic dream and seeing the real world for the first time.

Under the influence of this profound reverie, Marty felt an irrepressible urge to write about how he was feeling. He wanted to write for the reasons that a poet writes... to lay feelings – too large to hold inside – onto paper. He had never wanted to write for this reason before. It had just been his work... a job... a way to make a living. Whatever he was about to write, now, it mattered not to him, if any other eyes, besides his, ever beheld it. It wasn't for sale or for anyone but himself. He hastily clomped on his crutches into the cabin and dug out pen and paper. Back on his porch chair, Marty began to write a poem – the first poem he had ever written. He had always looked upon poets with suspicion and disdain – feeling that they were snobs... trying to be cryptic and mysterious... wanting others to believe they had knowledge of life secrets unknown to anyone else – writing verse that no one else would understand... with readers who would pretend they did understand, to claim membership in this elite inner-circle of knowledge. Marty now felt what true poets must surely feel. He wrote what he felt. He didn't try to be mysterious. He only tried to match words and rhythms to the contours of his being. If someone else were to read his words and try to feel his rhythms and didn't understand, that was all right... it wasn't for them. If it was mysterious to others... that was because they didn't understand – not because he wanted to be obscure. Marty became so engrossed in his poem that he failed to notice Art and Ben arriving home.

"Workin on a story, Marty?"

Marty looked up and quickly closed his tablet.

"No... just putting down some thoughts, Art. What did you get?"

"Six beaver... beautiful coats."

"Don't you sometimes feel bad?... trapping them I mean. I mean, they're such pretty animals and they must suffer in those traps before they finally die."

Art didn't answer. Instead, he sat down and took out his pipe, filled it, tamped the tobacco with his middle finger and lit it. As always, he took several puffs to ensure the coals were stoked, tamped it and lit it a second time. Snapping shut the metal lid of his Zippo with a muffled click and sliding it into his front right pocket, he looked out into the distance for a few moments. Having apparently resolved something in his mind – and still looking straight ahead – he began a story.

"When I first came ta this mountain, I never killed an animal before. I killed human beings. Shot four Germans in France... young boys my age... good lookin boys. It made me sick. I cried over and over about it. I never wanted to kill anything else again in my life. After spendin a lot of time up here, though… thinkin and rememberin and considerin… I finally put things inta perspective. I finally understood that killin, itself, isn't bad. It's *why* ya kill somethin that matters. I killed those four boys… probably good boys with a mother and father that loved em – boys that didn't know me… that had nothin against me, personally. They were drug out there just like I was… too young and stupid ta know any better. They were told ta kill us and we were told ta kill them. They were told we were bad people and we were told that they were the bad ones."

Art paused. The look on his face connoted that the story he was about to tell, held very painful memories for him.

"I was layin in some brush one day when these four boys come along. I was hidin. I heard em talkin and laughin… sounded just like me an my buddies when we got together. When they saw me layin there – I wasn't hidden very well – it scared the shit out of em – and me too. We all froze. They all just looked at me… and then at each other… didn't know what ta do. Neither did I. We'd all been practicing ta shoot someone… but at that moment, I felt like we should just talk ta each other or somethin… not shoot each other. I mean we were just five teenagers. I had never shot anybody and I'm sure from the way they were actin, they hadn't neither. From the look in their eyes, I could see they felt just like me. I started to get up ta say somethin… God knows what, since I didn't speak German… when one of em got scared and started ta grab for his gun… hangin over his shoulder. Without thinkin, I threw myself back down on the ground and started shootin… just like they trained me ta do. They weren't more'n ten feet from me. It was awful. The bullets were hittin em in the face and arms and legs… hit one of em right in the eye. I had one of these machine guns – Tommy Guns we used to call em – and they just had standard issue rifles, ya see. They didn't have a chance. They were all screamin and started to run. I just kept firin. Hit em in their backs and in the back of the legs and the back of their heads. They fell down… bleedin… parts of their heads and faces were missin. All four were layin on that dirt road… twitchin… bleedin… cryin… moanin. I finally got up and went over to em.

They had tears in their eyes. They looked really scared... afraid to die. They were tryin to say somethin to me and ta each other."

Overcome with emotion, Art's eyes glistened with tears. He cleared his throat and went on.

"I started tellin em I was sorry. I was cryin... sayin I was sorry. I bent down and touched each one of em. They'd stopped movin. Their faces were froze up... their eyes open and starin. That was the first time I ever seen a dead person – cept my gramma in her casket when I was a little boy – and I was the one who killed em. I started sayin out loud, 'What right did I have ta kill ya? What right?' I dropped my gun, right there, and started runnin – sayin over and over, 'I'm sorry, I'm sorry.' I'd been separated from my platoon... that's why I was hidin in the first place. I didn't know where I was runnin to. I coulda been runnin straight toward the Germans for all I knew. I ran and ran... cryin all the way, sayin I'm sorry. I finally came on some Americans. Damn lucky they didn't shoot me. I was just about hysterical. It wasn't until evening that I could tell anybody what happened and what platoon I was with."

Art relit his pipe and paused before he resumed the story.

"Well... I eventually got back to my platoon but I wasn't any good after that. I couldn't sleep... couldn't eat... was cryin all the time. They eventually sent me back to headquarters and from there to a hospital in England. I still didn't straighten out... was there for four months. They had these psychiatrists talkin to me. One soldier told me I better straighten out... said that blood n guts Patton had slapped a GI a few days before for cryin. They finally gave up on me and recommended a medical discharge. The day before they discharged me, on what they called a section eight – which meant they thought I was nuts – they awarded me the Bronze Star... for bravery... for killin those nice young boys. On the ship home, I threw it overboard. When I got home, I took off my uniform and dog tags and put em in the trash can... everything – even my boots and hat and even my GI underwear. I said goodbye ta my old man the next day and headed for the West.

And you know what? I even got a lifetime pension from the army... all for killin those boys and gettin nutty about it."

"With the money I had sent home while we were in combat, I bought me an old De Soto and headed west. Didn't know where the hell, exactly, I was goin. Just by chance I ended up in Bear Stump. One day, an old fellah, sittin beside me in the old diner – they tore it down years ago – said he had a cabin back in the mountains and he'd sell it ta me, real cheap. I bought it – sight unseen. This is it... well, this is where it was. The original one was fallin down, so I went ahead n pulled it down, rather than havin it fall on my head one night. I built this one here from scratch... and here we sit."

Art paused again, relit his pipe, and smiled at Marty.

"Guess this is a hell of a long way around ta answer your question, huh?"

"No Art... I'm enjoying it. Go ahead."

"Well anyway, back ta this killin thing. I was buyin all my food in town back then – cept for berries and such that I'd pick. Livin up here, though, I began ta watch the animals. They kill each other all the time... bears and eagles pickin up fish to eat... foxes eatin moles and mice... spiders trappin insects in their webs... mountain lions and wolves killin anything they damn well please. I started thinkin... now are they bad?... do they feel bad like I did about those German boys? That's when I realized they were killin because that's what they hafta do ta live. I realized after a few years – though it's as plain as a pimple on your face – that everything that's alive kills something else to stay that way... people included. Even when you eat plants and things... you're killin em so you can stay alive. I began ta see that the only bad killin is when you don't have to do it for livin."

Art turned his body toward Marty, indicating he was getting to the central point of the story.

"Killin those young German boys was bad killin. We were just told ta go kill each other... and we did it just because we were told. I coulda left those boys go by ta grow up, and they coulda left me pass, too. We didn't need ta kill each other. We just did it cause they told us to. Out here, I kill... just like the other animals... to make my way. There's nothin wrong with it... it's actually kind of a holy thing – livin things givin their life so somethin else can stay alive. That's why, every time I kill something ta keep me goin, I say to it, 'Thanks my friend.' No kiddin... no matter if it's a bear, a deer, or a fish or whatever – I say, 'Thank you my friend,' cause it's givin its life for me. That's more n most folks'll do. When's the last time you heard a fella eatin a hamburger thank the cow for dyin for em? If some mountain lion or wolf killed me, I'd bear him no bad feelins. As goofy as it sounds... I don't even get mad at germs when I get sick either. They're just doin what all the rest of us are tryin ta do... stay alive... have offspring. Course I'll take medicine ta kill the little buggers... but with no malice. It's them or me... their life or my life. I don't kill anything, just ta kill it. I mean it... you just watch... not a fly or spider or an ant, if I can help it. Course if I see a Black Widow crawlin in my cabin, I'll squash er. She might be climbin in my bed some night... uninvited."

Art paused again. His eyes searched the horizon to see if he had covered it all. From his final expression it appeared that he had.

"That's the story, Marty."

Art thought about it, laughed, and added to his sentence.

"... the long story."

"Quite a story... and quite a philosophy, Art. You might make an article after all."

"I don know, Marty... my whole story is the war and this mountain... that's it. Kinda borin if ya ask me."

"Well, you know Art, a lot of people think their story is boring...

only to find out that other people think it's fascinating. You never know."

"So whata ya workin on, my friend?"

Art pointed to Marty's yellow tablet.

Marty hesitated and felt the rising heat of embarrassment.

"Well… to tell you the truth, Art, I was starting a poem."

"Didn't know you were a poet, Marty."

"I'm not… I wasn't. This is the first poem I've ever started."

"What's the occasion?"

Marty looked away from Art, then stared for a few moments at the roof of the porch, then looked back at Art.

"I don't want this to sound dramatic… but a few minutes before you got back, I was ready to tell you I was leaving… going back to L.A. I felt as though I couldn't take anymore of this isolation on a mountaintop. I'm used to activity… lots of people and things to do. I was already to tell you all this."

"So? Did ya change your mind?"

"Yes… as a matter of fact I did. Well, I didn't exactly change my mind… my mind was sort of changed for me. It's weird, Art… and I told you I don't want to be dramatic."

Marty paused.

"As I was sitting here… thinking of how to tell you I was leaving… something happened to me. It's hard to explain. This feeling of quiet and peace came over me. I felt as though I slowed down all of a sudden. Rather than feeling like I was a prisoner on this mountain, like I was just before that, I felt as though I was free for the first time in my life. All of a sudden, instead of getting the hell out of here as fast as I could, I felt as though I never wanted to leave... never go back to that rat hole in southern California. I don't know, Art... maybe it's high altitude intoxication or something. Maybe it'll wear off, but at the moment, that's how I feel. Little weird, huh?"

"Oh, not so weird, Marty. I do some readin... an I remember certain things that seem true ta me. I'm thinkin of that Thoreau fella just now. He said that we all lead lives of quiet desperation, er somethin along that line. I think that's true... that's why I remember it. I look around at all the people in town and read about what goes on in the world and I think... most of these people are really crazy. They're in a helluva hurry all the time but don't know where they're goin. In a hurry ta get through college... ta get a job... ta get a house... a couple a cars... a bigger house... have a family... get them grown up as fast as they can... ta make as much money as fast as they can. I think to myself, what er they doin all this for? Most everyone I meet is miserable as hell. It's as though they think they're in a race – and after the race is over, they'll be happy. Problem seems ta be that the race never gets over with. Even these retired folks are in a God-awful hurry, Marty. I see em comin through the Stump, once in a while... and even though they have all the time in the world, they're in this big hurry ta drive as many places as they can... see as many things as they can... like they were racin somebody. Then they get cancer or a stroke or somethin and die. I just don't get the point."

Cocking his head to one side, it appeared that Art felt he needed to clarify some things.

"Now I'm not sayin that I have the perfect life, mind you. I told ya how I feel about that. I've missed a lot in life. But I never felt desperate. I felt sad and lonely sometimes... but not desperate. I never felt like I was in a hurry or in a race with anybody. Most everybody I meet has this desperate look in their eye... like they're kinda miserable but can't seem to figger out why. They look around and see that everybody else is doin what they're doin...

and figger they can't all be wrong. I feel sorry for people, Marty. You had that same desperate look, yourself, when I first met ya. I felt sorry for ya, but I also kinda liked somethin about ya ... maybe it was your singin."

Art smiled and Marty laughed.

"Anyway, probably what happened to ya... is this mountain. It's just so big and heavy that it sometimes grabs ya and holds ya still for a minute... long enough for you to get a gander at how nice things look when you're not in such a damn rush."

"Yeah... I think you're right Art. It sounds kind of funny to say... but this mountain is kind of big and heavy. The biggest, heaviest thing I've ever been around. I guess, given enough time, it's bound to slow you down."

"How bout some lunch, my young friend?"

Marty smiled. He realized, for the first time, that he loved this old man.

"Sounds perfect, old friend."

CHAPTER SIX

During the weeks that followed, Marty's growing confidence on his crutches provided him a corresponding increase in his range of travel, and he began to accompany Art on many of his daily duties. He fished for the first time in his life. Art nearly wet his pants watching Marty try to get a fish off his hook. Their friendship deepened, strengthened, and broadened. They even adopted special names for each other... a sure sign of intimacy. Sitting in their respective chairs, one Sunday afternoon in June – Sunday being Art's "day off" – Art surprised Marty by bringing up Malc MacDonald's name again. Although Marty had threatened to bring up the matter again, he hadn't, out of respect for Art's promise to Malc, and the consideration that comes from a true friendship.

"Remember I was tellin you about Malc MacDonald a while back?"

"Yeah... I do, Art. Why?"

"Well... I don't feel right keepin it all a secret from you. You're the honest-to-God first friend I ever had in my life and I always said that if I ever had a best friend I'd trust him and never keep any secrets from em. You're my friend, Martaroo... and I trust you. I know you'd never do the wrong thing."

Art's kind words instantly grew a lump in Marty's throat.

"That's a really nice thing to say, King Arthur. To be honest with you, you're the best friend I've had in a long, long time. Everybody goes around talking about their friends... but they're not really friends, they're just people you know or you work with or do things with. The last time I remember having a real friend was Ronny Anderson... in the fourth grade. He wasn't just someone I knew – I really loved him. Then we grew up. It was funny but when we got older we were sort of embarrassed about being such close friends when we were little... and then not being that way later on. It sounds kind of strange – but we both sensed it. We avoided each other when we got older, so we didn't have to talk or be embarrassed. But this thing about Malc MacDonald, Art... you really don't have to tell me about it if you gave your word on it. I was curious about it but – really – it's OK if you don't tell me... no big deal, King Arthur."

"Well it's a big thing ta me Martaroo... I don want any secrets."

"OK... what's the Malc MacDonald story, then?"

As was his custom before telling a significant story, Art filled his pipe... got it lit and tamped it just right... cleared his throat, looked up for a few minutes, and said, "Well..."

"Well... this was about... oh... let's see here... thirty or so years ago. One day a fella showed up here and introduced himself... Malcolm MacDonald, he said, was his name. Said he went by Malc. Was a mountain of a man... about six-five and built like a brick shit house. Strong as an ox... but a real gentleman and smart as hell. Was a Scotsman. Talked like it too. A real good lookin fella. Had reddish hair and a beard the same color... and these really deep blue eyes. Said he moved to the U.S. from Glasgow. He was a doctor. Said he had been a pricey surgeon from Boston. Apparently he screwed up on an operation on his best friend's little girl... a little two-year old. Was just a minor, little operation, he said, but somethin went wrong an the little thing died... was his friend's only child. His friend's wife took it so bad she killed herself with sleepin pills. His friend... never did tell me his name – and if he did... I forgot – anyway, he was another Scotsman... they grew up together... best friends... you know. His friend and wife. . . with their little girl... flew over to Boston from Glasgow cause they didn't trust anybody but Malc to operate on their daughter."

"Well... Malc's friend couldn't get over it and neither could Malc. Malc kept apologizin to em – over-n-over. His friend said he forgave em... but Malc, I guess, couldn't forgive himself. He said he just couldn't walk back into the operatin room anymore, an one day he just gave er up... everything. Kinda like what I did. He come out here, then. Knew the area pretty well, already. Was one of these outdoor types... campin, mountain climbin, and the like. He'd been around these parts quite a bit. He decided, he said, he was takin to the woods and never goin back. Now he didn't tell me all this the first day I met em... I guess he kept comin back until he decided he could trust me. One day he asked me for a favor. Said he had put some money in the bank in Bear Stump. Asked me if I'd be willin to get some things for em in the Stump once in a while. Said I could take as much extra as I thought I needed for my trouble. Said he was plannin on cuttin all his ties ta the rest of the world. Didn't wanna ever talk to or see anybody else the rest a his life. Kinda extreme, if ya know what I mean."

"I'll say. Was this Malc kind of loony?"

"Nah... not at all... just a really sad guy. I think he was servin a kinda penance for his sins, ya know?"

"So he was all by himself?"

"Well that's what I thought at first. Anyway, ta get back ta the story... I agreed ta do it... told him I didn't want paid for it... would just pick up things for him when I went into town... wouldn't cost me anymore one way or the other. He thanked me for it and said he'd leave the money thing up to me, but I was welcome, he said, to take whatever I needed. He signed this bank card, puttin my name on the account with him... and a letter ta the bank manager, and gave it ta me... ta use at the bank ta take out what money I needed for his supplies."

"The next day, he showed up with a woman... introduced her as his wife. Called her Ethy. She was real tall – like Malc – and thin and real pretty... a black lookin woman who said she was from one of those islands down near South America... the West Indies... or whatever you call em. She told the name of it, but I don't remember anymore. Had a funny way of talkin... course, so did Malc. She kinda sounded French, but not exactly. Malc said he had met her when he spent some time in a hospital down there... doin whatever they call that before you're allowed to be a doctor."

"His residency?"

"Yeah... I think that was it. Malc said that was the last time we'd likely meet face ta face. He had me walk with him to a place about two miles from here. There was this big rock formation with an overhang, way up on the cliff, n under this overhang, there was a cave that's about forty feet wide... and fifty feet or so into the rock. Malc told me if he needed some things, he'd hang a little red cloth outside this cave. Said he'd have a box in the cave with a lid on it, for me ta put the supplies in. Had a lid ta keep the critters out. Told me I didn't have ta check it everyday... about once a month was plenty, he said. We set the first day a each month as the day. Course I told em... come winter, I couldn't make it inta town every month... might get snowed in for a hell of a long time. He said he knew that. He said he'd put his list a supplies he needed in the box, then he made me swear I'd never tell anyone about him or this arrangement of ours... which I did... and which I'm breakin this minute ta my best friend. That was the last I ever saw a Malc MacDonald... that day... more'n thirty years ago."

"Wow, Art. That's a hell of a story. Are you still taking things to him?"

"Well... yes and no. I'm still takin things but I'm not so sure Malc's around anymore."

"What? What do you mean, Art?"

"This is where it gets a little screwy, Martaroo. Things went just as planned for the first two years. Malc'd order things like toothpaste and toothbrushes and shells for his rifles and huntin arrows... fruit and vegetables. He ordered a slew of books too... on everything you could imagine... but mainly, philosophy and religion and history. He was always askin for tablets and pens too. An then, later he began orderin picture paintin paint. Ethy'd order female stuff... a hairbrush now and then... ah... an well you know those things women need every month."

"I know, Art."

"Shoulda seen the look they gave me the first time I brought em to the counter at the Bear Stump Grocery."

"I could imagine. What did you say?"

"I said I was doin some shoppin fer some neighbors... which I was. Figgered it was none a their business, anyway. So... after about two years, Malc started, all of a sudden, writin down for cloth diapers... then about six months later he started askin for jars a baby food. Next thing I noticed was that about a year after he started askin for baby things, he stopped askin for anything for Ethy. That was it. Never asked for anything else for her again. I don't know what the hell happened... whether she got tired a livin in the wilds and left... or died... or what. Just don't know. Maybe she just stopped askin for things... but I doubt it. It's not like a woman, ya know. Well now... after about a year, Malc stopped askin for baby food and started askin for more fruit and vegetables. And asked for little kid books... the kind you'd get for a little boy. Funny thing... Malc never asked for any clothes for the boy. Guess he was makin his own for em or he was runnin around naked – one or the other. Never asked for any new clothes for himself, either. When he was orderin for Ethy, she'd occasionally ask for female underthings and the like. Now about... oh... maybe twelve years or so after I last saw Malc and Ethy, the writin on the note changed all of a sudden. It was a kid's hand – definitely a kid's hand. He started askin only for just fruit and vegetables and shells and arrows. Oh, and he started askin for drawin paper and drawin pencils... and then paint and brushes – the kind you do pictures with, like Malc used ta do years before."

"I'm guessin it was the kid, a course, that was leavin the notes. The food order was cut way down – a lot less than what a grown man and a teenage boy'd eat. Now there's the mystery. What the hell happened to Malc? I got worried. I figgered that if he was hurt and couldn't write... he could at least still eat... but there wasn't a big enough order for two. So I started goin up ta the cave and watchin for somebody... to ask about Malc. Never had any luck. Waited around all day, near the end of the month, a bunch a times. No one ever showed – but damn if that red cloth didn't appear again... and a note in the box. Isn't that somethin?"

"So... are you still getting notes?"

"Sure am... regular as always. The writin has changed... looks older now, but still the same person. He started askin for a lot of books when he got older, like the kind Malc used to. The day I brought you out here, as a matter a fact, I had just picked up an order for... whoever it is – Malc's son, I guess. Delivered it the next day. After breakfast. You probably didn't even notice. I kinda slipped out on ya... I was still keepin this from ya then. That's the story, Mart."

"Jesus, Arthur... that's one hell of a story. Make's me want to get back to writing."

"Now I said you'd do the right thing. You can't go puttin this in some national magazine... Christ almighty, Mart – they'd have a manhunt for this fella. Who knows, someone might suspect there was a murder or somethin."

"Yes, shit, you're right, Art. Fuck. Best story I've ever come across and I can't write it."

"Sorry, Mart."

"So how do you figure it, Art? I mean... what do you think is going on? Do you think that there's a guy up in these mountains that was born here and has lived by himself... all by himself... since he was something like twelve years old?"

"If you want my best guess – this is it. I thought about this a thousand times over the years... had lots of time, ya know. I figure... and this is strictly my guess... that Ethy had a baby boy and then died when he was about a year old... maybe from givin birth to another baby... I dunno. I just can't figger her goin away and leavin Malc and her baby. I also figger that when the boy was twelve or thirteen, Malc died. If he was just sick and then got better, he'd a started leavin the notes again himself... and probably would have left a little explanation as to why there was another handwritin on the list. So, yep, like you said... I figger there's a man up there... somewhere on this mountain, that was born here and has never talked to another human soul except his father in his whole life. I also figger he hasn't been with another human soul since his father died... some twenty years ago."

"Jesus! Can you imagine? What a story he'd have to tell. What would a person be like who's lived in the wilderness for his entire life and been alone for twenty years? Damn! That is something. How old do you figure he is... thirty or so?"

"Yeah... about that. Thirty... thirty-one or so. Maybe even thirty-three."

"When's the last time you tried to find out what's going on?"

"Oh, hell... it's been years."

"Can we try again?"

"I guess so, Mart... but you'll have a hell of a time with that cast... gettin up there. Doubt if you could do it."

"This is coming off in about three weeks. Can we try then?"

"Yeah... but it'll be a while after you get that cast off before you'll be doin any walkin. Ever see a leg after a cast comes off?"

"No."

"It'll look like the upper part of Popeye's arms."

"What do you mean?"

"Popeye? You know. Oh shit, never mind. In other words, it'll be shriveled and shrunk like a prune."

"No shit?"

"No shit."

CHAPTER SEVEN

Over the next several weeks, the mysterious mountain man was all Marty thought about or wanted to talk about. Finally, Art got so tired of it he told Marty to either talk about something else or shut up. Marty capitulated. To get his mind off his new obsession, Marty tried his hand at sketching. On their daily chores, Art would carry the sketch book he bought for Marty in Bear Stump, while Marty followed along on his crutches. He had gotten so accustomed to walking on them that... except for really rocky terrain or steep hills... Marty could just about keep up, without slowing down Art and Ben much. While Art would do his trapping or fishing or occasional hunting, Marty would find himself a good view and a comfortable seat, and sketch. As with the poetry, this was the first time Marty had done anything artistic. He turned out to be a fairly decent artist. Art told him so, anyway.

Eight weeks to the day, after he had broken his leg, Art loaded Marty into the back of the pickup and headed to Bear Stump Medical Center to get his cast off. Not only was Marty shocked to find a shrunken and shriveled leg under his cast but found that the prunish skin stunk to high heavens as well. Marty was greatly disappointed that he wasn't able to walk out of the office after his cast was off. That's how he had pictured it. As a matter of fact, he discovered that he had walked much better with the cast on, than off. Without it, he had no strength, whatsoever, in his left leg. The doctor told him he'd need physical therapy... a couple of weeks of it before he'd be able to do any walking at all. After much discussion, it was decided that Marty would stay behind in the Stump as an inpatient in the small, physical therapy wing of the medical center. Art persuaded Marty that there'd be no way he could get his leg back in shape on the mountain. Marty reluctantly agreed. As Art pulled away in the old pickup with Ben's big head hanging out of the passenger window, Marty felt his lower lip pucker up and tears form in his eyes. He was embarrassed to realize that he felt like a five-year-old being left at kindergarten on the first day of school.

Working with a female therapist, Marty was instantly reminded that he hadn't been around a woman in several months. As the first meal at Art's cabin became a culinary masterpiece by Marty's famishment – being around his first female in months, made her seem sublimely perfect and perfectly irresistible. Deprivation had honed Marty's senses to a razor's edge and to him, this woman's smell was sublime, her looks, exquisite. Her touch was electric to his skin, her voice – a symphony, her body – a work of art, her movement as graceful and seductive as a cat. Marty drank in her femaleness and reveled in her oppositeness. His flame lit, it compelled him to find a way to touch off a brilliant blaze before its inevitable extinguishment. Charm being the unprincipled ally of desire, Marty entertained, impressed, promised, amused, complimented, enthralled, captivated, and endeared... to the singular, impersonal, inevitable end. The flame – having blazed brightly unto total consummation – lifted the translucent, glowing veil of passion and the transient goddess fell to earth – he knowing she would – she pretending she wouldn't.

The instinctual demands of the species, thus honored, but the extended promise unfulfilled, Marty silently suffered his own guilt and embarrassment... and endured the woman's predictable anger and humiliation for the remaining days of his therapy. After the fact, as men do, Marty soon felt that the moment of white-hot passion wasn't worth the price inflicted by the woman scorned... knowing, full-well, as he thought this, that he would, unquestionably, do it again, given the same circumstances. Leaving the medical center with Art – walking stiffly with the assistance of a cane – Marty felt immensely relieved and liberated. He had never been happier in his life than when he saw Art and Ben pull up in front of the Bear Stump Medical Center.

For the first time, Marty rode in the cab... Ben grudgingly shoved into the middle of the seat, trying in vain to get his head out the window, drooling all over Marty's pants in the process.

"For Christ's sake, Ben... give me a break!"

Marty pushed Ben's head toward Art.

"You're in his seat, Martaroo."

"Look at my pants… he's drooling all over me."

"Just wants his head out the window. You're in the way."

Recognizing the hopelessness of the situation, Marty slid toward the middle of the seat and patted the now empty space beside the window.

"C'mon, Ben. Here's your seat."

Ben stepped across Marty, strategically placing one large paw and the full weight of his body directly onto Marty's groin, while retaking his rightful and traditional place at the window.

"Ah! Damn it, Ben… watch where the fuck you're walking! Christ!"

For a brief moment, Marty suspected Ben's step was intentional and malevolent. Looking at Ben's drooping jowls and hanging tongue, however, he quickly dismissed the thought. Watching these comic machinations between Ben and Marty, Art started laughing so hard he had tears in his eyes and could hardly see the road. Every time he thought he had it under control, he'd start all over again. The contagion eventually infected Marty, who added further momentum to the comic madness with his own laughter. Ben turned his head to briefly survey this uncivil interruption of normal truck-cab peace, then stoically returned to his lookout duties. Finally the comic kettle ran out of steam – enough, at least, to allow an attempt at conversation.

"Well Martaroo… how was your hospital stay?"

"Not too bad, Art. First few days were painful as hell. These therapists are a little bit sadistic, you know? You tell them it hurts and they smile and keep pushing your leg even harder. I swore at a couple of them. And..."

Marty flashed a coy smile at Art.

"And what... what the hell are you smiling about?"

Art mirrored Marty's smile as he spoke.

"Well... King Arthur... your boy got laid while he was there."

With this, Marty's smile transformed itself into the swaggering smirk of a conquering braggadocio.

"The hell you say. At a hospital?"

"Right in my private room."

"Get the hell outa here."

"I'm not shitting you, Art... it was one of the therapists. Took me about a week of charm... I was horny as hell. Course afterwards... when things got back to normal, she was nasty as panther piss to me. I couldn't wait to get out of there."

"That's the way it is with women, Mart. They know, all along, that what you're after is in their pants... but they go along with it – thinkin they can parlay that inta somethin more. When they can't, they're ornery as hell. If it wasn't for the fools men make outa themselves to get some pussy, women'd have no hold over em, whatsoever. Their pussy is the only thing that gets the man in the door... they know that... and they play that card all the way to the altar. But once they get their ring and house and kids and half interest in everything the poor guy owns, that pussy slams shut tighter than a banker's asshole. By then, it costs the man so much trouble and money to get outa the mess he's in, he resigns himself to it and makes his own life while she has hers. She's got her house and kids and furniture and your paycheck and lady friends to gossip with... he's got his job and the bar he drinks at... and if he's lucky, some female that's been around the track a time or two

– that'll be satisfied with a romp in the sack once in awhile with no strings attached."

"For a man who's lived on a mountain his whole life, you sure have women figured out, King Arthur."

"Well, most men are so close ta the page they can't read the writin. They're miserable as hell but can't figure out how they got that way. I've always been at such a distance from women that I could sorta study em – kinda like a specimen… thinkin about em with my big head… not the little one, like most men."

"Now that you bring it up, Arthur… how have you gotten along without a woman all these years… or do you sneak into the Stump for a little trim once in awhile?"

"Nah… I haven't been with a woman since the war, when I used to pay for a whore once in awhile. I told ya I didn't have the nerve ta talk to a woman… but those French whores… they come right up to ya and do all the talkin. They were real nice, actually… real friendly and considerate. They spent a lot of time with ya… talkin about anything ya wanted to talk about. After you had sex… they'd still be just as friendly… not lookin for anything else from you… not tryin to make ya feel guilty or make ya promise to call em again. It was a real, uncomplicated relationship between a man and a woman. If I could have that sort of setup with a woman, I probably woulda brought a woman up to the mountain with me… but what whore'd make that kinda deal? Not their cup a tea. The way I figgered it… I could go around bein horny and miserable all the time – or get over it like a bad rash. So that's what I did… I got over it. Most men won't believe it… chasin pussy all the time like they do… but it isn't that hard. That's a secret that women'd kill to keep quiet… it'd throw the balance of nature all outa kilter. If men knew how easy it was ta get over needin pussy all the time… ninety percent of em would never get married and the species would die out in nothin flat. The power would shift real quick. Women always think with their big heads… always plottin and plannin – never let horniness cloud their brains. Hell… you've seen women, Mart – they could go without sex forever if they haf ta, and it wouldn't bother em a bit. Yeah... once you get over needin pussy, you'd be surprised how much different the world looks. You start appreciatin other things in life... like women do."

Art shook his head up and down, appearing to be affirming the veracity of what he was about to say.

"When I was still a young guy... still fair game for the women in the Stump... they'd start their dance with me, then realize I wasn't addicted ta pussy. Made em madder n hell... like I was breakin the rules or somethin... not playin fair, ya know? But, it's like bein an alcoholic... you can get the disease, again, if ya take even a little drink. Ya can't let'm work on ya too long. They'll eventually find a way ta break ya down. I never stayed around em long enough to get infected again. Must be the way these priests do it... at least the ones who don't get some lunch as a side order, if ya know what I mean."

"So a man can get over his addiction to pussy... you're serious?"

"Yesiree... I'm livin proof. You won't find skin magazines layin around my cabin... and me poundin my turtle all day. That's like bein an alcoholic... no control... no self respect. If you can't get control over your urges... you're a sad case."

"Maybe you're just not as horny as most of us, Art. I mean... I can't imagine the average guy swearing off pussy for life. If it was that easy... we'd all do it so we wouldn't have to put up with all the shit we go through to get it."

"Not every guy wants ta swear off it. Some guys are satisfied in givin up their life for access ta that little honey pot. Most don't know what they're givin up ta get pussy, permanently, from a woman. They just end up with a ring in their nose one day and can't remember how it got there. Me... I made a outright decision ta get along without it. I was comin up here ta live on a mountain by myself an it just wasn't gonna work if I was pinin away for a woman all the time. Believe me... back then I was as horny as the next guy. I just made a choice not ta be... that's all. I'm not any superman... anybody could do just the same if they really wanted to."

"I'll take your word for it, King Arthur. I just don't know if I'm ready to swear off pussy at the moment."

"It's a free country Martaroo... you do whatever floats your boat."

No other essential topics surfacing, Art put on his country station and hummed and drummed while Marty was lulled into semi-sleep by the air, heat, movement, and music. About twenty miles back Old Log Road, Art remembered what he wanted to tell Marty. He tapped Marty on the side of the knee.

"Mart... Mart... I just remembered what I wanted to tell ya."

"What?"

"The red cloth was out this mornin. First time since the day I found ya. I went and picked up the order this mornin, before I came and got ya."

"No shit, Art?"

"Yep. Same sort of order... but no books this time. Just toothpaste, soap, shells, fruit, and vegetables, some coffee... and some writin paper. Was plannin on deliverin it when we got back."

"Can I go along?"

"If you think you can make it. You're not lookin real spry with that cane. It's a real healthy climb."

"I'll be all right, Art."

Back at the cabin, Marty changed into some jeans and a sweatshirt. Art got the cardboard box with the supplies, and they started out to the cave with Ben in tow. Marty very soon discovered that Art hadn't been exaggerating about the difficulty of the journey. They had to climb and traverse an assortment of rocks, hills, streams, and crevices to get to the stone formation. A few times, on the trek, Art had to put down the box and help Marty along.

When they finally arrived at the formation, Art told Marty he'd better just wait there, at the bottom, for him… that the climb would be too tough for his leg. Marty's curiosity being a stronger suit than his common sense, he insisted he wanted to see what the cave looked like. Despite Art's best efforts to dissuade him, he remained adamant about going up. Art finally, and reluctantly, acquiesced. Ben located some shade and lapsed into a deep dog-nap to await his companions' return.

Art took the box up first, then returned to assist Marty on the climb. He was very wary of Marty's attempting the climb, with his weak leg, given the perils of the direct, vertical drop from a number of places along the climb, where a slip could be a totally unforgiving, likely fatal, mistake. Anticipating the possibility that Marty just might be foolish enough to want to make the climb, Art, before they departed the cabin, had thrown a rope into the cardboard box. Standing at the base of the formation, he tied a rope around his waist and the other end around Marty's.

"Do you really think this is necessary, Art? I mean I'm not a mountain climber… but I'm sure I can climb these rocks without killing myself. I mean, you just did it, carrying a box in your one arm."

"Better safe than sorry, Martaroo. Ya ready?"

"All set."

"Just stay behind me and don't get too much slack between us. If you slip, I don't want ya fallin ten feet, then the rope jerkin me into a ten-inch waistline. OK?"

"All right. Jesus, Art, I'm not going to fall."

"That's good, Marty."

Art started up the jagged rocks… climbing at a slow pace… turning, like a mother hen to see if Marty was all right. Marty kept telling Art to keep going… annoyed at his lack of confidence in him. At about the halfway mark of the ascent, Art stopped and placed his left foot on the edge of an enormous rock. In front of him was a gap of about four feet to another ledge. Below the gap was open air, dropping vertically, several hundred feet, to the sharp rocks, piled at the foot of the formation. Art looked back at Marty.

"This here's a little tricky, Mart. Ya gotta push off your left foot and jump over ta that slanted, flat spot… see?"

"Yes… I see."

"Ya gotta be careful… it slants back some and it's real easy ta lose your balance. Almost done it a couple a times, myself. What ya gotta do is grab the edge of that flat rock there… where the crack is, ta keep yourself from fallin back. See it?"

"Yes, Art… I see it. Don't worry."

"Well as soon as your foot hits the rock, stick your hand out and grab a hold. It'll keep ya from fallin. All right?

"Yes, Art… Jesus."

"OK, watch how I do it. Give me enough slack to make the jump… and make sure you're not standin on the rope."

Marty stepped toward Art… slacking the rope. He made sure the rope was free from snagging onto anything, including his own feet. Art paused for a few seconds then jumped gracefully to the slanted rock… sticking his hand into the space between the vertical rises – grasping the edge to demonstrate how it should be done, although he really didn't need it for this particular jump. He turned back to Marty.

"Now I'm gonna move back some… so you have enough space ta get your foot on the rock when ya land. Go ahead and get yourself on the edge there. Put your left foot up there first, OK? You all right?"

"Fine, Art."

"Remember… the slant'll throw ya back a bit so grab for this edge here."

Art reached and patted the edge between the two rocks.

"See it?"

"You already showed it to me, Art. Yes, I see it."

"OK… whenever you're ready, Mart."

Marty looked down at his left foot, then across the gap at the slanted rock – then straight down at the considerable drop to the rocks below. Looking down, his heart began to pound and he was reminded, once again, that he was not a brave man. Art sensed his hesitation.

"If you don't wanna… there's no shame in it. Lot'sa people are afraid a heights. Your left leg isn't too good, anyway… might not have the strength to make the jump, Mart. We can go back down an try this another time when you're feelin a little stronger. How bout we just do that… OK?"

Marty sensed that Art knew he was afraid, which embarrassed and angered him… knowing Art was right. This was, he knew, one of those moments of truth in a man's life. He could overcome his fear in triumph or succumb to it and rationalize his cowardice, as he had always done, with standard adages – only stupid men take unnecessary risks… there are no old and bold pilots… discretion is the better part of valor. He looked at the slanted rock and he was ready to jump. He looked down and he wasn't. Back and forth he went. Art remained silent. He understood this poignant male moment. Suddenly Marty looked at the slanted rock with clenched teeth, narrowed eyes, and jumped. His atrophied left leg muscles didn't do an adequate job of pushing him across the gap and he landed on the slanted rock with only about the front four inches of his tennis shoe making contact. A moment of blind panic shot, wildly, through Marty's brain and body. He felt a scream emerging from his throat that couldn't find a voice. For a moment he was precariously perched on the very edge of the slanted rock with both his arms rotating backwards... teetering on going forward, toward Art... then backwards, down the precipice and down to his death. The backward movement began gaining momentum and he sensed he was going to fall. He glanced for one fleeting moment, backward and down, into terrifying chasm and felt certain he was going to die. Suddenly, something slammed into his chest. He turned to see Art's left fist grasping the front of his sweatshirt... pulling him toward the slanted rock. Art somehow overcame Marty's backward momentum and pulled him far enough toward him that Marty could get his right foot to join his left on the slanted rock. Tightly gripping the split rock's edge with his right hand, he pulled Marty further toward him... away from the slanted rock's edge. Slowly, Art edged backward... maintaining his vise-like grip on Marty's sweatshirt all the while... until he reached the level part of the rock. Mart kept edging, inches at a time, toward him. He finally got within a few inches of Art and threw his arms around him... his body trembling all over... his breath coming in loud sharp gasps. Art held him tightly... speaking to him in soft, comforting tones.

"You're all right, Mart. It's all over. Take it easy... just relax. Take a few deep breaths. You're all right, partner."

Slowly Marty relaxed. He eventually pulled his head away from Art's chest and looked at his face. Art smiled like a father, comforting a young son who had just awakened from a nightmare. He tried to lighten the moment.

"This savin your life stuff is wearin me out, Mart."

Mart began to half laugh... half cry. He sniffed... wiped his eyes and nose, and cleared his throat enough to attempt a reply that was intended to have been witty, but was betrayed by his hoarse, cracking voice.

"Just wanted to keep you on your toes, King Arthur."

Art laughed and hugged Marty in a tight, affectionate embrace. This was the love from a father, for which Marty had always yearned, and the son for Art. Art patted Marty on the back several times. They sat down on the flat rock for a few minutes to allow Mart to regain his composure and confidence. After awhile, Marty felt calm enough to converse.

"I can't believe you make this climb, Art... carrying that box."

"I didn't at first. I used ta tie a rope around my waist and make the climb... then pull the box up. I got so used ta the climb, though, that I could practically do it blindfolded. That little jump there is about the only tricky part a the climb... and it's not really so bad, once ya get used to it. You were just a little unsure of yourself, that's all... and that left leg a yours doesn't have much bounce to it yet. With a little practice, you'll be scamperin up these rocks like a mountain goat, Mart."

"That's hard to believe, Art. I'm already worried about goin back down."

"Well, Mart... it's like everything else... after ya do somethin for awhile it gets to be so easy ya can't believe how hard it was in the beginning. It's like shootin. When I first started, I couldn't hit the broadside of a pregnant elephant. Now, I can knock a squirrel out of a tree at a hundred yards... easy shot. It just gets easy after awhile."

"I guess, Arthur. Well... are you ready to go? I've got my legs again."

"Let's roll, Martaroo."

The rest of the climb was uneventful, though Marty's brush with death had left him shaken. The cave was a large opening in the rock formation, thirty to forty feet wide, that had a flat rock floor and an overhang above the entrance. Inside, the ceiling was about ten feet high, and the back of the chamber was forty feet, or more, from the entrance. The red cloth was tied to a metal stake that was pounded into a small crevice near the cave opening. The wooden box sat against the left side of the cave as you entered it… about ten feet back. Where it sat was about the maximum extent of the light that entered the cave and light diminished significantly from that point, on back… the farthest wall being just barely visible. Marty's journalistic curiosity was piqued by the scene and he instinctively dug for details.

"Is this the same box that's always been here, Art?"

"Yep… very same."

"So this has been sitting here for over thirty years?"

"Yep."

As they spoke, Art was taking the items from the cardboard box and placing them into the wooden chest.

"Doesn't look any worse for the wear."

"Well, not much gets to it in here. It's far enough back from the front, that it doesn't get rained on… and doesn't get much direct sunshine ta crack the wood. It's sorta in dry, cold storage back here. It could probably sit here a couple hundred years or more and still look perfect."

Art finished the delivery and closed the box lid… pressing the ornate brass bar that was hinged on the lid into the notch in the other brass attachment, screwed into the front of the box. It snapped in place with a sharp click.

"That'll do er Mart. Ready to go down?"

"Yeah... I guess."

They walked to the cave opening. Marty approached the edge a little too quickly for his urban brain, and suffered an instant case of vertigo. He grabbed for an imaginary handle in the air then quickly moved back a few steps.

"You OK, Mart?"

"Yeah... just got a little dizzy... that's all. I'm all right."

"Well... somethin I've learned about heights is that ya don't wanna be movin your head and eyes real quick. Just sorta look around, real slow and easy. That'll help."

Marty glanced at the red cloth.

"You gonna leave that up?"

"Yeah... I do. Don't know why. Probably would have made more sense to take it down so Malc... or whoever... would know I've been here. But that's the way we started... and that's been the system for more'n thirty years."

Marty reached up and felt the red cloth.

"Is this the same piece of cloth that you've always used?"

"You ask the weirdest fuckin questions sometimes, Mart. Well... lemme see."

Art went over to the cloth and rubbed it between his fingers.

"Looks like the same one to me... but who the hell knows. If you ever meet Malc's son... ask *him*."

Art grabbed the cardboard box, walked to the edge of the ledge, and dropped it. Catching the air, it floated and spun to the ground below. They started down the rocks. To Marty, it was much worse than the climb up. Going up, you had to make an effort to look down. If you didn't want to be reminded how high you were… you just kept looking up or ahead. Descending, the ground was in sight all the time and Marty's heart was racing the whole way down. He was naturally apprehensive, as they began their downward trek. . . nervously anticipating the infamous jump between the rocks. When they got to it, as before, Art went first and waited for Marty. Marty panicked momentarily… thinking, after his first brush with death, that he just couldn't do it again. He immediately pictured a humiliating helicopter rescue. Art sensed that Marty's fear was building to paralysis, so, as was his way, he joked with Marty to break the tension.

"Think you could do a three-sixty and land over here on your ass, Mart?"

Art's humor did the trick, and worked to lessen Marty's heightened state of anxiety.

"Well, I could probably do at least a one-eighty, Art."

Art laughed.

"Well… how bout gettin your ass over here, then… I'm about starved."

Their banter defused Marty's fear to the point that Marty regained the necessary confidence and courage to proceed. He took a deep breath and blew it out noisily through pursed lips. He then repeated this preparatory male ritual three more times. After the last exhalation, his eyes narrowed and his muscles tensed and he jumped… this time pushing off his right leg. The over abundance of adrenaline in his system caused his pushing leg to propel him several feet past the intended mark. Art had to quickly reach out and grab him, by the arm, to keep him from going over the far edge.

"Goddamn, boy… you goin out for the Olympics?"

"Guess I was a little pumped up."

Marty felt a great sense of relief when his feet finally touched the dirt at the base of the rock formation. He surmised it must have been how sailors would feel after a long voyage at sea. They both instinctively turned to look up at where they'd been. Art walked over and picked up the cardboard box, passing Ben along the way, and rousing him from his slumber. The three of them started home. Marty stopped suddenly.

"I have an idea, Art."

"What?"

"How would it be if I stayed behind here for awhile and watched for our friend… whoever he is."

"That's all right with me, Mart… but aren't you starved? I am."

"I'm hungry as hell, Art, but it'll be another month or so until I have a chance to try to see this mystery person. I just can't miss the chance. It's my journalistic training."

"All right, tell ya what. You stand guard and I'll go back ta the cabin and make us some lunch and bring it back. How's that?"

"Art… you're the greatest."

"That n two quarters'll get me fifty cents."

Marty smiled as he watched Art and Ben descend the hill, finally disappearing behind a huge jagged rock that stood on its edge… pointing its sharp stone fingers to the sky. Art was one of a kind, Marty reflected. He had never liked any person in his entire life as much as he did Art. Marty figured that if he believed in saints… Art would be one of them.

Marty hid himself behind some small rocks about fifty feet from bottom of the rocky slope… giving himself a clear view of the only route that anyone could take to make the climb. It was more than two hours before he heard Art's voice – singing one of his country songs… his vocalizing announcing his arrival before his actual person. As Art emerged from behind the large, finger rock, Marty issued a loud "shhhh!" at him, holding his right index finger in front of his lips to further emphasize the message. Art heard him and, realizing his mistake, shrugged his shoulders and turned up both hands in admission and contrition. He came up to Marty and squatted beside him. Ben disappeared… having a look of exploration about him. Art whispered.

"Sorry, Mart. I forgot you were on lookout."

He opened the brown paper bag and handed Marty a peanut-butter-and-jelly sandwich, an apple, and one of the resealable, ceramic-topped bottles, filled with cold tea, flavored with some lemon and sugar. Marty devoured his lunch in a matter of minutes. Art waited until he was working on his apple to talk to him. He continued in hushed tones.

"See anything?"

Marty's voice was equally as quiet.

"Nothing. Is this the only way someone can get up to the cave?"

"Unless they have wings."

"How long have I been here, Art?"

"Couple a hours."

"I'm getting sleepy as hell. Can you keep an eye on things for a while, while I take a little nap?"

"Sure thing, Martaroo. Rest all you like. I don't have ta be into the office for a little while, yet."

Marty laughed… putting his hand over his mouth to muffle it.

Marty was out for a long while. He dreamed he was on an old sailing ship. It was carrying a varied assortment of passengers on a long voyage. As he was standing at the ship's rail, a beautiful young woman he had never seen before, came up to him and stood beside him... gazing out at the blue ocean, but not looking at him. She didn't speak a word... just stood there with her shoulder and arm touching his. He could feel the warmth of her body. Without a word or glance, he knew she loved him... she knew the same thing about him. Though Marty knew in his dream that he was dreaming, he also knew he wanted to always remember the strength and purity of that moment... dream or not. Having resolved this, he awakened... the dream feelings remaining so strong inside him that they ached in his heart. He brought his hands to his chest... wanting to always keep that feeling there. Coming out of his sleep, he thought that if he could always keep this feeling in his heart, he'd never be unhappy or lonely, again, in his life. Art noticed Marty's opened eyes.

"I guess you were kinda tired, old paint."

"How long was I out?"

"I'd say about almost three hours."

"Wow. I had a really great sleep. I feel really good."

The business at hand pressed Marty back to reality.

"See anything?"

"I haven't seen so much as a gnat fart."

Marty sat up and looked at the rocks. His eyes followed the route of the climb... up to the cave opening. Suddenly he jumped up on his feet, and pointed up toward the cave.

"Son of a bitch!! Look!!"

Art's eyes shot upward. Marty shouted, his voice reflecting his exasperation, disappointment, and astonishment.

"The fucking flag is gone!! How could the fucking flag be gone, Art?! You sure nobody climbed those rocks?"

"Yeah, I'm sure. Never took my eyes off em."

"What the fuck?! How can this be, Art?"

"Goddamned if I know. There's no way you can get to that cave from the toppa the cliff… you'd kill yourself. Shit!"

The two of them stood, looking up and down the rocks, then at the other's bewildered face. Marty folded his arms across his chest and shook his head back and forth… looking at the ground for a while then back up at the cave entrance… his face contorted with puzzlement. Art kneeled down and picked up a small stick. He cocked his head and squinted his eyes, clearly deep in thought as he absentmindedly made scratches in the dirt. He would look up at the cave then back to his scratching, time and again. Finally he rose and looked Marty in the eyes… confidently shaking his head up and down.

"There's only one way you can explain this, Mart. He didn't climb the rocks cause he didn't have to."

"Whata you mean?"

"He came from the inside… he had to. I'll bet if you look around the backside of that cave, you'll find an opening somewhere."

"You think he got into the cave from somewhere inside of it?"

"I'd bet my bony ass on it."

"Hmm. Yeah, Art… you could be right. Can't see how else he could have gotten in there without us seeing him. Wow. Isn't that something?"

"Yes it is. All these years, me figgerin that he was climbin up there just like me… and never noticed any openings into the cave where somebody could get in, besides the front… but there has ta be one. I'll be damned."

"Are you sure that's the only way he could have gotten in there? I mean, I didn't see any openings in there, either."

"Just take a look up there, Mart. If he came from the ground, he'd a had ta have gone up this way. Now, do you see anyway he coulda climbed down there from the top?"

"Well, maybe he could have used a rope and scaled down that cliff. Of course that would be pretty stupid. How would he get back up, carrying a box of groceries? Also, why would he choose to get there in such a difficult way? That would be pretty stupid, too. Besides… if he wanted to stay hidden… scaling down a cliff wouldn't exactly be the way to do it. Yeah… coming from the inside solves the whole problem. Easy way in and out and stays hidden the whole time. Pretty clever, actually."

"I told ya, Malc was a smart guy… and an outdoors man. He probably found that cave on one a his hikes. That's probably why he picked it for this grocery thing. I never really gave it a whole lot of thought."

"You want to go back up, Art?"

"We're not ready, Mart. It's darker than the underside a midnight in there, near the back. There's probably a little tunnel or a small hole or somethin… and we'll need a flashlight ta find it. We'd end up fallin all over ourselves in the dark. How bout we get up tomorrow… early… bring a flashlight, and give er a try?"

"I'm not very good at waiting, Art… never have been, but you're probably right. Damn… this is exciting, isn't it?"

"Gotta admit… it's got my attention, Mart."

Art gave a whistle for Ben, who trotted into sight from among the pines. The three explorers started home.

CHAPTER EIGHT

As Art had grown to expect, Marty talked incessantly for the remainder of the day, and late into the evening, about the day's events and the morrow's possibilities. Art tolerated it until about 11:30... at which point he announced he was going to turn in for the night. Marty followed soon after but lay in his bed... wide awake. He tried to re-engage Art in further dialogue.

"What do you think this guy is like, Art? I mean we'd probably be the first human beings he's talked to in twenty years."

No response from Art.

"This guy has only known one person in his life. He'd have been too young to remember his mother... you know what I mean?"

No response.

"Can you imagine a kid taking care of himself in the wilderness from the time he was eleven or twelve years old? It's like an American version of Tarzan, you know?"

Silence.

"Well, I guess we'll just have to wait until morning... right Art?"

Continued silence.

"Goodnight, Art."

"Night, Mart."

In the morning, Marty wanted to leave immediately. Art understood the value of ritual and wouldn't be dissuaded from performing it. He made coffee... bathed in the lake... cooked breakfast. In Art's mind, you don't rush into anything... you do it right – nothing half-assed. Their early morning routine complete – being performed with precision and dignity – Art was properly prepared to face the day. Art, Marty, and Ben set out for the cave again, toting with them – rope, flashlights, and some food. They'd gotten only a few hundred feet from the cabin when Art stopped suddenly and returned to the cabin... telling Marty to wait for him. He came back with his hunting knife hanging in its leather holster from his belt.

"What's up, Art? What do we need that for?"

"Ya never know, Mart. We could be dealin with a real strange person here... considerin the life he's led. Don't like to take any chances... better safe than sorry."

"Aren't you being a tad bit dramatic, King Arthur?"

"You just don't worry about it. If I don't need it, OK... if I do, you'll want to kiss my skinny derriere. That's some French I learned."

"Whatever you say, Art."

They made it to the rock formation faster than before... both anxious about the adventure... Marty being obvious, Art, as always, maintaining his composure... always feeling the need to maintain dignity and calm – even when you weren't. They proceeded up the rocks as before... Art ahead with a rope around his waist... the other end around Marty. This time, Marty accepted the wisdom of the arrangement without question. Marty's anxiety increased as they approached the jump. Art cleared it again with minimal effort. When Marty took his position, Art spoke up.

"Maybe you should try pushin off your right leg this time, Mart. It's not as good a footing from your right, but that's your better leg."

"You think I should, Art? That's my outside leg and it'll put my left pretty close to the wall here... might jam me up a little. I guess I can move a little bit to my right, but my left leg still might catch on the wall. I'm not sure, Art. I'd feel more confident, pushing off my left and leaving my lead leg free."

"Whatever makes you comfortable Mart. I'll stand here and grab ya as soon as ya land."

"Don't stand too close to the edge... I need enough room to land... and if I jump too far, I don't want to run into you."

"All right... I'll back up a bit and be all ready to step ahead and get ya... OK?"

"That's good, Art."

Marty made his jump quickly... before he started thinking about the near-fatal experience of the last jump, and lose his nerve. This time it was a perfect jump and landing. Art didn't need to grab him. Safe on the other side, Marty thought of how he had heard that pilots were sent up again, right away, after they had had a bad experience. He decided, whether it was true or not... it now made perfect sense to him. If he had a long time to think about his bad jump... running it over and over again in his head... thinking of what could have happened... he probably would never have made that climb again. Art patted Marty on the back in congratulations and comradeship. Marty began to understand and appreciate something of the ancient bond of courage among men.

Inside the cave, they both immediately turned on their flashlights... shining them toward the inner reaches of the stone chamber. Art stopped at the wooden box and opened it. It was empty... as he expected. As they walked toward the rear of the cave, they continually swept the light beams back and forth... looking for an opening. None was apparent. They reached the back wall of the cave at about the center of it. They agreed to each take a direction and carefully examine the wall. Art went to the right... Marty, the left. As they walked, each shined his light up, down, back and forth... searching for an entrance, through which a grown man could pass. Marty made his way along his section of the wall... all the way back to the storage box... finding nothing. Art proceeded until he emerged into the sunlight on the opposite side of the cave... also unsuccessful. Both stood in the light... looking across the distance at one another, both wearing puzzled expressions. Art shook his head.

"Well, whata you make of it, Mart?"

Marty didn't answer. He was deep in thought... trying to figure out this apparent paradox. Art spoke again.

"Let's go back over it again, Mart. Maybe we missed somethin."

They retraced their steps... this time looking in all directions with an even more discerning eye. They met in the middle of the back wall – where they had begun. They decided to check out the other's work. As Art arrived at the wooden box and Marty in the sunlight at the far side, Art sat down on the floor of the cave and leaned his back against the wall. Marty did the same on his side. Both were silent... and deep in thought. Art had his head against the wall, the pointer finger of his hand tapping his closed lips to drum out some ideas. Marty leaned forward and placed his folded arms on his knees – his chin resting on his top arm. They continued their silence for a good while. Marty finally broke it.

"Maybe he *does* get in from on top. Maybe he comes down a rope."

"We already talked about that... how could he shimmy back up the rope with a box of groceries in his hand?"

"Yeah... you're right. Well how the hell does he get in here... fly?"

"Damned if I can figger it, Martaroo."

Marty got up on his feet and began to walk around.

"There's got to be an answer to this, Art. He's got to get in here, somehow."

Marty started looking all around again, with a determination, borne of frustration. Art got up and joined him. Without speaking, they snapped on their flashlights and went over the same territory once again. Marty began to move away from the wall a bit and shine the light on the ceiling. He became systematic, following a semicircle around the cave ceiling until he reached the sunlight on the other side, then moving a few steps inward, walked in the opposite direction until he arrived at the opposite position. By about the eighth pass, the semicircles had contracted to the center area of the cave ceiling. He stopped and studied an area in the very center of the ceiling.

"Art... c'mere. Look at this."

He moved his flashlight on a particular area in the very center of the cave ceiling, using a quick scribbling motion to show Art where to look. Art strained his eyes to examine the area in question. He looked at Marty then back up.

"What, Mart? Whatya lookin at?"

"Right where my light is. You see, it's been blackened up there... as though there had been a lot of fires right where we're standing."

Marty brought his flashlight down and shined the light on the stone floor below their feet. In a rough circle of about four feet in diameter, the stone floor was slightly blackened. Marty shined his flashlight back up to the ceiling.

"Look, Art... in the center of the blackened area. You can make out a circle that's a little different color than the rest of it. See?"

"Yeah... I see, Mart."

"Now just think about it, Art... if they used this, where we're standing, for a fire, wouldn't they have to have had a chimney?...

a place for the smoke to go out?... like the opening at the top of a tepee?"

"You'd sure as hell think so Mart. Some parts a this ceiling get pretty low. Whoever used this cave... probably Indians... would have smoked themselves out, if it didn't go out somewhere... couldn't just let it build up in here... they'da asphyxiated themselves, I'd think."

"I agree. So I'll just bet that area that's a different color was the chimney hole... and somebody has cut out a rock and put it in the hole."

"You think our friend opens that hole and climbs down here... gets his provisions and goes back up and puts that rock plug back in?"

"That's what I'm thinking, Art. Of course he'd need a ladder to climb down and up... then pull it back up into the hole with him."

"If that's what he's doin... he's slicker n hell. Pretty damn clever."

"Can you figure out any other answer as to how he's doing it?"

"Nope... that's the best I can see. That's the only way I can figger he's gettin in here."

"Well, there's not a damn thing we can do, right now. That's a good fifteen feet or more up there. How long's that ladder beside the cabin?"

"Should reach up there, I'd think."

"Shit, Art... that ladder won't work. It's just a single ladder. What's going to hold it up? We need... what do call those... with two sides, and a top... a step ladder?"

"Yeah... that's what ya call em. You're right... that's what we need. This could be a real challenge, Mart. We need a step ladder that's tall enough... and one that'll let both of us get up there, together, to push up on that rock... if it moves at all. It probably weighs a ton. How far across do you think that rock is?"

"I'd guess about three feet or so. Well... nothing more we can do here, right now. Let's go back to the cabin and start on a ladder. Are you hungry yet, Art?"

"Not a bit."

"Me neither. Why don't we just leave our lunches here and eat them when we get back. No sense lugging them back and forth."

"Good thinkin, Mart... you smart shit, you. We better stick em into the wooden box. No tellin what hungry critters get in here."

They put their lunches in the box, laid their flashlights on top, and started down the rocks.

Back at the cabin, they went immediately to work on a step ladder. They decided to construct a matching side to the one already made. The new side, they decided, would have to be a regular climbing ladder, also, since both of them would have to stand at the top to push the rock up. Art, being, by far, the handier of the two, did nearly all the skilled work... Marty willingly serving as assistant and go-fer. After they built the second ladder, Art bored holes near the top of each of the side pieces on both ladders with his ancient, hand drill. He then arranged the holes so each was aligned with the holes in the other ladder, then pushed two, handmade wooden dowel pins through the holes... forming a hinge that allowed the ladders to be pushed together, for ease of carrying. To keep the ladders from spreading too far apart when standing up, he nailed leather straps from one ladder to the other, on both sides, about a third of the way, down, from the top.

The ladder was completed by around noon. Marty wanted to get going immediately. Art wanted to sit down on the porch, a minute, and drink a glass of cool tea. Art won. He took two glasses and walked up to his "spring house" – a little stone chamber he had built under a small falls in the stream that ran above the house to keep his beverages cold. He took out the glass container of tea, twisted off the lid, and poured the cold tea, already slightly sweetened and with lemon in it, into the glasses. He replaced the container and rejoined Marty… already sitting in his traditional chair. They sat about twenty minutes – Art relaxing, sipping his tea with appreciation… Marty gulping his and, thereafter, drumming his fingers on the arms of his chair, making no attempt to conceal his annoyance at the delay his sedentary friend was causing. Unable to avoid noticing Marty's high state of anxiety, Art smiled.

"Thought you had slowed down, Mart… you know… relaxed… the big heavy mountain grabbin hold of ya… not so anxious to be runnin around anymore. Wasn't that you that said that?"

"OK… OK… I slipped a little bit. But, damn, Art, I'm anxious to get going."

"That fella isn't goin anywhere, Mart. Few minutes here or there won't hurt us. Art tipped his glass and let the last of the brownish-yellow liquid slide down the side of his glass and drip into his mouth. He reached to his left… picked up Marty's glass from the floor and stood up.

"All right – let's get on the road, Mart… before you develop yourself an ulcer over this."

Art took the glasses into the cabin and put them in the sink. He grabbed his long rope, hanging in a coiled loop, from a peg on the wall – slid his right arm through it – the coil resting on his shoulder. By the time he returned to the front porch, Marty had already picked up the back end of the ladder… ready to go. Art laughed to himself as he bent down and grabbed the front end with his left hand and stood up with it. He looked back at Marty.

"This sucker's heavy as hell… isn't she, Mart?"

"Sure as hell is. We need an aluminum model."

"Well… you wanna drive inta the Stump and get one?"

"Get serious. Let's go."

The three of them started out… moving at a considerably slower pace than they had that morning. Every ten minutes or so, Marty told Art to stop, so he could go on the other side of the ladder to use his opposite arm. Ben eventually grew weary of the delays and ran on ahead. By the time they reached the foot of the formation, Marty's arms ached like never before. His experience gave him an appreciation of the working man. Art hadn't switched arms during the entire trip and appeared to be completely without discomfort or fatigue at the journey's end. Marty's admiration for him went up yet another notch. They laid the ladder on the ground and looked up. Marty looked at Art.

"How are we going to do this, King Arthur?"

"Well… no way we can carry this up the hill, that's for sure. That's why I brought this long rope. We're gonna have to pull this ladder up from the ground and it'll take two of us to do it. Grab that end a minute and follow me."

They carried the ladder around the bottom of the rock formation to an area that was under the left side of the cave opening, where Art had dropped the cardboard box. From that point, it was a sheer, unobstructed rise to the cave. They laid the ladder on the ground, with the top end toward the rock formation. Art explained the options.

"Now… we can do this a couple a ways. I can climb up there myself with the rope and drop an end to you and you can tie it to the top of this thing… then climb up and help me pull it up. Or I can tie it on now… climb up with the rope… you'd have to keep the rope from tanglin up while I climb… then *you* come up. All depends on how good a knot-tier you are, Mart. Were you a Boy Scout?"

"Are you kidding? Do I look like a Boy Scout type? I'm kind of a klutz all the way around Arthur… you know. If it's not too much more trouble, I'd feel better if you tied it up."

"No prob Mart."

Art proceeded to tie the rope to the top of the ladder, wrapping it securely around each side of the top then tying it off to form a triangle so it would stay level as they pulled it up. He re-coiled the remaining rope and slipped it around his right shoulder and began walking to the base of the ascent with Marty in tow. Art explained as he walked.

"You stay down here and make sure this rope doesn't get caught on anything on my way up. When I get to the cave, we'll get the rope straight between me and the ladder… then you come on up to help me pull er up. You need me to come back down and help ya climb up? I can tie off the rope and come back down."

"That's all right, Art… I'll be fine."

"Sure?"

Art started up the climb then looked down at Marty.

"I'm gonna keep droppin off some rope for slack. You make sure it stays clear and doesn't get caught on anything. OK?

"You got it, Art."

Art took a few coils from his shoulder and dropped the slackened rope to Marty, then continued up the rocks… taking loops off of his shoulder as more slack was needed. Several times, the rope became snagged on the sharp-edged, chaotic rock structure and the two men had to work from both ends to free it. Marty held his breath as Art jumped the now infamous gap with quite a few pounds of rope still hanging on his shoulder, and the loose line dangling at his side. . . precariously near his feet. After he made the jump effortlessly, Marty wondered why he ever bothered to worry about Art. When Art reached the cave, he stood at the edge of the ledge and shouted down to Marty.

"OK, Mart... we have ta walk this rope around ta the left side where the ladder is. Back up some so we can pull it away from the rocks."

Marty backed up.

"Now pull it tighter so we can get er off the rocks."

Marty pulled. . . and the rope stretched taut between them, clear of the rocks.

"Now walk around to your right to the ladder."

Marty did as he was told. When he got to the ladder, he looked up to find Art standing directly above him. Art yelled down further instructions.

"I'm gonna pull the rope up some... to stand the ladder up against the rock. Guide it up."

Art pulled and Marty guided it as directed. The ladder now leaned against the side of sheer rock wall in a nearly vertical posture... the rope stretched tight, between Art and the top of the ladder.

"OK... good, Mart. C'mon up. You sure you're all right climbin by yourself? I can come down in nothin flat and climb with ya."

"It's all right, Art. I'll be fine."

Marty disappeared around to Art's right. Art went inside the cave and tied the rope around the wooden box so he wouldn't have to keep holding it, then walked out on the ledge to watch for Marty. He was able to catch only occasional glimpses of him as he climbed. In about fifteen minutes, Marty's head appeared at the left side of the ledge. His face beamed with pride... having, for the first time, made the climb by himself. Art untied the rope from the box and walked to the edge of the rock ledge, directly above the ladder. He looked down – then back at Marty.

"You ready, Mart?"

"All set, Arthur."

"It's gonna be heavy, partner. Tell ya what. Wrap the rope around your waist and keep backin up as I pull it in... kinda like reelin in a big fish. Keep it tight. OK?"

"Yep."

Marty did as he was told and stood ready. Art strained and pulled several feet of rope upward. The ladder left the ground and dangled from the rope. Art turned toward Marty... his voice reflecting the strain on his body.

"Back up and take up the slack, Mart."

Marty backed up until the rope was once again taut. Art cautioned him.

"You're gonna be holdin the full weight for a little bit – so get ready.

Art let go of his grip to reach down for more rope. Marty felt the pull. He leaned back with all the force he could muster to counterbalance the weight of the ladder. Art grabbed the rope and pulled... stepping backward several feet as he did. Marty backed up to stretch the rope taut again. They repeated this process until Marty was fifteen or so feet into the cave. Art called for a readjustment.

"OK, Mart. I'm gonna hold this tight. You get that rope off your waist and c'mon back out here."

Marty came within about ten feet of Art.

"Now wrap it around your waist again."

Marty did as he was told then backed up a few feet to pull the rope taut.

"OK, Mart, I'm lettin go again."

"Go ahead, Art… I've got it."

Art let go of the rope and went forward to continue pulling. The two friends repeated the same process a number of times until the top of the ladder finally reached the height of the rock ledge.

"OK, Mart… this is where it's gonna be tricky. I'm gonna keep pullin this ladder up… a rung at a time. You just keep the rope tight."

"I'm with you, Arthur."

Art began pulling up the ladder, according to his description. When a length of approximately eight feet of ladder extended above the ledge, Art grabbed a rung, as near to the top as he could reach, and pulled it toward him… the ladder rotating forward with the rock edge as its fulcrum.

"Pull with me, Mart."

The top end of the ladder continued forward, toward Art and Marty, and finally fell onto the ledge with nearly half of it still extending over the edge of the rock surface. Art immediately grabbed the top rung and pulled the remainder of the ladder onto the rock. With the bulky apparatus finally and safely up to the cave, Art sat down for a much-needed breather. Marty unwrapped the rope from his waist and joined him. Both were deeply panting from their task. Art's respiration slowed to normal before Marty's and he offered his commentary.

"That there was a hell of a job, Mart."

PAPA

"You're not shitting, Art. Christ! I'm so fucking worn out, I'm ready for a nap."

"If you're really that tuckered out, you go ahead and lay down a bit. You've been doin a hell of a lot for a man who's just gettin over a broken leg."

"Nah… just give me a few minutes… I'll be OK."

"You tell me when you're ready, Martaroo."

In about ten minutes time, Marty was ready. As he was resting, he was again reminded of how absurd it was that this man – in his seventies – was waiting for a young kid in his late twenties to catch his breath… especially when the old guy did all the hard work. Marty kept looking at Art as he rested, and the same recurring phrase passed through his mind.

"What a guy."

They carried the ladder into the cave and set it up in the center, under the designated area of exploration. Each climbed his side of the ladder until they met at the top. As usual, in matters of mechanics, Marty deferred to Art.

"How shall we do this, Arthur?"

Art studied the stone ceiling, only a few feet above their heads. He reached up and rubbed his hand over the circular area. From this close proximity, they could both see the small gap between the ceiling rock and the central circular rock. It fit quite well into the hole, but close inspection revealed imperfections. In some areas, the gap was nearly a half inch.

"It's definitely a plug, Mart. Damn well cut, too. If Malc did this, he's a hell of a mason. Let's both get up close under it and put both our hands on it. See if she even budges."

Their hands in place – and bodies positioned to give them leverage

– they pushed upward, on Art's command. The stone plug flew instantly, upwards as though it were weightless. A few seconds later it slammed back into place... nearly catching both sets of hands as it did. Marty pulled his hands back so quickly, he nearly fell backwards from the ladder.

"Damn! What the fuck happened, Art!?"

Art reached up and gently pushed up on the plug again. It inched upward. Allowing the rock to rest on his fingertips, he lowered his hand... the plug followed, back into place. He cocked his head and rubbed his chin... obviously "figgerin."

"She's attached to a counterbalance, Mart."

"What's that mean?"

"There's some kinda contraption up there that's takin the weight off it. Like this, Mart."

Art showed Marty with his hands how it would work. He closed his fist and stuck out his thumb and little finger in opposite directions to form a near parallel line with them.

"Now suppose I had a rope tied onto this here plug... and then the other end of the rope tied onto to a pretty thick tree limb... which is from one end of my thumb to the other end of my little finger, like this. The rope from the rock is tied to my thumb. There's a big rock under the middle of the limb... where it balances. On the end a my little finger... the other end a the limb... I got a rope that's tied to another rock that weighs just a little less than the plug. Just would take a little push up on the rock – on the thumb side of the limb – ta raise the plug outa the hole. I put somethin on the little finger side a the log... like a loop of rope to slip around something – to keep it open when I wanta keep er that way. Git it?"

"Yeah... hmmm. That's pretty ingenious, Art... fucking ingenious. That Malc was a smart fellow, indeed."

"Smarter n a bus fulla school teachers."

"How are we going to keep this open while we climb up?"

"Well... how bout I get up real high and push it up and keep it there til you get in... then you can hold it up for me. How's that?"

"Sounds good, Art."

"You got your flashlight?"

"No. It's down below. Guess I'd better get it, huh?"

"Unless you can see in the dark, Mart. Get mine while you're at it."

Marty returned with the flashlights. He stuck one in each back pocket to free his hands for the climb. Art got up onto the next-to-the-top rung and pushed upward. The plug rose several feet from its resting place. Marty climbed to the top rung and reached, apprehensively, into the darkness of the open hole, fearing what he might possibly touch. The ceiling of the cave, into which the hole was cut, was about two feet thick. He placed his hand onto the stone floor of the upper chamber. Not only was the stone cold, but he could feel damp, chilly air flowing downward from somewhere. Balancing on the top rung, he pulled himself up to a near-standing position... being prevented from full extension by the stone plug touching his head. In the two-foot space between the floor above and the hanging plug, Marty pulled himself up into the darkness. Once again, he was reminded that he was not a brave man. Ashamed of the thought, notwithstanding, he wished he had volunteered, instead, to push the rock and let Art climb up first. On his hands and knees, he reached into his back pocket for his flashlight... his heart pounding the beat of fear. The chromed flashlight threw a beam ahead of him to illuminate a stone and wood contraption... uncannily similar to that described by Art. He turned around, put his head down in the hole, and told Art about it.

"Just like you predicted, King Arthur. There's a beam with a rope holding up the plug. What a smart shit you are."

"Can't keep genius a secret, Mart… just has a way a poppin out."
"You're modest as hell, too, Arthur. Hold on and I'll go around the rock and see how to hold it up for you."

Marty got to his feet… shining the light in all directions to gain some perspective of the size and layout of the chamber. It was much larger than he had anticipated… at least the size of the lower chamber, the ceiling even higher. Marty walked around the rock over which the round wooden beam was balanced. On the other side… just like Art had predicted, a rope was hanging from the beam – tied onto a roundish boulder – some two feet in diameter. Near the top of the boulder, a hole had been bored – through which the rope was threaded and tied off in a rope stitch that indicated an experienced hand. Wedged into a small crack in the rock floor, was a metal stake, sticking up a couple of feet. Its top had been bent into a circle. From the metal circle hung a piece of rope… long enough to tie around the beam and hold it down – which Marty did. He returned to the hole and shined the light on the rock floor to illuminate Art's climb. Art pushed up with his feet as he pulled himself with his hands – gripping the rock floor. In one fluid movement, he sprang into the upper chamber. Marty handed Art his flashlight and, as Marty had done, he began shining it around to reconnoiter the chamber. Marty led Art to the other side of the rock fulcrum to show him the tie-down mechanism. Art shook his head up and down.

"That makes sense. Smart. Look at the workmanship on that rock. Bored a hole right through it. How's the plug tied on? Did ya look?"

"Didn't think to, Art."

Art returned to inspect it. The rock plug had clearly been chiseled into shape. On the upper side, the chiseler had cut a rock arch that extended above the upper surface about five inches and through which the rope was passed and tied off.

"Lookee here at this, Mart. Look at the workmanship. Either someone had a helluva lotta time... or was one hell of a craftsman."

"Now do you think Malc did this, Art... or was it already here and he just used it?"

"Hard ta tell. The underside had some black on it but, like you said, it looked kinda different than the rest of the black on the ceiling... like someone had rubbed it with somethin to make it blend in – so no one would notice... know what I mean?"

"I didn't really look that close, Art... but I'll take your word for it. So you think Malc made this contraption?"

"Wouldn't be surprised. Ya know, I was just thinkin... we haven't seen his ladder. He's gotta have one up here, somewhere, ta get up and down."

They both immediately began searching for the missing ladder. Art found it leaning against the wall near the wooden lever. He studied it.

"This is a well-made ladder, Mart. Each rung is hand carved... you can tell. They're pushed into these bored out holes. Not a nail or screw in the whole thing. It's just all stuck together with good workmanship."

Having completed their study and admiration of the ladder, Marty and Art got back to the business at hand. They both began shining their lights around... looking for an exit out of the upper chamber. Art found it.

"Look, Mart... over here."

Art started walking toward the cave wall on the opposite side of the chamber from the lever mechanism. There was a triangular opening... formed by a rock leaning at about a forty-five degree angle... under which someone could easily crawl. Art bent over and shined his light through the hole. It revealed a passageway that extended some forty feet... ending in a stone wall. He turned to Marty.

"You see any other way outa here?"

"I don't know, Art... haven't had enough time to really check it out."

"Well... let's look around first... before we start back this way. Could be a bunch of ways out. Let's see."

Walking together, they followed the walls of the chamber... looking up and down for other openings. They made a complete circuit of the stone room... finding no other exits. Remembering their experience in the lower chamber, they also searched the ceiling for holes – finding nothing. They concluded that the triangular exit was the only way out. Without a word of warning, Art disappeared through the open triangle. Marty followed and immediately sensed danger. He was now quite ready to kiss Art's bony butt for bringing his knife. Out of nervousness, he began asking Art questions.

"Do you think any bears could live in here, Art?"

"It's possible... depends if there's another way in. Sure as shit, they don't walk around carryin ladders... none that I've come across, anyway. If the way we came in is the only way inta here... we're safe."

"But, our friend must have another way in and out."

"Maybe... maybe not. He could drop his ladder down and go out the way we came in and just leave his ladder down there till he wants ta come back up. I don't know, Mart."

They had reached the wall at the end of the corridor. It continued with a near ninety-degree turn to their right. The floor began an upward grade. They followed it for a considerable distance... Art estimated it to be several hundred feet – where it came to a dead-end. They shined the lights around... then at each other's puzzled face. Marty spoke.

"Shit, Art... it's a dead end."

"Looks like it."

They both began shining their lights around again... not yet willing to accept defeat. Suddenly, Marty shined his light straight up.

"Bingo."

Art looked up. Another stone plug. Too high to reach... even on somebody's shoulders.

"I'll tell you, Art... I don't know who this guy is, but he's got more security than Fort Knox."

"Sure as shit does, Mart. Well... let's go git the ladder."

Reentering the top chamber, they walked to the hole. Art got down on his hands and knees – about to reach down for the top rung of the ladder. Marty stopped him.

"Wait a minute, Art. Why don't we just use his ladder? I mean, why pull that heavy son of a bitch up here when we can just use his? From the looks of it, it's got to be a hell of a lot lighter than ours."

"I dunno Mart. We don't know who this guy is. Could be real wild and real mean. Might be considerably pissed off if we'd use his ladder without askin. He'll probably be pissed enough with us just bargin in on him, uninvited."

Marty immediately recognized the wisdom in Art's words and got down with Art to pull up their cumbersome ladder. After a strenuous effort, spurred on by a wide selection of invectives and profanities issued by both parties, they finally got it into the upper chamber. They made their way with it to the end of the first corridor, only to discover they couldn't get it around the sharp right turn. Try as they may, the turn was just too extreme to get their ladder around it – and the ceiling wasn't high enough for them to walk it around on its end. Frustration overcame both men... Marty being typically demonstrative – Art undergoing a slow, silent burn.
"Fuck! Fuck! Fuck! Goddamn it! How fucking stupid can we be? If either of us had half a brain, we'd have seen we couldn't get this ladder around this bend before we carried this fucking monstrosity back here. Shit, Art. Now what?"

Art leaned his back against the stone wall, folded his arms across his chest, and looked up at the ceiling. He shook his head slowly back and forth.

"Not much choice, Mart. Gotta carry this heavy fucker back out go back to the cabin and make us a shorter ladder that'll get around this bend. Pain in the ass, huh?"

"Big fuckin pain. Wait... how about his ladder... think that would work?"

"Now use your head, Mart. It's the same length as ours or it wouldn't work to climb down to the lower cave."

"Yes – goddamn it – you're right. If I had a brain it would be lonesome."

The two men lugged their ladder back to the upper cave – put it down through the hole, stood it up, and climbed down to the lower chamber. Frustration had diminished the morning's enthusiasm to the extent that even the ever-talkative Marty Chapman had lapsed into a rare silence for most of the journey home. It was nearly five o'clock when they reached the cabin. Both were exceedingly tired, disgusted, and discouraged. They resolved to have dinner and get some rest… then resume their project in the morning. The silence and low spirits continued throughout the evening. Both retired early… still exhausted and disgusted.

After completion of the morning rituals – fully endorsed this time by Marty – they got busy on the smaller ladder… the new dawn having rejuvenated their spirits. Their renewed enthusiasm caused Marty to reflect on the phrase, "What a difference a day makes." He had fallen asleep with low spirits and a gnawing sense of unhappiness. In the brilliant sunlit morning, the previous night seemed a lifetime away and his depression of the previous evening was but a silly and slightly embarrassing memory. He thought of how some people – in the throes of depression – commit suicide, when, if only they had perhaps waited until the next morning, everything might have all looked so different and so much better.

With pieces of lumber lying around the cabin, Art quickly nailed together a short ladder. He had to guess on a size that would both pass around the bend, but also be high enough to reach the new stone plug. Being a single ladder and just slightly over half the length of their original ladder, they moved swiftly up the mountain to the rock formation. They decided it was light enough and easy enough to handle to allow them to carry it up the rock climb to the cave, which they did with ease – Marty having become so accustomed to the climb that his demeanor began edging toward cockiness.

Carrying the ladder, they entered the cave. They both stopped suddenly… shock taking the breath from even the unflappable Art. They stood rigidly… silently staring. Directly ahead of them, their step ladder lay on the stone floor under the ceiling hole, the stone plug having been returned to its place, filling the chimney vent. Art – in front – turned his head slowly to look at Marty, who was still holding the back end of the ladder. Marty's distressed composure was further eroded by reading a slight trace of fear on Art's face… the first he had ever seen there. Art bent down slowly, and quietly placed the ladder on the stone floor. Marty followed suit. Art unsnapped his leather holster and pulled out his large, and exceedingly unfriendly-looking, hunting knife. Gripping it tightly in his right hand, he moved it to a position – waist high, extended slightly from his body, and pointing straight ahead. He bent his knees a bit and his head leaned forward... his left hand moved away from his body for balance, his fingers spread – all of the motions clearly creating an unmistakable fighting stance. Marty was more afraid than he'd ever been in his life. This was the sort of thing that you only see in the movies, he thought – a guy with a drawn knife – ready to fight. "My God," Marty thought, "someone could get killed here."

Marty figured that if the perennially stoic Art took this situation this seriously, it must, indeed, be exceedingly dangerous. Marty had often written about danger in articles, but he'd never really experienced the feel of *real* danger. He immediately understood the fight or flight choice that fear presents. Personally, he was quite ready to flee, and Art was ready to fight. He wished with all his soul that he was like Art. He tried to imagine how brave men feel so he might achieve some measure of it. Failing, he was even more ready to run back down that rock pile, to put as much distance between him and whatever danger, real or imagined, might be poised to befall them. He was able to eke out only a small whisper to convey his point of view.

"Let's get out of here, Art."

Without taking his eyes from the dark interior of the cave – Art continued to search for any threat of danger. Finally he replied in soft tones.

"Just take it easy, Mart. Let's just see what's up."

Art reached around with his left hand and pulled the flashlight out of his back pocket. He turned it on and began shining it into the dark recesses of the cave. Marty watched Art... wishing Art would have succumbed to the same urges of flight that beckoned him. Suddenly, a shadow – cast from something, interrupting the shaft of sunlight behind him, moved into Marty's field of vision – beside him, and to his right. Marty froze... unable to move or speak. He could feel the hair rise on the back of his neck. The shadow disappeared behind him... moving to his left. Suddenly, Marty felt the presence of something very large, only a few inches behind him. Marty tried to find a scream but was able to emit only a low groan... loud enough for Art to hear. He spun quickly around... the light from his flashlight shining directly into Marty's eyes. Blinded, Marty could no longer see Art. The light beam moved slowly upward from Marty's face – to shine on something directly above him. With the light out of his eyes, Marty was able to see Art again. His face was a mixture of fear and wonderment. Art's mouth hung open as he stared at something very close to Marty. Slowly, Art moved his knife blade toward his body then forward in Marty's direction... repeating this several times... his eyes explicitly imploring Marty to come his way – and quickly – away from whatever was behind him. Feeling in danger of imminent attack, survival instincts overcame Marty's paralysis. He bolted suddenly from his position and ran to huddle behind Art... feeling very much like a little boy hiding behind his mother's skirts – but not caring.

Marty gazed upon the sight revealed by Art's light. There – some ten feet from them – with the glare of the sunlight shining behind him, creating a brilliant luminescence around his figure, stood a man, the likes of which neither Art nor Marty had ever seen. He stood at least six-foot-six in height – had enormously broad shoulders – eyes of a haunting, grayish blue – hair, a light brown covering of tightly coiled, kinky wool – a handsome, chiseled face possessing a dramatically square jaw line that was covered by a trimmed, full beard of the same light brown wool. Over his massive upper body was a sleeveless shirt made of tanned hides – sewn together with an obvious, high degree of craftsmanship. Around his waist hung a hide skirt – cut and shaped, very much like a Scottish kilt, that covered his legs to his knees. His feet were covered with hand-crafted boots, made of the same skin. Emerging from the shoulder openings of his shirt were enormous arms – dramatically defined by a deeply cut musculature. His calves were equally as well defined. His skin was a shade of oak-brown. He was clearly the son of Malcolm and Ethy – a beautiful composite of a handsome Scotsman and a striking black Islander.

The man stood erect, motionless, calm, and clearly unafraid – his arms hanging at his sides. He gazed at Art and Marty with as much wonder as did they at him. His face conveyed no danger or threat. Finally the look of wonder on the giant's face gave way to a warm and charming smile, baring large and brilliantly white teeth. He spoke to them in a pleasant, low tone – couched in a dialect that betrayed a profound Scottish influence.

"You're afraid."

Neither Marty nor Art could muster a reply... both feeling that the giant's description of their condition was a considerable understatement.

He spoke again.

"I won't hurt you."

Art turned to look at Marty... still slightly crouching behind him. Marty shrugged his shoulders... conveying his clear uncertainty as to how to proceed. Art took matters into his own hands – as was nearly always necessary in dealings with Marty. He slowly moved his right hand to his hip and slid his knife into its holster... realizing the futility in welding such a puny weapon against this modern-day Goliath. Art then managed a frightened smile.

"I'm Art Durbin and this here's Marty Chapman."

Feeling embarrassed, Marty finally stood to his full height, but still behind Art, and gave a small wave to their new acquaintance.

"Hi."

Marty immediately felt stupid for saying this – sounding like a little kid on the playground. His feelings about himself were reinforced when Art looked back at him, disapprovingly. Trying to salvage what little self-esteem he had left, Marty stepped forward to stand beside Art. Art spoke again.

"You Malc's son?"

"Yes."

"I don't suppose you like this light shinin in your eyes, do ya?"

"No."

"Well... suppose we all just walk out into the sunlight... so we can see each other."

Without replying, the man turned and walked toward the mouth of the cave and into the sunlight. Art started forward – Marty following a few steps behind him. In the sunlight, the stranger's appearance was even more striking than what the artificial beam of light had revealed. His gray-blue eyes were hypnotic, against the background of the brownish cast of his skin. Though he had the size and apparent strength that would have been more than enough to allow him to break the two of them like twigs, a sense of warmth and an almost childlike affection emanated from his being, which immediately disarmed both of the other men. Without understanding why, they found themselves smiling at him... both feeling very safe and welcome in his presence. They also felt an enveloping sense of security and protection, being near him... as though no harm could possibly come to them as long as they were near this sheltering man-mountain.

Marty and Art remained silent – but without self-conscious discomfort. Both felt peculiarly comfortable not to speak to this stranger they had just met... and who was looking directly at them. The man stepped forward to Art and gently put his hands on the sides of Art's face. The enormous extremities were so large that they not only covered the sides of his face but extended well beyond Art's ears. Through the warmth of the huge hands, Art could feel the unimaginable strength they must possess. The man gently lifted Art's face toward his. He smiled at Art... then took his right hand and moved it to the hairline on the right side of Art's forehead. In a slow and affectionate motion, he moved his hand over Art's hair… caressing it as it passed to the back of Art's head. He stood for a few more moments in that position… continuing his warm smile. Though he was more than twice this young man's age, Art felt he was but an infant, being caressed by a man, the age of the universe. The man then walked to Marty and did the same to him. Unable to control himself – tears flowed freely from Marty's eyes. Without thinking about what he was doing, Marty lunged forward, toward this imposing creature, put his face into his chest and began sobbing like a baby. The man put his arms around Marty and gently embraced him. The power Marty felt encircle him was unfathomable. Watching this scene brought a lump to Art's throat and water to his eyes.

When people meet for the first time, a dialogue usually ensues so that each may take the measure of the other. Without a word passing between them and this man, both Art and Marty felt they knew and loved this man more deeply than anyone they had ever known in their lives. Art and Marty felt more happiness in this man's presence than either had ever experienced. Neither Art nor Marty understood it, but neither did they care to understand it. This man made them feel good about themselves and about the world – this they knew. No further explanation was necessary.

The immense man then backed up a few steps and sat down on the rock ledge, crossing his legs in front of him. Marty and Art followed his lead and did the same. Even sitting, he towered above them. Sounding like a small child – but not caring – Marty spoke to the man.

"Who are you? I mean… I know you said you were Malc MacDonald's son, but that's not what I'm asking. Who are you?"

"I am your Papa."

"My papa? What does that mean… my papa?"

"My father, who raised me, was my Papa. One day, he went to our Papa when I was just a young lad. Our Papa is the father and the mother of all. Our Papa has come inside me, and I *am* Papa."

"Is this like... I'm not sure how to ask this. Is the papa... the one who your father went to... God? Is that what you're trying to say?"

"Yes."

"And that papa... God... came inside you... and so you're God?"

"Yes. I was born as the son of Papa's children, but Papa has come into me. He lives and sees through who I am... as I am."

"Papa... God... has come inside you... as a human being... and he sees and lives as a human being through you... but he's still God?"

"Yes."

"So do we call you Papa?"

"Yes... you may."

Marty looked at Art then back at Papa.

"Ummm, well... Papa... can I ask you... how you know all this?"

"Papa told me."

Art jumped in.

"You mean your father... Malc... told you?"

"No. Papa... the father and mother of all, told me."

Marty directed a glance at Art to remind him that interviewing was *his* business, then resumed the questioning with exaggerated authority.

"Papa... God... told you?"

"Yes."

"I see... Papa... the Papa that's God... talks to you."

"Papa did. Now Papa doesn't. I am Papa."

"So you're God?"

"I am. Papa is here, in this child, and I am Papa."

Marty's face clearly conveyed his intent to continue this cross examination. Papa smiled knowingly at him.

"Marty... you've traveled very far – from the West – to come to me... and I need you."

Hearing a total stranger, who had spent his entire life on a mountain top, who could have absolutely no way of knowing of Marty's point of departure, saying with absolute confidence, that he was from the West, and categorically stating that he had come to find him, stunned Marty into rare, momentary speechlessness. After a few moments, however, Marty's natural skepticism restored his voice.

"Please understand, Papa, this is all a bit much. First of all, how do you know I'm from the West?"

"I know."

"How?"

"I know."

"Is it possible you may have been around Art's cabin from time to time and overheard this information?"

"No."

Papa stood up and walked over to Marty. He bent his knees and squatted in front of him, reached out with his right hand and took Marty's hand, completely engulfing it in his. He then closed his left hand around it, also. Looking deep into Marty's eyes, he smiled – a father-to-son smile – conveying to Marty that it was time for the child to shut up and listen, which he did.

"Having become one of my children, I can feel much that I couldn't before. I am Papa… but I have taken on the weaknesses and fears of my children. I need you. Will you help me?"

"As Papa… can't you make me help you?"

"I could, but I won't."

"You're God… and you won't command me to help you?"

"No."

"What kind of help do you want?"

"I need you to write."

"Write… as in, professional writer?"

"Yes."

"Why do you need me as a writer?"

"There are things I must do."

"What sort of things?"

"I must try to help my children."

"Why me?"

"Because you're a writer, Marty."

"How do you know that?"

Papa smiled.

"I know."

Marty looked down at the stone floor for awhile to escape Papa's eyes in an attempt to derive some modicum of rationality from the bizarre situation in which he found himself. Finally he looked up at Papa and spoke quietly and respectfully.

"I really need to think about this for a bit… I'm feeling a little overwhelmed… if you know what I mean."

"I understand, Marty. There is much you will never understand. I can only speak to you in a child's tongue and there is much I cannot explain to you.

"When – if – I come back, how will I find you?"

"Just come back."

Marty was poised to inquire further about this – but stopped.

CHAPTER NINE

On their way back to the cabin, Marty and Art were both stunned beyond speech. There was a distinct feeling of unreality about this utterly fantastic encounter and they were both struggling to separate fantasy from reality. Marty reflected that this must be how people feel, who have had a UFO experience. What they had just experienced was just too far beyond common reality to place it into any rational context. Marty's head was literally swimming. It was all just too much for him. Meeting God! – he kept exclaiming in his mind. He realized he was feeling very much as he had after being in a serious car crash, outside L.A., a few years back – able to picture what had happened and knowing it had happened, but feeling as though it had all been a dream. The clash of reality and unreality hit him suddenly, and so dramatically, that he told Art he had to sit down a bit. Feeling as though he may actually faint, he lay on his back and covered his closed eyes with the back of his right hand. Ben – in his course of investigation as to the cause of the sudden stop – licked Marty's cheek. Marty, not up for such sloppy, canine affection at that particular moment, pushed his big head away. Moderately insulted by the rebuke, Ben sat down with tongue hanging and dripping, and panted hot air onto Marty's face. Too distracted to deal with the annoyance any further, Marty chose to ignore it.

Marty felt afraid. This encounter had shaken his life's perspective and cracked the psychic pillars that upheld his sanity. He felt an overwhelming urge to attack the source of his fear. Marty opened his eyes and found that Art had seated himself on the ground beside him.

"That guy is a nut, Art... a real fruitcake. Too much time in the woods. Ya know?"

Art remained silent – staring straight ahead, as though he hadn't heard him. Marty continued.

"He's one of those types like Hitler... so charismatic and mesmerizing that you're overwhelmed – like we both were. His appearance and voice... and those eyes... they throw you off balance... make you emotional."

Still eliciting absolutely no response from Art, Marty sat up and looked at him. His appearance startled Marty. He looked old... very old... like his grandfather – yet at peace. The youth and vibrancy of his face and eyes had, in a matter of minutes, completely vanished. His rugged exterior seemed to have melted into a pliable, elderly softness. A flood of possibilities ran through Marty's mind... a heart attack? stroke? shock? Marty put his arm around Art's shoulders and looked into his eyes.

"What's the matter, Arthur? You don't look so good. You feeling sick?"

Art smiled weakly at Marty.

"No... just tired... just tired."

Art's gaze returned, but focused on something so distant that it seemed to reflect in the infinitely deep pool of his mind. Marty was unable to rouse him. Concerned beyond reckoning, Marty helped Art to his feet and got him back to the cabin as quickly as he was able, given Art's sudden and pervasive weakness of body and mind. That morning, Marty had walked to the cave with a youthful, pulsing, strong man. Upon his return, he helped along an old and feeble gentleman who he barely recognized.

Marty put Art into bed as soon as they entered the cabin, and, despite the hot weather, covered him with several blankets, in an attempt to warm his chilled extremities. Ben sat close and attentively beside the bed... sensing, as dogs do, his master's distress. Marty quickly made Art some warm tea, which he refused. Art lay motionless, barely breathing, staring at the ceiling with a look of transcendence on his face. This distant countenance exacerbated Marty's already frantic concern to a state of near panic. He strived, admirably, however, to conceal his anguish as he spoke.

"We've got to get you to a hospital, Art."

Art looked at him with boundless affection, combined with inexpressible weariness.

"No Mart... I'm stayin here. I'm home now."

"C' mon Art... you're not well... you need to see a doctor. That crazy guy today was too much of a shock for your system. We've got to get someone to look at you."

"Mart?"

"What Arthur?"

"Promise me you'll bury me on my mountain."

Tears immediately rushed into Marty's eyes and ran down his cheeks. He threw his arms around his best friend and held him with all of his might and all of his love... as if he could, if he held on tightly enough, keep Art with him, forever.

"C'mon Art... please... please. You're not going to die. You're fine... you just need a little rest. Please Arthur... you're my best friend... don't leave me. I need you Art... I don't know what I'd do without you."

Marty lay his head on Art's chest – sobbing – saying "please," over and over, again. Art pulled his right arm from under the blanket and put it around Marty. For an instant, Marty felt Art's old strength return to his arm. Art leaned his head forward to Marty's ear and whispered.

"Help Papa."

Marty reared up – his eyes blazing.

"That son of a bitch! He's the one that did this to you! He did a real number on you – that bastard! Help him!? I'll kill him... that's what I'll do for him! I'll kill him!"

Art, tenderly, put his hand on Marty's cheek.

"No, Mart... no. He is who he says he is. He's made me not afraid to go. He's let me give up the fight... let me lay my burden down, Mart. I'm goin to join Malc and Papa."

"No you're not! No you're not! You hear me, Art?! You're talking crazy! That guy is no God! He's just some kook in the woods!"

"Stop, Mart, please. Just let me go. I'll always love you, partner. I'll always be with you. Anytime you feel lonely... old Art'll be there. C'mere, Martaroo."

Art put his hand behind Marty's head and pulled him down to his face. He kissed him on the cheek... then simply closed his eyes and was gone. Ben began to howl.

CHAPTER TEN

Marty eventually decided on a location for Art's grave... about halfway between the front porch and the edge of the cliff. He, at first, opted for a more remote spot... fearing someone may come upon it – if it was in an open area – then changed his mind. Art loved the view from the front porch and Marty decided that he'd be happy to spend his eternity overlooking his cliff. And, Marty resolved, it wouldn't really matter if someone *did* come along and discover the grave. What was there to worry about? Not likely that someone would try to rob the grave of some poor mountain man.

Marty got out the pick and the pointed shovel and went to work, first marking a rectangle in the dirt with the pick, as his perimeter, being about seven feet by four... figuring that should be large enough to accommodate Art's near-six-foot stature, and the broadness of his shoulders. The work went painfully slow – Marty encountering a plethora of rocks and pine roots in the soil. As he worked, Marty could hear Ben, who continued to howl for several hours after Art died... eventually declining to a plaintive whine.

Marty had always heard about people being buried "six feet under" and set that as his goal – using his own body as a measure. He realized, after two hours of work and only a knee-deep hole to show for it, that lowering the hole he was working on to a six-foot depth would be a yeomanly undertaking, indeed. At the rate of the current excavation, Marty calculated it would likely be dark before he had a six-foot-deep hole... and burying Art in the dark, he decided, would simply be unworkable. With these considerations in mind, Marty decided to stay at his task until about an hour before sunset – then bury Art, regardless of whether the hole was six-feet-deep or not. What was the significance in that depth, anyway?... he pondered. Probably just another stupid tradition without a practical rationale.

As he was digging, it dawned on Marty that he was probably doing something illegal. People don't just bury their dead in the back yard anymore, as they did on the frontier. You need somebody to do something official... like pronounce the person dead... or whatever they do. Then the person had to be buried in a graveyard. What would they say in a city if you started digging up your front yard and told people you were burying your wife there? It had to be illegal. After reviewing these matters, however, Marty decided that, frankly, he didn't give a shit if it was illegal or not. He loved Art Durbin and Art had asked him – on his deathbed – to be buried on his mountain. If it was a crime – fuck em! He'd pay the fine or serve the time... he didn't care.

With the sun going down behind Echo Ridge, Marty knew sunset was about an hour away. He was impressed with the depth of his work... the side of the grave now rising higher than the top of his head. It wasn't six feet deep, but it was deep enough. It was deep enough that Marty had to place a ladder down into the "head" of the grave to allow him to crawl in and out of it. Deciding it was time for the burial, Marty climbed out of the grave, for the last time, and pulled out the ladder. He went into the cabin to get Art.

Approaching Art's bed, under which Ben was lying and still mournfully whimpering, Marty had the absurd thought that he wished Art was there to tell him how he should do this. On the frontier, burial stuff was probably old hat, but as a modern man, he was at a total loss as to the practical considerations of interment. All he knew to do was simply call an undertaker. The first practical issue, with which Marty had to deal, was Art's jaw. It had fallen open while Marty was out digging the grave and gave Art's face a grotesque, howling expression which Marty felt he could not, in good conscience, allow Art to bear for all eternity. In an attempt to remedy the situation, Marty put his hand under Art's jaw and pushed upward, only to find it totally immoveable. He recoiled from the macabre coldness of Art's skin, then immediately felt ashamed of his reaction, but in his own defense rationalized that he had never touched a dead body before and, despite that fact that he dearly loved this man, it was simply an unexpected shock. Marty then put the heel of both hands under Art's jaw and pushed, leaning the weight of his body into it. Still, it remained in its locked and open position. Marty finally concluded that it would, literally, require a hard blow from some heavy tool, such as a hammer, to do the job... and he simply didn't have the wherewithal to do that – it seeming an unacceptably crude and undignified thing to do to his beloved friend. Thus, with Art's mouth still gaping open, he proceeded with the burial.

Moving to the center of the bedside, Marty put his arms under Art – one under his upper back – one under his knees – and lifted slightly – to gauge Art's weight. He was heavy as hell, Marty quickly calculated. As he lifted, Marty felt the rigidity of Art's body, feeling as though he were lifting a large log. Marty let Art's stiff body come to rest, again, on the bed, realizing that getting Art to his grave could be a daunting task, indeed – Art weighing a hundred eighty pounds or so.

Given the unwieldy shape and distribution of the body's weight, Marty didn't feel he had the strength to simply lift Art's body with the strength of his arms and carry him to his grave. While contemplating this dilemma, something came to mind that Marty had always heard about people dying... that their bladders and bowels relaxed and they wet and dirtied themselves. He didn't smell anything but wanted to check more closely. One thing he was not going to do was to lay Art to rest in his grave – covered in his own urine and feces. He pulled down the blanket and felt Art's crotch area for wetness, feeling a little odd at touching another man's genitals, even if he was dead. It felt dry. He wasn't sure how he should check for a bowel movement. He opted to merely smell. Bending down near Art's crotch area, Marty sniffed. Smelling nothing unusual, Marty was relieved... not relishing the cleanup if Art had moved his bowels.

After considering his task for awhile, Marty concluded that the only way he'd be able to get Art to his grave was by the undignified process of dragging him there. Looking around the cabin, he found some rope. He slid a four-foot length of rope under the blanket, below Art's upper back, then brought the ends together and tied them at Art's chest. He did the same around his thighs. With the blanket wrapped tightly around the body by the ropes, and Art's face peering out from the singular opening of the wrap, the corpse gave the grotesquely comic appearance of a mammoth papoose. Marty then lifted Art's legs and placed the lower end of his corpse on the floor His body now leaned, rigidly, from the floor to the bed like a wrapped, frozen side of beef. With the commotion above, Ben, at last, crawled from under the bed. He appeared agitated at this treatment of his master and began loudly barking to register his objections. With Art's upper body, balancing, tentatively, between the edge of the bed and the floor, Marty didn't have the time, nor patience, to deal with Ben's criticism... and told him so.

"Hush up, Ben."

Undaunted by the command, Ben continued barking. Choosing to endure the ear-punishing complaints for the moment, Marty moved quickly to Art's shoulders – lifting him up, then gently lowering his upper body to the floor – instinctively – and irrationally – trying, all the while, not to hurt him. Marty then stopped his work, long enough to comfort Ben... lamenting the unconquerable distance between man and beast in his futile attempt to offer solace to the grieving dog by words of explanation. Despite the fact that his words were in vain, Marty continued speaking softly to Ben while he stroked his head... hoping that perhaps his tone and affection would somehow translate into some degree of comfort for the poor creature. By way of the mysterious avenue through which dogs seem able, sometimes, to understand certain human communications, Ben's face and body eventually relaxed into resolute sorrow and, with his head hanging nearly to the floor, he walked, weakly, to the far, dark corner of the cabin and lay down to silently mourn the final journey of his master – from which he somehow knew, he would never return.

Marty returned to his task. He tied another, longer, length of rope to one already secured around Art's chest. Then, gripping the long rope firmly, he pulled on it and leaned backward. Art's body slid a few feet... meeting with considerable resistance from the rough, wooden floor. Marty continued this process – pulling Art's body a few feet at a time – then regrouping for another effort until it had reached the grave side. Again, Marty was undecided. Just how should he get Art's body into the grave? Just shoving it in and letting him fall, helter-skelter, seemed unforgivably disrespectful. He might land facedown in the dirt, for God's sake. Marty came up with a method that he was sure would have made Art proud of him – Marty being the mechanical dunce he confessed to be. Taking the free end of the long rope, he tied it to the rope that was wrapped around Art's legs. He then gripped the long rope just above where it was tied to both Art's chest and legs, one side of the rope in each hand. Marty felt bad about doing it, but, not having a free hand, he had to extend his right foot and shove Art's body over the edge of the grave side to begin the lowering process.

By alternating the tightness of his grip between his hands, Marty let the rope slide slowly downward, as evenly as possible, in an effort to keep Art's body level. Marty grimaced as the rough, rope fibers dug into the skin of his city dweller's soft palms. After a long and exceedingly painful descent, the body finally came to rest on the dirt floor of the grave. Marty looked down at Art, lying at the bottom of the grave, his face uncovered, wishing now he *had* closed his gaping mouth.

Marty gripped the shovel and prepared to push the loose, rock-filled mound of earth, piled beside the grave, into the hole. Just as he was about to begin shoveling, the obvious dawned on Marty that with Art's face uncovered, the dirt would fall directly onto it... and into his open mouth. He instantly resolved that he just couldn't allow this to happen. Marty returned to the cabin and retrieved Art's towel – the one he always took with him to the lake – to cover Art's face. Feeling the pressure of the rapidly approaching night, Marty returned to the grave at a quick step... and, without thinking, jumped down into the grave to put the towel over Art's face... lifting his head to tuck it behind. As he stood up, Marty came to the horrifying realization that he had forgotten to use the ladder and the hole was so deep that he couldn't climb out of it. Once more, Marty realized he had created a horrible predicament by his chronic haste. He looked around wildly... searching for a way out. A whimper... sounding much like Ben in his mourning for Art, emerged from his throat. He began leaping upward – grabbing at the loose soil, only to slide back down into the grave with hands full of dirt. With each failed attempt his terror grew. Time and time again, he jumped up toward the fading daylight. The full seriousness of his predicament finally overwhelmed his consciousness and he began to express his realization in piteous tones.

"Oh God... Oh my God... Oh my God. What am I going to do?"

At last, a full, blind, pulsing panic gripped Marty. He began clawing, like a madman possessed, at the earthen walls of the grave – dirt falling onto his face and into his mouth. Self-consciousness and composure having entirely disintegrated, Marty screamed and sobbed.

"Help! Help me! Please help me – please!"

As he reached upward to claw, again, at the collapsing grave wall that promised to bury him, alive, with his best friend, Marty felt something grip his right arm – just above his wrist. A moment later, he felt himself rising upward – so quickly that his mind could not possibly fathom the cause. He then found himself momentarily suspended, dangling by his wrist, several feet above the open grave. Something then wrapped around his waist from behind and he felt himself being pulled backward then pressed against something very large. He was then gently lowered until his feet met with the ground. The pressure around his waist was then released. Marty turned, tentatively, to discover that his savior was Papa. With his breath, still erratic and emitting whimpers, he was unable to speak. Before Marty could find words, Papa had disappeared among the pines.

Marty was so shaken by his ordeal that his drained body collapsed upon the ground and, lying on his side, he drew his knees up to his chest. His entire body quivered. After lying there, insensible, for an indeterminate period of time, his faculties were, at last, restored by the chill of the cold night air. Urged on by his growing discomfort, he compelled himself to his feet, and, on rubber legs, he made his way to the cabin to fetch his sweater. He lit the lantern and carried it back to the grave side. In the flickering light, he could see that Art's body had been partially covered by the dirt he had pulled into the grave. Marty reviled himself for his pitiful cowardice... that within minutes of finding himself in his predicament, he had been screaming and blubbering like a baby. Marty searched for an answer as to why he was like that. Why couldn't he be like other men?... courageous... strong. Were men born brave or made brave?... he pondered as he gazed down upon Art's body. Maybe his overly protective mother made him into a coward, he offered. He didn't want to be the way he was... and after each cowardly experience he would vow to be brave the next time... only to fall apart once again. "A coward dies a thousand deaths," was a phrase with which Marty had, on countless occasions, whipped himself in shame and punishment.

The task at hand finally regained Marty's attention. Art's grave still stood open. Marty put the lantern on the ground and resumed the task of completing the burial. Fortunately, the light emitted by the lantern didn't reach the grave floor so he was spared the sight of dirt falling onto Art's body. As he was shoveling the dirt into Art's earthen tomb by the flickering, ghostly light of the lantern, the perfectly bizarre nature of the scene suddenly struck him – poignantly reminding him of just how far removed he was from his former life in L.A. In his wildest dreams, he could not have conceptualized the scene in which he was now acting. His two worlds were truly separated by an entire universe. This thought provoked some practical considerations regarding his L.A. world. He hadn't called the office in over two months. His editor had no inkling as to what had become of him. He should have called weeks ago. Marty suspected that he may very well no longer have a job. He, frankly, didn't know if he still wanted his job. This life on the mountain had had a profound effect on him. He couldn't yet define it, but he felt it. He knew that this Papa creature had thrown his mind into an unknown, distant orbit... edging him precariously close to a flying off – into oblivion.

After several hours of furious shoveling, the grave was finally covered and Marty felt the wetness of his body under his sweater. Waves of moist heat escaped from the neck of his sweater, into his face, and the cold air was beginning to turn his warm sweat into chilled water. True to the wild-West movies he had seen, the finished grave was covered in a rounded dirt pile, rising some three or four feet above the ground level. It appeared to Marty that a hell of a lot more dirt went back into the grave than had come out of it.

Marty felt he needed to say or do something to dignify Art's burial and bring some sort of closure or attach some significance to Art's life and their friendship. Again, he realized how dependent modern people had become upon professionals to handle death. An ambulance takes the body to the mortician, who cleans it and embalms it, makes it up, and dresses it... all this for a corpse who's a total stranger to him. He meets with the family in a sterile, commercial showroom to peddle the latest line of coffins and death accessories. He then sets up the room at the funeral home for the viewing, filling it with flowers picked out and delivered by local florists. The funeral is conducted by a professional cleric. The cemetery owner digs the grave. The hearse driver transports the coffin. The loved ones, when all is said and done, do very little more for their dearly departed than passively watch the professionals at work.

How different this was. Marty had been a part of Art's life and now was a part of his death. He hadn't just watched Art's burial, he had done it. The work completed, he now had time to reflect on precisely *what* he had just done. He had actually dug a grave, lowered a body into it, and covered it with dirt. It felt good. He loved Art. Art had been the best friend he had ever had. Art was the best person he had ever known. He – not some greedy stranger – had buried him. It was so personal... so intimate... something they had done in private, together. They had even shared the same grave for a few terrifying minutes. This contemplation triggered a replay of those awful, suffocating moments he had suffered below the earth's surface, causing him to shudder at the thought of how very close he had come to burying himself alive. The recollection was so frightening he couldn't get it out of his mind. Try as he may to expel the horrific event, again and again his memory sadistically tortured him with it. Time, Marty hoped, would quickly do its job of sanding the sharp edges of this experience and allow him to relegate the unspeakable terror to merely an exceedingly bad memory. Eventually his subconscious mind was satiated with its need to inflict its torment and Marty was able to return to his desire to, in some way, ennoble Art's interment. He sat down beside the grave and began talking to his friend.

"I'm pretty much of a dumb fuck, huh, Art? Just about what you would have expected of me... jumping into a six-foot hole without a ladder. We could have ended up sharing the same real estate for a long time, old buddy."

Marty felt the thickness forming in his throat.

"I really don't know what I'm going to do without you, King Arthur... I mean it. You made my life make sense... and around you, I didn't feel like I was such a shit. Around you, Art, I knew I wasn't much... but you still liked me, no matter how stupid I acted."

Tears began to flow from Marty's eyes. He wiped his nose on his sweater arm.

"I don't know where you are now, Art. Maybe you *are* with Papa and Malc, like you thought you would be... or maybe you're just gone... but as long as I'm alive, so are you. You're inside me, King Arthur. You're there forever."

Hearing his own words, the true finality of the unconquerable distance between himself and Art became painfully manifest. Marty got onto his knees and put his hands over his face. He was overcome with an emptiness, so deep, that he felt his tears would surely fall back inside him. Instinctively, he began rocking and moaning. Time lost meaning for him. When he emerged from his mourning, two minutes or two hours could have elapsed... but he felt better. He had never truly mourned before, and he found it had helped close at least a part of the gaping hole he felt inside himself. He sensed that it had begun a process that would eventually grow new skin over the remainder of his wound through the power of his warm memories. Before he left his side, Marty wanted to clear up some final business with Art.

"Listen, Arthur… about this Papa guy. You asked me to help him. You think he is who he says he is. I'm having a real hard time with this. I hate him for what he did to you. I know you say he didn't, but… he did. Now he comes along and saves me. I'm all mixed up, Art. I know what you told me… but I don't believe this guy. But… well… it's like this. You asked me to help him. That's about the only thing you ever asked me to do… and you said it just before you died… so if it was that important to you, I'll do it. I'm not really wild about getting mixed up with this guy – but I'll do it. But listen… if he asks me to do anything really crazy… you know… you'll understand if I bail out. I know you don't want me getting mixed up in something really wacky, Art."

Although Marty was sure there was more he should say, nothing came to mind. He felt Art already knew what was in his heart. That's all that mattered. Marty signed off.

"Well… good bye, King Arthur. Wherever you are, you deserve the best. I'll always love you."

Marty picked up the lantern and walked slowly to the cabin. He stopped suddenly and returned quickly to the grave side.

"Don't worry about Ben… I'll take care of him. He's feeling awfully low right now, partner… but he'll come around."

Back in the cabin, Marty put the lantern on the table and looked for Ben. He was still lying in the corner and hadn't lifted his big head to investigate Marty's noises as he would have normally done. Marty opted to leave him alone to finish his grieving. Marty suddenly realized he was cold, very cold. The air had a premature touch of autumn in it. Marty built a fire and made himself some mountain coffee.

CHAPTER ELEVEN

Out of respect for Art, and feeling the need for the familiar, Marty faithfully performed the morning rituals... even reading one of Art's *Field and Stream* magazines with his coffee. His nervousness over encountering Papa, again, gave him diarrhea. As he sat on the toilet, he reviewed their previous meeting... talking to himself when emphasis or commentary was needed. Yes... he was overwhelmed by Papa's presence... but he made him feel happy and safe. He was an extraordinary person... his appearance, his life. But this God stuff... that was too much – too much to even think about. That was the part that had so terribly upset Art – Marty knew it was – so terribly that it had killed him.

How could anybody walk around, telling other people that he's God? Even half-believing it could make you crazy. Modern Christians believe that Jesus was the son of God... but only in the context of an ancient world, so long ago, so removed from their own world that it isn't real. Would they believe Jesus was God if he came to earth in this day of computers, X-rated movies, DNA engineering, and tabloid journalism? Would they believe some giant from the woods, dressed in a leather kilt, who said he was God?

The part of the story that distressed Marty, the most, was that Papa's presence was so completely overpowering. If any human being could be God, he felt it would be Papa. But to even entertain such a thought was to stand on a slippery slope at the edge of insanity. At this thought, Marty felt the fear returning... the same fear he had experienced in his first encounter with Papa. It had made him dizzy and faint. It made him feel as though he were losing grip of – albeit ugly and terrible – the real world... the world with which he was familiar... the world he had grown, not to like, but to at least tolerate. To accept, for even a single moment, that Papa was God... even entertain the thought... could not but fracture his sane, ordinary world into unrecognizable fragments.

Marty's ugly-but-real world didn't have a real, breathing, living God – wearing a leather kilt. In his world, God was a very safe concept – to be thought about when you're either very happy or very sad – like some imaginary and kind uncle... or as a concept, to be debated in a college philosophy class... but not to look at, face-to-face. Maybe that was it, he thought. Maybe Papa *was* God and that's why he had had this intense hatred and fear of him. Papa was to Marty, like some creature from an horrific nightmare who you feel is safely left behind upon waking – only to see him walking to the edge of your bed to say hello in the morning.

To Marty, the thought of meeting God... talking to him... touching him, was so fantastic that his mind simply refused to even consider the possibility. These things just don't happen in the real world. It's one thing to talk about God – like talking about aliens from outer space – but to consider him in a real, flesh-and-blood context was a far different matter. Marty knew he had often commented that it was quite possible that there were other intelligent creatures in the universe – but to actually be in the presence of one!... that would be more than his mind could accept. To actually meet an alien – or God – could knock the pins right out from under someone's sanity.

We can only be sane, Marty thought, in a world that somehow makes at least a modicum of sense. Meeting an alien would throw everything out of whack, but meeting God... that would surely crumble the common and fragile mind of any human being. Marty finally understood the terror Papa inflicted upon him. If he didn't reject Papa as God, he'd risk insanity... so he simply could not allow himself to pass even near that mind-sucking whirlpool. Being around him, he realized he'd have to be on constant guard not to – even for a fleeting moment – allow himself to entertain the thought of Papa as God. Maybe stronger people than he could deal with such a psyche-shattering concept, but he was certain he could not. He knew he couldn't. He knew he was a coward... even in this matter. He wished that he wasn't – but he was... and as such he had to protect himself.

But even stronger people, he pondered, how could they even half-believe they were talking to God? It just can't happen. You just can't look at God... and touch him... and talk to him. It can't be! Nobody has ever met God! Even Jesus said he was only the son of God... not God!... and he didn't actually say it... he just acknowledged that others had said that about him. Moses only said he talked to a bush that spoke as God... and these were stories from thousands of years ago and, more than likely just fables.

Here was a guy... in the twentieth century... not a character out of some ancient myth, safely obscured by the mist of antiquity. God was the creator of the universe... the ultimate force... timeless... ageless... all knowing... all powerful. No one could just walk up and talk to and touch this infinite essence. Marty had always prided himself on his logic, his rationality, his skepticism. Both logically and rationally, Papa could not be God. It was simply impossible. Marty's skepticism absolutely compelled him to reject any such claim. How could a logical person accept a clear irrationality? He couldn't. No one should.

Out of his commitment to Art, Marty would help Papa... but out of his own fear of Papa, he had to reject him as being God. Having resolved these matters, during his long perch upon the toilet seat, Marty felt he was ready to go to see Papa.

Before departing, Marty tended to Ben... and to Art's grave. Ben was still lying in the corner... appearing not to have moved since he lay down the past evening. Marty went over to him, sat on the floor beside him, and stroked his head and back... offering his sympathy with the kindness of his tone. Ben did not raise his head nor move his body. Marty fetched Ben's dog bowl and scooped out a portion of dog food from the fifty-pound bag. Then, to further entice Ben, he ladled out some bacon grease from Art's "lard can," as he called it, and mixed it in with the dry pellets. He laid it directly beside Ben's nose, but he had no reaction to its presence. Marty took a bit of the grease and touched it to the front of Ben's mouth. Still nothing. Marty filled Ben's water bowl with some fresh cold water and put it on the other side of Ben's head.

Apparently Ben wasn't thirsty either. Marty finally gave up the effort to rouse Ben and moved on to completing the finishing touches on Art's grave.

Staring at the undistinguished mound of fresh dirt, Marty felt it needed something to indicate what it was... and who it was... and what Art had meant to Marty. Marty went behind the cabin and located a wide board in Art's scrap lumber pile. He carried it to the front porch, laid it on the floor, and with Art's hunting knife, began carving words into it. In about forty-five minutes, it was finished. Marty propped it up against the door, stepped back from it, and read it aloud.

> Arthur Durbin is buried here.
> He was Marty Chapman's best friend.
> Marty loved him beyond words.
> Art's dog Ben loved him, too.
>
> Until we meet again, King Arthur.

Marty dug a small slot in the ground above Art's head – the end toward the cabin – wide enough for the board to slide in, and deep enough to keep it from falling over. He shoved the board down into the narrow opening then packed and tamped small stones into remaining space between the board and the dirt for support. Stepping back to survey his work, Marty concluded that the grave still looked too much like a mere pile of dirt... not sufficiently dignified for the great man who was buried there. He decided to mark the edges of it, using the rounded rocks that lined the creek bottom. He took the bucket up to the creek and filled it with the intended markers. In three trips, he had collected enough for the job. When it was completed, Marty stood, again, at the foot of the grave, and admired his work. For a guy who had virtually never in his life, done any manual labor, he felt he had done a capital job. It looked pretty damned good... and Art, Marty was sure, would have told him so. Of course, Marty knew Art would have told him that, even if it didn't look so good. That's one of the things he loved so dearly about his old friend.

Marty prepared for his return to the cave, gathering up only a flashlight, tablet, and pen. It seemed as though there were other things he should bring along but he couldn't translate the feeling into particulars. He figured that if Papa wanted him to write, he was at least ready for that. For lunch, Marty assumed Papa would surely provide some food. As he was walking to the cave, however, he began having second thoughts about the lunch idea... worrying that Papa – the primitive that he was – might eat only feral victuals, and such, that no civilized person would consider ingesting, but he was already too far from the cabin for a return to pack a lunch. As he neared the now-familiar rock formation, fear immediately began churning his stomach to nausea, as though some internal alarm had sounded. When he arrived at the base of the climb, he stood and stared up at the cave opening. His terrible dread of encountering Papa, once again, urged him to flee... as it had the day he first met him. His other self, however – committed to the promise he made to Art – tried to dissuade him, and another of his strong-guy, weak-guy soliloquies ensued.

"No! You're not going to run this time, Marty. You promised Art. Now just calm down. This guy didn't hurt you the last time... you survived. Just go and do what you need to do, then get out of there."

The dauntless self prevailed and after several deep and noisy breaths – intended to prop up his temporary feeling of bravery – Marty started up the rocks. He could feel his body beginning to chill and tremble... worsening with each step that drew him closer to the cave. The trembling escalated to a discernible body tremor as he neared the cave opening. When Marty finally set foot on the rock floor of the cave, he was so overcome with his impending sense of horror that he felt he would surely pass out on the spot. He knew himself, and he knew, alone, he just wasn't up to this much of a challenge. In a panic, he turned and began a rapid retreat.

"Marty."

He recognized Papa's voice, coming from within the depths of the cave. Marty froze... afraid to turn around. He could feel Papa approaching him, which caused him to mentally note that neither time Papa had approached him from behind did he hear him, but in both instances he could sense his presence. Within a few seconds, he felt Papa, immediately behind him. Marty spoke, without turning his head, sounding very much like a frightened school child, making excuses to a teacher.

"I don't really feel up to this right now. I'm feeling a little ill. Maybe I can come back tomorrow."

"Marty."

"Yes?"

"You're no more of a coward than any of my other children. All of you are lost and afraid. Even those who you think are brave."

Once again, Marty felt as he did the first time he encountered Papa – like a small child... protected and understood by a caring and tender father. Again, he felt his throat getting thick and his tears forming. He still couldn't bring himself to turn around but managed a few words.

"But I'm afraid of you. You make me afraid. I'm afraid of what you can do to me."

"A child is afraid of what he doesn't understand. You don't need to be ashamed of it."

"You said you're God. I can't accept that... I can't even think about it. It makes me feel dizzy and crazy to even consider it. I'm sorry... but I just can't listen to you say you're God. It just can't be. God can't be here... talking to me. You can't be God. I'm sorry. I'm sure you're a very special person, but you can't be God."

"Do you believe in God, Marty?"

"Only as an idea. It's safe that way... not scary. But it's very scary to have a real person tell you he's God."

"Look out at the world, Marty... the sky, the trees, the mountains. How do you think they got there?"

"You know... the Big Bang... stellar dust... planet formation... evolution – that stuff."

"And how did all that happen?"

"I don't know... it just happened."

"Does that make sense to you?"

"No. But people have been trying to make sense of the universe since they started thinking about it – and the harder you try, the crazier it makes you. I mean, something can't come from nothing... but everything had to start somehow. The universe had to start from something but if it did, where did that something come from to start it? It'll make you crazy to even try to think about it. Even time itself... it had to start sometime, but if it did, what time was it before it started? You see what I mean? Nothing makes any sense. I'm standing here and, as a human being, I have no idea how I got here, or why I'm here. That's why people are so screwed up... nothing makes any sense. You're right – we're all lost and we're all scared. I agree with you about that."

"The only thing that makes any sense is love, Marty. You don't have to understand anything to feel love. You loved old Art – your King Arthur. And he loved you, Marty. You didn't have to think about that... or understand it... but it meant more to you than anything else in your life, Marty."

Marty began to weep. Without thinking, he spun around and embraced Papa, his logic and fear, totally forgotten. Time and questions vanished. Papa was pure love. He felt it. Nothing else mattered. Marty looked up at Papa's understanding, kind face. In it he could find absolutely no trace of bitterness, fear, anguish, self-consciousness, distrust, or anger – all those scars that were traced on every other face he had ever looked into. Papa's face was pure love... nothing more... nothing less.

Papa smiled at Marty then turned and began walking into the darkness of the cave. Marty instinctively followed. He walked to the ladder and climbed it – the ladder Marty and Art had seen in the upper chamber. Marty followed. In the upper chamber, Marty snapped on his flashlight. The beam fell on Papa, pulling the ladder up into the chamber. He then walked to the lever contraption and pulled off the loop that was holding down that end of the wooden pole. The rock plug descended gently into place. He then crossed the upper chamber floor and exited through the triangular opening in the wall. Marty followed, and trailed Papa along the long passage that eventually made the sharp right turn. They climbed the sloping pathway to the dead end where – this time – a ladder stood, rising up into another ceiling hole. Emerging from the hole into the chamber above, Marty was rendered breathless by the sight that spread before his eyes. He was in an enormous cavern that was open on one side – an opening that had to have been over a hundred yards wide – revealing a spectacular view of mountain ranges that seemed to go on forever. The view from Art's porch paled in comparison to this nearly indescribable panorama. Between two craggy peaks, rising from a nearby mountain, was a waterfall that foamed and glistened as it fell from its birth stream... breaking into droplets as it descended. Clouds haloed many of the highest peaks. Thousands of feet below was a canyon that wound through the ranges... disappearing as it turned north. At least a dozen small lakes sparkled throughout this spectacular creation of nature. As Marty gazed upon this incomprehensible splendor, he realized that any man, greeted with such majestic beauty, each day of his life since the day he was born, could not help but be an extraordinary human being.

Marty turned to survey the interior of the immense cavern. The sun, moving into the western sky, was, at that moment, sending golden shafts of light into the innermost reaches of the stone mansion. It was several hundred feet wide... and at least that large in its depth into the mountainside. Numerous, smoothly-rounded, stone pillars – wider at the tops and bottoms than in the middle – connected the floor to the ceiling, looking as though they had been carved, with infinite patience, by some roaring, ancient stream that had once run through this grand chamber and probably cascaded in a great falls into the canyon below. In the back left corner of the cavern, as Marty faced away from the open side, was a small stream that flowed from an opening in the rock wall near the chamber ceiling, towering some twenty feet above their heads. It ran along some boulders that protruded from the back wall then fell about twelve feet, to form a small waterfall that splashed into a puddle below, then drained through a small crack in the stone floor.

In the center of the giant chamber was an area where the floor had been blackened from countless fires, and had, at that moment, several partially burnt logs lying in the middle of it. It was made in a circle – about ten feet in diameter – and was dug into the stone to a depth of a couple of feet. Marty, experienced, by now, with this fireplace configuration, looked, immediately, upward and found the round opening in the ceiling above the fireplace he had anticipated. This one, however, had no plug in it. A round, metal bar spanned the fireplace at a height of about five feet – supported on each end by upright, metal supports. The bar extended beyond one of the supports and, attached to that end, was a wooden crank, obviously used to rotate the metal bar. At a distance of about ten feet from the fireplace, toward the interior of the cavern, stood two beds. One was very large... six or seven feet wide and at least that long... the other was considerably smaller. They weren't of crude construction, like Marty and Art's, but instead, exhibited exquisite design and skilled workmanship. They were, in fact, pieces of finely made furniture – smoothly and artistically shaped and stained. Each bed was covered with a fur blanket.

Toward the open side of the cavern, only a few feet from the edge of the fireplace, sat three rocking chairs – also finely crafted – on a large fur rug. Two were of normal size and one was, unquestionably, made for a small child. To the right of the fireplace, as Marty faced the interior of the cavern, was a beautifully made table with three matching chairs. Between the fireplace and the table was a second table that appeared to be used for food preparation. Its top was at least four inches thick, and on the work surface, was a wooden knife block with a half dozen knife handles protruding from it. Some twelve feet behind the table, erected between two of the stone pillars, was an enormous set of bookshelves – eight feet high and at least twenty feet in length. Marty walked close enough to peruse the book jackets. It was immediately apparent to him that they were grouped according to content. He could discern sections of history, philosophy, religion, literature, psychology, geography, biology, art, and astronomy. On several of the nearby pillars, paintings hung from wooden pegs that had been driven into holes, bored into the stone. Some were landscapes – some abstract. All were impressive... as good, or better, than Marty had seen in many of the upscale L.A. galleries.

"Who did these?"

"My mother did the landscapes. I did the others."

"They're great."

"Thank you."

"This is a beautiful place, Papa... would have made Frank Lloyd Wright envious... you know who I mean?"

"Yes."

"Have you read all of these books?"

"Yes."

"Every single one?"

"Yes... several times."

"Cover-to-cover?"

"Yes."

"Did your father make all this furniture?"

"Yes."

"Wow. He was a hell of a craftsman."

"Yes, he was. He learned from his father, who was a furnituremaker in Scotland."

Papa walked to the three rocking chairs and sat in the one located in the middle. He extended his hand toward the other large chair, to his right, and looked at Marty. Marty sat down in it. Papa crossed his legs and folded his hands on his lap. He smiled at Marty.

"Have you come to help me, Marty?"

"Ah... well... um... yes. Yes, I guess so. I'm not exactly sure what you want me to do."

"I want you to write my story in your magazine."

"You keep referring to things – like my writing for a magazine... things you should have no way of knowing about. How do you know these things? It's frankly, very unnerving."

"I know all about my children. It frightens you, I know – but you have nothing to fear."

"Are you a clairvoyant? I did an article on some of the famous clairvoyants a few years ago."

"I told you who I am, Marty. Can't you accept that?"

"No... I can't. I'm sorry. You're a very special person... the most special person I've ever met in my life – bar none – but by saying that you're Papa... you're saying that you're God – and I can't accept that."

"If I performed a miracle, would you believe me?"

"Well... I guess that would help. Are you saying you can perform miracles?"

"Yes."

"Like what?"

"I can change the day into night."

"You mean instantly?"

"Yes."

"Go ahead."

"If I raised my hand and this bright day became as black as night, would it frighten you?"

"I'd be scared to death."

"Would you be afraid of me, then?"

"Afraid beyond words."

"Would you want your son to fear you beyond words?"

"No... of course I wouldn't."

"I want you to love me as I love you – not fear me."

Marty began to feel distressed – as he had, following his first meeting with Papa. He raised his hand and moved it to wave Papa off – turning his face from him as he did so. Papa leaned forward toward him.

"Marty?"

"Yes?"

"Can you just accept that I love you?"

"Yes… I feel that you do. I don't know why you should. You don't even know me… but, yes, for whatever your reasons, I can accept that you love me."

"Then I ask nothing more of you."

Marty derived an immediate sense of immense relief from this dispensation. Commensurate with this improvement in his well-being, he took his pen from his pocket… clicked the point into a writing position and appeared ready to begin work.

"Where shall we start, Papa?"

"Ask me whatever questions you need to write my story."

"Well… OK… how old are you?"

"Thirty-three."

"How tall are you?"

"I don't know."

"Weight?"

"I don't know."

"All right, let's get down to it. I'm going to do this like a reporter… you claim you're God, right?"

"Yes."

"Have you been God since you were born?"

"No."

"When did you become God?"

"When I was thirteen."

"How did you know – then – that you had become God?"

"Papa began talking to me soon after my father died and…"

"By Papa, you mean God?"

"Yes."

"Go on."

"Papa explained things to me – that he loved his children and he wanted to save them from their unhappiness. He asked me if he could come into me – so he could be among his children. I said yes… and he came into me."

"How did that happen?"

"The sun grew so bright that I was blinded and I was in the dark. A small star began shining in the distance. It came toward me, becoming larger and larger until it was larger than all of existence. It surrounded me with light. The light began pouring into my eyes until all of it was inside me. I then saw through the eyes of Papa and understood as Papa. I am one of Papa's children but I am also Papa."

"So you're completely human?"

"Yes."

"You're human but you're God?"

"Yes."

"Do you realize that there are many people who will read this article who will believe you're insane? I mean… hearing God's voice – talking to you – God entering your body. There are a lot of people in mental institutions who say the same sort of things."

"Yes."

"But you don't think you're crazy?"

"No."

"OK... ah... well, let's see... why have you – God – why have you come to Earth? I mean why... now?"

"My children on Earth have never been more unhappy. They are lost, alone, and afraid. My heart aches for them. Most of them will never come home to me, without my help."

"Is this the first time you've come to Earth... or have you come here before?"

"This is the first time."

"You've never been here before?"

"No."

"What about Jesus? He said – or at least his followers said – that he was the son of God."

"He was."

"But you said you've never been on Earth before."

"Jesus was my child. You are my child. He was my son. You are my son."

"But he was no different than any other person... or child, as you say?"

"No."

"Wow... you're going to piss off – I'm sorry – ah... you're going to make a lot of people very angry with you for saying that."

"Yes."

"OK... let's see... what else? Um... can you explain the big question? You know... like, why we're here... why the universe was created... that sort of thing?"

"I can tell you as much as you will understand."

"All right."

"I have always been. I was perfection."

"Was? What do you mean?"

"I was perfect. But my perfection was one and it was without love. One, alone, cannot love. Perfection cannot be love. Perfection is empty. Seeking love, I gave up my perfection and set it free. All that remained, after that, was my spirit. My body was no longer mine. It was free to become. It was free to be apart from me or come back to me. All that my body possesses of me is a memory of when we were one. With a parent's aching heart, I have waited for my children, who were born of my body, to come home to me – hoping that they will. Together we are not perfection – but we are pure love. I am now, not one, but many.

"This 'setting your body free in all directions'... is that what we call the 'Big Bang'? It sounds like it."

"Yes."

"So how does someone find his way back to you?"

"Through love."

"Loving you?"

"Love."

"If you wanted your children back so badly, why don't you just bring them back?"

"I gave my body complete freedom from me. My children are completely free to come home to me, or stay in their world."

"Papa... I've got to tell you – this is really wild. No kidding. Well, what else? Ah... are there other worlds beside the Earth?"

"Yes."

"With people – or children as you call them?"

"Yes."

"Many?"

"Yes."

"So why worry about the people on Earth? You've got children on all these other worlds."

"Does a parent stop longing for a lost child because the rest have come home?"

"I guess not. I guess you don't, huh?"

"No."

"So is this... what goes on, on Earth... your plan?"

"No."

"Whose plan is it?"

"There is no plan. The Earth and its children are completely free."

"We're on our own?"

"Yes."

"Could you intervene if you wanted to?"

"Yes. I am intervening now."

"For the first time."

"Yes."

"What do you hope to accomplish?"

"To have more of my children come home to me."

"And, how do you plan on doing this?"

"By helping them to love."

"What exactly is love, from your point of view?"

"Love is a feeling, already in my child's heart. All of my children can feel my spirit of love in their hearts. They feel that someone loves them and wants them near – but they don't know who it is. My children search for love, and love many things. They love other children, their own children, and those many other things my body has become."

"What does that mean… 'those many other things your body has become'"?

"Everything that you see is what my body has become."

"The rocks, the trees, the sky, the stars…?"

"Yes."

"Art really loved his dog, Ben… and Ben loved Art. Will Ben be with you?"

"No."

"Why not?"

"My children must be free to come home to me. I love Ben as a creation of my own body, but Ben cannot choose to be with me."

"Do you mean he doesn't have the free will to love you or not love you?"

"Yes."

"So, how do we know if we're loving you?"

"My children know when they love me. I know when they do."

"And what happens when they love you?"

"My child's spirit will come to me when it leaves its body."

"Do you mean when someone dies?"

"Yes."

"So, apparently, you don't think your children on Earth are doing too well."

"No."

"You want me to write your story for my magazine, right?"

"Yes."

"Why?"

"There will be some who will read it, who will understand it and believe it."

"And that's it… the end of the story?"

"No. Certain people, who believe, will contact you. You will bring them to me."

"People will contact me and I'm supposed to bring them to you? How in the world would I know who to bring?… I mean thousands of people might contact me."

"You'll know."

"I'll know?"

"Yes."

Are you sure about this? I mean… you ought to know if you say you are who you are, that I'm kind of a fuck-up – sorry – I screw things up a lot… just ask my editor."

"You'll know."

"Can you tell me how many people there will be in the group I bring to you?"

"There will be eight."

"Eight people… and I'll know who they are, even if a thousand people contact me?"

"Yes."

"You're positive that I'll know who these people are?"

"Yes, Marty."

"OK… I'll take your word for it."

Marty paused for awhile to ponder the astounding information that was bombarding both his mind and psyche… then got back to the interview.

"Well, all right… how about your life story… I mean the life story of Malcolm's son. You're Malcolm MacDonald's son?

"Yes."

"You were born here… in this cave?"

"Yes."

"Your mother's name was Ethy?"

"That's what my father called her."

"What was her real name?"

"Ethelia."

"She was born and raised in the islands?"

"In Martinique. In the city of Fort-de-France."

"Was she French?"

"French and African."

"Do you remember her?"

"No. She died when I was a wee baby."

"Do you have a picture of her?"

"No… but my father told me she was very beautiful. He loved her very much."

"How did she die?"

"In childbirth. She was giving birth to my brother. He died also."

"So your father raised you alone?"

"Yes."

"Have you had any contact with any other human being, besides your father, since you were born… until you encountered Art and me?"

"No."

"What happened to your father?"

"He was killed by a bear."

"A bear! Did you see it happen?"

"Yes. We were hunting. I was twelve years old. It was a female grizzly. She had cubs and we came too close to them without knowing it. She attacked my father. He screamed for me to run and I did. When I came back, he was dead."

"Did you bury him?"

"Yes."

"And you raised yourself from then on?"

"Yes."

"Haven't you been lonely?"

"Yes."

"Why didn't you come down off the mountain… to be with other people?"

"Papa came into me and I knew what I had to do. I had to wait."

"Wait for what?"

"For you."

"You knew I was coming here?"

"Yes."

"I didn't know I was coming here."

"No."

"But you did?"

"Yes."

"By the way… what was your name… you know… before you became Papa?"

"My father named me Ian."

"So you were born – Ian MacDonald?"

"Yes."

"So let me get this straight… you're completely human?"

"Yes."

"I mean completely."

"Yes."

"You could be killed like any other person… you have emotions – pain – fear – sexual urges – just like all the rest of us?"

"Yes."

Marty paused. He looked out at the magnificent view, but his thoughts were on his work. He tried to form a journalistic perspective of it. Had he covered the basics? What would be his slant?... "Mountain man claims to be God?" Could he get his editor to support the story? He was fairly sure he could. Even without the God thing, it was one hell of a story. Marty began, again, to feel the forgotten pull of ambition. He began to realize, at that moment, just how much he had missed his chosen craft. He realized that he truly yearned to be in front of a keyboard again... and see his name on an article.

"If I'm able to figure out who I'm supposed to bring to you, how do I do it? It's not as though you have a street address."

"Bring them to Art's cabin."

"You'll be waiting there?"

"No, but I'll know they are there."

"OK... I'm sure you don't want me to write exactly where you live in my article, do you?"

"No."

"Can I just say, Montana?"

"Yes."

The sun was disappearing behind the mountains. It suddenly dawned on Marty that he had better hurry... to get back to the cabin before nightfall.

"I've really got to get going, Papa. It'll be dark soon... and besides, Ben isn't doing too well."

"Ben is dead, Marty."

"What?! How the hell do you know?! I'm sorry but this all-knowing stuff is getting to be a pain in the ass. You've got a great story, Papa – and it'll likely save my job – but I told you... I can't accept this God stuff. I honestly don't believe you know any better than I do about Ben."

Marty stood up and angrily stomped across the stone floor to the ladder that led to the lower corridors. He climbed down, turned on his flashlight, and made his way to the upper chamber. He opened the plug by the lever mechanism – holding it in that position by tying the loop restraint around the pole. When he got to the outside opening of the lower chamber, it was nearing dusk. With the climb being, by now, second nature to him, Marty descended with confidence and speed. It was dark by the time he reached the ground... so black, it felt heavy around him.

Marty had never been this far from the cabin at night, and he was familiar enough with the mountain to have a realistic appreciation of the dangers that lurked in that nighttime wilderness. He knew there were wolves, wolverines, bear, and cougars in abundance on the mountain and that he could, easily, end up as a nocturnal snack for one of these large-toothed mammals. Marty, once again, began to regret his hasty decision. He realized he should have stayed the night in Papa's cavern. If Ben was dead... it was too late and if he wasn't – he'd still be OK in the morning. Just as Marty conceded his stupidity, the admission was given support by a wolf's eerie howl, emanating from somewhere, not far from where he stood. The ghostly wail, instantly sent chills down Marty's spine and gave rise to a tingling sensation in his groin. A second – then third – joined the chorus. Marty stopped – unsure of what to do. He had an hour's walk to the cabin – through a blackness that could be concealing some unspeakable terror. On the other hand, climbing back up the rocks, to return to Papa's cavern, with only the light of a flashlight, was also extraordinarily dangerous. He realized he was damned if he did and damned if he didn't. Marty's critical self was so distressed with his apparent, interminable propensity to make stupid decisions, he simply could not hold his tongue.

"You stupid fuck. You... stupid, stupid fuck."

The wolf chorus grew steadily louder and Marty was unsure if the increasing volume was due to the growing size of the pack or the diminishing distance between them and him. He actually wasn't positive if wolves really did attack people – like he'd seen in the movies – but he knew this was not the time to test the point. Feeling trapped and in danger of imminent, mortal assault, panic got the best of Marty – as it often did – and he found himself shouting.

"Help! Help!! Papa!! Help me!!!"

It became clearly apparent to Marty that it wasn't the increasing size of the wolf pack that made their howling seem louder – they were, unmistakably, getting closer to him… so close, in fact, he could hear their movement through the brush, all around him. He screamed louder. A sharp snapping noise, a few feet from where he stood, sent electric needles through his body. He instantly raised his flashlight, expecting to see the terrible red eyes of a wolf reflected in it. Instead, he saw Papa's enormous frame, moving swiftly toward him. His calm face made Marty feel both safe and self-conscious of his frantic state. Papa's voice paralleled the calmness of his face – but was laced with a degree of earnestness. He spoke as he turned away from Marty.

"Get on my back."

Marty didn't argue. Despite the danger, however, he felt a little foolish, riding piggyback on another man's back. Again, Papa instructed him in a businesslike tone.

"Keep your head behind me… and turn off your flashlight."

Marty immediately did as instructed. Papa broke into a fluid run, traversing the rocky terrain with the agility of a mountain goat. His moving body felt so massive and muscular to Marty's touch that he had the sensation of riding a horse. Papa ran, without stopping, for over ten minutes… finally stopping to lower Marty down to his feet. As soon as his feet made contact with the ground, Marty felt Papa's huge hand engulf his and felt Papa begin leading him somewhere at a steady pace. In the pitch blackness, Marty couldn't make out where they were going, but he felt the coolness of rock around him, and had a disturbing sense of being enclosed. He noticed that their footsteps echoed slightly. They made several turns and walked a few hundred yards before they stopped again.

"Turn on your flashlight, Marty."

The beam revealed a stone corridor that Marty had never seen before. They were standing at the end of a narrow passageway which appeared to be over seventy feet in height, looking as though it had been formed by a huge boulder splitting in half. A ladder leaned against the stone wall at the corridor's end, rising up to a ledge... some thirty feet above them. Papa took the flashlight from Marty, shined it up the ladder, and told him to climb up. At the top, Marty looked into the darkness of another passageway. He took a few safe steps from the edge of the rock shelf and waited for Papa, who was only seconds behind him. Papa pulled the ladder up onto the stone shelf, leaned it against the wall then started down the corridor. Several hundred feet later, the narrow walkway ended. To their left was a split in the wall beside them, about two feet in width. Marty followed Papa as he entered it sideways – left shoulder leading – and moved by side stepping through the narrow passage. They had only a few inches between the wall and their faces. It ended at Papa's cavern... just to the right of the small waterfalls.

The cavern was pitch-black, lit only by the singular beam from Marty's flashlight. Marty followed Papa – the flashlight shining the way – to the central living area. Papa handed the light to Marty. At Papa's request, Marty followed him with the light as he fetched some kindling of small twigs and broken branches from a nearby pile, and placed them in the center of the fireplace. Under the kindling, Papa shoved a handful of brittle-looking, razor-thin wood shavings. He then laid well-dried, split logs in a crossing pattern – two of them parallel on either side of the kindling – then two more, perpendicular and on top of these first two. He continued this pattern to a four-tier height. He then took two stones – and kneeled beside the log pile. He laid his left hand – palm up – with one of the rocks in it, immediately beside the shavings and struck it with sharp, glancing collisions with the other rock. Small sparks flew toward the shavings. Marty couldn't believe his eyes. He had read about ancient man starting fires with flint stones, but he couldn't believe he was standing there – in the age of computers and space shuttles – watching a man dressed in skins – actually doing it. The scene had a distinct, surreal feel to it. Marty had many historical pictures indexed in his mind – men killing saber-toothed tigers – slaves building pyramids – Hannibal crossing the Alps, but to him, they all had a mythical, cartoonish quality about them. To be watching one of these fables come to life, was a truly disorienting experience.

Within ten minutes, a roaring fire lit the cavern with dancing shadows and the radiated heat felt friendly and reassuring on Marty's body. In a scene that struck Marty as quite reminiscent of his first meal with Art, Papa took a metal pot, caught some water in it from under the waterfalls, and hung it from the metal bar that traversed the fire. Into it he broke some sort of whitish meat.

"I'm making fish soup."

Although Marty had never heard of such a thing, he replied, courteously.

"Oh… good."

It was ready in thirty minutes or so. Papa put two large wooden bowls on the table and two oversized metal spoons. In the center of the table he placed a basket of round biscuits and another basket containing apples.

They sat on opposing sides of the round table – facing one another.

"Be careful with the scones – they're very hard. You'll need to soak them in your soup, first."

"Thanks for the warning."

The soup was delicious, as were the biscuits, or scones, as Papa called them, which had a sweetness that surprised Marty. They were both hungry, and ate without conversation. Each had an apple for dessert. After the meal, Marty felt the stimulation of his lower bowel, alerting him to its need.

"Where's the bathroom, Papa... or do you go outside?"

Papa laughed.

"No... it's over in the corner there. I'll show you."

Papa shined the flashlight ahead and Marty followed. On the floor, near the wall, about twenty feet from the waterfalls, was a round, wooden contrivance, about eight inches high, capped by an oval-shaped top. Like everything else in the cavern home, it was a finely made piece of furniture – aesthetically contoured, smoothed, and stained. Marty, of course, immediately recognized its use. Before he asked, Papa pointed to the toilet paper – sitting on a nearby ledge – then returned to the living area... leaving the flashlight with Marty. Marty squatted down to make contact with the toilet seat. The wood, supporting his butt, was so smooth that it felt to Marty as though he were sitting on cotton. Marty could feel very cold air coming from the hole below him and could hear the echoing sound of moving water, deriving from the same location. He surmised that the water flow was likely the drainage from the falls. The height of the toilet was considerably lower than any Marty had ever been on but he immediately recognized the wisdom in it... the low, squatting position, allowing him to apply considerably more pressure on his lower abdomen, resulting in a far more efficient and effective bowel movement than was possible on the higher, conventional models.

When Marty had finished, he felt more familiar and comfortable in the cavern home – as though he belonged – as he always felt after he had defecated somewhere – be it the woods or a motel room. He never quite understood why he always had this feeling. He speculated that perhaps it had to do with the fact it's usually difficult to move your bowels when you don't feel comfortable or safe somewhere, and, when you finally do, you've apparently gotten over it.

When he returned to the living area, Papa was in his rocker. Marty sat in the one he had been in, earlier that day.

"Those were wolves I was hearing, weren't they?"

"Yes they were."

"Was I really in danger… or have I read too many Daniel Defoe stories?"

"You were in danger. Wolves don't kill people often – but each pack is different. There's a particularly vicious pack that lives near here. That was the pack, coming in on you. I recognized their voices."

"You can tell one wolf from another?"

"Oh, yes."

"Is that why we were in such a hurry?"

"Yes."

"Now… tell me Papa. . . are those killer wolves evil? I mean they'll kill your children if they get the chance, apparently."

"No, they're not evil. They do what they must do."

"So, if I understand the implication, if you have to have choice to be evil – and human beings are the only creatures on earth to have choice – human beings are the only creatures capable of evil. Do I have this right?"

"There is no evil. Many of my children are just lost."

"None of them are evil?! Not even Adolph Hitler?!"

"No."

With this response, Marty felt the hot flush of anger.

"There are a lot of Jews... including relatives of mine... who would take strong exception to that point of view."

"They hate as children hate."

"What's that supposed to mean?"

"A child who is bitten, hates the snake as being evil, which it is not. My children curse the flood, the drought, the heat, the cold, as evil. My body has become what it has become. It is free – but it doesn't know of its freedom until it is born as one of my children. Each of my children can choose to love or to hate. If the Jews can learn to love Adolph Hitler as they would love a lost child – they could find their way home to me. Now... if you'll excuse me... it's my turn for the bathroom."

Marty's voice dripped with angry sarcasm. "Oh, so God has to take a shit, too... just like everyone else, huh?"

Papa made no response and – without a flashlight – quickly disappeared into the dark recesses of the cavern. As Marty waited for Papa's return, he began to assess the situation – still in the heat of anger. Maybe he would just write this story as an exposé – quoting some of the rubbish that this self-appointed messiah was spewing – to show him for the idiot he obviously was – saying Jews should love Hitler! That asshole!

As his head cooled, Marty was obliged to factor into his assessment that Papa *had twice* saved his life. But he had also killed Art as far as Marty was concerned. There were just too many conflicting emotions about Papa at that moment to achieve any balance. He opted – as he often did – to sleep on it. When Papa returned, he told him so – and went to bed... taking the smaller bed.

CHAPTER TWELVE

An interruption in the steady flow of the waterfalls awakened Marty. He raised his head to see Papa showering under the falls. Well aware of the bone-numbing cold, visited upon those who brave the waters of these mountain streams, recently born of melting snow from the high peaks, Marty empathetically shivered in the warmth, captured under his deerskin blanket. Although self-conscious about staring at a naked man, the sight of Papa's exquisite physique overcame his inhibitions. This man had a body that looked to Marty, literally, like the Statue of David... and the glistening coat of water over the perfect contours of his brown torso and his squarely chiseled face made his skin shine like polished marble. Marty had never seen a more perfectly proportioned, beautifully muscled body. He mused, as he lay there watching him, that Papa could easily make a living as a world-class model. When he'd finished washing his hair and body, Papa reached for his leather kilt – hanging on a wooden peg that was driven into a crack in the rock – and rubbed soap on it. He then put the soap on a rock shelf and gripped a flat stone, with which he began rubbing the soapy hide. After scrubbing the kilt with the stone, he rinsed it under the falling water, and wrung it out. He then went through the same process with his hide shirt. Finished with his morning shower and laundry, Papa stepped out from under the falling water and dried himself with a large piece of a very pliable skin that gave the appearance of an enormous chamois. He hung the drying-skin on another of the wall pegs and began walking toward the main living area, carrying his wet clothing in his hand. Marty – his self-consciousness returned – laid his head on his pillow and feigned sleep.

Papa hung his clothing on the fireplace crossbar, to the side of the direct flames he had resurrected while Marty slept. He then walked about the cavern, performing morning chores, as natural about his nakedness as a wild animal. He returned to the falls and filled the cooking pot with water then returned to the fireplace and hung it on the cross bar, over the flames. Then, walking to a darkened carcass, hanging from a hook near the kitchen area, he sliced several cuts from it and placed them onto a wooden plate he had carried with him. He placed the plate of meat on the table and brought out the basket of scones and a jar of what appeared to be honey. He then went to a shelf, behind the table, lined with an assortment of cans and jars, and returned to the fireside with a small, square, wooden box, out of which he scooped a small handful of what appeared to be some sort of dried herbal mixture – and dropped the contents of his hand into the water, now profusely steaming in the pot. Papa noticed Marty's opened eyes – watching him.

"Do you want to get a shower, or eat first, Marty?"

Marty thought about the options. The morning air in the cavern was exceedingly chilly – although Papa's nakedness wouldn't bear this out to a casual observer – and he was so very warm under his blanket.

"I'll get a shower later on."

The breakfast meat was smoked venison – tasting very much like Art's... making Marty wonder if there was some sort of ubiquitous meat-smoking process practiced by all inhabitants of the mountain. The liquid in the jar was, indeed, Marty discovered, honey. The tea, which brewed from the herbal mixture in the boiling pot, had an odd, wild, taste to it... both bitter and sweet at the same time. Marty wasn't sure if he liked it or not... but it was warm and comforting, nonetheless. Papa continued all of his morning activities, including breakfast, in total nakedness. Marty was a bit uneasy about this... having never breakfasted with a naked man before. Several times during breakfast, Papa returned to the metal pot to dip more of the purple-colored tea into their cups. After placing Marty's third cup on the table in front of him, Papa spoke to him in a quiet voice.

"Do you have enough for your story, Marty?"

"Well, I'll need some pictures... of you... of your home here. Any problem with that?"

"No."

"After breakfast, I'll have to go and get my camera... down at the cabin. I forgot to bring it. I'll try to finish up my interview with you this afternoon."

Breakfast completed – and politely opting out of the cold waterfalls shower – Marty exited Papa's home through the now-familiar corridors and dual chambers... not being confident of the alternate route they had taken the night before. As he approached the cabin, Marty saw Ben lying on Art's grave and was pleased to discover that Papa wasn't infallible, after all, in his self-proclaimed omniscience. Bending down to stroke Ben, Marty immediately felt the terrible stiffness of death in his body. He was immediately overwhelmed by a mixture of emotions – a terrible sadness for Ben... and a hot resentment at the accuracy of Papa's prophesy.

Looking down at the ever-loyal Ben, Marty's heart swelled with love and admiration for him, then, a moment later, he wept, sorrowfully, for the passing of this wonderful creature who had, literally, died of a broken heart – unable to live without his beloved master. As his healing tears washed over the pain of his grief, Marty reflected on the thought of how few human beings ever loved anyone so deeply as Ben had Art – loved him enough to lie on his grave – to be with his master – at the moment of his death. The nobility and the tragedy of the act was so profound that by the time Marty had recovered his composure, he was totally exhausted from the extreme depth of his emotions. He never would have believed it possible that he could have felt such intense grief over the death of a dog.

Marty summoned his remaining strength and went into the cabin... returning to the grave side with a burlap sack. He lay the sack at Ben's tail end and lifted that part of the stiff body, then worked the bag around the entire corpse... tying it off with a small piece of rope. Marty then retrieved the pointed shovel from the cabin and proceeded to dig a small grave for Ben, a few feet to the side of Art's. Being considerably smaller and shallower than Art's grave, Marty was finished in a little more that an hour's time. He lifted the heavy burlap coffin and, on his knees, lowered it to the grave bottom. After filling it in, Marty returned to the wood pile at the rear of the cabin and found a suitable board for Ben's grave marker. Into it, he carved Ben's epitaph.

> Here lies Ben
> Always loyal
> Always loving
> In life
> and
> In death

Sweaty and dirty from his work, Marty took his towel and a bar of soap and walked to the small, nearby, bathing pond. As he waded into the chilly water, he, again, felt warm tears for Ben, streaming down his cheeks. Bathing in the crystal-clear lake, it felt good to Marty to be performing the familiar morning ritual he had adopted from Art and that had always been attended by their constant companion, Ben.

Back at the cabin, Marty located his camera and tape recorder – wanting to get a sampling of Papa's voice on tape. The camera's flash tested successfully. The discovery of the recorder's dead battery, however, was punctuated by a vociferous stream of profanities. Marty stuck two extra rolls of film in his shirt pocket and started back for Papa's cavern – the trip having, by now, become quite routine. As he ascended from the final ladder into the cavern home, Marty found Papa dressed and sitting on the outer edge of the cavern floor, looking out at the fog-shrouded vista, painted in breathtaking colors by the morning sun, rising from behind his mountain. Papa's feet dangled over the edge – hanging above the sheer drop to the distant canyon below. As Marty approached Papa, he was overcome by vertigo and stopped.

"I don't think I can come any closer. It makes me too dizzy."

Papa turned to look at Marty – his face expressing understanding and sympathy.

"We'll sit at our chairs, then."

"Before we sit down, I'd like to get some pictures of you, if it's OK."

Marty took two rolls of film… photographing Papa from a variety of angles and then pictorially canvassing Papa's enormous cavern home. When he was finished, they sat in their customary chairs to continue the interview. Marty got out his notes, and slowly rocking back and forth, reviewed them… pondering the story… searching for the missing questions and other essential pieces of the mosaic. Finally he looked into Papa's gray-blue eyes.

"What do you hope to accomplish by my writing this story… besides having some people come join you here?"

"To help my children find their way back home to me."

"And how will you do this?"

"By helping them to believe I am alive and that I love each one of them."

"And if they believe this… then what?"

"They will no longer hate or be afraid."

"Why?"

"Because they will no longer feel alone or unloved."

"Why don't you just do something big – like appearing in the sky with angels all around you… or by making the sun turn purple? Seems to me that'd be a heck of a lot more effective than the way you're going about it."

"If I did that, my children would worship me out of fear."

"You don't want to be worshiped?"

"No. All any parent wants from his children is love – not worship."

"But you could do things like that... the opening skies... the purple sun, if you really wanted to?"

"Yes."

"Is my friend Art with you now?"

"Yes."

"What does that mean, exactly?"

"His spirit is together with mine forevermore."

"So human beings have a spirit... just like you."

"Yes."

"What about a child who is born retarded... or dies at birth... does his spirit join yours?"

"No. The child hasn't yet had the chance to choose to come home to me. I only want my children to come home by their own, free choice."

"So what happens to the infant's spirit?"

"It joins with a new body."

"Like reincarnation?"

"Yes."

"Is that what happens to all spirits who don't join you?"

"Yes."

"Do you know if a particular child's spirit will be joining you?"

"A spirit who is love knows it."

"So someone won't be joining you just by going to church or synagogue or a mosque every week?"

"No."

"Will I be joining you?"

Papa's face saddened. His eyes glistened with tears.

"I want you to come home to me, Marty, with all of my heart."

"Will I?"

"Can you accept my love?"

"Do you mean – can I accept that you love me as God?"

"Yes."

"I don't think so... I'm sorry... I'm just that way. I'm a reporter. I'm a born skeptic. I'll do your story – but I've got to level with you... I don't buy the God part of it. I buy all the rest of it... born in the wilderness... living alone since you were twelve – and all that. But this God stuff... I really am sorry – I don't mean to insult you, but if I can be perfectly frank... I think you've just been out here in the wilderness too long. Isolation can do some very strange things to someone's mind. Don't get me wrong... I don't think you're faking it, or anything like that, I think you truly believe you are who you say you are. Maybe you are – who knows? I just can't accept it. I admit you're a remarkable guy... the most remarkable person I've ever met. But, to get back to the article, let me see if I get it. Is this the way it works? No one can come home to you unless they accept your love, right?"

"That's right."

"Why? Isn't that a bit harsh? I mean… you might have people who are perfectly wonderful, loving people who don't accept that you love them. Why can't these people come home to you?"

"My children's spirits are born of my own body. They can find their way home to me. I will wait, always. If they accept my love – their spirits will become love. Their lives will become love. They will no longer feel alone or separated. They will no longer fear. They will be complete. They will no longer hate. They will be at peace. They will be happy. They will be ready to come home."

"Do some of your children take many, many lives to come home to you?"

"Yes."

"Well… I'll give you this much – you seem to have all the answers. Of course… you've had a long time to think about it with no interruptions. Can we get back to this worship thing? You know… millions of people worship you… or God… which, in your mind is you, I guess… they worship you everyday."

"They don't worship me."

"They don't?"

"No."

"What do they worship?"

"Their fear."

"What does that mean?"

"My children are searching for what their spirit knows is missing. They are orphans, searching for their parents but don't know who they are or where they are. As frightened children, they create their own parents and pretend – like a baby with a doll. But the dolls aren't their parents and they eventually discover that they're still alone, unloved, and frightened. My children already know who I am. Each one has a memory of me. I am the familiar. I am simple, quiet love – not chanting, incense, and worship. I am the simple love of a parent. When my children feel love, they feel the yearning from the time we were one. Love has no time – no distance – no end – and no beginning. It is me. I am love. I wait with open arms for all of my children to come home to me so we can be together in a love without time or boundaries."

"And you can't just command them – like a dad calling his kids home at night?"

"If they were commanded – they would not be choosing to come home."

"What do you need these people for... the people you say will come to you, after I write my piece?"

"Only children can teach one another to love."

"And these people, these children, who come to you, will do this?"

"I hope so."

"You don't know for sure? I always thought God was all-knowing."

"My body is free from my spirit. My children are my body. They are free to choose."

"If they're completely free, does that mean they're completely on their own in life?"

"Yes."

"And you won't intervene?"

"No."

"Even if someone prays to you?"

"That's right."

"Excuse me for my bluntness... but what good are you then... if you won't help one of your children in need?"

"All I can do is comfort my children with my love. I won't take their freedom from them. I love them too much for that."

"Being entirely on your own is a scary thought... I mean that's why most of us pray to God."

"To be separated from your parent is frightening... but if you are in my love you are not on your own. I am embracing you and telling you not to be afraid. I'm telling you to be patient – that you will soon be with me. I am telling you that you are not alone and never will be. I am telling you that I love you always and will be with you always."

Marty made several more notes, then flipped back to the first page of his tablet.

"I think that's about it, Papa... I'm done. Oh... just a couple more things I just thought of. You've never seen a television... listened to a radio... ridden in a car... none of the things that everybody takes for granted? I know you said you've not been off this mountain since you were born... but I just wanted to clarify this for the story."

"I've never seen or done any of those things."

"But you know what they are?"

"Yes. I've read about them. I know how they work."

Marty got his things together and turned to bid Papa goodbye.

"Well… I'm off to L.A., Papa. I'll do your story. Actually it'll probably save my job, to be honest with you, so I must thank you for that. I'll take your word for it that I'll know who to bring to you, but you're far more certain about that than I am. Can I come back to see you sometime? I mean you know where I stand – about the God stuff – but I think you're a very good person… I mean I really like you… as a person. Besides you saved my life… twice."

"Yes. Come back to me."

Marty stuck out his hand to Papa. Papa, instead of shaking hands, tightly embraced him. He released him and put a huge hand on each of his cheeks – then leaned forward and kissed him on the lips.

"I love you, Marty."

Marty immediately stiffened and drew away from Papa. He turned and hurried away.

CHAPTER THIRTEEN

Leaving the cabin, for what could very well be his last time, Marty felt awkward and uneasy. As he stood inside and looked around, the details, that had grown so familiar to him over the past summer... that had blurred, through familiarity, into an indistinguishable mosaic, now reappeared, clearly and specifically. He noticed small things that he couldn't recall seeing before – cracks in the floor, a piece of sheet metal nailed to the corner of the ceiling, a small rolled up rug near the back wall. Departing this familiar home for a world that seemed a universe away, Marty began the necessary process of emotional weaning... readying his mind for the volcanic noise and frenetic movement of Los Angeles. As a part of this detaching process, he instinctively began distancing himself from this primitive cabin that he had called home for most of the summer... overtly striving to deny the deep attachment he had for it. In this frame of mind, Marty surveyed the inside of the cabin with a nostalgic heart and a stranger's eye. His heart warmly recalled Art sitting down to his morning coffee with Ben at his feet. His stranger's eye noticed, as if for the first time, the dilapidated condition of the table where he had sat. The familiar, homey smell, now seemed a bit musty and dirty.

For the first time in months, Marty was forced, reluctantly, to think in a businesslike fashion of some practical considerations, the resolution of which was necessary for his departure. Where were his car keys? Would his car start? Where did he leave his car phone and his address and appointment book? As he began packing his bag, Marty felt very much alone and curiously disoriented. He hadn't realized until that moment, just how much he had come to rely on Art to keep him organized and to generally take care of him. His feelings, as he searched for his things, were reminiscent of his first departure for college – a mixture of excitement, insecurity, and fear. Marty packed his notes, camera, exposed rolls of film, recorder, and clothes in his bags – most of which he hadn't worn all summer. He gathered together the drawings he had done and stacked them on the table. Looking at what he had assembled to carry to his car, Marty realized that he didn't really have that much to take with him... and that during the past summer he had existed, very nicely, with only a few changes of clothing. Returning to his urban life, he was reminded of the myriad of possessions he had grown to consider necessities in that world.

Marty looked around the cabin and pondered more practical business. The place wasn't very tidy – not as clean as Art would have liked it. Should he clean up? If he did, who for? It wasn't as though some new tenant was moving in. This thought brought new concerns to his mind – so many that he had to sit down at the table to deal with them.

Could he just get into his car and drive to Los Angeles? Art was dead. Marty was the only one who knew about it. Well, Papa knew too, but he didn't count, since no one but Marty knew he existed. People in Bear Stump had seen Art and him together. Sooner or later they'd begin to notice that Art hadn't come to town in a long while. If someone came out here to look for him – if they knew where his cabin was – they'd find the two graves. What would they think? They might suspect there'd been foul play. After all, he was a big city outsider – a stranger. They might think he had stolen money from Art, killed him, buried him, and taken off. Christ – they might think he had killed Ben, too, as a potential witness. What the hell was he going to do? He knew he should tell someone, but who? The police? Marty began to feel a cold sweat break on his skin and his stomach grow queasy. He needed some air and a cold drink.

Marty grabbed a glass, went outside, and climbed the small hill beside the cabin to the stream where Art kept his ice tea. He pulled the tea container from the cold water and poured himself a glassful. He sat beside the quietly gurgling stream and stared out at the distant mountains, slowly sipping the chilled beverage. He felt himself calming down and coolheaded reasoning returning. He decided he'd go to the police in Bear Stump and tell them what happened to Art and face whatever consequences that came with it.

If worse came to worst, and they suspected foul play, they could always exhume Art's body and do an autopsy on it. He wasn't sure about the burial thing. If burying Art, where he did, was a crime, then so be it. Marty was sure it wasn't a felony.

Out of respect for Art, Marty decided to tidy up the cabin, then, giving the interior one last visual going-over, Marty put a bag over each shoulder, tucked his drawings up under his right arm, and walked slowly out of Art's cabin for what he was certain would be his last time. He walked around to the foot of Art's grave – his back to the hazy mountain ranges. Once again, the realization of the insurmountable distance between him and wherever Art was, struck Marty and increased the depth of his loneliness. He said his final goodbyes to both Art and Ben – promising to come back someday – then started down the path to his car. He stopped suddenly, put down his bags and drawings and ran back to the cabin. Inside, he reverently lifted Art's pipe from the table and shoved it into his front pants pocket. Feeling it there made Marty's heart feel warm.

CHAPTER FOURTEEN

The certainty of action that Marty had resolved at the side of the mountain stream, disintegrated as he pulled into the parking lot of the Bear Stump Police Station – the details of reality… as they often do… overwhelming the simplicity of the original plan. It was an old red brick building that looked as though it had been, sometime in the past, someone's home. Inside was a thin, gray-haired, woman, seated behind a large wooden desk, speaking on the phone. From the discussion she was having it was clear to Marty that it was not an official police call. She was talking to someone named Janet and there was apparently a decision that Janet needed the gray-haired lady to make at that very moment. She held up her pointer finger to Marty while shaking her head up and down and smiling to indicate she would be with him momentarily. Her friendly demeanor reduced Marty's anxiety a few notches. Finally, with an air of command, the lady told Janet to order the cake – a sheet cake – and that she'd pick it up after work. Shaking her head and looking at the ceiling as she hung up the phone, the woman displayed her exasperation at having to deal with matters that she clearly considered to be a waste of her time and talent. Again, she smiled at Marty.

"Some people couldn't cross a street without asking if they should."

Marty smiled bigger than the circumstances demanded and spoke in an overly solicitous voice, hoping all the while that he didn't sound too much like a kiss-up.

"Isn't that the truth."

The lady didn't seem to notice the insincerity of his hyperbolic enthusiasm.

"What can I do for you?"

Marty decided to explain things to the gray-haired lady, first – as a rehearsal – before facing a man with a uniform and a badge... and a gun.

He walked closer to her desk and extended his hand across to her.

"I'm Marty Chapman."

As they were shaking hands, she introduced herself.

"I'm Annabelle Jackman. Nice to meet you, Marty."

"Mind if I sit down?"

Annabelle Jackman extended her hand toward the wooden chair in front of her desk.

"Please do, Marty."

Marty adjusted his body to the chair and took a deep breath, then wished he hadn't, since he felt it made him look nervous, and he figured that people who are nervous in a police station have usually done something they shouldn't have. He cleared his throat – again wishing he hadn't, for the same reason. Marty decided he had better get on with it, without any further bodily fanfare or the lady would probably start thinking he was there to confess to a murder.

"Do you know Art Durbin, Annabelle?"

"Oh sure – Art's lived around here for as long as I can remember. Are you looking for him?"

"No. Well... you see... I was living with Art this summer – after I broke my leg. I'm from Los Angeles and Art found me out in the mountains with a broken leg and brought me into the medical center, here... and when I found out that I couldn't work for a couple of months – with my cast on and all – Art invited me to come stay with him."

"That's odd. Art's always been such a loner. I don't know anybody in town that's ever even seen where Art lives."

"Yes... he told me that – said I was the first one to ever stay overnight in his cabin... first guest he'd ever had. Well, anyway... to get to the point. Art died a few days ago."

"Oh my goodness, Marty. What happened?"

"To tell you the truth, I'm not sure. He just got really weak and all white and was dead a few hours later."

"Do you need an ambulance to go get his body?"

"Well, that's what I've come here about. After he died, I wasn't sure what to do. Art had told me, just before he died, that he wanted to be buried up on his mountain... so that's what I did. I wasn't sure if I was allowed to do that – with the laws and all – but that's what he had asked me to do – so I did. And I buried his dog too."

"His dog died, too?"

"Yes. Not long after Art died. Just climbed up on Art's grave and died."

"Bless his heart."

"I came here because I figured I'd better tell someone what happened. I figured you can't just bury someone and drive away."

"You did the right thing, Marty. Wait here. I'll get Captain Thompson. We'll see what we need to do."

Annabelle disappeared into an office to her right. She was gone for several minutes. Marty figured she must be telling Mr. Thompson the whole story, herself. Annabelle returned and stood just outside Captain Thompson's door.

"Come on in Marty. The Captain would like to talk to you."

Marty didn't like the way she put that, nor did he like the looks of Captain Thompson – a large, overweight man in his fifties with a drinker's swollen nose and the piercing, skeptical eyes of a cop. Captain Thompson didn't smile nor greet Marty. He merely motioned with his head, toward the chair in front of his desk. He took out a tablet and immediately began asking questions in a curt and distinctly unfriendly fashion.

"What's your full name?"

"Martin J. Chapman."

"Address."

"2235 Bon Aire Boulevard, Santa Monica, California."

"Driver's license."

"Do you want to see it?"

The Captain's stare immediately indicated his opinion as to the immense stupidity of Marty's question. Marty fumbled through his collection of plastic cards in his wallet – passing over his license several times out of nervousness. Finally he located it and handed it – his hands shaking – to Captain Thompson, who copied down the information.

"What were you doing in Bear Stump, Mr. Chapman?"

Marty launched into a detailed explanation about his job and his writing assignment... the professor at Colorado Springs... the alleged hippie commune back the old mining road... the missing "Freaksville" sign... the snake... the broken leg... Art's rescuing him... the medical center – mentioning names for credibility – his stay at Art's cabin... how Art died... the burial... Ben's subsequent death and burial. Marty intentionally left out the whole Papa story, figuring it was a potential Pandora's box.

The Captain wrote furiously as Marty spoke, stopping him, from time to time, so he could get it all down... often reading what he had written for Marty's verification of accuracy. He asked for phone numbers – Marty's, home and at work... his editor's... friends' that knew Marty in L.A. He then telephoned the county District Attorney, apparently in a county seat some distance away – having to use an area code along with the number. Thompson asked the D.A.'s opinion on what to do... and requested him to run a criminal check on Marty. He hung up and told Marty they'd call him back with the information. Captain Thompson shouted for Annabelle, who quickly appeared at the office door. He told her to get out the Polaroid. Thompson had Marty get up and stand in front of the institutional-green office wall. Annabelle handed the camera to the Captain. He took a shot of Marty facing forward and waited until it developed. Comparing the photo to the corporeal image, his facial expression seemed to indicate that it was, apparently, a passable likeness. He repeated the same procedure with each profile then handed the three photos to Annabelle – telling her to open a file on Marty and put them in – then told Marty to sit down again.

Captain Thompson asked Marty if he was driving a car, whose it was, and for the registration card. The phone rang. Thompson began writing and shaking his head and repeatedly saying "OK." He hung up and gazed threateningly at Marty.

"They're faxing down an affidavit of death from the coroner's office. You need to fill it out and have Annabelle notarize it. You go on out front and have a seat until it gets here. Annabelle!"

She appeared again.

"They're faxing something down from Culver. When it gets here, have Mr. Chapman, here, fill it out and sign it, then you notarize it."

Marty and Annabelle went back to the outer office together. Marty was greatly relieved to be back in the singular company of this kindly woman. She offered – and Marty gratefully accepted – a cup of coffee, while they waited. To pass the time they started talking and somehow got onto the topic of Annabelle's quilting. Annabelle was, apparently, quite accomplished at her craft and had won a number of blue ribbons at the Culver County Fair. The fax machine finally went into action. Annabelle pulled the two sheets from the tray and handed them to Marty, along with verbal instructions as to how to fill them out. When the form was completed, signed, and notarized, Annabelle took it into Captain Thompson. She returned with a message from the good Captain.

"Captain Thompson wants you to stay in touch – just in case. He says if you change your address or job or phone number over the next year – let him know. OK?"

"No problem, Annabelle. It was very nice talking to you."

Marty extended his hand and Annabelle shook it.

"You take care, Marty. Are you driving all the way back to California?"

"Yes ma'am."

"Well, you be careful. That's a long trip."

"Thank you, I will... oh... by the way, Annabelle, what will become of Art's cabin? He didn't have a will or anything that I know of... or any family. I mean I just left it... just as it was. There isn't even a lock on the door."

"That's not really my department, Marty, but probably, it'll just sit there. We've got lots of places like that in the mountains around here... people just live there – then leave – leaving behind cabins and all kinds of belongings. That's just the way it is out there. Lots of strange people in these mountains."

"I can vouch for that, Annabelle."

CHAPTER FIFTEEN

Marty gassed-up at the Bear Stump Texaco, got a cup of coffee for the road, and plugged his mobile phone into the cigarette lighter outlet to charge the dead battery. He debated if he should call Marla before getting on the road, or wait. He opted not to call – waiting for a later moment, when he felt more confident about the potential outcome of the conversation. He, frankly, had no inkling as to whether or not he still had a job. He hadn't spoken to a single person in the office for nearly three months. It was late August, now, and Marty wouldn't be terribly surprised if Marla had replaced him. He was well aware that he wasn't exactly indispensable at the magazine – having been there only a couple of years and laying claim to no major stories as yet. He resolved that he'd call Marla when he got to Billings.

Job or no job, Marty, nonetheless, felt he had a great story – better than the one he had originally gone after – and great pictures too. He made up his mind that if Marla didn't want him, he'd sell the piece on the open market. Maybe that's what he'd do anyway, he considered... just sell it... to hell with Marla. That might be trouble, though, as he further considered this cavalier position. He'd done the work while still on the magazine's payroll – or at least on their workmen's comp account. If they really liked the story, they'd claim it belonged to them. If he shopped it out, they'd sue him – they were like that. What if he no longer had a job, but they still said the story belonged to them? He'd really be fucked, then. He decided he'd have to think about this for awhile. As he drove through the mountains, he rolled various scenarios over in his mind – considering what his best position would be. Finally he decided. He'd call Marla from Billings and ask her if he still had a job. If she said no, he'd shop the story around and sell it to the highest bidder. If they sued, he'd claim he was fired and didn't write the story until after he was fired. That might not win it outright for him, but it should be a strong enough position to get a good settlement.

Emerging from the peaks on the eastern side of the continental divide, Marty looked out over the flat country, ahead... becoming one with the horizon at some unimaginable distance. Plunging back into the real world – driving with his air conditioning on full blast to create a tiny, glass-enclosed refuge against the stifling, hot August air outside – Marty occupied himself with career planning strategies, then began thinking about his apartment in Santa Monica. His mind then drifted back to the summer. Now, away from the mountain, the whole summer – the cabin, Art, Ben, Papa – all seemed like a dream. Had he really lived on a mountain for the whole summer, he pondered? Made a best-in-life friend? Gone on a mountain climbing, cave exploring adventure? Watch his best friend die then bury him? Had he really encountered a bizarre, leather-kilted giant who lived in a cave and thought he was God? These events of the past summer suddenly seemed so out-of-context to his resurrected existence, that he was at a loss to integrate them into a singular reality... as though the Marty on the mountain had been a totally separate being from the newly reclaimed urban persona.

This profound sense of unreality, regarding his summer experiences, began to worry Marty in its possible bearing upon the potential reception of his story. If he, who had actually been there, now looked upon the events of the summer as utterly fantastic, how would the average reader regard them? Perhaps, he worried, the story was just too incredible for professional journalism standards. One of the tabloid rags might buy it, but they'd buy anything that would appeal to readers who believed in Elvis sightings and aliens in the White House. Money or not, Marty vowed that moment, that he'd burn the story before he'd sell it to one of the sewer-dwelling rags.

In Billings, Marty finally got up the nerve to call Marla, after gas and a McNuggets, fries, and Diet Coke dinner. It was nearly five, but Marla always worked late. He decided to call his department secretary, first, to obtain whatever intelligence she could afford him, regarding his continued employment at the magazine – or lack thereof. Connie told Marty that she really didn't know much, but did say that everyone in the department was wondering if he was alive or dead. She assured him she knew nothing about his employment status. Marty didn't try any other sources. He'd been in enough companies to know that if the secretarial grapevine didn't have the information, no one did. As Connie transferred him to Marla Kupetz' direct line, Marty could feel his heart pounding. He tried his voice out before Marla answered – not wanting to overtly disclose his insecurity.

"Kupetz."

"Marla?"

"Yes."

"It's Marty."

Silence. Marty continued.

"How are you?"

Silence. Marty waited her out and prevailed.

"What do you want, Marty?"

"Look Marla… I know I really fucked up. I should have stayed in touch… but it was a really weird summer. That's what I'm calling you about."

"You want to tell me about your really weird summer?"

"Marla… I need to know if I have a job or not."

"Well Marty, that all depends."

"On what?"

"On whether you have anything worthwhile for me or not."

"Have you replaced me?"

"That's irrelevant, Marty."

"Not to me it isn't."

"Do you have anything or not?"

Marty paused. It wasn't going according to plan. This could be a trap. If he said he had a great story, Marla could have him bring it in, take it, then fire him. He knew he'd have to just wing it from here on out.

"I have a fantastic story… better than the one I went out on… but I need to know the deal, Marla. If I still have a job… and we come to a firm understanding, you'll get the story. If not… the story's mine and I'll shop it to the highest bidder."

"What is this Marty… a hold up?"

"No… just my career and my survival."

"All right, look… it's Friday. You come in at ten on Monday and we'll talk about this. I'm not doing this kind of thing over the phone. All right?"

"I'll be there."

Marty got into Santa Monica on Sunday evening. The air inside his second story apartment – closed up for three months of southern California's hottest weather – felt as dead, Marty was sure, as did the ancient Egyptian tombs, opened for the first time in centuries. The atmosphere was so oppressively stifling that it instantly sucked the breath from Marty's lungs. He quickly turned the air conditioner on full blast, grabbed a six pack of beer from the refrigerator, and hurried onto his tiny patio, intending to wait there until the air inside was no longer life threatening. He sat in the white plastic lawn chair – the sole item of patio furniture – and sipped his green can of Rolling Rock.

It felt exceedingly odd to be back – as though he'd been gone for years. As he became more conscious of his surroundings, Marty quickly realized just how accustomed he had become to the undisturbed quiet of the mountain. The city noise, which had always been an unnoticed backdrop in his life, was now overpowering his senses. Having lived in nature's peace, for the first time in his life, Marty now recognized how unnatural and unhealthy this constant exposure must be... how insidiously destructive the perpetual cacophony of these modern-day urban centers had to be to the fragile psyches of the oblivious inhabitants. Pondering these thoughts, and three beers later, the two-room apartment was tolerably cool.

Marty's head was still moving, inside, from his twenty-eight hours on the road. Though exhausted and needing to get up early in the morning to see Marla, he knew any attempt at sleep, at that moment, would be futile. So, lacking a better idea, he decided to take a walk. He strolled, leisurely, to the bluff, overlooking the ocean – only fifteen minutes from his apartment – then continued south along the path that wound along the cliff's edge. He looked down at the vast Pacific and its calm waters, ablaze from the orange light of the setting sun. The living smell of the ocean air, in tandem with the rhythmic slap of the surf onto the wet sand, reminded him of the natural magnificence that still washed to the very border of the mechanized bedlam in which he lived. This ocean, he confessed to himself, he had missed. After a half-hour or so, Marty recrossed the street and walked a few blocks to the closed-to-traffic shopping area, and found himself gawking at the bizarre street people, like a tourist. He had actually forgotten just how strange they really were. Finally, Marty began to feel the moving road inside his head slowing down, gradually falling into synch with the rest of his body. Wearily, he made his way home and fell into his bed... sweet sleep quickly enveloping him.

On the way to the magazine office in the morning, Marty stopped at a Foto-Hut to drop off his summer film rolls for developing. He had already decided he wasn't going to let the magazine's photo department do the processing – not wanting them to gain possession of the film before his deal was cut. A moment of panic swept over him as he was driving away from the chain-store developer, worrying that something may possibly have gone wrong with either the film or the camera and he'd end up without any of the irreplaceable shots he'd taken. Recounting, however, the many faultless rolls of film he'd shot over the years, his paranoia gradually diminished.

Knowing he was in for a confrontation, Marty was a case of nerves as Marla's secretary picked up the phone to inform her that he had arrived. He was certain Marla was playing mind games with him – as she was prone to do – when she told Kathy to have Marty take a seat... that she'd be with him shortly. "Shortly" translated into twenty-five minutes, but it worked to Marty's psychological advantage by transforming his nervousness into anger.

Marla had on her game face as Marty walked into her large office. She got to the point immediately.

"OK, Marty, let's hear your pitch."

Marty told her the whole story... the missing sign... the snake... the broken leg... Art and Ben... the cave adventures... all about Papa... Art's death and burial, and Ben's... the photos. Though normally a very cool negotiator, Marla's excitement over the story was clearly evident. She asked Marty what deal he wanted. A guarantee of the byline, and the cover, was his response. Marla agreed so quickly that it threw Marty – ready as he was with all his arguments. He felt strangely cheated that he didn't get a chance to present them.

Marty got the September tenth cover. On the inside cover, Marla did an editorial background piece on him and his adventure. He got five full pages for his article, along with four photos – crediting him. A small, insert headshot of him accompanied the story. The cover was of one of the shots of Papa with his back to the spectacular view from his cave. Marty agreed with the selection, feeling it was one of the best shots he had ever taken. After the issue hit the stands, there was immediate talk within the magazine community about the cover being considered for one of the premier photo-journalism awards. Papa's imposing presence and loving tenderness were beautifully captured in the picture. Below the picture was the issue caption, "The New Messiah?" Marty also felt that the article was his best writing, to date.

The New Messiah?

By Martin Chapman

His story is the stuff of myths and legends. He was born in a mountain cave in Montana of a Scottish father and a Caribbean Islander mother. When he was one-year old, his mother and infant brother died in childbirth. He was raised by his father in total isolation from all other human contact, in a rugged world of mountains and forests – hunting wild game, drinking from mountain streams, cooking over an open fire. When he was twelve, his father was killed in a bear attack. Completely alone, he raised himself to adulthood. It was not until the age of thirty-three that he, again, came into contact with another human being – the first such contact in twenty-one years.

The man stands over six-foot-six – possessing a body reminiscent of an ancient Spartan warrior. He dresses in a sleeveless shirt and a kilt – both made of deer hide. He moves through the forest and mountains with the swiftness of an antelope and the stealth and power of a puma. His home is a very large, well concealed cavern, cut by nature into the side of a shear, rock cliff. It is filled, not with crude articles of a Neanderthal existence that one might expect, but with finely made furniture, magnificent paintings – done by his mother and him – and an impressive library, filled with volumes that traverse all aspects of human endeavor. He is highly intelligent, articulate, well-educated, and exceedingly handsome – an exquisite combination of a Celt and a French-Black African, having a light chestnut complexion and tightly curled, light brown, woolly hair and beard that dramatically set off his striking blue-gray eyes – so luminescent that they seem to project light from within.

The above story, considered alone, is a fascinating one, but there is much, much more. This man of the wilderness, born Ian MacDonald, who calls himself simply "Papa," also claims to be God, incarnate. In an episode in which Papa describes as a spectacular transition from darkness into light, he claims that God entered his body during his thirteenth year of life. Papa explains that this was voluntary on his part – God requesting – he acceding. Though being possessed by God, Papa explains that he is completely human – in every aspect. Papa, according to his own description, is both Ian MacDonald and God – an inextricable marriage of both mortal and divine beings.

The specific catechism (if you will) of Papa is both mesmerizing and blasphemous. According to Papa – speaking as God – this is the first time that he has visited our planet. Upon inquiry, he explained that Jesus of Nazareth was his son, but only in the sense that all of the people of the Earth are his children – Jesus not occupying any special status in the scheme of things. The universe was created, according to Papa's explanation because of his loneliness, he being, before the moment of universal creation, perfect, but entirely alone and without love. Seeking the love and companionship of others, he claims that he destroyed his own perfection – setting it free in every direction. All that remained of him, after this event, he says, was his spirit. His body was no longer his own, but the matter of all creation as we know it. It was free to "become," as he describes it. It was free, he says, to be apart from him, or come back to him. This destruction of his perfection and the setting free of his body has a scientific basis, according to Papa – being none other than the cosmic event we commonly refer to as the "Big Bang."

Papa explains that the sense of incompleteness and separation that all human beings (who he consistently refers to as his "children") feel is a vague recollection of the time when they were together with him as a single body and spirit. The fear and loneliness, that we all share, he says, is that of an orphan – alone and longing for his parents. To the anticipated satisfaction of the politically correct, Papa claims not to be a "heavenly father" but the "parent" – both mother and father – of all his children. The choice of the paternal term of familiarity, "Papa," is apparently used for convenience only. And to the vindication of UFO buffs, Papa explains that our Earth is but one of many worlds that his children inhabit – the Earth being, however, a particularly troublesome home, by his account. We, and all that exists, says Papa, are made of his body – from snails to comets.

Why has Papa chosen to make his very first appearance on Earth at this particular juncture in our planetary history? His earthly children are desperately troubled, he says. (A position, with which, it is difficult to take exception.) What does he wish to accomplish by this first-time visit? He hopes, he says, that through his coming, more of his children will return home to him. He doesn't plan on doing all this work himself, however. He believes that certain of his children will come to him after reading this article. As to where they will go to join him, it cannot be revealed by this writer, as per specific conditions agreed upon in giving the interviews for this article, but the number of disciples can be – being eight in number. According to Papa, he needs these disciples because, he says, only his children can teach one another to love.

Papa doesn't plan on any spectacular shows of might or power, by the way, although he claims he is perfectly capable of performing them. There will be neither opening skies nor angels on high, he says, but only his love and assurance that he does, indeed, live – and does, indeed, love his children. Why no miracles and sideshows? In his words, "If I did that, my children would worship me out of fear. All any parent wants from his children is love – not worship." As for his response to those of us who pray to and worship God, "They don't worship me." Who do they worship? "Their own fear," he says. "As frightened children, they create their own parents and pretend – like a baby with a doll. But the dolls aren't their parents and they find that they are still alone, unloved, and frightened. I am simple, quiet love – not chanting and worship. I do not want to be feared nor worshiped. I wait with open arms for my children to come home to me." As for praying, regardless of the goodness of the cause, Papa says he will not intervene in the affairs on Earth. "All I can do is comfort my children with my love. I won't take their freedom from them. I love them too much to do that."

Dr. Aaron Naylor, Professor of Psychiatry at the University of Pittsburgh, School of Medicine, views Papa's beliefs about himself as pathological and circumstantial, resulting from inadequate socialization. According to Dr. Naylor, "One needs, particularly during the formative years of adolescence, some boundaries, role models, and feedback to adequately ground one's psyche in reality. One who has been as isolated and deprived of human contact for as many years as has this individual, will almost certainly begin to confuse dreams and fantasies with reality, having acquired no ability to distinguish them, as is clearly the case with this man. Given an appropriate reintroduction to human society and contact, along with long-term therapy, this person would have a very good chance of achieving a psychic balance which would allow him to separate the realms of reality and fantasy. He is, to put it into simplistic, clinical terms – schizophrenic – having experienced a separation from reality to a degree that would be generally considered to be pathological – and I would treat him as such."

Rabbi Twerski of the Beth Shalom Temple in Chicago views Papa in both an historical and religious context. "One can never rule out the possible coming of the Messiah. It would, of course, be the greatest event in the history of mankind if this man were, in fact, the Promised One. His experience and revelation in the wilderness are very typical of the great prophets, as a matter of fact. Of course, there have been many pretenders throughout history, claiming to be the Messiah. Only time, and God, will tell if this man is truly the coming of God to the Earth."

Reverend James McAndrew of the First Baptist Church of Atlanta is not as gracious nor as open-minded as Rabbi Twerski in his assessment of Papa. "Any man, who states that Jesus Christ is not the Son of God, should be condemned by any believing Christian. His claims of being God indicate that he is either the unfortunate victim of a mental disorder – or it is possible he is the anti-Christ. Either way, his heretical claims are but a further demonstration of the degeneration of the fundamental moral fabric of American society."

An informal and random poll of passersby in Los Angeles indicates a wide variety of reactions to Papa's story, and the following are a representative sampling: "Ask him if he knows Elvis." "Join the group… first Jim Jones, then David Koresh… now Papa. Who's next?" "Tell him not to get Alcohol, Tobacco, and Firearms pissed off at him." "Hey… with as many people as there are who believe in UFOs, he shouldn't have any trouble getting a large congregation together." "It would be wonderful if he is, in fact, who he says he is. This world desperately needs somebody to save it." "I'm an atheist... so he better turn out to be wrong or I'm going to look pretty stupid." "Are you serious about this? I'd like to know more about it before I give an opinion. I would very much like to meet this man." "I give him two weeks before Geraldo has him on his show."

    Having agreed to certain conditions with Mr. MacDonald, this reporter cannot go into precise detail as to how or where I came to meet him. I can, however, relate my own personal perceptions of him. He has an overwhelming effect upon those who encounter him. For reasons I cannot explain, he made me feel very safe and protected in his presence, yet, at the same time, I also feared him, greatly. His presence, also, enigmatically, brought me to joyful tears on several occasions. He seemed to know things about me that I could discover no plausible way of explaining. The strength of his charismatic power may, in my opinion, be dangerous – having had such an effect upon an elderly friend of mine that I believe it may have contributed to his death. I do not believe he is insane. He is a strange, unique, frightening, yet wonderful person. As for the truth of his claims of divinity, I cannot, personally, accept them as being true – perhaps because of my own weaknesses. I told him this. He accepted my disbelief in him without any diminishment of his graciousness or love toward me.

    Whether you choose to call him Ian MacDonald or Papa, he is an easy man to like – or even love. He is unlike any other man I have ever encountered in my life. I will attempt to make no judgment of him, in this article, on behalf of the world at large. He may be merely a misguided and gentle giant who has spent too many years alone in the wilderness, or he may actually be who he says he is. In the words of Rabbi Twerski, "... only time and God will tell..."

CHAPTER SIXTEEN

Although Marty felt he had a great story, he could not possibly have anticipated the public's overwhelming reaction to it. Within days, the issue became the second highest selling in the history of the magazine – second only to the Kennedy assassination edition. Marty also could not have anticipated the unrelenting pressure he would come under to reveal Papa's whereabouts... nor the voracious bidding war that was declared to obtain the rights to exclusive interviews and appearances with Papa. Nary had a tabloid, newspaper, television network, cable company, nor talk show (both radio and television) failed to jump into the competition. When the bidding reached six million, Marla felt it was time to realistically reassess the firmness of Marty's commitment to Papa. She called him into her office and laid out the financial facts of life for him.

"Marty, look, I appreciate your concern for Mr. MacDonald's privacy, but... I've got a business to run here. The board is well aware of the deals we've been offered and Earl Montgomery is putting a hell of a lot of pressure on me to do something. This bidding hasn't nearly reached the top of the dike yet. We could easily drive it up to ten million or higher... who the hell knows how high. I think we need to talk about this, Marty."

"Marla... you know I'm as much of a whore as the next writer – but this is different. You just don't know what we're dealing with here. I just can't do this to this guy. I can't allow these media slime balls to violate this man. I just can't do it. I'm no hero, Marla, but I swear to God, I'll resign before I reveal Papa's whereabouts."

"Well, you may not have to. They may just find him for free. They've already traced your gas purchases to Bear Stump and have talked to the police there – who've told them some interesting parts of your story that I didn't even hear about, Marty."

"What! Who the fuck gave them my card number? I can't believe this!"

"You know this gang Marty – and everybody has their price. Nothing is confidential or sacred in this world. They probably had your account number and list of charges ten minutes after the issue hit the stands."

"Well I'll tell you what, Marla. They can look for Papa for the next two centuries… they'll never find him. They'll have a hell of a time even locating Art's cabin. I'd bet ten million they don't find that either. Fuck them!"

"Oh, c'mon Marty… they'll find him… it's just a matter of time. We might as well make ten million for the company as let it go for free."

"No fucking way, Marla… no fucking way. You can tell Montgomery I said so – that fucking whore!"

That night, Marty felt nauseous, thinking about a host of media scum, trampling on Papa's innocence and serenity. It would literally be, he thought, like the rape of an infant. He couldn't sit still… and paced, endlessly, around his apartment. Finally he went out to walk his usual circuit along the ocean-side bluff, hoping it would calm him down. He felt he was a part of an unconscionable complicity to violate Papa's purity, and could find no peace for his writhing conscience. He recited logical reasons why he shouldn't feel the way he did – Papa had asked him to write the article… he really didn't want to write it but Art had prevailed upon him… it wasn't his fault that the media was so Machiavellian. But he should have anticipated the likely response. He should have warned Papa about how these people operate… of what they would do to him. What did Papa know of the viciousness of modern-day media? How could he know they'd tear him to shreds for increased ratings or circulation? Marty knew they'd make a cartoon – a buffoon – of him, as they always do of anyone like Papa. They'll skewer him and ridicule him, he thought, just like they did to Shirley MacLaine when she started talking about her past lives. He'll become the material for Letterman's monologue... the butt of sick jokes and sarcastic humor... jokes that start – "Did you hear the latest about Papa?" Shirley MacLaine was streetwise and was able to handle the media cesspool. Papa was, in essence, a child... loving and trusting. What had he done to this good man? Marty asked himself. Oh, God... what had he done? But the deed was done... the article written... the dogs were on the hunt – so what could he do now? What could he do? Marty felt very protective of Papa. He felt he could not let the press get to him. Could they find him? He pondered. He had bet Marla ten million they couldn't, but he knew that was just bravado. He went over the possibility in his mind. How could anyone – not knowing about the ceiling hole or even the lower chamber – find it? He was sure they'd unearth the general vicinity of Art's cabin from the Bear Stump locals but no one from town had ever been to the cabin, from Marty's impressions. All the locals knew was that he lived somewhere back on Old Log Road. Marty then realized that someone from the Stump may have known the guy from whom Art bought the cabin. Someone may have visited the guy! Oh Christ!... the graves! Those vermin could be crawling all over Art's and Ben's graves at that very moment, violating their sacredness. The thought enraged and sickened Marty... causing him to walk faster, cursing louder with each emphatic step.

Marty walked for hours, into the falling darkness, until fatigue eventually wore his anger to despair. Exhausted and dejected, he sat on the wooden railing... looking out over the black, night water of the Pacific, dimly lit by a smiling sliver of the moon. He put his face down into his hands – seeking the peace that one's own palms can sometimes afford. For the first time since he attended synagogue, many years ago, he found himself praying.

"My dear God. Help me Father. Maybe it's you I'm talking to Papa, I don't know. I don't know how all this works or if anyone even hears me. I don't know what to do. I'm so sorry for what I've done. I shouldn't have written that article. I should have known better. Maybe I'm just talking to myself. I don't know. If you hear me Father... please tell me what to do. This is all beyond my puny mind. I know so little. I have so little wisdom. How do I protect Papa? How will I know who these people are who Papa said would contact me? This is all such a mess. Grant me wisdom, Father. Please grant me wisdom."

At around midnight, Marty stopped at a bar on the Boulevard and drank some draft beer – hoping it would give him some peace of mind – also hoping he wouldn't see anyone he knew. He was, at that moment, simply incapable of shooting the breeze with anyone. After five drafts and three bags of beer nuts, he headed home... his distress, mercifully blunted by a pleasant, foggy heaviness. He was fortunate enough to fall asleep before the protective shroud lifted.

By morning, Marty's emotions had run their course and their energy, and he was able to strategically assess the situation. He knew it was too risky for him to try to return to the mountain to warn Papa. The area would be crawling with reporters and he could, quite unintentionally, lead them right to him. He would just have to hope that Papa's cavern was as well hidden as he felt it was. He really did believe that it was nearly impossible to find, without help. The only clue as to the location of the cavern, that Marty could ascertain, was the photo of Papa, with his back to the mountain range. He worried that some clever shit might match up the view and figure out where someone would have to be standing to take the picture of the mountain ranges from that particular angle. If someone did that, it would just be a matter of time until they found him. But, then again, there were so many mountain ranges and angles of every view... what were the chances of someone matching it up with the photo? He just didn't know. On more immediate matters, he wondered what Marla was going to do. Fire him if he didn't cooperate? Assessing the situation, Marty felt he was in a pretty good position. With the success of the article, he was sure he could get another job, anywhere – and Marla knew it. He concluded her veiled threats were bullshit. She wouldn't fire him.

On the way to his cubicle, later that morning, Marty told Connie he wouldn't take any calls, except from inside the company – aware that an avalanche of outside calls waited to bury him if he allowed them in. She handed him a box, filled with pink phone messages – all from the media hounds. He dumped them into his waste can as soon as he entered his small, doorless, work area, enclosed by three-quarter walls, covered with rough, spongy, gray fabric. His phone rang before he could sit down. It was Marla. Had he thought about it? Yes... and Montgomery could still go fuck himself. Anything else? No. Goodbye. Marty cautioned himself not to let his confidence spiral into cockiness... that it might just rise up to bite him on the ass.

It had been a week, that morning, since his article had come out. Lacking legitimate sources, the tabloids were, as usual, already running stories about people who claimed to have met Papa. One man said Papa was his brother who he claimed had been lost as a toddler on a Montana camping trip. Another guy claimed there had been a UFO landing near Bear Stump around the time of Papa's birth. A woman from Brooklyn claimed to be his mother. In the afternoon, the beginnings of the mail barrage from self-proclaimed Papa-followers hit Marty's office. Seventy-five letters arrived in the first batch. By the end of the week, Marty had received five hundred more. Papa had said that Marty would know who to send him. Marty poured over the bin of letters. Many were clearly from kooks... making such representations as being the son of God, to being from another universe – claiming Papa was a former fellow resident whom the writer was commissioned to bring back to face intergalactic justice. But many were quite sincere – decent, levelheaded people, writing that they were willing to devote their lives to Papa. Marty had absolutely no way of sorting out the chosen-eight from the mountain of legitimate letters. It was impossible to come up with eight, he decided, except by random selection... and he was sure that was not what Papa had in mind to determine the final group.

Marty filled boxes, each day, and brought all of the letters home with him. He read them for hours every night, searching each one for some clue that might indicate something upon which to base a selection process. He began a system of two piles... one for normals – one for kooks. By the end of two weeks, the flood had slowed down to a trickle – typical for letter responses to an article. If anyone was motivated enough to write – they did so very soon after reading the article, or not at all. In all, Marty had a kook-pile of one hundred twenty-one and a pile of normals numbering eight hundred ninety-eight. Night after night, Marty read the letters, growing more frustrated as he read. Papa promised Marty he'd know, but he didn't. He still had no clue, whatsoever. Finally, after reading until dawn on Sunday morning, Marty's frustration finally got the best of him, after two weeks of steady reading. He kicked his foot straight forward, smashing into the side of the coffee table that was piled with the letters. The table flipped and the letters scattered across his living room rug. He jumped to his feet – angry and overtired.

"Fuck this shit! I don't care what you say, Papa, I don't know one letter from the other! I must be out of my fucking mind! Sitting here night after night – reading these goddamn letters – looking for true believers! No... I'm not out of my mind... you are Papa... and you suckered me! I'm an idiot! That's it – I quit! I'm done with this stupid fucking shit!"

Marty made his way to his bed and literally fell into it. He had one of those dreams that seem absolutely real... even though he knew he was sleeping. He was back in the cave and he was swearing at Papa – telling him how much of an idiot he had made of him. He told Papa that he was crazy. Papa didn't respond – except to smile with understanding. In the middle of Marty's tirade, Papa turned and walked to one of his paintings hanging on a stone pillar. He removed it from the peg upon which it hung, and brought it back with him. He held it directly in front of him as he faced Marty. Marty studied it. It was an abstract, done predominantly with reds, blues, purples and white. On the left side of the painting, as he faced it, was a single circle, outlined in red, having a solid blue center. In the middle of the painting were many small circles outlined in white, with blue centers. On the right was a single circle, outlined in red, filled with small circles, identical to those in the center. The entire background was a blackish-purple. Suddenly, Papa lifted the painting and broke it into two pieces, across his leg. He handed Marty the right half of the painting, then walked away, carrying the other half, and disappeared, down the ladder. Marty rushed after him and climbed down the ladder to follow. When he placed his foot on the stone floor below, he found himself in his own apartment – staring down at the letters, still strewn across his carpet. A wailing sound echoed throughout the apartment and Marty searched for its source. As he turned the corner to enter his bedroom, he saw himself sitting in his bed, listening to the sound of police sirens. The dreamer and the dream merged and Marty was awake, sitting up in his bed, listening to the annoying, discordant warble of sirens, passing outside his window.

Marty looked at his clock. The red digital numbers posted the time as eleven thirteen. During what seemed but a few moments time, he'd slept for over twelve hours. As he transitioned to the waking world, he vividly recalled each detail of his dream and replayed it, over and over, in his mind. It had felt so real to him – as though he had truly been with Papa and talked to him. As he pondered this captivating drama, written and directed by his slumbering brain, he became aware of his swollen bladder and gingerly walked to the bathroom to discharge the overnight accumulation. After peeing, he brushed his teeth – scrubbing away the gummy residue of a sleeping mouth, then made some coffee and seated himself at his kitchen table with pencil and paper. He quickly made a crude drawing of the painting Papa had shown him in his dream… then ripped it where Papa had broken it – taking the piece Papa had given him in his hand and pushing the remainder of the drawing away from him. His eyes moved back and forth between the pieces – seeking the message of the dream. He then repeatedly put the pieces together then moved them apart. Marty then recalled an old movie he'd seen on the classic movie channel in which two soldiers, sitting in a bar after getting home from the war, ripped a dollar in half. Each took a piece of it and swore they'd meet in that same bar in so many years, and bring their half of the dollar with them, so they would know one another… or something along that line. In a moment of unquestionable epiphany, Marty knew how to find Papa's eight disciples.

On a good piece of white paper, Marty redrew the painting – this time in very precise detail – then colored it with felt-tipped markers to match the dream painting as closely as possible. When he was satisfied with the likeness, he cut the picture, exactly where Papa had broken it in his dream. The next morning – Monday – Marty took the portion of the drawing that Papa had given him, into the office. He asked Connie to make him nine hundred colored copies of it. Her facial expression clearly indicated that she considered this to be a strange request, but, she said, if Marty was willing to sign for it, she'd do it. Marty had also brought the normal letters with him, and after Connie had finished the copying job, he asked her if she'd mind addressing envelopes to all the people who wrote the letters. He lied – saying it was for a follow-up article to the Papa story. He added that she should type his name on the envelope, under the company, return address. This time, her facial expression indicated profound displeasure at being asked to do such a monotonous, time-consuming task. Marty's promise to take her to dinner for doing it, not only softened her heart, but got the job done before the end of the day. Marty had intentionally delayed asking her to do the letter stuffing until the next day – not wanting to push his luck.

Marty frankly resented the stupid games they all had to play to get the secretaries to do work for them. It was, after all, to Marty's way of thinking, their job... but secretarial tithing was an accepted fact of office life. A pissed-off secretary could subtly make someone's life at the office, hell – lost memos, nasty rumors, being too busy to get to your work... but nothing you specifically could pin on the perpetrator. She could always win the battle, so the interminable and distasteful practice went on as a ubiquitous rite in corporate America. Marty figured it was probably the secretaries' way of assuaging their bruised esteem, borne of their unpardonable, low salaries and the abuse, invariably heaped upon them, as the lowest members of the organizational hierarchy.

On the following day, with a promise of yet another dinner, Connie agreed to stuff the envelopes with a folded copy of the picture, seal them, and send them down to the mail room. By noon, on Tuesday, the job was done and the letters were out in the late morning mail. Marty, as usual, began to have second thoughts about his actions. He began to think that, perhaps, he had reacted much too quickly to the significance he had imputed to the dream. Based upon a single dream, he had mailed out nearly nine hundred letters, containing as many copies, all under his cost code. The ever-present skeptic in Marty was, as usual, unrelenting. Who did he think he was – Richard Dreyfus in *Close Encounters* – connecting with a bunch of people who drew the same, flat topped mountain? Now that the letters were on their way, he began to feel idiotic. What would all these people think – receiving this drawing of his? What were the chances of someone actually sending back the corresponding half of the drawing? If he had only given this idea a few days' thought before he acted, he would have surely decided against it. Once again, he thought, the impetuous Marty screws up. Marty then rationalized the situation, as usual, for his own peace of mind. Probably, he conjectured, most of the people who received the letter would be a bit puzzled – but would chuck it and forget about it. What the hell, he minimized – it was only a few hundred copies and some postage. If Marla made a big fuss about the expense, he'd pay for it himself.

A week after the mailing, the only responses to Marty's mailing consisted of eleven letters, inquiring as to the purpose of the peculiar correspondence, plus six phone calls of the same nature. Marty was greatly relieved that this was the extent of the reaction to his bizarre correspondence, and also because of the fact that Marla had apparently not taken notice of his rather large copy and postage expenses. Things were, at this point, beginning to settle down, generally, on the Papa story. Apparently he had been right about the media not being able to find Papa – or for that matter – Art's cabin, as well. That was big country out there – the two needles were apparently safe in their rocky haystack. Marla issued a rare concession to Marty that he was right – they apparently weren't going to find Papa, after all. Given this, she renewed her efforts to have Marty reveal Papa's whereabouts, so the magazine could, in her words, cash-in before the information was yesterday's news… but Marty remained steadfast in his resolve to protect Papa.

Marty also began to sense that this entire experience with Papa – the summer on the mountain, Art's death, Papa himself, was gradually mitigating into just – albeit a once-in-a-lifetime experience – another story, another memory. The poignancy of his feelings about the experience was being gradually quelled by the inexorably flowing, stream of time. His life was slowly returning to normal. The city didn't seem so noisy anymore, and he was well on his way to resuming his previous, frantic pace. His evenings had, once again, become centered around bars – frequented by other young, equally shallow, upwardly mobile professionals.

On Friday morning, Marty's train, bound for what appeared to be an inevitable stop at total normalization, was instantly derailed by two, handwritten envelopes among his early mail. Both contained extremely accurate drawings of the missing part to Papa's painting... in colors that were uncannily precise. Looking at them, Marty immediately began to sweat and shake. The emotions he thought were safely tucked away in his file of memories came flooding back to him – as fresh as the first powerful moment. They were such an attack upon his recently reclaimed, normal reality that he felt dizzy, and had to go outside for some air. Walking along Wilshire Boulevard, Marty frantically searched for a way to regain equilibrium – for some way to rationally cope with the successful escape of a terrifying ghost he thought had been successfully relegated to a safe and nearly nostalgic memory.

Before that morning, Marty's mind was fairly well along in its task of rewriting the experiences of his summer into an acceptable memory. The story that was evolving was a warm and adventurous tale, and he was looking forward – after final editing – to telling it. It had a quaint, epic ring to it – Art, Ben, the rescue, the mountain cabin, their adventures, the tearful deaths and burials. The part about Papa was taking a little longer to pen, but was finally starting to gel. At this stage of the rewrite, the story line depicted Papa as a truly fascinating man of the wilds... reminiscent of John the Baptist... wearing hides... seeking his food in the wilderness. His life of isolation on the mountain, according to latest account, had done some strange things to his mind, causing him to believe he was God, and wanting Marty to write a story about him. The story and the pictures of Papa – Marty would conveniently insert into the narration – were not only enormous commercial successes but potential prize-winning material.

Once all the kinks were worked out, Marty would finally be ready to spin the tale at parties and bars. At this point, the end of the story had Papa, someday – coming to his senses about the God-thing, and about followers he thought would come to him, but never did. The harsh chill of reality would, according to the work in progress, inevitably prevail upon him at some point in his life. He'd probably never come down off the mountain, and he'd probably die there, as he had led his life – alone. Marty was just about ready to tuck Papa safely away, as a great memory and a great story.

And now this. These two, simple drawings that had arrived, so innocuously, had, in a moment's time, shredded this wonderful story he had labored, so assiduously, to draft. Just when his life had taken on the comfort of routine, familiarity, and safety, he was jerked back into the cold pit of terror, he thought he had left far behind him. The mind-bending possibilities of Papa being who he said he was were suddenly and frighteningly real again. The fear Marty thought he'd left behind on Art's mountain, had tenaciously pursued him – right into his sane and predictable Los Angeles world. It was, for Marty a nightmare revisited.

Marty's life in Los Angeles made sense to him. True, he would willingly concede, it was an egotistical, frantic, and obviously shallow existence… but he was used to it. He wasn't afraid of it. Marty knew, to the depths of his soul, that this macabre wind, blowing out of the repressed secrets of his past, had the power to utterly destroy his flimsy house of cards, and along with it, the fragile, frightened man inside.

BOOK TWO

THE DISCIPLES

CHAPTER ONE

VERONICA

As the oldest of five children in a home without a father and – except for rare, always unpleasant appearances – without a mother, Veronica Jones spent a good deal of her time trying to preserve some semblance of a family for her three young brothers and baby sister. Veronica wasn't sure of many things. For one thing, she wasn't sure why she was so responsible. While her friends were out in the "hood" every night, getting high, having sex, and hanging at the playground, she played "mommy" to her young siblings. She resented it but her love for these vulnerable, innocent children, kept her at home. She knew she couldn't enjoy herself if she was worried about them. That's just the way she was.

Veronica wasn't sure who her father was. During one of her mother's frequent heroin "highs," she told Veronica that he was a white advertising executive from Los Angeles that paid her for sex one night when she was working the evening, maid shift at the William Penn Hotel. She said his name was Steven Anderson... or Andrews... and that he owned his own airplane and drove a Mercedes Benz. Her mother had only mentioned it on that one occasion, when Veronica was twelve. Veronica made the mistake of asking her about it, a few days later. In response, Letitia, or "Shooter" as she was known on the street, punched her in the mouth with her fist... splitting open her lower lip. She never asked again but, since she was much lighter skinned than any of the other children in her family, and had thin lips, narrow nose, and greenish eyes, Veronica guessed it was very likely that her father was, in fact, white. Whether or not the rest of the story was true, remained, for her, unresolved.

By the time Veronica left Pittsburgh at age seventeen, she had been raped twice... once in her own bed when she was thirteen by her uncle on Thanksgiving night... and again, gang-style, when she was fifteen... outside a bar in her neighborhood by four men who pulled her into an alley... resulting in a pregnancy and an abortion. On the Greyhound Bus, bound for New York City, her heart ached for her brothers and sister. They were lost... of that she was sure. Her little brothers, who had giggled in the bathtub and played make-believe games in their bed at night, had already begun to run with the local gangs. They would soon be – or were already for all she knew – on drugs. All three – even little twelve-year-old, Paully – owned guns. Nicole, the baby, had just turned ten, but her virginity would be, in a few short years, no more than an inconsequential notch on the belt of a neighborhood homeboy.

The night before Veronica left for New York, Nicky had held Veronica with all her tiny might, not wanting to ever let her go... quietly sobbing in fitful starts and stops as she had when she was a baby. As she cried, she pleaded, piteously, with Veronica to stay. No one would take care of her after she was gone, she moaned... and she was scared... so scared. Veronica gave her the phone number of their Aunt Rita in New York City and told her to call there, collect, anytime she needed her. She also told Nicky that Annabelle, in the apartment below, had promised to look after her... and that if their mother, or anyone else tried to hurt her, she should run down there as fast as she could. Veronica promised Nicky that she'd send for her as soon as she was able. She had to go, she told Nicky. Someday, Veronica hoped, Nicky would understand.

Veronica was sure she'd made a terrible mistake in coming to Harlem as soon as her aunt Rita opened the back door of the white Cadillac limousine waiting for them, double-parked outside the Greyhound Terminal. Veronica recognized a pimp when she saw one. After she sat down in the back seat of the limo – its windows nearly opaque from the tinting – wedged between Rita and "Gatt," as Rita called him, Veronica instantly suspected Rita's motives for inviting her to Harlem. Gatt smiled at Veronica, exposing his large, white teeth, each outlined in gold. He reached out with his right, ring-laden hand and patted her left thigh.

"You a sweet piece of white chocolate, little sister."

Veronica grabbed the back of his hand at his wrist and squeezed it with all of her strength, all the while, digging her long, sturdy nails into his scarred, ebony-black skin.

"Keep your fuckin pimp hands off me."

A deep, raspy, smoker's laugh rolled out of Gatt's throat as he slid his hand along her leg toward her knee... then slowly lifted it from her.

"You just like your aunt."

Rita told Gatt to leave her alone. She and Veronica would talk when they got home, she said. Home was a large, well-furnished apartment in Harlem. Rita's tall, slender body and glamorous face had apparently paid off.

"Why didn't you tell me this is what you did for a living, Aunt Rita?"

"I thought you knew, Ronny. Your mother never told you?"

"My mother is always high... you know that. She never says anything to me except to cuss. All I knew was that Nanna said you were doing really well in New York."

"Well I am."

"Hookin."

"You listen, girl. We from the same neighborhood. I know by now you been givin lots of it away for free to those young black bucks at the playground... haven't you? I'm just makin em pay for it, that's all... just like all those married bitches that's lucky enough to have a workin man."

"I thought I was going to get away from that, comin here."

"Well what did you think was goin on in Harlem, girl? What you think you gonna do here? You with a tenth grade education... get hired as a executive? You either gonna bust your ass at some Mickey D's for minimum wage... or clean houses... or sign up for your check and stamps and live in the projects. Or you can hook like me... and live good. That's it. That's life, girl."

"I'm not gonna get my check and stamps like my mother... have babies and shoot up. If that's what my life was gonna be, I'd kill myself. I would Aunt Rita. And I'm not hookin either... havin those dirty dicks and bad breath and sweaty bodies on me."

"Whoa baby girl. That what you think?... I turn for the homeys and g's? Not me... I'm a champagne girl. Most my johns are middle-aged white men on Park Avenue and Trump Tower. Lotsa rich whitebread gets turned on by sweet black chocolate... don't you know that? Wouldn't look our way on the street... but can't wait to get into some black pussy the minute nobody's watchin. They don't take me out to dinner like they do the high-priced white girls, but it's real fine... room service, champagne... and they real polite and clean."

"White or black... I'm not hookin... and if that pimp Gatt or whatever the hell his name is, thinks I am... or you told him I would... you better go tell him different. I want more Aunt Rita. I don't know exactly what... but I'm gonna have a life that means something. I'm gonna be somebody."

Tears began to roll down Veronica's cheeks. Rita put her arms around her and held her, rocking back and forth as they stood, stroking the back of her head. She put a hand on each of Veronica's cheeks and wiped away the streams that had found their way from her eyes to her neck. Though Rita was only four years older than Veronica, she felt at that moment like her grandmother.

"Sweet baby... I wish things were different. I wish you could have everything you want. It's not fair, I know. Had you been

THE DISCIPLES

born white or if your daddy was some black doctor, you'd be gettin ready to leave for college next month. But you can't let that kind of thinkin drive you crazy. Envy is a green dragon that will eat you up and make you mean and bitter. You better off than a lotta girls. You are. How many your friends already got a couple of babies and is on crack? You got a beautiful face, honey... more white than black... and everybody likes that... black men and white men both. Why you think Diana Ross made it so big and Michael Jackson gettin whiter everyday? And you so tall and thin... be thankful for what you got, Ronnie. It could be a lot worse."

Veronica sat on the couch and was silent for a long while.

"If you're doin so well, how come you live in this neighborhood, Aunt Rita?"

"Well, in my line a work, it avoid a lot of trouble. Down here, the police don't give a fuck what you do. I move into some nice neighborhood and the nice people would soon enough catch on to what I was doin for a livin. Then it'd be nothin but a hassle."

"I'm gonna find a respectable job, Aunt Rita."

"You do whatever you like, sweet girl. Just don't expect too much. You settin yourself up for a big fall."

Within a couple of weeks, Veronica found a job, cleaning at a Citibank in Manhattan... working the evening, eleven to seven shift. She rode the subway to work the first few nights, against the advice of her aunt. The second night, a group of five "street niggers," as she described them to Rita, surrounded her just after she sat down in her subway car. They left her alone only after a security guard walked in. From that night on, she took the bus, even though it was slower and cost more.

Veronica made $4.35 an hour and, being the new girl, was assigned to clean the toilets. She immediately discovered that, despite the fact that these restrooms were used by so-called professional people, they still smelled just as bad as any other toilets. The white bankers apparently had no better aim than any other man did. She spent most of her nights smelling piss and cleaning gum and wet cigarette butts out of the urinals.

Veronica's first check was a net pay of $243.60 for two weeks' work. She had spent $50.00 on her bus fare... which she borrowed from Rita. After she paid her back – which Rita said she needn't – she had $193.60 to show for cleaning up toilets in the middle of the night for two weeks. It dawned on her that if she were living on her own, she wouldn't have had enough to pay for even a run-down room to live in... let alone food or anything else. Veronica showed Rita her paycheck. Rita smiled.

"I make this much in an hour."

"You make almost two hundred dollars in an hour?"

"I told you... I'm a champagne girl."

"What's Gatt get?"

"Half"

"That fucker."

"No, baby. If I didn't have Gatt, I'd be trickin for change. He good to me. He got the contacts and he run a good business. I only ended up with a few freaks in the three years I been workin. Never been hurt really bad... couple of black eyes and split lips... that's all."

One night, after she'd been on the job for about four months, Veronica asked an older Hispanic woman, who polished the brass – one of the "good" cleaning jobs at the bank – how long she had been there. Twelve years, was her answer. How much was she makin now?... if she didn't mind her asking. She didn't... and five-fifty an hour was her answer. The boss was making six an hour, she volunteered. Veronica asked her how she made it, having four kids and all. She said she also worked a day job in a garment sweat shop... and her husband parked cars at a Manhattan garage. They got food stamps and medical assistance and lived in a project.

On the way home from work that morning, at the tender age of seventeen, Veronica felt very old. She looked out through the grimy bus windows at the people walking along the downtown streets. It was a week before Christmas. The sky was gray and a few flurries were swirling among the buildings... with as many flakes going up as coming down. She saw young girls her age in designer clothing with smiles on their faces, bouncing along the wide, crowded sidewalks with gaggles of shopping bags, bearing the trademarks of upscale shops, hanging from their well-manicured fingers. She looked down at her own legs, covered by her heavy, gray, cotton work pants and suddenly felt a wave of panic, rising from her chest. She literally could feel the unbearable weight of her hopeless future descending upon her that very instant... years of hourly wages, babies she couldn't afford, an apartment in the projects... her stamps. She began to feel as though she couldn't breathe and knew that if she didn't get off that bus immediately she was going to start screaming. At the next stop she pushed her way against the flow of boarding passengers and leaped from the step onto the sidewalk and began running.

Veronica ran blindly... being nearly hit by an impressive number of buses and cars as she traversed the busy intersections. She had no idea how long she'd been running, or where she was when she finally gave in to exhaustion. She leaned against a brick wall for a while... then put her hands on her knees and panted like a dog in August. When she was finally able to stand up, she looked around to attempt to reconnoiter her location. She recognized nothing. Possessing the only black face in sight, however, she was absolutely certain she was nowhere near Harlem. Across the street she noticed a weathered sign over an equally weathered door that proclaimed, "Anthony's Lunch." With her throat parched from her mad dash, she crossed the street and went inside to get herself a Coke. Except for one elderly couple at a small corner table, everyone else was sitting, shoulder to shoulder, at the small counter... having their morning coffee and doughnuts. All heads turned her way as she entered.

Every patron looked very Italian to her. She stood for a few moments, unsure of what to do, then moved, cautiously, a few steps to her right to a stool at the far end of the counter. Deciding not to sit down, she remained standing behind the stool, looking at the large, overweight man behind the counter... mustached and topped with thick, black and gray hair. His permanently stained cook's apron told the story of a lifetime behind a lunch counter. He examined Veronica for a while then walked slowly in her direction, stopping directly across the counter from her and folding his fat arms across his wide torso. His large teeth showed through the gap between his fat lips... created by his malevolent grin.

"A little far north aren't you?"

Veronica froze. His smile had a frightening, cruel curl to it. She had heard stories about Benson Hurst and how they kill black people who wander there. She didn't know New York City very well and thought perhaps she may have ended up there. She immediately decided to forego the Coke. In a small, quivering voice that registered just above a whisper, she asked for directions.

"Can you tell me where I can get a bus back to Harlem from here?"

The large man turned his head and smiled at his patrons around the counter... all responding to him with expectant expressions... then returned his gaze to Veronica.

"Go across the street and watch for the bus that has a big watermelon on the front."

The customers instantly burst into mocking laughter. Veronica immediately darted out the door and ran across the street... happy to be safely away from Anthony's Lunch. She began to retrace her route. She couldn't believe how far she had run. It took her over forty-five minutes to reach the bus stop where she had jumped off.

Veronica got home at about 9:30 in the morning. Rita was still asleep. She and Rita had similar working hours... but while all Veronica had to show for her labors were urine-reeking work clothes, Rita came home in her fine clothes with four or five hundred dollars in her purse. Instead of going immediately to bed, as was her custom, Veronica made coffee and sat at the kitchen table.

Though the wave of panic had subsided, Veronica was still trying to divine its cause. She knew, now, that her life was a road to nowhere... and realized just how foolish her dreams had been. She was going to be somebody. She was going to make a difference in the world. On that bus coming home this morning, her dreams and her reality life had, in a single moment, separated from one another for the first time in her life. In a short four months, not even eighteen yet, Veronica had been cruelly jerked from her childhood... as a baby from the womb. She realized, as she sat, sipping her coffee, that only children dream and hope. Children can pretend, she thought, because they still believe that anything is possible. A child can imagine herself as an actress or a singer or married to a doctor or even as the president. Hope... that's what distinguishes a child. A child lives on the excitement of hoping that her dream world may actually be possible. No one could prove that it wasn't... so just maybe it was.

The most fun Veronica could remember having were the times when she and her girlfriends would sit around, talking and dreaming about what they were going to be when they grew up. None of them were sure, exactly, how it would all happen, but they were all quite convinced that it would. The greatest tragedy in life, Veronica realized, is the loss of those dreams. Hers were gone, she knew... entirely gone. She could feel the emptiness. She knew she would never again get that warm tingle in her stomach, just before she went to sleep... believing that somewhere, in the undefined future, something wonderful was waiting for her. Reality had coldly defined her future for her... and there was absolutely nothing wonderful about it.

Veronica had lost many things in her life but this loss felt so dark and heavy that it was almost more than she could bear. It felt much worse that when she'd been raped. That was terrible, but she still had hope then. Hope was the warmth inside her that made her want to go on. It gave color to her day... to ordinary things. How, Veronica wondered, does someone go on without hope? New, tormenting questions began to emerge from deep inside her, like vile worms, crawling out of her soul... each one making her colder and more afraid. What was there to live for? Why was she born... if only for this? How can someone keep living when there is no reason to get up in the morning?

Rita got up at around eleven o'clock to find Veronica staring at the kitchen wall, her eyes and face blank and expressionless. She had never seen her like this. Yesterday she was a little girl, full of spirit, love, and energy... even when she was tired. Today... she looked very old and very sad. Rita made some new coffee, poured herself a cup and sat down at the table with Veronica, who continued to stare straight ahead... as though she hadn't noticed her. Rita reached across the table, placed her hand on Veronica's left forearm and shook it gently.

"Ronnie?"

Veronica slowly turned her head to look at her. Rita was becoming frightened... fearing that something terrible had happened to her.

"What is it baby? What happened? Did somebody hurt you?"

Veronica continued to look at Rita... her eyes like those of a corpse, the green having taken on a grayish cast. Rita slid her chair around the table to Veronica's left. She put her right arm around her shoulder and with her left hand, she gently turned Veronica's face toward hers.

"Come on baby. Tell me. What's wrong? Should I call you a doctor?"

Finally, Veronica spoke in a weak voice.

"No."

"Then what is it? Tell me."

"I don't know. I don't feel anything. It's all gray. It's all gone. There isn't anything."

Bewildered, Rita took Veronica by the hand and led her to her bed. She gave her a couple of her sleeping pills and within a few minutes, she was asleep. Rita called Gatt and, purporting to be sick, told him to get a sub for her. Gatt was pissed off, but she knew he'd calm down. She was his best girl and he knew enough to keep his money-maker happy.

Veronica slept, almost without moving, until noon of the following day. Rita slept beside her niece that night, keeping an eye on her, as a mother would her sick infant, watching her chest to see if she was still breathing. She called in sick for Veronica, at the bank, for the second day in a row. Later in the afternoon, Veronica got up for a few hours, drank some coffee, ate a few bites of food at Rita's insistence... then went back to bed. Rita considered calling off work, again, but didn't want to push it too far with Gatt. She phoned a friend and had her come over to keep an eye on Veronica that night.

Once again, Veronica slept for over twenty-four hours... this time without sleeping pills. Convinced that something was obviously wrong with her, Rita got Veronica dressed and took her to her doctor... a high-priced, general practitioner in Manhattan that all her in-town clients said was the best. He knew Rita was a hooker but she had the money to pay his outrageous fees, so he treated her with the requisite professional courtesy. Dr. Friedman thoroughly examined Veronica and found nothing apparently wrong. He scheduled her for some tests at the hospital that afternoon... then referred her to an associate of his, assuring Rita that he was a top-notch internist.

The internist saw her the following day and told her that all her test results had come back, normal. He did a complete examination on her and, like Friedman, found nothing wrong. He told Rita that he felt Veronica was severely depressed and referred her to a psychiatrist. The psychiatrist concurred with the depression diagnosis and prescribed medication and therapy.

Veronica continued her pattern of prolonged sleep for several weeks, during which time she was fired from her job. Eventually she began to sleep less, but still had no appetite, nor any desire to get dressed or go outside. She began to look quite frail and even started to walk, bent over, like an old woman. Rita, though she truly loved Veronica, was beginning to run short on patience with her. After all, Rita was only eighteen when she came to New York. She got connected with Gatt and was turning tricks, full time, before she was nineteen... finding and paying for her own apartment. She learned to cope with the big cruel world... Veronica would simply have to do the same... or go home.

On a Wednesday afternoon, during the last week of January, Rita found Veronica, as usual, on the couch, in her robe, staring at the TV. She walked over to the television, turned it off... then sat in a chair, facing the couch. Veronica looked at her, expressionless, as usual. Rita had a look of business on her face.

"Ronnie, we got to talk. Sweetheart, I love you, you know that, but this can't go on. Maybe it's time for you to go back home. I know things aren't too good there, but maybe it'd be better for you. Maybe you just not cut out for the big city."

Veronica was silent for a while, looking out into space... then, suddenly, a focus came to her eyes, more so than Rita had seen in weeks. Not only was there a focus, but a never-before-seen bitterness, as well. Her sweetness was entirely gone. Veronica's voice was hard and it was business.

"Tell Gatt I'm ready to work."

CHAPTER TWO

Being what Gatt billed as "baby meat" to his clients, Veronica was immediately in high demand. In his business, Gatt found... the younger the better. By the time Veronica was twenty, she was a streetwise, seasoned whore who could command a thousand dollars for one night. She had quickly replaced Rita as Gatt's top girl. Rita took it remarkably well... but, then again, Rita was still pulling down top dollar for her tricks, as well. With Veronica's close-to-white looks, however, she was deemed acceptable by many of Gatt's, almost exclusively white clientele, to be "taken out"... often to the best restaurants in the city, the opera, the ballet, to Broadway plays, and occasionally to political events, including inaugurals and parties thrown for and by foreign ambassadors. This part of it, Rita didn't take well. She began to grow envious and resentful of Veronica's "whiteness," and the obvious privileges that came with it.

The childish, romantic dreams of Veronica Jones, oldest daughter of Letitia "Shooter" Jones, raped and abused child of Pittsburgh's Hill District, seemed another lifetime away to her now. This was real life. Her childhood dreams were of love... romantic love... of being somebody important... somebody that everyone respected and looked up to. She didn't dream anymore. She simply lived reality... and her reality was allowing men to use her body so she could have something better than the projects, stamps, and her check.

In her letters, Nicky told Veronica of the family and neighborhood news. Her two older brothers, James and Andre were both in prison, now, serving fourteen to twenty years. They were convicted of beating and robbing an elderly black couple, in their own home, to get money for crack. Apparently the couple, who used to let the boys play in their backyard when they were little, and would often feed them lunch at their kitchen table, told James and Andre they didn't have any money when the boys woke them up at two in the morning to ask for it. James and Andre apparently pushed them into their house and beat both of them, demanding to know where they kept their money. It turned out that they had a total of $2.43 cash in the house. The man's skull was fractured... the woman's nose and right arm were broken. He was seventy-eight, she was seventy-five.

Paully had passed the magic age of seventeen and all his trouble would be of the adult variety now. His juvenile record was long and varied... from breaking and entering to aggravated assault to drug and weapon possession. Veronica figured that the boys would all, soon, be together. Nicky was pregnant, expecting in four months. She had quit school and wasn't planning on going back. As soon as the baby was born, she'd sign up to get her own check and stamps... separate from Letitia's. She wrote Veronica that she knew who the father of her baby was, but hadn't told him the baby was his... and hadn't planned on telling him. She said he was a really violent "nigger" and she didn't want him coming around the baby.

Veronica never did send for Nicky. She was always going to, but just never did. She figured it had something to do with her hooking for a living. Even though it probably got back to Nicky, through Rita, what she was doing, Nicky never mentioned it in her letters or phone calls. Besides... the neighborhood where Veronica lived was even worse than back in Pittsburgh... and Nicky had all of her friends back there. Nicky had never even come for a visit in all the years, nor had Veronica ever returned to Pittsburgh... the old "hood" holding too many bad memories for her.

The news of her mother's death, when Veronica was twenty-two, had no effect on her, whatsoever. She died, as everyone knew she would, of an overdose. Veronica felt no different about hearing of her mother's death than she would upon reading about a stranger overdosing in the subway. Her mother had given birth to her and nothing more. She had mistreated and abused all of her children and was more interested in finding her next fix than feeding her babies. If it hadn't been for her grandmother, Nanna, they probably wouldn't be alive today. The good news was that Nanna, now sixty-eight, was still healthy and doing well... still singing in the church choir and playing bingo on Friday nights. She had developed high blood pressure but was taking medication for it and doing okay.

Veronica had a "good" life... all things being relative. Compared to where she could have been and where all her "sisters" in the old hood ended up, she was actually doing very well. It's funny, she often thought... because her mother needed a few bucks for dope and her father was away from home and horny – if the California executive with an airplane story were true – she ended up as a slender, attractive, very light-skinned black girl who made lots of money because of it. She realized that she really didn't do anything to deserve what she had. She hadn't studied hard, nor had she worked to develop any particular talent. She was simply born with a glamorous, almost-white face... and a tall, slim body that made men want to fuck her. She guessed the one thing she had to thank her mother for was for fucking her father. She figured she could, also, thank her for not having an abortion... but, realistically, Veronica knew her mother was probably just too stoned or lazy to go get it done... or just wanted a bigger check. She understood, also, of course, that if her mother had been light-skinned, attractive, and slender like she was, she may not have ended up as she did. Life was a toss of the dice and Veronica knew she had had the luck of the roll when it came to looks.

While she realized she was better off than many women, Veronica also knew that there were many women who had lives much better than her own. Despite all the fine things she had, she also had to put up with a lot that most women wouldn't want to even think about. How many women would be willing, she mused, to suck a different cock every night... often hanging on bony old white men with warts on their balls?... or have some young executive try to impress you with his power by slamming into you until the inside of your thighs were bruised – choking you all the while. One trick she recalled – a former American ambassador to Belgium... now a big shot with the U.S. Olympic Committee – paid her an extra $500 one night, to have her lie in the bathtub while he pissed and shit on her.

Life was, to Veronica, an endless series of hotel room beds and cocks to suck and fuck. Her life had both figuratively and literally fucked the spirit and love right out of her. She had things... but she knew she had nothing. She no longer loved anyone... not even her little sister . . not even her Nanna. Love – or any other emotion for that matter – had dried up and fallen from her soul like a parched blossom. She didn't hate anyone, either... not even her mother or her uncle or the drunks who raped her. She simply didn't feel anything, anymore. Something had gone out of her the day she jumped off the bus... never to return.

Veronica was pretty, intelligent... had beautiful clothes, a well decorated apartment, money to spend... but inside Veronica Jones was the same color gray that she remembered in the sky that December day on the bus... no warmth... no tingle... no hope. Veronica had stopped looking to the future. She just never thought of it anymore. She wished for nothing, she hoped for nothing. She lived in the moment, for the moment. If she were shot down in the street she would miss nothing... and she knew that no one in the world would miss her.

CHAPTER THREE

DAVID

He did what everyone expected of him... even attended the same seminary as his father. Reverend David Matthews, Sr. delivered the sermon for his son's ordination in the eighteenth century stone church where he had been pastor for the past twenty-eight years. David Timothy Matthews, Jr. married the daughter of another Presbyterian minister, a lifelong friend of his father. David was hired, directly out of seminary, through connections of his father, as the associate minister of a small church in Guildford, Connecticut, about twenty miles north of Branshire, his hometown.

The church, David often reflected, represented an archetype of a New England country scene, with a small stone fence enclosing both the church and an ancient graveyard, and the white-painted, original, wood siding – dating back to 1802 – still clinging to the body of the patriarchal structure. Two enormous oak trees stood in front of the church – one on each side of the cobblestone sidewalk that led to the ornately carved, red chapel doors. The bell in the steeple was still rung every Sunday morning for services.

Within three years of his marriage, David was father to two beautiful, hair-of-golden-fleece, cherub-faced daughters. His wife, Donna, was choir director and in charge of the Sunday School program. The church was one of the oldest and most prominent in the state and its congregation comprised a who's who of Connecticut society, including a United States Senator. David was quickly integrated into the social web of the community... invited to all of the "right" functions and named to several village boards.

David often considered that he lived as blessed a life as God had ever granted anyone. His marriage and his fledgling ministry were, in his view, but a continuation of such beneficence. He had never in his life wanted for anything... had never seen his parents argue... had attended a private boy's school... was always popular... was athletic, tall, blonde, and exceptionally handsome. And now he had what he considered to be a perfect wife... a petite brunette whose face would serve very nicely, he thought, as the cover girl for Vassar... which was, in point of fact, her alma mater. His daughters were a fortuitous blend of their parents' physical attributes... blessed with his blonde hair, height, and Grecian bodily proportions... her grace, beautiful facial structure, and flawless complexion.

The only real "blotch" on his life's landscape, was his younger brother, Roger. Not that his transgressions would be judged grievous by any current social standards, but Roger simply didn't meet the family's particularly high expectations – specifically, his father's. Roger didn't do well, neither academically nor socially, as he grew from childhood to early manhood. He got lousy grades and ran around with a gang of blue-collar kids from a neighboring town who drank beer and got into relatively innocuous trouble... occasional vandalism and some fights on Friday nights. Roger, as it would be expected, didn't end up with either the grades or the desire for college and, much to the final mortification of the good Reverend and Mrs. Matthews, got his girlfriend pregnant during his senior year of high school. They were married by a Justice of the Peace... and the two friends who served as witnesses, constituted the total sum of wedding guests. For their wedding reception, the four of them had wings and beer at a local tavern. In the last conversation they ever had, Reverend Matthews had informed Roger that they wanted nothing more to do with him, his "wench," or the "bastard child" – as he referred to each.

Roger was now living with his wife and three sons, somewhere around Allentown, Pennsylvania... repairing vacuum cleaners for a living. Roger would call David on occasion but the conversations always short and awkward. Although David felt some obligatory kinship for his brother, he couldn't help but look down on him... figuring that Roger had made the conscious choice to screw up his life and David saw no reason, therefore, he should be saddled with hearing about his problems. As far as he knew, there had been no contact, whatsoever, between Roger and their parents since the day the Reverend threw him out... and David was quite sure this arrangement was perfectly acceptable with his father. He knew his mother was bothered by how the Reverend had treated Roger, his wife, and their grandson, but she would never say so, nor would she do anything behind her husband's back. David suspected that his brother's fall from grace had proportionately increased the value of his father's stock in him. To a very large extent, David's exemplary life served to validate Reverend Matthew's own.

Each evening, warm enough to take out the children, the Matthews family would stroll about the town "green" – as they called it there – greeting and receiving the same from all passersby... basking in the obvious respect and admiration the town had for him, his position, and his beautiful family. He knew that only a few hours south was New York City... home to every despicable form of human life conceivable to the imagination... with sidewalks covered in excrement, urine, garbage, misery, perversion, and death. But he, his family, his town, his church, and his congregation were to him, proof that decency and proper living were still possible in a world that had become a modern-day Sodom and Gomorrah.

People all across the country, David often reflected, in cities, small and large, had lost their way. Life had, in the mainstream, become a social sewer. He had stopped watching the evening news, entirely, and only browsed the newspaper, looking for articles that concerned something other than murder, child abuse, drugs, divorce, and sexual perversion. Even the sports section had lost its appeal for him, having come to place more emphasis, it seemed to him, on the greed and personal foibles of the athletes than the games they played. What was the point, he asked himself, in watching or reading repetitious stories of tragedy and despair, over and over again? He knew most of the world was a garbage pile – he didn't need to be reminded of it every day.

Oftentimes, during the day, he would stop for a moment and silently pray to God, offering humble thanks for his "bountiful gifts." For whatever reason, God had chosen to shower him with every possible blessing. On a warm, breezy evening, in the last week of a beautiful June, as the Matthews were getting ready for bed... having just tucked in Sarah and Rebecca... David simply could not contain his sublime joy. With his heart beating the warm blood of love... the happiness pulsing through his veins... he embraced his wife and spoke with a voice that quivered with unbounded gladness.

"There is nothing I can think of that I could wish for, sweetheart. God has provided me with all that a man could ever want. I sometimes feel a little guilty, knowing there are so many who have so much less, but, I won't question God's wisdom and bounty. I just accept it with humble thanks."

In his private thoughts, David would sometimes ponder the possible rationale for his good life. His family, it was true, had been virtuous and had served God for many generations... but not all of his ancestors were given life's blessings as was he. There had been, in fact, numerous struggles and hardships for many in his family. Perhaps, he conjectured, his life was a sign to those who had gone before him, and who will come after him, that virtue does have its eventual reward.

David truly did, according to his own assessment, consider himself to be a virtuous man... trying his best to be objective about himself – considering vanity to be a flaw. He conducted, on a periodic basis, what he called his "personal moral assessment"... setting aside a specific day, each month, to reflect on these matters. He would ask himself... "In what way have I been deceitful or dishonest? Have I been covetous or selfish? Have I been vain or boastful? Have I served God to the fullest extent of my capacity?" He would try to answer these – and other similarly probing questions – in a forthright manner, avoiding as best he could, bias, self-serving, or false modesty. His reflections consistently indicated to him that, indeed, he was leading a virtuous life. He felt he was genuine in concluding that his life told the story of a man who – though not perfect – was nonetheless, decent, honest, loving, and who faithfully served his God. His constant supplication to God was that He allow him to serve His will and continue to bless him and his family.

It appeared that God heard David's constant prayer, and his tree continued to blossom... bearing more and more of life's succulent fruit. In his thirtieth year of life, David was blessed with a third child... a son, David Timothy Matthews III... and three weeks thereafter, when the senior minister retired from Guildford Presbyterian Church, David was named to head the congregation. David was also becoming a growing force in the national presbytery, being named to his region's council, and, a year later, as a delegate to the General Assembly... at which his networking was of a stellar caliber.

By his thirty-sixth year, David's pastoral reputation was of such note throughout New England that he was invited, or as David would characterize it, "called," to lead the congregation of the largest Presbyterian church in Boston... arguably among the most prestigious Protestant ministerial posts in New England, or in the opinion of some, in the Eastern Seaboard. He spent many hours in prayer... seeking God's will on this opportunity of service... and seeking also the opinions of his wife, his father, and his fellow clergy. It was, unquestionably, a wonderful opportunity for advancement in the church. From this Boston pulpit he would have a national platform – and international to some extent – to do God's work. While he had some influential members in his Guildford congregation, the church in Boston was the "major leagues" in terms of congregational wealth and influence... the church pews supporting the posteriors of key players in virtually every significant path of human enterprise.

On the other hand, there was much to be lost in leaving Guildford. The Matthews truly had an ideal life in this small, provincial, New England enclave. It was as nice a town as there was to be found, anywhere... safe and clean... and filled with good people. In Guildford, a drunk driver was still big news. There was, David was told, a town murder, some ten years before he moved there... apparently a lover's triangle... but having little interest in the matter, David had never pursued the details. Given the general state of crime in the country, however, Guildford was about as safe a town as a town could be. It was, clearly, a magnificent environment in which to raise his family. Women and children walked at night without the slightest consideration of danger. Heads turned and eyes followed anyone who didn't live there.

Although he didn't consider himself a racist, David found nothing wrong in the comfort derived from being among one's "own people," as he called them. Guilford was almost exclusively white... mostly Protestant, primarily of Northern European extraction... English, Scottish and German with some Irish and Scandinavians. There were only a few Eastern European families... Czechs, Poles, and Ukrainians, and fewer Italians, with nary a black or Hispanic living within the village limits.

David offered no apologies for liking these demographics. People, he felt, had a right to live within their own culture and to preserve it, separately and distinctly. Integration, in David's assessment, had been a colossal and inevitable failure. People in the United States had finally come to their senses, he felt, and were, at long last, willing to admit to the obvious truth that human beings universally desire to be with those who are like themselves. A little more common sense and a little less guilt-driven angst, he believed, could save the United States a lot of trouble in the future.

On the other hand, besides its prestige and potential influence, the Boston position had some financial benefits he could not ignore. David would be making, with the benefits package and the comparable worth of the free housing – which one could fairly describe as a mansion – a six-figure income. They were quite comfortable with the salary and house, provided them in Guildford, but as Donna pointed out to him, they had the future to think about... with three children to educate and the obvious consideration of what his family would do if something should happen to him. With the income they were offering in Boston, they would be assured of a solid financial future... allowing for investments and the purchase of a life insurance policy that would more than adequately provide for Donna and the children in the event of the unexpected. Also, as Donna pointed out, despite its many attributes, Guildford lacked a well-rounded cultural environment for the children and, in this regard, Boston offered so much more.

David expressed his concerns to Donna about the dangers and distasteful side of big city living. Neither of them had ever lived in a major metropolitan area and he wondered if they could adjust. Although the parsonage was in a very exclusive, upper class, suburban development, the church was in downtown Boston. They would, therefore, be in the city, a lot, he said, with its perverts and filth. Did they really want their children, he queried, exposed to all this?

After four weeks of agonizing, they finally decided on Boston. Donna closed the decision process by reassuring David that if they didn't like it, they could always come home to Guildford. With David's credentials, he was now in a position that he could virtually name his ministry… and Guildford, she was sure, would always welcome them back.

CHAPTER FOUR

During their first year in Boston, David and Donna were ready, every other week, to pack their bags for Guildford. David had even gone so far as to call Dr. Whitson, chairman of the Guildford Presbyterian Church Board, to ask him if they would be amenable to his resuming his post there. Dr. Whitson assured him they would be overjoyed to have him back. For just this reason, Whitson told him, they had advanced the associate minister to head the congregation on a strictly interim basis. Although they wished him well in Boston, in their heart of hearts they hoped David and his family would tire of the big city and come home to Guildford.

Sometime during their second year, however, Boston began to feel like home and they became slowly convinced that they had made the right decision. Again, David believed this was the Hand of God, working in his life and was a continuation of his bountiful blessings. In Boston, David and Donna were exposed to a life which neither had known existed... attending parties and events with some of the most powerful and famous people in the country... also some of the wealthiest.

In the late afternoon of July nineteenth in his third year in Boston, David was putting the final touches on Sunday's sermon. Donna had called for the third time, since noon, to remind him that he couldn't be late for his own fortieth birthday party... the big "4 – 0" as she called it. There were going to be twenty-two people there for dinner, including his father and mother. Rev. Matthews, Sr., had retired the previous year and was now finding the time to come visit David, which had never been the case when he was still working. At about ten minutes before five, David's secretary, Janet, came into the office just as David was getting up from his desk to leave for the day. She told him that a detective Bronyak from the Boston Police was outside, asking to speak with him. David was puzzled and a bit irritated, given that he needed to get home and, being rush hour, it was always an unpredictable drive.

Guests would be arriving for dinner by 6:30 and he simply had to get on the road as soon as possible.

"Did he say what he wanted?"

"No. He just said he would like to speak with you. I asked him if you were expecting him and he said that you weren't."

A surprising chill of fear ran through David's body. Sensing it, he laughed to himself. What is it, he thought, about people and police? As soon as you see a police car in your rearview mirror, you become paranoid and think he's going to pull you over for something. Even when an officer sits near you in a doughnut shop, you feel a wave of guilt... at least David did... even though you know you have done absolutely nothing wrong. He often mused that a police officer could make the Good Lord, Himself, uneasy.

"Well, OK, Janet... show him in, I guess."

Janet led Detective Bronyak into the office, leaving the door open, as was the custom. David stood up, came around his desk, and extended his hand to the detective... Bronyak introducing himself as their hands gripped. David tried his best to mask his irritation. Bronyak's expression and handshake were that of a person, anxious to get on with business. He glanced back at the open door.

"I think I'll close this if you don't mind."

David told him to go right ahead... then motioned for Bronyak to have a seat in one of the two, leather, wing-chairs to the right of his desk, separated by an oval, French provincial coffee table. Bronyak walked across the large and beautifully furnished, walnut paneled office to take a seat in the chair that faced away from the door. David sat in the matching chair, across from him... crossing his legs and folding his hands on his lap... his professional countenance magnanimously repressing his displeasure over this inconvenience.

"Can I get you anything, Detective Bronyak... coffee, soft drink?"

David hoped he didn't, so as not to prolong the visit, but, in his business, courtesy was the Gospel.

"No thank you, Reverend."

"Well, Detective Bronyak, what can I do for you? You're not here to arrest me, are you?"

David followed his words with a condescending and mechanical laugh... common to all clergy... whether in the pulpit or at a barbecue... using pedantic humor to suggest a relaxed equality with laymen – which no clergyman truly accepted.

Bronyak didn't respond... nor did he smile. Instead, he reached inside his suit pocket and pulled out a note pad... flipping the pages until he found the item for which he was searching. He pulled a ballpoint pen from his other inside pocket and clicked it down into its writing configuration.

"I have a few questions, Reverend Matthews... this is strictly voluntary on your part, of course. You don't have to answer these questions if you choose not to. You're welcome to call your lawyer first."

Adrenalin instantly flooded David's body, spreading its electric tingle into his chest and the lower part of his brain. He couldn't find breath nor voice. His palms felt immediately damp. David had never in his life been questioned in such an accusatory fashion by anyone... let alone a police officer. He was, after all, a man of God... a virtuous man.

"What... what is this... what is this about, Detective Bronyak?"

"Do you know a Valarie Steffey?"

"Yes... of course. She's the daughter of Dr. and Mrs. Steffey... members of my congregation. Why?"

"Miss Steffey claims you sexually molested her, Reverend."

David found himself on his feet, staring down at Bronyak, stammering.

"She... I... who..."

"Reverend Matthews... please sit down."

David slowly lowered himself back into his chair, using both hands for support. He was visibly shaking. Bronyak continued in his matter-of-fact monotone.

"Valarie Steffey claims that on several occasions, you had her stay late at the church... telling her that you wanted her to help you with some projects of yours. She says you molested her twice... says you apologized after the first time and said it would never happen again. She claims it happened again about two weeks later. This time, she says, you held her down on the floor, pulled off her panties and forced yourself inside her. Says you ejaculated in her. After you were done, she says you started to cry and pleaded with her not to tell anyone about it... said it would ruin your marriage and ruin your life. She got pregnant, as a result, and had an abortion a week ago, she says, in her third month. She just turned fifteen... makes it statutory rape, Reverend."

David spoke with a trembling voice, just above a whisper.

"I never... you've got to believe me... I would never..."

"If this checks out, Reverend, there'll be a warrant issued for your arrest, so don't take any trips... OK?"

David shook his head. Bronyak put his note pad and pen back into their appropriate pockets and stood up.

"Call your lawyer, Reverend."

Bronyak left the office, closing the door behind him. David sat motionless, staring. He felt as though his entire body were burning up, his head swimming. He felt that his life had just ended... in five minutes... ended. A faint tapping brought his vision into focus. He looked at the door.

"Reverend Matthews?"

It was Janet.

Tapping again.

"Reverend Matthews?"

The phone rang.

CHAPTER FIVE

Attorney Andrew Greenfield laid it out for David. Valarie Steffey was a very pretty, well developed, fifteen-year-old that any man could find sexually appealing. She had provided details about what happened that would make it hard for anyone to believe she had made them up. She described two brown birthmarks on David's abdomen just above his penis... one round, the other oblong. She had had an abortion, just as she claimed... he had checked it out. David did, in fact, have Valarie stay late at the church on three occasions over a one-month period... there were witnesses to this and David admits to it. David claims she was there to help him with some projects and to help him make some decisions about who should represent the church at the National Youth Council in May... and that's all that happened... they just talked. But that's just his word against hers. She has produced a pair of ripped panties that she claims David pulled off of her.

Greenfield continued. David had offered an explanation about the birthmark story. Valarie had accidentally walked in on him when he was in the cabana room, near the swimming pool, at a party given at the Steffey's home last August. He was completely undressed and facing toward her. She could have easily seen his marks then. Again... nobody but the two of them was there.

David broke in on Greenfield's soliloquy to ask about the fetus that was aborted. Couldn't they do some genetic testing on the tissues, he wondered, to see if it matched his? David said he had heard this could be done. Greenfield said he had already checked it out. The fetus had already been discarded.

Greenfield, returning to his verbal portrait of David's case, added the final touches. He was a veteran of twenty-five years of trial work. This case was, he said, a loser for David... no doubt about it. Yes, he said, he and David know that he didn't do it... but that's not what matters. He gave David about one chance in a hundred to win at trial. He said that they have to be practical. The D.A. would accept a plea of corruption of a minor... the parents didn't want this to go to court if they could avoid it... too much trauma for their daughter. It wouldn't make very good press for David if they went to trial, either... would be front page tabloid material all across the country... "Socialite Preacher Rapes Teenager in Church."

If David went to trial, Greenfield pointed out, and was convicted of statutory rape, not only would every person with an IQ above sixty know about it, but he was definitely looking at hard time in prison... and not at one of the white-collar country clubs, like where they put Jim Bakker.

"We're talking, if I could put it bluntly without offense to you, Reverend... the big house... with crack-head niggers and toothless white trash who'll size up your blessed asshole the minute you walk into the joint... if you don't mind me being perfectly frank, Reverend. And... you'll be going in as a 'tree jumper'... as the inmates call statutories in prison... which would make you the lowest scum in prison... and the first target of anyone looking to take out his frustrations on someone."

Fortunately for their sake, Greenfield explained, the D.A. was in a tough position... he wanted to "fry the good Reverend's ass," (sorry Reverend) but with the reluctance of the Steffey family to go to trial, he's forced to cut a deal... which pissed him off to no end (if the Reverend would excuse the language). Maybe the publicity would destroy the Reverend *and* the girl, the D.A. had told him, but goddamn it (sorry), he said, it would be a godsend in this election year... being hard on crime... willing to go after even big shot holy men... it would be beautiful. Greenfield's final brush stroke was to explain to David that if he'd plead, he could probably get him probation with community service and no jail time.

David repeatedly protested his innocence to Greenfield. Why, he pleaded, time and again, should he, an innocent man, a good man, a virtuous man, accept guilt for a crime he had not committed, nor could he ever conceive of committing? He had faith in God. His Heavenly Father would not allow his false accusers to prevail. He would fight... and God would be on his side. In response, Greenfield repeatedly assured David that he had no doubt of his innocence. He said he admired his faith, but religion was the Reverend's game and law was his. He explained that law had nothing to do with truth or innocence or justice. It was a game. It was the D.A.'s team against his. They get points for convictions, he said, and they don't give a shit (apologies) whether justice is achieved or not. The case was a solid one for them... a young, pretty, vulnerable, and very articulate victim, able to describe the Reverend's privates... the opportunity to commit the crime with no one else around... the pregnancy. Greenfield explained that his job wasn't to decide the Reverend's guilt but to advise him as best he could, legally. The Reverend had about a "snowball's chance in hell" of winning the case, in Greenfield's opinion, and the Reverend needed to be practical.

Greenfield recounted to David that he had seen many an innocent man go to jail who was convinced that justice would prevail. Justice never prevails, he told David... only the team with the best weapons... and they were outgunned by the opposition. If David insisted on a trial, he would, of course, represent him to the best of his ability, but they would lose... no doubt about it. But worst wouldn't be the conviction... it would be the press. They'd have a field day. He'd be front page news... cameras out in front of his house... reporters hassling his wife, or even his kids. He'd be national news. Greenfield made his final plea to David Matthews.

"Look Reverend... here's your choices. You can go through a trial and have your story carried all over the country, your reputation ruined for life, be found guilty, do hard time in prison... or we can arrange to quietly plead guilty to a reduced charge and get off with some probation and community service. I can't guarantee a complete news blackout... you know what scumbags the media are... they have eyes and ears everywhere and don't give a damn if they ruin somebody or not... you know... anything for a story. Anyway... your exposure, if you plead, will sure as hell be less than the made-in-heaven media event that a trial would be. You choose, Reverend, and I'll go with whatever you decide."

David, after another round of protestations and denials, surrendered to the inevitable. He realized he really had no choice, when it came right down to it, but to accept the plea. He knew he was in a no-win situation... it was now just a choice of lose small, or lose big. It was an absolute miscarriage of justice... but he saw no other way out. He told Greenfield that he needed to talk it over first, though, with his wife, before any final decision was made.

Donna, at this juncture, knew nothing of the situation. David had not wanted to unnecessarily worry her. He knew he had done nothing wrong and the Good Lord, he believed, would protect him. He always had. All through his fortieth birthday party, after just having learned of the problem, David had maintained a happy and gracious facade, while his nerves were churning the contents of his bowels into water. His ministerial training as a "vicarious happy guy" served him well over the next few days. His mask was flawless.

After the birthday visit from Detective Bronyak at his office, David considered seeking legal counsel, but did not. Instead, he knelt on his office floor and prayed for God's deliverance from these, his false accusers. He was a righteous man... and God would not allow any harm to come to him. Of that he was certain. He changed his mind about legal counsel three days later. Bronyak called him at his office, early on Monday morning, to alert him to the fact that the District Attorney was going to prosecute the case and a warrant was going to be issued the following morning. Bronyak, out of respect for the Reverend's position, told David he could turn himself in at the District Attorney's office, the next day. Bronyak, again, strongly urged the Reverend to get an attorney if he hadn't already done so.

In the evening following this last visit with Greenfield, David waited until after the kids were in bed, then approached Donna, who was sitting in their family room, working on her needlepoint that would be sold at the church's summer fair. She was listening to Mozart. Without announcement, David turned off the stereo. The sudden silence both startled and annoyed Donna. Her facial expression clearly conveyed her obvious vexation with David, for having interrupted her "quiet time." He sat in the chair to her right.

"Honey, we need to talk about something."

David's tone and expression caused Donna to stiffen.

"What? What is it?"

"We've got a very serious problem."

With this, Donna's eyes widened and her hand went to her mouth.

"What? David, what is going on?"

Her tone was quickly rising to near hysteria.

"Tell me!"

"It's something we can get through, Donna… we can. Can we pray together, first?"

"We'll pray later, David. I want to know, right now, what is going on."

David took a deep breath and blew it out with a whooshing sound. He looked up at the ceiling, down to his lap, then into Donna's eyes, which were not warm.

"Valarie Steffey has made up a story about me. She told the police that I attacked her."

David paused… waiting for some reaction from Donna. Her face was a study in frozen intensity. He continued.

"She says that I forced her to have sex with me. The District Attorney is going to prosecute. I've been to see a lawyer... Andrew Greenfield, you know, you've heard of him. He's supposed to be the best trial lawyer in Boston. He thinks I should plead guilty."

Donna's eyes narrowed and her voice shot at him like an aimed rifle.

"What?! What is this? What are you talking about? Are you telling me that you raped Valarie Steffey? Is that what you're telling me?"

"No, no, no, no. Donna, no."

"Then what are you saying David? Did you do it? Did you?"

"No. Of course I didn't. I can't believe you'd even ask me that."

"Then why are you pleading guilty?"

"Greenfield thinks I can't win it."

"Are you out of your mind David?! You say you are perfectly innocent. How could this lawyer think you can't win the case? Something's missing here, David. This doesn't add up. What are you keeping from me?"

"Well... apparently Valarie can identify some marks on my body... and I was with her a couple of times in the church... alone. Greenfield says that that will look really bad... and she got pregnant somehow."

"What marks? What marks are you talking about?"

David hesitated.

"David... what marks?!"

THE DISCIPLES

"I've got those two marks... you know... down here... just above my... you know."

"She's seen those marks?!"

"Well... she says she has. She's identified them pretty accurately."

"And just how would our little Miss Steffey have seen those?"

She pointed to his groin area as she posed the question.

"Like I told Greenfield... she saw me naked over at the Steffey's pool... getting into my suit in their cabana. You remember... we went over there last summer for that Labor Day party."

"That's funny, David... you've never mentioned this before. A young and pretty teenage girl sees you stark naked and you just forget to tell me? What else did you forget to tell me? What was this about being alone in the church with her?"

"We were getting ready for the Youth Conference last spring... you remember. We had all those programs to get ready... and posters. You remember how swamped I was, trying to get ready for that? Valarie volunteered to help, one evening, when I stayed late. Remember... I called you? It was just a coincidence that no one else was in the church at the time. I didn't even think about it. She helped me with some of the poster layouts. That was it. She was only there for about an hour and a half... then I gave her a ride home. The next week, she stayed again for... it couldn't have been more than forty-five minutes or an hour... to help fold programs and talk about who should go to the youth conference."

"I suppose, once again, no one was, coincidentally, in the church at that time?"

"No... I don't think there was anybody... what is this Donna? Don't you believe me? Do you actually think I did something to her?"

"Well, David... this is all just such a coincidence, Valarie Steffey can identify marks just above your penis... and then you suddenly remember that she accidentally saw you naked... which you had forgotten to tell me about until just now. She coincidentally is in the church, alone with you... twice in one week... and, what do you know?... she turns up pregnant. Quite a bunch of coincidences, David. I'll tell you what I think, Reverend Matthews... I think that sexy little slut with the well-developed body... which she shows off quite well with her low-cut blouses and short skirts that barely cover her butt... and I've seen you look at her, Reverend Matthews... was just too much temptation for the good Reverend. You're just like your brother, David... a loser. I knew everything was too good to be true. It was just a matter of time before you blew it... just like your brother. And now what... David? You're going to plead guilty to some sex crime? We're ruined! I won't be able to walk out in the street! You've ruined our lives, David. You might just as well have taken a knife and stabbed me... and the children... in our hearts. Their lives are ruined! Their father... a minister... a child molester... a pervert... a rapist. Our lives are over, David. Was that little bit of lust worth all this, David? You're a weak, sinful man, David Your life is ruined... our lives are ruined!"

Donna Matthews began to shake. A moan rose from her throat and emerged as a scream. She stood up... her eyes were darting around the room as though she had never been there before. Her needlepoint fell from her lap to the floor. She stared at David with wild, hate-filled eyes. Suddenly, she rushed at him with her arms flailing. Her nails scratched his face. David threw his hands in front of him for protection. She eventually exhausted her fury on him and collapsed onto the rug... sobbing weakly. After a while, Donna finally managed to get to her feet and quivering, walked silently out of the room.

In the morning, Donna packed bags for the children and herself and drove to Brandford... to her parents' house. A week later, David received a letter from Donna's lawyer, informing him of her intention to file for divorce and requesting that he cooperate in matters of child and spousal support. The letter also informed

David that Mrs. Matthews would not be amenable to allowing him visitation with the children and that she would strenuously oppose any action on his part, should he attempt to do so.

David had driven downtown, to Greenfield's office on the morning after his conversation with Donna. Together, they drove over to the District Attorney's office. There, David was arrested, fingerprinted, photographed, and given a formal arraignment date... two weeks hence. At the arraignment, David formally pled guilty to two counts of corrupting a minor. Later, at the sentencing hearing, as part of the plea bargain, David was given three years' probation and six months of community service... working at an inner-city soup kitchen. David and Greenfield felt luck was with them, concerning the media. Everyday, David would search the papers. Finally, about a week after the arraignment, it was there... the front page lead story. Somebody had leaked.

David mailed his resignation to the church. Waiting long enough for the letter to reach its destination, he phoned Janet and asked her if she would mind boxing-up his personal things from his office and mailing them to him. She consented to do it. Her voice was cold and professional... and did not inquire as to how he was doing.

Prior to the Valarie Steffey situation, the extent of David's drinking had consisted of an occasional glass of wine. Since the day he pled guilty, however, he had begun drinking heavily, to the extent that, a month later, he was routinely consuming a full fifth of bourbon in a twenty-four hour period. He wasn't able to eat, except for an occasional, forced bite of food. In the five weeks, following his first meeting with Detective Bronyak, he had lost over twenty-five pounds. His skin was gray... his eyes, sunken. His appearance had changed so much that he startled himself one evening upon catching a glimpse of his face in the dining room mirror.

One morning, about a week before his sentencing, David somehow worked up the courage to call his father... hoping that the senior Reverend Matthews could find it in his heart to forgive him and extend to him some modicum of the emotional and spiritual support, he so desperately craved. Passing the front door, on his way to use the phone in the study, a letter, lying on the floor, just below the mail drop, caught his eye... and saved him the trouble of making the call. He instantly recognized his father's distinguished handwriting on the envelope and with a sense of hope and due reverence for the epistle in his hand, he carried it into the study and placed it gently across the pages of an open Bible, lying on his desk. David sat in his chair and stared at the still-sealed envelope... feeling that, somehow, he might be able to divine its contents. He closed his eyes and prayed that the letter was one of forgiveness. Finally, he reached out and grasped the letter with his right hand and slowly turned it over. He slipped the sharp point of the pewter letter opener, topped with the head of a scotch terrier – a gift from his father's trip to Scotland – into the small opening at the corner fold. By fractions of an inch, he painstakingly separated the flap from the back of the envelope... trying not to unduly tear the cloth-fibered paper... intentionally prolonging the completion of the act. At long last, the flap was completely parted from its companion piece and rose slightly to reveal the ivory writing paper his father always used. After pausing for another moment of prayer, David summoned his courage and pulled the folded letter from the envelope. He flipped the top fold back and the bottom of it down, to expose the familiar hand of his father.

    David:

    I will get right to the point. There are inadequate words in the English language to allow me to express my feelings at this moment. Suffice it to say that from this day forward, I have no son by your name. I will make it my life's mission to erase any record of your having been a member of this family. I trust you will have the decency to, never again, contact me or any member of this family.

    May God have mercy on your wretched soul.

    Reverend David T. Matthews

The only remaining ember of hope that still smoldered in David's heart was thus doused cold by the venom of his father's pen. He had hoped, against all rationality – remembering how heartlessly his father had treated his brother for a far lesser offense – that he could somehow find the compassion within himself to forgive him. He believed that his father could extend him this small mercy – despite having lost everything else in his life – he could somehow go on. David sat at his desk, staring at what he knew would undoubtedly be, the last communication he would ever receive from his father. His mind drifted to escape the oppressive vacuum that was collapsing his soul.

The annoying din of a nearby lawn mower delivered his mind back to the palpable cruelty of his conscious existence. He glanced at the clock on his desk. He had been sitting in his chair for nearly three hours. He got up – feeling as though he were in a dream – and began to pace around the house... making the circle through the many rooms of the expansive first floor of his home. As he repeated his circuitous path, his mind was a jumble of thoughts and emotions... his thoughts, frequently returning to scripture. He found himself, understandably, thinking about the story of Job.

As David pondered Job's misfortunes, he began to see that Job was not a steadfast believer to be admired and emulated... but, instead, a naive fool. He had absurdly maintained his faith in the Lord while being sadistically tortured by cruel twists of fate. For the first time in David's life, he understood that Job simply never understood the big picture... he just never got it. David had finally seen the light, or, more accurately, the absence of it. All of Job's blessings – as well as his own – had created a false illusion of divine favor, when in reality they were nothing but mere coincidence. It was all so clear to David now. What he considered to be his blessings in life were but mere serendipitous happenstance. Things could have just as easily converged to create some dreadful existence for him. He could have, with but the slightest tweak of circumstance, been born his brother or some drug-dealing scum in a ghetto. The haze and shingles had finally fallen from his eyes and for the first time he saw through life as clearly as he did the clear pane of glass before his face. No God was looking out for him. Life was a game of chance whose promise of fortune was as fickle as the weather.

He had done nothing wrong, he repeated time and again... absolutely nothing wrong. That little Jezebel, for reasons he would never glean, had destroyed his life... taken away everything... just like that. One minute, everything... the next minute, nothing. There was obviously no grand divine plan... of that David was now absolutely sure. It was now all so apparent that he felt foolish for not having seen it before. Human beings are no more divine than a dog in the street. When a dog is run over, it doesn't matter... no one cares. Its carcass is picked up and dumped in a heap with the rest of the garbage. Human beings fool themselves into believing divine hocus-pocus because the truth – that there is no plan and certainly no God – is too hard to bear.

He thought back to all those Christian people who sat in his pews every Sunday... who shook his hand on their way out the door... who smiled at him... who wanted to be seen with him. All those good, caring, forgiving, compassionate Christians... where were they now?... now that he was down and in need of help... in need of Christian caring and forgiveness. Where were they all now? After he was visited with his tragedy, not one single person... either from his Guildford or Boston congregations... had ever inquired as to his well-being or offered their support. Of all those who joined him in "Christian Fellowship"... not one single person had called or written a word of support. Where were all those good Christians when you really need them? Didn't they sit in his pews and shake their heads in agreement when he sermonized about what a true Christian is? Didn't they all nod in remembrance that the Good Lord Himself administered to prostitutes and criminals?... that they should not be proud and arrogant as to their good fortune... but humble and thankful for God's bountiful gifts? Didn't they listen and agree with the scripture that commanded that those who are sick or down in spirit or lonely are blessed and should be ministered to by those of a Christian heart? Didn't they join in prayer and sing hymns about compassion and forgiveness in the world? Where were they all now?

He could now answer all his own questions with a searing forthrightness. His response was that all those good Christians who sat in his pews were nothing more than members of a Sunday morning country club... with a social pecking order for the best seats and open church board positions. They dressed in the designated club uniforms and sang the club songs. They saw and were seen. They were phonies and snobs... socialites at yet one more club event. They were nothing more. Their Christianity was an airbrushed sanitized, very white, perfumed box... tied up with coordinated, pastel bows. Their compassion for the dirty or black or smelly or poor or troubled people of the world was strictly a part of the mindless litany of the club... never to be taken literally.

As David looked about the rooms through which he was passing, they had the feel of a mausoleum... and he the corpse. He was already dead. His life was over. David considered, for a fleeting moment, ending it, there and then. This thought struck some part of his tortured psyche as perversely humorous. How does a dead man kill himself? His body was alive, yes... but it no longer contained a spirit. The spirit had been but an illusion. He needed a certain degree of enthusiasm about life – some little bit – to garner the energy just to take care of everyday needs. He needed to make money... have a place to live... buy food... and want to eat it. He now had no desire to do any of these things. At that moment, he felt he could have simply laid down on the floor of that room and never gotten up... just lay there until he died. He then realized that he didn't possess even the energy to kill himself.

Finally wearying of his first floor walking tour, David returned to his desk chair and dropped into it. He stared, but saw nothing. He thought nothing. Finally, around two o'clock in the morning, a need to urinate finally overcame his inertia. After peeing, he went to bed and fell immediately into a heavy sleep. On a number of occasions, he would awaken for a few minutes then, quickly, drift off again. Finally, he awoke, fully, and sat on the edge of the bed. The light from the window looked like evening. He had no idea how long he had been asleep. The clock indicated eight o'clock. He wasn't real sure if it were evening or morning. He looked out the window. From that window – which faced the north – he still couldn't tell which eight o'clock it was. He walked down the hall to his daughter's bedroom and solved the puzzle when he gazed out to the east and saw no sun.

David went down to the first floor, opened the front door, and picked up the three newspapers, lying on the porch... Sunday's, Monday's, and Tuesday's. He had laid down in his bed in the early morning hours on Sunday... and assumed he had slept until Sunday evening. He had, instead, he now concluded, slept, in fact, until Tuesday evening.

David abruptly realized that he now felt significantly different about things, than when he lay down in his bed on Sunday. Entirely gone was his sense of lamentation over his bad fortune and his destroyed life. A vague feeling began to find expression in his mind and he silently mouthed the simple declaration. "I don't give a fuck." This proclamation that had progressed from a thought to a whisper on his lips eventually emerged as a shout. He began running around the house... shouting his new credo... knocking things over... smashing fragile objects against the wall. Previous to this day, David had never in his life – not even in the days of youthful experimentation – used the word, "fuck." As he shouted it now, it felt good in his mouth, like a juicy wad of gum. It was liberating. He was no longer David Matthews, Minister, Husband, Father, Son. He was just David... who didn't give a fuck. He was simply a human being... an animal... about whom no one gave a damn and who no longer gave two shits about anyone else in the world. Fuck them... fuck them all... fuck the world... he just didn't care anymore. He no longer cared about anybody or anything... his old man, his soon-to-be ex-wife, his children, his brother, his mother... nobody. From this day forward, he would do whatever he wanted, however he wanted, with whom he wanted. He'd play the D.A.'s silly probation and public service game, but he wasn't going to hide. If he ran into a member of his former congregation, he'd walk right up to them and say, "By the way... fuck you." He laughed and clapped his hands together as he pictured the poignant moment. The word, from which he had abstained for all his life, had suddenly become his defining term for his life. He had found his true heart and his true feelings. His new answer to the world was simple and unambiguous.

"Fuck you… fuck you all."

CHAPTER SIX

DANIEL

After his third divorce, Danny Boscia had visceral insight that this was the last chapter of his matrimonial odyssey. Of course, when he reflected back, he'd felt the same way after his first two marriages ended, as well. Once again, as he had done after his first two conjugal derailments, Danny withdrew. He didn't answer the phone, came straight home from work, avoided making eye contact with anyone at the office, and drank more than usual. His friends and family had seen him this way before, so they weren't terribly concerned. It was his way of regrouping and pondering the course of his life. After such failures, he wanted, desperately, to understand why things had always gotten so consistently screwed up for him.

It certainly wasn't for lack of trying... of that he was absolutely sure. As far back as he could remember, he had tried harder than anyone he knew. When he was only eight, for instance, he trained, year-round, for his first little league try outs. He'd get up at six in the morning, put on his oversized, black, canvas sneakers and the hand-me-down, faded blue sweat suit his older brother had worn on Our Lady of Mercy's track team, and run around his neighborhood block. He had it figured... ten times around was two miles. He ran every day of the year... even Christmas morning. His mother called him "The Little Road Runner." In the winter, it would still be dark when he went out the door. In rain, or through a foot of snow, Danny would run. All the fathers, leaving for the seven o'clock shift at the Ford plant... their black, dented, metal lunch pails hanging from one hand and a chrome-topped thermos of coffee in the other, would make a "beep beep," Road Runner greeting to Danny as he dashed by. He'd giggle, wave, put back on his "game face," and continue on his way.

Danny was cut from the Knights of Columbus team that year, after the third practice. His dad told him not to take it too badly. He said the K of C had some of the best players in the whole damn Detroit City League. Danny took it badly, anyway. For two weeks, he stayed in his room, not wanting to talk to anybody, ignoring his three older brothers, no matter if they tried to be nice to him, or teased him for being such a "sissy." For the first few days he secretly cried... burying his face in his pillow to muffle the sobs. When the hallway was clear, he'd dash down the hall to the bathroom and splash cold water on his red, puffy eyes to camouflage his badge of shame. It would be a fate worse than death to have his dad or brothers know that he had cried over such a little thing. But, as would be a constantly repeated pattern throughout Danny's life, like the Phoenix arising from its own ashes, one morning, two weeks from the day he'd been cut from the team, Danny Boscia arose at six a.m.... donned his faded blue sweat suit and black sneakers, and The Road Runner was back in training. "Next year, I'll show them all," he repeatedly said to himself, time and again, to the pounding rhythm of his tennis shoes, slapping against the uneven, badly cracked, concrete, sidewalk squares of his blue-collar neighborhood.

The following year, he made it to the fifth practice before he was cut. Once again, after his period of mourning, he was back out again... circling the block. The third year, he finally made the team. He was only a second string, right fielder... but he was the most dedicated second string, right fielder in the whole damn Detroit City Little League.

And that's the way it always was for Danny Boscia. He never seemed to get a break... but he would never quit. Everything always came the hard way for Danny. It seemed to him that almost everyone else he knew got little "gifts" in life... some natural ability... somebody important to open a door for them... a special talent... a handsome face... something to give them a little edge in life. But Danny Boscia was just one of those people who was born average... average intelligence, average height, average looks, average talent, average everything. He was, in his mind, a four-door Chevy in a world full of Corvettes. For his just-above-average grades in school, Danny studied three times as hard as everybody else.

In Danny's blue-collar neighborhood... where sports ranked just below the Blessed Mother in life's priorities, a fair number of the neighborhood boys got full athletic scholarships to some pretty big schools... Michigan State, Purdue, Penn State, Ohio State. Two of his classmates had even been blessed with what was universally considered to be a mere step below entrance to heaven in his Irish-Italian, Catholic neighborhood... a football scholarship to Notre Dame. But with his just-above-average grades and low SAT's, the best Danny could do was community college. After two years, he transferred to Michigan State. He got no financial help, whatsoever... not a penny from his family. He wasn't angry... he knew his parents just couldn't afford it. Besides, they weren't a "college" family. His dad had gotten his older brothers jobs at the plant when they graduated from high school, starting at $9.50 an hour. Danny's dad admonished him to think twice about this "college stuff"... pointing out to him that he'd never make the kind of money that he could at the plant... teaching school or whatever he had in mind.

Clementine Boscia, Danny's father, was a practical man. He'd come to Detroit with his parents, from Sicily, when he was four years old and started working at the plant when he was fifteen. It was a good, secure job. To Clem, you take the sure thing... you don't gamble. In his mind, Danny was gambling with this college stuff when he could get him in at the plant and to him that was just plain stupid. Of course, he always kept his opinion of Danny's intelligence to himself. Clem really did think Danny was a little stupid, in general. Danny just never knew when to quit and, in Clem's mind, a smart person knows when to quit. Danny, he thought, always tried to get more than he was meant to have in life. Some people are born thoroughbreds... most are just work horses. In Clem's view, Danny was unquestionably, a work horse... who tried, desperately, to be a thoroughbred.

Although Mr. Boscia never actually told Danny what he thought about him, Danny knew. It was obvious to him. Clem would say things... like the year Danny announced he was going to try out for short stop.

"The K of C needs an equipment manager this year, Danny... keepin all the team stats, too... you'd be good at that, Dan... it'd be fun. I can put in a word for you if you want me to."

In high school, Clem tried to get Danny to sign up for Vo Tech instead of College Prep. Clementine wasn't a bad father, Danny realized much later in his life... he just wanted to protect him from disappointment. But that's all right, Danny would think... he'd show his dad, he'd show them all. That's the way Danny went through life... trying to prove to everybody that he was better than they thought he was. He was going to be somebody, get to the "top"... wherever that was.

To Danny, life was a series of plateaus, each one higher and better than the one below... and you had to scale a sheer cliff to get up to the next one. People who were lazy or had no guts, just stayed put, on the plateau where they were born. A few of these people tried the cliff, found it too difficult, and remained, thereafter... safely on the ground. Lots of people had advantages over him on the climb. Some were stronger, some smarter... some had others pulling them from above. All Danny had was determination... guts enough to not quit... no matter how slippery the rocks were from the rain... no matter how cold his fingers got from the wind. He'd hack his way out of an avalanche if it fell on him. If he crashed back to the ground, he'd heal up and start all over again. No matter what anybody said to him or did to him, he was going to the top. There, he'd look down at his detractors... at everyone who ever told him to quit... raise his arms to the sky and shout, "Danny Boscia is here!"

As would later become a standard practice in his life, during his senior year at college, Danny undertook a systematic assessment of his strengths and weaknesses in an attempt to determine the best course for his future. With as much objectivity as he could muster, he concluded that he was – tenacious, intelligent (but not brilliant), unafraid, very competitive, a very good writer and speaker, a voracious reader, and a person who liked to figure out problems and determine solutions. After much reflection, he came to the studied opinion that, given his attributes, he would be best suited to pursue a career in the law. The legal profession would also – from Danny's twenty-two-year-old vantage point – provide him with a certain degree of prestige and respect, which, after many years of being regularly subjected to dispersions as to his abilities from family and friends alike, would constitute some much-overdue vindication. Besides that, it appeared to Danny that lawyers always made a lot of money. The upscale neighborhoods were, after all, always filled with doctors and lawyers. To Danny's way of thinking, the top plateau had, among other things, lots of money laying on it. His mind made up, Danny steadfastly stepped to the foot of the cliff with the law degree at its top.

Not surprisingly, Danny ended up with slightly above average college grades... a 3.0 GPA... and LSAT's of about the same calibre. Although he tried for admission to the prestigious law schools, he was admitted to only one... Ohio Northern in Ada, Ohio. He figured that since he got in, they must take all of the average students in the country who wanted to be lawyers. His academic work in law school, one hardly need recount, was, of course, average. He found in law school, however, for the first time in his life, that he truly excelled at something. He won the trial moot court competition in his senior year, which pitted all senior students against one another in an elimination jury trial tournament. Danny was exultant... he had beaten them all... even those arrogant law review assholes. This was the first time in his life that Danny had come in first in anything. With this distinction, life suddenly took on a certain glow for him. He even thought he was somewhat better looking when he examined his face in the mirror. Not even his phone call with his dad – which he made the moment he got back to his apartment after winning – could ruin it for him.

"Dad, guess what?... I won the trial competition. Final round was this afternoon. I won it... the whole thing."

"Yeah? Hey, great Dan. Musta been on a really loaded up team, huh?"

"No Dad... it was just me... no teams. I was on my own."

"C'mon... who'd you have helpin ya?"

"What? I'm telling you I won... me... all by myself. Oh, fuck it, Dad... forget it."

Danny's new found sense of self-worth lasted until he got his first round of job rejections from the applications he mailed after graduation. He had sent out twenty-five letters of application... to corporate positions, the federal government, district attorneys, public defenders, Neighborhood Legal Services, private law practices – the whole gamut – and received twenty-five, standard form rejection letters. Danny then sent out thirty more and was again rebuffed in equal number. Many of his classmates were getting jobs through family connections but about the only real-life connection that Danny's family had with the law, to his recollection, was when his old man was arrested for punching another coach in the mouth during a heated exchange over an umpire's call.

To Danny, the challenges of this stage in his life were just another of the sheer cliffs he would have to scale. This particular climb, however, was shaping up to be exceptionally daunting. He was three months out of law school, owing twenty-seven thousand dollars in educational loans for college and law school – which he was required to start paying within three months of graduation. With what he made, delivering milk and cheese twelve hours a day for a local dairy, he was barely able to pay for his tiny, two-room apartment and his survival-level diet. He was also trying to study on his own for the bar exam... not having the money to pay for a professional prep course, in which nearly all his classmates were enrolled. When Danny thought nothing more could possibly be added to his life stress, two days before the bar exam his girlfriend informed him that she was pregnant.

Danny hadn't cried since he was cut from the K of C when he was eight, but a maniacal, crying laughter... as surprising to him as it was to his mother... erupted from his throat when she called him at around eight o'clock, on the evening before he was to take the bar exam, to tell him that his father had been diagnosed with terminal cancer and had about six months to live.

Loretta Boscia was sure it was simply the news about his father that caused her son to react as dramatically he did. Perhaps, she thought, she shouldn't have told him over the phone. What she could not have known was that Danny's near-hysteria was only partly due to the news of his father. It was more so the fact of Danny's mind finally registering its protest against his present reality. "How fucking absurd can life get?!" he thought. "Jesus Christ!... somebody has to be kidding here!" His life as he saw it was nothing more than a goddamn, second-rate soap opera. Nobody, he thought, could write such a stupid fucking script, such as this. Buried in debt... rejected by every job prospect... working twelve hours a day... studying for a bar exam... and, one day after your girlfriend tells you she's pregnant – the night before the most important test in your life – your mother calls to say your dad is dying of cancer. As he pondered it, Danny became convinced that a script, as preposterous as his present life circumstance, would be rejected even by the soaps.

Danny married his girlfriend, Miss Karen Chambers, daughter of an Ada, Ohio postal worker, in October... one week after getting his notice of failing the bar exam. It was a very small wedding... with ten people in attendance... neither family being thrilled about Karen's noticeably enlarged, lower abdomen. Wedding invitations were, thus, on a need-to-know basis only. "Why broadcast your daughter's lack of control?" Mrs. Chambers would posit, regarding the blessed event.

Karen Chambers believed that marrying a law student was her ticket out of lower middle-class oblivion, out of Ada, and into the country club set... where, she felt, she rightfully belonged. Danny was somewhat aware of her motives, but, in a perverse way, it was kind of flattering to him... somebody actually believing that he was going to amount to something. Karen was the best-looking woman Danny had ever seen in his life... actually a knockout in anybody's book... with long silky blonde hair, a sleek, athletic body with firm but squeezable breasts, hourglass hips, high cheek bones, pouting but very kissable lips, a milky complexion, and perfectly straight white teeth. Danny knew with her looks, given the right opportunity, she probably could have induced any guy into marriage, but, in a town as small as Ada, pickings were slim. Girls in Ada considered landing a law student a major coup. Antithetical to the provincial female ambitions, however, nearly all the male law students at Ohio Northern were from outside the local area and had blatant disdain for the female "townies"... particularly if they weren't university coeds... and Karen Chambers was not. Thus, despite her beauty, Karen Chamber's goal was not one that could be realized without great determination and stealth.

Karen hated school and was looking for the most efficient way to get herself the life she felt she deserved... without the distasteful burden of acquiring a higher education. For nearly all women, similarly situated, marriage was about the only career path... albeit a tenuous one. Tenuous, because she never knew, for sure, which card to hold, play, or discard. Women of this ilk are, of necessity, consummately practical créatures. Each is painfully aware that the fragrance of their bloom is but for a short season and that they must, therefore, choose very carefully... but not so carefully as to allow the petals to begin to fall before the bee is secured. Karen, as others in her position are prone to do, made her play as quickly as was prudent... calculated to yield as high a return as possible. Nevertheless, in this sort of game, no bet is a sure thing. One could never totally eliminate the possibility of a miscalculation.

Karen assessed Danny Boscia to be a pretty good bet. She considered him decent-looking but definitely not handsome. If she were to daydream of romance, Danny, most certainly, would not have been her choice as a leading man. He had a friendly face, though... but too short a forehead and too dark a complexion to appeal to her keltic bias. In addition to other features Karen found less than desirable, his nose had a slight bend to the left... and his teeth were a bit crooked. He wasn't ugly, mind you, she would say to her girlfriends, he had, well... pleasant looks. His heart also seemed, to Karen, to be in the right place. He was bountifully generous and dutifully attentive to her... doing everything he could to make her feel pretty and good about herself. He also had, she would always add, a good sense of humor, to boot. Above all, and most importantly, he was a determined, hard worker... the most determined person Karen had ever met in her life. He was, to her observations, hell-bent on doing well in his life... and his track record was, in her considered opinion, a good one, to date. Look how far he had come already, she would point out... from a blue-collar neighborhood to college to law school – never completely sure if she were trying to convince her friends or herself of Danny's desirability.

Ultimately, Karen Chamber's final decision, to make a play for Danny Boscia, was, predictably, a product of consummate practicality. Romance, good looks, passion – those were fine things for flings or dreams... but marriage was the real stuff of life. Will he be a good provider for me and my children? Will he be reliable? Will he be a good father? Those were the real questions that begged an answer in matters of matrimony. Contrary to the popular fiction that women are the romantics and men the practical sex... Karen knew the truth to be just the opposite. Men love sex, looks, and love... and will marry to keep them. They do it all the time. A woman, on the other hand, will use sex, looks, and love, strictly as part of the necessary weapons to keep a man off balance until after the ceremony... but marriage – not these ephemeral fancies – is always the clear goal... and she will maintain the steely composure of a wild west gun slinger to achieve her ends. Through this detached process of evaluation, Karen made her decision about Danny Boscia and she played her card... including the pregnancy trump for good measure.

It was early March and Danny would be graduating in May. With the sands of time running out, and with scant few grains remaining in the upper chamber, the pressure was upon Karen Chambers to expeditiously consummate her ambitions. Throughout the month of April, therefore, as per her matrimonial stratagem, Karen carefully placed joking, playful insertions into their conversations regarding the potential of their conjugal union.

"If we had kids, Danny, what do you think they'd look like?"

"Isn't that a beautiful ring, Danny?"

"If we ever decided to get married, honey, what kind of a house would you like to live in?"

This "getting him used to talking about it" tactic seemed to go quite well. Danny innocently and enthusiastically participated. The problem was, Karen couldn't get him to nibble hard enough to jerk the line. She could get him, before and after they made love, to say he loved her, and induce other encouraging pledges of commitment... that they would always be together... that he never wanted to be without her... that no other woman had ever meant to him what she had – but no firm proposal nor date-setting had come of it. Frustrated, Karen decided that the time had come for the clincher. She covertly discontinued her birth control pills and made sure they made love frequently during her ovulation. And... bingo! She didn't tell him until the latest date she felt she could wait... soon enough before he got any idea of leaving Ada... late enough that an abortion was out of the question. She picked July fifteenth, her birthday... her twenty-first... for the announcement.

Karen had been admirably prudent in executing her matrimonial scheme, but her weakness lay in her ignorance of certain esoteric characteristics of the legal profession. First, she was simply unaware that a lot of law school graduates flunk the bar exam. Next, it never dawned on her that there could be a bad job market for lawyers. She figured that, somehow, lawyers just walked out of law school into their three-piece suits, briefcases, and six-figure incomes. That's how the story went with the female townies, anyway. Karen also didn't know that Danny had borrowed all the money he used to go to school for the past seven years.

Christmas of that year found Karen's washboard abdomen, swollen beyond recognition, striped with what would become permanent stretch marks, ready to expel its precious human cargo at any moment. Her doctor had told her on her last visit that she had "dropped" and could "go" at anytime. They were living in Danny's two-room apartment at the time. He was getting ready to take the bar exam, again, in January... still driving for Holland's Dairy. Danny's dad was, by then, a skin-draped skeleton, too weak to eat, sit, or talk. He didn't recognize the family very often, anymore, and was mercifully asleep most of the time. He wasn't expected to see the new year. The only Christmas present exchanged between Danny and Karen Boscia was Danny's gift to Karen... an antique tea set which Mrs. Holland – aware of Danny's bleak financial fortunes – had given him, to, in turn, give to Karen. She didn't like it... and made no pretense about it.

As always, Danny viewed this multitude of problems in his life as just another cliff to be scaled. Karen, however, was inconsolably miserable... not only from her frequent physical discomfort and what she considered to be her grotesquely disproportionate body, but even more so as a result of her badly misplayed marriage hand. Karen eventually told Danny to his face, that their life together wasn't what she had bargained for. She flatly informed him that she could have had far better than what she had with him by marrying one of the local Ada boys... adding that she had had a thousand chances to do so. Their life circumstances *were*, in fact, about as bad as they *both* felt they could get, but Danny, of course, resolved that he was going to beat it. "I'll show them," once again returned to his lips, as it had so many times before in his life. Somehow, someway, he pledged to Karen, he would work his way out of the mess they were in. He'd give Karen the life she deserved. He'd succeed as a lawyer... and he'd be the best husband and father that there ever was.

Danny was getting there. He passed the January bar exam and, still without a job offer, he opened his own law practice... arranging to use a small back office of a local attorney's suite, free of charge, in exchange for doing research and filing for him. Danny, true to his promise, proved to be a wonderful father. He spent every possible, free moment with little Andy... named after

Karen's father. Danny wanted to name his son after his own father, who had passed away exactly one week before Andy was born. Karen not only rejected the suggestion but laughed, mockingly, in Danny's face for even proposing that they name their baby something "as stupid as Clementine," as she put it. Although Danny was not a violent man, it was all he could do not to smash in Karen's cover girl face for this insult to his father, whose funeral he had attended only four days before.

While Danny worked... often fourteen hours a day... Karen had Andy, perpetually, at her mother's house – everyday, all day – as she quickly dieted and exercised back to her former glory. She began to run with her old crowd, day and night. Danny would pick Andy up at the Chamber's house after work, take him home, feed him, bathe him, read him stories, and put him to bed. Karen would nearly always be gone – or going out the door – as he was arriving home. Danny would usually make himself a peanut butter and jelly sandwich dinner... too tired to do anything else... drink a beer, watch a little television, and go to bed... always alone.

Bernie Gardener, a local lawyer Danny had met at a bar association meeting, called him at his office one morning in mid-August, to let him know, as a matter of professional courtesy, that a divorce complaint was coming. His wife had retained him and he had filed it... said he was sorry to have to tell him so. Danny had heard rumors that Karen had been having an affair with Bill Turner, the owner of a local jewelry store... the Turners being an old, affluent Ada family. In October, Danny lost the custody hearing for Andy... receiving restricted visitation every other Sunday, from one o'clock until six. He figured he'd lose... being an outsider in the community. He was ordered to pay child support, even though he was sure, with Karen living at her parents' home, she'd undoubtedly use the money to go out partying, or to buy herself some new clothes.

By the time Danny was thirty, he had become a highly respected trial lawyer in Ada, making a very decent income... enough to pay off his educational loans and buy a decent house to live in. Karen married Bill Turner and had two more kids in short order.

They built a big house near the country club. At age thirty-one, Danny married a philosophy professor from the university. The marriage lasted four years. In this marriage, Danny discovered the true nature of academicians. He found that those stimulating, in-depth conversations about life, love, beauty, philosophy and art – that had attracted him to Dr. Nancy Colbert, Ph.D. – were the extent of her appreciative capacity. Until his association with Nancy, he hadn't realized that anyone could actually exist in a totally cerebral state, but Nancy truly did. She could describe love most eloquently, but never gave it nor experienced it. Her "anger" was of the nature of an extremely articulate, effete, opposing position. She considered sex a "fascinating topic" but neither wanted it nor when, on rare occasion, acceding to it, did she enjoy it. Danny had been looking for a wife who had intelligence and a broad range of interests. In pursuing this goal, to the exclusion of other essential attributes, he had ended up married, not to a wife, but to an intellectual colleague.

During their courtship, Danny believed that love would eventually spring from their many common interests – but dialogue proved to be the singular product. Their marital relationship was so void of passion, and so fraternal in nature, that at times, when they were together, Danny experienced the disconcerting sense that he was with another man. Danny's relationship with Nancy Colbert made him realize just how much he truly needed love and passion in his life. As might be anticipated in such a purely platonic match, Nancy and he had a very rational discussion about their problematic marriage... problematic, at least from Danny's point of view. Nancy, on her part, felt that everything was fine between them. In her undeviating pedantic style, however, Nancy assured Danny that she totally "understood his position on the issues"... and they parted so amicably as to be considered very peculiar by a number of associated spectators. Their marriage had been, as Nancy put it, "an existential experience," and she continued to call Danny for several years, following their divorce, to "discuss" their marriage and/or other current topics of interest.

And now, this last divorce. Carrie-Lynn's vulnerability drew Danny to her. She was so emotional, so passionate, so attuned to life, so empathetic... so unlike Nancy Colbert. She wouldn't discuss the interesting dynamics of a sad movie – she'd cry her eyes out. Carrie-Lynn had been through so much in her short life that there were few sorrows by which she had not been touched. Her father had sexually abused her and had beaten her mother. She had been dragged by her mother from town to town and from marriage to marriage. She dropped out of school and had started working, full-time, at age fifteen and was married by the time she was seventeen. She had two kids by the time she was twenty. She was beaten regularly by her first husband... and was divorced at age twenty-four. For the next four years, she had raised her two sons, entirely on her own.

Despite her hard life, however, Carrie-Lynn Taylor remained extraordinarily fresh-faced and full of spirit. At twenty-eight, she still had the spunky playfulness of a mischievous school girl. Danny felt she was, like him, a survivor. He honestly believed that with Carrie-Lynn he had, at last, found his intended soul mate. For the first three years of their marriage, Danny experienced the happiest time of his life. Carrie-Lynn was able to melt into the soft, sensitive flesh of his soul that had been insulated for so many years by the protective armor, necessary for cliff climbing. In Carrie-Lynn's engulfing compassion, Danny also discovered he was able to safely shed tears with her. Her two boys, Dawson and Barry – eight and ten when Danny and Carrie-Lynn were married – helped fill the void left from his painful separation from Andy. Karen had made his visitations so difficult and had so poisoned Andy's mind against Danny that, eventually, visitations devolved into nothing more than Christmas and birthday cards. Though Dawson and Barry were soothing balm, the loss of his son's love was a wound in Danny's heart that would never heal.

Because such memories had filled their first wonderful years together, the divorce from Carrie-Lynn was the most painful of Danny's marital failures. But with Carrie-Lynn, Danny had learned another of life's bitter lessons. Perhaps, he thought, what happened in his relationship with Carrie-Lynn was a result of a natural mistake that all human beings make. Although it flies in the face of rationality, Danny learned that nearly everyone is inclined to believe that someone will always be as they are when love is new. There is a common failure, he came to recognize, to grasp the obvious reality that what we see of our lover is but a moment's glimpse of a form and substance that is undergoing constant change from birth to death. A person at thirty-one, though bearing the same name, is in no regard, the same person encountered at twenty-eight. With Carrie-Lynn, Danny had finally learned the obvious truth of life – that the only thing constant in the universe is change... and that people are but indigenous pieces of the endlessly mutating cosmos.

With Danny's financial and emotional support... and with his unwavering encouragement... Carrie-Lynn earned her G.E.D. from Ada High School and enrolled at the university. Danny spoke with the provost, an acquaintance of his, and was able to have Carrie-Lynn admitted without taking her SAT's. Danny recognized Carrie-Lynn's innate intelligence and her irrepressible spirit of inquiry... and he was anxious to see her grow... trusting that "knowledge was the path to human fulfillment"... or whatever it was he vaguely remembered Plato writing.

Upon Carrie-Lynn's commencement of study at the university, Danny was, at first, vaguely amused by her almost immediate assumption of an imperious mantle that clearly connoted her belief that she possessed near-unfathomable knowledge. Four days into her philosophy course – taught, coincidentally, by Dr. Nancy Colbert – Carrie-Lynn was pedantically lecturing Danny at the dinner table on the nature of man... assuming that, apparently, he had never encountered such rarified and privileged erudition in his many years of schooling. Even more amusing were her orations on the constitutional rights of the accused – from the first chapter of her political science book – assuming, again, that apparently, in Danny's law school training, and fourteen years of trial practice, he must have, somehow, overlooked – or failed to fully appreciate – these concepts.

Danny's amusement slowly gave way to stoical toleration, sustained by his sincere belief that this was only a phase Carrie-Lynn was going through... a temporary syndrome brought on by "dangerous, little knowledge." Eventually, however, his toleration wore thin – then finally wore entirely out – giving way to repressed, then finally, expressed anger. Danny remembered one conversation, almost verbatim... being one of those exchanges that finally freeze fleeting thoughts and emotions into a palpable permanence in the mind.

During a Thanksgiving dinner at the Boscia homestead in Detroit, Danny's older brother, Dom, was in mid-sentence regarding the strike at the plant – then in its fifth week – when Carrie-Lynn abruptly cut him off. The point he was making was that, as a union member for some twenty-five years, who had weathered many battles that did not result in a strike, the current disagreement over health coverage and job safety that had provoked the current walk out, was so essential to their well-being that it was, as he put it, "worth going to the wall over." He had just gotten out the words, "Those greedy bastards..." when Carrie-Lynn brusquely piped in.

"Dom... come on now. It's a proven fact that auto workers are overpaid and that unions are ruining the country. If I were the owner, I'd fire all you union cry babies and hire all those thousands of people out there who want to work. That's what it's all about in a free market society... if you studied it, you'd understand."

Dom's eyes narrowed... his jaws tightened. Danny knew he was seething over the arrogance of this young woman, who knew nothing about union struggles, spouting off like a goddamn know-it-all and lecturing him as though he were a child. Danny also knew, however, that Dom would never violate the unspoken family understanding that you simply don't attack your brother's wife. But Carrie-Lynn had gone too far this time. Her big mouth around their own house had become intolerable, but at home, she was only insulting to Danny. To insult Danny's oldest brother... who had been nothing but gracious to Carrie-Lynn from the moment she met him... was just too much to tolerate. Danny had to do something on behalf of his brother since Dom could not defend himself. Carrie-Lynn had knowingly taken advantage of Dom's good manners and she knew it. Danny breathed deeply through his nose a few times to attempt to diffuse his anger before he spoke.

"Carrie... I think Dom knows a little more about this sort of thing than you do... don't you?"

"Oh... take his part, Danny, like always. You have no respect for any opinion I have. I'm just a woman. I'm just supposed to sit around and agree with all you asshole men all the time, right?"

Danny lost it.

"Why don't you just shut your big fucking mouth for once?! It's amazing, Carrie, how, in just three semesters in college, you've become an absolute fucking expert on every subject known to mankind! Absolutely-fucking-amazing!"

Carrie-Lynn was on her feet, screaming.

"You bastard! You fucking asshole! You've resented my going to college ever since I started! You're jealous! You're afraid of me learning something! You're afraid I'll learn more than you! You're afraid you won't be able to control me anymore! Well, fuck you, Danny... and fuck your whole family, too!!"

Carrie-Lynn stomped out of the small dining room, crossed the living room, opened the front door and clomped across the wooden porch and down the steps. Despite the frigid November day, she intentionally left the front door standing wide open. They all heard the car door slam and the tires dig into, and throw, the driveway gravel. The chilly draft from the open door poured into the dining room but no one moved or spoke. No one got up to close the door. Danny looked tentatively around the room with his eyes without moving his head. All the women had a hand to their mouth, as women often do in these circumstances, trying to conceal their shock but actually accentuating it by the gesture. His brothers and two uncles were looking at him with a mixture of bewilderment and compassion. They knew he had done what he had to do. They felt bad for Danny... being humiliated by his wife like this... in front of the whole family. The Boscias had had arguments at the table before... but no one had ever insulted anyone like this. It was just understood... you didn't do something like that to someone else in the family. No one knew quite what to say about it.

The Thanksgiving blowup was the beginning of the end for Danny and Carrie-Lynn... and they both knew it. Danny, as was his nature, did not at first, want to concede defeat, but he finally learned, at least in this situation, when to quit. He fell in love with a Carrie-Lynn that was passing through a certain part of her life that was everything that he was looking for at that time. There was a new Carrie-Lynn now... bearing virtually no resemblance to the former. Maybe it was his fault, he thought. Maybe he shouldn't have pushed the education thing. Maybe some people are better off, left in their natural state. He just didn't know. One thing he knew for sure... not only did he not love the presently evolved Carrie-Lynn, he didn't even like her.

Danny began his inevitable, introspective reflection about his marriage. Should someone remain married, solely for the purpose of not failing?... when that person makes your life miserable and makes you into a person you don't like to be?... when that person tells you, point blank, she wants a divorce? Not if you are in your right mind, Danny finally concluded. He asked Carrie-Lynn if she – or he – should file. She did, she said... adding that, after all, it was *she* who was wronged by *him*. He didn't argue with her. Danny felt very bad about Dawson and Barry. They were good boys and he cared for them very much. He figured, however – given Carrie-Lynn's new found vindictiveness – she would invariably keep the boys from him after the divorce. He was correct.

CHAPTER SEVEN

Each person concocts a simple story in his mind in an attempt to make at least a modicum of sense out of the unexplainable nature of life. Some stories are religious – some philosophic – some metaphoric. They serve as cupboards into which the observations and events of life can be arbitrarily placed, to create an artificial sense of order and logic to an existence which, in its primordial essence, has none. At times – often without warning and for reasons unknown – the story cupboard unexpectedly ceases to accommodate these life experiences. Significant trouble inevitably results from such a vacuum because the necessary level of order, required to preserve lucidity, can no longer be gleaned from the resulting chaos. Danny Boscia was, thus, in big trouble.

Following his divorce from Carrie-Lynn, for reasons he would never fully understand, his cupboard forthwith collapsed. The cliff-and-plateau story that had served him so well throughout his life, simply disintegrated before his mind's eye... and with its dissolution, gone was his constitution, his self-assurance, his compass. Regardless of what adversities he encountered, his story had always served to make sense of things... sustaining his will to press on. But without warning, he found himself, at age forty-four, in a moment of absurd insignificance, without his interpretive metaphor. It failed him as he sat... drinking a Rolling Rock draft in a local Ada bar... inattentively watching Monday Night Football. The Little Road Runner from Detroit who had never backed down from a fight in his life, who never quit, who continued against all odds from plateau to plateau, whose date with a glorious destiny was an accepted certainty, felt the grip of cold fear wrap suddenly around his heart in that common moment. He became, in an instant of time, during a lackluster, Dallas-Atlanta football game, literally frightened out of his mind. Such are the terrible consequences of losing one's story... without which, life becomes a black, impenetrable, chaotic mass.

Danny's body became immediately cold and clammy... his hands so wet that he was afraid his beer glass would slip from his grasp. Looking about like a frightened animal, his eyes darted all around the bar... searching for an escape from whatever had him in its terrifying grasp. The Fifth Street Tavern, which had been such a familiar and comfortable retreat for him for so many years, was suddenly a strange and unspeakably frightening chamber. He was in fear of everything, and everybody, in the bar. Danger seemed to lurk in the commonplace faces of the habitual patrons. He wanted, desperately, to get out of the room, but was so terrified, he was certain he could not make it to the door. Thus immobilized by fear, he sat, frozen on his bar stool, apprehensively glancing from side to side.

Danny felt a jabbing sensation on the inside of his arm, just where the biceps meet the forearm. He opened his eyes. A stout woman with short gray hair was looking at him.

"Well, you finally decided to wake up, huh?"

"What?"

"How are you feeling Mr. Boscia?"

Danny looked around. A metal tray was beside him... bright florescent light penetrated his eyes from behind a translucent plastic cover on the white-tiled ceiling. A faded green, floor-to-ceiling curtain entirely encircled his bed... hung by metal rings from shiny tubing.

He watched the woman remove a needle from his arm, to which was attached, a plastic, blood-filled cylinder. She pressed a cotton ball on the point of extraction then pushed his lower arm upward to maintain pressure on it. Danny studied the woman's plump face, in search of something he couldn't name.

"I'm in the emergency room."

"Yes you are, Mr. Boscia. Do you remember how you got here?"

"No."

"They brought you in about an hour and a half ago... picked you up over at the Fifth Street Tavern. Apparently you passed out and fell off a stool. You hit your head pretty hard."

With these words, Danny suddenly felt a strong, dull pain at the back of his head. He reached back to rub the large, throbbing bump.

"I wasn't drunk."

"We know. Bill Gates phoned the ambulance for you. He said you only had one beer... said you started looking really strange, turning your head back and forth, real fast. From what he says, all of a sudden, you started screaming at the top of your lungs... scared the hell out of everybody."

She laughed.

Danny spoke with an uncertain voice.

"Where's the doctor?"

"He's looked in on you several times... said to page him when you woke up. You've already had your X-rays. I'll go get him."

She jerked the cloth wall open, exited, then closed the momentary egress with another sharply executed pull. The fear that had gripped Danny in the bar began to return. He began to feel he was, truly, going to lose his mind. He was more frightened at that moment than he had ever been in his entire life... and had no idea why. Thoughts and questions flashed through his mind. What if I do lose my mind? He had visions of the horrors of lunacy... raving... losing contact with all the world... being closed into an Alice-in-Wonderland world where nothing made any sense and where no one could reach him... no one could help him. He was becoming frightened – almost beyond toleration – of being totally alone, shut off from the world, inside a private, insane hell. He felt himself beginning to swoon.

"Mr. Boscia?"

The voice repeated his name, louder.

"Mr. Boscia?"

Danny saw the face of a young man in his thirties, wearing a white lab coat with a stethoscope hanging from his neck. He was shining a beam of light into his right eye, moving it forward then backward. He then did the same thing to the left eye.

"Mr. Boscia?"

"Yes?"

"How are you feeling?"

"I… I… ah…"

"Do you know how you got here?"

"The nurse… ah… or whoever she was… the lady who took my blood… told me."

"Can you tell me what happened? Do you know what made you pass out?"

"It's… ah… it's hard to… ah…"

"Are you on any medications?"

"No."

"Have you had much to eat today?"

"About the usual."

"Has this ever happened before?"

"No."

As the doctor began forming another question, Danny reached out and grabbed his arm, squeezing it hard. He felt tears coming to his eyes.

"I'm afraid. I think there's something wrong with me."

Danny felt the fear growing inside him again.

"Can you help me? Please. I feel like I'm…"

Danny began to look agitated – his eyes became wild – his head began to turn from side to side. The world vanished.

When Danny awakened, he was in a regular hospital room with metal bars on each side of his bed. There was an I.V. inserted into the back of his left hand. A small light was on – attached to the wall above his head. Pinned to his pillow was a black cord with a red button on the end. Danny pressed it. Several minutes later, a nurse appeared. She told Danny that, apparently, he had had another spell… and that Dr. Trainer had admitted him.

Danny spent the next five days in the hospital, undergoing tests and observation. It was the opinion of Dr. Trainer and his consulting physicians that Danny's condition was not of an organic nature. They also concluded that Danny, as emotionally unstable as he appeared to be, was potentially a danger to himself. On that basis, they recommended he be committed to a psychiatric hospital for observation. Danny was given a choice… he could voluntarily agree to being admitted or, since they believed he could be a danger to himself, they would petition the court to have him involuntarily committed. Danny agreed to a voluntary admission.

Danny called his secretary on the second day he was in the hospital and asked her to have his three associates either cover his court appearances, or get continuances. With his commitment to a psychiatric hospital, his associates had no choice, under the professional rules of conduct, but to notify the courts as to his condition. His cases were assigned to area attorneys on an interim basis... until a prognosis could be determined.

Danny spent the next three months in the psychiatric hospital. Physically, other than being a little thin, he looked fine. Emotionally, however, he was a fragile shell... and he was the talk of Ada. The word was out that he had had a nervous breakdown. No one could believe it. He was universally known by his tough, aggressive reputation... often referred to as the "Pit Bull" by members of the local bar association... the attorney who never gave an inch. Whenever anyone wanted a tough attorney for court, Danny Boscia's name always came up. He was always under control, never blinked, and never panicked.

The "Pit Bull," at home, after his release from Western Psychiatric Institute, was afraid to even go out his front door. The medication he was on repressed his inclination toward panic, but the insidious, throbbing fear still had him in its grip. He was as puzzled as the rest of the town as to what had happened to him. A few months before, he was, according to his custom, regrouping and licking his wounds after his divorce... getting ready to go back to the cliff again. Now, without warning, his cliffs and plateaus had simply and suddenly vanished. His life's landscape had now become an endless, flat prairie where everything looked the same and nothing had any particular distinction. He had clawed his way, since he was a young child, day after day, believing he was moving upward toward something better... eventually to something great. Without the shadows – once cast by the great cliffs of his now vaporized, metaphoric, life paradigm – he began to see life as it really was... void of the stage sets he had constructed on it. He could now plainly see that there were no vertical climbs... and, consequently, no pinnacle.

Danny knew he had achieved a lot in his life. He was the first member of his family, ever, to go to college... had become a lawyer... had overcome great financial and personal hardships to establish a successful law practice... was making more money than anyone in his family had ever thought possible. He should, by now – according to the script he had mentally penned for his life – be standing on a high plateau, looking down and triumphantly shouting... "Danny Boscia is here!" Instead, at age forty-four, Danny Boscia was a broken, empty shell... completely alone and horribly afraid.

No one came to visit Danny. He became painfully aware that his lifelong commitment to total self-reliance had prevented him from cultivating any real friendships. His mother called him on occasion, but was now too frail to travel. Besides... her aging mind no longer allowed her to play a meaningful part in life's unfolding drama... relegating her dreams – and most of her waking hours – to oft repeated, reassuring memories of old familiar scenes of her life. His brothers were simply too busy with their own lives and problems, and didn't have the time, nor the energy, to deal with Danny's problems.

Danny had finally come to realize that the only happiness he had found in his life had been derived from a belief that his struggle would eventually bring him fulfillment of some sort... some meaningful and significant final chapter to his life. The real, final chapter found Danny Boscia a broken, unhappy, fearful, and lonely man. With his cliffs flattened to common earth, Danny Boscia found himself paralyzed, with no place to go. The climb itself, he discovered, had been the singular meaning to his life... and not the spoils he found at the top.

People could hurt him... turn him out... push him back... but he would fight back... he would show them... he would show them all. But as he now looked back, what was it he had shown them?... and who was he showing? As it turned out, no one, it seems, was even watching. All those people he was going to "show"... his dad... his brothers... the guys on the K of C... Karen. None of them, it seemed, even cared about what he did or did not do. It had all been for nothing... all the bloody hands... all the endless struggling... the healing and the regrouping... all for nothing.

With Danny Boscia's cliffs and plateaus, leveled into an endless plain, he found himself in the same flat dirt, along with everyone else. He was no longer able to define himself by his elevation above the masses. He had lost his markers in life. He no longer had any way of determining his relative meaning or worth. Without his cliffs, he was nothing. What is a man's meaning, he pondered, if not for his relative ascent above the rest? How can one find any meaning except by comparative elevations? Danny's life had, in that absurdly insignificant moment, during a Monday Night Football game, become totally devoid of meaning.

Danny Boscia was not a bad man. He had tried... tried so hard... to live a hardworking, honest life. He was never malicious and had never intended harm toward anyone. He had tried to be the best at everything... and he had ended up with nothing. But how could this be? he begged. Isn't hard work in life supposed to be rewarded? Isn't that what they always tell you? Hitch your wagon to a star... work hard... study hard... keep your nose to the grindstone. He had done all that... just like he was supposed to have done. Danny never accepted the average... the common. He could have. He could have taken the easy route in life – gone into the plant with his brothers – but he didn't. He could have taken the vo-tech curriculum that his dad wanted him to... and had an easy time of it... but he didn't. He did hitch his wagon to a star. He did keep his nose to the grindstone. He did endure endless hardships. He thought he had reached the heights that no one had ever expected him capable. He did everything he thought he was supposed to do... and where, now, was his reward?

Once Danny Boscia's story collapsed, he looked inside himself – then outside himself – for some other meaning to his life... and he found nothing. His whole life, he found, had been an exterior existence... spent doing whatever he had to do to be "successful." Throughout Danny's life, only that which he "did" had any meaning to him. He was a hardworking, honest, successful man. That should have been enough, in Danny's way of thinking... enough to make him happy... but it didn't. Danny had placed all his stock of happiness in what he had accomplished in life and found his hands and heart were empty at the end of the trail. Other than his familiar cliffs, Danny had nowhere else to look for meaning to his existence.

Religion is often the path for those who find themselves as forsaken as Danny Boscia... but such a course held no promise of redemption for him. He considered those who were religious to be either phonies or weaklings. To Danny, the only way you got anything in life was to go get it yourself. No one had ever helped him in his life, nor did he ever want anyone's help. He certainly wasn't going to pray to some god for help. To him, that was about as stupid a thing as anybody could do. Did any truly rational and emotionally stable human being, actually believe he was really talking to a god when he prayed? It was perfectly clear to Danny that all prayer was merely the expression of a hope, from yourself to yourself... and nothing more. Did anyone truly believe that some divine being, like a celestial operator, was listening in? To Danny that was just plain silly. Sure, it might make you feel better... talking yourself into not being afraid of something or making yourself believe you could do something you were about to try... but a god listening in, like a genie in a bottle, granting you three wishes?... that was utter nonsense.

The deep, cold, frightening pit in which Danny now found himself, was a special hell, reserved for those who lose all dimension in life. Danny had lost his ability to define himself and the world in which he lived. He could no longer describe himself by his climb, nor by any other artificial designations. Inside himself, he found a meaningless void. Not even the thought of death brought a sense of relief to Danny. He had no divine beliefs about death, but neither did he have rational assurance that his anguish would be relieved by blessed oblivion. For all he knew, death could be a conscious, anguished, inescapable eternity... much like his present life.

After forty-four years of life, Danny Boscia... the Little Road Runner... the Pit Bull... had finally been handed the world's reply to his lifetime of hard work.

CHAPTER EIGHT

SUSAN

Some seem to know from their earliest moments in life, what they're meant to be. Susan Atherton did... always did. While the life ambitions of her childhood friends fluctuated among actress, nurse, teacher, and recording artist at least twice a month, Susan's remained constant. Much to the dismay of her ambitious mother, all Susan wanted to talk about, from Adelle Atherton's earliest recollections of her daughter's conversations, was of being a wife and a mother. Adelle guiltily regarded her daughter's obsession as an unfortunate result of their own, considerably less-than-perfect family circumstance.

Adelle had met Susan's father when she was only eighteen, while working as a receptionist for the Chamber of Commerce in Jackson, Tennessee. Bob Wilson was a thirty-two-year-old salesman for Walker Brothers – a paper product wholesaler out of Memphis. Adelle told her mother that Mr. Wilson was the handsomest man she had ever laid eyes on... in person, anyway. She said he was every bit as handsome as the male models she had seen in the Sear's Catalog... even as handsome as a movie star. She said she "turned to butter" every time he came into the office. Adelle would rave about Bob Wilson to such extent that her mother would laugh and say that Bob Wilson "musta hung the moon" to get such wonderful praises.

Bob would periodically stop in at the Chamber to get the names and addresses of new businesses in town. Bob and Adelle's small talk eventually broached the personal, and after about a half-dozen visits to the Chamber, Bob asked Adelle out on a date. After dinner at Al's Steak and Ale House on a warm, mid-August night... and a few drinks at the Jackson Holiday Inn, where Adelle lied about her age... what may have been the sole, remaining eighteen-year-old virgin in Jackson, was, by 1:10 a.m., no longer... via Room 124 of the Jackson, Tennessee, Knight's Inn.

Adelle told and retold the story of her date, ad nauseam, to her mother and all her girlfriends... leaving out, of course, the Room 124 part. Bob was so suave, she would say... so handsome... had been everywhere... was so mature and attentive... knew about everything... could dance so well... and on and on. Every night Adelle would lie in her bed, trying to recall, and fix for all eternity, every detail of her evening with Bob Wilson. She was a very pretty girl, but only just out of high school, and for someone like Bob to take notice of her – let alone take her out on a date – was, to her young mind, an undeniable honor. Adelle had always planned on saving herself for the night of her wedding, but to her way of thinking, this kind of opportunity seldom knocks twice on a young girl's door... especially one who is, in her own opinion, a nobody.

In September, Adelle missed her period. The blood test was positive. She was going to call Bob, but decided to wait until he came to Jackson in November. Adelle was certain that someone as mature and attentive as Bob Wilson would do the right thing. When he finally showed up, during the last week of the month, she asked him if they could have lunch... saying she needed to talk to him about something. Bob said he had too many customers to see, and lunch was, therefore, out of the question. Adelle said she really didn't want to discuss what she had to say, right there in the lobby... could they, maybe, step outside for a few minutes to talk? Bob guessed so, but she'd have to make it quick.

In a voice, quiet, shaking, and reverent – as Adelle believed was appropriate in addressing someone as god-like as Bob – she gave him the news, trying to straighten the small proud smile, working to curl up at the corners of her mouth. Adelle tried, but couldn't conceal her pride in carrying Bob's baby and she was absolutely sure, even though she was very young and inexperienced, she would make him a good wife and mother to his child. His few words, that would change the course of Adelle's life, burned into her mind like fragments of white hot shrapnel.

"Listen sweetie... if you're going to be big enough to go to bed with a man, you can be big enough to take care of yourself. Haven't you ever heard of the pill? I've got enough on my mind without this kind of chicken shit stuff. It's your problem, sweet cheeks, so handle it. I don't have time for this kind of crap... I'm already late for an appointment."

Without another word, Bob Wilson turned abruptly and walked down the steps and out of Adelle Atherton's life, forever. She watched as he crossed the street, got into his car, and drove away. She waited in front of the Chamber building for over an hour... convinced he would change his mind and come back to her. The next month a new salesman came in Bob's place. He explained that Bob had been given a new sales territory in East Tennessee.

Adelle had her baby, two days before she turned nineteen and named her Susan... after her own mother. Adelle's mother had a day job, cleaning houses, and couldn't watch the baby. Her Dad was on permanent disability from the Tennessee Authority and couldn't, or wouldn't, watch her... so Adelle quit the Chamber and took a nighttime, waitressing job at an all-night diner, leaving the baby with her mother for the night. Adelle had, since her experience with Bob, formulated a dramatically new way of looking at things. Men were, in this new perspective, selfish jerks... and life was nothing but an unfair struggle. Guided by her new vision, she was determined that she would, never again, be exploited by another man... and would, never again, depend on anyone.

Adelle began taking classes at the community college, getting baby sitters when she could afford it, taking Susan to class when she couldn't. She earned her associates degree in accounting and went on to get her bachelor's at Union University. After passing her C.P.A. exams, she landed a job with the accounting department of the Jackson division of USX. She did very well, climbing to assistant comptroller by her early forties. True to her pledge, she had never depended on a man... and never would. Susan's obsession with a husband and family, understandably therefore, drove Adelle to utter distraction. Logic and cajoling, having failed to dissuade Susan from her singular domestic ambitions, Adelle played a mother's universal trump card – guilt.

"I'll be very disappointed in you if you throw your life away, Susan. You have so much potential. I'd be so proud of you if you got your degree... it would have meant a lot to Gramma to see you become successful."

The best Adelle could coerce from Susan was her agreement to go to college... and finish... before she got married. That was it. The way Susan looked at the deal... college was an excellent place to find a good husband. In keeping with the theme of her plans, she majored in early childhood development.

Susan's wedding was three days after she and her fiancé graduated from college. For months before the wedding Susan would walk around her dorm room, play-acting. "Hello, I'm Mrs. Davenport... this is my husband, Roger." "Honey... could you pick up some wine on your way home?... the Andersons are coming over tonight." "Now give Daddy and me a big kiss and off to bed, sweetheart."

Roger was pre-med in college, and was accepted at Vanderbilt's School of Medicine. His family was well-off and Susan's mother was generous to them as well... so life was good. Roger was exhausted, nearly all the time, but Susan made it tolerable – even nice at times – with lots of affectionate doting and home-cooked meals. Finding herself in her life's dream, she adored every moment. Susan particularly loved decorating their apartment. She'd read home magazines... she'd bring back color swatches for Roger to see... she'd go from showroom to showroom... she simply loved it. Susan worked tirelessly to create an apartment motif that could, in her opinion, measure up to anything she'd seen in *Better Homes and Gardens*.

During Roger's third year in medical school, Susan got pregnant... as per their agreement. Melannie Ann Davenport was born on Memorial Day at 3:10 a.m.... a week after Roger's graduation. Roger, Jr., was born the following summer... Andrew, the next spring. Roger did his residency in Memphis. He became board-certified in internal medicine and joined a private practice in Nashville... catering to the social elite of the community, including many of the country and western stars. They built an impressive antebellum-style home in the exclusive subdivision, north of the city.

Life was better than Susan had ever hoped. She wanted for nothing. She had a husband who was an excellent provider, attentive to her needs, respected in the community, and good-looking. She had three beautiful and intelligent children... a wonderful house... great in-laws... good neighbors and friends. Susan could never understand why any woman, who could be at home and live for her husband and children, would ever want to do anything else. A number of her friends had jobs for "fulfillment," as they put it. She questioned how anyone could be more fulfilled than she. What could be more meaningful than to provide a wonderful home for your children and husband... to watch your children grow... to see their first steps... hear their first words... to hold them, sleeping in your arms in a big rocking chair on the front porch on summer evenings? No job could give her these things. She often suspected that her working friends, if the truth be told, just didn't want to be a homemaker like she did. They were, for reasons beyond Susan's understanding, satisfied to have a nanny do all those wonderful things that a mother gets to do. In her opinion, they just didn't know what they were missing... but why make a point of it? – she would say – it was their life.

Every summer the Davenports would travel. By the time Melannie was ten, they had toured twelve countries and been on three continents. The children attended an exclusive private school. Melannie was given music, dance, and riding lessons... the boys went to soccer, tennis, and swim camps. Melannie became an accomplished dancer and was asked to join a summer ballet, touring company, when she was fifteen. Roger and Andrew became top-notch swimmers for the "Willow Grove Aquatics"... Roger a backstroker... Andrew, butterfly. Each boy held a club record in his event.

CHAPTER NINE

Adelle was never comfortable with her daughter's life. She no longer lectured her about the evils of men, and the desirability of the professional life, but she was constantly waiting for the other shoe to drop in Susan's domestic heaven. Adelle knew that anything too good to be true, simply wasn't. She knew the shoe would fall one day and wanted her daughter to be prepared. Adelle tried to bring Susan around to facing reality about life – and men. When Roger would travel out of town for medical conferences, Adelle would ask Susan, "Why doesn't Roger want you along?" Are there female doctors and nurses at these things? Have you ever called Roger's room in the middle of the night?" On other visits she would question Susan about what she would do if, "... something happened to Roger?" or "... what are you going to do with yourself once the kids are grown?" Susan would accuse her mother of "looking for trouble." She'd also accuse her of being jealous of her having all the things Adelle had never had. What Susan never understood was that Adelle was trying to protect her by creating little cracks in her flawless mirror, so when life inevitably smashed it, she wouldn't be mortally wounded by the flying shards.

Adelle knew no life, as perfect as Susan's, could continue indefinitely. She knew life for what she frequently called it – "... a shitty struggle." Adelle looked at Susan as someone who was on a "high"... intoxicated by some cruel and peculiar cruel twist of fate that was setting her up for an inevitable fall... from such a height that it could, like Humpty Dumpty, break her into so many pieces she could never be put together again. The perfection of Susan's life terrified Adelle. As every front has a back, every up a down, every beginning an end... Adelle knew that for every heaven there was a hell.

And hell came.

On Valentine's Day, Roger, Melannie, and the boys, drove to Knoxville for the finals of the Miss Tennessee Pageant. With her preliminary scores, Melannie was in good position to possibly win it all. The finals were scheduled to begin at seven in the evening, but they left early in the morning so Melannie could have plenty of time to get herself ready. She was the type of girl that didn't do well if she was rushed. She wanted time to compose herself... then go through her ballet routine several times before the pageant began.

Susan had been up the entire night before the pageant with diarrhea and vomiting. She tried, several times, to get herself together for the drive to Knoxville but would end up running back to the bathroom. Finally, she told Roger to go on without her... that she'd be more trouble than she would be worth. She said she'd just watch the pageant on the television. Besides, she told Roger, Melannie didn't need anything more on her mind... that she was agitated enough as it was.

By about ten in the morning, Susan finally fell asleep. It was one of those exhausted sleeps when a sickness has finally passed and the return to mere normalcy takes on a golden glow. She dreamed of Melannie's birth... reliving her inexpressible joy of seeing her for the first time. From the hall, outside the delivery room, the phone began to ring – the annoying sound cruelly shattered Susan's ecstasy. She began to yell at the nurses to answer it... they all began to laugh at her. Susan began to sob... asking why they were all being so mean to her.

Susan found herself sitting up in her bed, weeping... the phone on the night stand, ringing. Finally separating her bedroom from the delivery suite, she picked up the receiver.

"Hello?"

"May I speak with Susan Davenport, please?"

"This is she."

"Mrs. Davenport… are you the wife of Mr. Roger Davenport… 133 Oak Wood Lane… Nashville?"

"Yes… who is this? What's this all about?"

"Mrs. Davenport… this is Trooper Johnson… Tennessee State Police… I…"

"What happened?… what's happened to my Roger?… oh God… oh God… please… please God…"

"Mrs. Davenport…"

"I know something's… I know…"

"Mrs. Davenport… please… Mrs. Davenport?…"

Trooper Johnson could hear Susan's wailing. He had a secretary get on the line and monitor it while he phoned the Nashville police on another line.

Officers Dalton and Latimer of the Nashville Police Department banged on the door of the Davenport home… loudly calling out Susan's name. When they entered the house, they could hear a female voice, screaming, from the upper floor. They hurried up the stairs and found Susan crouched in the corner of her bedroom. She had a look of madness in her eyes. She continued screaming when Dalton and Latimer came into the room… appearing not to notice their presence. Her voice had the raspy grate of vocal cords, stretched beyond their intended limits. Dalton bent down, placed his hands on Susan's shoulders and looked into her eyes. They flickered momentarily with some indication of recognition. Finally, her screaming began to wind down to become a steady, anguished moan and her body lost some of its rigidity.

Dalton stood up and spoke quietly to Latimer.

"Get some EMT's over here. I'm not going to tell her anything... I'm afraid she'll flip out again. Let somebody else do it. I just can't handle this kinda shit."

Latimer left the room and Dalton sat down beside Susan, his back against the wall. She stared at him with the eyes of a terrified child. She stopped moaning.

"I... I... he was going to tell me something bad... I can't let him... don't let him say anything bad... please sir... I'm a good girl... he's bad... he's so bad..."

Susan stuck her thumb in her mouth, curled into a fetal position and lay her head on Dalton's lap. Dalton instinctively brought his hand up and began stroking her hair. When the EMT's entered the room, Susan sat up and immediately began to scream again. The closer they came to her, the louder she screamed. Dalton told them to go back outside the room. He said he'd talk to her.

Dalton put a hand on each of her cheeks.

"Shhh... Shhh... you're all right Susan... it's OK... they're gone."

The scream faded. When Susan was quiet again, Dalton spoke softly to her.

"Will you walk with me, Susan? I won't let anyone hurt you. OK?"

Susan stared at Dalton, not responding. Dalton quickly decided upon another strategy.

"Will you let one of the people give you something to make you feel better? I'll stay right here with you. Let me have your hand, Susan... you just squeeze it if you're scared. OK? Will you take some medicine?... please?... will you take some for me, Susan?"

After a long pause, Susan slowly shook her head up and down… then held out her hand to Dalton. He held it for a few minutes, while he continued to sit with her, to gain her confidence.

"You wait right here, Susan, OK?… I'll go and get someone with some medicine that'll make you feel much better… OK?"

Susan nodded. Dalton gently released her hand, got up and very slowly and quietly walked out of the room. He asked the female EMT if she had a sedative she could give Susan. She said she did. With Dalton in the lead, the two of them re-entered the room… walking very slowly and very quietly toward Susan. Her eyes began to get big again. Seeing this, Dalton immediately halted… extending his hand behind him to stop the female EMT.

"It's all right Susan. I'm here… this is…"

Dalton turned his head to read the plastic, blue and white name tag.

"… Andrea. She has some medicine for you. Can she give it to you? It will make you feel a lot better. OK?"

A nod. They continued forward. Dalton resumed his place beside Susan. He took her left hand in his right. The EMT pulled the plastic cap from the needle of the syringe in her hand. Susan's eyes went from the needle to Andrea's face to Dalton's. Andrea took an alcohol swab and gently rubbed Susan's right arm. Skillfully, she slid the needle through Susan's skin, then emptied the contents of the syringe into her underlying tissues. In a matter of seconds, Susan's eyes began to gloss over. Her head began to fall forward. Dalton caught it and directed it onto his shoulder. Andrea told him she'd get a stretcher.

After putting Susan into the ambulance, Andrea asked Dalton what had happened. He told her that, apparently, Susan's husband and three children had been killed in a car accident, just outside Knoxville… only about an hour before. The Tennessee State Police had called her, he said, and she had flipped out. Dalton added, "what a fuckin' tragedy it was... her whole family being wiped out."

Susan was kept in the hospital for a week... under heavy sedation. The doctors advised Adelle that, given her condition, Susan not be allowed to attend the funeral... suggesting it could do some permanent psychological damage. Roger's family handled just about everything. Adelle went to the funeral on Susan's behalf... the only relative on her side in attendance. Adelle was, in fact, Susan's only remaining blood relative in the entire world. Adelle brought Susan back to Jackson to stay with her for a while. A year later, Susan was still there.

Between Adelle and the Davenports, the business associated with death... the insurance, the will, the banking... paying the charge cards... putting the house up for sale... was managed. They all concluded that Susan didn't need to be in a house so large – with all the memories. They felt it would just reinforce her sense of loss and loneliness. They had the furniture and other household items auctioned off... selling just about everything except Susan's clothing and personal mementos. They put all the family pictures and albums into safekeeping... waiting until Susan's condition was more stabilized to return them to her.

During that first year, Susan was, for all intents and purposes, a child... eating when Adelle told her to... going to bed at the set time... not questioning anything. Adelle began to worry that Susan would never return to a normal life. During the day, she would sit and stare blankly at the TV. Adelle would turn it off in the evening, hoping Susan would take an interest in something else... but to no avail. She would take Susan out for occasional car rides... to movies... to the zoo... to the beauty parlor. Nothing seemed to reach her. Adelle would brush Susan's hair for her... put on her makeup, draw her bath, lead her to the tub, and help her wash. Susan would not talk to anyone. She had remained wholly silent since those few words she had spoken to Officer Dalton. Roger's family visited her often, showing great affection and concern for her. She would smile, slightly, when she saw them... but maintained her unbroken silence.

During the early summer of the year following the accident, Susan began to incrementally awaken. Adelle first noticed, to her great relief, that Susan was beginning to exhibit slight, occasional, irritation with her. When Adelle would call Susan to the table to eat, she began, much like a teenager, to lift her upper lip in a partial sneer, shake her head in disgust, and heave a peevish sigh. Susan's growing intolerance of Adelle finally drew out the first words she had spoken in nearly a year. Despite the fact that it was a criticism aimed at her, Susan's voice was such a symphony to Adelle's ears that she cried tears of joy and embraced her. The soul, or whatever it was, named Susan, had, at long last, returned to inhabit this still young and lovely body. What a grand sight it was for Adelle to finally see this spark of life, glowing in Susan's eyes, that had, for so long, been inanimate... often resembling the lifeless stare of a dead fish.

Adelle's joy was short-lived. The Susan that returned to inhabit the body living in Adelle's house had virtually no similarity to the pre-accident Susan. She even looked different in some indefinable way. Perhaps it was something in her eyes... or the way she carried herself... or her tone of voice... but Adelle knew something was dramatically different about her daughter. Adelle felt oddly uncomfortable with this new person... as though she were living with a stranger.

The new Susan was, as Adelle would – for lack of a better description – characterize her, utterly professional. She began to ask endless questions about all that she had missed over the past year... the details of the accident... the funeral... the coffins... what dress was put on Melannie... the suits on Roger and Andy... the sale of the house... the insurance policies. Her demeanor in these matters was not that of a grieving widow, nor an inconsolable mother, but very much akin to a tenacious reporter, brusquely probing for the details. There was not even a suggestion of grief or sadness in her countenance... only a detached, factual interest. Adelle also noticed other new, small but revealing signs of change. For instance, when Susan would see a baby, her eyes no longer would light up with the glow of love and tenderness as they always had in the past. She now seemed to merely study it... as though it were some variety of specimen.

Adelle's mother had often told her not to wish for something too hard... because she just might get it. Adelle had always wished for Susan to become an independent career woman, like her – professional... dependent on no one... carving out her own future. Susan had, since her awakening, become the archetype of Adelle's dream... to such an extreme that it frightened Adelle.

Susan took her considerable estate – some six million in total assets – liquidated it, and went into business for herself. Her first purchase was a small wholesale paper products company in Memphis – Walker Brothers Inc. – the very same company for which her father had worked at the time of Susan's conception. Bob Wilson had long since left the business, of course, having moved north to Cincinnati, the last Adelle had heard of him. Susan told Adelle that this particular transaction gave her a distinct feeling of satisfaction... a sense of getting back at that "rotten bastard of a father" she had. The new Susan, incidentally, cursed quite frequently, while the old Susan would just as soon have had her tongue cut out as to use profanity.

The woman who had never had any interest, whatsoever, in the family finances and who had considered money and business "men stuff," had, inexplicably, emerged from her soul's year-long hiatus as an exquisitely ruthless businesswoman. Immediately after taking over Walker Brothers, Susan asked Adelle to do an analysis of the salary structure and benefits programs of the company... wanting to know how to get rid of the "deadwood" around the place... particularly those who had been with the company a long time and were, as she characterized it, along for a "free ride." Adelle gave her a list of those employees who were costing the business the most... adding the unsolicited observation that these people had families and that a large number of those on the list were getting close to retirement. As for the added, unrequested information, Susan responded to Adelle in a condescending tone, more appropriate for an unruly child.

"If I want a commentary on something, I'll ask for it."

Susan gave some thirty, long-term company employees, the axe. Many were in a position and stage in life that finding comparable employment was a near-impossibility. Their medical benefits were immediately cut off. Quite a few of them had only partially vested pensions and came away with next to nothing. In short, Susan had coldheartedly destroyed the lives of a good many honest and loyal employees – and their families. Adelle, unable to hold her tongue any longer, finally gave Susan her opinion of what she had done. She told Susan that running a business was more than just dollars and cents... that she had the lives of human beings at stake, as well. Susan's curt reply was that, first of all, Adelle had never run her own business, and secondly, she wasn't running a charity. In business, she informed her mother, one factor, and one only, mattered... what came out on the bottom line. If these ex-employees wanted a piece of the bigger pie, let them take the risk and go into business for themselves, she said, and then see how generous *they* would be when *they* were paying the bills.

Under Susan's shrewd and unforgiving leadership, within three years Walker Brothers grew to be one of the largest businesses of its kind in south-east United States. Susan's phenomenal success was totally incomprehensible to Adelle. Susan had never had a single business course in her life... never had even a flicker of interest in the field of commerce. Now, here she was... making astute judgments with the precision of a surgeon and the coolness of a professional assassin. In time, Adelle's feelings toward Susan eventually devolved into a love-hate ambivalence... the biological compulsion of a mother to love her child, intertwined with her hatred of a truly despicable human being.

Susan, eventually tiring of her mother's progressively more frequent moralizing, moved out of Adelle's house and purchased a relatively small condominium in Jackson – small, considering what she was capable of buying. It had the ambience of a bear's cave – hardwood floors void of rugs, a bare modicum of furniture, consisting of simply a kitchen table with two chairs, a television, one chair in the living room with a pole lamp beside it, one single bed, one small dresser, and a desk with a computer, printer, and phone. Heavy gray curtains were perpetually drawn across the windows. She had no friends, nor did she aspire to have any. Her only occasional visitor was her mother. Her employees hated her. Her business associates respected her capabilities and feared her ruthlessness.

Adelle bore a sense of guilt about her daughter. Perhaps, she thought, all that advice she had given her as she was growing up – about independence and career – had caused all this. She had, perhaps, planted a seed that had suddenly sprouted... then had grown into a tangled, ogreish mass during her post-traumatic incubation. But then again, she would consider, what was there about which to feel guilty except, perhaps, for Susan's victims? Certainly not for Susan. Her daughter seemed entirely content. She never looked happy... never smiled nor joked nor exhibited any warmth whatsoever... but neither did she seem unduly unhappy. She certainly wasn't coming to Adelle and telling her she wanted to go into therapy because of her sorrowful life.

Under Susan's unmerciful command, her business empire grew steadily. She expanded into other fields... the furniture business... an investment firm... a small radio station. Her most recent sights were on the commercial insurance field. Her mode of acquisition had, over the years, become standardized. She'd find relatively small companies – often family-owned – that had promise, but were having cash flow problems. She'd then make deals to bail them out, and through legal and financial machinations, end up entirely controlling the business. The previous owners were, uniformly, left out in the cold with nothing to show for a lifetime of struggle.

When Susan would detail these operations to Adelle, she didn't gloat, nor was she egotistical or arrogant about her exploits. She was... as best as Adelle could describe it... like a rapidly expanding virus... mindlessly growing... wreaking havoc, destruction, and misery in its path.

Occasionally Adelle could not contain herself. She'd blurt out challenges to Susan, asking her how she could do the terrible things that she did. Susan was consistently unresponsive to these admonitions of Adelle's. She'd simply stare at her for a few seconds... then continue on as though Adelle's words had never been spoken.

Susan Atherton Davenport, at age forty-three was friendless, unloved, unloving, and exceedingly wealthy. She was named, that year, by three financial magazines, as the most successful business woman in the southeastern United States.

CHAPTER TEN

HENRY

Henry Butler shook his head, and with a self-effacing smile, recalled how, in his earlier decades, he had often sworn that no one would ever catch him sitting around McDonald's when he got old. He took the last sip of his coffee just as the McDonald's coffee hostess came by and filled his white Styrofoam cup. She was just about as old as he was, he figured. He asked her for two creams as she started to walk off.

He finished reading the *USA TODAY* and reassembled the various sections in appropriate order. It was a sunny, but brisk, fall morning... only early October, but you could already see the vapor condensing out of the mouths of passersby and rising in small clouds from the car exhausts. As was his pattern in the morning, he began to wax reflectively... rerunning parts of his life... still trying to derive their essence and meaning. As he looked around McDonald's that morning, he thought of how far in the distance his stage of life seemed to the younger people there... and how close their time of life was to him.

This particular morning, Henry was, once again, reflecting upon a theme that frequently dominated his contemplative passages... that life seemed to flash by with such breathtaking speed. The stages came in quick succession... childhood, teenage years, twenties, thirties, forties, fifties, sixties, and now he was in literal disbelief to find himself halfway through his seventh decade of life. He would sometimes shake his head and mentally subtract his birth date from the current year to see if, perhaps, there might not be some mistake in his calculations.

When Henry was younger, he'd always viewed life as he had a book or a movie. He was positive that in the end there would be a climax and a conclusion... a point where everything came together and made sense – an end to the story. If only there were, he thought. Here he was, seventy-four years old... and still trying to make some sense of his life – and find at least *some* degree of closure.

Henry looked around at the people in the restaurant and remembered, vividly, when he was their age. Kids, three or four years old, sat close to their parents... asking a million questions... looking to their mother and father as all-knowing... all-protective... openly affectionate toward them... totally lacking self-consciousness about anything... infinitely happy and comfortably languishing in their small, safe, simple world. Boys, nine or ten, would run by the table... loud, and looking for mischief. Groups of girls, thirteen or fourteen were clumped together, looking at a group of boys their age... giggling and clustering even closer when one would return their glances. Teenage couples, sixteen or seventeen, stood at the counter... the boys broadening at the shoulders and possessing men's voices, self-consciously trying to act like an adult, one minute, then lapsing into childish antics, the next... their girlfriends, clearly ready and anxious, physically and emotionally, for the next stage of life, desperately wishing their boyfriends were, as well.

As a McDonald's daily patron, Henry became a student of observation – focusing, in particular, on the common elements of life stages. He observed that the late-teens and early-twenties group, who had gone away to college, would invariably parade around in their fraternity and sorority jackets and college sweatshirts... trying, with overt pomposity, to demonstrate to old friends that they had moved on... beyond their provincial roots, their insignificant former lives, and old relationships. Those who hadn't gone to college took on an immediate, aged look – derived from working with men and women twice their age... resigned to dead-end jobs and unfulfilled lives... anxious to mercifully forget the bloom and promise of their teen years. The young college grads would brag about their new jobs... the importance of it and of their destiny as a consequential person of the world. Couples, in their mid-to-late twenties, just married – or about to be – would

THE DISCIPLES

beam with the anticipation of a perfect life... to be much improved over that of their parents. They would assure one another how they would overcome all obstacles... how their life together would be just as they wanted it to be.

Not many years later, Henry would see these same couples... looking dramatically older... the men having gained weight and showing early signs of balding ... the women, thin and frazzled, trying to cope, physically and emotionally, with their screaming toddlers in tow. The thirties crowd would meet... usually with business associates – energetic and displaying unabashed self-importance – hatching plans for every imaginable type of venture... obsessed with making their mark in the world. The forties group would have that look of exhausted resignation... talking more of their children and the state of the world than their business... no longer looking for windmills to joust. Those in their fifties would show the signs of winding down their professional lives. They'd sit with their spouses, now... openly avoiding business associates. They'd talk quietly together with secrecy of communication, borne of a private language, created through many decades of shared joys and tragedies.

The retired, sixties generation took on a look of renewed youth... more energetic and healthily skin-toned than they had been in many years. They would, in an almost childlike fashion, plan outings, often with some rather sizeable groups of other couples their age... laughing, joking, and having a hell of a good time.

At Henry's age, the party had just about wound to a close. People were getting sick, losing energy, getting brittle, having pain, and dying. Just last August, Henry's wife of fifty-two years had passed away – breast cancer – having had both her breasts removed, but still unable to outmaneuver the grim reaper. A lot of his old friends were either dead or in nursing homes. Still in relatively good health, Henry lived each waking moment, now, waiting for his turn. He had begun, lately, to wake up at night in a cold sweat, tormented by visions of being in a nursing home... bony and semiconscious... being fed softened food while he drooled onto his pajamas.

And, most bothersome of all, Henry had, at seventy-four years, no more idea of what to make of life than the eight-year-old, sitting at the next table, eating her Happy Meal. Life had had its moments, of course, good and bad... falling in love with Margaret... their wedding... their first house... watching their three kids grow up... Jimmy being killed in Vietnam... Annie's three divorces... Tommy's second child, born with Down's Syndrome... the trips he and Margaret had taken together... making full professor. Mainly, though, if someone were to ask Henry what his main impression of life was, after more than seven decades on earth, he'd have to say that its essence was work, routine, and worry.

Henry had spent nearly all his time and energy, from his twenties on, trying to get ahead... moving up the ladder at the university... trying to scrape enough money together for his family's needs... constantly worrying about deadlines and expectations that, he felt, had to be fulfilled. Added together, there were, in Henry's assessment, perhaps a couple-dozen significant events in his entire life... significant enough to put a blip on his life's chart. On the whole, however, as he considered it, his life was primarily meaningless repetition... rising at the same hour... teaching the same courses... traveling the same roads... saying the same things... eating the same meals at the same time, at the same table.

Like everyone else he knew, Henry had always been so busy in life, doing the mundane, necessary things that there was really no time nor energy for the truly "meaningful" things of life, whatever they were supposed to be. He and Margaret were just as busy after he retired, as before... always going somewhere... taking care of the house... club meetings. Throughout his life, Henry had always had this unshakable faith that at some point he would get off the treadmill of the everyday bustle and his existence would take on some specific meaning... something, at the least, more than simply tedium. At seventy-four, he was certainly off the treadmill. The problem was, he would say, that by the time you're no longer up to your ass in alligators, you're just about out of the time and energy to do anything else.

THE DISCIPLES

Henry had spent most of his life, searching for some meaning to the everyday motions that human beings go through. Though he did all the things in his youth that were expected of a young boy... baseball, fistfights, paper routes, girls... he was a closet philosopher... something he, of course, would never have admitted to his neighborhood buddies. He would nearly drive himself crazy, pondering everything he saw... where did everything in the world come from?... how could there be an infinity?... what would it be like to be a dog?... do other living things like ants or bumblebees know they're alive?... are they afraid when someone tries to swat them?... is there a God?... why do bad things happen to people? He sometimes tried to engage his friends in discussion of such lofty considerations, but they thought he was plain goofy. They'd rather find a girl and get their hand up her dress than discuss the divine purpose of why boys and girls were so different.

Henry's contemplative obsession led him to study philosophy in college... and eventually get his Ph.D. at Johns Hopkins, specializing in nineteenth-century German philosophy. He took a faculty position at the College of William and Mary, fresh out of his doctoral program, in the Philosophy and Religious Studies Department, where he spent his entire career, spanning thirty-eight years. The problem he encountered after he joined the faculty was that he spent more and more time doing "stupid stuff," as he called it, than the profound inquiry of life's "meaning." He had to get tenure and promotion and that required committee work, grinding out meaningless research papers and articles that said more and more about less and less, and finding the right tricks to get his students to favorably evaluate him.

After getting tenure and, ultimately, a full professorship, Henry was relegated to teaching the same dull classes, semester after semester, that all, eventually, ran together like watercolors on wet paper. He read an endless stream of essay exams, authored by less-than-inspired and quite less-than-brilliant undergraduate students, the bulk of whom were taking his courses by required curriculum fiat. The rest of his time was spent on the everyday stuff... paying the bills on a professor's salary... mowing the lawn... dealing with the kids... getting the car repaired – all that meaningless stuff that fills the days. Throughout these "treadmill" years, as he called them, Henry remained convinced that the day would come when he would write his "great book" that would explain the meaning of everything in life – sort of a final word on all those questions he had pondered since childhood... as soon as he had the time and energy – and quiet – to do it.

The problem was, Henry found, the time had just never come. He had started on his "great book" at least a dozen times over the past twenty years, but had never gotten beyond the introduction. Henry discovered that when he would finally have a few discretionary hours, he was just too tired – or too frazzled – to be lofty. Now, with unlimited time and absolute quiet, and still plenty of energy, he no longer felt he had anything to say that was worth writing. Life no longer inspired heavenly emotion – nor even lofty thoughts – in Henry. He had come to see life as a very rapid, empty journey... that left loose ends lying everywhere in sight... totally void of sublimity.

To his eight-year-old fast-food neighbor, Henry knew that from her point of view, he was an infinite journey from her station in life. But from Henry's vantage point to hers, it was but a short step. You look in the mirror, one day, and you're a father... you blink and you're a grandfather... open your eyes again and you're not there anymore. Young people look at you as though you have always been that old... as though you know how to be old. Funny thing is, Henry reflected, old age feels as though you've found yourself at a Halloween party, wearing an old man's costume that you can't take off. The young, vibrant you is inside but no one can tell... and about all you can say is that you still feel young – like all old people say... the young people failing to realize that you really mean it. Henry had just never gotten the hang of acting like an old person. He sometimes felt that old age was like a bad joke that someone had played on him.

Henry often recalled a particular afternoon, a few years past. He was having lunch with an old friend that had come to William and Mary the same year he had... and retired the same year. They started talking about how quickly it had all gone by. They both recalled, as though it were last week, the day they met, and how they looked... both in their late twenties... heads full of hair... skin ruddy and tight... both with firm, athletic bodies. Frank started laughing, out of the blue, to the point of tears. Henry did too, just looking at him. Frank finally got out his words, still laughing.

"How the hell did we get so old, Henry?"

Henry responded amid his laughter.

"Damned if I know, Frank."

Frank continued.

"Christ... look at us, Henry... we look like shit... wrinkled... skinny... a few strands of what used to be hair on our heads... liver spots. We're ugly as sin. When did all this happen to us, Henry?"

Henry was now laughing so hard, he couldn't answer, and felt sure he was going to pee his pants if he didn't get a handle on it. He trotted to the men's room with people staring at both him and his loony friend. Henry laughed every time he thought of that day.

Funny, Henry thought, but those few minutes with Frank were one of the high points of his last ten years. Not really funny, though, on further reflection... actually pretty pathetic. A few laughs... a high point of a decade? What a life. Of course, he was better off than a lot of people. He had a good pension... his old job was about the best work anyone could have had... teaching twelve hours a week, summers off. Life could have been a lot worse... and it was for most people. So if his life, as good as it was, qualifies a few chuckles as a high point of a decade, what about all those other poor slobs, who have had so much less than he... and so much more trouble?

Henry began thinking about his daughter. Martha had attempted suicide three times in her life. From the earliest time in her life she had been overly sensitive and prone to internalizing everything. She was, in Henry's opinion, an unfortunate exaggeration of himself. He was sensitive, he admitted, but Martha was like a peeled grape. Criticism, to Martha, was always like a knife through her heart. Henry remembered how she had burst into tears and had run from the room, in kindergarten, when the teacher – responding to her question as to whether or not she thought her finger painting was the best in the class – told her it was good… but that the other students' paintings were good, as well.

Martha always had to be perfect. She once bloodied her own lip with her fist when she got a "B" on a junior high social studies test. Henry and Margaret began taking Martha to a psychologist when she was a mere eight-year-old. The doctor told them she was obsessive-compulsive. As with most psychological interventions, however, they now had a fancy label, and could tell everyone what was wrong with their daughter, but possessed no solution to her problem. The doctor would merely say that "… it would take a lot of work…" to help resolve Martha's deep-rooted problems. The years of "work," however, failed to produce anything even resembling a resolution. As a matter of fact, Martha's condition significantly worsened over the years of expensive therapy.

Martha's extremely attractive looks had compounded her problems. In his experiences with Martha, Henry discovered just how truly simpleminded, instinctually imprisoned, men really were. No matter if the woman were an obvious nut case – which Martha was, he was sorry to say – let the woman have a beautiful face and a curvaceous body, and a man will marry her with no further questions asked. Martha's marital record was three-up… and three, quickly down. Henry knew that no woman who walked the face of the earth was as stupid as the average man when it came to marriage. He guessed that the only providence that could save a man from a disastrous marriage was just, plain luck.

Martha's three disastrous marriages were, Henry would readily admit, entirely her own fault. By the unfortunate luck of the draw, the men who foolishly married her were, in Henry's opinion, quite decent human beings... conjugally impaired, but decent. Martha quickly drove each of them to frenzied distraction. It was the same story each time. Nothing and nobody was ever good enough for her. The only stroke of luck in the entire repeating course of marital calamities was that Martha was barren. Mercifully, therefore, Henry solaced himself – her madness would end with her.

Now in her early fifties, Martha lived alone in a small apartment, not too far from Henry's house. She worked in the college bookstore – a job Henry arranged for her. She had lost her alluring looks, completely, and now constantly wore a twisted, somewhat deranged expression on her face, and in her eyes. Her appearance seemed somehow off-center... something akin to the look of a stroke victim. Her behavior was seldom, now, between the lines of normalcy and people politely and consistently avoided her. They continued to keep her on at the bookstore, strictly out of respect for Henry, working in the back room, tracking stock. Her only companions in life were her three cats. Henry was always fascinated by the looniness-multiple-cat syndrome, but could never quite fathom the essence of the connection. Martha and he no longer had any communication between them, whatsoever. She had nothing to say to him and he guessed, if he got right down to it, he really had nothing to say to her, either.

Tommy had earned an engineering degree from MIT and had moved to southern California after graduation... eventually landing a good job in Silicon Valley. He'd been out there, now, for over twenty years, and had come home for a total of five visits with Henry and Margaret during that time. Henry had always heard that daughters were the ones who always stay close to their parents. He guessed in his case, he'd struck out on both scores. Of course, he had to admit, he was probably the primary cause of Tommy's distance from him.

While Tommy was growing up, Henry had always been just too busy to spend much time with him. Consequently, instead of love growing between the father and son, a respectful courtesy evolved in its place. Their dialogue was always strictly limited to impersonal matters... world events, careers, sports, science, history... always avoiding matters of the heart by tacit agreement. Whenever Tommy felt in need of parental guidance or affection, which, for boys is, of course, rare... he would, invariably, go to his mother. Thus, having never nurtured a shared emotional life, and also by simple virtue of being two males, neither Henry nor Tommy would pick up the phone to call one another, except when absolutely necessary... and males, of course, rarely consider calling to merely see how someone is doing a necessity. The communication between the two of them eventually became, therefore, ritualistic. Tommy would call Henry on Father's Day, Christmas, and New Year's Day. Henry would call Tommy on his birthday and Thanksgiving. Their conversations were consistently short, routine, and always self-conscious – both awkwardly searching for something to say, beyond the initial salutation. For Henry, having a son had become a mere fact... in response to demographic inquiries. They had, in fact, Henry would sadly admit to himself in bare moments of painful honesty, no real relationship beyond their shared genetic material. Henry found this lamentable, but dealt with it stoically, as water over the dam... feeling it was much too late to do anything about it.

Age and experience had, by now, tarnished the shine of Kant, Nietzsche, and Heidegger for Henry Butler. He now regarded his former philosophical champions as mere ordinary men, who had tried, in vain – as he had – to make sense of a nonsensical life. All their tortured logic and endless rumination didn't add a day to their life nor a moment's happiness to their existence... nor anyone else's for that matter. In the end... and Henry was just about at his own... Henry had grown to view his former love of philosophy as just a lot of unnecessary fuss... much ado about nothing, as the old bard had described it. What, he often mused, had all his anguish over the great questions of life gotten him but a headache? Henry now understood that philosophy was a young man's game... young enough to think it all mattered.

Despite his newfound disdain for philosophy, however, Henry simply couldn't keep himself from pondering his own life. Eventually, Henry came to recognize that the measure of his life was to be found in his heart and not within his rational faculties... and his heart was sad and it was empty. He was a very intelligent man, who had risen from a common birth to that of a distinguished professor in a well-regarded institution of higher learning. But, when all was said and done, he knew he was really just another ordinary man who had lived. . . and would soon die... and be sooner forgotten. What was the point?... Henry would ponder, time and time again. What was the point to his life?

For a short time, in recent years, Henry had begun to think that, perhaps, the meaning of life was not in rationality... but spirituality. He soon abandoned this line of thinking, however. For Henry, religion was a blessing... but only for the simpleminded... simpleminded enough to accept, without rational dissection, some story that gave life meaning beyond itself. In his later years, however, Henry had grown to envy these simpler people of the world. They weren't endlessly tormented, like he was, by all the interminable pondering. They had found a way of accepting plainly mundane, meaningless existence with grace. To them, the meaning of their lives would be found at its end. Henry aspired to the peace that these people exhibited, but how would he – a man whose nature it is to question all he encounters – acquire and sustain this comforting, blind faith? Henry believed that men such as he were destined, never to dwell in this enviable spiritual nirvana... whether on this globe or beyond.

Henry, the rational every-man, now found himself looking forward to death. He had put in his time... the job was done... it was time to quit. His greatest sorrow was not for himself... but for mankind, in general. All these poor people, he would anguish... striving, worrying, working so hard... all, in the end, for naught. He still had no idea as to how or why human beings found themselves as the only creatures with consciousness on this tiny ball of soil-and-water-covered rock, whirling through space.

If there were, in fact, some force or being that created the universe, Henry believed it must have been an exceedingly sadistic entity, indeed. He could think of nothing crueler than human existence... inquisitive creatures somehow awakened to their own being with absolutely no idea as to why. What a rotten joke, Henry thought. It was as though some whimsical omnipotent decided, in a moment of boredom, "OK, I'll wake em up and let em walk around, helplessly trying to figure out how they got there, who put them there, and for what purpose... that'll do for some laughs." It's no wonder, Henry thought, that humans invent religion... what the hell else were they supposed to do?... go nuts trying to figure things out? Go nuts... yeah... not hard to do if you keep trying to play it straight like Henry had... holding out against all those implausible sacred stories, offered to explain the unexplainable... believing that the answers to life could be found through pure, rational thought.

In his forties, Henry had dabbled in Buddhism for a while. It was the one religion that he found to have the potential of surviving the bright light of rational inquiry. As he understood it, Siddhartha Guatama, the Buddha, had been born into affluence... had everything he could want in life. Apparently, Siddhartha then took a walk into the countryside, one day, and discovered that his life was an obvious fluke – that contrary to his former perspective, indicating to him that life was a bowl of cherries – it was, in actuality, almost universal, unabated misery... from the moment of birth to the instant of death. To make matters worse, Sid concluded, you keep getting reborn every time you die... so you were thus trapped in a circuitous hell on earth. Well, Sid said, only one thing to do... keep yourself from being born again and take yourself out of this unending, diabolical cycle. How to do that? Well... you're born again, the Buddha said, because you cling to life and the things of life, so stop clinging and let go of life. If you let go, you enter Nirvana... a nebulous state of eternal detachment and you are thus spared the endless agony of rebirth.

This made some sense to Henry... at least more sense than the story of a Jewish carpenter who walked on water and arose from the dead and somehow, by being hung upon a standard apparatus of capital punishment of the time... died for the sins of all mankind. This Jesus was, in Henry's opinion, a brave, highly principled and compassionate man, but accepting this son-of-God stuff was a bit too much to ask of a rational man. All the other religions, save Buddhism, were, to Henry, just about as implausible as this Jewish carpenter story.

What eventually disenchanted Henry with Buddhism was his conclusion that Sid went a bit overboard in his assessment of the condition of life. Henry figured that what Sid saw on his walk, in the utterly miserable countryside, was just as unrepresentative of actual life on earth as Sid's own bowl-of-cherries existence. Life just wasn't quite that bad. People have a lot of problems – true – but they don't go on, in general, unabated, without some bright spots... or just spots, bright or not. No, Henry had to say... life wasn't unending misery... it was just, well, in his view... pointless. Maybe Sidhartha would say that leading a pointless life was endless misery too, but Henry didn't buy it. Most of the time, people are too damn busy to know it's pointless. It doesn't really dawn on you until you totally slow down... and then you only have to put up with it for a few years, then... poof!... the end of the story.

It's really too bad, Henry thought, that life is the way it is... a maddening swirl of hollow days, terminated without any meaningful closure. If only there really were something... some ultimate being... some higher design to existence... that could give all the meaningless stuff of life some purpose. If only there were something that intelligent, thinking, skeptical people, like Henry, could believe in. But if there was one thing of which Henry was sure it was that miracles don't happen in real life and, unfortunately, life is what it is... no magic... no miracles... no god... no meaning.

CHAPTER ELEVEN

PAULO

Rikers Island is considered by those who seriously pursue a career of crime, the capstone of any such calling. Paulo Mandos had worked his way from juvenile detention centers, to Attica, to Soledad, before being finally delivered into the ranks of the true "big house." He knew, upon his arrival to the Island, that his reputation would go only halfway in ensuring respect and, in turn, securing his ticket to do "easy" time. The rest, he'd have to resolve in quick order. If any of the brothers thought he had a soft piece of flesh on him, they'd be instantly eyeing up his Chicano ass for a conjugal visit... maybe even group love. The first chance he got, he knew he'd have to make his move.

Paulo had made a costly mistake in Soledad... waiting too long to draw blood, and he paid... paid big time. Considering him "easy meat," a group of some Soledad brothers got him in the back of the laundry room and tried to see just how loveable his Chicano mouth really was. On his knees with three brothers holding him... one on each arm and one with a forearm around his throat... the biggest brother, standing in front of his face, pulled out his penis, that – erect – was nearly twelve inches in length... and unceremoniously shoved it into Paulo's mouth. Paulo allowed this penetration for his own purposes. As soon as he felt enough of the hardened flesh inside his mouth for his intended mission, he instantly squeezed his jaws together – tighter than he ever had in his life – dug his teeth into the intruding organ, then turned his head sharply to his left... in a motion, much like a dog ripping a piece of meat. For a stunned moment, the big brother stared down in disbelief at the remaining portion of his penis... then began screaming in the discordant wail of a man who had gone out of his mind. Blood squirted like a pumping hydrant from the remaining, torn flesh... soaking Paulo and the writhing man's cohorts.

Startled by the scene, the man with the hammerlock across Paulo's throat let go of him. Free, Paulo jumped to his feet, pulled the six inches of flesh from his mouth... looking in his hand like a small length of black sausage... then threw it into main man's face. Instead of running, Paulo stood there... covered with blood. He raised his face to the ceiling and began howling like a crazed animal. He then bared his teeth and gazed at the brothers with wild, blazing eyes. They all immediately backed away... then ran, leaving their mutilated brother writhing in a pool of his own blood. After their encounter, all four brothers became a part of Paulo's harem and his oral surgery on the big brother earned him the lasting prison handle, "Loco Cocka Roacho."

Most of the guys on the bus ride out to Rikers, tried hard to conceal their fear. They were all hard-timers, or they wouldn't be heading out to the Island, but Rikers had a mythology that scared even the hardest of the hard... with stories told of the guards as horrific as those recounted of the inmates.

Paulo, alone, felt no fear. The last time he remembered being afraid in his life was when he was three years old... sitting in a high chair. He could still vividly remember watching his father smash his mother's head in with a large, black, iron skillet. He remembered screaming and crying... looking down at his mother, lying on the floor, motionless, with a pool of dark, red blood rapidly enlarging around her head on the cracked, pea green linoleum floor. Paulo could still distinctly recall the look in his father's eyes and the smell of his liquor breath when he grabbed him from the chair by his two little arms... shook him... screaming for him to shut up, then threw him, his frail little son, his only child... crashing against the wall. Little Paulito... as his mother called him... still remembered the trip to the hospital... the young man in a white jacket looking down at him... looking very worried.

Paulo's old man, Jesus Mandos, was convicted of second-degree murder and Paulo was placed in a state orphanage. He spent the next twelve years there... being routinely beaten or, alternately, molested, by the older boys and various members of the staff. At age fifteen, he ran away.

Those who don't know about "bad men" would have a hard time understanding that Paulo didn't consider himself to be "evil," despite the fact he had, by the time he was twenty, killed four men, beaten at least another thirty men into critical condition, been a heroin addict, sold drugs, committed armed robbery, stolen cars, plus a laundry list of other crimes that, added together, would cover a substantial portion of a crimes code. What Paulo had never done, however, was to hurt anyone or commit a crime without a purpose. Unlike some he had known he had never hurt anyone merely for the fun of it. He was, in his mind, simply a hard guy living a hard life. When he killed, he did so as would a shark or a wolf. He never took any joy in it... it just had to be done. If a member of a rival gang in the barrio is gunning for you, you take him out before he does you. If a brother puts a knife to your throat, you kill him. It was simple as that. He had never raped a woman nor hurt a child. Paulo had often thought that if he had been born into another life – that didn't require him to hurt people – he probably would never have done all the terrible things he had.

What he now had to do in Rikers was just another example of something he simply had to do. He had seen what happens to those in a big house who won't fight. They're literally enslaved by the predators. They're made to take a penis up their ass, or in their mouth, anytime their old man tells them to... whether it's for him or his favorite brothers. A weak man would be made to wash the clothes of his man, run his errands, turn over his money or anything else he would get in the mail that was worth having. It was either that or fight. Paulo would fight. To him, death was far better, by comparison, than such a dehumanized existence.

After being processed into the Island... strip search, warden lecture, an initial beating by five or so of the guards... Paulo was taken to his cell. On the Island they had four men to an eight-by-ten cell. Paulo looked his roommates over... he was already looking for the right target... somebody that looked "bad"... that would be considered a "good score" and make his reputation.

THE DISCIPLES

One guy was white, the other two black. The white guy looked to Paulo like a typical white, inmate degenerate... skinny with grayish skin... missing most of his front teeth... those remaining being brownish-black with decay. He was probably a "tree jumper," Paulo guessed. He looked the type. One of the black guys was short and well-built, with arms the size of most men's calves... a result of pumping iron – for hours every day. The other black was an older guy... probably sixty or more. He had a tired, but pleasant, look in his eyes. Paulo figured he was one of those repeat offenders... nothing too serious... but added together, was enough to win him a long-term stay on the Island.

None of the three inmates of Range B, Cell 212, knew Paulo... but they knew of him. Paulo had that look that immediately frightened other people. Paulo's face and eyes told a long story... of hurt and hurting. Looking at Paulo, his cell mates knew, instantly, that he would, if necessary, kill any one of them in a heartbeat. No one spoke to him. Paulo returned his stare to the degenerate, sitting on the lower bunk, across from the blacks. Without a word, the white-trash convict got up and moved his things to the upper bunk... then sat on the floor with his back against the bars... the ceiling being too low to allow him to sit on his newly acquired, top bunk.

The old black guy was sitting on the other lower bunk, next to the younger man. He avoided looking at Paulo... putting his head back down, ostensibly studying the magazine on his lap. He was obviously a man who wanted no more trouble in his life. The younger black continued to look at Paulo – but in such a way so as not to convey a challenge. He was big, but Paulo was dangerous... too dangerous to even consider fucking around with. Finally he spoke to Paulo... afraid too much silence might be misconstrued. In a very deep and gravelly voice, he spoke his own name.

"Gerald... they call me Pumper."

Paulo looked at Pumper. Paulo's face remained expressionless. His eyes moved to the old man... who, feeling it, looked up.

"Bill."

Paulo didn't bother to find out the white guy's name... he didn't care to know.

Paulo spoke.

"Call me Loco."

Pumper spoke.

"I heard a you. You the crazy dude dat circumcised a brother out at Soledad. We heard you was comin."

Paulo shook his head... acknowledging Pumper. Pumper issued a solicitous smile, knowing well that a friend like Loco could be priceless in the savage world of the Island. Paulo sat down on his lower bunk and looked around the cramped cell. It was about as bad as they get – four men in a small cage. There was only about four feet between the bunks. They went, end to end, from the bars to within about two feet of the inside wall. The stainless steel toilet, with no lid, was against the inside wall, within a foot of the bunks. It smelled of shit and piss, both new and ancient. Beside the toilet was a metal sink that hadn't been cleaned in a very long time. Above the sink and toilet were three metal shelves where the few items, that these men could call their own, were stored... the only outward symbols that distinguished them as individual human beings from the rest of the warehoused carcasses, stored in this island hell hole.

Paulo looked at Pumper.

"You know what I gotta do."

Pumper shook his head.

"Who's ripe?"

Pumper put his finger to his mouth, thinking. After careful

consideration, he spoke.

"I'd take out Snow White if I was you."

Paulo didn't respond... waiting to hear more. Pumper continued.

"He mean, man... mean. He in for some bad shit. They say he tortured seven young girls... raped em then cut all their throats. Say he raped them again after they dead... bad man... real bad man. He hate everybody... everybody hate him. But nobody fuck with Snow White... he a blonde devil. A brother on C Range challenged him in the yard once... couple a years ago. Snow White grabbed him by the throat... and tore his wind pipe right out. Shoulda heard it. The brother couldn't talk or even scream... all you could hear was all this wind comin out of the hole in his throat. Blood ran down into his pipe... he drowned on his own fuckin blood. Dat Snow White... he one fuckin scary dude. You take him out... you run the Island... an I be your best man... you bet.

Paulo lay down on the bunk and closed his eyes.

CHAPTER TWELVE

Two days after his arrival, as they stood in the yard, Pumper pointed out Snow White to Paulo. He was about six-foot, lean, with hard-looking muscles rippling across his body... not an inch of fat on him. His blonde hair hung to his shoulders and deep blue eyes stared out from tight slits. Pock marks – grotesque artifacts of a lost battle with acne – covered his face, chest, and back. His mouth was formed into a permanent sneer. He definitely looked bad... real bad. Paulo would have to give this some thought. He wasn't afraid of anyone... but he wasn't stupid either.

His period of consideration was cut short... the very next day. A message was delivered to Paulo by one of Snow White's slaves. The skinny, white inmate was shaking when he delivered it.

"Snow White says to tell you he dug up your dead mother and fucked her. He says he wants her baby boy now."

Skinny beat a hasty retreat... not hanging around to get a response.

Snow White, obviously, wasn't going to give Paulo any choice. One or the other was going down. The inevitable carnage was immediately the talk of the Island and bets were placed with anything they had to wager... from cigarettes to blow jobs. The guards knew all about it and were just as anxious as the inmates to get in on the action. They formed a betting pool, with each guard drawing a piece of paper from an empty coffee can. Each chit had either Paulo or Snow White as winner, a given number of minutes the fight would last, and whether or not one of them would be killed. There was a palpable air of anticipation permeating the Island.

Snow White was bad... so was Paulo... but Paulo was smart... really smart. He had lived by his wits from the time he was three years old. Every con, every fade, every trick... Paulo had seen it, and he was going to give himself every advantage. He kept his distance from Snow White for a few days... just to watch him... how he walked... how he talked... how he stood... how he carried his hands and arms. Snow White was at least three inches taller than Paulo... had long arms and legs... big, strong-looking hands... strong enough to tear out another man's throat. Paulo arranged to get himself a four-inch shiv. No one was better and quicker with a knife than he was... and Paulo had already concluded that Snow White was slightly clumsy and not nearly as agile as he was.

On Saturday morning, Pumper, Bill, and the white degenerate knew, instinctively, that it was time. Paulo was up early. He sat on the edge of the bunk... looking almost serene. No one spoke a word to him, or to one another. They moved around the cell as quietly as possible. Pumper had to take a shit – really bad – but didn't... not wanting to disturb Paulo. Paulo didn't go down to breakfast. Everybody who passed the cell, did so reverently... moving silently by... daring only to look at Paulo out of the corners of their eyes. The entire cell block was quiet. Everybody knew.

Paulo would use his most successful strategy... countering. He would let Snow White make a move and commit himself, then counter it. It was, of course, an inherently dangerous strategy. Paulo had always been very successful with it, but there was always that chance that the first, free move that Paulo spotted his opponent could be lethal. But Paulo was quick... and countering was a good strategy if you were quick. Paulo just hoped he was quick enough to handle Snow White.

As Paulo entered the yard for the after-lunch exercise period, he kept his head forward but moved his eyes from side to side. Snow White always got to the yard before Paulo... but today he was no where in sight. Paulo knew Snow White would have gotten the word that this was the day. He apparently was going to alter his routine to psych-out Paulo. Paulo didn't like it. He always liked to have his opponent in view. He had been both knifed and shot in the back before, by unaccounted adversaries. Snow White was definitely fucking with him. Paulo went to the farthest wall and leaned his back against it, so he could visually sweep the entire yard. Everybody kept their distance from him. Forty minutes passed. The return-to-range horn sounded. Nobody moved. The loud speaker blared out... ordering the residents to assemble for return to the ranges. Slowly, they began to move toward the doors... disappointment written on every face. They were up for the event and Snow White had failed to appear.

Paulo's hairs were up on the back of his neck as he passed through the doors into the east wing. Snow White could come out of anywhere in this crowded corridor. He reached into the front of his pants and slid out the shiv with his right hand. With his right arm beside his body he held the shiv with his thumb – the blade concealed by his stiffly extended fingers. He continued to hold it as he came up to the search point for re-entry into the range. He wasn't surprised when the guard waved him by without a search. He had to have known what Paulo was carrying. Paulo figured he had money bet on him.

Back in the cell, Paulo continued his silence... as did his cell mates. He lay on his bunk and closed his eyes. The muffled conversations about Snow White's no-show wafted through the air of the range. Paulo suspected that Snow White had something in mind for dinnertime. To counter-psych Snow White, Paulo stayed in the cell when the dinner horn sounded. After dinner, Pumper told Paulo that Snow White was there and he definitely looked like he was up for some action... just had that look. Paulo smiled and lay back down.

Entering the dining area the next morning, Paulo looked immediately to the far right corner of the room. Snow White's range got there before Paulo's... and Snow White always sat at the corner table, facing the door, his back to the food line. He wasn't there.

Just as Paulo started to sweep his eyes to the other side of the hall, he felt a tremendous impact on the back, right side of his head. His knees buckled and slammed onto the concrete floor. Sparkles of light danced before him. Everything sounded as if it were coming from the far end of a tunnel. The room felt to Paulo, as if it were tilted on its side. Suddenly he felt two powerful arms lock around his throat... one on the front... the other on the back. They squeezed together like a hydraulic vise. His windpipe closed shut. He was going to black out.

No one can truly explain the ultimate essence of a human being. Someone who had been hit on the back of the head with a piece of hard wood, the size of a small baseball bat, moving with the speed and force that could impel a line drive to the center field wall... then choked by human vise grips... should, by all rights, lose consciousness. Some people... the great ones... seem to be able to do what, by all rights, appears to be simply impossible. Something inside them... something without name... something extremely rare... rises up inside such men in their moments of greatness. This moment in the Rikers Island mess hall was one of those rare moments that proves there are great men – even among convicts. It was one of those moments that gives rise to legend.

Just as it appeared that Paulo was going out... his eyes beginning to roll back into his head... it happened. Suddenly Paulo's eyes regained their focus and his face took on a look, quite inappropriate for the circumstance. It was a look of calm... and utter confidence. It was so strange that it was frightening... even to the hardened spectators. It was as though Satan, himself, had slipped through some unguarded opening to take possession of Paulo's soul.

In a movement that could best be described as graceful, Paulo rose from his knees to his feet... pulling the clinging Snow White with him. He then calmly reached up and gripped Snow White's right hand and began to bend it backwards. A sound like rubber bands snapping issued from Snow White's wrist. He howled like a wounded dog. In obvious and excruciating pain, Snow White let go of Paulo entirely, then backed up a few steps. His right hand flopped around, freely, like the head of chicken on a wrung neck. Snow White had a look of sheer terror in his eyes. He put his arms up in front of him... his right hand falling forward, to lay completely against his forearm. Paulo's face took on a countenance of something that was not of the earth. He began to walk slowly toward Snow White. With each step Paulo took forward... Snow White took one backward. His backward movement was finally halted by the yellow tile wall of the mess hall.

Paulo moved to within inches of Snow White's face. Then, moving so quickly that no one saw Paulo's right hand coming up, he locked it onto Snow White's throat. Paulo then began to slowly move his hand upward... Snow White's body moving with it. Paulo continued his motion until Snow White's feet were a foot off the floor. Judging from the relative size of Snow White and Paulo, it seemed almost impossible that this could be happening... but... it was.

Paulo turned suddenly to his left and, still holding Snow White by the throat, he catapulted him through the air. He landed on the nearest table and slid across it... falling off the other side... knocking over the metal chairs as he fell. His limp body draped itself over various parts of three overturned chairs. Paulo walked calmly around the table to where Snow White lay. His head was at Paulo feet.

Most of the people in the room that day were accustomed to brutality. They had seen hundreds of fights and gallons of blood spilled on the floor. Paulo's next move, however, made even such veterans squeamish. He reached down toward Snow White's head with his right hand. In a movement identical to picking up a bowling ball, he put a finger on each of Snow White's eyes and pushed them into the sockets. His thumb rested on Snow White's forehead. Paulo then lifted Snow White's head in this bowling ball fashion, and with his right arm hanging down at his side, he began walking down the center of the long hall with Snow White's head in his hand... his body dragging behind, on the brown-painted concrete floor.

The assemblage opened before Paulo like Moses parting the Red

Sea. They stood in awe of the pure animal viciousness of that which they beheld. Paulo's face was serene... looking as though he were out for a Sunday stroll in the park... while carrying a man's head in his hand like a ripe melon. Everyone appreciated the almost sublime nature of the scene. Rarely is one a witness to such unapologetic and surgically executed carnage.

Paulo continued his processional toward the chow line. The tray slide was some thirty feet of stainless steel, protruding from the bottom of slanted glass, behind which sat the food containers and servers. Nearing the line, Paulo took one long step and then flung Snow White's body upward and onto the tray slide. It hit the steel with a loud, thudding jolt. Paulo slid his bloody fingers from Snow White's eye sockets. He lay there, motionless, but still breathing... his right arm, limply hanging down from the tray slide. Blackish-red ooze was seeping from his empty sockets.

Paulo turned to face the totally silent, transfigured multitude... gazing upon him in wide-eyed reverence. It wasn't just the grotesque mutilation that so transfixed the cons... it was Paulo himself... his almost papal countenance amid the blood and gore. What he had done to Snow White was performed with an air of ritual ceremony, without anger or words. His demeanor and movement were as graceful as that of a ballet dancer. His face, as he surveyed his flock was possessed by a continuing serene bearing. After some thirty seconds or more of worshipful silence, Paulo took it upon himself to end the hushed tranquility... speaking in a soothing, but firm voice.

"It's over."

He paused. Then spoke again.

"Go back to your tables and sit down."

Silently, several thousand prisoners obediently returned to their tables and sat down as commanded.

Looking back and forth at one another... they slowly began to pick up their forks and spoons, resuming their breakfast in continued silence... nervously awaiting Paulo's allowance to speak. Looking directly ahead, Paulo strode, gracefully, down the long aisle between the tables... returning to his usual seat. He sat down... the only man at the table. His usual tablemates were standing at a distance from the table, unsure of whether or not they should risk the audacious act of sitting at the same table with this newly ordained, Island god. Finally, Bill came quietly up to Paulo and asked him if he could get him something. Paulo told him just some coffee. Bill returned with the black coffee and put it down in front of Paulo and remained standing. Paulo thanked him. Bill and Pumper walked up to the mess line and asked the servers for some breakfast. Snow White was still lying there. A large pool of blood was forming under the tray slide where he lay. The servers looked at the guards behind the counter, who nodded their consent. Others, who, also, had not yet gotten their breakfast, followed suit. The remaining service of breakfast proceeded with Snow White still lying there. All the cons acted as though he were invisible... no one daring to even chance a glimpse of him. All the conversation, during the entire breakfast period, was conducted in whispered tones... sounding more like a church than a prison mess hall. No one dared to venture a seat at Paulo's table. When the horn finally sounded for return to range, Paulo remained at the table... sipping the remains of the last of several cups provided by Bill. He knew he'd have to pay for the bloody mutilation... and he was ready.

After the cavernous room had completely cleared, the guards – eight of them, for their own sense of safety – slowly approached Paulo, standing around him in a semicircle. Paulo continued to look into his coffee cup. After an awkward silence, the senior guard finally spoke to him in a low, respectful voice.

"C' mon Mandos... we gotta do our job."

Paulo stood up. The guards instinctively backed up a few feet. Paulo continued to look down. He put his hands behind his back... knowing the routine. He had been there before. They put the cuffs on him and led him away to solitary confinement, where he spent the next four months. Paulo was tried and convicted on aggravated assault. Several guards testified, during the trial, that Paulo had acted, for the most part, in self-defense. The judge, in the non-jury trial, found Paulo, nevertheless, guilty... saying that Paulo went far beyond what was "reasonably necessary" to defend himself. In the sentencing, however, he took into account, the guard support of his actions and the provocation by Snow White. He sentenced Paulo to six-to-ten years for the conviction, but, allowed him to serve it concurrently with his present, ten-to-twenty term he was already serving for voluntary manslaughter. What it all boiled down to was that it didn't cost Paulo a minute more time in prison to permanently blind Snow White.

Snow White was sent to a special facility in Franklin, upstate New York, for the blind, and other variously handicapped inmates. The blonde devil's diabolical reign over Rikers Island had ended. The former killer, rapist, and torturer was now a helpless blind man, depending upon everyone for everything. After Snow White had been in the state correctional facility in Franklin for about nine months, the word got back to the Island that a member of his former harem – who had developed debilitating arthritis and was transferred to Franklin – had slit Snow White's throat. The story went that, before he cut his throat, he had gagged Snow White, and tied his hands behind his back. He then buggered Snow White with a broom handle and whispered in his ear the whole time... recounting every sadistic, demeaning act that Snow White had forced him to do, during his years on the Island.

CHAPTER THIRTEEN

For the remaining eight years of his incarceration on the Island... until the day he was paroled... Paulo reigned as the undisputed, crowned sovereign of Rikers. His destruction of Snow White had become a Riker's legend... passed on to new arrivals as soon as they stepped onto the Island. The story had become embellished, of course, as it was repeated over the years. Some even had Paulo pulling Snow White's eyes from his head and eating them like grapes. Those who had actually seen the great Island event, however, would never forget it. When a person is pure he is revered... whether purely saint or purely satanic. No one who had seen Paulo that morning would ever forget his demon-like mutilation of Snow White – like a shark devouring his prey – without emotion or apology. Paulo was a savage... but a pure savage. Both the inmates and guards alike, gave him his due respect and space. Paulo Mandos was one of those rare human beings that come along, only once in a very long while, whose greatness is intuitively sensed by anyone in his presence.

Paulo was paroled from Rikers after serving eight years of his sentence. He was issued a set of new, out-of-style clothes, a prison check for $150 and a $200 travel voucher for purchase of transportation to his chosen point of destination. He was also given a check for what was left of the money he had earned at the rate of twenty cents an hour, working over the past eight years at Rikers – amounting to sixteen hundred dollars. He caught a bus to Washington D.C. for no other particular reason except that he'd never been there before. Having no family or friends, he had nowhere, in particular, to go. Paulo casually walked around the city... checking out the monuments... spent one whole day walking through the Smithsonian. It became clearly apparent to him that people were staring at him. It wasn't his clothes, he decided. They certainly weren't G.Q. but, then again, they weren't sufficiently remarkable to cause such a sensation, either. It was just him. He knew it. He could, like a dog, sense their fear. No one knew what, exactly, he had done in his life but somehow... in some unexplainable way... they knew him. They knew he was dangerous. Paulo's mere presence conjured up vestigial memories – still lurking in the primordial shadows of modern man – of inexpressible fear of the savage predators that roamed the black nights of the ancient forests.

Paulo found a cheap hotel just outside the city and paid for three nights. He spent the next three days in the room... trying to decide what to do... where to go. His only obligation was to make arrangements, within two weeks, for a parole contact. He was now thirty-five... and over the past twenty years, he had spent sixteen of them, incarcerated. He had no family, no friends, and no home. He had no trade and a sixth-grade education. He had never held any real job. The only money he had ever had was from stealing or drug dealing. He was smart. That he knew. He learned anything he ever wanted to learn... fast and well. He knew people. He could see through any line anyone could ever think of throwing his way.

Paulo knew that many people thought of him as the devil... as the epitome of evil. But he knew he wasn't. He was hard... but that wasn't evil. Life had just never allowed him to have any soft spots. But he, alone, knew of his one secret place of tenderness. Within the rock he had to have for a heart, tucked away among the crevices, in a small, dark, but warm spot, was a space that allowed him to cry in the secret darkness of the night. Inside that hidden place was the tiny boy who still loved and longed for his dead mother... the only human being in his life who had ever shown him any kindness or love... the only human being who had ever cared if he lived or died.

To Paulo, mankind was his adversary. He trusted no one and loved no one. Everyone he had known in his life, except his mother, had invariably tried to hurt him in some way. He had been lied to, cheated, beaten, and abandoned throughout his life. To Paulo, life was a cruel journey from one end to the other. He had discovered that even mothers could be heartless and sadistic to their own children. Some of the kids he had met in the orphanage had had their hands burned by their mothers for taking a dollar to buy some food... girls whose mothers had sold them for sex to men when they were twelve years old for drug money... mothers who had beaten their babies into a bloody pulp. Having the memory of one good human being in his life, Paulo figured, made his life better than many.

Paulo truly did not want to, ever again, hurt anyone. If there were a way to survive in his life without ever doing harm to another person, he would do it. But Paulo wasn't naive. He was a con... a lifetime con. That would follow him wherever he went. With no marketable, lawful skills, and a grade-school education, he'd be stuck doing menial work for the rest of his life... cleaning out toilets... picking fruit with his wetback amigos. People doing this kind of work were hard, dangerous people. It was only a matter of time before he was forced to hurt someone, again... which would buy him his return ticket to Rikers.

Freedom, Paulo knew, was a relative term. He was now, in essence, out of one prison and into another. There were actually more limitations on his life, outside prison, than inside. Inside he had respect and power. He could command others. That structure gave him a great deal of latitude and freedom. Outside, he didn't have the freedom of eating decently or the freedom of a reliable roof over his head. In a few weeks he'd be broke... with no job... and any job he could get wouldn't pay him enough to live decently. On Rikers Island, he would be considerably freer to enjoy life. But, on the other hand, what kind of a life was it to be human cargo in a warehouse?

Inside or outside, Paulo was trapped. He had been dealt a lousy hand at birth and had never had a fair chance from the start. Thus, as the clock ticked off the passing moments of his life, Paulo Mandos – Loco Cocka Roacho – wished, desperately, for another path to follow, but knew in his heart he was damned by the inexorable, indifferent, immutable nature of destiny.

CHAPTER FOURTEEN

AARON

After drifting in and out of the conscious world a number of times, Aaron was finally anchored there by the cruelest pain he had ever felt in his life. He lay there for quite a while, trying to orient himself. Finally, through the lifting haze, it all began to return to him, and upon putting it all into context, his personal reality brought with it a sense of insufferable emptiness. Aaron Tyger's intention, when he finally got up enough nerve to pull the trigger of the gun he had inserted into his mouth, was to never again face the prospect of enduring another day of life. He had, with all his remaining energy, longed for oblivion. Now, here he was, again, with his day, his life, stretching out before him with the maddening promise of continued, unabated unhappiness. Christ, he thought to himself... I even fucked-up my own death.

Aaron touched the general area from which the bone-thumping pain seemed to emanate... near the right side of his jaw and head. The thick bandages covering the entire area prevented his touch. The pain was so bad that he felt a wave of panic. He didn't think he could endure it for much longer without going out of his mind. He had the urge to run... to try to get away from it. It was another one of those times in his life that he wished he could, somehow, climb out of his body and into another that was more of his liking... or even better... be completely free of a body altogether. He began to feel cold sweat on his skin and the muscles of his chest tightening. Just then a nurse walked into the room.

"How are you feeling, Mr. Tyger?"

Aaron attempted to speak to the young, tight-faced woman in the green smock. He had his thoughts... but his mouth was unable to deliver them. Finally he began to put together fragmented sentences in a voice that sounded like somebody else's.

"The pain is... the pain... is terrible... I need something... the pain is..."

Aaron's right jaw ached, cruelly, each time he tried to move it.

"The doctor will be in to see you, shortly... he can prescribe something for your pain."

"How long... will it... will it be?"

She began to wrap the blood pressure cuff around his right arm. Once the Velcro stays were secure, she pumped it full of air.

"He won't be long, Mr. Tyger... he's on his rounds, right now."

She then put the black plastic ends of her stethoscope into her ears and pressed the cold metal disc against the inside of his arm. Aaron remained silent until she had completed the procedure and had recorded her readings on his chart. Before she moved onto whatever she was going to do next, Aaron spoke to her.

"Do you know... why I'm here?"

"You had surgery, Mr. Tyger... you're in the recovery room."

"That's not what... that's not what I mean. Do you know... why... they brought me here?"

"I just came on duty Mr. Tyger... but your chart says you had a gunshot wound. Dr. Van Dyke apparently did some extensive surgery on you... on the right side of your face and the lower right side of your skull. You're lucky to be alive."

Despite the extreme pain, Aaron managed a small, groaning laugh.

"I'm lucky... to be alive? Don't they tell you... anything?"

THE DISCIPLES

"What do you mean?"

"Can you please tell the... the doctor... to hurry... to hurry up?"

She hung his chart on the end of his bed. She looked at Aaron and screwed her mouth into a tight and disingenuous smile.

"Dr. Van Dyke is on his rounds. He'll be here when he gets here."

Giving a final tightening to the professionally formed lips, she nodded slightly, narrowed her eyes for an instant and strode, with an obvious air of authority, out of the room.

Aaron could feel the pain synchronizing and building with each beat of his heart. If he could, he would get over to the window and throw himself out. After getting over the fear of pulling that trigger... and knowing it would blow his brains out... he no longer had even the slightest fear of death. He had faced it and had gotten past all the uncertainties of the unknown that usually keep people from killing themselves.

As he lay there, the line, "Death, where is thy sting?" kept repeating itself in his mind. Aaron couldn't remember its source but it accurately summed up his feelings. Pulling that trigger reminded him of how he used to fear the high dive at the community pool back in Newton, Iowa. After years of being terrified of it, one day he unceremoniously climbed up the long metal ladder, walked to the end of the abrasive metal board, and before he lost his nerve, jumped off. In the water, he looked up at the diving board and laughed at how he had anguished, for so many summers, over what proved to be an insignificant experience. Once you do it... it's nothing. Once you have the guts to pull the trigger, you've been to the edge... and jumped. It was really no big deal.

It all seemed so clear to him, now. Here he was... alive... with excruciating pain pulsating throughout his head and neck. What is better, he thought, this, or nothing? Pain or no pain? All these people had worked hours… at great expense… to keep him in a world where he no longer wanted to be. He had given life its chance. Thirty-eight complete trips around the sun was enough. He had used up all the sayings and mini-philosophies that keep people going – things have got to turn around sometime… when the going gets tough, the tough get going… God only burdens those who have the shoulders to bear it… God works in mysterious ways.

Aaron had decided that, for whatever reason, there are lives that simply should not have come into being… as though someone had simply screwed up, and, by accident, allowed certain people to have life who should not have had it. Of course, he realized, lots of people have less-than-perfect lives… but most of them seem to have at least a few things going for them that make living worthwhile… kids, someone who cares about them, a job that provides a sense of self-worth… something.

Aaron Tyger hadn't started out in life with this forlorn view. He was, in fact, a very happy little boy. Up until age eleven, life couldn't have been better. His dad worked for the local granary… operating a chaffing machine… and his mother was a housewife. Aaron was an only child… and the perennial apple of his parents' eyes.

Newton was a small, farming town of about ten thousand. The people were very conservative… but that was good. They had solid families, and good and bad were very clearly defined. A divorce was still a scandal in Newton… a window, broken by a boy's baseball, was town knowledge by day's end. Newton, Aaron always thought, could have served well as a setting for a Mark Twain story. Baseball and basketball were the paramount interests of the town's boys. If they weren't playing one of the two games, they were hanging out at the Mobil station on Washington Street or, in summer, swimming at the town pool. Aaron was never an outstanding athlete, but was able to get by without embarrassment. He had lots of friends… and life had a perpetually warm feel to it. He belonged. His dad was good to him and his mother loved him without limitation, and his family, having been there for four generations, was accepted and respected by the townsfolk.

Aaron had been raised to be an honest and truthful boy... and he was. He had, literally, never told a lie to anyone throughout his entire childhood. He was taught to be polite and considerate to everyone... even to the three black families who lived in the small, run-down houses at the edge of town. He played ball with Clyde and Billy Johnson who hailed from there. Of course, he wouldn't have thought of asking them home to dinner. That was just the way things were, his parents would tell him. The Johnson's were just as good of folks as they were but, they would explain, they just didn't house-visit with them, that's all.

In every person's life, there are moments when intersections are encountered and decisions must be made... actions taken, or words spoken, that change the course of the journey for all time. Such was the case in Aaron Tyger's eleventh year of life.

By the time he was eleven, Aaron sensed that something wasn't quite right with him. Later in his life he would hear other gay men proclaim that they knew they were that way from the time they were very small children. Aaron didn't feel that way. When he was a small boy, he loved the boys he ran around with... but they loved him, too. None of them ever really said they loved one another, but they all knew that they did. They felt it. In the summer, they would spend the entire day together... from early morning to late at night... playing games, telling stories, doing mischief, scaring girls, lying on the grass, trying to find elephants in the passing clouds. They were inseparable. In school, they were in the same classroom... sharing a common fear of Miss Shockey's wrath, chasing girls at recess when they weren't showing off for them, copying from one another's test paper, covering for each other when they were in trouble. They would often walk down the street with their arms around each other's shoulders, giggling and skipping. Young boys of such tender years... loving one another... was as normal as green grass. For the rest of his life, Aaron would never love anyone as much as he did his boyhood friends during those innocent years.

By age eleven, though, Aaron sensed that his friends were moving on while he stayed behind. They began to talk about girls in a different way than they ever had in the past. Before, they would make fun of them and talk about how annoying they were... how boys were so much better at everything... and truly wonder what actual purpose girls really served in life. The only function they could garner was that they were easily annoyed by boys... which was grand fun. Now, his friends were meeting at their hideout in the woods to study pictures of naked women, clandestinely removed from the lower drawers of their fathers' dressers... usually tucked in the back right-hand corner, beneath the underwear. Howie Miller seemed to always discover some tantalizing cache of his father's, and the boys, except for Aaron, eagerly anticipated his arrival.

Aaron simply didn't get it. He didn't feel any differently about girls, now, than he ever had... and he still felt the same about the boys with whom he had grown up. He still loved them. He had noticed of late, however, that when he'd put his arm around their shoulders, they would give him a new and strange look... screwing up their mouths in an expression of disdain at his continuance of this tacitly terminated childhood practice. Their coldness was very upsetting to Aaron. He loved his friends and he still wanted to touch them as he had since they were toddlers.

One Saturday afternoon in July, Howie rounded up all the boys in the neighborhood and led them to the second floor of his garage that his family used for storage. From behind a large cardboard box, he proudly pulled out a whole stack of naked women magazines. He had found them, he said, in old man Winter's trash, that very morning. Their juvenile sexuality was encouraged by the sweltering heat of the small, slanted roof enclosure, heated by the radiant warmth from the tar paper roof and the brilliant beams of sunlight, streaming in through the window that faced the alley behind the garage, cutting sharp, white shafts into the dusty air.

Howie told all of them to sit in a circle and he'd show them something. He distributed a magazine to each of them and told them to open it to a really good picture. He said that Timmy

Williams, a boy in the eighth grade, had shown him something... said it was called a "circle jerk." Howie stood up and pulled down his pants and underwear to his knees then sat back down. He told the other five boys to do the same. They all looked with uncertainty at one another. In attempting to overcome their obvious reticence to participate, Howie prodded them. "C'mon... you'll really like this." Finally "Red" McConnell stood up and started to slowly unzip his pants. The rest, except for Aaron, eventually acceded to Howie's instructions. Save Aaron, they were now all sitting with their pants down to their knees and their bare butts spread on the warm, splintery floor boards. Aaron continued to resist, always having been very modest about his body... particularly his privates. Not satisfied with having a dissenter among their lot, they all began goading Aaron to follow suit, and reluctantly, he gave in.

Howie took his left hand and encircled his penis and told the other boys to do the same. As before, after some hesitation, they did... Aaron being, again, the last to conform. Howie told them to watch what he was doing. In his right hand he held his naked woman magazine and while looking at it, his left hand began to make a sliding motion... toward the head of his penis then back toward the base of the shaft. Each of the boys met with varying degrees of success with this odd procedure. Ricky Waters didn't get the idea at all. He was sliding his hand along his penis with too little grip, allowing it to slip off the end. Howie corrected him, telling him to hold on harder. Soon, all of them were masturbating with acceptable proficiency ... given their novice status.

All the boys, but Aaron, were staring at their pictures. He was otherwise entranced, looking at the enlarged, stiff penises, around the circle... feeling a strange longing he had never before experienced. Tommy Miller was the first to ejaculate. Except for Howie, none of the other boys had ever seen this before. They looked on in wonderment and fear at the creamy geyser... wondering if Tommy had hurt himself with all that pus – or whatever it was – coming from the end of his penis. Frightened, Tommy's eyes got big, and he looked at Howie with his face contorted as if he were going to cry. Howie laughed at him and told him that that was supposed to happen... said he had done it lots of times – despite the fact it was only his second time. Tommy looked immediately relieved. Red spurted next, followed by Howie. The rest didn't make it. Howie, Red, and Tommy all started talking about how good it felt. The other boys listened in awe and envy.

Lying in bed that night, Aaron reviewed the garage scene in his mind. His focus was on the enlarged penises. Visualizing them, he felt his own grow stiff. He began to stroke it as Howie had instructed, and as he did, the images of the penises distorted in both size and color. His mind displayed a scene of him reaching out and touching them. His passion grew... his breathing became erratic. Finally he erupted and hot fluid gushed out of him and onto the sheets, soaking them. He panicked... fearing his mother would find the mess in his bed the next morning. He fretted most of the night over the imminent discovery of his nighttime activity... terrified as to what his mother might do to him. Finally... sleep catching him in a momentary lapse of vigilance... he was temporarily spared his torment. When Aaron awoke in the morning, he immediately ran his hands over the sheet around him. To his amazement, everything was completely dry. He jumped out of bed and pulled back the top sheet. Try as he may, to his utter disbelief, he could find absolutely no evidence of the previous night's watery explosion.

After lunch, Tommy Miller came by to walk with Aaron to the swimming pool. On the way, Aaron – being the honest boy he was raised to be – told Tommy about his experience the night before. He told him everything... even the part about his imagining that he was touching the other boys' penises. Tommy didn't respond... just glanced at Aaron sideways, his eyes narrowing, his lips pursed. At the pool, Tommy pulled the other boys aside and told them Aaron's story. By the end of the day... everybody had been told that Aaron Tyger was a "queer." None of his friends would sit with him or play with him or even talk to him. That was the first day of the hell that would dominate the rest of Aaron Tyger's life... right up to the moment he put the .45-caliber revolver into his mouth and pulled the trigger.

From that moment at the Newton Municipal pool, forward, Aaron Tyger's life was never again the same. The warmth and love and belonging he had felt, constantly, from his earliest recollections in life, had, on that sunny afternoon, entirely vanished... as though it had all been a dream. He walked home from the pool by himself that day, sobbing, looking down at the sidewalk, his hands in his pockets. He really didn't understand what had happened.

Growing up, Aaron had always been sheltered from life's problems. He was, consequently, overtly naive and trusting... believing everything his parents told him. They had told him to always tell the truth... even when it hurts. That's what good, honest, little boys should do, they said. So he did... and that's what he had done with Tommy Miller. He told the truth... and now nobody liked him. He truly had no idea why. Aaron, in fact, had no idea as to what a "queer" was.

Aaron had always loved the boys he grew up with. His mother and dad had told him that love was the most important thing in life. Everybody hated him now. What had he done? He told Tommy the truth... that's what good people do. He loved his friends... that was good, too. Aaron had never before, in his entire life, felt unloved. Its sudden absence hurt him terribly. It hurt his heart. Even though it was a hot, July day, Aaron felt cold. The way he felt was how he had always imagined the lost dogs must feel that he'd sometimes see walking along the side of the highway into Newton... scared, cold, alone, unloved... their heads down and tails between their legs, their eyes darting about in fear of every passerby.

When Aaron got home from the pool, he ran to his mother, buried his face in her bosom and wept harder than she had ever seen him cry. Miriam Tyger was, naturally, quite alarmed. He was always such a happy boy... always smiling... always loving. She stroked his head and held him tight. When his tears finally stopped and his body went limp, Mrs. Tyger led Aaron, gasping in irregular breaths, to one of the chrome and red vinyl kitchen chairs. Although he was eleven, Aaron was small and slight of build, so he still didn't look too big when Mrs. Tyger gently pulled him onto her lap. He laid the left side of his head against her chest, just below her neck. Miraim waited until Aaron had calmed down, then she gently pushed his body several inches from hers, putting her left hand on his hip and her right hand on his cheek. Aaron continued to look down. Softly, Aaron's mother crooked one finger under his chin and slowly lifted his head. His eyes continued to look down. She spoke to him, tenderly.

"What is it, sweetheart? Tell Momma what happened."

Finally, Aaron looked into her eyes. As he did, Miriam's heart ached... his appearance being, still, so similar to what it had been as an infant... innocent, soulful, hurt... seeking out love... his lower lip protruding. She could barely restrain herself from sweeping him up in her arms and carrying him around the room like a baby. He spoke in his small, still childlike, voice.

"Everybody hates me, Momma."

Mrs. Tyger smiled slightly, relieved to discover that it was apparently just one of those first-of-many-to-come minor crises of a preadolescent.

"Oh now, Aaron... your friends don't hate you. What happened... did you have an argument with one of them?"

"No."

"Well then, c'mon sweetie, tell Momma what happened."

Aaron proceeded to tell his mother exactly what had happened... the whole story... the circle jerk, the magazines, the eruptions of the three successful boys, and finally, his dream of penises and his eruption into the sheets the night before. He went on to tell her about the situation with Tommy Miller and the swimming pool and how they had all called him a "queer." As he spoke he felt his mother's body stiffen and back away from him. Her face conveyed unmistakable disapproval of what she was hearing. She continued to look at him... her eyes showing she was thinking about what and how to say something that was on her mind. When she finally spoke, her voice had a cold hardness that Aaron had never heard in it before. It frightened him.

"I'm not happy with you Aaron. We're a religious family. It's bad enough that you and those boys were abusing your bodies and looking at sinful pictures, but what you were thinking about last night... about other boys... is very bad... very bad, Aaron. God meant for boys to love girls... it's a very bad sin for boys to even think about doing anything with other boys. I don't want you ever to even think about such a thing again. Do you hear me, Aaron?"

"Yes Momma... but... but... don't you love me anymore, Momma?"

"Yes, I love you Aaron, but that doesn't have anything to do with it. We follow God's law in this family. God punishes people who don't follow his law. I want you to be a good boy Aaron. You want God to love you don't you?"

"Yes Momma."

"Well then... you do what you're supposed to do. I don't want you looking at those sinful pictures ever again. You can like girls... but looking at pictures like that is different. Looking at pictures like that is a sin Aaron. And don't you ever think about other boys that way, again... or touch yourself like that, again. That's awful Aaron. You're a very bad boy to do that."

From that day on, Aaron Tyger never again felt the same about himself or his mother. Before that day, Aaron had always felt good about himself... felt he was a good boy. His mother and father had always told him he was. He always felt his friends loved him. Beginning with the swimming pool experience that day, he never felt that way again.

After his conversation with his mother, Aaron was very confused. His parents had always told him to tell the truth. They said that was always the thing to do... no matter what. Always tell the truth. He had... both to his mother and to Tommy Miller. Because he had done what he had been told to do, none of his friends liked him anymore and his mother told him he was bad and was cold to him for the first time in his life. Aaron had learned a new, important, life lesson... telling the truth was stupid... it could destroy your life. It did his.

Aaron was also very confused about God. In Aaron's mind... right up to the moment that his mother told him that God thought he was bad... he had felt that God loved him and always would... no matter what. That's what his mother and dad and Reverend Victor had always told him. He remembered... they said God's love was everlasting. Now, because he had thought about boys' penises, God didn't love him anymore. Aaron didn't understand that. It was an awful feeling to know God thought you were bad. He couldn't even look at himself in the mirror... not wanting to see the awful face of a sinner. He figured, now that he was a sinner, he must look different... and that other people would be able to see the sin in his face, too. In Sunday school, when they talked about sinners, he had always pictured awful-looking people... ugly and scary. Now, he felt that that's the way he must look.

The most painfully confusing thing about the pool experience, to Aaron, was his total inability to understand that just because he loved his friends, they hated him... and had called him names. They kept calling him a "queer" at the pool. He didn't know what that meant, but since they said it in such a hateful way, he figured it must be something really bad. He had no one to ask about the word. He knew he couldn't talk to his mother about it and he didn't have any friends left to ask. Aaron just couldn't understand how loving other people could be bad. He had been taught to be loving to everybody... and he was... even to Eddy Willis, the kid who everybody else hated and made fun of. While everyone else would tease Eddy because he had funny ears that stuck out, and because he was kind of stupid... Aaron would always take his part and play with him when no one else would. Even on Valentine's Day, when no one else would put a Valentine in Eddy's box in school, Aaron always did. Eddy would always give him a big smile from all the way across the room. And when you love people you want to touch them. His friends looked at naked women and wanted to touch them... why was it bad that he felt the same way about naked boys?

Every day, until the day Aaron left Newton at age seventeen, he was tormented by all of the kids in town... and sometimes by certain adults as well. The kids in school would write words like "faggot" and "fairy" on his locker. In the locker room they would snap his bare bottom with their towels and call him names. Once, during his sophomore year in high school, when he was taking a shower, a group of boys surrounded him and pissed on his legs. Aaron did not have a single friend during the entire six years he remained in Newton following the pool incident. He was utterly alone. For fear of being considered "queer" by mere association, no fellow high school student dared even talk to him.

Following the conversation between Aaron and his mother on that July day, she never brought up the topic, again. Also, after that day, Aaron, never again, felt the same way about his mother or father. It was as though a cold wind had frozen their previous warmth into perpetual winter. Aaron could sense that his father was embarrassed when they were out in public together. Newton was a small town and Randy Tyger knew what everyone said about his son. Once, about a week after his mother talked to him in July, Aaron's dad asked him about it, saying that his mother had mentioned it, but he wanted to know for himself. He said he wanted to know if Aaron really felt that way about boys... that he wanted to touch them like that. Aaron anguished over his answer. Telling the truth had proven to be a very bad thing for him to do. Despite the obvious response he would get from his father, old habits die hard. He answered, "Yes." As anticipated, Aaron's father looked at him with great disappointment, shook his head, and walked away. He never brought it up, again... nor did he feel the same way about his only son, ever again.

During the spring of his junior year of high school, Aaron decided he could no longer bear his life in Newton. He could not abide the thought of, yet, another year of high school... trapped in that lonely, friendless hell. He knew, by now, what a "queer" was. He checked out several books from the Newton Public Library on human sexuality and had read all about it. He had concluded, according to the definition of a homosexual, he definitely was one. He may go to hell, as his mother warned, but he couldn't help his feelings. He loved males. He loved to look at them... he longed to touch them. While he knew that he felt this way, he also hated the fact that he felt this way. He hated himself. He was, in his estimation, a sickening pervert. His self-loathing reached the point that when he would get an erection in bed, then masturbate while thinking about naked boys, he would, afterwards, run to the bathroom to vomit.

In his seventeenth year, the first serious thoughts of taking his own life entered Aaron's mind. One of the reasons he didn't act on it was that he still believed in God and Satan... heaven and hell. He was afraid that if he killed himself... being the disgusting pervert that he was... he just might go to hell. He could still vividly recall the horrific pictures of hell, assiduously burned into the impressionable minds of the Newton youth by the dedicated teachers of the First Baptist Church Sunday School. He recalled the description of the flames and the eternally burning skin and remembered being told of the screams of pain and the gnashing of teeth. He was never completely sure exactly how someone gnashed his teeth... but he was sure it made a very unpleasant sound.

According to a particular issue of *Newsweek* that Aaron read in the school library during the first half of his junior year of high school, there were more homosexuals in San Francisco than anywhere else in the United States. Although he looked upon all queers as loathsome deviates, he figured that misery loves company. At least in San Francisco, he wouldn't be the only queer in town. His mind made up, as soon as school let out in June, at the end of his junior year, Aaron packed a few things in his green canvas gym bag, walked out to Route 33, and stuck out his thumb... heading west to San Francisco. He didn't tell anyone he was leaving... not even his mother. He simply left her a note saying that he had to go... and not to worry about him.

The first thing Aaron discovered about San Francisco was that, despite being in California in June, it was cold... cold all the time. On the Oakland side of the bridge it was almost ninety degrees. By the time he had crossed the bridge into San Francisco, it was about sixty-eight degrees and clearly sweater weather. On the second day he was there, he located a small, one-room apartment about a block from Market Street. He had, when he arrived in San Francisco, his life savings of five hundred thirty-two dollars in his pocket... saved over the years of working odd jobs in Newton.

Three days after arriving, Aaron found a job... bussing tables in an upper crust restaurant in the North Beach section of the city. It only paid minimum wage, but it was a job. Aaron quickly discovered what was meant by the term "openly gay" in the *Newsweek* article. On his very first day on the job at the restaurant, a waiter – introducing himself as "Bobby" – asked Aaron his name, where he was from and, as though he were asking his shoe size, if he was gay. Aaron was dumbfounded by the blatant inquiry. Without thinking, Aaron instinctively said, "No." He wasn't sure why he answered that way... he supposed he just didn't have enough time to think about it. He had, after all, spent every day of his life since he was eleven, trying to be invisible and hating himself for being a homosexual. To openly admit to a total stranger that he was gay was just too much, too fast... so he lied. His life experience had, long ago, extinguished his belief in the virtue of truth-telling.

Aaron found that homosexuals were, literally, everywhere in San Francisco and he saw things he could never have imagined back in Iowa. It seemed that the gay men were considerably more noticeable than the lesbians. Maybe, he thought, the lesbians just weren't as open about their homosexuality... or maybe there just weren't as many of them... he wasn't sure. One thing for sure, though, he was absolutely shocked the first time he saw two men walking down the street, hand in hand. The first time he saw two men kiss... right on the mouth... right on Market Street... he thought he was going to faint. He just couldn't believe his eyes. Aaron had imagined himself doing these same things, many times, over the past years, but to actually see it was shocking... too shocking to be erotic.

Once, after about two weeks in San Francisco, as he was passing a small park just off of Market Street, he was so astonished that he stopped and stared, too mesmerized by what he saw, to be aware of how *he* must have looked to passersby – staring, openmouthed at the sight. The sun was going down and the park lights had just come on. Two men were standing under one of the park lights with their backs against the light pole. Both had their pants down around their knees. In front of each man was another man, down on his knees. The men on their knees had the penises of the standing men in their mouths. The kneeling men also had one of their hands around the base of the standing men's penises. Their heads were going forward and backward – toward, then away – from the standing men, while the hand that grasped their penises was making a twisting sort of motion. Aaron's eleventh-year fantasy flooded back to him. They were doing exactly what he felt he wanted to do just before he ejaculated that first night. The scene seemed so extraordinary to him that it took on a surrealistic air. The four were going about their business... right out there in public... as nonchalant as they could be, with people walking right by them. As he watched, Aaron could feel himself swelling... the crotch of his pants stretching tight from his erection. He felt the way his boyhood friends must have, he thought, when they looked at the naked women pictures. He suddenly felt like masturbating right there as he stood on the sidewalk. He hurried back to his room and did.

The next day at work, he approached Bobby and admitted to him that he was gay... and also admitted that he was a virgin. The admission of virginity appeared to visibly excite Bobby. He suggested to Aaron that, after work, they do something together. They ended up going to a restaurant in Chinatown. Aaron was quite tense – this being his first real "date" – and was able to force only a few bites of his sweet-and-sour chicken into his quivering stomach. Bobby, Aaron found out, was twenty-seven... ten years older than he was. Aaron, being somewhat slight in build and only five-foot-seven, looked even younger than his seventeen years.

THE DISCIPLES

What Bobby didn't tell Aaron was that he was, sexually, very experienced, and quite a hustler of young boys. Aaron, being the hick from Iowa knew no better. To Aaron, Bobby seemed to be a very nice and considerate young man. By the end of the evening, Aaron had a vastly different opinion of him.

After the meal, Bobby persuaded Aaron to come home with him... saying that he had some great music he wanted him to listen to. Aaron, feeling he finally found a friend, nervously accepted the invitation, being flattered that someone as sophisticated and good-looking as Bobby would take an interest in him. Once inside the apartment, Aaron's happiness quickly turned to horror. Bobby told Aaron to have a seat, saying he'd be right back... then disappeared into his bedroom. He returned a few minutes later, totally naked, with a large erection protruding from his crotch. He walked straight to Aaron... still seated on the couch... and pushed his penis toward Aaron's mouth. Aaron turned his head and Bobby's penis collided with Aaron's cheek. It had all seemed so much more erotic to Aaron in his imagination... and the real thing was grotesque and frightening. It was all too much, too fast for the virgin boy from Iowa. Aaron started to get up from the couch but Bobby grabbed him by the hair and pulled him back down. Bobby screamed at Aaron to open his mouth. Aaron, too frightened to know what to do, obeyed. Aaron felt Bobby's huge penis push into his mouth... all the way to the back of his throat, blocking his air supply. Aaron panicked, feeling he was going to suffocate. He tried to move his head but Bobby pulled even harder on his hair. Aaron found that when Bobby would pull his penis slightly outward, he could take a quick breath before Bobby violently thrust himself into the back of his throat, again. Focusing on the task of trying to breathe during these very brief intervals, Aaron had no idea as to how long the rape of his mouth went on.

At some point, Aaron was startled by a huge gush of hot fluid shooting into the back of his throat. He started to gag and choke... and tried to push Bobby's hips away from his face. Instead, Bobby pushed his penis even further into Aaron's throat. Somehow, Aaron was able to swallow the thick liquid to avoid choking. Moments later, Bobby fell onto the couch beside Aaron...

his body limp, his eyes closed. Aaron glanced at Bobby... then at the door. He got to his feet and ran across the living room to the door... grabbed the knob, turned it and pulled. The door was key-locked with a dead bolt... and the key was gone.

Aaron turned his head... looking back at Bobby. He was still lying on the couch. The door of the bedroom suddenly swung open. A large, heavy man with a beard stood in the opening, nearly filling the space with his enormous body. He walked toward Aaron. Terrified, Aaron put his back to the door. He wanted to scream but couldn't push any noise from his throat. The man had an excited look on his face. He appeared to be several years older than Bobby. He spoke to Aaron in a threatening tone of voice.

"C'mon with me."

As he spoke he motioned to Aaron with his right hand.

Aaron stood rigidly... he could feel himself shaking. The man spoke again.

"You don't want me to get rough with you... do you?"

Aaron managed to slowly shake his head, once to the left, once to the right.

The man grabbed Aaron roughly by the hand and led him into the bedroom. He closed the door behind them... then told Aaron to take off his clothes. Aaron slowly acquiesced. The man then told him to lie down on the bed. Aaron did... on his back. Seeing this, the man, with a look of disgust on his face, put a hand under Aaron's right shoulder and right leg, and flipped Aaron's slight body onto his stomach, turning him as easily as if he were a rag doll. Aaron could feel the terrible strength of the bearded man's grip. With a stern voice he commanded Aaron to stay where he was. Aaron heard the bathroom medicine cabinet open then close. A few moments later he felt the same, large, strong fingers at his rectum... rubbing something that felt very greasy on him. He then felt a well-lubricated finger intrude his anus. Apparently finished with his preparations, the man climbed on top of Aaron. He could feel the large man's erection bumping into his legs and buttocks as he mounted him. Suddenly, Aaron experienced the sensation that his entire lower intestinal tract was being violently torn apart. Spurred on by this inconceivable, tearing pain, Aaron at last found his voice and screamed.

Aaron's next recollection was a feeling that something was moving upwards, along both his legs. He opened his eyes to see Bobby and his friend pulling his pants on him. They looked at him, noticing he was coming to. Aaron was lying on the bed on his back with his pants halfway up with no shirt on. Bobby spoke to him in a tone that dripped with revulsion.

"Get dressed and get out."

Having said this, Bobby and his friend both walked out of the bedroom. Aaron got quickly dressed and walked, timidly, into the living room, where the two men were sitting. Bobby was on the couch... his friend in a nearby chair, drinking a bottle of beer. Aaron walked cautiously by them. Just as he was passing Bobby, Bobby stuck out his leg and stopped him. He hissed out a threat.

"Keep your mouth shut about this, chicken-little."

Aaron nodded slightly. Bobby dropped his leg. Aaron tried the door and found it was unlocked this time. He opened it, stepped out into the hallway, and closed the door quietly behind him. Aaron walked down the long hall, through the double doors to the landing that led to the stairs... and started down the three flights of steps to the street below. He was shaking so violently, he could barely walk. On the way down the stairs he began to feel wetness in the back of his underwear. On the second floor landing he stopped. After looking up and down the stairs to see if anyone was coming, he quickly unzipped his pants and pulled them down to see why he felt so wet. As soon as he saw the blood, soaking the entire back and bottom of his underwear, his knees gave out. On his hands and knees, he vomited.

After throwing up the remains of his few bites of sweet-and-sour chicken, Aaron began to convulse in dry heaves. With great effort, Aaron grabbed the stair rail and pulled himself up onto his feet. He pulled up his pants, zippered them, and fastened the catch. Wiping the remains of vomit from his mouth with the back of his hand, he continued down the remaining stairs and out into the cold, foggy San Francisco night. After two hours of walking, he somehow made it back to his room. His whole rectal area was, by then, screaming with pain. He took some aspirin… a whole handful of them. It helped a little and at dawn, exhausted, he fell asleep.

A profound, tearing pain awakened Aaron at about two in the afternoon. He felt wet again. He reached his hand down and felt the sheets. They were drenched. He sat up and apprehensively lowered his eyes. His lower body was surrounded by a large, fresh blood stain. Aaron gently swung his legs over the edge of the bed and slowly lowered his feet to the floor. He could feel that his buttocks and back of his legs were soaked. As he began raising his body to a standing position, he felt an unbelievably sharp, tearing pain in his rectal area. One excruciating step at a time, he slowly made his way to his dresser on the far side of the room. Each step created the nauseating sensation that he was tearing his skin.

Aaron had a small, square, hand mirror that he used to trim the back of his hair. He picked it up from the dresser and took a few deep breaths. His intention was to bend over and examine his rectum. He began to do it three times… each time stopping… afraid of what he might see. Finally, during a fleeting moment of courage, he rapidly bent over and looked between his legs into the mirror.

Aaron's rectum was torn… about two inches above and below his anus. The tear was fresh, with blood still seeping from it. He was instantly overtaken with a wave of nausea and light-headedness… requiring him to grab the top of the dresser to keep from collapsing onto the floor. Aaron slowly and methodically packed several of his clean, white socks inside of a pair of clean underwear and pulled them on. With extreme difficulty, he finished dressing, and through extraordinary efforts, he somehow made his way down the stairs, out the front door of his apartment building, and over to the nearby bus stop... feeling more and more light-headed as he walked.

After twenty minutes of waiting, the bus finally arrived. He knew that this bus passed the hospital, since it was the one he took to work everyday. He got off at the hospital stop and walked into the emergency room. For insurance purposes, he gave his father's name, address, and employer. It must have checked out, since they passed him on to the next square in the process. Aaron was admitted by the emergency room physician and taken immediately into surgery.

After he had recovered from the anesthesia, the surgeon told him that there was extensive damage both internally and externally to his rectal area... mentioning that there was sperm throughout his lower anal cavity and intestine. He said he was putting him on a broad course of antibiotics to prevent infection. Aaron was released after three days. His life had reached another significant turn in the road.

CHAPTER FIFTEEN

As the only queer in Newton, Iowa – at least to his knowledge – Aaron had come to San Francisco to escape his loneliness. Even though he felt he, and all other queers in the world, were an affront to common decency, he, at least, didn't want to be the only freak in town. In San Francisco, he had, after a short time, begun to feel that, perhaps, his eccentric sexual passions weren't quite as sick as he had been conditioned to believe. He began to feel that maybe, he was entitled to sexual love just like any other person. In a matter of an hour or so, however, Bobby and his bearded accomplice had dashed his fresh hope for happiness, for all time. After being raped in both his mouth and rectum, Aaron would never again think of a man's penis – or body – without fear and revulsion. He was, once again, all alone in the world... and consumed with an even greater sense of self-loathing.

Aaron spent the next twenty years of his life, desperately searching for a reason to live. He also spent those years, totally alone. He had no natural desire to be with a woman... and after San Francisco, even less to be with a man. The experience in Bobby's apartment left him with a sense of shame he could never put behind him. Even with those few people who had, over the years, tried to befriend him, Aaron was too ashamed to let them get close to him. For a time, he turned to religion, searching for a god who was more understanding and compassionate than the one Aaron's parents had told him about. Trying Christianity, and hoping to discover a different divinity than they worshiped in Newton, Aaron strived with all his will to accept Jesus and to open his heart to the Holy Spirit. Despite a few episodes of self-induced euphoria that were short-lived, he wasn't able to find any real happiness or hope or love in the Christian life. The preacher exclaimed that Jesus loved him. Maybe he did... but Aaron couldn't feel it.

Aaron read about Buddhism, Judaism, Islam, Hinduism, Confucianism. He read philosophy books. But neither religion, nor philosophy, could lift the oppressive sadness that was crushing his fragile spirit. Despite his depressing life... moving frequently from one city to the next... working minimum wage jobs... living in small, dirty, one-room hovels, Aaron still retained a small, warm – but faint – glow... somewhere deep inside himself. Maybe it was, he thought, just a part of his brain that could still recall the wonderful radiance of life before Tommy Miller and the pool incident. Whatever it was, that one remaining faint, flickering candle inside him, was all that kept him going for those many years.

On his thirty-seventh birthday, as his windup alarm clock awakened him with its cacophonous clamor, Aaron knew something was terribly wrong. He didn't feel sick. He sat up and looked around the room. The cracked, water-stained walls looked just as distasteful as they had the night before, but on this morning, the walls, the room, the view outside his window was not only exceedingly ugly, but wholly unacceptable. As he sat there, pondering this vague sense of loss, he knew that something was fundamentally different that morning. When his mind finally sorted out the cause of the change, the revelation went through him like an arrow through his heart. During the night, while he slept, Aaron discovered that a foul wind had somehow made its way to the innermost sanctum of his being, and had blown out his small, life-sustaining flame. With the extinguishment of this – the sole, nourishing light upon which his spirit fed – he found himself in total darkness. There was now nothing left inside him to cast any flicker of hope or gladness upon his dark and ugly life.

During that entire day, as he swept the halls of Saint Theresa's Elementary School in East Chicago, he tried, in vain, to shake the weight of the dense blackness that engulfed his soul. Hoping it might be the cold and gray November weather that had him in its grip, he quit his job that very day and got on a bus to Corpus Christi, Texas... to the sun and warmth. But Aaron quickly discovered that the warmth and light of Texas, bathed only his skin, and couldn't penetrate into the cold, forbidding depths of his being.

Aaron found a job cleaning off the decks of fishing boats, after they docked for the evening. Two months later, the darkness had still not lifted. He had lost all desire to go on. Aaron came to understand that, when a person loses all hope in life, everything becomes a great effort, since there is no longer any motivation to do anything. Food loses its taste and sleep becomes impossible. Eventually, the only motivation he found he had was to find a way to see to it that he no longer had to face another day of life.

On his way to the gun shop, Aaron felt, for the first time in many years, a true sense of purpose. He had never, in his life, had a gun in his hand. His dad was against guns, and one of the few men in Newton who didn't own one. Aaron asked the man behind the counter what kind of gun he would recommend for protection. Aaron said he wanted something that would kill somebody in one shot. The guy, Mel – according to his name tag – handed him a forty-five caliber semiautomatic pistol, saying it would "… stop a fuckin elephant with an attitude." Aaron asked him to show him how it worked… admitting to Mel he knew absolutely nothing about guns. Mel told the other salesman to watch the counter… he was going back to the range for a few minutes. He motioned for Aaron to follow. Mel showed Aaron how to load the clip with bullets and how to put it into the stock of the pistol. After showing Aaron a few basic features of the gun, he aimed and fired the gun at the range target… demonstrating to Aaron the proper way to hold the pistol and squeeze the trigger. Mel then handed the forty-five to Aaron and positioned his hands into the proper configuration to grip the weapon. The first time Aaron pulled the trigger, the gun reared up and back so violently that it nearly kicked out of his hands. By the time Aaron had gone through several clips, however, he was feeling fairly confident with the pistol. Aaron bought the gun, along with three boxes of ammunition. He really didn't need so many rounds, but Mel had been so nice to him, he wanted to make the sale worth his while.

Back in his room, Aaron took the boxes containing the pistol and ammunition out of the plastic bag, and placed them on the dresser. He then lay down on the bed and stared up at the ceiling… studying the patterns made by a mosaic of cracks, hanging plaster, and water spots. His eyes finally wandered back to the boxes. Suddenly, the thought of actually loading the gun and using it on himself sent an electric tingle of adrenaline flushing through his body, producing sensations of both fear and excitement. It struck him as bizarre that the first real feeling he had about anything, in months, had been generated by the thought of blowing his own brains out.

After taking several deep breaths through his nostrils and blowing each loudly from his mouth, Aaron sat up in the bed and placed his stocking feet on the splintered floor. He put one hand on each thigh and deeply inhaled and exhaled again... this time, deep-breathing through his mouth. He locked his glance on the gun box and took more deep breaths, trying to clear his head. Aaron then stood up and, determinedly, took the four steps to his dresser. He picked up the revolver box and one containing ammunition then returned with them to his bed. He sat down on the edge of the bed and placed the boxes to his right. Aaron opened the revolver box and took out the forty-five, then opened the ammunition box and dumped out a dozen or so rounds on the bed. He popped out the clip and filled it... feeling an odd sense of pride for having loaded a gun by himself, for the first time in his life... despite the ultimate purpose of his act.

It was reality time. Was life truly so bad that he could actually put that bluish-black, steel barrel into his mouth and pull the trigger? He didn't know if the gun-in-the-mouth method was actually the way you were really supposed to do this sort of thing, but he had seen it in several movies and guessed it probably was. He breathed deeply again. Maybe, he thought, this might, after all, be a mistake. His life had been nothing but meaningless anguish... but was there, perhaps, still some possibility of hope? He supposed, logically, there was... but hope was a feeling and not a logical inference. Inside, he knew his soul was cold and lifeless. He was, he realized, in a sense, already dead... so what was the difference? He tried to look into the future... searching for any possible scenario to give him reason not to end his life. He saw nothing and he felt nothing.

As bizarre as it may seem, the idea of his own death suddenly began to stir a sense of warmth inside Aaron – a feeling he hadn't experienced in many years. It was a sense of control. He hadn't felt in control of his own life since he was a little boy. Life had been – since age seventeen – a cruel taskmaster to Aaron... driving him from town to town, job to job. Aaron had been running and hiding for his entire adult life. He had run, unceasingly, but had never gotten any closer to anything that had made his life worth living.

Aaron had spoken to his mother only once in the last twenty years... the day after the incident in Bobby's apartment. He had called, collect, from the hospital after the doctor had sewn together what was left of him after the bearded guy's sexual frolic with his rectum. It was immediately obvious to Aaron that his mother was not happy to hear from him. Miriam and Randy Tyger had moved on in their lives since Aaron had departed Newton. After he was gone, they had adjusted to it, rather quickly. Life, without a boy like Aaron, in a small, mid-west town like Newton, Iowa was, frankly, much easier for them. Aaron wasn't accepted by the town, and though the Tygers were pleasant to him while he continued to remain there, their love for him had, over the years, dwindled... then died altogether.

Had someone come to Miriam Tyger, when Aaron was a little boy, and told her that, someday, she would no longer love her little Aaron... her darling... the central meaning of her life, she would have considered that to be absolutely inconceivable. She had discovered with Aaron, however, that everything in life changes... even the way you feel about your children. She was just never able to accept Aaron as a homosexual. Queers were, to both Miriam and Randy Tyger, degenerate human beings, and an abomination to God... even if the particular human being happened to be your own son. When the Tygers discovered that Aaron had run away, they mentally wished him well... but sincerely wished he would stay away.

Aaron had cried, after he hung up the phone that day... and never called home again. Over the years, while he was still in Newton,

Aaron had felt the coldness between his parents and him grow, but he continued to believe that, in their heart of hearts, they still loved him. It was like an icicle through his soul when he came to the realization, during this, his last phone call with his mother, that not even his parents loved him anymore... nor even cared about him, for that matter. He hadn't even told his mother, during their short conversation, that he was in the hospital. Quickly realizing that his mother's love for him had died. . . and that she, clearly, did not want to be on the phone with him, he politely ended his painful attempt at dialogue and said his final good-bye to his mother.

His mother had often talked to him about the loneliness and desolation of being outside "God's flock." Aaron had never really understood what that meant until that moment on the phone. He now knew what it was like to be outside "love's flock." If being outside "God's flock" was as painful, he pitied anyone so abandoned. It was awful... the most awful feeling he had ever had in his life.

As he sat there on the bed, it struck him that, besides his building manager, no one in the entire world knew, nor cared to know, where he was at that moment. His entire adult life had been defined by what he, alone, knew about himself... where he was... what he felt. One thing he knew, for sure... no one would shed a tear if he *did* blow his brains out. He had once read an article about suicide that said the most common suicide was what was called anomic suicide, from the French term, *anomie*, meaning, as he recalled, being entirely alone... without contact or relationships with anyone. Most of the unsuccessful suicides, the article said, were by people trying to get attention, hoping to be discovered before they expire. With Aaron, there was no one's attention to get. The final, explosive discharge of his gun would be like the proverbial falling branch in a forest. In Aaron's world, no one would be there to hear it.

Aaron picked up the gun with his right hand and studied it. He realized that he held in his hand, an instrument that had the power to end all his suffering. Aaron had learned that loneliness was a physical pain that eventually numbed the mind and heart. If no one cares anything about you... what you are doing... if you are sick... if you are unhappy... if you are afraid... eventually you don't care, either. If no one else cares, then why should you? Aaron finally decided that he could pull the trigger by asking himself if he could face another tomorrow... another tomorrow of loneliness... of emptiness... of meaninglessness. He decided he could not. Not waking up to another of his tomorrows would be better... happier... than waking up.

His mind made up, Aaron brought the barrel up to his mouth. He swallowed hard and licked his lips, then opened his mouth wide enough to accommodate the metal cylinder. He inserted the steel barrel, four or five inches into his mouth then closed his lips around it. The metal felt cold and had a taste that made saliva start running into his mouth and out the corners of his lips. The end of the barrel momentarily touched the back of his throat and made him gag, so he pulled it slightly outward. He gripped the thick, gridded, plastic covering on the pistol's handle with his right hand. He then wrapped his left hand around the fingers of his right hand and rested his right thumb on the trigger. His heart began to race. He felt cold sweat beginning to leak from his hands and head. His mind went back to the high dive at the Newton pool... don't think about it... just do it. Do it now... or you never will.

And he did it.

CHAPTER SIXTEEN

Aaron spent two months in the hospital. He had blown away a section of his skull at the lower right side of his head... and his right ear was, other than a small remaining piece of earlobe, completely gone. The surgeon replaced the missing piece of skull with plastic, and had, in a series of operations, grafted pieces of skin from Aaron's leg to help close the gaping wound. An ear, that was inoperative but passable in appearance, was also constructed from various components of his body.

Aaron's injuries, being a result of a suicide attempt, prompted the physician to order a psychiatric workup, and around-the-clock observation. Aaron was placed in a room directly across from the nurses' station, equipped with a video monitor. There was also a large observation window on the interior wall of his room. Privacy was, thus, nonexistent for Aaron. The many precautions were a result of the consulting psychiatrist's opinion that Aaron was a "very determined suicide"... and highly likely to try again in the very near future, if given the opportunity. The doctor recommended an involuntary commitment to a psychiatric facility... suggesting Eastbridge Psychiatric Institute because of its having on its staff, several of the best suicidologists in the business.

At Eastbridge, Aaron was, once again, placed on twenty-four hour monitoring and was administered bountiful dosages of very potent drugs. Under the effect of these drugs, Aaron was literally reduced, emotionally, to a human cipher. Along with the course of drugs, Aaron also underwent a series of shock treatments, as well. After several months of intensive treatment, his attending psychiatrist concluded that very little progress had been made in Aaron's case. Dr. Burner felt, however, that if Aaron were released, he'd be dead by his own hand, within a very short time. Aaron was, in his opinion, one of the most determined suicides he had ever treated. Were they still in psychiatric vogue, he would have seriously considered Aaron a prime candidate for a lobotomy.

Dr. Burner brought in several other consulting psychiatrists to evaluate Aaron. They came to the same conclusion as had he... that Aaron was a most determined suicide. Burner was torn. If he released Aaron, he would, most assuredly, kill himself. The only other course of action was indefinite commitment... to warehouse Aaron for many years... maybe for the rest of his life... forgotten in the bowels of some state mental institution. After talking with the legal staff and, despite his ethical qualms to the contrary, he opted for warehousing. Releasing him – with such a high probability of a successful incident of suicide – could incur, in the opinion of the legals, just too much potential liability for Eastbridge. Aaron was, thus, transferred to the state psychiatric hospital in Mayview – an old and underfunded fossil, constructed in the 1930's – on an indefinite basis. Dr. Burner mailed Aaron's file to the hospital, and promptly put this pathetic case behind him... as one of those dismal failures of his professional career that he just didn't want to, ever again, think about.

Aaron Tyger was, at age thirty-seven, a perpetually drugged, and forgotten, zombie. No one knew him... no one cared about him. Besides the staff who fed, medicated him, and occasionally helped to bathe him, no one in the world knew that Aaron Tyger existed. His parents hadn't heard from him in many years... nor had they wanted to. They suspected he might be dead. The only mention of Aaron's name in Newton was at high school reunions when someone would, from time to time, ask where the "school queer" was these days... usually followed by crude jokes that cruelly suggested his whereabouts.

Aaron was now light-years away from his tender childhood world... from the warm arms of his mother that held and protected him... from the smiles and giggles of those little boys who clasped their arms around his shoulder and glowed with the innocence of youthful friendship and love.

There are those who will say that one needs a reason to live. The mass of flesh and pumping blood, confined indefinitely to the Mayview State Psychiatric Hospital, processing food and cycling through days and nights of waking and medicinally induced sleep, distinguished only by a medication schedule and vacantly recorded numbers on a chart, could well serve as a compelling retort to that proposition.

CHAPTER SEVENTEEN

KATHERINE

The moment Antoinette Deville looked into her newborn daughter's eyes, she knew Katherine was very special. She was her fourth child... her second daughter. Katherine somehow looked familiar to Antoinette... as though they had met in another life. Though most newborns have a milky, bluish cast to their eyes, even the nurses remarked how strikingly green and clear Katherine's were. Even as a newborn, her gaze had an uncanny, knowing quality about it. In checking over her newest arrival – beyond the instinctual toe and finger count – she found herself drawn to Katherine's face. It was, discounting a mother's bias, beautiful... smooth and serene... not wrinkled, red, and puffy like her other children had been. But there was also some indefinable and distinctly unnerving – even unnatural – quality about Katherine. With a sense of guilt, Antoinette would later tell her husband, Emile, that she immediately thought of the demented children in Henry James' *The Turn of the Screw* when she first looked into Katherine's eyes. It was as though she wasn't really looking at a baby at all, but staring through tiny windows, at an adult hiding inside who had, somehow, hitched a ride into life, inside this tiny, corporeal carrier.

Emile told his wife that when he was a young boy in Rheims, he remembered his grandmother telling him about her sister who was also very "special"... that she, like Katherine, from the moment of birth, had an extraordinary, unnerving presence. The story, he said, was one of those peculiar little things of early childhood that, inexplicably, stays with a person throughout his life... despite remembering little else of many more ponderous events. Emile could remember, in great detail, sitting on his grandmother's lap on a particular summer afternoon when his family was visiting his grandparents' farm. His grandfather and grandmother had always spent their summers on a small farm, just outside Paris, that his grandfather, being the oldest son in the family, had inherited. Emile could still distinctly recall the smell of his grandmother's talcum powder and the warm breeze blowing through the window of the kitchen... where everyone always sat to visit.

His grandmother told him, that day, about her sister – Agnes – who, she said, was much too pretty, too smart, and always wanted too much from life. She could, his grandmother said, do anything – and do it well. She danced, she sang, she played the piano... she could tell marvelous stories. She was the center of attention wherever she went. In school, she mastered everything so quickly so as to become such a nuisance to the teachers. Finally, when she had attained the age of ten, their parents were told not to send her to class anymore. She could speak several languages by the time she was eight years old. Emile remembered that his grandmother then grew silent and began staring out the window... stopping in mid-sentence. He still remembered, word for word, what she then said to him. She turned his face toward hers and spoke to her favorite grandchild in a tender – yet pleading – tone.

"My darling child. Don't ask too much of life. Be satisfied with what is put on your plate. Eating too much candy can make you very, very sick."

Emile had no idea, at the time, what his grandmother meant by her soulful admonition. As the years passed, however, he heard more storied bits and pieces of his Great-Aunt Agnes. After she was grown, she had, apparently, traveled the world... China, Africa, South America, United States. She had worked as a school teacher, a newspaper reporter, a nurse, and at a wide assortment of other vocations. She'd also had, according to the stories, a great many lovers – both men and women. One day, Agnes' mother received a letter from a woman in Peru that was, from that day forward, kept as a revered relic in the family Bible. On a boring Sunday afternoon at the farm, when Emile was twelve, he took down the huge and ornately decorated, leather-bound Bible from its place on the living room mantle. It opened, automatically, to the location where the letter had been placed among its pages. The envelope, yellowed and brittle, had, beside the name and address of Emile's great grandmother, a quote written in a different hand than the author of the letter. Above the quote was written the name Maurice Maeterlinck and the words, "Our Eternity." Beneath was written a quote...

> "All our knowledge merely helps us to die a more painful death than the animals that know nothing."

Emile turned the envelope over, lifted the flap and took out the letter. The old, crisp paper crinkled as it unfolded.

My Dear Mrs. DeComte,

I am sorry to be writing this letter. I bring you the sad news of your daughter's death. Agnes was my dear friend and had lived with me for nearly two years. She was most brilliant and beautiful, yet was the saddest person I have ever known in my life. I am assigned here, in Peru, by the Catholic Mission of Buenos Aires, to bring the word of God to the remote villages of the mountain regions. Agnes appeared, one day, at my door, asking if she could stay awhile. She told me little of her past or even of how she had found me. I know of your name and address from a small book she carried with her. She told me she was searching for something but did not know the nature of her quest. I tried to bring her peace through the knowledge and grace of God. She made a sincere effort to accept His peace, but was unable.

Agnes would often go, alone, into the mountain jungle, sometimes staying away for days at a time, taking neither food nor water with her. Her eyes were often deep pools, reflecting her lonely soul. She would sit for hours each day on the stone cliff that juts out over the waterfall known as the Agua de Dios, reading, sketching, or just thinking. Two days ago, when I returned from my daily missionary duties, I found a note on a table, from her, in my small mountain home. I have copied it below for you. I have kept the original for myself, since it was addressed to me. I hope this will not be objectionable to you.

My Dear Sister Margarita,

I have seen and learned all that I can or wish to learn of life. I am, I know, a freak of nature, destined for inescapable unhappiness. Life has simply not met with my expectations. The world and its people, I am sorry to say, bore me to a point of desperation. I say this in truth, not vanity. There simply must be more. I am, by now, convinced that I will not find what I seek in this existence. Though one can never be sure, perhaps I shall find my fulfillment in another world. Perhaps not. But I have given this world its fair chance.

Please do not grieve for me. I am far better off that I am no longer of this world, whether by the time you read this I am elsewhere, or merely nowhere. Either is better than my present circumstance. Being nothing is better than being somebody who is constantly filled with despair.

You are a very good person, my dear friend; the best I have ever known in my life. You tried very hard to bring me peace when you had no obligation to do so. But it was not to be. It was not your fault, nor mine. It was the fault of my cursed nature. I have felt in your presence, your peaceful happiness. You are blessed. If your peace is a gift from your God, he is, indeed, a benevolent deity. I am sorry that, for whatever reason, my nature is such that I could not receive His love.

Well, my dearest friend, on to my next adventure.

Your friend and companion,
Agnes

After reading Agnes' letter, I went immediately to the waterfalls. There I found her clothes and shoes lying on the cliff where, I had mentioned, she often sat. I ran to the nearest village to seek help. The men of the village descended the many miles necessary to reach the foot of the falls. When they returned, nearly ten hours later, they carried with them, Agnes' lifeless body. I must tell you that her face had a look of peace; the first I had ever seen there. Despite her professed absence of faith, I conducted a Christian burial for her, nevertheless, and marked her grave with the Cross of our Lord. She is buried near the crest of the falls, under a lovely tree.

Again, I apologize for being the bearer of such sadness. Would that I had been spared such an obligation. May the Love of God be with you in your sorrow. I shall pray for you and for the soul of our beloved Agnes. May God, at last, bring her the peace for which she so longed.

In God's Love,

Sister Margarita de Cortigon

Over the years, Emile often took out Sister Margarita's letter – understanding more of its message as he matured, and with this came a gradual comprehension of his grandmother's words to him. As he recalled all of this, his wife's description of their infant daughter sent a chill down his spine. He silently prayed to God that this small child be spared Agnes' curse.

A curse and a blessing are often difficult to distinguish and Antoinette and Emile quickly forgot their fears about Katherine. They would soon laugh about these early concerns they had for their daughter when one or the other would remember them in the safety of reminiscence. They soon basked in carefree joy, in celebration of their strikingly beautiful infant daughter. The news of Katherine's uncanny beauty spread through the Deville and Bordeau family networks with impressive speed. Relatives arrived, daily, at the Deville household to bring congratulations, praise, and gifts. They made the trip to Montreal from all across Quebec, Nova Scotia and the Western Plains... with a few relatives even making the voyage from the Old Country to greet this new, wonderful addition to their large family.

Katherine's cradle became like a shrine, and the liturgy was quickly established. Relatives would arrive, exchange greetings, share in a glass of wine, then climb the stairs, in near-reverence, to view the much-touted child. Katherine, lying in her cradle – finely decorated in ribbon, lace, and flowing satin – never failed to delight... as though knowing to perform on cue. She would lock her eyes on each visitor, gurgling and smiling... appearing to study them, more than they her. Antoinette could not help but notice an air of uneasiness that came over many of the visitors who met Katherine's gaze. While she had grown accustomed to Katherine's unsettling countenance, she had not forgotten her first reaction to her and empathized with the relatives' uneasiness. There was really nothing she could think to say to prepare Katherine's visitors for her... so she simply allowed them to experience her uncommon presence for themselves. Often, while viewing the infant, the guests would commence a nervous sort of laughter then, to further relieve the tension, would initiate inane small talk... the delivery, her birth weight, how her siblings felt about the new arrival... all the while, avoiding Katherine's intent gaze.

Although Katherine's childhood was a near-parallel story to Agnes Decomte's, Emile and Antoinette were so overcome by Katherine's beauty and charm that they were made either blind to the similarities or simply denied the obvious. Katherine was speaking full sentences by the time she was a year old. She was reading at age two and singing complete songs that she had heard only once.

Katherine warmed every heart she touched. Love, intelligence, charm, and joy radiated from every fiber of her being. Emile would often refer to her as, "the light of his eyes." And, indeed, she was like a beacon. Upon her entrance, she would immediately make any room seem magically brighter. Katherine just seemed to possess an inner energy that permeated into every corner of any room she occupied.

On Sunday afternoons, when Antoinette and Emile would take their four children to the park, other children and adults, alike, would be invariably drawn, quite unconsciously, to Katherine. She would dance and sing for them in voice and rhythm and with grace and style not altogether unlike that of an accomplished and seasoned performer. She would make polite but inquiring conversation with strangers of any age... but preferred adults.

Although Katherine received constant attention... much more so than her sister and two brothers... her siblings were remarkably absent of jealousy toward her. Katherine had a way of making everyone with whom she came in contact, feel very special... as though each person was her very best friend. Despite being consummately charming, however, there was no trace of insincerity about Katherine. It was apparent that she truly did love people and she truly loved life... and everything about it. She couldn't get enough of it. She never seemed to stop. Katherine would read late into the night, sleep a few hours and then be back at it again. She literally wanted to know everything there was to know. By the time she was eight, she was well beyond her parents' capacity to provide her with adequate answers to her never-ending – and increasingly more complex – inquiries. Her teachers, also, were at their wits' end with her. The Devilles finally decided to employ a tutor from the university to teach Katherine, privately, in addition to her parochial schooling... to help alleviate the pressure that her all-consuming passion for knowledge brought to bear upon everyone with whom she had an association.

As with Agnes before her, Katherine excelled in talent as well as intelligence. In August of her ninth year, Katherine declared to her family that she was going to play the violin. By Christmas, she was able to entertain the family with an impressive repertoire of songs from folk traditional to classical. The following year she mastered the piano, next the flute, then the cello. In her tenth year, she became interested in art. Working with several university art professors, she quickly mastered oil painting, acrylics, pastels, charcoal, pen and ink, then watercolors. She did a portrait of her parents, that year that was, according to her oils instructor, "just short of a masterpiece."

Antoinette and Emile were both exceedingly proud of Katherine but were also, at the same time, frequently exhausted by her constant, voracious appetite for new horizons, as well. She had, by this stage in her life, established a distinct pattern to her pursuits... initial interest, swift mastery – bordering on obsession – boredom, then invariably – abandonment. Once Katherine had mastered something, it held no further appeal to her. Antoinette and Emile were often disappointed, and frustrated, by Katherine's disdain for that which she had previously conquered. They would, at family gatherings – desirous of showing off their gifted daughter's repertoire – ask Katherine to perform one or more of her many talents... only to be curtly refused by her if she had moved on to new interests.

By the time Katherine was twelve, her most frequent complaint to her parents was, naturally enough – given her insatiable appetites – that she was bored. In an effort to appease her, the Devilles exhausted a liberal retinue of offerings. She was given, for instance, a myriad of pets... a cat, a dog, tropical fish, guinea pigs, an ant farm, a boa constrictor, a pony, and a horse... each abandoned after a short time. Antoinette and Emile began to dread Katherine's inevitable report and subsequent query, "I'm bored. What is there to do?" Katherine's parents eventually ran out of suggestions. Her next interest, following pet animals, proved to be the most challenging of her childhood for the Devilles.

Commensurate with her first menstrual period, Katherine newest fascination was, as might be anticipated, sex. For the first time, Katherine broke with her inviolate routine and returned to a previously abandoned talent... painting... but, with a new focus. She began, at first, to paint simple nudes... male and female. Her subject interest then quickly turned erotic. With impunity she painted, in graphic detail, renderings of all imaginable sexual activity... and in every combination and partner, from a ménage a trois, to two men, to several women, to elaborate orgies... to atrocious scenes of bestiality, using liberal amounts of blues, reds, pinks, and purples. She left virtually no sexual stone unturned in her art, including every variation of oral and anal sex, bondage, and sadomasochism. Much to the mortification of the Devilles, Katherine blatantly displayed her works on her bedroom walls, and they suffered Katherine's blossoming anger when they drew the line at her attempt to hang her favorite renderings on the living room walls.

As one could assuredly expect, erotic painting quickly became inadequate for Katherine and it wasn't long until stories began to make their way back to the Deville family about Katherine's sexual exploits. The first story about Katherine, by then, thirteen – and a fully developed, beautiful young woman – was reported by a nun at Saint Bernard's Academy, where Katherine was a pupil. It seems that Katherine had been caught in the boys' rest room, totally nude, except for a pair of black, patent leather heels, dancing erotically, to the great pleasure and amazement of some twenty or more very appreciative boys. Katherine had, according to Sister Constance, charged each boy a two-dollar admission for the performance. Katherine's exploit was not only without precedent in this century-old parochial institution, but quickly assumed the mantle of legend among both the staff and student body. Katherine was summarily dismissed from the Academy and was, thereupon, enrolled, the following week, in the local public school... where the comparatively liberal culture was much more to her liking.

Although Katherine's prodigious sexual activity stunned the entire Deville family, she was undaunted, and her extraordinary behavior frequently presented her parents with a wide array of problems. One problem it did not present, however, was that of deceit or fabrication. Whenever asked any question of any nature from anybody, regarding reports of her endeavors, Katherine responded with such forthrightness that it often made questioners blush... and with such blatancy as to give the appearance of arrogance. When her parents confronted her, for example, about her nude cabaret performance for the boys of Saint Bernard's, she not only admitted to it, but provided many more details than Emile and Antoinette cared to learn. They knew the uselessness of forbidding her to do this sort of thing again, for she would do, regardless, as she had always done – which was exactly as she pleased.

Katherine quickly moved from sexual exhibitionism to actual intercourse. Their first report of this activity was from the Lafferty's... a neighborhood family with a sixteen-year-old son. Apparently, Mr. Lafferty, a trial attorney, had returned home to retrieve a forgotten file he needed for court that day, only to find his son, Timothy – who was to have departed for school by that hour – lying naked, on his back, on the living room rug, with an equally naked Katherine Deville straddled across his loins, engaging in spirited sexual intercourse, giving every indication, according to Mr. Lafferty, of appearing to know exactly what she was doing.

Mr. Lafferty, in utter amazement, related to the Devilles that when he marched up to the totally absorbed couple and demanded to know what they thought they were doing, his son froze in shock, while Katherine continued her motion without breaking rhythm... and answered Mr. Lafferty's inquiry in a matter of fact tone. Mr. Lafferty inserted here, in his account to the Devilles, that his question to them as to what they thought they were doing, was, of course, of a rhetorical nature and not solicitous of a factual response. He went on to relate that Katherine replied to him that she was – he quoted her – "fucking his son." He said her tone of voice and facial expression was of a nature to indicate that she felt he had asked a terribly stupid question. Mr. Lafferty said the activity stopped only when his son sufficiently regained his senses to literally throw Katherine off of him and dash, naked, for the upstairs. In Mr. Lafferty's opinion, had his son not done this, he was convinced that Katherine would have, no doubt, continued her activity, unabated. Katherine, then, according to Mr. Lafferty's account, proceeded, with complete composure intact, to get dressed right in front of him while engaging in absolutely casual conversation, as if, he said, they were at a tea party. She attempted, unsuccessfully, he said, to engage him in a dialogue regarding his law practice and as to how he felt about lawyers having such a bad reputation among the general populace. The Devilles would later relate to family members – when retelling the story – that Mr. Lafferty was so incensed by Katherine's audacious behavior that he could barely get out his words during his telling of the tale.

Although other stories of Katherine's sexual odyssey made their way back to the Devilles, most did not. It wasn't that Katherine sought to hide her adventures, she simply saw no reason to volunteer the details of the encounters, unless asked. Katherine's interests eventually moved on from boys to men... from men to women... to combinations of both. On several occasions, she charged men for sex... just to see how it would feel. Katherine's curiosity about sex enjoyed the greatest longevity of any of her life interests to date... continuing as a primary preoccupation for several years, until she was seventeen.

On Christmas Eve, following Katherine's seventeenth birthday, she matter-of-factly informed her parents that she was pregnant. With this event, Katherine's sexual adventures ended. She was going to have, she explained to her parents, what was the naturally intended end product of sex and was anxious to, as she put it... "experience parenthood." She named her son Jean Paul Sartre Deville – having developed an intense interest in philosophy during her pregnancy. He was born July 13th... a blonde-haired, blue-eyed beauty, with a round face that was too pretty for a boy, and skin that was, and remained throughout his childhood, a warm pink. He had, one could see, his mother's spirit... but would, thankfully, prove to be possessed of more love than intensity.

Katherine had plenty of free time for her baby, having just graduated with honors from public school, a month before Jean Paul's arrival. She was, from the moment of his birth, totally devoted to her infant son... putting as much energy into perfecting motherhood as she had all of her other previous pursuits. Her parents asked her, only once, about the child's father, to which Katherine replied that it was, as she calculated it, one of four men, but... given Jean Paul's blonde hair and blue eyes, she deduced that it was, most likely, Harold Blatherwick, the principal of her public school... a married, forty-eight-year-old man, with four children. She had not informed him of Jean Paul's birth, nor did she intend to do so. She added that she found Mr. Blatherwick to be quite sexually appealing... but otherwise, rather a bore.

For the next two years, Katherine was the perfect mother. She tended, meticulously, to her son's every need... feeding, bathing, dressing, napping, strolling, teaching, playing, singing, and loving. Everywhere Katherine went, Jean Paul was her constant companion. Katherine took every opportunity to read or talk to him... resulting in Jean Paul's precocious ability to talk in full sentences by fifteen months. Overcoming their shame of having an unwed mother among their brood, the moment they lay eyes on their first grandson, Antoinette and Emile were filled with love and pride for Jean Paul, and took every opportunity to show him off. They were also equally proud of the fine mother their daughter had proven to be. With a sense of great relief, Antoinette and Emile began to accept – for the first of many times to follow – that Katherine's life course had, at last, swerved toward a path of normalcy and that her past history of extremes was but a symptom of her highly spirited youth. But this was not to be.

As instantly as Katherine had devoted herself to motherhood, in one day, she detached herself from it. On a night in April, she went to bed after rocking her two-year-old son to sleep... a picture of domesticity... only to wake in the morning to announce to her parents that she must move on in her life. She told them that she loved Jean Paul, dearly, but that she could not possibly devote any more of her life to his care. There were "other mountains" she was "compelled to climb," she explained... and she simply must get on with her life's destiny. They could, she told them, take Jean Paul as their own to raise or she could, she offered, arrange other accommodations.

With their hearts, heavy with sadness and disappointment, Antoinette and Emile Deville told their daughter they would, of course, take Jean Paul... adding that they could never abide the thought of anyone else raising one of their own. Katherine told them she was leaving Montreal in the very near future... as soon as she had made a few decisions and arrangements. She said she was not sure when she would return... perhaps not for a very long time. Katherine told her parents that they were free to use their own judgment as to what to tell Jean Paul about her, as he grew older. She would trust, she said, that they would make the right decisions.

Within the week, Katherine had resolved on traveling to Paris, to enroll in the Sorbonne. She would study philosophy.

CHAPTER EIGHTEEN

Antoinette expected that Katherine would be absent from the family for a time. She was nearly twenty when she left, and had never before been away from home. It was that time in life, Antoinette understood, that the young – if they are of a healthy spirit – need to explore the world and unfold their new wings. They did not expect, however, a thirteen-year absence. The only communication from Katherine, during that time, was by letter. Never once had she telephoned. She occasionally enclosed photographs of herself, her various associates, and her surroundings, so at least the Devilles had some idea as to how she had changed over the years. Jean Paul studied each picture intently, as if, possibly, he could derive some feeling of his mother by touching her image. He held each letter in his hands, sometimes for hours, repeatedly reminding his grandparents that his mother had held these same pages in her own hands and had pressed against them as she wrote. He ritualistically placed each photograph and letter into an album he had especially purchased for this purpose... covered in dark leather with gold edges and impressed designs and bearing his mother's full name, Katherine Sainte-Bueve Deville... that had more the appearance of a Bible than a picture album.

Katherine's letters read like an odyssey... each unfolding a new adventure in another part of the world. Katherine had graduated with honors from the Sorbonne... concentrating in philosophy and religious studies. She had supported herself by waitressing in an assortment of bistros, modeling nude for art classes, and eventually landing an acting job with a professional theater company which toured throughout Europe during the summers. After graduation, she accepted a position as a social worker in the slums of New Delhi, where for the next three years, she worked in a Catholic orphanage... tending to the physical and emotional needs of children who had been found abandoned in the streets. It was at this orphanage where she met the man who would become her husband... a physician from a wealthy New Delhi family. Katherine enclosed photos of their exotic wedding. She looked tanned, radiant, and stunningly beautiful in the brightly colored, flowing Indian fabrics. Her husband, Dr. Madan Krishnan, was a tall and slender man, dark and mustached, with a kindly and compassionate face. They went on an extended honeymoon of some six months, traversing much of the globe – from Tibet to the islands of the South Pacific.

Upon their return to New Delhi, Dr. Krishnan announced, much to his family's dismay, that he had decided to accept a position as chief of internal medicine research at a large hospital in Rio de Janeiro. While on their honeymoon, Madan explained, he had made the acquaintance of a gentleman, a Manuel Ortega, administrator of Rio Del Grande Hospital. Actually, he clarified... Katherine met him, first, aboard the deck of the Norwegian Princess, during their South Seas cruise.

What Madan did not know was that Mr. Ortega was immediately taken by Katherine, and that it was for that reason, alone, he had invited Madan and Katherine to his table for that evening's dinner. Manuel was immediately struck by Katherine's eccentric and compelling beauty, charm, and wit. In fact, he was immediately overcome by a true obsession for her – which was quite unlike Manuel. He was a man of forty-four, married, with six children... a conservative man who planned everything in his life in great detail, leaving as little to chance as possible. He could not understand, nor explain, the flames of passion that Katherine instantly ignited inside him. Despite his finely orchestrated life, upon encountering Katherine, had she so much as hinted at their escaping and spending their lives together, he was sure he would have abandoned everything he had, and that very instant, gone away with her.

Manuel Ortega did not care to analyze his determination to have Katherine. He knew, only, he could not live without her... and that he must, somehow, find a way to have her. Not normally a gregarious man, after meeting Katherine, Manuel exhibited a newfound charm and wit at the first dinner with the Krishnan's, and the days that followed, that utterly flabbergasted his wife. Intuitively sensing a natural strategy, Manuel immediately ingratiated himself with Madan... empathetically inquiring of all his interests, dreams, and ambitions... designing in his mind, as they spoke, a future that would accommodate these... and his own, as well. Madan, he unearthed, had grown tired of the standard practice of medicine and was inclined toward engaging in certain research interests... specifically, the effect of emotional trauma in the generation of disease. Madan had long held the opinion that western-style medical practice was far too organic in nature and inappropriately disdainful of the spirit. He wished to pursue the exploration of this forgotten, and much maligned, link to health.

As Madan related the story of their chance meeting with Mr. Ortega to his father, he openly pondered, with great wonder, the highly unlikely, serendipitous opportunity it had presented. What were the chances, he posed, that he would, on a honeymoon cruise in the South Pacific, encounter a man who ran a large hospital that just happened to be seeking someone to head up a research project into an area of medicine that precisely fit his long-held dream? It seemed, as he reflected upon it, almost too good to be true. His father pointed out that those things in life, too good to be true, usually aren't. Madan disregarded his father's comment as the cynicism of an old man who, selfishly, wanted his son to stay at home to provide him with company in his advanced years.

Katherine was certainly not as naive and trusting as her husband. She instantly sensed the true nature of Mr. Ortega's feelings toward her. If his obvious infatuation with her would achieve for her husband what he wanted in life, however, she would, she vowed, willingly allow it... and, if necessary, encourage it. She fell in love with Madan because of his innocence and kindness. He was the gentlest, most caring person, she had ever met. While he could have been making a large salary in private practice within his family's affluent, social network in New Delhi, he chose, instead, to treat orphans without compensation. Katherine had never encountered anyone so entirely selfless and was, thus, immediately fascinated with him. Being a shrewd and astute skeptic, however,

Katherine studied Madan for many months, frequently engaging in sometimes brutal examination of his purpose in doing what he was doing... searching for his hidden agenda. Despite her determined efforts, however, she could find no other purpose to his work than the apparent. He was, in fact, she concluded, a kind, beneficent man... desiring nothing more than the satisfaction of easing the suffering of others.

Falling in love with Madan – and true to her nature – Katherine totally dedicated herself to love and to loving Madan. She would become, she vowed, the perfect lover. She searched out his every physical and emotional need and fulfilled it. To Madan, Katherine became his life... his breath... and the mate to his soul. Upon their marriage, Katherine dedicated all her talent and intelligence and emotion to becoming all that a wife could possibly be to a husband.

Settled into Rio, in a luxurious apartment, leased for them by Manuel Ortega... conveniently located only a few blocks from his own, spacious home, Ortega wasted no time in pursuing Katherine. She was faced, for the first time in her life, with a true moral dilemma. If she did not accommodate Ortega's desires, he could, potentially, take it out on Madan and possibly even terminate his employment. Ortega had been, to that point, completely true to his word – pledged in his promises to Madan. He had assembled several other medical researchers for this holistic research project, hired a highly qualified support staff, and had allocated a generous budget... and Katherine resolved that she would do nothing to deprive Madan of this, his dream's fulfillment.

Madan was ecstatic with what he found in Rio. It was far more than he had truly expected. He immediately threw himself into the research project... meeting with colleagues and staff... designing research models and objectives. It was a joy for Katherine to witness Madan's childlike, bubbling spirit and enthusiasm. Every evening he would excitedly describe his day to Katherine with the joy of a child at Christmas. Seeing this, Katherine renewed her resolve to do whatever was necessary to preserve Madan's wonderful, newfound world. She knew she could not tell him about Ortega. It would surely destroy him, she felt, if he knew Ortega had only offered him his situation, solely to bed his wife. Katherine also knew, full well, she could not risk disappointing Ortega. She would do, therefore, whatever she *must* do.

Ortega quickly began the practice of phoning Katherine at the apartment as soon as he would see Madan arrive at the hospital. After a number of such calls he finally got, bluntly, to the point. He said that he knew Katherine must be aware of his feelings toward her... that it was so obvious she could not have mistaken it. Katherine did not lie to him. She forthrightly acknowledged that she was aware of his feelings, and intentions, from the first moment they met. She asked him, point blank, what, precisely, his intentions were. He told her that he must have her. She asked, precisely, what that meant. He said he wanted her for himself... that he would do anything to have her. Katherine made it clear... she would give herself to him, sexually, but that she loved Madan and had no intentions, whatsoever, of leaving him. Ortega said he would find a way to make her love him. She assured him that he would not. Undeterred, Ortega said he would... if it took him to his dying day to do so. With their understandings and differences out in the open, Ortega was ready to move forward on consummating his long anticipated fantasies... and find a way to sway Katherine's love from Madan... and to make her his own.

During Madan's third week at the hospital, Ortega, unable to wait any longer, showed up, unannounced, at Katherine's apartment. Without ceremony, he passionately embraced her... kissing her face and neck, all the while proclaiming his unfathomable love for her. Katherine remained silent, yet compliant. Ortega slid Katherine's deep purple, satin robe from her shoulders. It fell into luscious folds around her feet. Her naked body rose from the soft, shiny pedestal with the perfection of a Venus. Her milky-white flesh – as smooth as polished marble – defied blemish. Her beauty was such that it rendered Ortega breathless. In the presence of such unearthly splendor, his passion bowed in subservience to the higher order of adoration. He stood, speechless, in awe of her perfection. She was, he realized at that instant, too much for any man to possess. She was meant to be worshiped... not touched. Her countenance was of a nature that bordered on the divine. Her ivory flesh seemed to radiate starlight from some heavenly glow within.

Katherine continued to stand before Ortega... her gaze steady, and straight into him... her posture erect... her demeanor unashamed and unshakable. She made no effort to cover herself. She looked as serene in her nakedness as a wild beast in the forest. She was, Ortega realized, a strange and powerful creation of God... unlike anything he had ever seen before. His hands shaking, Ortega knelt humbly before her. He reverently lifted the robe from around her feet and raised it, slowly, up to her shoulders, then closed it across her. He lowered his eyes from her gaze and backed away several steps, turned, then, slowly and quietly, walked to the door and departed without looking back.

From that moment forward, Ortega made no further advances toward Katherine, and his demeanor toward her became noticeably rigid and awkward. He behaved toward her, almost as one would in the presence of a nun... polite and proper to a point of self-consciousness. Madan noticed the change in Ortega toward both Katherine and him. He was no longer gregarious and solicitous of their needs and interests as he had been, but rather cold and mechanical. Madan asked Katherine if, perhaps, she thought he had done something to Ortega that may have upset or angered him. She assured him that he had done nothing, and that what he was noticing was very likely just a change in circumstance. When they met Mr. Ortega, she reminded Madan, it was on a cruise ship, and in the festive atmosphere that colored every day and night. They were back in the real world, now, and at work, where Ortega had a demanding job and where Madan was merely another member of his large staff of hospital employees. They couldn't expect, she explained, the magic of the cruise to affect their relationship with him, indefinitely... especially once they were back into the grind of everyday life. Mulling this over for a bit, Madan granted that Katherine was surely right and he never again raised the issue.

Fortunately, Ortega's return to his normal temperament did not affect Madan's job. Ortega remained true to all of his promises, and dealt with Madan in a consistently polite and professional manner on all occasions, both social and professional.

Katherine's letters to her family told of her happiness as Madan's wife and with marriage in general. Katherine threw herself into domestic chores with the dedication of a true, familial zealot. She decorated their apartment in a beautiful and tasteful manner... became a cook of the highest order... cleaned tirelessly... provided Madan with a constant stream of affection... was cheerfully available for his sexual pleasure upon demand... and was a delightful hostess to Madan's friends and colleagues. Though Antoinette and Emile had suffered through innumerable disappointments with Katherine's constantly shifting interests, they both felt that this time, at last, she had found her place and her happiness in life... and that her frenzied need for constant change and new circumstance had finally been satiated. After three years of marriage, her letters contained not even an inference that she was tiring of it. For these reasons, the Devilles were stunned beyond all expression by the letter they received from Katherine, written one week after her thirtieth birthday.

> Dearest Mama, Papa, and Jean Paul,
>
> This is the most difficult letter I have ever written in my life and I hesitated to write you of the news it bears, but I believe you should know of it. As you know, I turned thirty last week. That event had an unanticipated and profound affect upon me. I came to the realization that my youth was all but gone and my years of life ahead were becoming very precious. Faced with this, I realized I could not continue what I had been doing. Though I had spent the years of my life with Madan in happiness and serenity, it had become, I realized, routine and unchallenging. I came to realize that I could not face a lifetime of this, as pleasant as it was. There were just too many things I had not seen and done, and too much I had not learned of the

world. I knew that I could not go to my grave with so much untouched.

I knew Madan loved me without limit but, tragically, I did not know to what end such a love may lead. Madan took me out to dinner for my birthday to my favorite restaurant; a small and intimate place, tucked into a mountainside overlooking the ocean. We had champagne and he gave me a diamond necklace that was stunning. As you may recall, Mama, I had wished for such a piece of jewelry since I was a little girl. He was so wonderful to me that I almost felt I could not say what I needed to tell him. Knowing that I must, however, and aware that putting it off was, in itself, a cruelty, I summoned up my courage and told him of my need to move on in my life. I searched for the right way of telling him, but there was none other than merely to say it. He took it badly, very badly – much worse than I had anticipated he would. He cried and pleaded with me, telling me he could not live without me. He told me I was the meaning to his life, the reason he drew breath. I assured him, over and over, that his life would go on without me; that he had his research and his many friends and that the wound would, in due time, heal. He could not be consoled.

When we got home, he continued his sorrowful pleading, but eventually became very quiet. After a while I told him I was going to bed and asked him if he was coming. He said he would be in, shortly. He asked me, in a whispering voice, if I could, somehow, find it within my heart to change my mind. I told him that I loved him, and that for his sake I wished that I could feel differently about things, but I simply could not. He smiled and kissed my cheek and told me he loved me. He told me that he understood. With this, I felt somewhat better about the situation. At about four o'clock in the morning, I awakened to find that Madan still had not come to bed. I went to the living room to look for him. He was asleep in his chair, his eyes closed and head back. I rubbed the top of his head and softly spoke his name. I touched his cheek and felt the cold. On the table beside him was an unfinished glass of water and an empty prescription bottle of sedatives. I put my hand to his chest and felt no heartbeat and put my hand in front of his nose and mouth and felt no breath. Madan was dead. Beside the prescription bottle was a piece of paper with a note written on it. The words were, "My darling Katherine, I know I am a coward but I cannot face a life without you. Forgive me, my love."

Madan's funeral was yesterday. My heart is breaking with grief and guilt. Madan was the kindest person I have ever known and I doubt if I will ever love anyone as much as I loved him. My nature, my dearest family, is, I believe, a curse. Being who I am and what I am, I understand now that I should never allow anyone, ever again, to love me or depend upon me, for I shall surely disappoint them as I did my beloved Madan. If there is a God, may he forgive me the tragedy, wrought by the restless nature of my soul.

Yours with love,

Katherine

The Devilles did not hear, again, from their daughter for an entire year. During that time, Antoinette was sure Katherine was dead. She told Emile that she sensed her desolation and her inconsolable guilt in her last letter. She anticipated, any day, receiving a communication confirming her fear. When a letter arrived, postmarked on Katherine's birthday, and addressed in Katherine's own handwriting, Antoinette was beside herself with joy.

Katherine wrote that she had entered a convent outside of Rio. Her guilt over Madan was more than she could bear. She felt a need to serve a penance for the tragedy she had caused. She wrote of finding inner peace among the Sisters of Mercy. She was, she wrote, seriously considering the possibility of taking her final vows in marriage to Christ and dedicating her life to God and the service of mankind. Katherine related that her Mother Superior was a native of Paris with whom Katherine spoke French, and who knew of some of their family in the old country. Mother, Katherine wrote, was favorably impressed by her exceedingly zealous devotion to the order... and by her ability to learn her prayers. She was confident that Katherine could, when she was fully prepared, take her vows and join the order.

True to Katherine's nature, she excelled in all that one could, within the narrow confines of the extremely structured world of a convent. She was never late to prayer, kept the rules without a hint of deviation and did her chores with unflagging energy and impressive results. As the most recent devotee to the order, Katherine was assigned the most mundane of tasks... washing floors, cleaning toilets, polishing the brass. Never had the floors, toilets, and brass of the Sisters of Mercy Convent shined as when Katherine did them... and despite the Order's vow of modesty, the Sisters could not help but praise Katherine's work to her face. She quickly became the favorite of the order.

In pursuing penance for what she now considered to be her murder of Madan, she pushed herself, unmercifully, in everything she did, to the point of pain. She would scrub the floor until her knees and knuckles bled... sometimes working at her task for an entire night and day without rest or food... turning a deaf ear to the Sisters' pleas that she sleep and eat. Mother understood Katherine's need for this penance and instructed the Sisters to refrain from their understandable – yet misguided – interference, which they tried to obey but, upon seeing this angelic, yet pitiful, creature driving herself beyond exhaustion, they could not help themselves but to stand in violation of Mother's order.

For two years, the Devilles received letters from Katherine that filled their hearts with joy and hope. Katherine was happy with the Sisters of Mercy, but more than this, she was cloistered behind the walls of the order and sheltered from the outside world's endless temptations. This was, perhaps, they thought – at last – Katherine's natural and final destination... the only refuge for a woman such as she, whose drive, intelligence, and talent knew no limits, and if unbridled, would certainly drive her, without mercy, to a tragic end. She needed protection from herself. Her spirit, if set free, would, like a riding crop, beat her, unmercifully, into such a long, furious ride that she would, inexorably, run herself to death.

Too much talent and intelligence, Katherine's parents had come to realize, is a terrible burden for one to bear... a taskmaster with neither pity nor compassion. It was a beast that simply would not leave their daughter in peace. Antoinette and Emile prayed to God to protect Katherine and keep the terrible beast from penetrating the walls of the Sisters of Mercy. "Give our daughter peace," was their constant supplication. But apparently, not even Almighty God had the power to restrain the will of this ungodly force.

A week before Katherine was to have taken her final vows, she appeared at Mother Superior's chamber door, near midnight. Mother knew from the pleading, yet resigned look in Katherine's eyes, that she was leaving the order. She did not allow Katherine to speak... it wasn't necessary. Mother drew Katherine to her bosom and held her like an infant. She whispered in her ear.

"You cannot deny your nature, my sweet child. We all have our life's burden. We can hide from it, but it always finds its way to us. God has his purpose, Katherine. I pray He will give you the strength to bear your life's work with grace."

Katherine drew her head away from Mother. Her mouth formed to speak but Mother pressed her finger against Katherine's perfectly formed lips.

"No one needs to explain God's will, Katherine. No one can. Don't feel you have failed me, or God. We travel many streams in our lives. I am blessed that for a short time, our waters ran together. This is where we go our separate ways, but you take with you, my love, which I pray will warm and strengthen your soul against fear and loneliness. That is my gift to you, Katherine, which no one can take away from you. You're a good person, Katherine, and God loves you. Go and do what you must do. Don't be sad for what you are leaving. Be happy for what you have had."

Katherine leaned to Mother's ear and whispered, "I love you."

In the morning, Katherine's room was empty.

CHAPTER NINETEEN

After a six-month lapse in communication, a letter finally arrived from Katherine, postmarked from New York City. She recounted to her family that, following Madan's funeral, she had telephoned a college friend with whom she had stayed in contact through the years, and who had often encouraged her to come to New York. Katherine's friend, Amy Whitmer, was an associate editor for the *New York Times* and had always believed that Katherine would make a splendid art and entertainment critic – given her knowledge and love of the arts – and also being possessed of her boundless energy, her intelligence, and her exceptional writing abilities. Besides, Amy would always remind her, Katherine was the best friend she had ever had in life and would cherish being with her again. After leaving the convent, Katherine called Amy to inquire if the offer still held. It did. Katherine accepted.

Amy and her husband, Robin Forbes, an off Broadway playwright, producer, and director – born Scottish, raised English, and Oxford educated – lived in a fashionable condo in Central Park West. At Amy's insistence, Katherine moved in with Amy and Robin, until, ostensibly at least, she could find her own place. Besides, Amy told Katherine, with four bedrooms and just the two of them, they had more than enough room for her.

This was the first face-to-face meeting between Katherine and Amy since their Sorbonne graduation. They had been close friends since their second week in Paris... sharing classes, lovers, a cold-water Latin Quarter flat, and intimate thoughts, throughout their academic and social tenure at the Sorbonne. They helped pay their bills by waitressing at the same bistro and by utilizing their considerable physical beauty for profit, posing nude, singly and together, for the Sorbonne human figure-painting and drawing classes. Amy was one of the few Americans at the Sorbonne and Katherine, a rare Quebecois. As two North Americans in a foreign land, the two girls felt an instant kinship that would not normally exist, except for the phenomenon of the distances between homelands shrinking in inverse proportion to the distance traveled away from them. To reinforce this contrived commonality, they always spoke English to one another, despite French being the native tongue of the northernmost comrade.

Katherine and Amy embraced when they were reunited in New York as only old friends do... as though affirming the existence of a palpable incarnation of mutually shared, ancient secrets. They instinctively checked one another from head to toe... and were pleased. To the eyes of both women, it was apparent that the hands of time had been mutually very gentle. This was a welcome pleasure – as it is for all old friends – to discover that time had not yet obliterated the corporeal reality of their memories. Given the kind preservation of their youthful appearances, they were not yet compelled to reflect on their shared past as "the old days... when they were young"... talking as though it were some mythical time and place, far removed from their present world. Except for some changes in hairstyle and clothing fashion, it was easy for either to picture the other, without any sympathetic glossing of the eye, sitting at one of the sidewalk cafes they frequented... sipping espresso, engrossed in a discussion of the particular philosophical or political issue of the day... seriously believing that their ideas and solutions to world problems, borne of their newfound university enlightenment, had been somehow overlooked by the preceding generations.

As would be expected, Katherine took to her newspaper job, immediately – tirelessly traveling from one artistic event to the next, covering not only the standard art, theater, ballet, symphony, and opera events... but the avant-garde and bizarre as well. Among the cutting-edge performances Katherine reviewed, were such artful performances as a full ninety minutes of on-stage love making, to the accompaniment of a high-tech sound and light show. Her reviews were immediately met with high regard by the readership – considered by nearly all to be entertaining, knowledgeable, and insightful. Her talent and intelligence were immediately recognized by the editorial staff and Amy was repeatedly congratulated on her fortuitous "find."

Given their commonality in interests, Robin and Katherine fast became friends. In her "off" time, Katherine began visiting the theater where Robin worked... and was part owner. Deferring to her unquestionable sense of artistry, Robin would frequently ask her opinion on sets and scenes and other such theater matters... and seriously consider them. Their rapport reached a point that Katherine, eventually, began offering even unsolicited suggestions. Robin's respect for Katherine's abilities grew to such an extent that, during rehearsal of a particular play he had written, he asked her to try her hand at rewriting a particular scene that just didn't seem to be working. She did, and he often used it, verbatim... even following her inserted, unsolicited blocking suggestions.

Their mutual interest in the arts broadened to a general social relationship and Katherine began frequenting the late-night Soho parties with Robin. She was taken by the rainbow of talent that bowed across her new horizon... painters, sculptors, actors, dancers, directors, musicians, writers, came and went... careening from one party to the next. It wasn't unusual for the sun to be making its appearance before Katherine and Robin returned home.

Amy was, by this stage of her marriage to Robin, quite accustomed to his lifestyle. He was a "theater person" and she understood that unconventionality was intrinsic to his nature. She had never known anything different with Robin – he, already being a major player in New York theater when they met. While Amy liked the arts, and admired the talent of its creators and performers, she wasn't consumed with a passion for it, as was Robin. Consequently, the parties quickly lost their appeal, and she was, thereafter, quite content to stay at home while her husband romped through the Soho all night.

Katherine felt she had possibly found a world, sufficient to accommodate her soul's restless nature... and was hopeful that her obsession with change and perpetually new horizons had, perhaps, found its means of satiation. The life she discovered in New York City swiftly transmuted her into metaphoric pinball... dizzily bouncing from bumper to flipper on an endlessly changing game board of every imaginable color, bauble, and bell. A new horizon or challenge or point of view was there with a twist of the head. Such a match was this life to Katherine's nature that she eventually reached a state of perpetual euphoria... unable to sleep for more than an hour or two a day... fearing something new or remarkable might occur without her being present to witness it. Here, in this axis of the art world, was to be found, a seemingly endless source of knowledge, talent, and creation. Katherine would entirely immerse herself in the perpetually lapping waves of fascinating conversation, representing all manner of human endeavor. New York City, she found, was a modern-day version of Athens of the Golden Age... the world's gathering place. Here, it would not be unusual to find an ambassador from Russia discussing the latest in computer graphics with a kid from MTV... or a classical violinist from Japan jamming with a heavy-metal guitarist. Almost anything that anyone could imagine was eventually extant in New York City.

Robin actively encouraged Katherine's exploration of her newly discovered world... and he guided a steady stream of talent, fame, intelligence, wit, audacity, and perversion in her direction. This constant stimulation showed in her work at the newspaper and her column gained an increasing audience and critical acclaim from her press colleagues. After only fourteen months on the job, Katherine was the recipient of a Golden Quill Award for art criticism – an unheard-of honor for a rookie writer – almost exclusively bestowed upon seasoned veterans of the press corps.

In her never-ending voyage of life exploration, Katherine also pushed the boundaries of her personal senses. Normal means of perception became mundane to her and she thus, sought out new ways of experiencing the world... and Robin was happy to accommodate her. He introduced her to cocaine... which she embraced with characteristic zeal. Under the spell of the white powder, her appreciation of the sights, sounds, smells, and feel of the world reached new heights of ecstasy. With her brain, bathed in this chemical highball, she felt she could understand and appreciate meaningful nuances she'd been missing, theretofore. Her use of the drug became ubiquitous to all aspects of her life. At work, she felt she could write better with it. At artistic events, she believed her appreciation and specific recall was greatly enhanced by it. Combined with sex, she found it to be a psychosexual experience she had never imagined possible – and in this regard – her relationship with Robin inexorably evolved from friendship to passion, with cocaine as the perennial third party of their ménage a trois. Of course, they were not exclusive to one another in this infidelity... nor was it expected. Given the assortment of flesh available in this glitzy, throbbing, menagerie of carnality – exacerbated by the aphrodisiac of fame and talent – sex was as common as casual conversation.

LSD was the next prevailing wind in Katherine's pharmacological quest for new perceptional horizons. While cocaine had been an enhancer of her senses, LSD brought them through doors of which she was unaware of possessing. On a "trip," Katherine was, at last, completely free of mundane, bodily limitations in her appreciation of the surrounding environment. LSD bridged the gulf between the stimulus and the sensor and allowed them to become one. On her new drug of choice, Katherine could "see" the music floating upward from the orchestra. Colors became tastes and textures. She began to recognize how the color, red, differed, in sound, from that of blue... and how they felt on her tongue and hands. Watching a play on LSD, she became the characters, the props, and the set. On one particular trip, one Sunday afternoon, though friends told her she was only "gone" for about two hours, she spent twenty years in a particular room... watching herself and the world go by... becoming, alternately, a part of the wall paint, and a rose vase.

So frequently did Katherine "go away" on her LSD escapes that the line between reality and her drug-scapes eventually blurred to inconsequence. Her work at the paper became increasingly affected. Her witty and creative phrases progressively devolved into unpublishable gibberish. Amy, unable to persuade Katherine to take sick leave before irreparable damage was done, was powerless to save her inevitable termination from the paper.

It became apparent to all who knew her, that Katherine had literally pickled her brain through a constant soaking in a bath of acid. She began having bad trips on such a regular basis, that it was no longer safe for Amy to allow Katherine to be alone in the condo. Amy became convinced of this when, at the last second, she stopped Katherine from "flying" from the rail of their twenty-sixth floor condo to join, as Katherine explained it, some friendly pigeons in the park below... claiming they called out her name.

Amy and Robin, who felt a mutual sense of responsibility for Katherine's condition – particularly Robin – were able to have her placed in a high-priced, private clinic... secluded in the Connecticut countryside. Her insurance from the paper, which Amy and Robin had the foresight to continue on an individual basis, paid a portion of the costs, and Amy and Robin – out of a mingled sense of guilt and responsibility – picked up the tab for the remainder. It was more than six months before the medical staff felt it safe to release Katherine... much to the relief of Amy and Robin. Although they had great affection for Katherine and felt they shared some responsibility for her condition... even guilt-laden devotion has its limits when the price tag is in excess of ten thousand dollars a month.

Katherine had undergone dramatic change during her six-month stay. Her obsession for change had been, at long last, satiated by a prolonged trip that lasted almost four months, during which she traveled, endlessly, in her mind... to all dimensions and times... as everything and nothing. The magic carpet inside her head carried her to every imaginable world... outward and inward. She felt she had touched infinity at the outward limits of the universe and the divine core at the inward limits of matter. After four months, Katherine began, in sporadic, brief intervals, to return to the real world. The balance eventually began to shift in favor of tangible reality, and except for the occasional flashback, she had finally returned from her immense, psychic journey.

Amy and Robin visited Katherine regularly, although their early visits served only to fulfill their sense of obligation, and as balm for their guilt... having no real value to Katherine. They would invariably find her either sitting in a chair or lying on her bed... eyes wide open and mind elsewhere... totally unaware of their presence. As distressing as this was to witness, Katherine's final return to reality was even more so. She had come to New York, a vibrant youth... full of energy... thirsting for knowledge and experience. She returned from her extended mind-trip, although still beautiful in appearance, an empty ship, void of both spirit and energy. Her eyes were now but vacuous globes of membrane and water, no longer possessing their previous sparkle of inner-light. She was interested in nothing. She had no enthusiasm for anything. Amy and Robin tried, valiantly, to find something that might strike a spark in her mind. They'd tell Katherine about her old New York friends and a selection of the more titillating stories that were constantly bubbling up from the Soho cauldron. They'd read articles from the paper to her, of which she would have had, previous to her stay at the clinic, great interest. They'd show her pictures of new art... and discuss new plays in rehearsal. All failed to provoke, in Katherine, even the slightest degree of interest.

Amy had considered calling Katherine's family during her confinement, but did not. She felt that the news of Katherine's deteriorated condition would be very hard on Katherine's parents – who were now both in their seventies – and on Jean Paul, even more so, who was now fifteen and who continued to idolized his mythical mother. Another reason Amy hesitated to call the Devilles was that Katherine had told them that she had not spoken with her family since she left Montreal and that she preferred to communicate, exclusively, by letter. Katherine explained to Amy that the telephone was, for her, too open-ended... too confusing a mixture of past and present... particularly when it came to Jean Paul. Amy decided that if she called the Devilles it would be, first of all, a shock to them... and secondly, a violation of Katherine's highly valued privacy. Katherine's impending release from the clinic, however, caused Amy to reconsider her position. Katherine would have to go *somewhere* after her release, and both Amy and Robin felt that, frankly, they had done *more* than their part in helping Katherine and did not want her back in New York with them. Their lives were just too busy to take on the responsibility of caring for her, and, if the truth be told, Katherine had become rather an embarrassment – and a liability – to both of their careers, and their social network. Several days before Katherine was scheduled to be released, Amy finally got up her nerve and got to the point with Katherine.

"What are your plans, Kathy? We understand that they're going to release you next Thursday."

"I don't have any plans, Amy."

"Well sweetheart, you've got to go somewhere. Robin and I would love to have you with us... but under the circumstances, it just wouldn't work out. You're not completely yourself yet and the doctors say you need some... well, not exactly supervision... but to be with someone. You've been here for over six months now and you're just not ready to go out on your own, just yet."

"Amy... I don't really care where I go."

"Do you want us to call your parents?"

"If you wish."

"Well... I only want to call them if you want me to."

"Yes, then... go ahead... I understand it wouldn't work out with my coming back to New York with you."

Amy's heart began to ache. She came over to Katherine, who was sitting in her chair, got down on her knees in front of her and took both of Katherine's hands in hers. She then reached up and stroked Katherine's hair.

"I'm so sorry, Kathy. I'm so sorry things turned out the way they did. You were doing so well... you were so happy."

Amy rose up to Katherine's face and kissed her lightly on the lips.

"Honey... you're my oldest and best friend. I want you to get better... and then we'll get together, just like old times. Real soon. OK?"

Katherine smiled weakly and spoke in a voice that matched her smile.

"Sure... I'll be OK, Amy. You've both been wonderful to me. We'll all get together again... real soon."

Katherine's mouth smiled at Amy and Robin, but her eyes betrayed the impenetrable blackness of her soul. Something precious was gone. The darkness that could be seen through the windows of Katherine's eyes gave the observer the feeling of staring into the cold, charred remains of a campfire that had, only a short time before, blazed so brilliantly.

CHAPTER TWENTY

The uncommonly warm, early March air was colliding with an Arctic breeze that was pushing its way into Canada... determined to return things to normal. The airplane that carried Katherine to Montreal, shook, lifted, and dropped as it was tossed about by the thick, gray violence around it. Brilliant flashes of blue-white lightning added the finishing touches to the high altitude chaos.

In times past, Katherine would have been thrilled by this spectacular display of life-threatening natural violence. This time, however, she was not. She had not seen her family in over thirteen years. Her mother had, over the years, enclosed photos with her letters, but they had, eventually, taken on a sense of unreality. She could rationally accept that these were photos of her family – that the tall, strikingly handsome, dark-haired young man was her son. But in her heart, Jean Paul was still the round-faced, rosy cheeked toddler, crowned with long blonde curls, she had last seen in the arms of her mother as she boarded her plane for France, those many years ago.

In her mind's eye, her parents were still the robust, energetic, middle-aged couple she left behind in the terminal that day... unable to accept that the thin, gray creatures in the photos could possibly be them. Emotionally, she simply denied that it could be true. Her oldest brother, Jacques, was now in his mid-forties, with four children. His oldest son would be graduating from Cornell University in two months. Her sister would turn forty in August. Her youngest brother had just turned thirty-five. Both were married, with children. Collette had three daughters. Andre had two sons. The last time the four Deville children were together, they were all in their twenties... just kids starting out on life's journey... full of hope and ambition.

Katherine, finally returning to Montreal, now understood that, truly, no one can ever go home again. Nothing was as she had left it. Her old world had moved on without her. As with most who have been away for a long time, Katherine preserved home, unchanged, in her heart... and felt selfishly and irrationally angry that things had been transformed without her consent... that they should have had the consideration to stay the same as when she left... to await her return.

Katherine was, of all the things she would face upon her return, most anxious about Jean Paul. Her mother had written her of his album... of how he worshiped her and followed her life and stories as though she were some mythical goddess. Katherine knew she would be a certain disappointment to her son. Few can, she knew, while still alive, measure up to a legend. Such a worry was, however, but one source of Katherine's concerns. She also felt that returning home was, perhaps, a tragic mistake. Jean Paul could very well be, in the long run, better off with his dreams and his aggrandized imagination, than with the reality of a broken, disappointed, and disappointing woman just out of a drug-recovery clinic. Yet, where else was she to go? For the first time in her life, Katherine had no meaningful point of destination.

Life, to Katherine, had had meaning only through her ever-changing vistas... be it art, music, sex, drugs, travel, marriage, career, fame, knowledge, religion, or having a child. Once she had become familiar with these newfound worlds, however, she could fathom no further purpose in remaining there. To stay would be to Katherine, to die. She could never understand how anyone tolerated everyday life. It was so... common. Passing the days, repeating the same meaningless acts, was Katherine's concept of hell. As a matter of fact, when she was a little girl, and still attending mass with her family, she would try to imagine what this hell and purgatory – about which the parish priest was so fond of referring – was all about. The underground world of eternal flames and torment seemed a bit cartoonish... even to her very young mind. No... in Katherine's way of thinking, hell would be more along the lines of being condemned, for all eternity, to be ordinary... to work the same job forever... to always be around the same people... to return to the same house everyday... to the same family. She could see no more purpose in such a life than in being a tree stump. What meaning or purpose could one possibly find in constantly repeating the same day, over and over again?

Yet, as Katherine surveyed the world into which she was born, she saw just that sort of hell, everywhere she looked... ordinary people with ordinary intelligence, with ordinary talent, thinking ordinary thoughts, saying ordinary things... aspiring to the mundane. This, she knew from the moment she was capable of reason, she could never tolerate. The very thought of it struck unthinkable, claustrophobic fear into her mind... and panic into her heart. The fear of this unspeakable horror had unmercifully driven Katherine from horizon to horizon... leaving each scene the moment it became familiar... running from the hell hounds of the ordinary who were always but a hot breath behind her heels.

Now here she was... descending into Montreal airport... plunging back into the world of the ordinary... having no new horizon as a destination. The hounds had finally run her down. Katherine had seen all she had desired to see... and found nothing that had any lasting meaning to her. With panic rising in her chest, at the same rate the plane descended, Katherine knew she had finally been damned to the insufferable hell of commonplace.

CHAPTER TWENTY-ONE

JOHN

Rachael E. Hennessey

Survived by her son, John, her daughter Elizabeth Hennessey McGrath, and three grandchildren.

John Hennessey read the black marque with the push-on white letters, standing just inside the entrance of the Geible Funeral Home, then quickly glanced at his watch. Six fifteen... viewing until seven... services at seven fifteen... out of there by eight at the latest. He'd make his flight back to California.

Stepping inside the viewing room, John spotted his sister... sitting with her husband and children on the far side of the room, a few feet from the casket... dealing with a mixed stream of true mourners and obligatory appearances. Her face was pale, her eyes, dark circled and sunken... her eyelids, red and puffy. This was her second day of this duty and she looked much worse for the wear. The room was full of friends and relatives and the curious... talking in hushed tones... careful not to let a smile slip through their mindful death faces. John hated this sort of "crap," as he called it. His mother was dead... she was a good and kind lady... let it go at that. As John saw it, this funeral "bullshit" was a grand waste of time – and money. Had his mother left him and his sister the cash she had prepaid for the funeral and had just been cremated, they would have each pocketed about seventy-five hundred dollars.

From where John was standing he could occasionally catch a glimpse of the grotesque, porcelain doll profile in the casket that was to have resembled his mother's face. The mortician must have been an admirer of Picasso, John figured, judging by the surreal mask he had painted on her corpse.

"Your mother looks wonderful, John. She was a fine woman."

John stared at the bony, elderly man with a lump protruding from the left side of his forehead, extending his hand in John's direction. John had no idea who he was, but shook it anyway.

"Thank you."

Other than a handful of visits to his parents' home, John had not returned to his hometown nor stayed in contact with anyone else he had known in Springfield, since he left for college some twenty years before. He had no interest in his family and no friends with whom he wished to stay in contact.

John Hennessey had had only one friend in his entire life... Donny Broad. He and Donny were both too immature for kindergarten and had both cried for the entire first week. This, John supposed, was some weird kind of bonding, but, thereafter, they were inseparable. When they returned from Christmas vacation, John had brought in a toy motorboat his mother had given him as a Christmas gift... the only gift he'd received. It was made of plastic that looked like wood and had a battery-driven propeller. There was a front seat, into which you could place the two passengers that came with the boat... one with hands that wrapped around the steering wheel. Donny's eyes lit up when he saw it. It was, he said, the neatest toy he had ever seen. He wondered aloud to John, if he could borrow it and play with it in his tub. John had not yet, himself, put it into water... saving the christening for a special time he had planned, but Donny was his best and only friend, so he reluctantly gave it to him.

A week later, Donny still had not returned the boat and had not mentioned it, either. John was anxious to get back his only Christmas present, but didn't want to bring it up to Donny... afraid he might take it the wrong way and stop being his only friend. Finally, after two weeks, John mentioned the situation to his mother. Unfortunately for John, his father overheard the conversation. John, senior, asked John, junior, if he was aware how much that boat cost. John was not, he said. His father told him he should be. Mr. Hennessey demanded to know Donny's last name and where he lived.

On the way over to Donny's house, John's father kept his eyes directly ahead, on the upcoming road, as he laid out the facts of life for John's enlightenment. It was time they talked, he told his small son. Friends, Mr. Hennessey explained, are those people who are able to get close enough to you, to knife you in the back. All friends are, he said, are people who want something from you. No one is nice to you, he explained, unless they want something. This situation with Donny Broad was a good learning experience for him and John should feel lucky, he said, that he was learning this lesson so young. All it had cost him, this time, was a couple of weeks without a toy boat. He, on the other hand, had learned about friends the hard way and it had cost him dearly. It wasn't too early for John to learn about the true nature of life, he said.

Mr. Hennessey went on to explain that life was a simple situation... you're born, you live, and you die... that's it... nothing more. He told his small son that people would try to feed him cock-and-bull stories about heaven and hell and love and flowers but in the end, you're on your own... nobody's going to look out for you, but you... and when you're dead, that's it... the end of the show. Fifty years after the two of them are gone, he said, nobody would even know they were ever alive. John interrupted.

"But Daddy... Mommy looks out after you and me and Elly. She loves us doesn't she?"

"Well John, it's a long story. Everybody, you see, has a job... it's what they're supposed to do. Your mother is a woman... she was born to have children and look after them. That's what she's supposed to do. It's just like the way Heidi looked after her puppies or the way that robin outside your window last spring sat on her eggs then fed her babies worms after they hatched. Nature makes animals do things so they can survive. Nature, understand, is selfish, too. All it cares about is surviving. We humans like to call this sort of thing love – but it's just nature... people doing what they're born to do. If nature has to allow the weak animals to die for survival... it will. Remember that only one of those baby robins lived?"

"I cried when those babies died, Daddy."

"There's nothing to cry about, John. It's just the way nature works. Apparently there was a reason that those three robins didn't make it."

"But people aren't animals, Daddy. We wear clothes and drive cars and stuff like that."

Mr. Hennessey laughed. "We don't like to admit we're animals... we like to pretend that we're something special... but we're not. We're just a little smarter and, for now, pretty much run the show. But don't forget, John, not that many generations ago, our ancestors looked like apes and, further back, all living things can trace their family tree to the same pond slime."

At this point... with the pond slime and all, Mr. Hennessey had totally lost his young son, but as John grew, these lessons were repeated time and again... and they had their inexorable effect... and as they did, Rachael Hennessey grew increasingly distressed at seeing her loving, kindhearted Johnny become his father's son.

When Rachael Woodland was a high school sophomore and John Hennessey was a senior, she fell in love with the brilliance of John Hennessey's mind, the strength of his character, his athletic physique, and his exceptionally handsome face. He seemed to know everything about anything and was the most determined person she had ever met... not a weakling like her father – who drank too much, cried too often, never got ahead at work, and who, in a crisis, left her mother to be strong for the family. She wanted a man... a strong man... for a husband and father to her children... a man destined for success, who didn't know the meaning of failure.

Rachael Woodland got her wish. John received an academic and athletic scholarship to Carnegie Tech and, five years later, graduated magna cum laude in architecture. After graduation, John was immediately hired by a prominent architectural firm in Houston, Texas... one of some two dozen job offers he received. He married Rachael and took her to Texas with him. Within four years, he had left the firm and had founded his own practice, which was, in precious few years, one of the leading firms in the Houston area. John had proven himself to be what Rachael had anticipated he would be. He was strong, decisive, determined, ambitious, and successful. She wanted for nothing... except love.

It wasn't long after they married that Rachael Hennessey realized that men possessed of great brilliance, strength, ambition, and determination have little left for anything – or anyone – else. It was a trade-off, she guessed, and she wasn't sure which was worse. Her father was a failure and a disappointment whom she disdained and often pitied... but she had loved him without limit, nevertheless. Despite his many faults, he had loved his family... and loved life. He loved music and poetry. He would cry over a sad movie. John had none of her father's faults... but neither did he possess any of his attributes. Desperate, Rachael got pregnant... over John's objections. He couldn't see, as he put it, the "necessity of children." As he saw it, things were fine as they were.

Johnny's birth filled the void in Rachael's lonely heart. She was, she discovered too late, very much like her father... needing love and family more than anything else in life. After several years of marriage to John, she would have traded all that she had... the big house, the cars, the status, the money... all for a word of love from her husband. She finally concluded that John was simply, incapable of love. He was, without question... talented, intelligent, reliable, good-looking, and a wonderful provider, so much so that Rachael was the envy of many of her friends, but her covetous friends failed to take into account what she did not have. John Hennessey was, at his core, an exclusively rational and emotionally detached human being. The only emotion she had ever seen him express was anger... usually as a by-product of his not having achieved some objective as soon, or in the precise manner he had desired.

Rachael became consummately resolute that her precious son would not become like his father. Johnny would have a heart... she would see to that. Rachael, in pursuing her ends, showered her little boy with love and constantly talked to him of feelings, and families, and the beauty of the world. She read him stories about puppies and bunnies, and mommies and daddies and children who all loved each other. She strolled him through the parks and the zoo... taking every opportunity to point out the love and beauty of the world. Rachael's heart swelled to near-bursting each time Johnny would, without being asked, kiss her and tell her he loved her. Rachael taught Johnny to pray and he would ask God to bless his Mommy and Daddy and his grandpa and two grandmas... and after her arrival, his baby sister, Elly, too. Not long after the Donny Broad matter, however, Rachael began to notice some small but disturbing changes in Johnny.

With Elly aboard in her car seat, Rachael picked up Johnny on his last day of kindergarten. To celebrate the occasion, Rachael had promised Johnny they would eat at McDonald's then go to see *Bambi* playing at the mall theater... Johnny's choice. Rachael had initially hesitated to take Johnny to see *Bambi*. She was afraid some parts of it... particularly when Bambi's mother is killed... might upset him, but all the other kids in his class had seen it and faced with this compelling rationale, she, of course, gave in. As unobtrusively as possible, she monitored Johnny's reactions to the sad scenes of the movie... ready to provide comfort as needed. To her dismay... no comforting was necessary. Throughout the entire movie, Johnny's expression remained stoical... appearing more to be studying the movie than feeling it. She waited until she was tucking him in bed to say something.

"Did you like the movie, honey?"

"It was really good, Mommy."

"Weren't some parts of it really sad... especially when Bambi's mother was killed? I hadn't seen it since I was a little girl, but I got tears in my eyes. Did you?"

"No."

"Didn't you think that was sad?"

"No. That's just the way things are, Mommy. Men shoot deer to eat... it's nothing to cry about."

Johnny's words were so much an echo of her husband that after she recovered from the anguish that knifed through her heart, hate pumped hot blood through her brain. She felt that, had her husband walked through the door that very moment, she would have surely killed him... as surely as he was killing their son's kind, loving heart. At that moment, Rachael Hennessey mentally declared war on her husband for Johnny's soul. The next morning at the breakfast table with Johnny still in bed, she proclaimed it.

"John... I'm not going to let you destroy Johnny."

"What in God's name are you talking about, Rachael?"

"You're turning him into an automaton like you... I'm not going to let you do it. I'm going to fight you every step of the way, John. I mean it. Johnny was a caring, sensitive, loving, sweet child... and you're trying to make him into a cold, calculating bastard like you."

"What's this all about?"

"Johnny didn't cry during *Bambi*."

"What?!"

"He didn't cry during *Bambi*... and he should have."

"I'm a coldhearted bastard because John didn't cry during *Bambi*?!"

"First of all – you insensitive prick – don't try to make a joke out of this. Secondly, our son is five years old... he's too young to be 'John'... that makes him sound like he's an adult. I've asked you a thousand times to stop calling him that. The point is that *Bambi* is a very emotional movie with some very sad parts. A child with normal emotions would get upset... most children Johnny's age would cry or at least get tears in their eyes during the movie. Johnny was like a rock. He had no emotions... no expression. Last night I asked him about it and he sounded just like you. He told me that things are the way they are... deer get killed... there's nothing to be sad about. It's you... I know it's your influence on him... and I'm not going to let you ruin him. I want a son who has a heart and feelings... a son who's not afraid to cry or to fall in love... who's not a block of wood with a stone for a heart... like you."

"OK, Rachael... well... first of all, I'll call my son whatever I think is appropriate. I've always hated these cutesy little names with e's at the end of them. His name is John and that's what I'll call him. Secondly... it seems as though you aspire to have our son become a weakling like your beloved father. Are you hoping he'll become a blubbering drunk, too?"

Rachael was instantly on her feet. She threw her half empty coffee cup and saucer at John's face. A quick athletic move of his head barely averted a direct hit, but the saucer glanced off his left ear. The collision of the breakfast porcelain with the marble tile floor echoed sharply throughout the spacious kitchen. Rachael Hennessey was enraged.

"You fucking prick! How dare you criticize my father! He had his faults but at least he had a heart! When they cut you open they're going to find nothing but a cold piece of granite!"

Rachael was so angry she was shaking. Tears came to her eyes and she ran from the kitchen... not wanting John to have the satisfaction of seeing her cry. John dispassionately surveyed the results of Rachael's "tantrum," as he considered it. The cup and saucer were broken into slivers and spread out over the floor in a wet, brownish spray. The left sleeve and shoulder of his white shirt were brown-speckled, as well. He methodically cleaned up the floor mess... then proceeded upstairs to get a clean shirt from their bedroom. Rachael was sitting on the edge of the bed... her back to him... staring out the window and dabbing her eyes and nose with a tissue. As he was departing the bedroom he spoke to her, nonchalantly.

"See you after work, Rachael."

Rachael replied, her voice exhibiting the hoarse aftermath of her tears.

"I meant what I said, John. I won't let you ruin Johnny."

"Whatever you say, Rachael... whatever you say."

Rachael lost her battle for Johnny. She was never completely sure whether it was John's influence or simply genetics. When sadness or guilt overwhelmed her, she would opt for the latter. There came a day, however – when Johnny was fifteen – that changed her life and her relationship with him, forever. For years, under the influence of her own self-delusion, she remained convinced that, despite the coldness that eventually pervaded Johnny's personality, she loved him still. He was, she would remind herself, still her baby... her son... her firstborn.

As a disease is sometimes, for a while, kept in check by the sheer will of one's body – only to erupt one day without warning or ceremony – her real feelings toward Johnny emerged one morning from the recesses of her soul, just as she awakened... in that vulnerable and tender valley between dreams and life. She sat on the edge of her bed and mouthed her escaping thoughts – loud enough for her to hear their recital.

"... I don't love Johnny."

Having heard herself speak these secret words, kept buried for many years, in fear of allowing herself to even think them, Rachael wailed as a woman whose son had just died. As if at Johnny's wake, she tore at herself, beat her legs and arms with her fists... hating herself for not loving her own, her only son... her firstborn child. She knew that when a mother comes to not loving her own son, he is for her, dead, and that the part of her heart, dedicated to him from the moment she first felt his movement in her womb, dies along with him. What kind of a woman, she asked herself a thousand times that morning, does not love her own son? Only a woman, who is not fit to be a mother, was her answer. Is not a mother's life... a mother's being... her reason for living... to love the children who grow inside her very body... who feed at her breast... whose very smell and breath she memorizes at birth? A mother who no longer loves her child, she concluded, is a woman undeserving of any further sustenance from the world. She is, and rightly should be, she felt... a pariah among women.

Rachael's rites of death and penance went on for the entire day. When her husband found her that evening, she was more unconscious than asleep. She was lying, naked, and face down on the cold, dark blue tiles of the bathroom floor. Her arms were covered with blood. John quickly rolled her onto her back, noticing as he did, the large puddle of blood on the floor that her body had been covering. The entire front of her body was crimson with wet blood... still oozing from the deep scratches that covered her body. Rachael's fingernails and palms were painted in dried blood and skin scrapings. John called an ambulance.

Rachael, the medical staff reported to John, was in a state of shock from excessive loss of blood. She required several immediate blood transfusions. She remained in intensive care for two days. Her attending physician felt her physical injuries were, though quite serious, not life-threatening. Her vital signs, however, remained alarmingly weak. Dr. Hernandez questioned her will to live and began treating Rachael as an attempted suicide. He asked John if she was depressed or extremely upset about anything. He told the doctor that he was totally unaware of anything unusual that had occurred. He could think of absolutely nothing that had happened that day or, for that matter, for as far back as he could remember, that could have set off such a dreadful act of self-mutilation. Rachael, he said, had been doing what she had always done. There had been no big arguments... no big problems of any sort, of which he was aware. John told Dr. Hernandez that he was totally at a loss to explain Rachael's vicious attack – carried out against her own body. The kids, he said, were doing fine... good students... never in any real trouble. Rachael was tending to her duties as a mother and wife as she had always done... washing clothes, cooking meals, attending P.T.A. meetings, driving Elly to her lessons, John to his games. She had, her husband explained, a good and happy life... many friends... great children... a beautiful home. This self-mutilation was so bizarre and out of character for Rachael that he was, he said, absolutely flabbergasted over its occurrence.

Rachael spent two months in the hospital. She had some very bad bouts with infection and her fingernails had torn off so much of her skin that she required a number of skin grafts. By the time of her release, the wounds were substantially healed, but had left behind ugly scarring across the entire front of her body and face, giving her the appearance of having been a burn victim. Several psychiatrists talked to her about why she had done this to herself... but to no avail. She refused to discuss the matter with anyone. During her entire hospitalization, the only comment she made about the incident was in response to her husband's inquiry... and then saying only, "It's between my God and me."

Upon her return home, given the circumstances of her departure, life returned to normal, in remarkably short time. In Rachael's heart, she felt she had suffered, as she had deserved, for a mother's greatest sin. She had suffered the pain and would, deservedly, bear the scars of her sin – for all the world to see – for the remainder of her life. Her ivory white, youthful skin had been replaced by a course hide, garnished with ripples, creases, bumps, craters, and enlarged pores. Out of her continuing need for atonement, Rachael steadfastly refused the suggested plastic surgery that offered her promise of a much-improved appearance.

Rachael resumed her normal activities around her home and in her life with such an uncanny, everyday demeanor, it was as if the frenzied, self-mayhem had never occurred. She took up doing exactly what she had always done... in the manner she had always done it. Only Johnny knew there was something fundamentally different. No words had passed between his mother and him that proclaimed the death of his mother's love for him, but Johnny knew. And he didn't care. In his view, this new relationship with his mother made it actually "cleaner"... by eliminating the messy emotions that unnecessarily clutter-up associations within a family. If anything, the withdrawal of his mother's love merely reinforced his now thoroughly ingrained life view... that love is just a silly "hearts and flowers" creation that clouds over the true nature of a purely biological function.

According to the chapter and verse John had memorized – benefit of his father – nature compels the females of certain species to care for their offspring for prolonged periods of time. This compulsion had been glamorized and romanticized... attaching aesthetic and even metaphysical meaning where none belonged. The fact that his mother appeared to be fine – and that he was fine, as well – was proof to Johnny that one could certainly live without "love" – that daydreamer's fancy, liberally attached to a horde of mundane biological functions. It really made no ostensible difference in his life. He still had a roof over his head and his mother continued to cook meals for him and wash his clothes. Nothing that really mattered had changed.

Like his father, John was an intelligent, determined young man. He graduated as his high school's class valedictorian. His graduation address was one that would be remembered by all those who heard it, or heard about it, for many years to come. It was, as was everything with him... short and to the point.

> I won't bore you with flowery words and grand visions. I am valedictorian of this class for one reason and one reason only... I have achieved the best grades of the entire graduating class. I was able to do this for two reasons. First of all, I have an I.Q. which is considerably higher than any classmate in this auditorium... and, secondly, I am more determined than any other student in this class.

While valedictorians typically stand before their classmates, relatives, staff and faculty and thank many people for their success, I will not. What I have achieved has been strictly because of my own innate ability... and there is no one here to thank for the random and uneven distribution of genetic materials. I have found the teachers in this high school to be of average intelligence, at best, and to be considerably lacking in commitment and professionalism. The administrators are possessed of these attributes to an even lesser degree. I leave behind in this school, no one whom I would call friend... and without regret. I have gotten from this experience what I need... a diploma, a top-of-the-class ranking, and a full scholarship to Harvard.

I will recommend a particular reading to you, my fellow graduates, which I doubt that many of you have read – Charles Darwin's *Origin of Species*. This, I believe, will help you make better sense of your life... your successes... your shortcomings, far better than any other book you may select for such a purpose. Make no mistake about it... the principles of natural selection, as described by Darwin, are as applicable to us in this day as they were to the first slime that floated upon the stagnant water of an ancient pond. The strongest among us will survive... and the weak will fall. This is the way of life. It is not cruel... it is not unfair... it is not evil. It is merely life as it is and nothing more.

Do not make more of life than what it is. It is a struggle... each of us against one another – a struggle for the limited resources and pleasures of this earth. Don't allow silly romantic notions to distort the true nature of life... for it can weaken you and confuse you. Set your sights on whatever you want and achieve it by any means within your power. Rely on your strength and don't look for a helping hand. That extended paw may look inviting... but a close examination will surely reveal its hidden claws... ready to tear into you and hold you in its selfish grasp the moment you reach out for it.

You have but one life to live. Derive from it all that you can. Don't be lulled into complacency and mediocrity by weaklings who rely upon fairy tales to explain life and their personal failures. Believe me... you are not storing up treasures in heaven during this life. All you will ever be after your death is what the dead of every species has been since the first spark of life appeared on this planet... recycled chemicals for use by future life forms... nothing more... nothing less.

So, my fellow classmates... my final admonition to you is a simple one – "Eat, drink, and be merry, because tomorrow we die." Believe me my dear classmates... one thing we will all do... and this is the only promise I will make to you... we will all die... and much sooner than we like to imagine. A few years after we are gone... very few will remember us. All of your great anxiety and handwringing will have been for nothing. One hundred years from now... no one in this entire assembly will be either alive or remembered.

Enjoy your lives. There are no reruns. Good luck and good bye.

At Harvard, John Hennessey quickly stood out among his colleagues... for both his intellect and his extreme views, and, consequently, he quickly acquired a number of critics as well as admirers. During the second semester of his freshman year, John established a club which he named, "The Cognitive Society," which had among its stated purposes, "... to attack the false, misleading, and perverse romanticization of reality." The Cognitive Society held weekly meetings, first in John's dorm room, then, as the club grew, in the back room of a local bar. The meetings were informal at first, with John serving as the facilitator of the discussions. As with most groups, however, given the human compulsion for order – habits, then rituals, then rules developed. Dues, officers (John, president), planned events, and a publication (*The Foglight*), evolved in due time. *The Foglight* was initially distributed on the Harvard campus, only... then, as membership grew, resulting in more dues, to a number of other colleges.

In the first issue of *The Foglight*, John, in the "President's Message," set forth the views of the Cognitive Society.

> As rational human beings, the members of the Cognitive Society believe that much damage is done to the advance of the human race and its potential by the distortions of reality by weaklings and fools, passing under the name of artist, poet, lover, and holy-man. The Society has dedicated itself to resisting and opposing these deceivers. We are committed to the truth of reality and will do whatever we can do, within our power, to reveal and preserve it.
>
> We hold the following to be true: Human beings are animals who represent, to date, the highest life-form to have evolved on this planet. Human beings do what they do because of their instinctual drive to survive and propagate, as does every other life-form, and for no other purpose. Neither humans beings, nor any other form of existence, organic or inorganic, nor the totality of existence itself, is divine or of divine creation. The existence of the universe is a random occurrence which is physical in nature and which follows no plan. The physical universe is the beginning and end of existence. There is nothing beyond it and there is no meaning beyond physical existence.
>
> "Love" is merely a chemical process affecting the brain and other organs of the body, serving the evolutionary function of propagation and of child rearing. "Beauty" is but a cultural bias. "God" is a fictional creation, serving to explain life and death to those neither intelligent enough nor strong enough to accept reality as it is. "Art" is but an evolved instinct to manipulate physical materials – as in painting and sculpture – having no more meaning than the

"art" of a spider web, or the design of a honeycomb, or a bird's nest. The so-called "art" of dance is instinctual movement, having no more significance than the mating rituals of many other species. Music is nothing more than organized and repetitive sounds which have no higher purpose than the calls, quacks, squeals, chirps, whistles, and buzzes, of other animals. "Good" and "Evil" are but labels chosen by groups of human beings for behaviors that they wish to encourage or discourage, widely differing from group to group. "Evil" is no more applicable to a human than it is to a Black Widow spider, a rat, a maggot, or an illness-causing virus. As for "Good"... is a gorilla who tends to her young for years, "good," while a fish who eats hers, "evil?"

We have joined together in the Cognitive Society to shine a collective light through the thick fog which has been spewed into the clear air of reality by misguided romantics whose only accomplishments have been to obscure the vision of truth. You are invited to join us in our mission.

By the end of its third year, *The Foglight* had a distribution of more than ten thousand readers, spread over twenty campuses and John was frequently invited to address colonized chapters of the Cognitive Society across the country. Within this association of extremists, John had achieved his first celebrity.

The Society was not, of course, John Hennessey's only interest at Harvard. He was, after all, by his own definition, an "animal"... highly evolved, albeit. As such, he had his "instincts" and his "needs." As a handsome, athletically sleek, intelligent, and articulate young man, John did not lack the ready availability of what is required to satisfy the paramount "instinct" of male youths. One feat of John's, in this instinctual regard, became legendary among his "associates" – John still laying no claim to any person as a "friend." During the course of a Valentine's Day bash in John's junior year – designated as a lingerie party – he became an immediate icon among his male peers by the extraordinary feat of having had sex with seven women in one evening. Actually, the truth was that it was only six women... John having had sex with one coed twice, constituting the first and sixth episode. This particular "repeat" coed, some weeks later, loudly confronted John as he was exiting a chemistry lab. She animatedly expressed to John, her shock and total lack of awareness that she had been a part of this, "perverse sexual daisy chain," as she referred to it. She had been his date to the party and told him she felt entirely demeaned and dehumanized by his behavior. She told him he was a "... totally reprehensible and amoral degenerate." She, Candice Kaplan by name, told John he should be ashamed of himself... ashamed to even look at any of the females he had so debauched.

John waited until Candice had completed her tirade. His smirk then broadened into a full-faced smile, erupting, finally, into an uninhibited howling laugh... whereupon Candice burst into tears. John laughed long and loud, the sounds reverberating down the long, concrete, basement corridor of the science building... having no care about the scene he was generating for the benefit of curious passersby. With some effort, John was finally able to regain a sufficient demeanor that allowed him to speak... occasionally broken by remaining bubbles of laughter, still finding their way out.

"Look... Candy, isn't it?"

Candice's sobs ceased instantly and her eyes narrowed at this additional, new insult, hurled by John's feigning to be unable to recall her name. Unbeknownst to her, however, the lost name was actually genuine on John's part.

"Well, whatever your name is... get real... OK? You gave me sex twice in the space of a few hours on the first date we were ever on. Now, all of a sudden, you're the Virgin Mary? You spread your legs for me for the same reason that women have always done it... hoping I'd like it enough to come back for more so you could tangle me up in the 'relationship' web. If it had worked, we would have been 'making love'... if it hadn't – like it didn't – I'm a selfish, perverted bastard. Face it, sweetie, you're every bit as mercenary about sex as I am... just not as honest."

Candice's right hand shot out, fist closed, and slammed into John's cheek. She screamed.

"You fucker!"

Candice Kaplan ran, crying, down the corridor and exited out the first set of doors she could find. John rubbed his cheek... his temper aroused. He shouted after her before she traversed the doorway.

"Asshole!!"

CHAPTER TWENTY-TWO

As he fully expected, John graduated from Harvard with honors... receiving his Bachelor's Degree in structural engineering. As had his father before him, John received dozens of job offers from top engineering, architectural, and construction companies from all across the country. He decided upon a position with a company in Los Angeles that engaged in worldwide, large scale, construction projects. John was assigned to the dam building division. He worked at dam construction sites in more than two dozen countries over the next five years... quickly rising to assistant director of the division... the youngest person ever to hold that position.

Though John's knowledge of the world was greatly expanded by his travels, his long-held view of life remained unchanged. He was out to get what he could in this life... before his "chemicals" fed the next generation of organisms. Although his talent and intelligence partially accounted for his meteoric rise at Anatel Construction, his exquisitely designed and faultlessly executed treachery played an equally important role. John's shrewd and calculating mind quickly assessed the culture, traps, chutes, and ladders at Anatel and he expeditiously formed plans for his climb to the top – over, around, or through anyone in his way. He used whatever strategy necessary for any given situation... be it charm, talent, intimidation, deceit, character assassination, or outright theft of another's ideas. True to his nature, John did not have anyone he considered a friend at Anatel... though a fair number of his colleagues were entirely convinced that they were. John's mode of dealing with people who could help or hurt him could be summarized by the classic entreaty that advised of the prudence of "keeping your friends close... but your enemies closer." John moved forward expeditiously – unencumbered by either conscience or moral principle. The only two questions that John Hennessey ever considered in any contemplated plan of action were – will it work, and if it involved a potentially damaging moral or legal transgression, what is the likelihood of being caught?

John's attitude toward women also remained unchanged as his knowledge of the world grew. Women continued to be, in John's assessment, good only for the most obvious thing. He had no desire for children but, like any other healthy male... he required sexual servicing. In this pursuit and not trusting anyone – women, of course, included – John had a vasectomy to protect his interests. He understood the plotting mind of the female and he would allow no "pregnancy trap" to close on him. On a couple of occasions, a few women tried out the "I've missed my period... what are we going to do?" ploy to ferret out his true intentions. In response to such amateurish schemers, John would, in cruel humor – intended to humiliate these amateurish schemers who had the audacity to believe that he was blockheaded enough to be manipulated by such an obvious plot – take on a look of great concern, walk slowly out of the room, and return with a medical file folder which contained the details of his vasectomy operation. Still clutching the folder in his hands, he would then address these unknowing targets with affected distress in both his voice and demeanor.

"First, there's something you need to know about me. I don't know how to tell you this."

Finishing his sentence, he would then hand the poor woman the folder while feigning a look of unforgivable guilt. A look of sheer terror would invariably come over his victim as she received the green, manila folder – fearing certain discovery of having been infected with some horrific disease by him. It took several frantic minutes for each woman to read through, decipher, and finally glean the meaning of the very technical documents. John knew the precise moment of epiphany by the unmistakable death-wish expression each of them directed toward him. The joke completed, John laughed like a hyena... bounced in his chair, and clapped his hands in a fit of near-uncontrollable mirth, whereupon each and every woman proceeded to engage in one or more acts of violence, including slapping, clawing, biting, and screaming obscenities at him. After these experiences, John was absolutely convinced that nothing could anger a woman to a greater degree than being outfoxed by a man in the mating game.

THE DISCIPLES

John found his prestigious job, large salary, expensive clothes and car, and his expansive, beautifully decorated condominium in West Los Angeles to be just the right bait for foraging females of the species. He had a highly recommended interior designer decorate his condo which included, strictly for the effect, the strategic placement of numerous pieces of expensive art. John still viewed art as meaningless "crap"... but he found it worked well for entertaining business clients and also for "bedding down the females" as he described it.

John's seductions became so routine that he could run it on a woman, almost without thinking. Most of his conquests were "meat," as he referred to such women, from the L.A. clubs. Going on a "hunt," he'd wear obviously expensive suits... buy drinks for targeted game... relate his experiences from around the world... (he knew after a while, which played better than others... which to drop and which to embellish)... imply the enormity of his salary... flash his expensive rings... suggest he was tired of the bachelor life and was looking for a permanent relationship... invite her to drinks and the hot tub at his condo... entice her with the possibility of landing all this for herself... then let her take the hook. John's sexual performance was what would be expected of such a devout egoist. He had not the slightest care about the woman's satisfaction... but, he discovered, few women actually minded. Their focus was on where the sex would lead, not on the quality of the conduit. Given all that John could apparently offer, a small thing like failing to achieve climax could be indulgently overlooked.

John would continue to be involved with a particular woman until it became patently obvious to her that she had been used, whereupon she would create a quite predictable scene and whereupon John would move on. To John's initial amazement, it took some rather intelligent and sophisticated females, weeks – sometimes months – to figure out his game. He eventually connected the length of time to the woman's level of desperation. He discovered that women in their late-twenties to late-thirties, who had not as yet had their offspring, were unquestionably the most desperate of age groups. They wanted a husband and children so badly that John felt a level of disgust at how easily they took the hook. He found he could treat women like this in a blatantly rude manner and still get sex, as long as he dangled the domestic bait before their eyes. Despite clear, obvious signs that indicated he was overtly using them, women as desperate as these would very often continue on – in denial – blinded by nature's unbending will.

On the other hand, John found most women who had reached their forties, as yet unmarried, to be fairly well resigned to being childless and grudgingly accepting of life without a husband. No longer desperate, they were just too hard to get into bed and John, thus, avoided them. Women who were divorced, with children, were cautious, as well... and not as likely to take his bait without thorough consideration of the circumstances and demand for concrete assurance of promise fulfillment. Consequently, John avoided this group as well ... except in dire sexual emergencies – which were rare.

On occasion, John would connect with married women who would claim to be looking for sex alone, and nothing more... much to his appreciation. Initially, he believed the professed motivations of such women. He eventually discovered, however, that most were, actually, dissatisfied with their husbands and were looking for new before dumping the old – or in the alternative, cheating on their husbands to get even for *his* cheating. John found that the women, of the first instance, would eventually initiate implicit, then finally, explicit dialogue on "the future," as would any other woman who was seeking the apprehension of a permanent mate. At least with these women, John knew he could self-righteously defend their inevitable complaint of "being used" with the retort that it was they, in fact, who misled him... which he invariably offered with great satisfaction. In the second case, the woman would cheat on her husband to the extent that she felt the score had been significantly more than evened... after which – satisfied, and without fanfare – she would return to the exclusive bed of her mate. Though unpredictable, John grew to appreciate the easy-exit aspect of these particular liaisons.

Eventually, however, as John entered the third decade of his life, the grind of the hunt became wearisome. He was, therefore, faced with a dilemma. He had a biological need for sex but had grown tired of the effort required to get it. He considered prostitutes as a solution, but concluded they were too expensive, too risky, and, in general, not very appealing. Next, he weighed the pros and cons of keeping a mistress. This, he decided, was altogether too expensive... with the apartment, stipend, clothes, etc. John's final deliberations were upon the possibility of either a female live-in, or marriage.

The problem with a live-in, as John saw it, was that she would, he was convinced, initially agree to the arrangement, but all the while intend on parlaying the deal into marriage. He didn't want to be forced to contend with the constant ploys and games that would come with this sort of relationship, and so, in the final analysis, John opted for marriage... but for reasons beyond the easy availability of sex.

There were advantages to marriage and family life that John had eventually come to recognize. He had begun to notice that successful men frequently used both their wives and children to their distinct advantage... not only in business but in the political arena as well – a field which had begun to arouse his interest. Unmarried and childless men, he came to realize, are often at a disadvantage in these circumstances... and John was not one to concede an advantage to anyone. The right woman, he decided, and – if it fit his needs – a couple of good-looking kids, could greatly enhance his future, if he played it right, regardless of his chosen career path. The issue resolved, John set about – in his standard, calculating way – to accomplish his objectives.

After much consideration, John systematically established his criteria for a spouse. She must be very attractive... from a good gene pool... mentally noting that he needed to get a good look at her mother before things went too far. There could not, obviously, be any history of infertility or other health problems. She needed to be intelligent enough to be of use to him, but not to the extent that she would be personally ambitious. She must possess sufficient social poise to handle the appropriate occasions, but be sufficiently insecure to ensure that she would be dependent upon him and subservient to the degree that he could maintain rigid control over her. John realized that his criteria was quite expansive and specific and would, therefore, severely limit the potential marriageable pool, but he was determined, nonetheless, to achieve his objectives.

One particular aspect of the marriage arrangement that John wanted to absolutely guarantee was protection of his financial estate. If the marriage turned out to be a mistake, he did not want his wife to benefit from his error. In pursuance of this end, he sought out the best divorce lawyer in the Los Angeles area for counsel. Armed, therefore, with an ironclad pre-nuptial agreement, John began his search.

John knew, setting out, that finding a woman who would fulfill his criteria and who would, also, be willing to sign a pre-nuptial agreement – stripping her of everything in the event of a divorce – would be a challenge, indeed. A woman with the looks and adequate breeding he sought, could very likely drive a hard bargain. With this consideration in mind, he added to his criteria that she must, also, be quite vulnerable and naive. This added criterion dictated that, very likely, he would have to search among women of relatively tender years, who were not, as yet, of independent means.

In pursuit of his objective, John volunteered to participate in an undergraduate, executive mentoring program at USC. The executive volunteers were to meet, once a month, to advise undergraduates on their career planning. Each executive was assigned a group of about twenty students – a new group each month – who were to be provided guidance on interviewing for a job, preparing a resume, job searching, networking, corporate politics, and other such information of practical note. Of course, John's only purpose for entering the program was to search for a potential spouse… caring not in the least if he fulfilled the university's intended objectives.

John was sorely disappointed. Nearly all of the women in the program were business majors... all much too analytical and aggressive to suit his needs. With his third group of students, however, he had a stroke of luck. A very attractive accounting major engaged him in conversation after the meeting. She would not do, he immediately concluded. Despite her pleasing physical attributes, her demeanor clearly demonstrated to John that she suffered from the same disqualifications as all the other business majors, with whom he had dealt. As he was in the process of ending the dialogue between them, the coed timidly asked him if he would like to see how campus life had changed since his college days. His curiosity piqued, John asked her what she had in mind. There was a sorority formal in two weeks, she explained... and she thought, perhaps, he might possibly consider going with her. In an instant, John assessed the proposal, screening it for any possible advantages it could offer him. The accounting major didn't qualify... but other females of her acquaintance might. To her astonishment, he accepted.

John felt downright silly knocking at Nicole Fischer's apartment door... a thirty-year-old business executive picking up a school girl for a sorority party, but his plan was set and he'd do whatever it took to carry it out. The door was opened by a young girl in a sweatshirt and very short shorts who could not have been more than eighteen. She ushered him into the living room – with walls decorated in posters of tan, muscled men in bikini briefs, and pictures of cuddly kitties and flowers. Three other young women emerged from the bowels of the dwelling to blatantly stare at John. He stood looking at the mute females... mentally shaking his head at what had the clear signs of an impending debacle. Just as he was about to excuse himself, and bail out, Nicole emerged from the same area, dressed in a formal evening gown with her hair up. She made a stunning appearance. Encouraged by this development, but still unsure of proceeding, John gave clear body signals of his skepticism about the evening – quickly sensed by Nicole. Feeling the need to break the oppressive silence, Nicole introduced John to her awestruck roommates... stating his professional title along with his name. Each young female managed only to eke out a "hi" then continued to look at him as though the slightest provocation might cause all to bounce up and down where they stood. John was exceedingly thankful that he had left Nicole's corsage in the car... the presentation of which would have been, he was sure, simply too much for the juvenile entourage.

Besides finding the antics of the college boys at the formal, amusing – standing in packs to stare, slander, and laugh at John... a tactic John recalled last seeing in junior high school when the school boys were confronted with another, clearly superior male – he also found Emily Hughes. Emily was a strikingly beautiful, statuesque brunette with a bright and engaging smile, exposing a set of brilliantly white, perfectly shaped teeth. She was, he found, upon initiating a conversation with her, an early childhood education major and from a small town in Nebraska, on a full academic scholarship. Her family was blue-collar... her father a foreman on a tractor assembly line... her mother an aide at a Head Start Center... two brothers and one sister... she was the second oldest. She was graduating in May and said she wasn't exactly sure, as of that moment, what she was going to do thereafter. At his inquiry, she showed John a picture of her family... a recent one – pleasantly surprised at his interest. Her mother was in her forties and was still very young-looking and quite attractive. Her father was tall, also nice-looking, with a full head of hair. The genetic pool had promise.

Emily had a buoyant personality... smiling a lot and possessing a pleasant and positive attitude. She was genuinely interested in John's life and his life views, and held very few strong opinions of her own. She talked with John for most of the evening, much to the displeasure and chagrin of Nicole and Emily's date. The latter pair danced together most of the night in a very juvenile effort to spur John and Emily to jealousy. John and Emily set a date to meet the next day for coffee.

Never one to procrastinate when convinced of something, after only nine dates John made the decision to marry Emily Hughes – then proceeded directly to his urologist for a vasectomy reversal... the initial procedure having served him well but no longer fitting his new plans. Emily met his established criteria, almost perfectly. She was beautiful, with a pleasant and very accommodating, submissive personality... was sufficiently intelligent for his purposes... had well-developed social graces... was not personally ambitious... was greatly desirous of having children... was in good health and promising fertility, as far as John could determine... performed well, sexually... was very willing to be a homemaker... and, very importantly, could be easily put into a state of total dependency on him.

Emily accepted John's offer of marriage with childlike joy... and was so absolutely trusting when signing – without reading – the "small agreement," as John described it, that he was taken aback by it. Not that John had any pity for her naiveté and childlike trust... he just found it rather fascinating that a woman of such high intelligence, possessed of a college education, could be... much to his great fortune... so totally lacking in cynicism. Somehow Emily had, at age twenty-two, still retained the frail and easily broken purity of trust and hope normally found in only the very young. The last John recalled being in so pure a state was when he was still in kindergarten. How could anyone, John wondered, have lived such a life that did not, long ago, burst this flimsy bubble of innocence?

John and Emily were married in Hallwell, Nebraska in a very brief ceremony and modest reception. John had offered to pay for a large and lavish affair but Emily's father insisted, as a matter of pride, on doing his duty as the father of the bride. John's parents, Elly and her husband, and their two children were the only wedding guests attending for the groom. Elly served as one of Emily's bridesmaids. Her son, Jeffrey, was the ring bearer and Elly's husband, Arnie, held their baby, Jeanine, during the wedding ceremony. On Emily's side there were one hundred fifty guests, spread out on both sides of the aisle so as not to accentuate the meager size of the Hennessey clan.

After the ceremony, held at the Hallwell United Methodist Church, the wedding party and guests retired to the Hallwell Volunteer Fire Station for the reception... featuring a cafeteria-style meal on paper plates, catered by the ladies auxiliary, and music by Bobby Walker... Hallwell's only professional D.J. The almost-exclusively blue-collar crowd was loud, uninhibited, and friendly. John and his father were barely able to tolerate these "working class ingrates"... as they privately concurred they were. John's mother, Elly and her husband – himself a blue-collar worker – on the other hand, felt quite welcome and at home with the bride's clan and had great fun all evening. Emily could not have been more gracious to all her guests. She made a point to spend some time with everyone in attendance. Despite her humble roots, Emily had somehow developed into an elegant hostess with an impeccable sense of social decorum, that appeared to be completely natural and sincere and in no way flaunting. She seemed to know just what to do or say in any given situation... able to make a ditchdigger or corporate executive feel equally welcome and special. Observing this, John was reassured that he had made the right choice.

Elly and her mother discussed John's marriage, at length, during the reception. They were both shocked, initially, when they learned of John's intention to take a wife... given his life philosophy and his general disregard for both women and children. They both felt that this was a positive sign that a certain sense of humanity was finally taking root in John's life. He must have, they surmised, come to recognize the need for an emotional side to his life and they were delighted that John had finally discovered the beauty of love. Rachael, having given up on John's heart when he was only a teenager, was particularly ecstatic at this, his emotional resurrection. She was so astounded, in fact, that she found herself doubting that something this wonderful could actually be true. But, as with anyone who wants, desperately, to believe something, she alternated between denial and rationalization to sustain her faith. In her rationalizations she would sometimes set forth the possibility that, perhaps, the apparent victory for John's heart only appeared to have been won by her husband and that the seeds of love she had so carefully planted in the virgin soil of her son's young heart had remained in a dormant state and had, with the shower of love his new bride had rained upon him, finally germinated. Neither Elly nor Rachel allowed themselves even a fleeting thought of other, more pernicious motivations that John may possibly have had for his marriage to Emily Hughes.

Fortunately for John's mother, she didn't live long enough to be disappointed in her belief in John's newfound sense of humanity. Six months after the wedding, John's father died of a brain aneurysm. A year later, Rachael was dead – the final victory of diabetes, which ate her organs, inch-by-inch, until it, finally, killed its accommodating host. Rachael lived long enough to learn, to her immense joy, that Emily was pregnant. Emily was in her eighth month when Rachael passed on and, despite registering her strong objections with her obstetrician, Emily followed his advice and did not make the long trip with John to attend the wake.

In her final weeks, Rachael often asked for Johnny. Elly called him a number of times... telling him of their mother's rapid decline and of her oft repeated wish to see him. John promised, each time, to come. He never did. He had entered the congressional race in his district and was – as he explained to Elly – "up to his eyeballs in campaigning." Emily wanted, on many occasions, to go visit Rachael but John insisted she stay to help him with his campaign appearances. John's campaign manager told him that Emily was absolutely essential to his campaign. Married men have a distinct advantage, he explained, but having a beautiful, charming, gracious wife – who was pregnant to boot – was an edge they simply had to exploit to the hilt. John had bet right on Emily's loyalty to him. She stayed by his side... doing all that he asked of her, but who also cried, quietly, each night, for Rachael. She called her nearly every day and was, occasionally, able to get a reluctant John onto the phone with her for a few minutes.

John put in an appearance at Rachael's funeral and was able to get back to California for a fund-raiser, scheduled for that evening... using his mother's death to great advantage, enabling him to raise considerably more money than they had anticipated. John's campaign manager played Rachael Hennessey's death with flawless cunning and skill.

Just before John's arrival at the Hilton, upon his return from his mother's funeral, Jimmy Parling informed the Hilton audience about John's recent loss... apprising them of the likelihood of his being slightly delayed. When finally John appeared at the banquet room door – following Parling's instructions to him – he smiled weakly at the guests then kept his eyes on the floor as he walked, mournfully, to his place at the head table. The guests were respectfully quiet during his entrance and throughout the entire dinner. Though he was famished, John followed Parling's script and didn't eat his dinner nor did he converse with anyone at the table. When it came time for John to speak, he approached the podium... glanced about the room, welled-up the scripted tears, then turned away from the crowd and wept. One could have, literally, heard a pin drop in the cavernous banquet room. As orchestrated, Jimmy Parling walked over to John... put his arm around his shoulder and gave the appearance of consoling him. Then, with his arm around his waist, ostensibly to support him, he escorted John down from the speaker's platform and out the door to the left of the platform. After about thirty seconds, Parling reappeared, ascended the platform, and walked to the podium. He apologized for John's inability to speak... explaining that he was simply too overcome with grief to do so. Jimmy then went on to read John's speech... which focused on family and values. It was received with a standing ovation and a substantial increase over the expected level of contributions. John was, during all of this, in a room on the fourth floor, devouring a meal and drinking a beer, ordered from room service.

Jimmy came up to the room, immediately after the guests departed. He entered with a broad smile. John rose, expectantly. Jimmy threw his arms around him and shouted.

"Bingo!"

John was now matching Jimmy's grin.

"How good?"

"You're not going to believe it."

"C'mon... what was the take, Jimmy?"

"One hundred eighty-five thousand dollars."

"You have got to be shitting me!"

"You want to count it?"

"Goddamn... not in my wildest dream did I ever..."

"We're on our way, Johnny boy."

And they were. John Hennessey easily won the primary and just as handily defeated his opponent in the general election. John quickly discovered, during the campaign, that he had a knack for oratory... able to dramatically and convincingly deliver whatever message was required to gain favor with any group he was addressing. It mattered not that he would often walk out of one gathering to another, to deliver a speech that entirely contradicted the one he had just delivered. Whatever he needed to say, he said... with totally believable forthrightness. Immediately after the election, John named Jimmy Parling as his administrative assistant and sent him down to Washington to start getting things ready... picking and furnishing an office, hiring a staff, finding housing, and all the other matters that need attention in setting up a congressional office. Before he left for Washington, Jimmy also located several locations for district offices and found some good people to get them staffed and ready.

Emily had her baby on December 14th in San Bernadino, California. John was in Washington at the time... interviewing potential staff members. Emily's mother came out to stay with her for a while. John Hennessey, the third, was two weeks old before his father first laid eyes on him.

Emily proved to be a true enigma to John. He was certain that after being married to him for nearly two years, she would have surely, by then, figured out the actual deal with the marriage and the baby... but she apparently never had. She continued to believe in John and to love him as devotedly as the moment she first fell in love with him. Even with her childlike trust and naivety, John simply could not believe Emily had not seen through all the smoke and mirrors. After all, almost as soon as the wedding was over, he had dropped the charm and resumed his true, calculating persona. Other than having sex with Emily and expecting her to show up wherever he ordered her, he had virtually nothing else to do with her. He often did not even maintain a professional politeness toward her.

In John's mind, he and Emily had made a deal, even though she had no idea what it really involved. Emily got a big house, access to more money than she had ever seen in her life, a new car to use – in John's name, of course – a country club membership, and now a baby. The way John saw it she had benefited very nicely from the arrangement and should appreciate it. If she wasn't satisfied, he had it figured that Emily would stay with him, anyway, via the "small agreement" she had signed. If she walked out, she'd have nothing... and would be just another single mother, struggling to support her baby. John's assessment was – he got a wife that he needed for sex and social appearances and a necessary child... and she got the things for which women marry. But, despite John's unwillingness to believe it, Emily Hughes had married, truly and purely for love... and stayed with him for that sole reason. John knew she had married for love, but never believed her feelings for him would survive, once she understood his real motivations for marrying her, which, he felt, anyone of even ordinary perception could not fail to do. But, for whatever reason – and constituting an everlasting mystery to him – Emily's feelings toward John remained resolute and unshakable.

John had always anticipated ending up in a marriage like his father's. He knew, very well, that his mother didn't love his father, and vice-versa. She was a woman who desperately wanted love... this he knew... and after her love for him had died, she had showered it all on Elly. Nevertheless, their marriage had survived until death ended it. His father was content with it... his mother put up with it. This was the sort of marriage John was convinced he would have... and was satisfied with the expectation.

Contrary to John's anticipation, however, Emily didn't give up on loving him. She defended him to her mother and to all other critics. Regardless of how cold he was to her, she never faltered in her warmth toward him. She would call him, every day, at the congressional office – much to John's annoyance – and lovingly ask him about his day... was he all right... was he eating right? She'd tell him not to get too exhausted. She'd tell him about Johnny... how he'd smile... funny things he'd do... what he looked like asleep... how he said Da Da. Before she would hang up, she would always tell him she loved him... to which, John remained invariably mute. John simply didn't know what to make of Emily. Was she faking this affection to make a mockery of him? Was she just plain stupid? He just didn't know.

According to John's original strategy, he would maintain control over Emily by the threat of taking away all that she had, if she started bitching at him or about her life. He came to realize that he may never have to play that card. For reasons John could not fathom, Emily remained entirely loyal and devoted to him and continued to act like a woman in love. John knew he was a complete prick to Emily. He knew it, and he didn't care. But, given his demeanor, how could Emily, or anyone for that matter, love him? Love to John, of course, was just a bunch of "bullshit"... just a selfish survival mechanism. Emily didn't have to love him to keep what she had, so what was it all about? What was she up to? After considerable pondering – and still unable to come up with a satisfactory explanation for Emily's persistent love for him – John eventually abandoned the matter, dismissing it as a true enigma... and a waste of good energy.

As John became increasingly immersed in the political world, he spent less and less time at the family home they had purchased in Arlington... eventually reaching the point that the only time he spent with Emily or Johnny were the occasions when he needed the family image. For these, he'd direct Emily to dress up Johnny and show up at the event... just enough ahead of time to allow them to walk in together as the happy family, with Johnny, proudly borne in his father's arms. Almost immediately after the endearing, expertly staged, familial entry, mother and son were summarily returned to the home front until their services were again required.

John sublet a condo at the Watergate from a member of the Venezuelan consulate. It was a sweet deal for the Venezuelan... with his country's government paying for the place and the consulate member living cheaper, elsewhere, and pocketing the difference. John began staying there nearly every night. By this stage in his political career, John had discovered that he no longer needed Emily for his regular, sexual gratification. Power, he found, was a stronger aphrodisiac than he had ever imagined possible. On any given night he had legions of extremely attractive young women at his disposal... and never a night went by that he did not take advantage of this abundant resource. To John, this was a wonderful arrangement. These women didn't want marriage or a long-term relationship... they just wanted to be screwed by power... and John was most accommodating.

Emily filled her days with Johnny and in attending the charitable events and social gatherings that John arranged for her. She dutifully carried out John's directives, working the wives of power and other operatives of the Potomac social scene. She served him well. Her charm, grace, and beauty played nicely on the circuit and substantially contributed to the growth of John's political capital portfolio. John discovered Emily to be an effective tool for making some necessary connections. He often gave her specific assignments... to make contact with a certain person... to warm certain waters before he dove in.

Emily's mother was not, in the least, taken in by John's public facade and was most unhappy with his treatment of her daughter and grandson... and repeatedly informed Emily of her opinion. Shirley frequently asked her why she stayed with John. She regularly pointed out to Emily that she didn't have any life with John... that he was never home... that he treated her like a pet dog... and Johnny, too. Searching for an understanding of her daughter's motivations, she posed the question during a phone conversation of whether it was the luxurious life she was leading in Washington... and all the rich and powerful people she was meeting... that was keeping her with her husband. Emily responded with her unsinkable optimism.

"No Mummie... I really don't even like these Washington people. I love John, Mummie. I know you don't understand that... but I do. He's a good man underneath that hard shell that you see. In his own way, I know he loves me too. He's just all caught up in his career right now. It won't always be like this. Don't worry Mummie, I'm OK."

Shirley Hughes shook her head... knowing Emily was wrong but also realizing she could not convince her, otherwise. Shirley was particularly distressed about her grandson. Other than the show he put on at events where he needed the family image, John had virtually nothing to do with his young son. Johnny was growing up without a father... or any male influence for that matter. On occasion, her husband, Tom, would accompany her to Washington, when he could get off work, and would spend time with Johnny, but that just wasn't sufficient in Shirley Hughes' mind. Despite Emily's, oft repeated pleas to her mother to stay out of their relationship, Shirley showed up at John's congressional office, one afternoon, unannounced, and without Emily's knowledge. She informed the receptionist that she was John's mother-in-law... and was shown directly into John's office. John was visibly angered by this unsolicited intrusion and his voice was coldly professional toward her.

"Hello Shirley... what can I do for you?"

"We need to talk, John."

"Did Emily ask you to come here?"

"Heavens no. Emily, for reasons only known to God, is very happy with her life... and if she's happy... well... I'll leave well enough alone – though I'll never understand it for the life of me. It's Johnny I'm worried about. If Emily wants to throw her life away, that's her business, but Johnny is a different story, John. You have a wonderful little boy, John, who needs his father.

Emily tells him grand stories about you all the time and he asks his mother 'Where's Daddy?' all the time. He misses you and he needs you, John. Don't you care anything about him?"

John's face instantly flushed with hot blood. His voice quivered with the urgency of his anger.

"Who do you think you are, Shirley?... coming over to my office and lecturing me about raising my son. You have a lot of fucking nerve, you know that? I don't tell you how to run your family, do I?"

John was on his feet, screaming.

"I suggest you get up out of that chair and get the hell out of my office! As a matter of fact... get the hell out of my house and don't come back! Stay the fuck away from me and my family!"

Shirley's face turned white. She began to shake. Never in her life had anyone talked to her like this. She was so stunned she couldn't move. With her mouth hanging open, she stared at John. John leaned his hands on his desk... his body bent toward her. His face had the appearance of being chiseled stone... his eyes ripped into her soul. He spoke, just above a whisper.

"Shirley... did you hear me?"

Shirley nodded.

"Shirley... I want you to stand up..."

She did... unsteadily.

"... pick up your purse."

Slowly she reached down for it... her eyes never leaving John.

"Now walk over to that door... open it... go out... and close it behind you... you understand?"

Shirley nodded again. Clasping her purse to her chest, she did as she was told... never looking back. She proceeded in the same mindless fashion through the outer office and into the cavernous marble corridors of the Rayburn Building. She walked slowly toward the elevator. Suddenly feeling unable to walk any further, she sat on a padded leather bench along the wall. She stared ahead... expressionless. Her lower lip then began to arch and quiver, and tears welled in her eyes, finally overflowing. She felt a shaking sensation rise from her lower abdomen and climb into her chest... bursting forth from her throat as anguished sobbing. She lowered her face into her cupped hands... her chest and back heaving.

After Shirley left John's office, he immediately dialed home. Emily answered.

"I just threw your mother out of my office. I don't ever want to see that bitch again... not in my office... not in my house. Do you understand Emily?"

"John... what happened? What was my mother doing at your office?"

"She was lecturing me on how to raise my son."

"Oh God. I asked her to stay out of things. Please, Johnny, she didn't mean any harm... she just worries about things. I'm sure she's sorry she upset you. Please sweetheart... wait until you calm down... things won't look as bad. You're just angry now, honey. Please wait a little bit before you decide anything. OK, Johnny? Please?"

"Emily?"

"Yes?"

"I meant every word I said. As soon as she gets home I want her packed and out. Understand?"

"Johnny… please."

"There's nothing to 'please' about, Emily. Do what I told you."

John hung up the receiver.

Emily stood with the dial tone buzzing in her ear. Though miles apart, mother and daughter shed tears together.

CHAPTER TWENTY-THREE

John's political star was on the rise. His shrewd, calculating strategies were beginning to pay considerable dividends. He won his first congressional re-election in a landslide and was already being openly mentioned as a top contender for the Senate seat, vacant in two years. John formed an exploratory committee and began fund-raising.

John Hennessey glowed with success and promise. He was thirty-four, handsome, wealthy, well-liked, respected, and had a beautiful wife and son. John lived a life that most only read or dream about. He met and partied with the rich, the famous, and the powerful. He slept with a selection of some of the most beautiful women inside the Beltway. He was powerful... and was growing more so every day. No one ignored his call... from Hollywood to the White House. John had quickly and skillfully weaved an intricate political web with the deadly cunning of a hungry spider... and he was just beginning.

John felt that he was living proof of the stark truth delivered in his valedictorian address. He was strong... most were weak. He had much... most had little. He was, in fact, the grudging envy of his entire high school class. They saw John Hennessey on television... read about him in newspapers and magazines... about his life with the rich and the powerful and the famous. He had taken his graduation address and shoved it in their faces. He had proven his point. They were stuck in their everyday ruts... their nine-to-fives... driving the freeways back and forth to their three-bedroom-suburban houses to face overweight, bored spouses. He was glamorous... they were miserably plain. The higher he rose... the lower they felt. They envied him. They hated him. John, on his part, felt nothing but contempt for his old classmates. They had what they deserved... he had what he deserved. Life was good. In John's mind, he lacked for nothing. His life was full of luxury... the finest food and liquor... the finest women... the finest clothes and cars... the finest living.

As John Hennessey drove in the sticky heat of summer through the Washington slums to Capitol Hill, he looked with disdain at the broken, graffiti-covered hovels, lining the garbage-strewn streets... crawling with human vermin... smelling of unbathed bodies, urine and excrement of both dog and human origin. He reacted with revulsion to this, such as one might experience upon finding a spoiled piece of meat, teeming with maggots in one's own refrigerator. The loathsome sights pushed a tremor through his body, ending with a brief quivering of his head and a closing of his eyes.

After a nonstop day of Fourth of July appearances, John Hennessey sat, sipping brandy, gazing through the wide living room window of his Watergate condominium, surveying the Washington panorama twinkling below him in the early morning hours... his hand stroking the silky hair of a young Department of Agriculture staffer, asleep on the couch, her head on his lap, her knuckle pressed between her slightly open, gently sucking lips... wearing the scanty negligee, into which she had slipped, before – and after – they had had sex. He felt vindicated. The world was as he claimed it to be... full of weak fools... looking to the heavens or writing romantic drivel to compensate and forgive their disabilities... searching for meaning beyond their pathetic lives.

No supreme being orchestrated this uneven distribution of life's pleasures... of that he was sure. No... like rats searching the garbage dumps for food, or ants crawling through the grass on a mission for the colony... human beings scurry about the earth's surface, scratching for survival... nothing more. The mystic and divine imaginings of these pathetic human creatures were but desperate attempts to append fictional dignity and meaning to a life which has none. Despite all the prayers offered in the multitude of holy places, or poems penned by hopeless romantics, his life – earned by brutal force and brilliant treachery – was considerably brighter, and filled with many more pleasures and abundantly more happiness than those common, dirty, ugly lives, borne by most of the human swarm.

In fifty years or so, John knew he would be surely dead... as would a good many of those sharing the same air he was now breathing. Their carcasses would be, by then, a putrid mass of skin, bone, hair and formaldehyde, fermenting in an overpriced casket... or as ashes, scattered by the wind and indistinguishable from street dirt. Despite all the fantastic hopes of these pathetic hairless beasts, all that really mattered were those few years spent between birth and death. Life is all that anyone would ever experience... be it miserable or pleasurable. There would be no reward for a virtuous life except in someone's imagination... and an imagination is but a screenplay written by chemicals and electrical sparks swishing through the gray flesh of the brain... ceasing forever with one's last breath.

John finished the last of his brandy... feeling the warmth flow down his throat and through his chest. He breathed deeply through his nostrils and exhaled through his mouth. A luxurious drowsiness fell over him. His eyes were growing heavy. He felt himself smile. He slid his hand under the satin negligee and his fingers enveloped the lusciously smooth, firm breast, offered beneath. As he passed into slumber, three words formed in his mind.

"Life is good."

BOOK THREE

THE MINISTRY

THE MINISTRY

CHAPTER ONE

As was his habit, Marty thought over his situation at his favorite bar on the strip. His immediate instinct was to run... drop the whole situation... forget about the unexplainable pictures... forget about Papa... forget about the whole damn thing. He was back into his familiar routine – where he was before this whole Papa thing ... and he liked it. The past summer had just been too overwhelming for someone like him. He had come to admit to himself, to his disgust and chagrin, that despite his aspirations to the contrary, he was still the little, quaking, cowardly Jewish kid on the playground – just older. He didn't like himself very much, but he was stuck with who he was... and had to settle for that instead of constantly beating himself up about it, wishing he were different. This Papa thing frightened him, terribly. Marty supposed that some brave-hearted adventurer might look upon his situation with envy... as a chance of a lifetime... a real-life mystery... but he didn't. He wished it would all just go away.

As per the mixed blessing of alcohol, each succeeding beer further simplified Marty's circumstance until he was able to express its essence by the unadorned, common vulgarity, "fuck it." He muttered the expression repeatedly – each time with more conviction and enthusiasm. He had gotten what he wanted from the Papa story. He was a feature writer now, with a substantial pay raise... and up for some awards. He had done his bit for Papa... at least the major part of it. Hadn't he written the piece, and told Papa's story to the entire world? Hadn't he remained true in his loyalties to Papa by refusing to disclose his whereabouts, despite constant pressure and bountiful financial temptations? How much did the guy want for nothing? Why should he now serve as organizer and tour guide for some eccentric, misguided band of loonies? Why should he allow himself, again, to be tormented by the maddening possibilities presented by this man of the wilds? If Papa truly were God, he'd find another way to accomplish whatever the hell he had in mind. If God is omnipotent, why the hell did he need some cowardly, Jewish magazine writer to do his work for him? So, fuck it... just, fuck it.

His succinct, exculpatory resolution bore a sense of welcomed emancipation in his hazy, simplified, beer-colored world... sufficiently freeing his spirit to allow him to engage in his former pastime of "pussy-chasing," as he called the sport. She was a secretary for an L.A. law firm, she said... originally from Pittsburgh... tall, leggy, very attractive... in her late twenties. Marty embarked, posthaste, upon his well-practiced routine... painstakingly designed as a fail-safe strategy for getting women out of their panties, to wit – show great interest in her life, flatter her, empathize and support her in her strongly held opinions, and make himself appear affluent, fascinating, and quite available. Marty, having dedicated much of his life to this art, had, by this juncture – at least in his opinion – honed it to a science, and very rarely failed in his mission. This time, however – to his utter astonishment – it just didn't go at all. Marty encountered a rare, stone wall across his path to the bedroom. Curious as to the cause of this remarkable and total failure, Marty's mental focus moved upward, from the juncture of the woman's legs, to her eyes. They narrowed enough to tell him to drop the bullshit – but smiled enough to show him she had a good heart. Instantly, Marty knew this was not one-night-stand material. This, his heart instantly sensed, was a woman who could change his life.

Her indefinable power over him, sobered Marty, immediately, and as the haze lifted, the oppressive weight of his temporarily forgotten circumstance descended upon him, once again. Marty had, to that moment, trusted absolutely no one with the complete story of Papa. However, after a fifteen-minute acquaintanceship with a total stranger named Ginny Allen, originally from Pittsburgh, he was telling her everything... right down to the recently received pictures, and his contemporaneous resolve to abandon the cause... all with an absolute conviction that he *should* tell her.

This woman had a familiar feel to Marty... such as he recalled having had with only one other person in his life – Joan Kellar – in the third grade. Marty thought Joan was the prettiest girl he had ever seen, at least at that youthful juncture of his short life. He had had crushes on other pretty girls, but all had ended in painful rejection and esteem-shattering humiliation. After months of yearning, Marty finally got up the nerve to write Joan a note... expressing his feelings for her. He slipped it, surreptitiously, into her spelling book while passing her desk on his way out to recess. He was well aware of the risks of such a rash move, and anticipated the great likelihood of being ridiculed by her. Instead, she was very kind and understanding to him about it and became, in time, his best friend. When the playground bullies would beat him up – which they did as a regular pastime – she would dab his tearful eyes with the lilac-fragranced, rose-embroidered hanky she always carried with her. She'd put her arm around his shoulder and gently rub his arm. She was that blend of beauty, tenderness, sexiness, compassion, understanding, and friendship that men, and little boys, recognize as rare and special... and so very female. Her family moved to South Carolina at the end of that school year and he had never seen her again... but Marty had never forgotten how she had made him feel. Throughout the years since then, he had often thought of Joan Kellar... particularly when things got him down. The mere memory of her kindness had gotten him through many a crisis.

Ginny Allen immediately made Marty feel the same way that Joan Kellar had. He had lost Joan Kellar through the tyrannical nature of a child's derivative fate... but he determined, within minutes of meeting Ginny Allen, he would not lose her. As he talked, his troubles became hers. They were finishing sentences for one another from the early moments of their conversation. If there were such a thing in life as a soul mate, Marty was absolutely certain that Ginny Allen was his. Sitting with her, it felt as though they were, as his grandmother used to say, "two peas in a pod" ... so comfortable... so safe... so familiar. Ginny went home with Marty that evening. In bed, he held her tight until he fell asleep. They didn't have sex. She was more than that. He needed to know the depth and breadth of her soul before he learned the secrets of her body. In the morning, Ginny and Marty both called in sick. They went to the beach and walked for miles – talking incessantly with mutual, voracious appetites for knowing all there is to discover about the other. Marty quickly sensed that Ginny was much stronger and more courageous than he – but it didn't embarrass him, as such a comparative deficiency with a female normally would have. Marty felt the freedom to be just who he is… gutless as he is… loyal as he is… compassionate as he is.

Ginny revealed to Marty that she had read his Papa article and had found it riveting. After reading it, she said, she felt compelled to learn more about this magnificent man. She also confessed that she had seriously considered phoning Marty about it but couldn't get up the nerve to do it. She told him she would have undertaken the next step in the story in a heartbeat. She wanted to understand his hesitation.

"Why are you so afraid of this story, Marty?"

"It's the man himself, Ginny. He's so powerful that you can't easily dismiss him as a kook. Being with him makes you believe it's possible that the story's true… then you get away, and you realize it *can't* be. It's really disorienting. It kind of undermines your entire sense of reality. To me… that's scary. It's hard to explain. You'd just have to meet him to understand what I'm talking about. He's not like anyone I've ever met… and in my business I've meet a lot of unusual people."

"Can I meet him, sometime?"

Marty walked on in silence, looking into her face then back down at the sand.

"I don't know, Ginny. He didn't say… 'well bring your friends out to meet me sometime.' He only mentioned the eight. And that's another thing… these eight. It's just another thing that makes you think, for an instant, that the story could be true."

"Why can't it be true?"

"Think what you're saying, Ginny. This man claims he's God…

God!... not his son or a prophet... but God! Just think of what that means, Ginny... the creator of the universe... the ultimate source of everything... living in a cave in Montana? This man who claims to be God dresses in a leather kilt, takes showers, cooks dinner, takes a crap, and talked to me face-to-face... he's God? I'm sorry Ginny, that's too much. That's more than my mind can accept. Maybe I'm just too weak or something, but I can't even allow myself to consider the fact that it could be true."

"Is he a frightening person?"

"No... no... not at all... not himself, personally, anyway. As a matter-of-fact, he's one of the kindest and gentlest people I've ever met. But look at what happened to old Art. Accepting him as really being God literally killed him... put him into shock... dead within a few hours. That's how fundamentally dangerous this sort of thing is if you take it seriously. It can, literally, kill you... or make you crazy. I'm not going to go even near it, again. I'm serious, Ginny. I'm afraid I could lose my mind. That may sound a bit dramatic... but that's exactly how I feel."

"Well, I'm not going to try to argue with you, Marty. You've met him and experienced all this. I haven't."

They walked on in silence for a while, but it became apparent to Marty that Ginny wasn't ready, as yet, to give up on the subject.

"Are you so afraid of this man that you won't ever see him again?"

"I don't know Ginny... I honestly don't know right now."

"All right. We'll talk about it when you're ready."

They sat in silence on a sloping hill of sand – rock cliffs to their backs – and watched the sunset. It was December now, and even though the day was unseasonably warm, the early evening air off the ocean carried with it, winter's chilly bite. Their light sweaters were soon insufficient to cope with the penetrating breeze and they hurried back to Marty's apartment. He made her hot tea, then made her dinner… then, later that night, made love to her for the first time. This was the first sex Marty had ever consummated that he could honestly describe as having made love. Before this night, he had always secretly doubted that the act – at least for a man – could be more than a simple, carnal experience. That's all it had ever been for him, before Ginny. Of course, he had always obliged the woman with professions of love, before and during the act, but was quite cognizant of his overt disingenuousness. He had always figured that the term, making love, was probably coined by a woman as an expression of what she hoped would result from the physical union.

After the final explosion, Marty held Ginny even tighter than he had during their passion, and rather than moving away from the hot sheets and the wet spot to find his own, cooler, drier space, as had been his previous, consistent practice with other women, his space was her space, was their space. The wetness under their bottoms and the wrinkled hot sheets, chaotically twisted around their bodies, rather than constituting an irritating annoyance, was, instead, a tangible proclamation of their first tender passion, and they reveled in the feel of it. Sleep came to Marty, that night, more softly than it ever had in his adult life… so softly that no line could be drawn between waking and slumber… blending together without distinction.

Papa visited Marty's dreams, again, that night. The bullies were, as usual, taunting him on the playground. They all had schoolbooks in their hands and were hitting him on the head with them… calling him a sissy Jew. He started to cry. As he looked at the cruel, twisted faces of the bullies, he realized that these weren't the usual boys who had always tormented him – but total strangers, and three of them were girls. They pushed him down into the hot dust and he could feel the fine, dry dirt filling his nostrils… mixing with the water that ran from his nose, onto his upper lip. He wiped the muddy flow with the back of his hand. They all then began to kick him and he drew his legs up to his stomach to try to make himself as small as possible. Suddenly they stopped. After a few uneasy moments, he looked cautiously up at them to see why. They appeared to be staring at something behind him – their eyes,

THE MINISTRY

large, and filled with wonder. Their lips began to pucker and tears began flowing down their cheeks. Marty sat up and turned his head to look. Coming across the schoolyard was Papa, with Ginny holding his hand, leading him toward Marty and the bullies. As Papa grew near, the bullies ran to him and hugged him. He tenderly stroked their heads then kissed each one of them. He then spoke to them in words too quiet for Marty to discern. Then, one at a time, each of the bullies came to Marty, bent down, held him then kissed his cheek. Their faces were full of both remorse and love. Afterwards, they all walked away, leaving Marty alone in the dirt.

Looking around him, Marty noticed that their books had fallen from their hands and all were lying, face up, and open to the same pages. On the two visible pages was Papa's painting – half on each page. Marty looked up… toward where Papa and Ginny had been standing, to find only Ginny. Papa was nowhere in sight. On the outside of the school yard fence, stood a boy, staring at the two of them, his fingers intertwined among the twisted wire. His face was void of expression and emotion. When he noticed Marty looking at him, he turned slowly, and walked away. Ginny came over to Marty and sat in the dirt beside him. She put her arm around his shoulders and rubbed him like Joan Kellar used to do. She smelled of lilacs. She put her lips close to Marty's ear and whispered, "My Marty… my sweet, sweet Marty."

Marty looked over at Ginny. She was asleep with her lips next to his ear. He could feel the warmth of her breath. He had awakened as he had gone to sleep – without any demarcation between the two worlds. Ginny opened her eyes and smiled – the same smile she had offered Marty, moments before, on the Morphean playground.

"Ginny?"

Marty spoke very softy.

Ginny smiled even bigger. She brought her lips close to his ear again and whispered to him.

"My sweet boy."

Her specific words instantly knocked the dust from Marty's awakening senses. His eyes narrowed and his body stiffened. An uncanny wave of fear, anger, and suspicion swept over him. He sat up. Ginny joined him, her face expressing puzzlement over Marty's instant change in demeanor.

"You have to tell me the truth, Ginny."

"What is it, Marty?"

"You have to tell me… has Papa sent you?"

"Why are you asking me that?"

"Don't ask me… just answer the question."

Ginny was silent. She looked into Marty's eyes, then down and away, then back to his eyes.

"I'm not sure how to answer the question."

"Just tell me the truth."

"In a way, yes, I guess he did."

"What's that supposed to mean?"

"After I read your article, I felt that I needed to do something… something for him. I wasn't sure why… and I didn't know what… I just felt I did. Then, when I met you in the bar, and found out who you were, I knew it couldn't be just a coincidence… that whatever I needed to do for him, it would be through you."

"Why didn't you say something?"

"I should have… but it was one of those things that you think about – that you know will sound really silly to actually say it.

Besides, I could see how upset you were, already, about all this. All you would have needed was for me to tell you that I was somehow involved with it. But really, maybe our meeting *was* just a coincidence... I mean millions of people read that article of yours – thousands right here in this town. And I'll bet a lot of people were moved by the article – it was well-written and really touching – and they probably felt just like I did. So the odds of you running into someone who had read the article and felt moved to do something about it were probably pretty good. Don't you think?"

"I don't know what to think. Are you here with me because you want to do something for Papa or because you want to be with me?"

"Both, I guess. I'm here for you because you're you – but I still feel this need to do something for him. What made you ask me about all this, anyway?"

"This dream I had."

"When... last night?"

"Yes."

"Will you tell me about it?"

Angry with Ginny for her lack of disclosure, Marty remained stonily silent. Ginny waited him out... and he finally gave in... offering his response in a tone that clearly demonstrated his lingering annoyance and disappointment in her.

"Yeah... I guess so."

Marty waited until his emotions had subsided a bit more before proceeding. Ginny continued to wait, patiently and silently... suffering from a guilty conscience, borne of her lack of forthrightness. Finally, he began.

"All right, well... the dream... it was kind of strange. I was having another one of my 'Marty gets his ass kicked in the playground' dreams – that I have at least once a week. The kids were hitting me with their schoolbooks then knocked me down and were kicking me and calling me a sissy Jew. But when I looked up at them, it wasn't the bunch of bullies that used to always kick the shit out of me. I have no idea who they were – never seen them before – and three of them were girls. Anyway... they stopped kicking me all of a sudden and were looking at something behind me. I turned around and you were standing there with Papa."

"Was I a little girl?"

"No... you were just like you are now."

"Go on."

"The kids around me all started crying and ran over to Papa. He rubbed their heads and kissed and hugged them, then talked to them... but I couldn't hear what he was saying. Then the kids came back over to me and bent down and hugged me and kissed me. They all looked really sorry for what they'd done to me. Then they all just walked away. Then you came over and sat beside me and put your arm around me and said nice things to me in my ear."

"What did I say?"

Marty was embarrassed and showed it.

"C'mon Marty."

"You said something like... sweetheart or my sweet Marty... something along that line."

"Ahhh."

"And that was about it."

"What happened to Papa?"

"Oh, I forgot… after the kids all hugged and kissed me and left… I looked over and Papa was gone… you were standing there all alone. Wait! I almost forgot the strangest part. While the kids were kicking me, they had all dropped their books. They had fallen open when they hit the ground and were lying face up. Every one of them was open to the same pages that had the complete painting of Papa's… the one that I mailed out. Isn't that weird?"

"How many kids were there?"

"A lot of them. Let's see… there were three girls and the rest boys."

"Were there five boys?"

"Could have been… I'm not sure. Oh… one more thing. When I looked over and saw you were by yourself, I also saw this little boy standing outside the fence, watching all this go on. He was a really nice-looking boy – looked like a rich kid – but had this stony face – no emotion – and was just staring at us. When he noticed me looking at him, he just turned around and walked away."

"What do you make of it, Marty?"

"You mean the whole dream?"

"Yes."

"Oh, it's probably just one of those dreams all about the things on your mind that day. We'd been talking about this stuff, all day long… and I'm sure it was on my mind when I went to sleep… even if I didn't realize it. Actually, not much was on my mind when I went to sleep last night… if you know what I mean."

Marty donned an impish smile that paralleled his words. Suddenly understanding the twin communications, Ginny giggled and playfully slapped Marty's thigh. Having thoroughly enjoyed their private communion, Marty continued.

"I'm not one of the 'dream people,' like Joseph, who thinks they're something mystical with all kinds of deep, hidden meanings. I think they're just brain waves... sorting things out."

"I think they're much more than that, Marty. Carl Jung did too... and he's not some weirdo."

"Some people say he was more of a mystic, than a psychologist."

"Whatever... I think dreams are full of guidance and wisdom from other dimensions. I learn a lot from my dreams... a lot that's helped me understand things that I wouldn't have otherwise."

"I don't have to remind you that I'm an incurable skeptic, do I? I told you I was. If something can't be proven by some rational method – I don't buy it. I'm sorry."

"Well, your dream made you question me."

"Yes, but that was probably a question that was in my subconscious, anyway, that just came out in my dream... and then the first words out of your mouth when you woke up were almost exactly what you had just said to me in my dream. It just sort of shook me up at first... that's all. I'm starting to clear out the cobwebs and get my head on straight now."

"Even so... your asking me if Papa sent me shows that you must at least have some suspicion that strange, unexplainable things can happen. I mean... you know very well he's never laid eyes on me. Why else would you have asked me?"

"I guess it was just because I was waking up, and not thinking very clearly. You know how it is... when you first wake up. I actually feel pretty stupid, now, having even asked you such a ridiculous question. I mean, what was I thinking? ... that Papa's some omnipotent being that can make people do things... that he speaks to people in their dreams?

Marty hummed the theme song for the *Twilight Zone* to which,

Ginny sportively punched his arm and shook her head in mock reproach.

"Can't you allow for any possibility that there are things beyond the everyday, three-dimensional world, Marty?"

"No, I honestly can't. I'm just not the type."

"Can't you have faith in anything that you can't touch or see?"

"No... I'm sorry, Ginny, I can't. Maybe it's because in my business, you run into so many kooks and frauds who want to get their story into print. You just become hardened toward accepting anything you can't substantiate."

They sat in silence. Ginny broke it.

"Want to hear my theory about your dream?"

"Why not? Go ahead, Joseph."

"Papa is telling you that he understands what torment this situation – with the eight people – is putting you through. That's why they were beating you up and hurting you. I walked into the playground with him because he wants me to bring you and the eight others to him. The kids ran to him so he could comfort them with whatever problems or sorrows they have. The open books, with the painting, were showing you who these people were. I'll bet if you thought about it hard enough, there were eight kids, altogether... the same number as those who sent you the other half of the painting. The little boy outside the fence... I'm not sure who that is... no idea. From the way you describe his face, though, he's probably not a very positive addition to the story... but I can't even guess about him... have to just wait and see. Well... what do you think? Does it make sense to you?"

"I guess so... if I was into dream interpretations. What are you trying to say, Ginny... that Papa is communicating with me through my dreams?"

"I think it's obvious, Marty. Besides, you must give *some* credence to dreams. You mailed out that picture on the basis of one – and got results... the exact results that Papa told you, you would – eight people on the nose. That's a little bit too much for a coincidence, don't you think? How many of the eight who returned the picture were women? I'll bet you know."

Marty didn't respond... but he knew three were women. The situation was becoming too bizarre for Marty's liking. He got out of bed, went into the bathroom, and closed the door. They both called in sick, again, and went back to the beach.

CHAPTER TWO

The issues on the Papa story had been discussed so many times between the two of them that Marty was becoming exasperated. He sensed that if it continued, he and Ginny were about to have their first argument. It was very obvious to Marty that Ginny was pushing for him to become involved, again, in the Papa situation… and he was strongly resisting. Finally, he lost his temper.

"What is this, Ginny!? What is the big fucking deal about me getting involved with this story, again!? What are you, Papa's press agent or what?!… for Christ sake!"

Ginny didn't want an argument. She answered softly.

"Sit down, Marty."

She sat down and gently patted the sand beside her. Marty – still fuming – resisted.

"C'mon… don't be angry, sweetheart. Let's just cool down for a while, OK?"

She patted the sand again. Despite his anger, Marty cherished Ginny's softness, and also, it didn't escape him that this was the first time Ginny had used a term of endearment towards him, signifying, in his mind, a durable intimacy. The two elements, combined, were more than he could resist. He sat, as requested – embarrassed at his outburst. Not only had he screamed at this sweet girl, he'd cursed at her as well. If she had screamed back at him, he thought, he wouldn't have felt nearly so bad about it.

"I'm sorry Ginny… I really am. I shouldn't talk that way to you. You don't deserve it. I just have this temper that makes me say stupid things sometimes… and hurt the people I shouldn't."

Ginny put her arm around him and smiled with an understanding that made Marty feel much younger than she. She rubbed his left shoulder, up and down, as she gazed out at the water. They were quiet. Marty decided to wait for her. Fifteen minutes later she spoke.

"I'll say what I have to say, one last time, Marty. And I'll never bring it up again – that I promise you. Then you make whatever choice you feel is right for you. I'm staying with you either way. OK?"

Marty nodded in assent. Ginny continued.

"There's no logic to how I feel... no way of proving anything. But I feel you need to do what Papa asked of you. There's much more to this than just some crazy eccentric living in the woods. I know there is. I can't say, for sure, what it's all about... I just know that it's very important that you do this. I've never felt more strongly about anything in my entire life... and never more sure of what should be done. This is hard for you, Marty, I know. But I'm asking you... I'm pleading with you... please just have faith in my intuition about this. I promise you... it's the right thing to do."

Marty looked away from Ginny and gazed out at the Pacific, searching the vast watery expanse for his feelings. Ginny waited, knowing this was probably one of the most difficult decisions Marty had ever made in his life. She knew he wasn't a brave man. He was, however, courageous enough to come right out and tell her he was not, which she knew was a very hard thing for any man to tell a woman. And she knew he was possessed of a morbid fear of becoming involved with Papa again. And now the woman he loved was asking him to do it. Her heart ached for him – knowing the enigmatic position into which she had put him – but she truly had an overpowering, undeniable feeling that he must do as Papa had asked him... and having absolutely no idea why she felt this way. She would, also, she knew, be true to her word if his answer was that he could not do it. She would immediately put it behind them and never look back. She was a woman who considered promises to be inviolate. Finally, he turned his head and looked deeply into her eyes. Ginny's heart was pounding in unison with his.

"I trust you Ginny. And I'm putting myself on a high wire without a net, and it's not like me. I'm leaving myself wide open – but with you, I'm not afraid. If you say it's what I should do… I'll do it. God help me… I'll do it."

They embraced and cried together. If there had been any lingering doubt, before that moment, there was none now. They both knew they were deeply and irrevocably in love.

CHAPTER THREE

Marty quickly discovered that Ginny was a woman who made command decisions – and executed them with the single-mindedness of a field marshal. She informed Marty she was quitting her job, moving in with him, giving up her apartment, and going with him, wherever the Papa story took him. Her confidence and self-assurance was breathtaking to a man as indecisive and disorganized as Marty. It was, to him, a thing of beauty. He loved her, but he quickly grew to admire her, as well. And, as all who so deeply love, he soon came to realize that he was now terrified of losing her.

It was readily apparent that Ginny would also organize Marty's life, in general... but he didn't resent it as he had when his mother had, so often, tried to do the same thing. Ginny wasn't arrogant about her usurpation of Marty's life-structure and functioning... nor autocratic. She did what she did because it needed to be done to improve the life of the man she loved. She also did it with a self-deprecating sense of humor and humility. She clearly had neither a hidden agenda nor troublesome pathology requiring domination. With Ginny, Marty immediately realized that his undisciplined talent may finally find a much-needed focus and direction. And, along with this structural renovation of his life, Ginny also fulfilled Marty's lifelong yearning for an ever-elusive sense of peace and safety.

After being together for only a week, Marty and Ginny knew one another as well as many lifelong companions... both learning that such profound, intimate knowledge was more a function of the depth of their trust than the length of their time together. In his life, as in his dream, Ginny made Marty feel, for the first time, unafraid. Since he could remember, he had always carried in him, a dark ball of fear... forever floating in his stomach... and Ginny had, somehow, exorcised it... compelling its return to its black, cold chamber. Somehow, she had chased away all those demons that had always been but a step behind the frightened Jewish boy. With Ginny in his life, the playground bullies could no longer find their way into his dreams. Marty supposed that some men would have ridiculed him for finding his safety and protection in the arms and love of a woman, but he didn't care. He didn't know what he had done to deserve such a godsend as Ginny, nor, frankly, did he understand what she saw in him, but, for whatever reason, he was able to accept this magnificent gift without his normal doubts and tortuous self-recriminations. Ginny was light, strength, and love. Ginny had become his life. With Ginny, the everyday world took on a radiant glow – as did his heart.

In consultation with Ginny, Marty decided to write each of the eight picture people... give them his home number and ask them to call him there, after seven o'clock in the evening. They decided he shouldn't do this sort of thing at work. As far as the magazine was concerned, the Papa case was a dead issue, and would remain so, unless Marty decided to do a follow-up piece. After they mailed the eight letters, every evening they sat at home, waiting for the calls, and, sure enough, one by one, all eight phoned him. He explained the story to each of them... that Papa said he was to bring eight people to him... that the eight of them had accurately returned the missing half of Papa's painting. Marty asked each of them how they were able to do this. All had the same reply – they didn't know. They said they had opened the letter from Marty... seen the copy of the painting... and immediately pictured another half... drew and colored it, and returned it to Marty. None could explain how or why they were able to do this. Marty asked if any of them had had dreams of Papa. None had. He asked them if they wanted to see Papa. All replied that they *must* see him... but none understood the compelling sense of their urgency. Marty also asked each of them about their lives.

Before meeting Ginny, this increasingly bizarre tale would have panicked Marty. He was, therefore, quite astonished, by his newfound sense of calm and lack of fear as he reentered it. He still didn't accept the purported, divine aspects of the story – but, at least, he was no longer afraid of it. He told each of the eight that he would soon be in touch with them about meeting Papa and got a phone number where they could be reached. After each conversation, Marty would recount the details to Ginny... who waited with childlike excitement for each new installment. She eventually learned that they had quite a crew – an old, depressed, retired philosophy professor... a convicted felon on parole... a lawyer who had suffered a nervous breakdown... a prostitute from Harlem... a ruthless female industry magnate... a very talented, but morose, French-Canadian woman... a male, homosexual resident of a state mental institution... and an ex-minister – and full-time drunk – who claimed to have been falsely convicted of a sex offense against a teenage girl.

Marty began to seriously question whether or not he had the right eight people. Frankly, he told Ginny, he wasn't so sure he wanted anything to do with most of them. In response to his manifestly haughty deprecation of the group, Ginny inquired of him as to what sort of people he had expected. He said he wasn't exactly sure... but certainly not convicts, sex offenders, prostitutes, and gay, mental inmates. "Who would need Papa more than people like this?" she posed to him. He reflected and understood... contrite for his unseemly arrogance.

Marty and Ginny were now faced with some very practical considerations in the Papa saga. The preliminaries were over and even Ginny was a bit unsure of where to go, beyond this juncture. They both found themselves procrastinating about having the necessary and inevitable conversation about these matters. Innately, they realized they were hesitating, as one always does, to take the first, actual step of a long journey. Finally, the moment came in which they sensed they must either step forward or turn back. Marty made a pot of coffee and they sat at the kitchen table at 7:30 on a Wednesday evening and began.

"I have to say something, first, Ginny."

He paused, searching her eyes.

"You need to understand exactly how I feel about Papa before this goes any further."

Again he paused for a possible response. None came.

"I'm not really afraid of this Papa situation, anymore. I think you know that. It's because of you... you know that, too. I don't know if I'm a braver man with you – probably not – but at least I'm not afraid all the time, anymore. Maybe you are my courage... who knows? But you need to know how I feel... how I have to feel – to think – about Papa."

Marty sipped his coffee as his eyes searched for the right words. He always felt clumsy and imprecise in speaking his thoughts. That's why he became a writer... so he could ponder his words before anyone else encountered them. In writing he always appeared so very confident and articulate – precisely how he aspired to speak.

"I know we've gone over and over this... but I feel I need to say it... one final time. I can't deal – emotionally – with even the possibility that Papa is God. I simply can't do it. I've told you why a dozen times, but, maybe for my own peace of mind, I need to say it again, tonight... before we go any further on this."

Marty tapped his pointer finger on the side of his coffee cup several times – then looked into Ginny's eyes with a business-like gaze.

"I think he's a remarkable man... a totally unique person who's lived a very strange life. He's a good man... kind and innocent and well-meaning. An intelligent man... talented and articulate. I think he absolutely believes – with no pretense about it – that he is who he says he is. In my opinion, it's purely a result of the eccentric life he's led... living all alone since he was a child... reading all those books... living in that wild, magnificent environment. I also think he has certain exceptional abilities... beyond the normal realm. I mean, like, extrasensory powers. You know what I mean?"

Ginny didn't respond… so Marty went on with diminished confidence – interpreting Ginny's lack of acknowledgement to constitute disagreement… or at least skepticism.

"Well, that's what I think they are… his appearance in dreams… his knowing about people before he should… knowing about things before they happen… reading thoughts… influencing how people think. There are lots of people in the world like that… hundreds of cases – telepaths, clairvoyants, that sort of thing. That's how I explain the prediction about the eight people and how they knew what to draw. He has a very powerful mind. I've read about these mystics who live on mountaintops… who have powers like this. They're extraordinary people… but they're not divine and they're sure as hell not God. That's how I think about this, Ginny. There's a rational explanation for everything that's happened so far… there always is. Everybody likes to believe in the supernatural – in fairy tales. It gives some meaning to this everyday, bullshit existence we put up with. We all want to think there's something more – or somebody who can rescue us… who can cause it all to make sense and give it some glory. People have probably been searching for answers like this since mankind first realized his own ordinary existence. Face it, Ginny, other than the thrill of being in love, like we are, and a couple of other things in life, life's pretty mundane. We go to movies to pretend for a few hours that there's something more to life than the same old grind we face everyday. But only children can afford to pretend all the time, everyday. I think responsible adults have to give up fairy tales and be rational – cynical is probably a better word. Life is tough and cruel and demanding. You can't walk around with your head in the clouds – as tempting as that is – and survive. I've known some people who are so anxious to find some excitement and meaning in life that they believe in every new hoax that comes along… UFO's, extraterrestrial abductions, ghosts, crying crucifixes, Big Foot… and even Elvis and Blessed Virgin sightings… or they climb mountains or jump out of airplanes to get a momentary adrenaline rush. I think of these kind of people as kids who never grew up. In my mind, when you grow up, playtime is over. If there's going to be meaning and excitement in your life, you need to find it in your everyday life – not in some supernatural mumbo jumbo. I accept life for what it is – not for what I would like it to be... and it's mostly a pain in the ass... the same routine at work, paying bills, trying to inch ahead, buy a few nice things every now and then. Once in a while, some wonderful things *do* happen... you fall in love, have children, do something that's exceptional. That's where you have to find meaning – in the real things of life – not in the latest tabloid rip-off. Do you understand where I'm coming from, Ginny?"

Instead of answering, Ginny went over to the counter and brought back the coffee pot and the pint of Half-and-Half. She filled their cups and added the correct portion of cream to each – particularly Marty's... knowing the importance that men attribute to such small things. She returned the pot and carton to the counter then resumed her seat. Her eyes reflected the depth of her thoughts and the importance she had accorded Marty's opinion. She offered him a smile of love and wisdom. As it often did, Ginny's knowing smile made Marty feel, once again, the younger of them. She reached across the table and covered the intertwined fingers of Marty's hands with her right hand, then, giving his hands a parting and gentle squeeze, she slowly brought it to her right cheek and rested her slightly tilted head on it.

"I think most people are just like you, Marty. They're practical and logical... and if they can't see it or touch it or prove it, it doesn't exist. I think that's why most really aren't very happy. If you believe that the whole world consists only of the things that you can see and understand, then it's bound to be a boring, small, sad world. That isn't the way I look at things. I have – or had, I should say – my job. It was so routine – typing, filing, answering the phone – and so uninspiring that if I thought that's all there was to life, I'd end it all... I really would. As a matter of fact, with as many people who look at life like you do, Marty, I'm surprised there aren't an awful lot more suicides."

Ginny paused on that thought for a moment before going on.

"I look at life as though it were an iceberg. I can only see the top of it, but I know that there's a much bigger part of it, invisible to me. I can't see under the water to prove it's there, but I feel its existence. I just don't believe that the world we can see and touch is all there is to life. I *know* there's so much more… just like I know that your going to Papa is the right thing to do. I don't know how I know these things… I just do. Not everything in life is logical or provable, Marty. I can't prove to you that there's a wonderful world all around us that we can't see or touch, but I know there is. I don't know if Jesus was who he said he was, but one thing he said that I always think about, is that he pitied those of little faith. I don't think he meant just those who didn't have faith in him. I think he meant those who were strictly logical… who dismiss the possibility of anything that their weak and limited eyes and minds can't grasp or prove. I know there are things in this world that we can't even imagine – most things in the world. I love you Marty. You have a good heart – a kind heart. But I also feel sorry for you, my sweet love, because you live in such a small, logical world. To me, Papa's story could very well be true because I trust my heart more than my brain. When I meet him, my heart will tell me the truth – much more clearly than my mind."

Marty's eyes welled with tears. His voice was thick with emotion.

"God, Ginny, I wish, so much, I could be like you. Your world is so much bigger and fuller and happier than mine. But I don't know how to be anyone except who I am. My parents were very practical, logical people who looked at everything with a jaundiced eye. My dad would always warn me to look out for the flimflam man… the shyster. His message was always – don't trust anybody. That's how I was raised. That's how I am… who I am."

"Do you trust me, Marty?"

"Yes, of course I do."

"Why?"

"I really can't explain it. I just do."

"You just feel it, right?"

"Right."

"Well that's how I feel about the world, sweetheart. I just know there's so much more than what we can see. All that's keeping you from feeling the way I do is fear, Marty. It's as though you're always sleeping with one eye open... having no trust in the world."

"That's exactly right, Ginny. I only feel safe if I hold on tight. I'm afraid of letting go, and trusting in the world. I just don't have any faith. I honest to God wish I could – but I don't think you can understand how hard it would be for someone like me to accept anything except what is logical."

"I understand, Marty... I really do. If I had been raised like you, I'd probably be the same way. But my parents were just the opposite of yours. They both always had this sense of magic about the world... that there's so much that we don't understand."

"Can I meet them, sometime, Ginny?"

"They're dead, Marty. They were killed in a car accident three years ago – in Pittsburgh. That's when I came out here."

"Oh Christ, Ginny, I'm sorry. I didn't know... you never said anything. I'm so sorry."

"You didn't know, sweetheart... nothing for you to be sorry about. They would have been happy that you wanted to meet them."

"Can I ask you something?"

"You can ask me anything you like."

"I don't want this to come out wrong, but I don't understand why you're just a secretary – not that there's anything wrong with it – but you're so intelligent and so articulate. You could have been anything. You could have gotten a Ph.D. if you wanted to. I mean, talking to you... if I didn't know you were a secretary, I would never have believed it. You're just really smart, Ginny."

Ginny laughed sweetly.

"I've always had faith that I would find what was right for me... so I just waited patiently... and here you are. I've always just followed my heart."

Marty's heart swelled in his breast. More than ever, he feared losing this rare and precious woman. He now understood the agony and ecstasy of love. He was happier than he'd ever been in his life, finding Ginny – and more miserable than ever, in fear of losing her.

CHAPTER FOUR

Having clearly stated their feelings about Papa, and the world in general, Marty and Ginny plunged into the practical planning, necessary for the next step of their endeavor. The general concept of bringing eight people to Papa was simple. The details weren't. Should they all fly to Los Angeles, then use both their cars to transport them to Montana? What if some of them didn't have the money for a plane ticket? What should they bring with them? It was winter, now, and the roads to the mountains were very likely impassable. Should they wait until spring? How long were they going to be with Papa? How about the gay guy in the mental institution... how were they supposed to get him out? Could Marty get off work for this venture... and for how long? Where were they supposed to get all the money for this? Should Marty propose to do a sequel to the story and ask for an advance? The more they talked, the more they realized just how complicated the situation truly was.

One by one, they addressed each issue. First... when to go to Montana. From what Marty recalled of Art's description of winter in that area, the roads were just about impossible to travel for months at a time. Besides the roads, the trails would be equally as difficult. There was also the cold to consider. Maybe Papa and Art were adept at survival in the wilderness, in frigid cold – but their group was just a bunch of ordinary people... used to central heat and hot showers. Eventually it became abundantly clear that they simply had to postpone the trip until spring. The next logical question was, therefore... when did spring come to the Montana mountains? When were the roads passable and the temperatures tolerable? How could they find out? Marty had an almanac that gave this sort of information in a very general way but, obviously, not specific enough to indicate when Old Log Road would be open. Who could he ask? The only person who came to mind was the police department secretary in Bear Stump. She was nice and seemed to know everything about the town. She'd certainly know about the snow situation. For the life of him, however, Marty couldn't think of her name. He racked his brain but simply couldn't come up with it. He decided just to call the office and hope to get her.

Marty called information and got the number. He dialed and a woman answered who sounded about like what Marty remembered.

"Bear Stump Police Department."

"Hello there. This is Marty Chapman... I don't know if you remember me or not... I was the guy who came over to see you about Art Durbin last August."

"Oh sure. How are you Marty?"

"I'm fine, how are you?"

"Just fine."

"How did everything go with the situation with Art? Any problems?"

"No. Everything went fine. The Chief drove out to check out the scene at Art's cabin but..."

She laughed good-naturedly.

"... he couldn't find it. He was sure he knew where it was... said he'd been out there when he was a boy... when Billy Wilson owned it – before Art – but spent the whole day and came back empty-handed. He was fit to be tied. By the way, that was quite an article you wrote, Marty. I have it cut out and in my scrap book. The chief was kinda mad that you didn't tell him the whole story when you were here... but he was so proud that Bear Stump got mentioned in a big-time magazine that he got over it real quick. The town was like a three-ring circus for weeks after that piece... news people all over the place... even foreigners... askin questions... takin pictures. They tried like the dickens to find that cave and Art's cabin... but they didn't have anymore luck than the Chief. They even had helicopters out there. It was really kinda funny. Everybody in the Stump was givin them their theory on how to find the place... and everybody had a different story. They were runnin around in circles."

She laughed again.

"Finally they just quit and went home. Oh my... it was something. So why'd you call, Marty?"

"Well, I was thinking about bringing my girlfriend out that way, this spring, to show her where I lived last summer, but I'm not sure about the weather. When can you usually get back into the mountains and not get stuck or freeze to death?"

"Oh... to be safe, I'd wait until at least May. You should be safe by then."

"Well, I'll tell you what. I'll bring Ginny by, to meet you, when we come out."

"Why that'd be just lovely, Marty. I'd be real happy to meet her. I'll have to get you to autograph my article when you're here, too... if you don't mind."

"Happy to. First time I've ever been asked for my autograph. I feel like a rock star."

She laughed again.

"OK. We'll probably be out that way this spring, then. I'll look forward to seeing you."

"You take care, Marty."

They now knew the trip was literally – and figuratively – on ice until the following May. Next, they turned to the question of how to get the people to Montana. Marty wanted everyone to fly into L.A.... then drive from there to Montana. Ginny favored everyone flying into Great Falls, Montana. She'd looked at the map and said they'd be only a few hours to Bear Stump from there. She didn't see any purpose in everyone coming to L.A. first, then driving for two days, backtracking to the north. She won.

They moved on to costs – cars, hotels, food, plane tickets. They certainly didn't have the money to finance this excursion out of their own pockets. That realization resolved another question. They had no other choice but to get the magazine to pay for it... and to get them to foot the bill, Marty would have to promise to do a sequel. Marty promised he'd talk to Marla about it the following morning. He was certain she'd go for it. She'd love it, as a matter of fact, he said. The sequel, *The Disciples* – Marty's instantaneously coined, working title – had, in his estimation, the potential of being even bigger than the first installment. As he considered it further, however, Marty had some reservations as to whether Papa would want him to do it. He had told Marty that he wanted him to write his story... but Marty wasn't certain just how far that went. After extended discussion, they decided that Marty would get the money from Marla on the promise of a sequel... then, if Papa didn't want the story written, they'd just have to cross that bridge at that time. If worse came to worst, they vowed to find a way to reimburse the company.

As for how long they'd be with Papa, and just what he had in mind for the disciples, they decided they'd just have to play it by ear, since there was, obviously, no way of answering that question at this time. They'd tell the eight the same thing and let them decide what to bring and for how long to prepare. The question of the guy in the mental institution was, clearly, a sticky one... and beyond their field of expertise. The only thing they figured they could do was to contact a lawyer from a town nearby the institution and get some advice. The bill for Marla was going up, rapidly. As a final matter, they resolved to keep the whole project completely confidential. They were acutely aware that with even a small leak, the media would be on their trail like a pack of hungry wolves. Marla would have to agree to this also... and stick to it.

One by one, Marty called the eight disciples. To his surprise, they all accepted the four-month delay, quite well. He had anticipated frustration – possibly anger – at such a lengthy postponement, but they all seemed to have almost expected it. Marty didn't want to read anything unusual into this and simply speculated that they could look at a map as easily as he could – and figure out that the mountain roads, at that northerly latitude, would be blocked for quite a time in the winter. He told them that, pending a successful meeting with his boss, he would be able to furnish them all with plane tickets to Montana... and that they'd all meet there then drive to the mountains. Several told Marty that he didn't have to send them tickets – that they'd be very happy to pay their own way. Marty insisted, however... and they acquiesced. When he told them that he had no idea as to how long the anticipated stay with Papa would be or what, exactly, the purpose would be, they all seemed to have a much more concrete view of this than he did. Each of them said that they would be with Papa for quite a long while... for as long, they said, as he needed them. Marty was rather surprised by this very uniform response and inquired as to why they felt this way. As with the painting, none could say, for sure, exactly why. Given Marty's ever-suspicious mind, in order to rule out any sort of ongoing complicity, he asked each of them if they had any idea as to who the other disciples were and if they had contacted any of them. None had, they said, and to his chagrin, Marty conceded that his conspiratorial notions were obviously asinine.

Marty had some special questions for Aaron – the gay man, confined to the institution. Marty asked him if he were free to leave the institution. Aaron wasn't completely sure, but he said he didn't think he was. Did he know how to go about getting out? He didn't... but felt sure it would have something to do with the courts, since that was the process by which he was initially confined.

The following morning, as Marty had promised, he met with Marla. As he had predicted, she thought the idea of a Papa sequel was a wonderful idea. Would she fund the trip? Yes... but what, exactly, would he need? Marty swallowed hard and began his pitch. Besides the usual travel and subsistence, he said he would need some additional funding. What exactly? Well, he replied, it was a long story. Marty went on to explain all about his dream, the half-of-a-picture mailing, the eight correctly completed drawings, and his conversations with the "disciples"... along with a brief summary about each of their backgrounds. Marla was beside herself with excitement – more so than Marty had ever seen her – so much so, she had to stand up and pace as she talked. She searched for adequate superlatives. Sensing the momentary heat of the iron, Marty knew it was the time to strike the hammer for the additional expenses. He did... and he was resoundingly successful. He came away from the meeting with a virtual carte blanche commitment, ". . . whatever it takes," she had said. For future purposes, he didn't ask for any further clarification. In response to Marla's question as to when he would get started, Marty explained to her about the weather delay. Marla rolled her eyes in profound disappointment, shook her head, then resigned herself to this realistic impediment and her need to overcome her chronic impatience with life in general. She was the type of person who would speed-read books and articles on how to relax and live longer... then anguish over the lack of immediate results.

Marla was now on the money hook and Marty determined he would utilize his own liberal construction of her words. He had, for a brief moment, considered riding her euphoric crest into a pay raise for himself, as well, but decided not to push the envelope that far... fearing the additional demand might screw up the rest of the deal. Ginny was thrilled with the results. That evening, they selected a date for arrival in Great Falls – May 1st – for no particular reason other than it sounded right... and called the group of eight with the decision. None had any objection to it. Marty said he would mail each of them their tickets in plenty of time. They'd be one way, he explained, pending developments, but assured them he'd pay for their way back, if – and when – they were ready. Marty also informed them that the whole trip – travel, lodging, food, etc. – was on the magazine. He then went on to reveal the reason the company was willing to cover the trip – that he had agreed to do a story on this next phase of Papa's life... his life with them – the disciples. He asked each of them if this presented a problem... also waiting for a response to his trial-use of the word "disciples" in referring to them. None objected to the use of the term. Only one said the sequel could pose a problem. Paulo, the ex-convict felon, explained that, as a condition of his parole, he wasn't supposed to go out-of-state for more than four days per month and he was required to visit his parole officer once a week. If he disappeared and Marty wrote an article about him and where he was, they'd come pick him up as a parole violator. Marty told Paulo that he'd check with the magazine's attorneys and see what could be worked out. He assured Paulo he was certain they'd come up with something.

Over the next several months, Marty and Ginny worked on the details of the trip. Marty met a number of times with the attorneys and had also started working on the first segment of the article... chronicling the events leading to the return trip to Montana with the disciples. Each night, in preparing for this segment, he'd spend several hours on the phone with various disciples – asking questions about their lives and attitudes and expectations. He took notes, and Ginny would transcribe them... saving them on computer discs – a separate disc for each disciple. As they amassed information, Marty became increasingly paranoid about the security of his files. He was working, primarily, at home now, and keeping all his papers and files there, as well, and he was poignantly cognizant of the disaster that would ensue if some media maggot – as he was prone to call them – was somehow able to come into possession of his research. It could ruin the whole project – not to mention the lives of the disciples, and possibly Papa. In this frame of paranoid mind-set – like some member of the French Underground – Marty designed a "safe place" for his materials. Drawing from a scene in an old spy movie, he pulled up one corner of the wall-to-wall carpeting, loosened several floor boards, and began the practice of hiding his materials in the space below. Ginny couldn't help laughing at him as he was creating his clandestine cache. He finally joined her, realizing how funny this would all seem in the years to come. Despite the *Get Smart* quality of his clandestine antics, however, Marty truly believed his extreme measures were justified, given the possible catastrophic ramifications of having his materials stolen. So, each night before bed, or whenever they'd go out – with a sheepish smile on his face, and to the lyrical accompaniment of Ginny's giggles – he'd pull up the rug, lift the boards, and hide his secrets.

On the legal front, the attorneys were able to make arrangements for Paulo to temporarily report to a designated law officer in Montana – the Police Chief of Bear Stump, specifically. As for Aaron, it was considerably more complex. They had to retain local counsel from a town near Mayview State Mental Institution. The local attorney quickly determined that Aaron was under a court-ordered, indefinite involuntary mental commitment. To be released, it would require a petition to the county court and the production of convincing psychiatric testimony, establishing that Aaron was no longer in need of confinement. The attorney located a very expensive, well-respected, accommodating psychiatrist who, after meeting with Aaron for a total of fifteen minutes, was able – as per the objectives of his forensic commission – to professionally conclude that Aaron had sufficiently recovered from the effects of his previous pathology to allow him to live, safely, without any further inpatient treatment. At the hearing, Aaron's attending institute psychiatrist, having little personal interest in Aaron's case, made a very feeble objection to the private assessment – but then conceded that it was, of course, a matter of opinion, and deferred to the eminent qualifications and opinion of his esteemed colleague. On this basis, Aaron was ordered to be released from Mayview. The attorney set Aaron up in a room at a local Motel Six and gave him two hundred dollars, each week, for his subsistence. The total cost for the attorney and the psychiatrist – billed to the magazine – was slightly over ten thousand dollars. Additionally, the attorney submitted the motel and subsistence outlay for reimbursement at the rate of $420 per week. These items drew Marla's immediate and rapt attention... and her corresponding ire... requiring Marty to remind her of her carte blanche commitment, which, in turn, and in the heat of the moment, spawned her fiery admonition that the piece had better be a blockbuster or Marty's ass would be in a painful sling.

By late April, via the extensive communications between Marty and the eight, both Marty and Ginny felt they knew each disciple quite well, despite having never laid eyes on a single one of them. Largely due to the information, garnered during these many conversations with the disciples, Marty was pleased with his introductory segment of the sequel. Final details of the trip were now becoming firm. Everyone had received their tickets. Marty told them he would be standing at the Great Falls Airport arrival gate holding a sign that read, "Papa." Marty and Ginny would drive both of their own cars to Great Falls. Marty wanted to fly there and rent cars, but Ginny reminded him that they had no idea as to how long this trip might last, and that it would be, therefore, both impractical and prohibitively expensive to have rented cars for what might be a very long time. He agreed. With a week to go before the big day, the anticipation fluttered in both their stomachs and their sleep became light and erratic. They departed Los Angeles for Great Falls, Montana on the 27th of April... giving themselves, they thought, plenty of time – in case of car trouble or other unforeseen delays – to get there before the first of May.

CHAPTER FIVE

Allowing five days for the trip turned out to be a wise decision, indeed. Six miles from Cedar City Utah, Ginny began noticing an unusual noise, emanating from the rear of her car... which rapidly escalated into an exceedingly loud, clunking sound that shook the entire back end. She pulled over to the shoulder of the road – Marty pulling in behind. They decided to try to make it to a service station in Cedar City. After driving into – and out of – four gas stations, they realized that very few of these places work on cars anymore... this being a revelation for both of them. Finally, they found an old Sunoco station that proclaimed "Full Service" on a battered, crookedly hanging metal sign. From the black, shiny coating on the cracked and potholed concrete in front of the station, it was apparent that many a car, with big problems, had graced its oily portals. In the tool-and-tire-laden service area of the station, a very short, stocky man in overalls, stained to the same shade and condition as the station concrete, was hunched over the side of an old Chevrolet, climbing around under its gaping, mouth-like hood. According to Marty's and Ginny's rapid reconnaissance, he appeared to constitute the total sum of human presence within the entire greasy premises. He either didn't hear them come up behind him, or didn't care to acknowledge their presence. Finally, Marty uttered, with overly done solicitude, "Excuse me." No response. Marty repeated his plea. The man slowly retracted himself from the depths of the automotive bowels and turned around to look at the two of them... his face crunched into unquestionable annoyance at the interruption, as well as displaying an utter lack of interest in either their presence or any possible problems they may be experiencing. He said nothing. To call an end to the uncomfortable staring duel, Marty smiled and stuck out his hand.

"Hi, I'm Marty Chapman."

Without any softening of his aloof, nettled facial presentation, he raised his grease-covered right palm toward Marty as an answer to his salutation. His mostly grease-obliterated name patch appeared to spell out the name, "Bill." Marty continued.

"My girlfriend's car is making a really loud noise and the whole back end is shaking."

Bill glanced briefly at Ginny, then out at their two cars, parked directly in front of the station. Just then, an old model truck pulled up at the gas pumps – the tires compressing the black hose, ringing the bell twice, as each set passed over it. Without apologies, Bill walked directly between them, wiping his hands on a rag that had, ages ago, apparently been red. Marty and Ginny looked at one another... their faces mirroring mutual bewilderment and growing concern.

When Bill returned, he spoke to them in a curt, clipped fashion.

"Which one is it?"

Marty answered... pointing as he did.

"The red one."

Bill glanced at it for a fleeting moment... his face continuing to wear its intense apathy. He then proceeded to instruct them in a tone, clearly indicating that in his grimy kingdom, he was accustomed to unilateral command.

"Pull it over there against the fence and leave the keys."

He then turned and, without further elaboration, plunged, once again, into the depths of the presumably ailing Chevrolet. Before he was totally inserted, Marty leaned awkwardly over the posterior of the partially immersed body and meekly requested of him, information that he felt was obviously pertinent.

"Do you know when you can get to it?"

Without retracting himself, Bill's muffled words found their way around the Chevy's innards to the befuddled couple's ears... echoing from their metal-enhanced journey.

"As soon as I can get around to it."

Marty looked at Ginny. Her eyebrows raised in synchronization with the upturning of both her hands. Her eyes mirrored Marty's look of utter helplessness. Marty shrugged his shoulders and nodded his head to the side, motioning for their retreat. Marty pulled Ginny's debilitated car up to the partially fallen, weather-beaten, once-green fence. He returned to the office and laid her keys on an old oak desk, strewn with an assortment of dirty papers and automotive magazines. Pulling out of the Sunoco station, Marty and Ginny looked at one another... then, simultaneously, burst into spontaneous laughter at the same instant. They continued their indecorous howling for the next four blocks... rendering Marty barely capable of operating his vehicle. Marty regained his composure first – only to intentionally sacrifice it.

"Wasn't that guy on the *Andy Griffith Show*?"

The remark immediately refueled the comical tempest, as Marty knew it would. After a few more minutes... when the caterwauling had finally degenerated to intermittent bursts and giggles, Marty was finally able to ask Ginny if she was hungry. She was, she said. At Ginny's instance they pulled into an old-fashioned diner they spotted... Ginny saying she liked the classic looks of it... that it reminded her of a place, in front of which her dad had once posed for an old photograph she had of him. The counter was lined with men wearing tractor-labeled ball caps, blue jeans, flannel shirts, chains on their wallets, and work shoes. From the stares, with which Marty and Ginny were greeted by the counter assembly, both felt as though they had the letters, "L.A." stamped, in large letters, across their foreheads. They took a seat at a booth that had Formica seats on either side of a Formica table – sporting a chrome box on the wall with numerous pages of songs that could be flipped by the shiny, metal tabs extending below.

A high school-age waitress with very crooked teeth and a name tag reading, "Heather," gave them the one-page, poorly mimeographed menu, then water, without asking if they wanted it or not, then asked, as though the question were actually a declaratory statement, "Coffee"... then appeared slightly annoyed by the couple's declination of the diner's clearly presumptive beverage. Instead, Ginny ordered an iced tea with lemon... Marty, a Diet Coke. The daily special, doubly underlined on the menu with red marker, was a meat loaf dinner. They both ordered it – neither of them having had meat loaf in a long time. Expecting an L.A. delay, they were shocked to find the waitress back, within two minutes, bearing two enormous platters of food. Besides the huge piece of meat loaf, rising over an inch thick from the plate, there was a pile of mashed potatoes – so large that it reminded them both of the Richard Dreyfus dinner scene in *Close Encounters* – succotash, coleslaw, apple sauce, a salad, and an immense basket of bread and butter.

The communication that immediately ensued between the two sets of eyes, nearly set off what both knew would be a completely uncontrolled, and totally inadvisable, renewed fit of laughter. As they ate, they continually swallowed their interminable rising mirth along with the food, to the point of mutual indigestion. Both were desperately afraid to make even a passing comment to one another – about anything – for fear of setting the other off. Each of them was able to eat only about a quarter of their meals, after which Marty asked, mercifully, for the check. The waitress studied the mostly uneaten food and inquired, suspiciously, if everything was all right. Marty assured her that the food was excellent... but they just weren't used to such generous portions. As he spoke, he could feel a rogue laugh, gurgling up from around his midsection, trying its level best to emerge into the common air. Ginny instantly recognized the telltale symptoms and straightaway cautioned him with a gentle kick on his ankle and a compelling, wide-eyed reproach. Back in the car, they started again and laughed until their sides hurt and forgot what was funny.

They found a new-looking Holiday Inn, just outside town and checked in for the night. It advertised an inside, heated, swimming pool which they both found inviting, but, not being on an actual vacation, neither had packed a swimming suit. Marty called the front desk in the hope they might have some suits that the two of them could borrow. They didn't. Marty suggested they both put on a pair of his boxer shorts... and Ginny, one of his T-shirts for a top... and go on down to the pool. Barefooted and clad in their jury-rigged swimming apparel, with hotel towels in hand, they rode the elevator, down to the lobby and followed the signs marking the route to the pool. They made a final left turn into a narrow, cement block passageway and walked the final yards to the pool through the provocative, thick, wet, chlorine-laced air, wafting from the warm water... entering the tropical room through a condensation-obscured glass door. As soon as Ginny got the white, well-worn top, wet, the shape and pinkness of her breasts and nipples stood out like bumpers on an old Buick, which, once again, rekindled their seemingly unquenchable laughing jag. A middle-aged couple, with three teenage boys, stared at them... actually, just Ginny. The boys – and their dad – were blatantly and demonstratively appreciative of her considerable attributes. The mother, on the other hand, clearly, was not. In response to the obvious – and intolerable – interest her males were unabashedly exhibiting in Ginny's shining, shapely, and clearly discernable torso... with overt disgust, she quickly gathered together the family's poolside accouterments and commanded the men to follow... which they did... with clear reluctance... the boys continuing to stare back, longingly, at Ginny, until they finally disappeared through the steamy door. Ginny and Marty gazed warmly at one another as mutually delighted conspirators in the creation of this comical, intra-family fracas. They silently agreed, at that moment, that they were a team, as well as they were lovers.

The entire day had been like a honeymoon for the two of them, and the roots of their love had attached more firmly to that invisible flesh that grows between lovers... fertilized, that day, by shared laughter. They both grew to understand that the ability to laugh together was the touchstone of true love. That night they made tender, and very friendly, love.

The following morning, after breakfast, and with hopeful hearts,

THE MINISTRY

they swung by Bill's Sunoco. Surprisingly, he was already working on Ginny's car... at least they assumed the feet sticking out from under the rear of Ginny's car belonged to Bill. Apparently spotting *their* feet, Bill slid out from under the car on his wooden sled that rolled, smoothly, on small, black, swivel wheels. He announced the automotive diagnosis with conspicuous certainty.

"It's your universal."

Feeling odd – talking directly down to a man, lying flat on his back, Marty squatted beside the sled.

"Do you know how long it will take?"

"I've got to get some parts."

With no further explanation apparently forthcoming, Marty continued his inquiry.

"Do you know how long that might take?"

"Ray might have them."

"Who?"

"Over on Maple."

"Oh."

"Do you think you'll have it fixed today?"

"Wouldn't count on it."

"Tomorrow, maybe?"

"Yeah. Tomorrow sometime."

"Well... OK... I guess we'll check with you tomorrow, then.

What time should we stop in?"

"Afternoon."

Reality's glare had suddenly emerged from the soft haze of yesterday's merriment. It was the twenty-ninth. They wouldn't get Ginny's car until the afternoon of the thirtieth – if they were lucky – and they still had at least forty hours of straight driving ahead of them. At the rate they were going, they'd be lucky to make it to the airport on time, even if they drove straight through, of which, neither believed they were capable. Yesterday's giggles were totally vanquished by today's consternation.

Life had always seemed to be this way to Marty... like a constant roller coaster... up one minute, down the next. He guessed that was the reason he always had a nervous stomach. All the while something nice was happening, his ears were constantly busy – straining for the sound of the next, dropping shoe.

On the following day, they returned to Bill's at twelve, noon. To their delight – and astonishment – the car was done. To their even greater amazement, Bill didn't take credit cards. Marty simply couldn't believe it. In his version of the world, nobody refused to take a credit card. The bill was $147.50. Marty had about fifty dollars in cash on him – Ginny, twenty. Marty asked Bill where the nearest ATM was... then had to further clarify his question, explaining that he meant an automatic teller machine. Bill understood this more proper term, and directed him to the "... national bank – down on Market." Marty withdrew two hundred, returned to the Sunoco, and paid the bill. By one o'clock in the afternoon of April thirtieth, the two cars were back on the road and the luxury of time – and a relaxed drive – had vanished.

Marty and Ginny agreed to drive in three-hour segments – take a fifteen-minute break – then back on the road. At the end of nine hours, they would stop for food. At midnight, they'd find a motel, get a few hours' sleep, then back on the road. The plan was carried out without a glitch, and they pulled into a motel, just outside Salt Lake City, at five minutes past midnight. They could both still hear the sound of tires in their ears and feel the motion of their cars inside their heads. After quick, hot, showers, however, they fell instantly asleep, on opposite sides of the bed, just like an old married couple... but fatigued beyond the point of caring.

The alarm at five-thirty a.m. was cruel. Only with extraordinary effort did they succeed in not falling back asleep. After breakfast, and several cups of regular coffee, they were somewhat revived. After their first three-hour segment, however, they were both already so tired, they feared for their own safety. Unwilling to press their luck, they pulled over at a roadside rest and slept in Marty's car for two hours – his having more room. She slept in the front... he in the back. Marty set the alarm on his watch and hoped it would be loud enough to awaken their overly tired bodies and minds. It was, and the two hours seemed to do the trick. They used the rest rooms... peeing... then washing their faces with cold water. They now felt much better, and ready to go. At 2:00 a.m. on May first, the utterly exhausted pair pulled into a motel in Great Falls, Montana. They thanked the merciful heavens that the plane wouldn't arrive until 11:30 that morning... allowing them the sleep they so desperately craved.

As they lie in bed, awaiting delivery into the benevolent respite of slumber, their minds and bodies were pulled in opposite directions by fatigue and excitement. Excitement finally got the edge and, giving in, they sat up and talked for the next three hours, after which fatigue finally overcame its rival. Their road-spinning, exhausted heads had slightly intoxicated them and they literally babbled on without self-consciousness, sophomorically speculating on a host of trivialities, pertaining to the following day's events, pursuing each topic with manic delight. What would the various disciples look like? Despite his otherwise thorough interviews with each of them, Marty had, absently, failed to get physical self-descriptions. Would they somehow recognize one another during their common flight from St. Louis to Great Falls? Would they get along? Would one of them emerge as a leader... as Peter to Jesus? What would the former minister think of Papa's view of Jesus? The sportive speculation filled the hours until five in the morning – just before sunrise – when they were finally overcome with blessed sleep.

Despite their brief slumber, anticipation stoked their energy to the extent that neither of them had any trouble in answering the bell at nine. Marty was excited to the point of diarrhea... which was not uncommon for him under such stimulating circumstances. Ginny was literally bouncing, as she walked and giggled around the room in her bra and underpants. An English muffin and coffee was the most that either excited stomach could tolerate for breakfast. They left the motel at 10:10 for the fifteen-minute drive to the airport.

As they were approaching the airport entrance, Ginny suddenly remembered that they didn't have the "Papa" sign that Marty said they'd be holding at the gate. She beeped her horn to get Marty to stop... reminding him of their forgetfulness. They turned their cars around and drove back, a few miles, to a small shopping area they had passed on their way. In a Rite-Aid Drug Store they bought a piece of white poster board, a black magic marker, and a cheap pair of scissors. Laying the poster across the hood of her car, Ginny printed the four letters on the top half of the poster board, as best she could, given the time factor and the uneven curvature of the hood. She then cut off the bottom half of the board... both of them concurring that a full-sized poster might be a bit much.

They were in the airport parking lot at 10:45 and at the assigned gate by 11:05. As they waited, the tension was building to a near-unendurable crescendo. Neither of them could sit still – taking turns going to the bathroom or looking out the floor-to-ceiling windows for the arriving plane. Marty was so overcome with the significance of the moment, he worked himself into light-headedness, wondering, as always, if he were up to all this. Seeing Marty's flagging composure, Ginny reached inside herself and brought forth the necessary courage, confidence, and calm for both of them. As had quickly become an intimate and accustomed practice between the lovers, Ginny put her arm around Marty's shoulders and rubbed him... to the intended effect... allowing him to recover his equilibrium just as the flight arrival was announced over the public address system. They took their places, just off to the side of the gate door… close enough to be seen, but far enough away to allow adequate space for the anticipated gathering.

Holding the sign, Marty could feel the wetness between his trembling hands and the cardboard. Fortunately, he looked down at the poster, suspended at the level of his chest, to notice he was holding it upside down… and quickly reversed it. As the large group of deplaning passengers began emerging from the gate door, Marty and Ginny both anxiously searched the oncoming faces for clues as to who, in this diverse, moving crowd, might be members of the long-awaited band of disciples… not knowing, however, what characteristics, precisely, they were seeking. Shouts, smiles, reunions, kisses, and hugs abounded between the travelers and their welcomers… followed by the inevitable question regarding the quality of the flight. All consistently responded that it was fine… except for a little bumpiness during the landing.

The first passenger to show a response to their sign was a rather stocky, dark-haired man, looking to be in his late forties. He jerked his head upward to acknowledge them, and made his way to them through the arriving throng. He put down his small, black, leather carry-on bag and extended his hand to Marty. The man's smile was warm, but his face showed a great weariness and dearth of spirit.

"You must be Marty."

Marty shook his hand, immediately recognizing the Detroit dialect, of which he had become so familiar during their many phone conversations.

"I'll bet you're Danny Boscia."

"Good guess."

Marty introduced Ginny. She extended her hand… Danny shook it gently.

One by one, the disciples joined the group.

Amid the introductions, Marty tried – for purposes of his article – to make mental notes of his initial impressions of each disciple. He would have taken Danny Boscia, he noted, to be a blue-collar worker had he not already known his professional background. He had an ambling, clumsy carriage, a weathered-looking, no-nonsense face, and a rather large, squarish head. His speech, though articulate, had a raw-edged, streetwise bite to it. Marty decided that if he were ever to cast a welder in a movie, he would have picked Danny Boscia.

Veronica Jones was next to join them. She was a stunning beauty and entirely different in appearance than Marty's preconceived image of her. Marty had expected that she – being a hooker – would likely have a rather trashy, gaudily bejeweled, heavily made-up appearance. Instead, before him, appeared someone who could have easily passed for a corporate executive, or a world-class model, who had been dressed and made-up by Cosmo fashion consultants, and possessed of the carriage and delicate manners of a debutante. Her speech, with which Marty was already familiar, by way of their interviews – to his initial surprise when they had first conversed over the phone – instead of the anticipated, coarse, grammatically abortive language he expected of a hooker from Harlem was a delightful work of practiced elocution and grace. Marty reasoned that – given her socially elite clientele and their willingness to "take her out" to their upper-crust functions – she must have quickly mastered the language and style as an occupational necessity. Despite her chic fashion and beauty, however, an air of hopelessness seemed to possess her. What struck Marty the most about Veronica was her striking, physical similarity to Papa. They could have easily, he judged, passed for brother and sister. Both had tall, strong physiques, light-chestnut complexions, fine features, and coarse hair. Both also had an animal-like balance, confidence, and stealth in their gait.

Aaron Tyger looked terrible… as one might expect for someone who had been institutionalized for several years and daily drugged. Marty immediately pondered whether he could tolerate the journey and crude living conditions that lie ahead. Aaron was exceedingly thin and sickly. His light-brown hair was very fine, straight, and thinned. His complexion was pale and unhealthy. His right ear was noticeably deformed – an obvious product of a less-than-artistic plastic surgeon. He had long fingers that moved delicately. His movements were cautious and insecure – his voice soft. He had a vacant look in his eyes that often comes of being confined, too long, behind closed doors.

Marty was drawn to Katherine Deville's eyes. They were playful, spirited, engaging, and searching at certain moments – distant and blank at others... as though constantly passing between two worlds. She was in her thirties, but still youthfully pretty with a girlish bloom in her cheeks and a certain sparkle that betrayed a coquettishness and sexuality. One could sense her energy. Despite the obvious fire inside her, however, she also had an unmistakable air of desperation and fear... like that of a trapped animal.

Henry Butler's appearance was the only one of the eight that Marty had accurately anticipated – probably because the characteristics of men in their mid-seventies have usually narrowed down to a fairly predictable range. He had pale, delicate-looking skin with some liver spotting... thin, mostly gone, gray hair... a creased narrow face with sharp features, and a stiff, bony body. Henry also had the countenance, vocabulary, reserve, and genteel nature of a professor but, like Veronica, he suffered a haunting hopelessness in his eyes that seemed to be looking at the approaching face of death and seeing nothing beyond it.

Marty found Paulo Mandos immediately frightening, perhaps because he knew of his history of murder and mayhem, but he sensed it was more than that. Like a large dog, Paulo seemed, to Marty, to exude a clearly discernable aura of potential danger about him... giving no signs of attack, but who could, at any moment and without warning, lunge for the kill. He was short and very powerfully built – the obvious product of a lifetime spent pumping iron in the penitentiary yard. He had on a black T-shirt which was stretched to its limits by the rippled body and large, defined biceps. His handshake had the force of a hydraulic press.

His big and stunningly white smile – topped by a black mustache – seemed to issue an unmistakable warning which read, "I'll be nice, if you are... if you're not, God help you." Marty was convinced, straightaway, that he never wanted to see Paulo when he was angry.

The first word that came to Marty's mind, in meeting Susan Atherton was *hard*. She was still a statuesque and attractive blonde as she approached her mid-forties, but clearly lived behind a social, glass wall. She was there, but impossible to touch. Her words were measured and emotionless. One could not mistake her for anything, save the predatory and heartless industrialist she was. Unlike the others, Marty could read absolutely nothing in her eyes... no hate... no loneliness... no fear – nothing. An odd metaphor struck Marty in Susan's presence – that she was a machine... only made of flesh and not metal. Marty was at a loss as to why such a woman would feel compelled to reach Papa... at a loss to believe that she could, in fact, feel anything. If there were ever a body without a soul...

David Matthew's face told his story. It traced a tale of a once pampered, well-educated man, who had, in times past, been accustomed to fine things, and to being the object of reverence. The formerly smooth and blushing, aristocratically white skin of the once-handsome man, was now hacked with the creases and furrows of bitterness and too much alcohol, and was a mere shell of the distinguished person he had once been. He still possessed, however, a public countenance... characteristic of men of the cloth... just cautiously short of arrogance, defined by the impeccable manners, the suspiciously zealous solicitude toward others, and well-oiled social graces. But the craters, pocking his countenance – left by the acid of bitterness – could not be camouflaged. As with a forgotten movie star, however, one could sense David's still-lingering former eminence.

They went, as a group, to retrieve their bags. Knowing their destination, all had packed lightly, in wilderness-ready bags. Several brought sleeping bags. Veronica and Susan looked particularly odd, walking through the terminal in designer clothing and heels, carrying their all-terrain duffle bags and back packs. At the parking lot, they divided into two groups for the trip back to the motel. Once there, Marty gave each of them their room key... having already rented their rooms that morning. Each was assigned separate lodging. Marty asked them to join him in his room in about an hour.

At the get-together, Marty outlined his proposed itinerary. They would leave in the morning – around nine – for Bear Stump. He told them he needed to stop at the Bear Stump police station for a short time, then, they'd be on their way to Art's cabin. He warned them about the possibility of media detection... and the disaster that could ensue if they were discovered. He suggested that it may be advisable that he and Ginny drop them off... perhaps somewhere, back on Old Log Road... then the two of them would drive back to Bear Stump in one car. He told them he didn't want them to think him paranoid but he explained that he knew the media very well and it wouldn't be beyond the realm of possibility that they had paid informers in Bear Stump... keeping their eyes open for any signs of Papa-type activity. Ten very noticeable outsiders arriving at one time, he pointed out, would certainly not go unnoticed in Bear Stump. Paulo stopped Marty.

"I'm supposed to report to the chief in Bear Stump... right?"

"Yes... damn... I'd completely forgotten about that. I guess you'd better come with Ginny and me and get things set up."

The rest of the group looked back and forth between Marty and Paulo... clearly wondering what this exchange was all about. Marty knew he had an immediate decision to make – to maintain certain confidential information he possessed about all these people, or get the secrets out on the table. He decided to put the question to them, directly.

"Look... we're going to be together for a good while, probably... and I have a feeling it may be very important for all of us to get to know one another... and to trust one another. I already know quite a bit about each one of you... at least what you were willing to tell me in our interviews... but you know virtually nothing about one another. I can already see that you're wondering what Paulo and I are talking about. I'll play this anyway you want to. I'm certainly willing to keep confidential information to myself, but you need to decide if you want to know about one another or not. You all have at least one thing in common... you feel compelled to meet Papa... and somehow the eight of you, out of the hundreds of people who wrote me, knew what the other half of Papa's painting looked like. So I..."

Paulo interrupted again.

"Look, man... I don't give a shit *what* you people know about me. I am who I am. I'm a convict on parole. I been a drug dealer, a mugger, a killer, and a lot of other nasty things in my life. I spent most of my life behind bars. That's my life story... OK? I gotta go see the man in Bear Stump cause it's my parole. If I don't go... they'll throw my ass back in the big house."

Paulo looked around at the others... his head cocked, mouth set, and eyes narrowed – ready to pounce on any problems that anyone might have with his short autobiography. Veronica broke the silence.

"I don't want to do any pretending. Paulo... you're a convict – I'm a hooker... from Harlem. I get paid a lot from uptown johns... but I spread my legs for a living – just like any other streetwalker. I've been a working girl since I was a teenager. That's my life... nothing more."

After a short, uncertain silence, Danny went next.

"Nothing very exciting to say about myself. I come from a blue-collar family in Detroit. I busted my ass to try to be a big shot. I became a lawyer... then went nutty and lost everything. Haven't worked in three years... and I'm broke. I've been through three marriages. I have one kid – a son – who I haven't seen since he was a baby. That's my story in a nutshell."

THE MINISTRY

David.

"I'm a former Presbyterian minister. I had the world by the tail... a large church in Boston... beautiful wife and daughters... a wonderful home... big income... respect. A teenage girl in my congregation accused me of raping her. Despite the fact that I didn't do it, I was advised to plead guilty to a lesser offense. I did. As a result, I lost my wife, kids, and church... and was suspended, indefinitely, from the ministry. I've been working in a canning factory for the past five years – mopping the floors. I'm also an alcoholic... trying to recover... been sober for four months."

Katherine.

"I'll go next. I'm a Canadian from Montreal. I live at home with my parents and son... who's seventeen. I'm virtually a recluse and I very rarely venture outside. I've lived a very fast life – always looking for something new – but came up empty-handed. That's it."

Aaron.

"I've spent the past several years in a mental institution. I'm gay and I've had a miserable, lonely life... and I tried to blow my brains out by sticking a gun in my mouth and pulling the trigger. I missed my brain... but I blew away a part of my skull and my ear. That's why it looks so funny."

Henry.

"Well, as you can tell... I'm old. I've worked all of my professional career as a philosophy professor at a college... out east. Been retired for ten years. I have grown children... a daughter and a son... and two grandchildren. I very rarely see or talk to any of them. My wife is deceased. I spend my life at McDonald's and in my apartment. I'm at the end of the road, and still don't know what it's all about. I have this sense that Papa does. I hope he does."

Susan.

"I really don't have anything to say."

Paulo erupted.

"What the fuck! Everyone of us has owned up to our lives, admitting to a lot of shit… and after listening to everyone else tell it like it is, you don't have anything to say? That's bullshit!"

Marty tried to intervene but Paulo cut him off in an instant, and scared the hell out of him. With this, Marty had had his first, small taste of Paulo's potential fury.

"Hey! Who are you… the man here? If I need someone to tell me what to say – I'll go back to the big house."

Susan looked at Paulo with passionless eyes and a steady voice.

"My life is my own. It's nobody else's business."

Paulo jumped to his feet.

"You fuckin bitch!"

He walked to the door, opened it, and walked out… slamming it shut behind him.

A tense silence followed. Everyone was clearly uncomfortable, except for Susan, who appeared completely unmoved by the experience… almost serene. Marty felt the responsibility, as host, to restore good will. He tried humor.

"Well, I guess we can rule out a career in mediation for Paulo."

Only David and Aaron felt obliged, out of courtesy, to offer half-smiles. Unsuccessful with his humorous approach, Marty tried another tack – to move on as though nothing had happened.

"Well, anyway... for tomorrow... as I said – if no one has any problem with it – we'll meet in the lobby around nine and get on the road. Bear Stump is only a couple of hours drive from here. Ginny and Paulo and I will take care of our business then we'll set out for the mountain. That's a good drive too... back Old Log Road... about sixty miles... most of it, a one-lane, dirt road. That'll take another couple of hours. Anybody have any questions... or anything else they want to say?"

There was a pause... then Ginny spoke up.

"I just want to say that I hope no one has a problem with my coming along. My only claim to being here with you is that Marty is my boyfriend, and I asked him if I could come along with... ."

Marty broke in.

"Now wait, Ginny. Everyone needs to know what part you actually played in this whole situation. I was ready to scrap the whole deal... this whole Papa thing. It's a long story, but it was just too much for me and I didn't want to deal with it any longer. If it hadn't have been for my meeting Ginny – and falling in love with her – none of this would have happened. I'm very serious. I wouldn't have called you... and you wouldn't have had a chance to meet Papa, if it weren't for Ginny."

Henry spoke.

"First of all, Ginny, I, personally, have no problem, whatsoever, with your being here... and I am thankful that you influenced Marty... but, on another subject, Marty... can I ask you something? What is Papa like... beyond what you wrote in your article? You're apparently the only living person to have met him since his father died."

"All right... it's truth time. I had someone else with me when I met Papa... a guy about your age, Henry, the specifics of which I intentionally left out of the article – other than by vague reference. I don't know if you want to hear this or not, Henry, but it's a part of an answer to your question. Papa had such an impact on my friend – Art was his name – that the shock killed him within a couple of hours. He may have been just too old for it – sorry Henry – but that just may have been the case. And he was in great physical shape, too... could run circles around me. I have to admit that Papa had quite an effect on me, too. I'm very glad I didn't have a weak heart."

Veronica.

"What is it about him?... Papa, I mean."

"I don't know if I can describe it... he's... I don't know... almost like meeting someone who's more than human... like meeting some character who just stepped out of Greek mythology. Just his looks, alone – he's massive... tall, muscular... dressed in that leather kilt. He's just so much out of the ordinary that your mind takes a turn when you meet him. You see him... but it doesn't quite register. And his voice... it's very soothing and reassuring... like talking to your grandfather – yet it's powerful – as though he's speaking with absolute authority. Connect all this with the claim he's making – being God and all – and you have a very mind-altering experience. I don't want to sound theatrical, but the experience isn't for the fainthearted. I mean, look..."

Marty paused to look at Aaron.

"... I don't want to be an alarmist, but Aaron, you've been in an institution for a good while and – to be perfectly frank – you're not looking too terribly strong right now. I honestly hope, for your sake, that you're up to this experience."

Ginny interjected.

"Marty... for goodness sake – you're going to scare all these poor people to death."

"I'm sorry if that's the way it's coming across... but Henry and Veronica asked me about him... and I'm telling them the truth.

THE MINISTRY

Meeting Papa is a powerful experience – at least it was for Art and me. Maybe – with my getting all of you ready for it – it won't have as much of an effect on you. I mean… Art and I just bumped into him – totally unprepared. It was one hell of a shock – and I'm not exaggerating… or trying to scare anyone."

Veronica.

"I'm not afraid, Marty. I hope he's everything you describe him to be. I want to believe he is who he says he is. I need him to be."

Danny.

"Whata you think, Marty? Is he, who he says he is?"

"I was kind of hoping this wouldn't come up, at least not this soon, because I don't want to sway anybody, one way or another… or burst anyone's bubble… but… OK… no – to be honest – I can't accept what he says about himself. Ginny and I have been over and over this but, for my own reasons, I just can't accept it. Who knows?… maybe he is… but I simply can't buy it. Maybe it's just too much for my puny mind. I mean it. It just won't fit into my version of the world… and I've gotten kind of used to my version."

Danny, again.

"So you're saying he might be God… but you can't accept it?"

"That's right."

Danny looked around at the faces of the assembly.

"How about the rest of you? What are you expecting?"

Katherine.

"What about you, Danny?"

"I don't know. After I read that article of Marty's, I felt some really strong emotions... as though the story sounded familiar... as though I'd heard it before. I felt this need to meet this man... regardless of who he is. This whole situation has helped me, already. I was... who can explain a mental breakdown?... but I was a hollow person, living in terror of... I don't know what... afraid of everything – living or dying. I've been in hell, the last three years. My need to meet this man... and coming all this way to do it has helped me already. It's given me some meaning to my life... a purpose, if you know what I mean. Somehow I feel I need to be some part of this man's life. The final piece of this, for me, was that picture Marty sent us. It looked so familiar... as though I had seen it everyday of my life. I knew every color and line – the whole thing... what was there... and what was missing. I knew it as well as if I had painted the whole thing myself. That convinced me that something special was going on here. I don't know what – but I have an open mind. This sure as hell isn't one of your run-of-the-mill life experiences. Whether Papa is God or not... I'll just have to wait and see, then judge for myself. Who knows? I might get cold feet, like Marty, and not be able to deal with the whole possibility... I'll just have to wait and see."

David.

"That's exactly how I feel about everything. I was bitter and hopeless and hated everybody... I even hated my own children... and that article did something to me. Maybe I'm just desperate for something to make my life worthwhile. Like Danny, the picture was the thing that did it for me, too. I have no idea where I had seen it before, but I knew it like the back of my own hand. I didn't know Papa had painted it until Marty told me over the phone. I had completely given up on the concept of any divine being in this universe. I've been in that business already... with the Sunday Christians who compete for the best pews and the prettiest kids to parade down the aisle... who feel so clean and pious for an hour... then drive through the inner city on their way to their suburban bubble... disgusted at being forced to look at all the street niggers and white-trash winos littering their way. I used to think I was one of those blessed people – blessed by the benevolent, upper-middle-class, Caucasian God... until I found out that the whole thing had nothing to do with divinity. Money and social standing was the name of the game... that was it. Without the two, you're out on your own, just like any other poor scumbag. Without money and social standing, you can't get in to even see their designer God. But this Papa person is something different. I sense it. He's not even totally Caucasian. My father would despise him. He'd never worship what he would call a half-nigger God. In my mind, if there were a divine being, he'd be something, just like this Papa... humble, loving, strong. I'm open and hopeful. That's all I can say. I hope I'm not disappointed. This is the first sense of hope I've felt in years. I'd be really shattered if this all turned out to be a giant farce. You're not setting us all up, are you, Marty... for another big story? You're going to break a lot of hearts and souls if you are... at least mine, you will."

"I can't believe you'd even think I'd consider doing something like that. Of course, you don't know me from Adam and, given the reputation of the media, I guess that's not an unreasonable suspicion... but I swear on all that is holy to me... I swear on my love for Ginny... I'm not setting any of you up for anything. I told you, I really didn't even want to continue on with this thing. I was all ready to give it up. I'm only doing a sequel for the money... the money for the trip. I'm not independently wealthy, you know? I need the salary and the expenses. This is a wonderful experience, but there *is* a practical side to it... like Ginny and me eating, and keeping our apartment in Santa Monica."

The door opened and Paulo walked in, a lit cigarette in his hand. He didn't speak, but crossed to the far side of the room and sat on the floor... away from the rest of the group – his back resting against the metal air conditioning cabinet. He didn't look at anyone. He concentrated on the lit end of his cigarette and noisily blew the smoke straight up into the air... watching it rise above his head. Marty hated cigarette smoke – not only the sour smell... but because it often gave him asthma. Despite his revulsion to smoke, however, he wasn't about to ask Paulo Mandos... Loco

Cocha Roacho... killer of men, to put out his cigarette. He began to feel toward Paulo as he had the bullies on the playground. He wanted to say something to them too, but was afraid. He felt the tyranny of Paulo's domination over him, and he hated it and hated himself for feeling it. It made him feel less than a man. For another countless time, he wished, once again, that he were a brave man. Cowards, as he had come to know so well, were always prisoners of their circumstance. He looked over at Ginny and was even more ashamed... feeling that primordial urge of every man to show bravery for his woman... and suffering the humiliation because he couldn't.

Aaron.

"You're right about my health, Marty... both physically and mentally. I'm not in very good shape. I don't know if I can handle everything that lies ahead of us, or not. But I have nothing to lose. I've already tried to kill myself once – and I probably would have done it at Mayview if I hadn't been drugged-up all the time. I still can't believe that your article had such an effect on me... with the stuff they had me on. I would usually read the newspaper and have no idea what I had just read... but every word of your article was as clear as light to me. It made something inside me come alive, again – that had been dead for a long, long time... a kind of warm spot... a spot of love. I started feeling as though I was a person again... with a soul. I started sticking the drugs they gave me in my pocket instead of taking them... then flushed them down the toilet. They used to watch me take them, when I first got there... then, after a while, I guess they figured I always would – so they stopped waiting to see me swallow. I started thinking again and feeling again. That's when I decided to write you a letter. I felt the same way as everyone else about that picture. I recognized it immediately... from somewhere. After that, like everyone else, I sensed that something special was going on. I don't really believe I was chosen or anything like that. What God would choose a skinny, worthless faggot for anything special?... and I'm not looking for any sympathy, that's how I honestly feel about myself. I'm still not very strong... those drugs take everything from you. And I'm still a little shaky and fragile in my head... but the way I look at it, if Papa is who I hope he is, it will be wonderful… if he's not, or the shock kills me, I'm not much worse off than before all this started. Either way, I'm already better than I was. Am I making any sense? I still get mixed-up when I'm talking, sometimes."

Katherine – sitting beside Aaron – placed her hand on his shoulder.

"I understand you perfectly, Aaron. We're in about the same boat… you and I. I had reached the point, just like where you were, where life was all gray… and had no meaning… no feeling to it. You were locked up in an institution… I had locked myself away in my own prison… and numbed myself – day and night – with my own drugs. I'm surviving on the first glimmer of hope I've seen in many years. I feel the same way that David does. If this doesn't pan out… I'll be broken… for the last time. I – literally – have my life riding on this trip."

Veronica.

"It sounds like we're all a bunch of losers… hoping this Papa will be our ticket to somewhere or something."

Paulo.

"Did the tight-ass bitch tell any of her secrets yet?"

Without replying, Susan stood up and quietly walked to the door and went out of the room… softly closing the door behind her. Danny spoke up.

"Hey Paulo… why don't you just get off of her ass for a while? Maybe she just doesn't want to talk, OK?"

Paulo shot back.

"Hey – fuck you… whatever your name is. She's a tight-ass bitch that thinks she's better than the rest of us. I got no time for people like that."

Danny turned to look, again, at Paulo. Marty envied his bravery.

"What are you doing here, Paulo? The rest of us are looking for something from Papa to give us a reason to live... how about you? Looks to me like all you're looking for is a fight."

"To be straight with ya... I don't know what the fuck I'm doin here. All I know is I'm here. I read this guy's article and felt like I needed to come here and meet this Papa dude... don't know why... don't know what I'm lookin for... or if I'm lookin for anything at all. I had the same goofy fuckin thing with that wild-ass picture as the rest of you. I knew I seen it somewhere before... the whole thing... don't know the fuck where. Look man... I ain't here to cause no trouble with nobody. I just don't like nobody lookin down on me or tellin me what to do. I had enough fuckin trouble in my life to last a thousand years."

With the conversation appearing to have run out of steam, Marty adjourned the meeting.

"All right, well, let's all meet down in the lobby around nine tomorrow... and we'll get on the road."

The group filed out. Paulo was the last one to go out the door. He stopped and came back to Marty.

"No hard feelins, man. It's just this prison shit... always watchin for someone tryin to get over on me. It's a habit. I'll be cool. Don't worry... I ain't gonna smoke ya... not unless you fuck with me. And that tight-ass chick... she'll chill."

Paulo grinned with his last words and winked at Marty. He stuck out his hand to Marty. Marty took it and Paulo led him through the intricate hand-dance of the big house. Marty couldn't keep himself from matching Paulo's childlike grin.

After Paulo left, Marty and Ginny sat silently on their bed... each trying to put the meeting into some perspective that would allow comment. Both unsuccessful, they looked at one another, then burst into a good-natured laugh over the remarkable clan of devotees. Shaking his head, and with a warm smile, Marty remarked, "What a crew."

Ginny mirrored his smile and nodded in agreement.

CHAPTER SIX

With the exception of Paulo, the group that assembled in the lobby was dressed, unquestionably, for a camping trip... Levis, flannel shirts, hiking shoes. Paulo still had on the same outfit he was wearing at the airport... tight black T-shirt, form fitting jeans, and sneakers. Hanging around his neck, outside of his shirt, was a gold chain, supporting a sizeable, ornate, Spanish-style crucifix. Marty discovered that he had failed to discuss breakfast arrangements during the previous day's gathering. Four of the eight had already gone out for breakfast – the motel not having its own restaurant – and four had not – expecting they would go as a group. Marty and Ginny were aligned with the latter faction. The ten of them resolved to go to the Denny's next door. The four who had already eaten would go along... but would just have some coffee. By 10:15 they had all eaten and were on their way to Bear Stump.

The spring weather was beautiful... the bright sun sharing the sky with only a few feathery, white wisps... the temperature in the mid-seventies with a playful breeze blowing. The earth was in bloom again and its perfume was in the air. None in the group – save Marty – had ever been to Montana before and, consequently, spent most of the trip to Bear Stump looking out the windows... open, to allow in the fresh fragrance. The morning had the feeling – at least to Marty – of a summer holiday. The spirits of all his passengers were high. Ginny was riding with him. Danny had volunteered to drive her car – sensing she would prefer to be with Marty. Marty was unconcerned with how the rest of the group divided up, with the exception of Susan and Paulo, who he subtly arranged to be in separate cars. With Marty, besides Ginny and Susan, were Katherine and Aaron. David, Veronica, Henry, and Paulo rode with Danny. Marty found the self-selected travel arrangements – excepting, of course the contrived, Paulo-Susan separation – to be fascinating. Already, the factions were lining up, he observed, as they always do in any group... at least for the time being. He wasn't yet sure what to make of it and refrained

THE MINISTRY

from any premature judgments.

Just after one o'clock in the afternoon the cars passed through Bear Stump. After turning onto Old Log Road, they drove about four miles to a grassy area that was pleasantly shaded by a cluster of large, friendly trees. Paulo got into the car with Marty and Ginny, while the remainder of the party made themselves comfortable under the trees... each with their submarine sandwich and soda they'd gotten just outside Bear Stump at Larry's Subs and Suds. Each had also made a prudent toilet stop at Larry's... knowing they were heading into the woods.

As soon as Marty saw the friendly face of the secretary behind the big desk at the Bear Stump Police Station, he instantly recalled her name.

"Hi Annabelle!"

Annabelle Jackman looked up from a report she was proofreading and beamed.

"Marty! How are you?"

She got up from behind her desk and gave Marty a sturdy hug... as though he were a long-lost friend.

"This must be your girlfriend!"

"Yes... Annabelle – this is Ginny... Ginny – Annabelle."

Annabelle shook Ginny's hand with a firm grip and a pump handle motion.

"So nice to meet you, Ginny! You must be proud of Marty... his article and all!"

"Yes... I am. It's very nice to meet you, Annabelle."

Marty turned to Paulo, on his left, then looked back at Annabelle.

"Annabelle… this is Paulo Mandos. He's supposed to be reporting to Captain Thompson, for a while."

Annabelle extended her hand to Paulo… who shook it gently… and in a standard fashion.

"Nice to meet you, Paulo. The chief told me about your reporting here. He'll be back in a couple of minutes. He's down at the Cozy Corner having his lunch."

As he shook her hand, Paulo nodded his head forward in respectful deference to the gray-haired Annabelle… exhibiting that somewhere in his upbringing he had learned proper manners and due respect for his elders.

"Very nice to meet you, ma'am."

"He's a very nice looking young man, Marty."

Marty wiggled his eyebrows and smiled at Paulo. Paulo grinned sheepishly and studied his shoes.

"I've got my magazine, Marty… had it here for the past month… waitin for you to stop by."

"You want my famous autograph, huh?"

"Sure do. Would you?"

"I try to keep my fans happy, Annabelle."

Annabelle giggled girlishly, then fetched the magazine from her top drawer. She had it paper-clipped open to Marty's article.

"Sign it under your picture and write something nice."

Marty pulled the pen from his jeans pocket and angled his lips into a sportive smile.

"What shall I write?... ah... let's see... how about, to the sexiest lady in Bear Stump?"

Marty grinned. Annabelle laughed and kiddingly slapped his forearm. He wrote something under his picture then turned it around for Annabelle to read.

"Oh, aren't you a sweetheart. If I was thirty years younger... you hang on to him, Ginny."

Ginny smiled.

"I'm planning on it."

Captain Thompson walked through the door. It was immediately and abundantly clear to Marty that his thoroughly unpleasant deportment hadn't improved any since their last meeting. He concluded that the chief's excitement over seeing Bear Stump mentioned in a national magazine obviously didn't carry over to the author, himself. He nodded his head stiffly to Marty, touched the brim of his western style hat to Ginny, narrowed his eyes at Paulo and walked through them... disappearing into his office. Annabelle shrugged and smiled at the same time to explain that that was the way he was so don't be disturbed by his lack of civility. She then turned and followed him into his office. A few moments later, she reappeared.

"Captain Thompson will see you and Paulo now, Marty."

Marty looked at Paulo. About to face "the man"... Marty could tell his bristles were up. He looked ready for trouble. It worried Marty. He didn't want trouble and wanted to communicate that to Paulo before it had a chance of getting started.

"Be cool, Paulo... OK?"

Paulo stared at him with hard eyes. Finally he nodded slightly... and Marty felt a little better. Marty went into the Captain's office, ahead of Paulo. He proceeded to the front of his desk and stood stiffly. Paulo joined Marty and stood to his right. The Captain was writing something and didn't look up. Marty could see Paulo's eyes burning and his temper rising over this obvious act of disrespect. Marty sincerely hoped, for everyone's sake, that the Captain would get on with it very soon. He didn't. They stood... both feeling like lackeys... for at least another minute and a half. Finally the Captain put down his pen and looked each of them up and down, like a drill sergeant in a full dress inspection. He cocked his head to the right – looked at Paulo – then leaned back in his wooden, swivel chair.

"You're Mandos."

"Yeah."

The malignant intonation of Paulo's reply left no question in Captain Thompson's mind as to his opinion of law officers. Thompson instantly returned Paulo's obvious animus.

"You have a problem, Mandos?"

Paulo paused. Marty held his breath. To his great relief, Paulo decided to let it slide.

"No problem, chief."

"Call me Captain Thompson."

"No problem... Captain Thompson."

Marty was waiting for Thompson to tell them to sit in the two chairs, a few feet behind them. He didn't. It became clear to Marty that the Captain was playing a demeaning, control game with Paulo and he had been pulled into it by association. He began to understand Paulo's hatred for lawmen.

Thompson leaned forward over his desk and began flipping through a thick stack of papers. As he perused the documents, he spoke without looking up.

"You got quite a biography here, Mandos. You're a real altar boy, huh?"

Paulo didn't answer.

Thompson looked up and leaned back.

"All right. You come here, every Friday, at ten o'clock in the morning. Don't be late, don't drink, don't carry a firearm, don't get so much as a parking ticket. You fuck up even a half-inch and your ass is mine. I'll have you back where you belong... quicker than your mother can bang out another spic-ito. Comprende?"

Out of the corner of his eye, Marty could see Paulo begin to move forward. His heart raced and his breath stopped. Paulo's movement halted. Marty breathed. Paulo spoke.

"Sure thing, Captain."

"How long you planning to be out here, Chico?"

Another pause for Paulo's response and Marty's resumption of breathing.

"Not real sure, Captain."

"Let's not make it a long visit... OK?"

"No problem, Captain."

"Where you stayin?"

Marty interjected.

"Out at Art Durbin's place... I wanted to show Ginny where I stayed last summer. Thought we'd stay a while. I asked my friend Paulo, here, to stay with us."

"Who's Ginny?"

"My girlfriend. You saw her in the office out there."

"You, your girlfriend, and Chico here… out in a cabin in the woods… real comfy arrangement, sport."

Now Marty was hot.

"What do you mean by that, Captain Thompson?"

"You gettin smart with me, Chapman?"

Marty had to counsel himself as he had Paulo. He calmed down.

"No sir. Do you need anything else from us, Captain?"

"Not right now. Don't take me lightly, Chico. You might think I'm some hick son-of-a-bitch… but don't fuck with me."

"No sir."

Thompson looked down and began putting Paulo's papers into its file. Marty took this to mean they were dismissed. He turned to his right, tapped Paulo on his forearm, and they walked quietly out of the room.

Ginny saw the expression on Marty's face and squinted her eyes to ask what the problem was. He shook his head to say… wait until we're outside. Annabelle thanked Marty, again, for his autograph and reiterated how happy she was to meet both Ginny and Paulo. They said their good-byes.

As soon as they had closed the outside door behind them, Marty muttered under his breath… afraid that, somehow, the Captain might hear him.

"That motherfucker."

Paulo supported the description.

"You got that right, boss."

Ginny waited until they were in the car to ask her questions.

"What happened?"

Marty spit out his words as though each was laced with bitter herbs.

"That fucking pompous prick."

Marty shook his head… searching for a sufficiently superlative, derogatory expression to do the Captain justice.

"That arrogant asshole did everything he could to insult Paulo and get him to do something… then the prick started in on me."

Paulo chuckled.

"Welcome to my world, Chico."

"If that's the way the law is to people like you Paulo… it's no wonder you hate them. I swear to God… if I had had a gun in my hand in there… I'd a blown that fat fucker's brains out… I swear to God I would."

Marty vented during the entire trip back to Old Log Road. Finally Paulo intervened.

"Hey man… I been livin with this shit since I was ten years old. You just gotta get over it, man… can't let it get under your skin. That's just what the man wants… to piss you off so you do somethin so he can beat the shit outa you and throw you back in the house."

Paulo's seasoned perspective humbled and silenced Marty.

It was nearly three-thirty when they finally rejoined the others. Although they'd been stranded for nearly two hours, given the beautiful weather and pleasant surroundings, none seemed to be the worse for the wear. Marty continued to find the groupings fascinating. Danny, David, and Henry were sitting together... Veronica, Katherine, and Aaron were in the other group... and Susan was sitting by herself. As the three returnees approached the trees, under which the other seven sat, Danny stood up and came to Marty.

"We were just talking about provisions. Do you realize that we don't have anything with us... food, soap, plates, silverware... nothing?"

Marty was embarrassed and felt immediately incompetent in his role as the ostensible group leader. Leadership simply wasn't his cup of tea, he rationalized to himself. He had spent his entire adult life taking care of only himself... and not doing that great a job of it. What did they expect? He admitted his shortcoming to Danny.

"You're absolutely right, I hadn't even given it a thought. Well, what shall we do... go back to the Stump and load up?"

"The where?"

"The Stump... that's what the people around here call the town."

"Oh. Yeah, well, I guess we'd better. But we'd better sit down first, though, and make out a list."

The ten gathered together and sat cross-legged in a circle while Danny wrote on one of the many tablets Marty had brought along. As items were mentioned, he wrote them down... bread, coffee, dry coffee creamer, sugar, toilet paper, canned goods, eggs, a can opener, towels, plastic plates, spoons, forks, knives, flour, butter. After about ten minutes, they had a fairly sizeable list. Marty mentioned that they might be buying a hell of a lot of things they might not need, pointing out that Papa had most of the provisions they were buying... plates, silverware, and quite a bit of food but, of course, there were ten of them and that was a lot of mouths to feed. Besides, he said, no one was sure what the arrangements would be... if they would be living with Papa in his cave or in Art's cabin... or something completely different. Either way, he guessed they had better be prepared. They could always drive back into town, he offered, if they needed more.

Again, not wanting to unnecessarily arouse the interest of the locals, Marty and Ginny volunteered to go back to the Stump, alone, and do the shopping. In town, Marty had to go to the one and only ATM to withdraw cash – knowing they wouldn't take a California personal check at the Bear Stump Food Mart... and knowing further that – at least as of last summer – the Stump hadn't entered the credit card age for grocery shopping. Before starting back to the Stump, they had shifted the luggage from Marty's trunk to Ginny's to make room for the shopping bags. It was good that they had... the bags filling up Marty's entire trunk. Buying for ten was a new experience for both of them. They figured they had enough, roughly, for a week. If they needed more by then, they'd just have to make a return visit.

Upon their return, they found the same groups together, as before, except that Paulo had, by then, joined with Danny, David, and Henry. Susan was still alone. At six o'clock, with the sun going down, they began the arduous, two-hour journey to Art's cabin, back Old Log Road. Nobody came out and said it before they got into the cars, but there was a general sense – Marty included – that it wasn't such a good idea to be setting out for an obscure mountain cabin with night rapidly approaching... a dark which Marty recalled as being pitch blackness. A few miles back the road, Marty looked over at Ginny. Her expression affirmed his concern. He braked the car to a stop and got out... asking everyone else to join him... telling them that they needed to talk. In the light of Ginny's car headlights, they discussed their situation. The obvious issue was whether or not to go on in the dark, or stay the night somewhere else... and start out in the morning. The immediate and unanimous consensus was to stay somewhere for the night. Marty said he knew of two motels outside Bear Stump, and recommended the Betty Miller Motel. The other – The Pines Motel – was directly behind Carl's Tavern and was usually, according to Marty's information, full of drunk, horny couples from Carl's...

taking advantage of the Pines' special two-hour room rate.

At Betty's, there were six rooms available... obviously requiring subdivisions of the larger coalitions. Danny roomed with Paulo, Henry with David, Veronica with Katherine, and Marty with Ginny. Susan and Aaron each took their own rooms. This seemed to please Susan... and upset Aaron – no one having volunteered to room with him. He was sure – he lamented to Marty in private – it was because he was gay. Marty asked the heavyset woman behind the desk, dressed in a pink and purple, flowered house dress, who was alternately listening to him and trying to watching a funniest videos program on the television set behind her, in the living room that directly connected to the front desk, if there was somewhere, nearby, they could get something to eat without going back into Bear Stump. She said that Carl's was about the only place that was still open at this time of night... that the food was great... great steaks... that they would cover their whole plate... and real cheap, too. They ate at Carl's... going in, in twos and threes – Marty still paranoid about drawing attention to their group. They sat at four different tables. Ginny told Marty she thought he was carrying this clandestine-operation stuff a bit far. And, as he looked around, noticing that everyone in the entire place had no doubt they were all together, and from out of town, he conceded the point and felt stupid. The seating arrangements at Carl's paralleled the motel plan... except that Aaron sat with Marty and Ginny and Susan sat with Katherine and Veronica. Everything the flower-frocked motel mistress had told them about Carl's food, turned out to be entirely true.

Back at the motel, they agreed to meet at the cars at nine o'clock in the morning. Marty was the only one who had brought along a portable alarm clock and he said that after he got up, he'd go around and knock on their doors at around seven-thirty... Betty's Motel not offering the luxury of clocks, phones, or a wake-up service. They would eat breakfast at Carl's then get on the road.

As they lie in bed, Marty complained to Ginny that he was quickly tiring of this group situation... of being the leader... of being responsible for so many people. He had always been a loner, he explained, and responsible only for himself. Ginny offered consolation by reminding him that as soon as he had guided the eight disciples to Papa, his responsibility was through – at least it should be. Ginny's small qualification at the end of her sentence was enough to touch off the insecure, distrusting aspect of Marty's psyche. He suddenly sat up in bed. He could feel the familiar tightening in his stomach and moisture on his palms.

"What if he's gone?"

"Who?"

"Papa... what if he's not there any longer? I haven't seen him in almost a year. Maybe he gave up on me and decided to try something else... some other plan. Maybe he's come to his senses, after finally talking to someone from the real world, and realized how crazy all of this is... you know? What am I going to do then... with all these people with me... all expecting something great. You heard Katherine – it's virtually a matter of life or death to her... Aaron too... for all of them, for that matter. What would I do? They'd all think I made this whole thing up. I've dragged all these people out here to this wilderness... got Marla to pay for all this. Oh God... what would I do, Ginny?"

"Just have some faith, Marty. Everything will be fine. Wait and see. C'mon... lay down, honey... I'll tickle your back."

To encourage Marty's acceptance of her offer, Ginny slid her hand under Marty's T-shirt, as he sat, and drug her fingernails, in a gentle, scraping fashion – up and down his back. She could immediately feel his muscles begin to relax.

"C'mon, sweetie."

Slowly, she withdrew her hand from under his shirt, grabbed the back of it, and gently pulled him backwards, onto the bed. She then pushed his left shoulder upward and away from her... Marty ending up, lying on his right side. Ginny resumed her tickling, and as she did, began softly singing the Peter, Paul, and Mary song...

"Hush-bye, don't you cry… go to sleep little baby. When you wake, you will find…"

Marty's heart swelled with such love for this sweet, kind, loving woman that joyful tears formed in his eyes. This brief, private time in the darkness of a small room in the Betty Miller Motel was, to date, the happiest moment of his life.

Despite his gentle passage into slumber, Marty was tormented by a horrific nightmare. He was standing on a precipice, towering over what seemed to be a canyon of infinite depth… so deep that if he would slip he knew he would fall forever… eternally feeling the helplessness of plunging to one's death, without ever reaching the bottom… all alone… beyond anyone's help. He was frozen with fear on a narrow edge of rock… trapped between the two hells of infinitely falling… and remaining forever, frozen in place. He began screaming out for Ginny. From the depths of his soul, he yearned for her protective arms.

Marty awoke, soaked with sweat, to find Ginny holding him. After several minutes, she gently pulled her arms from around him, climbed out of bed and crossed the room to the light switch on the wall, to the right of the door. She flipped it upward and the overhead bulb, attached to the ceiling at the very center of the room – the only light in their lodging – glared insolently down upon them, filtered only by a dirty square of translucent glass that served as the final resting place for many generations and species of insects. As she approached the bed, Marty was startled to see that Ginny looked as pale and frightened as he felt.

She climbed under the covers, moved close beside him then looked imploringly up at his face… Marty now sitting up and leaning his back against the laminated wood headboard. Marty could feel Ginny's body trembling against him.

"What's the matter, Ginny?"

"I had a nightmare… I guess you did, too."

"Oh, Christ… I haven't had a nightmare that horrible since I was a little boy. I was absolutely terrified. I'm not kidding. My heart is still racing. I can still feel the fear. God – it was awful. What kind of a nightmare did you have?"

"Mine was awful, too. I can't ever remember being so scared – ever."

"What was it?"

"I was on the edge of this jagged rock. I don't know how I got on it… but it was above this valley that seemed to be a thousand miles below me…"

Marty interrupted.

"And you thought if you fell, you'd fall forever."

"Yes… as though I'd never reach the bottom and be put out of my misery."

"I had the same dream… exactly."

"The exact same dream?"

"Exactly. I was afraid to move on the rock… for fear of falling. I was stuck with no one to help me. I started screaming for you."

"I started screaming for you."

"This is really scary, Ginny. I can feel my stomach quivering. This is still a nightmare… even when we're both awake. I don't like this kind of thing… I don't like it one bit. Maybe it's an omen… a sort of warning… that there's danger ahead… or maybe that we shouldn't go on."

"I don't know, Marty. I've never had anything like this happen to me before."

"This is the way that this Papa thing made me feel last summer… just like this… sort of out of control."

"If this is how you felt, I'm really sorry if I've made light of it, honey. Look at my hand. Look… it's shaking."

It was four o'clock in the morning. Neither Marty nor Ginny wanted to go back to sleep… afraid they might return, again, to the same, hellish precipice. Ginny ran a hot bath in the exceptionally deep and long, old-fashioned, claw-footed bathtub. They both got in. Being the gentleman, Marty took the faucet end… putting a towel over it to support the back of his neck. Ginny lay back against the comfortable slope of the other end and slid down into the water, up to her chin. Marty leaned the outsides of his bent legs against the worn porcelain. Ginny was able, given the length of this antique tub, to fully extend her legs, directly in front of her. Under other circumstances, she mused, she would have, no doubt, played mischievously by wiggling her toes, but neither of them felt safe enough, at that moment, to be flirtatious. They both just needed a good friend. The warm water and the brightness of the bathroom helped restore their spirits and courage. After about an hour they emerged from the water with their hands and feet looking like the skin of some exotically wrinkled show dog. They climbed back in bed and fell comfortably asleep.

At breakfast, they all sat together – Marty dropping the spy routine. The nightmare conversation went around the table like falling dominoes. All ten, it turned out, had suffered the same nighttime horror. Every detail of the ten dreams was identical. Even Susan was sufficiently distressed to join in… though in a very reserved and limited fashion. With the spirited animation of their dialogue, they barely noticed the food they consumed. Marty was particularly surprised at the candor with which Paulo – who Marty had, theretofore, presumed fearless – admitted to his fright. Despite his violent past, his demeanor, in so forthrightly admitting to his horror, made him appear very childlike, vulnerable, and endearing – a side of Paulo that few in his life, Marty was entirely certain, had ever witnessed, or thought possible.

THE MINISTRY 505

This common, frightening experience immediately bonded the entire group together – each drawing comfort from the warmth that flows from learning that in at least one of life's many terrors one is not alone. They searched for perspective and meaning to their common experience. Was it some sort of a warning? Should they go on? How was such a thing possible? The whole situation was so bizarre and frightening that it had a sense of unreality for all of them. Marty explained to them, as he had to Ginny, that the way they were feeling about this episode was the way that Papa had affected him. Their faces offered a newfound empathy and understanding toward him.

The shared, nighttime experience completely and irrevocably changed the trip's ambience. The holiday mood was now entirely displaced by caution, suspicion, and fear. Veronica, as she had shown the propensity to do, brought closure, once again, to the discussion.

"This is how I feel about it. This whole situation is becoming very scary, I admit… but if any of you are thinking about turning back, ask yourself, what is there to turn back to? For me?… nothing. My life is an endless string of miserable days… one after another. If I had had the courage, I would have done the same thing Aaron tried to do to himself… a long time ago. I've got nothing to go back to – nothing. So… scary or not, I *have* to go ahead. I don't have any other choice."

Each of the other seven disciples shook their heads in appreciation of having someone find and express their true feelings for them. Marty and Ginny, however, didn't feel the same as the rest. They had just fallen in love and, like most new lovers, were beginning to dream of a life together… of a future of ever-growing love… wanting to share everything, even the smallest things, together. Also… their lives, to that day, weren't the best… but neither were they the worst. They had at least tolerably good lives to which they could return… and a future together, for which they now desperately yearned. Unlike the rest, their lives had not become one-way streets. They were not desperate people, like the disciples. If this bizarre dream-of-ten foretold of great danger…

perhaps death for all of them... Marty and Ginny didn't want to risk it. They felt they had just too much to lose. They couldn't afford, they felt, to deal with this potential danger in the same, fatalistic manner as the others. They explained this to the other eight. The eight said they understood... but... without Marty, they wanted to know – if he and Ginny turned back – how were they supposed to find Papa?

Unable to find an acceptable way of responding to the question, Ginny and Marty excused themselves. They needed some time – alone – they said, to discuss things. They found several picnic tables between Carl's and the Pines Motel and sat on top of one, their feet resting on the bench. For a while they both just sat in studied silence... staring down at the sparse spring grass. Both felt the shame of covetousness – wanting so much for themselves that they were willing to deprive the others of something they so desperately needed. This moment was, they both understood, a trial of their beings. And they knew their collective decision would set a fundamental precedent for their future life together.

They silently traveled across reasons and rationalizations for a decision – searching for the foundation stone upon which each of their characters was set... hoping, for the sake of their future together, that both would prove to be of the same element. It was. Neither of them, they found, could do something that took so much away from so many. Despite the danger, they resolved they would go on. The recognition of this common nature of their characters drew them, once again, even closer to one another.

Their decision gained them the unmitigated respect and appreciation of the other eight. Even Susan, uncharacteristically, spoke up and said that she wasn't sure, had the circumstances been reversed, she would have been as benevolent as they.

At ten-thirty they were, once again, back on the road. Though no one articulated it, there was now, among the ten of them – like soldiers going into battle – a new sense of allegiance, empathy, mutual protection, and a growing affection toward one another. As of that morning, they were no longer strangers and the previous factions lost the strictness of membership.

At one o'clock that afternoon, they pulled in behind the trees where Art always parked his truck. The old pickup was still there, where Art had last parked it before he died. The sight of it immediately gleaned a flood of forgotten details and commensurate emotions from Marty's memory. Their recollection, in turn, washed his eyes in poignant tears... recalling anew, just how very much he had loved Art Durbin... and how very much he still missed him. Fearing his emotions would overwhelm him if he paused for even a moment Marty climbed swiftly out of his car, opened the trunk, grabbed a sizeable box of provisions, and started toward the path, leading to the cabin. The others immediately followed suit, a bit puzzled at Marty's hasty and unceremonious departure. Ginny hastened to catch up with him, but, seeing the anguish drawn across his face, and guessing its likely source, she left him to the solitude he was running ahead to preserve.

As he made his way up the winding path to Art's cabin, Marty could feel the emotion rising in his chest until finally, as he reached the crest of the hill and the two graves came into sight, he burst forth in loud, mournful sobbing. Ginny quickly closed the gap between them and embraced him. The other eight allowed the two of them to have their private time... remaining silent and at a respectful distance from them. Having never seen Marty like this, Ginny was torn between sobbing along with him and remaining strong for him. She chose the latter, and tried, as do all consolers, to find the words that can heal a tearing heart, but realizing, as do all consolers, that there are none. Nevertheless, she spoke in tender tones to him, for what comfort the sound, itself, could offer. Ginny knew his grief would have to run its course and would not be shortened by anything she could do. The rest waited patiently for Marty... putting down their loads and sitting or leaning against the rough pines. At last, with uncertain voice, Marty tried to explain his tears – which everyone had already surmised – pointing weakly toward the graves. Adequately recovered, Marty offered apologies to all. They were uniformly declined as unnecessary. Their procession began again, but as they neared the cabin, Marty veered off to his left, to visit the graves. The others continued on, knowingly, to the cabin.

Marty squatted at the gravesides... his eyes sweeping over the now-settled, flattened earth where, nine months before, were two large mounds. He looked at the falling and slanted grave markers, then out at the great, familiar expanse. His mind traveled back to the previous summer and, with his grief spent, he dwelled for a time on the many happy moments that he, Art, and old Ben had spent together... and felt himself smile. The others left Marty alone with his memories... even Ginny... this being a part of his life that she respected as being his, alone. As he reminisced, it seemed another lifetime to Marty that he and Art had sat on the porch – looking out over these mountain ranges – talking and laughing about life. The caring and comical sound of Art's voice returned to his mind's ear... and his knowing smile, his wrinkled, timeworn understanding face, to his eye. The constantly moving river of time, Marty discovered, had already washed away some of the clarity of the deep love he had felt for Art. At his grave, it returned, once again, as clear as the morning... so clear he could almost see Art coming back from his morning swim and could smell the friendly, sweet smoke from his pipe. Oh, how he had loved that old man. He had been both his father and his best friend. Marty vowed, that moment, that he would, never again, allow time to rob him of the small details that preserved the flesh and blood of his memories.

As his mind traveled through the gone and golden summer, Marty recalled that Papa had told him that he and Art were together, after he had died. Marty clearly was not an easy believer, but he wanted, desperately, to believe this comforting story. Whether it was rational or not, he needed to feel that the soul of that kind old man still existed, somewhere... that his unique light and warmth had not been forever snuffed out, like the wick of a burnt candle. But he could not allow himself even this small piece of mythical balm. If only, he anguished, he were capable of a mere shred of faith, he would be so much happier in his life. Marty knew it was a missing piece of his humanity – carved away by distrust – and he was reminded, once again, of his ambivalence – contempt and envy – toward the faithful.

When Marty had finished his communion... and had straightened and reinforced the grave markers by stamping down some new stones around their bases, he joined the others who were sitting on all aspects of the old porch. Seeing them there, a curious wave of resentment pulsed through him... feeling that a very private, sacred place had been invaded by outsiders, having no right to do so. Aaron was sitting in Art's chair... Veronica sitting in his... both innocently unaware of committing the most particularly offensive transgressions of the invaders. Like a host, grudgingly accepting his guest's appropriation of his well-worn areas of comfort, however, Marty pressed stoically on with the business at hand, magnanimously repressing his indignation. Almost sounding like a tour guide, he addressed the group, beginning with the plainly obvious.

"This was my friend, Art's, cabin... where I spent last summer. That's Art's grave over there... the smaller one is his dog, Ben's. I buried them both."

As he said these words, Marty could feel his tears rising again, and turned his head for a few moments. He cleared his throat and resumed.

"Art and I both spent time with Papa. Actually, Art knew Papa's father... and mother. He used to buy things for them in town. Art's the one who first told me about Papa. Now... where we go from here... I don't know. Papa told me to bring you here. He said he'd know when we're here. That's all I know... and I've done it. Whether he'll come here to find you... or if we'll have to go to his place... I just don't know. I guess we can plant ourselves here for a few days to wait and see. There's room enough for all of us inside. It's probably still a bit nippy to sleep outside, up here on the mountain. You'll see what I mean, as soon as the sun goes down. Not everyone will get a bed – there are only two inside... at least when I left there were. Anybody have any suggestions or questions?"

Henry spoke up.

"How far is it from here to Papa's cave?"

"It's a good walk... could take us an hour or more. Getting in is another matter... if we have to do that. One way up is really dangerous. You could get yourself killed, trying it... I almost did. There's a hidden, back entrance... but I don't know if I could find it or not. This will sound strange... but Papa carried me there one night when I was surrounded by a wolf pack. I know that sounds like something out of a Daniel Defoe novel... but he actually saved my life a couple of times. Anyway, I really doubt if I could find the back entrance... and the front way would be really risky... so I guess we'll just have to wait it out for a while... and play it by ear."

All accepted Marty's explanation and logic... then went inside to reconnoiter potential sleeping accommodations. To Marty's eye, the cabin was untouched since he had left it. As often is the case, however, his memory had enlarged it substantially. Now seeing it through his corporeal eyes, it seemed to have substantially shrunk. All were impressed with Art's ingenuity in the cabin... particularly the hot shower arrangement. There wasn't much wood left for a fire so Henry, Paulo, and Danny volunteered to go gather some. The women decided, after a fire was started, to try out the warm shower setup... saying they felt in great need of it. The males – probably as a vestige of a young boy's natural aversion to bathing – failed to express any enthusiasm for this late-day, watery experience. Ginny volunteered to start dinner. David and Aaron volunteered to return to the cars and retrieve the remainder of the gear and supplies. Marty went out to the smokehouse to check on the condition of the meat. It was still there, untouched... but being a city boy, he was totally in the dark as to whether or not the meat was still safe to eat. He returned with this inquiry. Aaron said he knew a little about smoked meat and returned with Marty to the shed. Inspecting it, and smelling a small cut he sliced from one of the hanging sides, he said it was, in his opinion, perfectly good to eat – adding that as well-smoked meat it was probably good for another year or more. Marty returned to the cabin and asked those still there... Ginny in particular, since she was the chef for the evening... if they would be interested in eating some smoked meat. He described his memory of its fine taste. Ginny said she was game... and the rest reservedly acquiesced to try this exotic cuisine. He took a platter from the cupboard and returned from the smokehouse with a large portion of venison slices.

A backwoods feast was partaken that evening. Ginny threw potatoes, carrots, celery, and onions into the pot with the venison... and the combination of the pure mountain air, the woods, and the smell of the open-fire cooking piqued appetites to a near-frenzy. They opened some cans of fruit – peaches and pears – put out a block of Swiss cheese, a loaf of whole wheat bread and a stick of butter, a jar of apple butter, and three pies – cherry, blueberry, and pecan – for dessert. Given the copious amount of food consumed during this, their first meal, Marty had immediate concerns as to just how long their grocery supply would actually last.

They placed an assortment of seats around the table. Besides the two dining room chairs that were always there, the two rocking chairs were pulled in from the porch, as well as two small benches, dragged from the rear wall of the cabin. Marty, his host-like magnanimity waning, possessively and immediately claimed his rocker.

At Ginny's request to set out some beverages, Marty climbed the small rise beside the cabin to Art's ice tea cache... on the long shot that there might still be some tea there. Opening the mountain stream cooler box... its top submerged below the rapidly flowing, crystal clear, frigid water, Marty was surprised to see the iced tea container was still there, in tact, and full of tea. He had assumed, somehow, that it would either be gone or burst by the cold of winter. It turned out to be still quite tasty and, obviously, quite cold. Along with the delicious spread of food that was laid out... both coffee and beer were – besides the tea – also served. Paulo particularly savored his can of beer – in secret violation of his parole – picturing all the while, Captain Thompson's face, and smiling broadly as he took his first long, frothy swallow.

The large meal, shared by the ten, served as a celebration of their newfound camaraderie... something akin to the affirmed sense of family at a Thanksgiving dinner. For the disciples, who had all reached a point of utter desperation and meaningless in their lives, the evening was also a kind of emotional resurrection... giving life to warm feelings they had long presumed dead within themselves. Marty's view of responsibilities also underwent change that evening... happily abandoning the onerous duty of host and leader... sensing that he and Ginny had, by then, become accepted as simply peers. Even Susan was beginning to tentatively smile and respond on occasion. Regardless of what was to happen with Papa, this adventure had already proven to be a life-changing event for the eight.

The misty, near euphoria of the previous evening was cleared away by the clarity of the sparkling sun and crystal-chilled, morning air. The group awoke to face the mundane practicalities of sharing a relatively small space in which to accommodate the diverse morning rituals of ten human beings of mixed gender. All needed to use the toilet, brush their teeth, shower, and eat. To help facilitate matters, Marty prevailed upon the men to join him in bathing at the nearby lake. He had, unfortunately, failed to consider the dramatic difference in water temperature in early May as compared to the mid-days of summer when he and Art had last bathed there. The contrast was, literally, breathtaking... a moment that the men would remember and laugh about in times to come. The water was so remarkably cold that Marty truly feared for Henry's heart. Of course, being an assembly of men among men, all did their best to conceal their reaction to the pain caused by the bone-numbing cold water. The six men, out of their instinct for survival, completed their bathing in an absolute blur of speed and efficiency. As they walked back to the cabin, fully dressed, they were still chilled so deeply that their insides quivered uncontrollably, despite the warming rays of the sun radiating down upon them.

Representing the antithesis of the male bathing experience – the heat from the remains of the previous evening's roaring fire, having maintained the warmth of the stone water chamber – the women enjoyed the friendly and familiar feel of a warm, albeit short, shower. The mountain-style coffee was made, according to Art's method – passed along to new converts by Marty – by the time the men arrived back at the cabin. Several cups were necessary to control their bodily tremors. For breakfast they had another culinary delight, consisting of a fried concoction of eggs, venison, potatoes, and onions with sides of sliced bananas and strawberries, along with toast with butter and jam.

After breakfast, Marty led the group on a tour of the surrounding area, eventually making their way to the steep rock slope that ascended to the front entrance of Papa's cave. After surveying the climb from the ground, all agreed that Marty had not exaggerated its danger. Being this close to Papa's home, their senses were naturally heightened by the possibility of Papa appearing... particularly Marty's, who had had personal experience with his stealth and propensity for unanticipated appearances. Marty pointed up at the gap between ledges that had to be leaped in making the climb, followed by the story of his near-fatal fall. He also went on to tell of the upper and lower chambers and the well-concealed hole in the ceiling with its stone plug and the clever mechanism by which it was raised and lowered. He recounted his adventures with Art in their search for Papa... and their first surprise encounter with him. With Papa so near, the story was particularly compelling and anxiety provoking, like a ghost story spun in a graveyard. They walked around the bottom of the shear, stone rise, climbed the rising path through the thick forest of pine, and arrived at the general area where Papa had carried Marty on the night of his wolf problem. They all began to immediately search for the entrance... Marty providing as much recollection as he was able, which wasn't much, given that he was carried there in pitch blackness. About all he remembered was the general direction Papa had carried him and the appearance of the entrance from the inside. They searched, in vain, for over an hour, but the hidden entrance remained so.

Tired from their hike and searching, they rested on some rocks – warmed by the brilliant May sun. Everyone noticed that Aaron didn't look well. Although he hadn't complained during the trek, his pale face and labored breathing betrayed its effect upon him.

Veronica asked him if he was OK. He replied with an unconvincing nod of his head and an accompanying weak smile. Unspoken concern registered on all faces, each questioning Aaron's ability to withstand the experience they were facing. Henry was also looking exceedingly tired and was added to this mutual consideration.

Reality displacing anticipation, they began reassessing their plans. Being this close to Papa had put things into a new perspective. Katherine suggested that Marty – having had experience with the front-entrance climb – should go looking for Papa and let him know they had arrived. Marty smiled at this suggestion, saying he was sure that if Papa was still here, he knew they were here. Also, he added, Papa told him to bring them to the mountain, and he would come to them. Stimulated by the excitement of the adventure, Katherine's innate impatience experienced a rebirth. She pressed.

"We could be waiting around here, indefinitely, Marty. What's the big problem with you telling him we're here?"

"It's not a big problem... I'm just telling you that he said he'd find us... and my experience with him is that he'll do just that... when he's ready."

"But, good God, Marty, we could be sitting around for weeks – and what did you mean, by the way... *if* Papa is still here? Is there some reason you think he may not be?"

"Look, Katherine... I haven't seen Papa since the end of last summer. He said that I'd be bringing eight people to him, and I have... it's just that it's been a long time – almost a year – since I've seen him, that's all."

David spoke up.

"Why don't we give it a couple of days... and if he still hasn't made an appearance, then maybe Marty can go looking for him... how about it Marty?"

THE MINISTRY

"That's fine. All right, look... it's Monday. If we haven't seen Papa by Wednesday, I'll go to his home and see if he's there. OK?"

David looked to Katherine in search of her assent. She offered it, grudgingly, with very apparent exasperation, turning her palms upward and giving a negative shake of her head.

Uncertainty bred nervous tension among the group – similar to those awaiting a jury verdict – and dinner was unusually quiet that evening. The atmosphere changed dramatically, later that night. As a means of escaping the anxiety of their circumstance, the entire group elected to turn in early – around eleven o'clock. The warmth and the dancing shadows of the large fire lulled them quickly and pleasantly to sleep – the group consensus allowing Henry and Aaron to have the two beds – the rest lying on their floor-level, blanket-beds. At 1:30 in the morning, almost as if someone had rung an alarm, the entire cabin awoke simultaneously... all in terror... some screaming... some too frightened to scream. Everyone found themselves sitting up, looking around at the other faces in the cabin – their expressions revealing the soul-shaking horror that had followed them from the land of their dreams to ravage their consciousness. The scene was overtly bizarre... ten people awakened in horror at the same moment, all bathed in the surreal light of the flickering fire. For a short time, they sat in silence, searching the other faces for simple, primal comfort.

Without speaking, one by one, they came to the table, until all ten were assembled about it... seeking the warmth and security, derived from both the fire and their common humanity. Without exchanging words, they all knew what had happened. The same horrifying dream had, once again, invaded their slumbering worlds. But this time, something was different, rendering the common experience far more terrible than the first episode. This time, they all specifically recognized the area in their dream, nearby the endlessly deep valley. They had all, in fact, been there that very afternoon, while searching for the rear entrance to Papa's home. They all now knew where the horrid valley lay – if it was actually real – and how to get to it. The merger of dream with reality added a cruel dimension to their terror, not allowing escape in waking... denying them the safe place where human beings hide from their nighttime monsters. Paulo was able to capture their collective emotions of the moment.

"I came lookin for this man cause he was something to me... the father I never had... the one we all need. He was love to me... somebody who cared if I lived or died. But this dream stuff is scarin me, man. Scarin me, real bad. It can't be just for nothin that we're all havin this same dream... and now we know where this terrible place is. It's up there – for real – we all know it is... right up on that mountain... right up where he lives. It's makin me think again about this man... you know... *who* he is. This dream isn't about love. It's the scariest thing I've ever felt in my life... worse than I ever felt in any rat-fuck jail I been in. At least in the house, I knew what I was dealin with and I was ready for whatever came down. This kinda shit makes me feel like a little scared baby. I never have felt so all alone and helpless in my life... like sombody's puttin an icicle right through my heart. Maybe somebody's tryin to tell us all somethin... like, you know... stay away from this dude, or somethin. Maybe he's powerful... but maybe he's walkin the other side of the street... you know, man... maybe he's, you know... the reaper – Diablo. Maybe we're all bein set up... you too, Marty... set up by this dude. Maybe he don't wanna help us at all. Maybe he got somethin else in mind... you know?"

No one was certain enough of the meaning of this event... it being so far beyond everyone's experience and comprehension... to take issue with anything that Paulo had said. It was simply too far beyond the pail of human experience to allow them to grasp any meaning from it – at least with their tired, terrorized, and confused minds of that moment. Rationality impossible, they sought merely the animal comfort, derived from being physically close to one another... and sat silently together like a litter of frightened puppies. Eventually, however, overwhelming fatigue was their brother and led them back to a merciful sleep – this time without monsters.

THE MINISTRY

The virginity of a new and beautiful morning bolstered courage and lessened the grip of the previous night's terror. At breakfast, they were able to, at least, attempt a rational dialogue regarding the experience. Marty offered a delayed response to Paulo's, previous night's hypothesis.

"There's no denying that something very strange is going on here... and I'm as scared as everyone else. But I can't buy the idea that Papa might be Satan or anything evil. I can't say for sure, just who he is, but I'm absolutely certain he doesn't intend us any harm. I'm as sure of that as I've been about anything in my life. Look... my friend Art lived a long life and knew about people. He loved this man. If Papa was evil... Art would have known it. If I trust anybody's judgment, I'd trust Art's."

Paulo jumped in.

"But you told us that Papa killed Art... that's what you said, man."

"I shouldn't really say that... I'm not sure why I do... maybe just for the effect... I don't know. The shock of meeting Papa – and who he claimed he was... and Art believing it – was simply too much for Art to deal with. That's what killed him. He was old. I was pissed off at Papa for doing it, at first, but I came to realize that he didn't intend any harm to Art. He truly loved him... I'm sure he did. And he didn't do any harm to me. Christ... he saved my life, twice, as a matter of fact. I'm telling you that this idea that these dreams we're having is because something is trying to keep us away from Papa, so he can't hurt us in some way, just doesn't make any sense to me. I'm not saying I know what's going on – but I don't think that's it."

Danny spoke.

"It has to mean something, Marty. If it's not a warning, then I don't know what it is."

Veronica closed the matter, according to the apparent, acquired role which she undertook in moments of group indecision.

"We can all talk about this, forever, and never get anywhere. We all think we know where this valley is. Either we should turn around now and go home, or go see what this is all about. None of us, except for Marty and Ginny, has any reason to go home, so there's really not much to talk about... is there?"

The total absence of response signaled resigned, tacit agreement with Veronica's assessment. Without any further discussion, they cleaned up the breakfast remains and stoically began their journey... toward a valley that none of them had ever seen before, except in their collective dream – but were as sure of its existence as though it were a familiar street in their own neighborhoods.

The cold hand of fear instantly wrapped around each heart as they neared the area where they had searched for the back entrance. They were certain that, only a short walk from there, they would come to face the very same valley that had inspired in them, previously unknown depths of terror. Each step they took, as they walked toward the anticipated valley, sent electricity from their feet, up through their bodies and brains. Each of them experienced a sense of walking, wide awake, into a dream. They continued toward their fate with a sense of numb resignation.

As they reached the top of the rise, the ineffable valley loomed suddenly and majestically before their eyes. Their hearts instantly raced and their heads collectively swooned. They looked into one another's faces, seeking an answer each knew was not there. The spectacularly deep valley lay below what appeared to have once been some sort of rock bridge between two large stone plateaus. Most of the narrow stone bridge had, apparently, collapsed... leaving only a sharp, chiseled edge between the rock tables, which stood several hundred feet apart. They were all afraid to go any closer to the edge of the plateau... fearing they might fall – or worse – afraid they could not resist throwing themselves off, to fulfill some fiendish destiny. Stepping, awake, into their common nightmare was more than their mortal hearts or common courage could bear. They could all sense the panic, mutually rising among them and they knew they were, as a collective pack, about to run like wild animals from a fire. Just as they were turning to begin their mutual flight, a voice stopped them instantly. Marty immediately recognized it.

"Come to me."

The voice was filled with both authority and compassion. They turned to see an enormously large man, wearing a leather kilt and shirt, standing on the distant stone plateau, his arms outstretched to them. They all knew who he was.

CHAPTER SEVEN

Papa's mere presence immediately answered all the disciples' questions about him. Their hearts recognized him, as a child might sense his own mother. He was, for them, who they had desperately hoped he would be. They felt bathed in the glow of his limitless love, reaching out to them from across the terrible divide. They yearned to be in his arms. But, as a child can be pulled to the verge of tearing by warring parents, they were all undergoing emotional evisceration by the terrible, opposing forces of love and fear. To be embraced by him, they must walk into a waking nightmare and face a fear, more horrid than any of them had ever imagined possible. They stood, close together, at the edge of their plateau… staring across the chasm… like small children on the edge of a swimming pool, wanting to leap into their mothers' arms, but paralyzed by their fear of the water. Crossing the sharp edge of rock that connected the two plateaus was akin to walking several hundred feet of stony, uneven tight rope over an enormously deep canyon, absent a net. Papa could see the piteous ambivalence in their faces. He smiled with kindness and spoke to them.

"Don't be afraid. Come to me. Trust me and believe me that everything will be all right."

For an infinite moment, they all weighed the option… fall captive to their fear and stay forever behind, trapped in their pathetic lives… or traverse a hellish nightmare to reach inexpressible love. This time, none looked at one another, but only within. It was a solitary trial. Each realized that this was a birth process. To be born into a new life with Papa, they must undergo the fear and pain of birth. At this moment, each was his own mother.

Katherine was the first to move. She stepped onto the jagged edge of rock and began, without hesitation, walking toward Papa – her arms outstretched to her sides like a high wire performer – her feet trying to feel their way along the flinty rock – her eyes, moving up and down between Papa and her impossibly narrow path. Marty couldn't bear to watch and turned away. Papa's words of the previous summer returned to his ears. He had told Marty he wouldn't intervene in any of his children's lives. These eight people were, thus, completely on their own, facing death. A slight, indecisive movement or a moment of vertigo would condemn them to that horrible cavern of death. They had all been warned, in their dreams, that it could happen. The insanity of the moment suddenly struck Marty. These people, he realized, were risking almost certain death to reach a lunatic. Even a skilled high-wire performer would consider this crossing far too dangerous to attempt. He turned and screamed at Papa.

"What are you doing to these people, Papa?! Tell them! Tell them what you told me – before they kill themselves! Tell them they're on their own... that you won't lift a finger to save them if they start to fall! Tell them! Good God... tell them! At least let them know!"

Katherine stopped. She glanced back at Marty, momentarily, then, with a questioning expression quickly turned to look at Papa. He spoke to her.

"Katherine... what Marty said is true. You are on your own to come to me. You can fall... and you can die. But if you trust me, you will be all right – no matter what happens. Do you believe me, Katherine?"

Marty shot back.

"You don't know who this man is, Katherine! He could be God or he could be a kook! Are you willing to kill yourself to find out?!"

Without looking back, Katherine responded.

"How does he know my name, Marty? Did you tell him?"

"No... I didn't. How could I?"

Katherine spoke to Papa.

"How do you know my name?"

"Wouldn't a parent know his own child's name?"

"Are you who you say you are?"

"Yes."

"What will happen to me if I fall?"

"You'll die, Katherine."

"Then what?"

"You'll be home with me. We'll be together again. You've been looking for me all your life… and I've waited for you… and you'll come home."

Tears began running down Katherine's cheeks. After a while, she resumed her crossing.

Marty refused to give up.

"Are you willing to kill yourself on this man's word, Katherine?"

"Yes."

One shaking step at a time, Katherine moved toward Papa. Several times, she appeared to have completely lost her balance and seemed destined to fall… her arms waving madly… only to finally regain her balance. Marty was so overwhelmed with fear for her that he was nauseated. As she reached the halfway point and, once again, it appeared certain she would fall, Marty dropped to his knees and vomited.

After some twenty minutes of stops and starts and near falls, Katherine, at last, stepped onto the distant stone ledge to Papa. He embraced her tightly. Her face beamed with the innocence and unquestioning joy of a newborn. Her expression spoke encouragement to the rest.

Paulo went next. He crossed the canyon with the adroitness of a cat... never once hesitating or showing any uncertainty or lack of balance. He was with Papa in a matter of minutes. Susan was next.

Her look was that of a person who felt she must move, quickly, before she loses her nerve. As she began her crossing, her expression wavered, back and forth, between trust and abandonment. At about twenty feet from the beginning edge, she appeared to have completely lost her courage. She was stuck... afraid to go forward but could not turn around on the narrow edge and return to safety. Papa spoke to her.

"Come, Susan. I'll never leave you alone. I am always with you... now and forevermore. You'll never lose me as you lost your family. You can believe me and trust me and I'll never let you down. I promise you... my poor hurt child. I'll never hurt you. Come to me and come home."

Susan tried to step forward but her legs were frozen. She remained there, perched on the rock edge, like a statue, except for the slight, balancing movement of her outstretched arms. Marty couldn't take it any longer and, again, he screamed at Papa.

"She's stuck, for God's sake! You got her out there, Papa... you come get her! Look at her... she can't move... she's frozen out there. Get her before she falls!"

"She'll be all right, Marty. She's coming."

After a long pause, Susan finally moved her right foot and swung it slowly out around and in front of her left foot, placing it carefully on the sharp rock edge. She repeated this motion with her left foot. With excruciating slowness, she stepped the long path across the edge to Papa.

Danny moved to the edge. He looked down into the canyon then looked at Papa. He then appeared to be studying the clear blue sky above. After a while, he took a loud breath and blew it out, as do athletes before their event. Completing this pre-competition, ritual, he placed his left foot onto the rock edge with overt determination and certainty... then moved forward with a bullish, ungraceful but steady, gait. Without stopping or hesitating, he plodded his way to Papa.

Henry advanced toward the edge of the stone ledge. His eyes caught Marty's. He was, clearly, very frightened. Marty went to him and put his arm around his shoulders.

"You don't have to go, Henry. That's a hell of a trek for you, my friend."

Despite his advanced age, Henry's face had the appearance of a young child... desperate for an answer. He sat down on the plateau's edge... his legs dangling over the untold thousands of feet that stretched below the soles of his shoes. Marty sat beside him and focused on Henry's face... unable to look into the canyon's depths.

"Why don't you just think it over for a while, Henry? Wait until the rest go over."

"Marty... either I'll go now – or I won't go at all. I know myself. I'm not a terribly brave man... never have been. That's why I spent my life reading about life and not living it. I've never had the courage to do it. All those philosophers and all their talk – that's all it was – talk. They were just like me... paper tigers. None of us academics are worthy to even carry the shoes of a brave man. All my degrees... and I envy any high school dropout with an ounce of courage."

"A lot of us lack courage, Henry. I do... I just don't have what it takes when it calls for guts. I don't know why. I don't know why some people do and some people don't. Maybe it's like eye color... I just don't know... but you don't have to do this to prove something to yourself. It's just too big of a risk. It's not worth it, Henry."

"I know a lot of us lack courage, Marty, but that doesn't make it any easier to live with. Dying a thousand deaths is a hard life to live."

Henry stood up... Marty joined him. He turned toward Marty and embraced him.

"Marty... I'm not brave for what I'm about to do. I'm more afraid of going back to MacDonald's and my empty apartment than I am of falling into this valley."

"So you believe him... who he says he is... enough to lose your life?"

"Yes... as crazy as it probably sounds to you, Marty... I believe him. It's the first time in my life I've ever followed my heart and not my brain... and it's the first thing in my life I've ever been willing to die for."

With those words, Henry formed a warm, parting smile on his face... then turned to look into the great chasm. He closed his eyes for a few moments then stepped onto the sharp rock. It was immediately apparent that his stiff, aged body, wasn't up to the task, but he continued, rigidly and painstakingly, along the razor-like edge. By the halfway point, he was, unmistakably, exhausted. His movement had slowed and then had stopped, entirely. Everyone knew he had nothing left. Henry glanced slightly back over his left shoulder to try, unsuccessfully, to find Marty, then, with all of the energy he could muster, he tried to bring his back foot forward. It made it halfway, glanced across the side of his planted shoe and shot straight out to his right – seeking balance. For a frozen moment, he stood on one foot – his free leg perpendicular to his body, moving up and down, instinctively searching for his center of gravity. Suddenly, the fingers of both hands reached out and clawed the air for a nonexistent handle. Henry stared for a brief moment into Papa's eyes – then fell suddenly to his right. His body bounced several times off of the sloped rock that rose to form the crossing, then found the open and direct drop to the distant canyon floor below. He fell in deafening silence – his body becoming a mere speck in the air before disappearing altogether.

All stood in silent and unbelieving shock. It had happened so quickly that it hadn't yet caught up to their minds and emotions. Ginny's shriek signaled its first arrival. Marty fell to his knees and pounded the rock... moaning, "... no... no..." Veronica had her hands to her mouth, her eyes shouting her disbelief. Aaron had his arms wrapped around himself – rocking back and forth with a vacant stare. David looked – back and forth – at Papa, then into the yawning mouth of the voracious canyon that had just swallowed Henry as live prey. Like everyone else, he was searching for some explanation for this death.

Those on the other side had backed slightly away from Papa and were looking up to him for an answer. He gave it so that both groups could hear.

"Death is not what you think it is. The passage is frightening, only because it is unknown... but it is crossed in a brief moment. Henry is my child and is home with me now. He'll never be lonely or unhappy or afraid again. He was never a coward... he was only afraid – like all of my children."

He held his arms out.

"Come, Veronica."

Marty shouted.

"Leave her alone... you crazy fool! How many more of these good people do you want to kill? You may believe this stuff about yourself, but don't – for Christ's sake – don't take these poor people with you. Stop and think! You don't really know, for sure, if any of this stuff you say about yourself is true or not. Just give it the benefit of the doubt that you might be wrong. Is the gamble worth another life? Please... stop this before somebody else is dead!"

"Marty, I am who I say I am. I can't force you to believe me. That's your choice. If you come to me, Veronica... whether you fall or not... you are with me and will always be. I promise you that what I'm saying is true."

Marty intervened.

"I know you think it is, Papa... I know that. And you're a good man... I know. But you're asking these people to risk their lives on your promises."

Papa didn't reply. He looked at Veronica. She looked with uncertainty to Marty then to Papa... then back to Marty again. Marty had said all he could say. He looked at her beseechingly.

Veronica looked at Papa and turned her palms upward – seeking direction. He held his hands toward her. She paused, looked once more at Marty and then stepped forward onto the rock bridge. Marty had the urge to grab her or shout at her but was afraid he'd frighten her and cause her to fall. Her movement along the rock edge was that of a ballet dancer, possessed of consummate grace and balance. When Marty saw the liquidity of her motion, he relaxed a bit. If anyone could move along this rocky rope of death, he judged, it was obviously Veronica. She literally danced along the bridge and safely reached Papa.

David and Aaron looked at one another... waiting for the other to step forward. Aaron paused for lack of courage – David for lack of trust. Neither moved. Papa spoke.

"You come next, David. Everyone has turned their back on you. I never will. I'll never walk away from any of my children. Trust me, David."

"But how can I be sure? Can you make me sure? I'm afraid of dying... afraid there isn't anything there. My god deserted me. How can I be sure of you?"

"Have you told me your name, David? Have you told me that everyone deserted you? I know because I'm your father and your mother. I know the hearts and minds of all my children. I've felt every breath you've taken since the moment you were born. But you're a free child, David. I won't make you do anything. I can tell you that if you come to me, you'll find what you've always known was missing in your life – but you must choose. I won't force you to be with me."

David stared across the divide... trying to find his feelings. Marty could feel his uncertainty. Finally his resolve came.

"I'm in your hands, Papa. I'm trusting you. I'll trust you enough to die. Just stay with me in my fear, Papa. Give me courage, please. I'm so terribly afraid."

"I'm with you, David. You have nothing to fear. You will never, again, know fear for as long as you live. You're in my hands and in my love... now and forevermore."

David began the crossing of birth and death. Fifty feet from the launching edge, however, his resolve was discernibly wavering. He appealed to Papa.

"I'm afraid, Papa! I'm so afraid!"

David's body was visibly shaking, with his voice quivering in tandem.

Papa's voice was calm and soothing.

"You're fine, David. Just look at me and come to me. You have nothing to be afraid of... not now... not ever."

David began, again, with renewed courage, and it carried him over the treacherous path to Papa. Only Marty, Ginny, and Aaron remained on the home plateau. Papa called out to Aaron.

"It's your turn, Aaron. You'll be fine. Everyone you've known has

THE MINISTRY

hurt you. I've cried for you many times... hoping you'd come back to me. I'm here for you now and I've always been here. Can you be brave for me?"

Aaron's lips were quivering... his eyes were filled with frightened tears.

"I don't think I can. I feel so weak and sick. If I try, I'll fall. I know I will. Please don't make me. I just can't do this... I just can't."

Marty came to Aaron's side and put his arm around his shoulders. He spoke to Aaron with a newfound perspective.

"I'm not going to tell you what to do, Aaron. I'm here for you on this side... Papa's there on the other side. That's about all I can say to you."

Aaron looked at Marty with eyes that had seen too much sorrow.

"Will you always be here for me, Marty... always?"

The directness of Aaron's question demanded truth – not tact – and Marty supplied it, without garnish.

"Aaron... I'd like to say yes... but I have my own life... Ginny and I do. I could say I'll always be here for you, but I'd be lying. I'll move on and so will you – and my life will be my own – and yours will be your own. Someday, under the right circumstances... it's possible I could turn my back on you. I'm not God and I'm not perfect... and I can't say that I won't. I'm sorry. I wish I had a different answer for you, Aaron, but that's how life is... you can't be responsible for everybody you meet. I only have so much time and energy. I'm sorry. That's the best I can do for you... or for anyone else... but Ginny. I can say I'll be your friend, but I can't say I'll always be there for you. I'm only human, Aaron."

Aaron looked at Marty with understanding and resignation.

"You're no worse than anyone else in the world, Marty. Everyone has their own problems and they can't look out for everybody... especially someone like me. And I'm not looking for sympathy. I don't think any more of myself than the rest of the world does. I'm pathetic... a pathetic faggot and I know it. I don't expect anyone else to feel any differently about..."

Papa interrupted him.

"Aaron... listen to me. You are precious to me... a precious, beautiful child. You're a part of my body. You were born of me. I care about you and I will always have time for you... as much time as you need. I will have time for you, forever. You come to me and you'll never be alone again. I promise you that."

The choice became abundantly clear to Aaron. On his side, no one who would care... not always. On the other side was a promise of love, for always. But to get to that promise, he'd need more courage than he'd ever had... more courage than he had within him... and he would literally have to cross a valley of death, which he knew from his dream held the promise of an unthinkably horrible fall.

Although the choice had become very clear to him, the question of whether or not he possessed the requisite bravery to carry out his choice was not. Just standing on the edge of the flat rock, he could feel the overwhelming pull of the depths below him... making his head swim. He had never been so frightened in his life. He forced himself to move forward... trying his best not to think about what he was doing. He put his left foot ahead and placed it carefully on the jagged rock edge, then shifted his weight slightly forward onto it. As soon as his foot was planted, he could feel the loss of balance under it – his weight bending his ankle right and left, like that of an inexperienced ice skater. He immediately returned his weight back to his right foot, still resting on the plateau. He looked at the several hundred feet of jagged rock ahead of him, and the steeply sloped sides of it, down which, he had watched Henry plunge to his death, and he felt he just couldn't do it. He looked at Papa with tearful, pathetic, childlike eyes... appealing to him.

THE MINISTRY

Papa smiled warmly at him.

"Everyone is afraid, Aaron... but you are only afraid of life because you don't understand it. Life and death are the same – only separated by a valley. You're afraid of the valley because it's deep and you're not sure if there is anything on the other side. My children live their lives with this constant fear. You have only to open your heart to find me waiting on the other side of death, Aaron. I've always been there... always waiting for you to come across. Our love for one another is all you need to cross over. I have made you free – but with a memory of when we were together. Open your heart, Aaron, and you'll remember when you were with me and surrounded with a love that never ends – that never turns away – when we were one. Do you remember, Aaron? Do you remember your first parents?"

Aaron's eyes poured out tears of happiness.

"I do remember, Papa. I remember in my heart. It's a feeling. It's just what you describe. I never knew what it was. Why haven't you come to find me before? Where have you been through all the awful years of my life... when I had lost all hope?"

"I reached out to your heart, Aaron... but it had hardened and couldn't find me. I have suffered every terrible moment of your life with you, Aaron. I love you without limit... and want you to come home. Please come home to me. I can't make you do it. You have to come to me by your own choice. Death is but a short step to me if you come my way. You needn't fear falling because you'll land in my arms, at home. I promise you that, Aaron. I promise you that – as your first mother and father who have always loved you every moment of your life."

"Can you give me the courage to step out on this edge, Papa?"

"I can't give you anything but my love and my promise that if you come to me, you'll be home, whether you make it to this side or not."

"Can you make me not afraid?"

"You are only afraid because your heart hasn't accepted me. If you accept me, there is nothing to fear. No harm can come to you."

Aaron wiped his wet eyes with the backs of his hands. He spoke with the voice of a frightened child.

"I'll try, Papa."

"You come to me and everything will be all right."

"Can you promise me that if I accept you as my father and mother and love you – I won't fall?"

"No. I can only promise you that we'll be together whether you make it to this rock or not."

"You promise?"

Papa smiled.

"I promise you, Aaron."

Aaron covered his eyes with his hands for a while and held his head downward. The heaving of his chest told of his deep, sharp breaths. He again put his left foot on the edge and looked across to Papa.

"You promise?"

Papa merely smiled and held his arms out to him. Aaron put his full weight on his left foot and lifted his right foot from the plateau. His left foot began to immediately wobble back and forth. His entire body then joined in the pendulum-like motion. His fall appeared imminent. His left foot slid suddenly to the left side of the narrow rock path and his body fell directly downward – his crotch colliding with the jagged edge with bone-jarring impact – one leg straddling each side of the chiseled peak. He screamed out in excruciating pain. Marty rushed forward to grab him but he was just beyond his outstretched arms. He shouted at Aaron.

"Give me your hand, Aaron! I'm right behind you!"

Aaron glanced back over his shoulder – afraid to remove his hands from their frozen grip on the sharp stone.

"I can't move! I can't move! I'm going to fall, Marty! I know I'm going to fall!"

Marty spoke again.

"Just don't move, Aaron. I'm coming."

Marty sat on the edge of the plateau and put one leg on each side of the jagged rock... intending to straddle it and attempt to slide himself along the rock to Aaron. He put both hands on the sharp rock ahead of him. It dug painfully into his palms. He leaned forward on his hands and tried to pull his body to follow. It didn't work. Besides the pain of the sharp rock digging into his hands, the peak was so jagged that it was virtually impossible to move forward... the rock digging and tearing into his legs and the crotch of his pants. He spoke softly to Aaron to keep from scaring him.

"I can't get to you, Aaron. I can't slide along this edge... it's just too rough."

Marty backed his bottom onto the flat ledge behind him. Aaron cried out to Papa.

"Why do I have to do this?! It's too hard... it's too cruel! I thought you loved me! If you loved me you wouldn't make me do this! It's hurting me! It hurts so bad! I can't go anywhere. I'm stuck. Please save me Papa! Please come get me! I don't want to die!"

Papa spoke as a father would who knew his son was in need of a command.

"Aaron. I won't save you. You can choose to come to me or you can be alone. You have to choose."

Marty could hear Aaron lapse into deep, heartbreaking sobs... and also noticed urine dripping from Aaron's pant leg. Ginny wrapped her arms around Marty and they both, helplessly, wept for him. Marty felt a burning hatred for Papa. He was cruel and unbending – not loving as he said he was... but Marty knew it was in vain to argue with him. He always had an answer. After several minutes, Aaron's breathing became less erratic. He sat in silence – staring at Papa. He resigned himself to the reality that he was completely on his own... to live or to die. No help was coming. He began looking around – as though he was searching the air for a plan to extricate himself from his hopeless position.

Slowly, Aaron began to slide his hands forward as his feet dug at the sides of the rock for traction. Eventually they made their way, backwards, to the top of the sharp edge. He was now lying with the entire front of his body, flat along the edge. He then brought his right knee, slowly forward – his foot sliding up to nearly his waist. While slightly rolling onto his left hip, he placed his right heel on the rock edge and then carefully pushed the top of his body upward – his hands pushing hard against the sharp rock... his body balanced precariously on his right foot. Very slowly, he brought his left leg forward... placing its heel behind his right foot – each foot now pointing outward and bringing him to a squatting position. Marty began to realize what he was attempting to do. He was going to try to stand up from a crouched position while balancing on his two heels. Marty was absolutely certain that Aaron would fall as soon as he began standing up. It would take a miracle, he felt, for him to balance on that sharp rock edge on just his heels. His feet were simply too close together. He would have nothing but his waving arms to balance his entire body while moving upward. Neither Marty nor Ginny could bear to watch. They covered their eyes to avoid seeing the inevitable fall. After fifteen or twenty seconds, they peeked between their fingers, fully expecting to find Aaron gone. Instead, they saw him standing, fully erect – his arms waving slightly... his feet, closely together in a duck footed stance. With his arms straight out to his sides he slowly moved his left foot forward and placed it ahead of his right foot – in the same, outward-pointing position as it had maintained before he moved it. His right foot remained outwardly pointing, also. It seemed to Marty that Aaron had hit upon a method of balance that gave him some sense of stability. He moved his right foot forward and, again, placed it duck footed, ahead of the left. With each step, he seemed to gain a little more confidence in his system. It began to look as though, except for some unusual happenstance in his awkward-looking traversal of the canyon, he just might make it. Marty felt himself silently cheering for the poor, frail, brave soul... so alone on that ribbon of death. Marty was proud... very proud of this frightened, small man... proud that he was able to find such courage within himself. Marty also envied him. He felt he could never have ever been so brave. As far as Marty was concerned, Aaron was the bravest of the entire lot of those who crossed over, for the simple reason that he was the most frightened.

After what seemed an eternity, Aaron finally set foot on the far plateau with Papa. Papa embraced him... not only with the unqualified love for a child, but with an unmistakable fatherly pride in him, as well. Papa's face beamed with it. The rest of the onlookers broke into spontaneous cheers for Aaron... Marty and Ginny included. There was something very wonderful about witnessing such bravery. Marty's hate for Papa was swept away by his happiness for Aaron. Marty was sure he could never have asked his own son to do what Papa asked of Aaron... but then, he wasn't Papa. Marty didn't know who Papa was... but he knew he was an extraordinary person... one for whom – on pure faith and love – eight people had faced a terrible death... and one had found it. Seven people had crossed the valley and were now with Papa. Marty could not help but envy every one of them. Even across the distance of that great chasm, their appearance was noticeably different than before they had conquered death to reach the other side. It was as though, by crossing this valley, they had been given new life. They appeared almost childlike – innocent – standing close to their proud, beaming, self-proclaimed parent. Looking at

Papa, it was undeniable that he loved these people... these children. He wasn't God – at least not to Marty – but he loved these people... and they loved him. Of that, Marty was sure.

Papa's next words sent an immediate sparkle of adrenaline, tingling through Marty's veins... along with the nausea of terror.

"Will you come to me, Marty?"

Papa spoke these words with his arms outstretched... as he had with the other eight – those warm words and arms having led one of them to an unspeakable death. Marty was stunned at Papa's invitation. He had always considered himself as an outsider... merely an observer in this story... the delivery boy... the reporter. Papa's words instantly demolished this comfortable wall he had tenaciously maintained between himself and the others. Papa was now inviting Marty to become an actual player in this grand, bizarre story... to step out of the audience, onto the stage. Even the possible consideration of such a thing was overwhelming to him. He was entirely unable to form words... and stood there, blankly staring at Papa. Papa spoke again.

"You're not a coward, Marty. You have just never allowed yourself to trust with your heart... that's all. I am who I say I am, Marty. I know you, and I know your heart. You're lost and alone like all my other children. If you can believe me and trust me, Marty, your fear will have no power over you."

A chord was struck that pried a small burst from Marty.

"I'm not alone. I've found Ginny and I love her. With her, I'm not lost and I'm not alone."

"Yes... I know you love Ginny, Marty... and she loves you with all of her heart. But even your love for one another can't overcome the question of your creation. You are of my body and will remain on this earth with a remembrance of me... always sensing the loss... always searching for your first parent, until we are together again. I love you, Marty... I don't want you to go on, apart from me, for untold lifetimes. None of my children on this earth have ever seen me or touched me before. You and Art were the first... and Art crossed over to me. You can see me before your eyes, Marty... and feel my arms. All of you are very blessed. I will not join with the body of one of my children, ever again, on this earth. I have done this in the hope of helping my children find home. Freedom has been particularly hard on the earth's children and I have come, this once, to call for all of you. Will you come home, Marty? Will you, please, come home to me?"

The collision of Marty's sane, simple, rational world with this utterly fantastic scene was more than his mind could bear. The protective curtains blackened his stage. His eyes rolled back into his head and his body went limp. His knees buckled and he dropped to a squatting position then fell to his right... his head striking the rock plateau solidly. Ginny was instantly at his side. She gently lifted Marty's head and cradled it in her lap. Blood began running from the corner of his mouth. Ginny began to scream.

"Help me! Please help me! He's bleeding! He's hurt really badly! Oh God! Oh God!"

Papa spoke to Ginny with calmness and compassion.

"He's all right, Ginny. It's just his tongue. Look inside his mouth... he's just bitten his tongue. Go ahead... look, Ginny."

Papa's words calmed Ginny to the point of allowing her to at least follow his directions – though with shaking hands and teary eyes. She gently slipped her right forefinger into Marty's slightly parted teeth and... putting the palm of her left hand on his forehead to allow opposing movement, she pulled down his jaw. Her concern for Marty's condition had overcome her initial panic and she peered into his mouth with coolheaded concentration. As Papa had predicted, the left side of his tongue was bleeding from a wound that appeared – from its location – to have been caused by his teeth clamping together. Instinctively, Ginny pulled her blouse from her jeans and used the tail of it to press against the wound. After a short time she released it and watched for the results. The flow stopped for several seconds… then began again. She returned to the wound with more pressure and more time. The second attempt was successful. Marty began mumbling unintelligibly then opened his eyes. He stared at Ginny and blinked as though he was trying to make sense of his situation. Ginny spoke tenderly to him.

"Hi sweetie."

She stroked his cheek.

"How are you feeling?"

Marty continued to stare into her eyes… searching for answers. Finally his eyes focused and his eyelids tightened – announcing his recollection of events. He smiled weakly and spoke in a private whisper to Ginny.

"I love you."

Ginny responded in a matching whisper.

"I love you, my sweet darling."

They loved one another, for a time, with their eyes. Ginny finally brought it to her voice.

"Are you OK, baby? I was so scared."

Marty nodded slightly several times.

"I'm OK, Ginny. I just went out. First time in my life I ever fainted."

"You feel like sitting up?"

"Yeah… I do."

They sat beside one another… Ginny's arm around Marty's

THE MINISTRY

shoulders. With her other hand, Ginny instinctively straighten Marty's tussled hair – her movements exhibiting an unmistakable fulfillment of innate maternal compulsion. She spoke softly to him in private conversation.

"Do you remember what happened?"

"Yes… it was just all too much for me. All this is just too much for me. I'm not like these other people. I just can't buy all of this, Ginny. I just can't risk my life on his promises. I just can't do it, Ginny."

"Marty… if you can't… you can't. It's all right."

Ginny's acceptance returned Marty to familiar ground. He rose slowly to his feet – Ginny along with him. Holding hands with Ginny, he spoke with a steady voice to Papa.

"I can't cross over, Papa. I'm sorry. I wish I could believe like the rest do, but I can't."

Papa's face saddened with compassion.

"I'll wait for you, Marty. I'll miss you very much. Always remember that I love you. Maybe someday, you'll find your way home."

A great sense of relief came over Marty… similar to being excused from a big test for which he wasn't prepared. But his respite was short-lived. Papa spoke again.

"Will you come over, Ginny?"

Marty immediately shouted at him in hot anger.

"Oh no… oh no! You leave her out of this… you son-of-a-bitch!! I brought her along and I'm responsible for her. I'm not going to allow you to kill *her*! No way, Papa! No way!!"

Papa shook his head and smiled at Marty.

"You just don't understand, Marty. You think you're being loving to Ginny, but by keeping her from joining me... you're depriving her of the greatest happiness possible. You can love her for your lifetime, Marty... but that's all. If you keep her from joining me, she'll wander through many more lonely lifetimes. She won't remember you or this moment when she is born into the body of another child. She may not be loved, again, by someone like you. My children, in their fear and loneliness, sometimes do terrible things to one another. Will you allow that to happen to this woman you love, Marty?"

"Goddamn you, Papa! You're a master deceiver, you are... a man of clever words. Hitler had people march into death with smiles on their faces... so did the emperor of Japan. Those poor young boys trusted those crazy men so much, they were happy to be torn apart by bullets or intentionally fly a plane into a fucking aircraft carrier! You aren't the first person to try this shit, man! Charlie Manson... how about him, Papa? One of your kiddies?"

Papa responded with a quiet voice.

"It's hard to risk the loss of someone you love so much, Marty. I know. I risked losing all of my children when I gave birth to them and set them free. It constantly tears at your heart. I know. I ache for every one of my children... despite what they do or how badly they turn out. Yes, Marty, Charlie Manson is one of my children and I ache for his lost and misguided spirit and lament all of the pain and suffering he caused my other children. I ache for you, too, Marty... and I ache for Ginny. Love her enough to let her go, Marty."

Marty's anger gave way to confused tears. Despite his tenacious, self-imposed need to disbelieve Papa's words... he could not deny their compelling force. Papa spoke in such a way that, if he allowed himself – even an instant of vulnerability – he'd be overwhelmed by him. Marty's body stiffened suddenly when he felt Ginny's hand slide from his grasp. His eyes searched hers for an answer. Hers replied by begging for his forgiveness. She closed them for an instant then turned and stepped forward to the great, deadly breach. An overwhelming sense of abandonment overcame Marty. He loved this woman more than life itself. He felt as though she were being literally torn from his body. He felt the deep, black, painful despair of emptiness. He pleaded with Ginny.

"Oh please, Ginny. Don't leave me... please. You're tearing my heart out. You're the first woman I've ever loved... the only woman I'll ever love and I'll love you till the day I die. Please, Ginny... I want to marry you and have children with you and grow old with you. I want to watch our kids grow up. I want to die in your arms. Please don't cross over, Ginny. If you die... I'll die. I'll have no reason to live. Oh God, Ginny... please stay with me..."

Papa said nothing. He raised his arms toward Ginny. Ginny moved her right foot toward the sharp edge of rock... then stopped suddenly and looked at Papa with the same plea for forgiveness she had begged of Marty, moments before. Papa understood and forgave her.

"I'll always love you, Ginny."

Ginny responded.

"I'll always love you, Papa... but I can't leave Marty, all alone. I'm sorry. You have your other children. Marty only has me. I can't do this to him. I'm sorry."

"One day, you'll come home, Ginny. I'll wait. One day you'll find your way. Try to remember my love."

CHAPTER EIGHT

One by one, Papa brought the seven back across the treacherous rock path – carrying each of them on his back, as he had Marty, the night of the wolf encirclement. He walked along the sharp rock edge with the calm and balanced stride of someone on a leisurely Sunday stroll along a wide forest path. None of his passengers gave any indication of having the slightest concern for their safety or doubt in the ability of their carrier. All together on the home landing, Papa began walking away from them. He stopped for a moment and motioned to them with his hand, saying merely, "Come," then continued on – striding ahead of them in his fluid, athletic movements.

They followed him to the rear entrance of his cave, for which they had searched the day before. They had thoroughly examined this precise area of the mountain during their search, but now discovered that the sheer, flat rock rising hundreds of feet into the air that appeared to them, yesterday, to be flush with the mountain, in fact, wasn't. Instead, at the base of it, was enough room for bodies to enter into the dark passageway that led to Papa's cavern. Although Marty had seen Papa's home previously, his memory had failed to preserve its true magnificence. He was in nearly as much awe of the revisited sight as the rest of the group, experiencing it for the first time. The panoramic view that spread itself before the open end of the cavern was almost beyond the capability of human appreciation. Its size and beauty were so overpowering that it was almost necessary to divide them into comprehensible portions to perceive the sum of its totality.

The group began freely wandering about the enormous cavern home. Marty and Ginny walked together, hand-in-hand. Besides the extraordinary sights and fine workmanship and interesting items in the home, Marty noticed that Papa had built a number of new beds – crafted with the same fine skill as was employed in the making of all the other furniture in the home. There were, besides the large and small bed that Marty had seen the previous summer, eight more. They noticed that a pot containing some sort of bubbling stew hung from the metal bar, near the low burning fire, and that the table was already set for dinner. Ginny told Marty to count the place settings. There were ten. They exchanged quizzical glances. Ginny verbalized the question.

"What do you make of this, Marty… ten beds… ten plates?"

"Either Papa isn't eating with us and he planned on the two of us sleeping together… or he knew there would only be nine guests."

"Nine of us… with Henry the missing guest? Maybe he didn't know about my coming along with you, Marty. That would be the simple explanation."

"I don't know, Ginny… we'll just have to wait and see."

They didn't have to wait long. Only moments after this exchange, Papa called all of them to the table for dinner. He joined them, sitting at the head. If Henry had made it, they would have been one plate, short. Marty, being the writer he was, immediately asked the obvious question.

"Why only ten plates, Papa? If Henry had made it, we would be short, wouldn't we… or is it because you didn't expect Ginny?

"I knew Ginny was coming, Marty."

"So you knew Henry wouldn't make it?"

"Yes."

"How?"

Papa smiled.

"If I told you that I knew because of who I am – would you believe me?"

"No."

"Then I have no answer that would satisfy you."

Marty got up from the table and walked slowly toward the open end of the cavern. He sat on a ledge of rock, jutting out from the stone wall... looking out at the hazy mountain ranges. Ginny followed him and sat down beside him.

"What is it, Marty?"

"I think it was a mistake... my coming here... bringing you here. Every time I turn around there's some new, unexplainable mystery. Papa knows all about everyone's life without ever having met them. He knew eight people would come out here. He knew you would be along. We all have the same dream at the same time... a dream about that terrible canyon – then we find Papa on the other side of it, the next day. Henry is killed, and beforehand, Papa has already set the table with one short. There's got to be some rational explanation for all this, Ginny. We can't be sitting down to have dinner with God... it can't be! As simple as that... it can't be."

"Marty... listen. I believe him. I believe he's God. I really do. If it hadn't been for you, I would have walked to my possible death to be with him."

"Can't you concede that there may be some other sort of explanation for all of this? I mean... maybe he's clairvoyant or something. I did a lot of research for my article on this sort of thing, Ginny. The U.S. government and the Russians spent a lot of time and money studying people like this. We had a program that went on for twenty years or so... trying to use these kinds of people for military intelligence. They had these "distant viewers" – they called them – who could sit in a room and see what was going on anywhere in the world. They'd just give them the coordinates and the viewers would look and see, in their minds... as though they were up in the air above the spot. They could actually see it... I mean specific things – buildings, lakes, people, weapons. They could even see inside of buildings. They tested them out... and they were very accurate. They were still using these people during the Gulf War. I mean... there are lots of people around who do these unexplainable things – know what is going to happen – read thoughts – see into the past – move objects with their minds – all kinds of things. Can't you accept the possibility that Papa is one of these kinds of people... and not God?"

"Marty... I know there are people around like that... but how many of us would cross that valley to get to one of them? Look, honey, my belief in Papa isn't a rational thing... not some logical decision. I can feel inside – in my heart – that he is who he is... and I can't tell you how and why I know it. I'd say it's women's intuition – but the men seem to know it the same way. I can't explain a belief. I can't prove anything. Papa could probably perform miracles for someone who's looking for rational proof and he'd probably still think there was some trick to it. I know in my heart that he's God, Marty. That's all I can say. He's not just some magician or somebody with ESP – that, I know."

Marty buried his face in his hands for a while. He then moved his palms far enough away to be heard.

"I don't like this, Ginny. I feel like such an outsider. All of them – even you – believe this man... and I can't. Maybe I should just leave. Seriously. I really don't belong here."

"If you go, Marty... I go."

"But Ginny... you believe in him."

"I do... but I couldn't give myself to him like he wanted me to. I've given myself to you, Marty... for better or worse. I'm yours, baby doll. Where you go, I go."

Marty dropped his hands and embraced Ginny and whispered in her ear.

"God, but I love you, Ginny. You're giving up being with God for me?"

"Yes, Marty, I am… but let's not talk about it anymore. I'm hungry, sweetheart… and that stew smells great. Want to go eat?"

"OK… but I need to talk about this with Papa."

"About what?"

"About my leaving."

"If you need to… go ahead, Marty. You know where I stand."

Papa ladled some stew into Ginny's and Marty's bowls. They each took a hard biscuit and some of Papa's tasty tea. When they had all finished eating, Marty raised his concern to all at the table.

"Listen, folks… I'm thinking of leaving. Don't take this the wrong way… I'm not angry or anything – but – I… ah… well… I just don't feel as though I fit in here. All of you believe in Papa… and that's OK. I'm the only one who doesn't… and I just don't feel right about it. I feel as though I'm crashing a wedding reception, if you know what I mean."

Papa replied.

"I want you to stay, Marty. I need you. I'm not going to be with you for very long."

At Papa's words, all faces instantly formed into expressions of puzzlement.

"One of my children will soon kill me."

Several asked in unison.

"Why?"

"Out of fear. Many of my children will fear me. Children fear the new and the unknown... enough to kill their own parent, sometimes."

Marty could not resist.

"I've got to say this, Papa. This is sounding an awful lot like the New Testament story... you know... Jesus telling his disciples at the last supper that he will soon be taken away from them... the Judas thing, the olive grove, and all. Are you sure you haven't become obsessed with the crucifixion story? I've seen the books in your library over there... the Bible... religious treatises on the life of Jesus, that sort of thing."

Papa laughed.

"And would you be Thomas in this story, Marty? Would you need to place your hand in my wounds to believe?"

Marty joined the laugh.

"Yes... I suppose I would, Papa. Forget I mentioned it."

After a singular chuckle at his own expense, Marty resumed his line of questioning.

"Do you know who will kill you? You seem to know everything else."

"Yes, I do."

"Who?"

"You'll have to trust me that it's best that you don't know."

"Oh, come on, Papa... let's cut this mysterious bullshit. Who is it?"

Paulo looked at Marty in anger and in respectful defense of his adopted parent.

"Let it go, Marty!"

"OK... whatever. If you people want to buy all of this hocus-pocus mysterious crap... be my guest. That's why I said I shouldn't be here. All I'm going to do is piss everybody off all the time. What do you need me for, Papa? I delivered these people to you – like you wanted me to – minus one, of course. My job is done. I'm supposed to be on a magazine assignment here – but I don't think it's going to work. I'm going to get in the way of whatever you've got in mind for these people, Papa. That's obvious."

Papa responded.

"I need you to write the whole story, Marty. That's why you ran out of gas on Old Log Road last summer. That's why you're here now. You'll tell the story, truthfully... without exaggeration... and through the eyes of a skeptic, like many of my children who will read it. They will be able to learn about me and decide, without embellishment, whether or not to join me. They'll decide of their own free will. If their hearts are open to me, they'll understand when they read the truth. You're here because you *don't* believe in me, Marty... but I don't love you any less because of it. You're just not ready yet... but I won't give up trying or hope."

"Will I actually write the story, Papa?... since you seem to know everything."

"You'll answer that for yourself when the time comes."

"I could just refuse to write it... to prove you wrong."

"Yes, you could. I won't make you do anything, Marty."

"Well, look... if you can't force me to do anything... and we all have this supposed free will, what about this mystery person who's supposed to kill you? Can't this person change his mind and decide not to do it?"

"Yes."

"Then you can't say, for certain, that this person is going to kill you, right?"

"This child's heart is set on it... but a heart can be changed."

"Then it's possible that this person won't kill you?"

"Yes."

Late that night, Marty and Ginny lay in the large bed which Papa insisted they take. As she was prone to do, Ginny fell asleep, almost immediately. Marty had too much on his mind and although he seemed to be the only one awake, he didn't mind. It was such a pleasant scene, he was actually glad he wasn't missing it by sleeping. Out of the open end of the cavern, he could see distant mountain ranges, bathed in moonlight... while inside, the stone, all around him, reflected the red, flickering glow of the large fire and echoed the crackle of the burning embers. This collage of color and sound was accompanied by the steady, rhythmic splash of the falling water, at the rear of the cavern – where Papa took his morning shower. Ginny's warm, naked body touching his, under the soft, deerskin blanket, completed this incredibly warm, idyllic scene.

The feeling he had that night reminded Marty of summer nights when he was a little boy... when big thunderstorms would roll through, one after another, all night long. He loved the power and magnificence of the lightning and the thunder... and the security of the steady downpour of the rain on the roof. It always made him feel, for some reason, wonderfully cozy and protected. He was never quite sure why. Maybe, he surmised, it was because the sight and sound of nature's enormity seemed to block out the rest of his ordinary world – making it all seem so trivial in comparison to the majestic force of nature. When he got older, he took to sleeping with a loud fan in his room at night – in both summer and winter – that gave him the same feeling. He sometimes speculated that, perhaps, being surrounded by large, comfortable, reliable sound aroused some remembrance of a forgotten time, long before he had actual memory... perhaps, he guessed, in his mother's womb, where there surely must have been the steady sound of her heart and the gentle, steady rushing of water all around him. As a little boy, during the storm, he would hug his pillow and, surrounded by warmth and safety, would be overcome with sleepiness, but would fight it, so he could continue to hear the delicious sounds. He felt the same luxurious comfort on this night and, as in his childhood, he was torn between enjoying the lavish serenity... or accepting the sleep it enticed.

As he lay there, Marty tried to imagine what it must have been like for Papa to sleep there, all alone, as a young boy, after his father and mother were gone. He imagined that the cave and fire must have become like a parent to him... lulling him to sleep each night. He realized how such a life would have produced a very extraordinary person – and Papa was, without question, very special. Nature, itself, must have become his parent. Perhaps, he thought, that was the key to understanding why Papa began to think of himself as God. Perhaps Papa's young persona eventually merged with nature... becoming one in the same with it. He became the magnificent mountains, the lovely streams, the powerful storms, the sleek, stealthy mountain lion, the graceful deer. Perhaps, also, he somehow gained – or regained – powers that mankind once had, then lost, in its separation from nature. Perhaps, at one time, he pondered – when mankind was still one with nature – it possessed some of the unexplainable powers still retained by the animals... knowing how to build nests without ever being taught... finding a nectar-rich flower miles away from the hive by watching another bee dance... caring for their young without a baby book. Perhaps, Papa reentered nature, so to speak. Perhaps, he regained the secret knowledge of the world, long-lost to the human race. Perhaps, this was the key to unlocking Papa's mystery. This... Marty could accept. This... made some sense. Perhaps, he reflected, at some stage in its evolution, mankind was able to do these unexplainable things, of which Papa was capable, as a regular course of life. Perhaps, human beings could read one another's minds before they could speak. Perhaps human beings could, at some time in the ancient past, look into the future and the past. Perhaps, this was a plausible explanation for someone like Nostradamus... who could look centuries into the future. Maybe the ancient stories of prophets and mystics were quite real accounts of what human beings were once able to do at some point in the long-forgotten past. Perhaps Papa misunderstood his own powers. Maybe they were simply a natural result of an inextricable mixture of inherent abilities and extensive book-learning. With the new powers and insights he began to have, and his rediscovered, natural aspects emerging, he, perhaps, used the stories he had read – the Bible, Greek mythology, and science... to explain life to himself. In this way, he may have begun to view himself as God... even weaving such scientific concepts as the Big Bang into the expositive mosaic.

These thoughts about Papa provided Marty with the beginnings of a rational foundation, upon which he could craft a much-needed perspective about him... a way in which he could lucidly deal with the fantastic events he was witnessing. Having come to a somewhat plausible context in which to perceive Papa, he moved on in his thoughts to the seven remaining disciples.

Papa's extraordinary effect upon these seven people was undeniable. Marty had never witnessed such a rapid and radical transformation of any group of people. Not only did their attitudes and outlooks seem drastically different after they made their death-defying walk to join Papa, but their actual physical appearance was noticeably altered. They somehow seemed younger, happier... more innocent. They had returned from their crossing, possessing the undeniable countenance of young children... trusting, loving, innocent, wide-eyed. Before their walk, they had the appearance of virtually every adult human being, who has suffered the inevitable slings and arrows of life's outrageous fortune... skeptical, angry, distrusting, expectant of disappointment, hurt, calloused. Those inevitable life wounds of the disciples now seemed to have been totally healed. Their eyes and faces seemed almost to glow with love – a love for everything and everybody – a timeless, endless love. Their absolute change begged explanation – and Marty had none. His return-to-nature model was workable for Papa... but not for these seven people. They were now clearly different people. Ginny said she believed in Papa but she was still laboring under the same fears and weaknesses as was Marty... afraid of losing one another... concern for their future together... uncertainty. These seven had been the victims of life's unrelenting cruelty... and here they were – after having merely entered the presence of Papa – washed clean of their scars. It was both wonderful and unnerving to witness. Marty envied them... as he had often envied the happy innocence of children... but he felt compelled to find some rational explanation for this wonderful new lease they seemed to have been given on life.

Perhaps, Marty considered, someone could, if they wanted to badly enough, join Papa in his unspoiled natural happiness by sheer force of personal will. These seven certainly had the motivation. Life had dealt them every bad card from a sadistically fixed deck. They had every reason to wish for a new life. Perhaps Papa's strength and happiness were so apparent and appealing to them – even across that wide canyon – that they were willing to risk their lives to be like him. Maybe the experience of near-death was enough to literally shock their splintered psyches into a new vision of life – like being struck with lightning – and they, as do many others, mistook this sort of dramatic life-changing event for the hand of God. Regardless of the cause, Marty had to concede that if everyone on earth could be changed in the wonderful way these seven were, by believing in Papa, the world would be a far better place in which to live. Even though Marty was convinced Papa wasn't God, if people truly believed that he was, that's probably all that mattered. The belief alone, perhaps, could change a person's life. While pondering the last of these questions, the winds of slumber carried Marty, in mid-thought, to the Land of Nod.

CHAPTER NINE

Marty was awakened by the sounds and light of morning. Ginny was already up and dressed, sitting near the fire in one of the rockers, sipping a cup of coffee. Susan was in the rocker beside her, also with coffee. Looking around at the sizeable assembly of beds, Marty discovered that, besides being the last to fall asleep, he was also the last to awaken. Marty scanned the cavern for Papa and found him near the waterfalls, drying himself. The immediate question on Marty's mind – based on last summer's experience – was answered in the next moment. He hung the drying hide on a peg, grabbed his wet, washed kilt and shirt, hanging from other nearby pegs, and walked – as naked as a newborn – to the fireplace and hung his clothing on the metal bar to dry. Marty was stunned at the sight. It was shocking enough to see him do this when it was just the two of them… but with so many people – four of them women – was absolutely extraordinary. Marty searched the faces – particularly the women – for their reactions. All of them – men and women – appeared to be as taken-back as he felt. Marty wasn't sure if the reactions were more result of seeing a naked man walking about with such comfort and lack of inhibition, or the striking beauty of Papa's physique. His genetic inheritance, enhanced by his life in the hand of nature, had combined to produce a living work of art.

Papa went about making breakfast – entirely oblivious to his own nakedness. Into the hanging pot, he poured a mixture of flour, water, honey, and blackberries… preserved from the previous summer. This cooked into a thick, delicious pudding that Papa served them, still warm, for breakfast. Over the dark purple pudding, he poured milk… which Marty later learned was squeezed from the udders of the wild goats that roamed the higher elevations of the mountain ranges. Papa had also churned the cream of this milk into butter, which he placed on the table in a large wooden bowl. They used it, not only on their biscuits, along with raspberry preserves, but in their pudding, as well, following

Papa's lead. The culinary masterpiece seemed almost miraculous, given the wild environment from which it was extracted. At the breakfast table, as he had during the past summer with Marty, Papa ate with them, still naked.

After breakfast, Papa put on his, now-dried and warm, kilt and shirt and, as they sat around the table, he began to tell them of his plans. They would set out, he said, on foot, and walk to Los Angeles. Marty, of course, immediately interrupted.

"You have got to be kidding me! Walk from here to Los Angeles? Christ!... that's over twelve hundred miles from here! That would take us... months! And if you go by way of Route Fifteen, you're talking about crossing the desert at the hottest time of the year! Papa... you can't be serious!"

Papa was unperturbed.

"Everything will be fine, Marty."

Before Marty had a chance of a rejoinder, David spoke up.

"When will we leave, Papa?"

"Tomorrow."

Susan, uncharacteristically, posed the next question.

"Why are we going?"

"To meet my children and give them hope."

Paulo looked at Aaron.

"You think you can make it, amigo?"

Aaron smiled broadly.

"After crossing that valley, it'll be a stroll."

Paulo laughed and slapped Aaron on the back... a little too hard, given his strength and Aaron's frail frame, but Aaron bore the impact with the balm of the intended camaraderie. He hadn't been pounded in good-natured, male friendship, since his boyhood... during those golden years before his dream confession to Tommy Miller... and the pain felt wonderful to him.

David was next.

"What will we take along, Papa? That's an awfully long walk."

"Just the bare necessities, David... blankets and some water."

Marty jumped in, before he could, again, be preempted.

"Blankets and water? That's it? No food... nothing else?"

"Everything will be fine, Marty."

"I've got to say this. I feel like I'm with a bunch of crazy people... like the Jim Jones bunch that drank the poisoned Kool-Aid when he told them to. Papa... we could die out there. That's a long, long, hard walk."

Papa stood up and extended his hands to Marty.

"Come here, Marty."

Marty hesitated... looking around the table... uncertain and delaying. Finally, he rose slowly and walked to Papa with a skeptical, suspicious expression on his face. Papa pushed back his chronically falling hair from his forehead and embraced his face with his hands. He bent toward him with a gentle, good-humored smile.

"My Marty... so little faith. It will be all right. Will you trust me?"

Marty's emotions and thoughts were so jumbled and confused that he couldn't manage a response. He continued to look, shyly, into Papa's warm face and smiling, fatherly eyes. Suddenly Marty's rational defenses seemed to melt, and his heart found voice and spoke with a slight nod of assent and a boyish smile. Papa's eyes twinkled and his smile widened. He gave Marty's face a gentle squeeze with his enormously powerful hands.

"That's my boy."

Marty couldn't deny the warm feeling in his heart that Papa's touch, face, and words brought to him. For a brief moment – before his cold rationality reclaimed him – he felt a part of the family that sat around the table… and felt a distinctly childlike love for Papa.

For the remainder of the day, there was a sense of excitement and anticipation about the journey. None, save Marty and Ginny, seemed to have any fear or concern for the likely dangers that lie ahead for them. On another note, Marty, in fulfillment of his practical commitment to author another magazine story about this phase of the Papa saga, searched for an opportunity to speak, alone, with David. He needed to gain some understanding, from their point of view, as to how, exactly, these seven disciples now felt about things… and why they appeared so different than they had before their crossing. David was, by far, in Marty's judgment, the most articulate of the group… and he felt that if anyone could put their present state of mind into words, it was him.

Marty approached David and asked him if they could walk together, for a while, and talk. David was very happy and cordial to oblige. They left the cavern by way of the back entrance and walked along a shaded path that led to a nearby ridge, overlooking one of the many small, beautiful lakes that abundantly adorned the mountain range. They sat down on some flat rocks that had been warmed by the morning sun. After they both made a few irresistible comments on the breathtaking beauty of the view, Marty began his interview.

"David… all of you – the seven of you – are noticeably different since you crossed that valley, over to Papa. Do you know what I mean?"

"Of course, Marty... we all feel much differently than we did before."

"Just... how do you feel? Can you describe it to me?"

"I can try, Marty... I'm not sure if I can do it justice. Umm, let's see... I think the change... at least for me... began when I was crossing that valley. You were there... you know how scary it was – and we had all had those terrible dreams about falling, that made it even worse. You remember how frightened I was... terrorized, is a better word. I was absolutely sure I was walking to my death. I had just seen poor Henry fall... and I was petrified. I could feel myself falling before I even started out on that rock. People can say they believe in something... I used to hear it every Sunday in my congregation... but to face that horrible death on the sole basis of someone's promise to you is an extraordinary experience. *That*... walking to your likely death, on the basis of your belief in somebody... *that*, is faith. I preached about faith, every Sunday, for years... and had listened to my father do the same thing... from the time I was old enough to understand. I thought I knew what it was all about. I found out that I knew nothing about it. Anyone can claim faith when it's safe. I wonder how many of those Christians I used to minister to would cross over that valley to reach Jesus Christ on the other side? Would they risk falling to their death to be with him? Would they have enough faith in him to do that? I'd venture to say... very, very few of them would do it."

David picked up a small, brittle twig and began, unconsciously, breaking it into tiny pieces as he pondered his next words.

"I feel as though I walked through death and came out on the other side of it... as a newborn. I know... some Christians call themselves born-again – but I mean it in a literal sense. All of what these Christians do is symbolic... nothing real... very safe... no real sacrifice or danger or threat to them. It's all pretty and musical with dresses and ties. It was as though I left all that I was, on that flat stone behind me... all my hatred, fear, loneliness, personal ambition, my ego, my lies... everything. I have no rational explanation as to why I was willing to face death for Papa... other than to say that once I accepted him as God and believed the promises he made me, I felt very different about death, myself... everything."

Marty searched for a journalistic focus.

"Can you tell me, specifically, how you feel right now... how you're different than before?"

"Well... even before my life went down the toilet at the hands of that young girl – when I was a golden boy in the world – I still had nagging doubts and fears. I would secretly worry about losing what I had... about my career climb... about pleasing my congregation. Now, I have no sense of worry or climbing or needing to explain myself to anyone. I guess the best way to describe how I feel, now, is to say that I'm at total peace with everything and everybody... with the entire world. I feel complete. I feel I'm one with Papa... with God."

"Is it possible that this is just some sort of temporary religious euphoria?... you know... the way some people react at revival meetings. They say they're full of the Holy Spirit – when all they're full of is mob hysteria... like the ex-preacher talked about in the *Grapes of Wrath*, you know? Then... a few hours after the meeting, they're back down to earth again. Isn't that a possibility?"

"No... really, it's not. I've experienced religious euphoria before... at some retreats I went to as a young man – but I knew what it was when it was happening. I think everyone, deep down, knows it's only temporary... but while it's happening, why spoil it? The way I feel now isn't that manic high that makes you feel all pumped-up for a while... it's just the opposite. I'm calm... the calmest I've ever been in my life... as though I've gotten off of some racetrack and laid down in the grass to rest. It's a very quiet, peaceful feeling. It's love... that's what it is... that's the best word I can use... love. I feel completely loved and completely loving... but a quiet, steady, happy love – not some passionate, energetic thing."

"David... look, I've got to ask. I'm doing the story on this and I've got to be a journalist and dig for the truth. Are you absolutely sure that Papa is God? Isn't there even a remote reservation in your mind that you might, possibly, be wrong?"

"No... there isn't. Do you actually think that if I had the slightest doubt in my mind about Papa, I would have walked across that valley? I told you... I was sure I'd be killed. I'm not being arrogant about my belief... it's just that I know... not in my brain but in my heart. I've never been so sure about anything in my life."

"What do you think your purpose is with Papa?"

"I asked him that last night. He said I would know."

"And you just let it go at that?"

"Yes."

"You'd never make it as a reporter, Dave."

"Not with Papa, I wouldn't."

"Doesn't this twelve-hundred-mile trek worry you a bit... especially with taking no provisions along?"

"Papa said everything will be all right. That's all I need to know. You know, Marty... I wish you could join us. I don't mean on the trip... but as one of Papa's believers. I know you're afraid to let go and totally trust someone... I was too... but this feeling of love is so wonderful that I'd like to share it with everybody. It's almost indescribable. You can't appreciate how different you feel after you've given yourself – totally – to someone you trust to always love you. After you do, the whole world seems completely different."

"Maybe the reason that Papa chose the seven of you was that... well... no offense... but all your lives were, basically, for shit. None of you had anything to lose. You had no where to go but to him... nothing to go back to. Maybe it's just a lot harder for those of us who feel we have something to lose... a lot harder to risk everything you have on a promise."

"You're right, Marty. Maybe you have to reach the bottom of the barrel before you can truly find peace."

That night, Papa displayed a talent, and a side of him, of which Marty had been completely unaware. After dinner, as the sun was setting behind the mountains, and they were all gathered around the fire, Papa disappeared for a few moments and then came back with an old-looking, handmade flute. He explained that his father made it, years before he was born, and had taught him to play. He then commenced playing a wide variety of songs... from Scottish ballads to island ditties, to selections from Bach and Brahms. Although Marty and Ginny weren't true believers, they were, nevertheless, fundamentally affected by the scene... the loveliest that either of them had ever, in their lives, experienced. The love was so strong among Papa and his seven special children that Marty and Ginny could literally feel it – as distinctly as the touch of a soft summer breeze. The beauty of the mountain ranges – silhouetted by the limitless colors of the halo, cast by the setting sun – performing to the accompaniment of the soft, breathing music from Papa's flute... their bodies bathed by the friendly warmth and color of the crackling fire and the steady, reassuring splash of the waterfalls in the background... all merged into a soul-touching symphony. Both Marty and Ginny felt that, regardless of the final outcome of the Papa story, their lives had been privileged and blessed and permanently enriched by that night's experience.

Anticipation drew everyone from their beds, early the following morning... barely dawn, and all were wide awake – even Marty... the chronic late-riser. Marty and Ginny were worried... the others, excited. After breakfast and morning rituals, Papa filled seven goatskins with water and distributed them. They each rolled up the deerskin blankets from their beds and tied them with rawhide strips. Inside their blankets they had each put a few personal items they wanted for the journey. The only food Papa packed was a large portion of dried meat strips and some hard biscuits, which he put into a leather sack with draw strings, along with the wooden plates and cups they had used at the table. Papa slid the metal pot from the bar over the fire, slipped a long, leather strap under its handle and tied it into a loop to allow for a shoulder carry... then handed it to Paulo who pulled the strap over his shoulder – the pot hanging at his side like an oversized army helmet. The whole situation struck Marty as so bizarre that he had to laugh – in spite of his concerns. This made Ginny smile responsively and question him with puzzled expression. He explained.

"I feel like I'm in some documentary about the nomads of the Steppe lands... goat-hide water skins... deer-hide blankets... a few strips of meat and biscuits... and a pot... setting off on a thousand-mile journey, on foot, with the clothes on our backs. This is just unreal. Did you notice how little food he packed? That'll last us a day or two... at the most. Then what?"

Ginny shook her head in empathetic agreement. Marty continued.

"I wonder if Papa really appreciates just how far Los Angeles is from here? I mean... he's never been off this mountain, for Christ's sake! I can't believe he's doing this. I can't believe *we're* doing this! I mean... we must be nuts, Gin... really... it's just crazy... absolutely crazy. If you want to get out of this now – seriously Ginny – I'll understand. As a matter of fact, I wish you would... then I'd only have myself to worry about. I have a bad feeling about this trip... that it's going to be a very strange and very dangerous trip – especially once the word gets out about us on the road... and that won't take long. A few days after we pass through Bear Stump, the world's going to know about this... mark my word. Really, Ginny, how about it? Why don't you just get in my car and go home and wait for me? I'd feel a lot better if you did. I'm worried... really worried. If something happened to you, I couldn't live with myself. Honestly. How about it honey?"

"You know my answer without asking. Where you go – I go. I told you that... and that's it, sweetie... you know better than to even ask me."

"Are you sure, Gin?"

Ginny pursed her lips and tilted her head to the side... theatrically reacting to the immense stupidity of Marty's question. He acknowledged it.

"OK, honey."

As with the commencement of every long journey, there was a quiet, reflective moment before the first step was taken... as though all were awaiting some particular signal to begin. All, but Papa, were congregated in the general area of the fireplace... their senses peaked, as though anticipating a loud noise. Papa was standing, alone, at the wide cavern opening... staring out at the great expanse. They all sensed what must be going through his mind. This was the only home he had ever known. He had spent every night of his life in this beautiful mountain place. The mountains that he drank in with his eyes must have become a part of him. If what he said about his inevitable murder were true, he knew that this would be the last time he would ever look upon his beautiful mountains, or be in his beloved home in the mountainside. They looked at one another, questioning whether someone should go to him. Veronica volunteered without speaking and walked, tentatively, to his side. She talked quietly to him for a few moments, then gently raised her hand to his face and wiped the tears from his cheeks. Everyone instantly felt the anguish and helplessness that children always feel when they see their parents cry. Veronica stroked the side of Papa's face then gently kissed it. When she rejoined the group, tears were streaming from her eyes. All overcome with profound emotion, they avoided one another's eyes.

Finally, Papa walked over to join them – his eyes showing that tears had been shed. He found his voice and spoke very softly.

"It's hard to leave home."

All eyes welled with empathy tears for this loving man.

With his private farewell concluded, Papa left his home in the mountains – for the last time.

CHAPTER TEN

As they filed out of the narrow fissure between the mountain and the towering rock, Marty stopped suddenly. He had forgotten, he announced, his notepads... under his bed. While the rest of the group waited for him in the grassy area just outside the back entrance, Marty rushed back into the cavern. Entering the enormous cave – knowing it was now deserted – was both sad and eerie. He walked as quietly as he could – as though someone else had taken possession of the space and he was an intruder. Marty got down on his knees to reach his stack of tablets, under his bed – bound together by several large rubber bands. He grabbed them and stood up quickly – so quickly that he was momentarily light-headed. In that moment he thought he saw someone standing in the same spot where Papa had been when he was saying good-bye to his mountain. It looked like a small boy... who was staring at him. As the blood returned to his head, nothing was there. Marty felt the hair rise on the back of his neck and adrenaline pulse through his body. He instantly turned and ran, in fright, from the cave. The distress and paleness of his face and his discernable rapid breathing was immediately apparent to Ginny as he rejoined them. As soon as she got the chance to talk to him, privately, she asked him about it. He hesitated... then explained.

"I thought I saw something up there... when I stood up... after I got my notepads from under the bed. I was down on my knees and stood up really fast and was light-headed for a minute... you know? I thought I saw this little boy standing at the edge of rock... where Papa was just before we left... looking right at me. It looked just like that little boy I saw in that dream I had... you know... about the playground?... the one outside the fence?"

"I remember."

"It scared the shit out of me, Ginny. I'm not kidding you. As soon as my head cleared, though, there was nothing there. I was so scared I ran out of there as fast as I could."

"Isn't that strange? You think maybe you were just dizzy and thought you saw something?"

"I know I was dizzy... but I'm also sure I saw that boy... as sure as I'm looking at you right now."

Ginny puzzled, and Marty scared, they walked for some time, in silence, at the back of the column. As they passed Art's truck and their cars, Marty had an overwhelming urge to jump into one of them and, with Ginny, just drive off... away from all this craziness. Papa must have sensed it because he looked back at Marty at the very moment the thought passed through his mind. As they rounded the end of the tree line to head toward the road, Marty took one last look at the motorized means of escape he was leaving behind. He sighed, audibly.

The day was beautiful... bright sun and cool air. Everything was now in bloom and a chorus of sweet smells filled the air. There was little conversation among the group... everyone preoccupied with the gorgeous scenery adorning both sides of the road. Papa walked ahead of them... striding in lengths he had shortened to allow his column to keep up with him. Across his back was a large wooden bow, a quiver of hunting arrows, his rolled deerskin blanket, and his leather food sack. Into one side of his kilt's waist was tucked a large hunting knife... his flute on the other. He looked, Marty thought, very much like a Scottish Highlander, heading into battle. All that was missing was a piper to lead him.

They stopped for the day at around five o'clock. In all, having spent about a half-an-hour for the lunch, provided from the contents of Papa's sack, they had walked about nine hours that day and covered, Marty estimated, about eighteen miles, or so... much farther than Marty felt they could travel in a day. Of course, he reflected, this was the first day... with everyone fresh and strong. As the toll of the journey wore on, the mileage could very well be substantially reduced. Everyone was exhausted by the time they stopped for the day, except Papa, who looked as strong and fresh as he had that morning.

They found a shaded area near a stream where they spread their blankets and immediately collapsed upon them... their bodies drained from the lengthy trek. Papa took off his blanket roll and food sack and immediately disappeared into the woods with his bow, arrows, and knife. He reappeared in about forty-five minutes with a small deer slung around his neck... a set of legs hanging down from each shoulder. He tied its hind legs together with a strip of hide and hung it from a branch. The gaping red cavern in its abdominal area revealed that its innards had already been removed. The group was fascinated by this primitive hunting display. Papa then asked for help in gathering fire wood. Everyone, anxious to be a part of this frontier meal preparation, immediately spread out in search of the requested timber and, within ten minutes, there were more sticks and limbs piled up than could be burned in a week of campfires. Papa arranged the wood in the same fashion Marty had witnessed the previous summer and then bent down to employ his primitive fire-starting method. Paulo squatted beside him and pulled out a red Bic lighter. Papa laughed and leaned back... deferring to Paulo's modern, fire-starting method.

Papa then disappeared, again, into the woods and returned with three fresh-cut branches. Two of them, he cut with his knife – leaving a "Y" at the top of each. He then sharpened the bottom of these. The third branch – which was straight – he sharpened at one end. He pushed the two "Y" branches into the ground on opposite sides of the fire and then took the straight stake with him to the hanging deer. He laid the stake on the ground, then proceeded to cut the deer's head and legs from the torso. After this, he stripped off all of the hide. What remained hanging looked like a side of beef in a meat market. Papa pushed the straight end of the stake all the way through the torso, from end to end and then carried it back to the fire and laid the ends of the stake into the "Y" of each standing branch. Papa looked down at his blood-covered hands and arms and walked to the stream to wash them.

Papa came over and sat down with them. They talked... but all were hungry to a point of distraction... having had only a few strips of Papa's smoked meat for lunch. Occasionally, Papa got up to turn the cross-stake – rotating the roasting torso to another side. Paulo got up suddenly and, without a word, started toward the woods. He then stopped and inquired sheepishly.

"We got any toilet paper, Papa?"

No one had packed any. Papa laughed... then walked over to the just-cut deer skin, lying on the grass. He knelt on one knee and cut a number of square pieces from it – eight-or-so inches across. He took one in his hand and walked toward the stream – Paulo following. He bent down and washed the blood from the hide side of the skin with a rock then dipped the whole piece into the water and shook it, then handed it to Paulo. He told him that, when he was done using it, to wash it out, shake off the water and keep it with him for future use. Paulo stared vacantly at Papa for a few moments... then suddenly smiled as he got the idea. Now equipped for his mission, he disappeared into the woods. Papa came back to the group, carrying the other pieces of deer skin... so each of them could have their own "toilet-hide," as he called it... telling them they all needed to clean the back of them, as he had – which they all proceeded to do – each of them then storing their hide in select places for future use.

After about an hour's time, Papa began cutting juicy portions of the blackened flesh from the roasting animal with his large hunting knife... laying the succulent meat on the wooden plates for his traveling companions... the first fresh-killed meat any of them, save Papa, had ever tasted. To an outside observer, the dinner scene would have, unquestionably, appeared to be something akin to a gathering of stone age primitives – all sitting about the fire... eating fresh-killed meat with their hands... wiping their mouths with the backsides. They all felt an exhilarating sensuality... devouring freshly killed, wild flesh in this crude, animal-like fashion. Given the circumstances, with all normal table etiquette and manners abandoned, they experienced a palpable connection with their primordial ancestors. Dispensing with utensils – which distance modern man from his food and prevent the complete communion of the eater with the eaten – they devoured the flesh, roasted while the body still retained proof of life through the natural heat of its living spirit. The sum of the experience gave rise to something very similar to a pure sexual experience. The juice of the deer's body, that only an hour before had sustained his surging muscles and beating heart – now ran through their fingers and dripped to the ground. They shoved their faces deep into the succulent warm flesh as their lips parted and their teeth bit and tore at it, with animalistic abandon. So soon after its death did they devour its flesh, they seemed to taste the very life that still lingered in its body. Marty reflected on the pure sense of joy that his ancient parents must have felt about living – before rationality and self-consciousness held a mirror before their faces, artificially reflecting their natural sensuality and nakedness and forever, thereafter, casting shame on their innocent pleasures.

The ropes of inhibition were untied for the moment by the flesh-eating experience and set free the unbridled passions of Papa's companions and, unabashedly, they disappeared into the lush forest to seek consummation... the coupling tacitly accepted as though predestined. Marty went, of course, with Ginny... Paulo with Veronica... David with Susan... Danny with Katherine. Aaron, as he had done so often in his life, went alone – but this time with no sense of bitterness or abandonment. Papa smiled at the innocent happiness of his children.

The same couples slept the night together – falling asleep to the lullaby of Papa's flute. He was already awake when the rising sun opened their eyes, having brewed a breakfast tea with select wild flowers and bark he had foraged. Along with this odd, delicate tasting brew, they finished-off the biscuits from Papa's sack. After they had toileted, then washed themselves in the creek... brushing their teeth and swishing their mouths with the ice-cold water... they gathered together their sparse nomadic possessions to continue their journey. Papa sliced some of the hard, cold, blackened flesh from the previous evening's dinner and put it into his sack. As they began the second day of their walk, the troupe quickly realized they were not conditioned for such a bodily challenge, and struggled to lift their stiff, aching, lead-laden legs. As Marty had anticipated, fatigue became a factor and reduced their mileage to less than eleven miles that second day.

To everyone's great surprise, and relief, Aaron was able, during the following days on the trail, not only to keep up with the rest of the group, but do so with abundant energy. Ever since his crossing over to Papa, his health and self-image were completely changed for the better. His appetite had become almost voracious – already putting onto his bone-protruding frame, some much needed weight... and color into his cheeks. Strength and energy quickly followed. Gone was the vacant, forlorn look in his eyes – replaced by a sparkle of enthusiasm and the steadiness of self-confidence. Of the seven disciples, his physical change, after meeting Papa, appeared to be the most dramatic. If he were, at that moment, to walk into his former mental institution, Marty was convinced that nary a person would recognize him.

As with any other repeating activity in life, their journey quickly fell into a routine – setting camp... starting the fire... Papa, killing dinner... falling asleep to his flute... wild flower tea in the morning. The post-meat-eating passion did not become routine, however – such special moments remaining special – but the coupling arrangements did continue... talking, walking, and sleeping together.

For variety in their diet, and berries not yet in season, Papa located a variety of tender and tasty vegetable treats... including dandelion greens, wild onions, and tubers which only Papa could identify. On the evening of the fifth day, they were camped only one day's walk from Bear Stump. The following morning, they would enter the tiny village and everything, they all knew, would change, forever.

CHAPTER ELEVEN

All through the night before they walked into Bear Stump, Marty's mind was preoccupied with business at hand. As was often the case with the two of them, Ginny was sound asleep at his side while he pondered various matters in the privacy, provided him by being the only one awake in a sleeping world. Before the morning arrived, he knew he had to make some important business decisions. As an experienced journalist, he knew that as of the next morning, the cat was out of the bag about Papa. Word would get to the media, almost as soon as they hit the Stump. Traveling with Papa was, also, he had to sometimes remind himself – besides being a life-altering experience – his assignment... his job. As of the next morning, he'd no longer have exclusivity to the source and would be in competition with an avalanche of rapidly descending media.

Marty speculated that, within an hour of their arrival, someone in the Stump will have contacted the media, and some would begin arriving as soon as that afternoon or early evening. Allowing for some delays in details and confirmation, it would very likely be the following day before the media really got a firm hold on the story. If he could get his story to Marla, immediately upon hitting town, he'd be able to scoop the rest of the media. The magazine could sell their exclusive to the wire for immediate release... then do the full, in-depth piece in the following week's issue. He'd have to get to a fax machine and send out his notes immediately, he decided, after they got into town. The Bear Stump Police Station had a fax, he remembered, and unless Chief Thompson was being a real prick – which wasn't an improbability – Annabelle would, for sure, let him use it.

Another matter of business – and a real problem – was Paulo and his parole meeting. Tomorrow was his scheduled appointment with Thompson at ten o'clock in the morning. Marty had nearly forgotten about it until Paulo reminded him that very afternoon.

The problem was, it was probably a five-hour walk into the Stump from where they were camped, just near the end of Old Log Road. They'd have to leave at five in the morning, at the latest, to get to his appointment on time. Paulo didn't seemed terribly concerned... but Marty was. If Paulo missed the meeting, Thompson – sure as hell – would come looking for Paulo and, having technically violated his parole, Thompson would do everything he could to have Paulo back to prison... of that, Marty was sure.

Marty slid from beneath the warmth of their deerskin blanket and walked as quietly as possible over to where Paulo and Veronica slept. Under the full moon and clear sky, he could easily see his way. He knelt beside Paulo and gently grasped his shoulder, shook it slightly, and backed up a bit – not knowing what to expect from an ex-con, being suddenly awakened. Paulo awoke with a slight jerk... his eyes straining to discern the identity of the person looking down on him. Marty assisted him.

"Paulo... it's Marty."

"What's up, Marty?"

His voice contained the gravel of sleep.

"I'm really worried about your appointment with Thompson tomorrow. If you don't show up on time... he'll come looking for you. It's a violation of your parole. He could send you back to prison."

Paulo was silent for a few moments... then finally responded.

"You're right, Mart. I guess I better get my ass in there, huh? Whata you wanna do?"

"I want to get you there on time. We need to leave about four-thirty or five o'clock to make it, I figure."

"What time is it now?"

Marty looked down at his watch.

"I can't tell."

Paulo pulled out his Bic lighter and sparked it. The hands indicated one-thirty. Marty set the plan.

"Keep that on for a minute and I'll set my alarm... for... let's say... four o'clock, for safety sake. OK?"

"OK buddy."

Marty set the alarm and returned to Ginny... the warmth of the blankets and her body, at once, pulling the chill of the cold mountain air from his body. She awakened for a moment and asked him what the problem was. Not wanting her to be alarmed by his being gone in the morning, he told her the plan.

It seemed to Marty that he had just laid his head on his rolled-up-sweatshirt pillow when his alarm buzzed. He quickly turned it off and told Ginny – who had stirred at the sound – to go back to sleep... which, having not irrevocably emerged from her slumber, she acquiesced, posthaste, without further inquiry. He went over to Paulo and awakened him for the second time that night. They both peed, got themselves dressed, and started down Old Log Road in the cold, wet air and blackness of the night. Marty asked Paulo if he had told Veronica he was leaving early... so she wouldn't be worried in the morning. He had, he said. Given their utmost significance, Marty, as he walked, repeatedly touched the bulge in his jacket to reassure himself that he had, indeed, remembered to bring along his notes for faxing. This earlier-than-anticipated jump on the media would be even better than his original plan.

It was still dark when they reached the highway. At about five-thirty, gray light began to appear on the eastern horizon, giving way, within fifteen minutes, to the crystalline blue Montana sky. Both their faces were chilled from the night air and the touch of sunshine on their skin was a welcomed pleasure. Only a few old pickups passed them by during their four-hour walk along the highway. It was nine o'clock when they reached the outskirts of Bear Stump. With an hour to kill, they decided to get some breakfast at the Cozy Corner before going to the police station... both hoping they wouldn't encounter Chief Thompson there... which they didn't. Although Papa's breakfasts were delicious, out on the trail, the taste of juicy bacon, pancakes with butter and syrup, and brewed coffee was, in the opinion of both men – with no offense intended to Papa's cooking – pure gastronomic bliss. They arrived at the police station at ten minutes to ten.

Captain Thompson wasn't there... having responded to a call about a Peeping Tom at the Pines Motel. Annabelle editorialized – giggling – that it was probably some man looking for his wife. Thompson had told her, she said, to have Paulo wait there for him. Annabelle was, as always, friendly as ever to both of them. Marty decided she was, without a doubt, one of the most unaffectedly cordial human beings he had ever met. She asked about Ginny... to which Marty gave a positive report and added that she'd be along, shortly... which appeared to please Annabelle, immensely. Asked about their stay at Art's cabin, Marty – not wanting to be blatantly disingenuous to this kind, gentle woman, for whom he had developed a great fondness, but also not wanting to open a discussion which would generate untold questions and explanations – said simply, that it was just as beautiful, up there, as he had remembered... and that they had all really enjoyed their stay... feeling guilty as soon as he had committed this fraud by omission.

Taking advantage of Thompson's absence, Marty asked Annabelle if he could fax something to his magazine, to which he knew she would, of course, graciously accommodate. Having made over thirty pages of notes, he knew it would take a good while to complete the faxing process... and sincerely hoped Thompson would not return until the job was finished. As he was tapping his pages on their various edges, to square them for the feeder tray, Annabelle couldn't resist asking.

"Another big story, Marty?"

Marty quickly assessed the situation. He really did like Annabelle... and didn't want to lie to her any further. In a matter of hours, the rest of their party would come walking into Bear Stump, with Papa in the lead, and she'd discover the truth for herself, anyway. He decided to level with her. He put the papers into the feeder tray, dialed the office fax number, waited for the warble of the computer dialogue and then pressed the "send" button. After the paper began to successfully pass through the machine, he sat down in the chair, next to the fax, and searched for an understandable way to begin the incredible story to Annabelle.

"Annabelle... I haven't told you the whole story about what I'm doing here... and I'm sorry... but there were reasons that I couldn't. Everything is going to sort of bust loose here, later on today, and I don't want you to feel that I didn't trust you with what I'm about to tell you."

Marty paused before he began the actual story... pondering how to begin.

"It's a long and kind of strange story that's going on here... kind of hard to know where to begin, actually. You remember in my magazine article... the guy who thought he was God?... this Papa person?"

Annabelle, so enthralled by the potential of the forthcoming tale, merely shook her head in acknowledgement... her eyes open wide.

"Well... I didn't tell the whole story about him. Actually... he also told me that eight people would contact me about the story... and I would bring them here – to him. Well, that's what I'm doing here... not what I told you last week. I've brought these people out to meet him, and now they're on their way here... with Papa... and should be arriving sometime this afternoon. Believe it or not, we're on our way to walk to Los Angeles. Won't be long until the media catches wind of it... then all hell will break loose around here."

Marty stopped to entertain any questions. Instead of a question, Annabelle merely proffered an exclamation.

"My gosh, Marty! Isn't that something?"

"Yes... and there's something else, too. I kind of hesitate to tell you about it... but I guess I'd better. I went out to the mountain with eight people... and only seven are returning."

"Why, Marty?"

Marty's words stuck in his throat and required an effort to retrieve them.

"Well... one of them... Henry... Henry Butler... was killed."

"Oh my goodness, Marty. What happened?"

"He fell from a... a... ah... a kind of stony bridge... that went between two ledges. Fell into a really deep canyon. I suppose I'd better tell Captain Thompson about it, huh?"

"You'd better, Marty. Did Henry have any relatives that should be notified?"

"A daughter and a son."

"Oh my... are they just youngsters?"

"Oh, no... Henry was in his mid-seventies. They're all grown up... both in their forties, I think."

"Do you know their names, Marty?"

"You know... I can't say that I do. Don't even really know, exactly, where either one of them lives. Henry used to teach at William and Mary... as a philosophy professor... and his daughter, as I recall, works in the college book store... and doesn't live too far away. I guess the bookstore would be our best bet for getting in touch with her... then she could let her brother know. He's somewhere in southern California... Silicon Valley, I think... but I have no idea how to find him."

"That's a good idea, Marty. We really should notify his next of kin... and we can't just leave his body out there, either. You may have to go with the Captain and show him where he fell."

"Oh geez... just what I wanted to do. I hate to say it, Annabelle, I know you work for him... but Captain Thompson is a real jerk... I'm sorry to say."

"He can come across like that... I know. But it's just with people he doesn't know. Folks around here really like him. He'd do anything for you."

"Well if that's the case, Annabelle, he's a real Jekyll and Hyde, then. With Paulo and me... he was a jerk... a real jerk."

"I know, Marty... I heard him talking to you. I told him so, too – after you two left... that he shouldn't have been so mean to you boys... and that I thought you were two really nice, young fellas... but he just won't listen. Says you need to keep outsiders on their toes... to avoid trouble before it starts. He's hopeless, I'm afraid."

Just as Annabelle finished her sentence, the object of their discussion walked through the door. He nodded to Annabelle, ignored Marty and Paulo, and disappeared into his office. By some apparent signal, unseen by Marty and Paulo, Annabelle was summoned. She excused herself and joined the chief. Ten, or so, minutes later, she stood at the chief's door and asked Paulo, only, to come in – which he did. She closed the door behind him and returned to sit behind her desk.

Marty immediately asked Annabelle if she had said anything to the chief about Henry Butler. She hadn't, she said... felt it was best coming from him. He then proceeded on another matter.

"We've got another problem here, Annabelle. I'm sure, with my track record, you're not surprised."

Annabelle smiled good-naturedly and tilted her head to the side, as if to say, "Oh, not really."

"Well, as I told you... we are – believe it or not – walking to Los Angeles from here. I know... it's crazy, but nevertheless, that's the plan. The problem is Paulo's parole. We won't be coming back here, anytime soon, if ever... and I frankly don't know exactly where we'll be over the next few months. I calculate that it'll take us a good three months to walk to L.A.... which'll put us there around the beginning of September... if we make it, that is. Personally, I have my doubts if we will. Anyway... Paulo has this special arrangement with Captain Thompson for his parole, you know?... and I don't know what we're going to do about it, after today."

Annabelle looked concerned and squinted her eyes in thought. She spoke while still shaking her head back and forth.

"That's a tough one, Marty. I really don't have any idea what to tell you."

"You think we should say something to the chief about it?"

"Oh... I would, Marty. If Paulo just doesn't show up next week, the chief will take it really bad. He's got quite a temper when people don't do what they're supposed to."

"You don't have to convince me of that, Annabelle. I'm sure you're right... it would be best if we told him... no matter what."

Annabelle shook her head in agreement and sympathy. Paulo emerged from Captain Thompson's office, looking none the worse for the wear. Marty searched his eyes for a more definitive response but was unsuccessful.

"How'd it go?"

"No problem, Mart. I just answered all his questions... didn't break any laws... didn't have any firearms... didn't drink any alcohol..."

With this last answer, Paulo smiled broadly and winked at Marty... not hiding it from Annabelle, borne of his trust in her. She smiled along with him, as if to say... "Your secret's safe with me."

Marty stood up and walked to a corner of the office where he was sure the captain couldn't hear him and jerked his head to the side to beckon Paulo. With their faces toward the window, Marty explained the purpose for the caucus.

"We need to tell the chief about our walk to L.A. You're not going to be here next week... for your appointment... and he'll come looking for you... sure as hell. Annabelle thinks it would be better to tell him ahead of time, so he doesn't have any unpleasant surprises. We also have to tell him about Henry. He's got a son and daughter... and eventually they're going to wonder about him. Besides, we owe it to Henry to tell *someone*. And, as Annabelle just pointed out to me, we just can't leave his body out there... you know?"

Paulo reflected on Marty's assessment of the two situations and agreed with him on both. He inquired, further, about his.

"What, exactly, are we gonna tell him about my parole? I can't believe that man would just let me walk out... knowin I'm gonna break my parole... you know what I mean?"

"Yeah... you're right, Paulo... you're right. Shit."

They stood in silence... both at a loss for a solution. Eventually Marty tilted his head to the side, squinted his eyes, and made a humming sound in his throat. Paulo looked, expectantly, at him.

"What if we tell him that we'll call him every week... every Friday... from some police station... letting the police verify that we're where we say we are... and letting them ask you the questions that Thompson would? What do you think?"

"Might work, amigo. Can't hurt to try."

Marty and Paulo returned to Annabelle's desk and asked her if she'd tell Captain Thompson that they'd like to talk to him about something. She did, then ushered them into his office. He looked up at them, suspiciously. They were heartened, somewhat, when he told them to sit down. Although the invitation was issued in an overtly gruff tone, it certainly constituted a substantial improvement over their first three-way encounter. Marty hoped this meant that either they weren't considered outsiders, as much as before... or, perhaps, Annabelle's admonitions about his lack of cordiality possibly had some effect on him. He began to lose this fragile hope when Thompson merely sat and stared, coldly, at the two of them... not inquiring as to their intended business with him. Assuming he was waiting for them to begin, Marty obliged him.

"There's a couple of things we need to talk to you about Captain Thompson."

No response.

"Well... first of all... ummm... I'm not sure where to start this."

No response.

"I wrote that magazine article. You read it?"

Thompson's head nodded... so slightly that the purpose was unclear. Taking it to be an affirmation, Marty continued.

"I wrote about this man who thought he was God... well... there was a little more to the story than what I wrote. This man, Papa, had me bring some people back here to join him... and that's what I'm doing here. I took them up on the mountain to meet him. Well... to make a long story short... and I already know this is going to sound crazy... but we're all walking from here to Los Angeles... on foot."

At this, Marty paused to assess the Captain's reaction. His stony countenance had altered itself, and he was now looking at Marty as though he were a lunatic. Marty, happy to have produced at least some effect on Thompson, went on.

"Problem is... Paulo's parole. Once we start out, he won't be able to come here for his meeting with you... obviously. We wanted to be up front with you about it and tell you ahead of time... to avoid any trouble, if we can. We had an idea that we'd like to suggest – if you think it's workable."

Thompson leaned his head to the side. His face clearly said, "OK... let's hear your stupid idea."

"We were wondering if it would be possible to arrange, every Friday, for Paulo to check into a police station and call you from there. They could verify to you that we were there... and either they, or you, if you'd like, could ask Paulo the necessary questions. That's what we were wondering, Captain."

Marty wanted to keep it brief. They waited. Thompson leaned back in his chair and looked slowly back and forth at them... appearing to be assessing their credibility. He cocked his head and spoke in a stern voice.

"I'll tell ya what. I'm gonna check with Mandos' central parole office and see what they say. If it's all right with them, then, OK. I don't much care, one way or another. I'd just as soon not have to deal with this bullshit, anyway. Anything else?"

"Well... yes. As I said... I took some people back to the mountain... eight of them."

Marty hesitated – thinking how what he was about to say was going to sound.

"One of them... Henry Butler... fell into a canyon and... ah... was killed."

Thompson's eyes drilled into Marty's.

"People seem to have this way of dying around you, Chapman... don't they?"

"I guess that's kind of the way it looks, Captain... but this was strictly an accident... completely accidental."

"Where's the body?"

"Still there. He's still on the floor of the canyon. I, frankly, have no idea how anyone would get down in there. You might need a helicopter."

"All right. You go out there and write me a complete statement about how this happened. You write everything that happened. If you farted, you write it. Get it?"

"Yes sir."

"While you're doin that, I'll check in with Mandos' parole people."

In the outer office, Paulo found a very out-of-date *Field and Stream* magazine and sat in a chair near the window – vacantly moving his eyes alternately across the pages and the view outside. Marty relayed his instructions from the chief to Annabelle... about writing a detailed account of Henry Butler's death. She gave him a legal pad – he had a pen. He sat in a chair on the opposite side of the room from Paulo so he could compose his thoughts without interruption. He needed to make an immediate decision. Thompson wanted the whole story... and the whole story could prove to be a problem. The whole story would describe Papa encouraging these people to walk across the stone bridge. The whole story would explain that this encouragement is the precise reason why Henry Butler lay dead on the floor of that canyon. This account might, very well, lead to legal problems for Papa – as an accessory of some sort. He could lie about what happened, but Thompson would be sure to question the rest of the party about it. If they told a different story, it might look as though he were trying to cover up what really happened... which might cause Thompson to suspect foul play. Then they'd all be in deep shit. After due consideration, Marty decided that the best course of action would be to tell the whole truth... which he did. It took nearly an hour to complete it – eight full pages. Looking it over, he realized the document could have been much briefer... but he was a professional journalist and took great pride in his work product... be it an article, a post card, or an accident report.

Marty handed his lengthy epistle to Annabelle who, in turn, took it into Captain Thompson. Marty waited nervously for Thompson's reaction. In about twenty minutes he got it. It wasn't good. As he sat in Thompson's office, he greatly regretted his decision to opt for the whole truth.

"So this... Papa guy... talked all these people into risking their lives? Is that what you're trying to say here? And this Henry Butler was killed because this man got him to walk out on this rock?"

"Well... not exactly."

Thompson pointed to the legal pad.

"Isn't that what this says here?"

Thompson began reading the relevant section of the report... his words framed in accusatory intonation.

"... Henry was afraid to cross over to Papa, but Papa encouraged him – telling him everything would be all right..."

Thompson laid the tablet on his desk and glared at Marty.

"Seems to me that's just what you said here, Chapman."

"Yes... that's what I wrote... I know. But you'd have to have been there to really understand how it was. Believe me, Henry walked out on that rock of his own free will. He wanted to do it. He believed in what Papa told him."

"This... Henry... believed this Papa guy was God... that's what you're telling me? And he went out and killed himself because he thought he was talking to God?"

"Well... he didn't actually go out to kill himself."

"Tell me, Chapman... would Mr. Butler have walked out on that rock if this man hadn't told him to do it?"

Marty paused to decide, again, between truth and lies. Never having been a very good liar, he stuck, once again, with the truth.

"No... I don't suppose he would have gone out on his own. Look, Captain Thompson... what's this all about? Where are you going with all this?"

"I've got a second man – dead... up on that mountain, Chapman... in less than a year... and they're both connected with you. In that thing you wrote in that magazine, you said Art Durbin's death was connected with this Papa guy, too, right?"

With the question, Marty could immediately feel his scalp beginning to sweat. The ball of yarn was starting to unravel and he could think of no way, at this point, to keep it from coming completely undone.

"It was... in a way, I guess."

"In what way?"

"Jesus..."

"C'mon, Chapman. Let's get this story out on the table before it gets any worse for you."

"Oh, fuck... look... Art was an old guy... you know that. He met Papa in a very unexpected way. And... it was the whole situation... Papa's appearance... what he said... everything, that did it."

"Tell me about it."

"Oh man... all right... shit. Papa is a really big guy... six-six... six-seven... really muscular... has a beard... he wears leather... leather kilt... leather shirt... deer hide actually. And he said he was God... and he seemed to know all about both of us... when he had no way of knowing. He has this effect on people. It's overwhelming. He makes you happy, afraid, confused... all at once. Art was really affected by him. I was too – but I didn't believe him... about the God thing. Art did. It was just too much for Art, you know? I think he may have had a heart attack or something. He was dead within a couple of hours after meeting him."

Thompson picked up his pen.

"What's this guy's real name?"

"Who... Papa?"

"Yes."

"Ian MacDonald."

"How old is he?"

"Early thirties."

"Where's he from?"

"He was born up on the mountain... lived there his entire life."

"Who were his parents... do you know?"

"Malcolm and Effie MacDonald."

"Where'd they come from?"

"His father was originally from Scotland... then moved to New York. He was a doctor. The mother was from... ah... one of the Caribbean islands... can't think of the name of it at the moment... a French island. You know, Captain Thompson, a lot of this stuff was in my article."

"This is a police report. Parents still around?"

"No."

"Dead?"

"Yes."

"All right. I'm gonna have to talk to Mr. MacDonald."

"Oh Christ... do you really have to, Captain? I mean... it wasn't his fault and he's... he's not used to dealing with the outside world. He's spent his entire life up on that mountain. He's never been in a town before – let alone, interrogated by the police."

"Chapman... by your own account, there'd be two people still alive if it hadn't been for this guy. I'd say that makes him a potentially dangerous person – and I'm gonna find out. Now... where can I find this Mr. MacDonald?"

Marty lowered his head and shook it dejectedly – wishing, so much, he had never opened his mouth or picked up his pen about any of this stuff. He finally looked up and spoke in a quiet, defeated tone.

"He'll be in Bear Stump in a few hours."

"Well, I'll be waiting for em. On Mandos' parole... his case officer said that as long as I stay on as the contact person, they'll go along with it. But you tell Mandos that if he misses a single call… they'll pick his Chicano ass up and take him back where he belongs."

CHAPTER TWELVE

Cars slowed to a near stop as they passed Papa and his companions, walking along the side of the highway – gaping out their windows at this strange and magnificent giant in skins. Some of the young males shouted at him, issuing an unimaginative selection of obscenities and vulgarities, characteristic of the social impairment of that age and gender. Papa simply smiled at them, while the rest of his party reacted with protective anger. At around three o'clock in the afternoon, the travelers entered the main street of Bear Stump. They spotted Marty and Paulo in the distance... coming toward them at a rapid pace. As the two drew near, the distress, written on their faces, was clearly evident. They walked directly to Papa... Marty, shaking his head, his eyes apologetic and his face begging forgiveness for his yet-to-be-revealed transgression. Paulo wore an expression of both compassion and worry. Marty undertook the responsibility of briefing Papa on the troublesome developments.

"Papa... I'm sorry... but there's trouble. I had to tell them about Henry... and now the police want to talk to you about it. I'm really sorry... I shouldn't have said anything. I should have just kept my big mouth shut."

Papa's face remained unperturbed, reacting to Marty's words with no more animation than one might expect to his having reported to him, the local temperature. He patted Marty on the cheek, affectionately, and shook his head in forgiveness and understanding. His voice was pleasant and upbeat.

"Well then, let's go see Captain Thompson, Marty."

"Do you know him?"

"We've never met in person... but I know him."

The answer intrigued Marty... but no longer having the gumption to pursue such matters with Papa, he left it go. The entire group walked along the sidewalk to the Bear Stump Police Station – Papa, Marty, and Paulo in the lead. They were clearly attracting the attention of the townsfolk, as Marty had predicted they would. None of the curious was yet brave enough to talk to anyone in the group, but it was obvious from their spirited exchanges, they knew who Papa was. They had all seen Marty's article... and according to Annabelle, Papa's picture adorned walls and refrigerators all over the Stump. Papa had become something akin to the Loch Ness Monster of Bear Stump – a new local legend – and by far the most interesting thing that had happened in the Stump – again, according to Annabelle – since Larry Moore's murder, back in 1977.

Papa, Marty, and Paulo went into the police station, with Papa in the lead. His head touched the top of the door frame as he entered. Annabelle's eyes opened wide – her jaw dropped – her face froze in position. Papa walked to her desk and smiled warmly at her. She slowly rose to her feet – speechless, overwhelmed, and afraid. Papa, as was his custom in greeting, reached out and gently stroked the side of her face with his massive hand. He leaned down toward her face and spoke in a reassuring tone.

"Do you know who I am, Annabelle?"

Annabelle opened her mouth, even wider, to attempt to form words – but none came out. Papa spoke again.

"Don't be afraid of me. You know who I am."

Annabelle remained speechless, but managed a childlike smile. Thompson's voice boomed from inside his office.

"MacDonald?!"

Papa turned his head slowly to his left and looked at the scowling face, glaring at him from behind the large wooden desk in the adjoining office. He stood up to his full height, turned, and strode

THE MINISTRY

fluidly into Thompson's office – stopping just in front of his desk. Papa looked down at the seated man's, still unpleasant, face... then playfully cocked his head to the side and smiled as a parent would in attempting to coax an improvement in the mood of an angry child. Thompson didn't respond. His features, in fact, hardened even further.

"You're Ian MacDonald?"

"I was born Ian MacDonald."

"Oh yeah... that's right – you're God now, right?"

"Yes, Dennis, I am."

"Who told you that name?"

"That's the name you were given at birth."

"I haven't used that name since I started school. Only a handful of people in the world know that name. You've been snoopin around, haven't you? Who'd you talk to... Chuck Williams... or maybe my brother... huh?"

"No. I know your name, Dennis."

"Are these some of the parlor tricks you do, MacDonald, to get people to think you're God? Gotta come up with one better than that for me, buddy. As far as I'm concerned, you're just some weirdo from the hills. Were you, by any chance, connected with that hippie bunch that we ran outa there a few years ago?"

"My poor Dennis... so angry. I'm so sorry."

"What! You think I give a rat's red ass what you think about me?! Who the fuck do you think you are!... givin me that bullshit. Sit down, MacDonald!"

Papa paused, then slowly lowered himself into the wooden chair...

his body dwarfing it and his expression and posture, that of an exceedingly patient parent. He continued to smile pleasantly at Thompson. Thompson didn't like it.

"What's so funny, MacDonald? You think this is a big joke?"

"You have so much to learn, Dennis. If you'd open your heart, you'd be so much happier."

"Oh, Christ... who the fuck are you... Billy Graham?"

Papa didn't respond. His face took on a look of sadness and he quietly sighed.

"OK... look, MacDonald... let's cut the bullshit. You're here because according to my information, you're directly connected with two deaths – Art Durbin and Henry Butler..."

"Art and Henry are with me now."

"What?"

Papa didn't respond.

"What's that supposed to mean? Is this some more of your God stuff... or are you a grave robber, too?"

"You could understand if you wanted to, Dennis."

Thompson's face reddened with anger.

"All right... I've had about enough of this shit from you, Mr. God. Suppose I just detain you for a good long while about this... think maybe you'd be ready to give me some straight answers then?"

"What would you like to know, Dennis?"

"First of all... don't call me Dennis. I hate that fucking name...

always did. You call me by the name you see on that name plate – Captain Thompson."

"Your father was very cruel to you, Dennis... but he lived with a lot of pain and sorrow, too. He gave you his name on the day you were born... and he loved you very much. He loved you until the moment he died. Your name was the last word on his lips."

Captain Thompson's face instantly softened and looked younger and more vulnerable. A faint glistening appeared in his eyes. He struggled to stem the flow of tears. He looked painfully sad, frightened, and confused. In that unanticipated instant, when his guard was momentarily down, he slipped between the moments into a forgotten world where his heart was still unscarred... and when the warmth of love still bathed his tender, young soul... glowing with the sweetness of a lullaby. His eyes pleaded with Papa to spare him the pain that a heart – opened to the world – could suffer. He lost the struggle. He began to openly weep – his tears instantly washing away years of stony hardness. Papa went to him. He knelt on one knee beside his chair and put an arm around him. Dennis turned to him and buried his face into his broad, protective chest, as would a lost child who was found. Every sob set free years of stored-up hatred and sadness. He cried until the demons that had plagued him since childhood were, at long last, exorcised. Finally, his body gave up the fight and softened like the opening of a tightly clenched fist. Papa stroked the back of his head.

Annabelle had watched the entire, remarkable scene from her desk. Tears ran down her cheeks. She knew she was intruding upon a secret moment but could not force herself to turn away. She watched as Dennis slowly pulled his head from Papa's chest. His eyes spoke the love and gratitude to Papa that his voice could not. Papa leaned forward and kissed his forehead. The scene was one of such love that Annabelle felt her heart could not help but burst in her chest. Marty and Paulo could hear, but would not allow their eyes to invade Dennis Thompson's moment. Annabelle watched Papa as he spoke softly to him – their faces very close together. He then rose to tower over Dennis – making Dennis appear very small... almost childlike. He reached down and softly touched his cheek a last time, then walked quietly out of the office. The Captain got up from his desk and walked to the door. For a brief moment, his eyes met Annabelle's. His face wore a tired, calm joy that comes of laying down a lifetime's burden. He smiled at her with an innocence she had seen, only on the faces of the very young. Very softly, he closed his door. A few moments later they heard his weeping.

CHAPTER THIRTEEN

They spent the night, just south of Bear Stump. By that time, some of the Stump inhabitants had overcome their reticence of approaching the travelers and showed up at their camp site. They brought with them, food and drink for all… and cameras to capture the event for their scrapbooks. It was patently apparent that their initial interest in Papa and his companions was motivated by pure, mundane curiosity… but once in Papa's presence, it became, for some of them, much more than that. As always, Papa instilled in their hearts, a mixture of both love and fear. Some who came – like Papa's disciples – had the trust and courage to open their hearts to him, and accepted him… while others – like Marty – simply could not.

The encounters with some of the visitors were extraordinary… of a nature – Marty would later say – no other word but, miraculous, was apropos. He was witness to lives in spiritual metamorphoses… lumbering, earthy souls, transmuted into buoyant forms of ethereal resplendence. Marty didn't know the true nature of Papa's ultimate essence, but, being near him, he clearly recognized that he was in the presence of greatness… the like of which, he felt, may only occur once in a millennium. He felt both pity and empathy for those who maintained a wall around their hearts – like him – hiding, in fear of letting go… and profound admiration and envy for those who had the courage to believe. Regardless of who Papa was, those who believed in him were clearly and wonderfully affected. Watching this remarkable process, Marty began to understand the powerful, soul-changing nature of true belief – founded or unfounded. It seemed to give instant meaning to life, regardless of how mundane that existence may previously have been. He remembered reading somewhere, that the happiest of all people were those who had a cause in their life, and that, without a cause, life had no true colors. Perhaps, he speculated, Papa was somehow able to provide these very ordinary people with a cause… so much larger, more meaningful, and more urgent than their daily, insipid routines, that its pulsing spectrum bathed their gray existence in a rainbow of life... bringing with it a sense of glory to a commonplace world.

As Marty lay awake that night, he thought of what would likely transpire in the coming days. His notes were, by now, in the hands of the wire services. The next day the story would break – worldwide. Soon thereafter, there would be a crushing onslaught of media... and with that, the intimacy of their small group – that they had all grown to cherish – would be gone, forever. They – and in particular, Papa – would soon become mere players in an enormous media event. The whole story was out there now... the names of the disciples... their backgrounds... their walk across the valley... Henry's death. It was all out – and around the world in a single day.

Marty was plagued with a palpable sense of impending invasion... and the inevitable exposure of something very private and beautiful, held before the vulgar glare and microscopic inspection of the news world. The thought made him nauseous. He knew what was coming... but was sure that neither Papa, nor his followers, had any idea. Cameras and microphones would be shoved in their faces. They'd be asked rude, moronic, insulting questions. Before many days, there'd be Papa T-shirts and Frisbees on the market. Throngs of curiosity seekers would flock to see them – creating a circus, amid the media frenzy. Every talk show would have on their "experts" to analyze the "Papa phenomenon." And worst of all... all of this would bring out the kooks... and many kooks were very dangerous people. Among the disturbed people in the world, Marty was sure that at least one of them might imagine himself playing Judas to Papa's Christ, feeling compelled to carry out the divine mission of making Papa the sacrificial lamb for the sins of mankind. These thoughts plagued Marty to the point that sleep was impossible. He got up and sat near the fire. As he watched the flames turn the dead wood into beautiful, living light, he thought of how Papa was able to do the same thing to, seemingly, dead lives.

As the night wore on, another problem presented itself for Marty's consideration. He began to think about what, exactly, he would say when they stuck a microphone in *his* face. The most obvious question would be to ask if *he* believed that Papa was God. He would have no choice but to say... no, he didn't. Being a journalist, he already knew the follow-up question. Did he think, then, that Papa was a fake? He would be walking right into an interviewer's trap. Once he said he didn't think Papa was God... he must, logically, therefore, think Papa was a faker. He would be stuck, then, with offering weak qualifiers – that while he didn't really believe in Papa as God... Papa himself believed it – so he wasn't really a fake. How blatantly sophistic that would sound! He would try to offer ameliorating observations on Papa's – albeit non-divine – qualities... his great love for mankind... his effect on people... his preternatural ability to know the names and backgrounds of all the people he encounters. Despite all the exculpatory additions he would offer, they would still use Marty's denial of Papa's divinity to impeach Papa's credibility. Even if he said, "No comment," they would use it to the same end. In his mind, he could already hear the questions they would ask Papa... "Sir... Mr. Chapman thinks you're a fake... how do you respond to that?"

He thought of how the others would answer the same questions. They would say – yes – they believed Papa was God. Even Ginny might. Then they'd ask for evidence they had seen of his divinity. Had they seen him perform any miracles? Has he cured the sick... raised the dead? The media would make them look like fools... like cultists... like kooks... like buffoons. All they could really say was that they believed in him... that he had caused a fundamental change in their lives... that he made them lose their hate and fear and made them feel embraced with love... that they were willing to die for him. What more could they say? But nothing they could offer would stand as proof of anything more than this man was a charismatic... linking him to the likes of a David Koresh, a Jim Jones... or even a Charlie Manson.

Marty was pulled from his lamentations by the graying of the morning sky. Everyone would be up soon... and they would be, that day, walking into the tabloid snake pit that had stolen a night's sleep from him. At around noon, as they walked by a service station, Marty read the headlines on the papers through the plastic window of the metal newspaper boxes. It confirmed his previous night's fears. The headline of *USA Today* read, "Self-Proclaimed God walking to L.A." He pulled two quarters from his pants pocket and dropped them into the slot. The rest had walked on to some shade trees near the station and were sitting down for their lunch break – consuming the remains of the food provided by the Bear Stump visitors. Marty sat with them and quickly read through the article. It had the whole story... names, backgrounds, Henry, the valley, their journey. Marty shook his head. It was only a matter of time, now – and not much of it.

At around two o'clock, as they walked south, along the two-lane highway, the first wave of the invasion came from the air. A helicopter with television call letters from Great Falls had spotted them. They could see the cameraman in the hovering craft – filming them as they walked. The aircraft landed a few hundred yards ahead of them and they continued to roll the camera as they approached. A woman jumped out with a microphone in her hand... the cameraman immediately after her. She hurried toward them. Marty audibly expressed his feelings.

"Oh fuck... here we go."

The blonde – a stereotypically dressed and coifed reporter – ran toward Papa. She stopped about fifteen feet from him and did her setup... pressing on her ear piece and concentrating with obvious intensity on whatever communication was coming through it. She looked into the camera and appeared to be composing herself for the shoot. On some cue, unheard by all but her, she commenced with typical, hyperbolic, news reporter animation and gravity.

"That's right Tom... I'm just outside Bear Stump, Montana... and I'm standing a few feet from the man who made headlines, last year, by proclaiming himself to be God. According to our sources, this man – who refers to himself simply as Papa – is leading his group of disciples on a walk from here in Montana... all the way to Los Angeles, California."

As Papa drew near to her, she asked a question then pushed her microphone to his mouth... the foam noise-baffle pressed against his lips. The cameraman zoomed in for a close-up on Papa's face.

"Do you claim to be God?"

Papa reached up and engulfed in his, the small delicate hand that held the microphone. He gently moved it to a comfortable distance from his mouth... then smiled warmly at her.

"Do you think I am, Sharon?"

From the reporter's puzzled reaction, Sharon was apparently her name. She quickly recovered from this mild surprise. Marty surmised that, very likely, she rapidly assessed the situation and probably concluded that Papa had seen her on television... thus memory – not magic – was to account for the accuracy of her identification. She posed the same question again... this time allowing a respectful distance between Papa's mouth and the mike cover.

"Your baby brother's death wasn't your fault, Sharon. It's time you forgive yourself."

Sharon eyes widened. She struggled for words but found none. The hand that held the mike began to visibly shake. Marty noticed that the cameraman had moved his focus from Papa's face to hers. A number of times, Sharon's mouth appeared to be working on the formation of words, but none materialized. Her entire body began to shake... her eyes then rolled back into her head and she collapsed in a dead faint. Unconscious on her feet, her knees buckled and struck the dirt. Her limp body then fell onto its side... her fragile hand still clasping the mike. Papa immediately bent down and scooped her up... as easy as if she were an injured bird. He carried her to the trees that lined the road, laying her, gently, in the grass and putting one of his water skins under her head as a pillow. He knelt beside her and tenderly stroked the side of her face in the fatherly manner, to which his band had become accustomed. Papa's face wore an expression that one would expect of a parent – seeing his child in distress.

As Marty watched Papa – bent over the small blonde reporter – he was, once again, in awe of the overwhelming affect he had on people. He could not accept Papa as God but it was undeniable that he was extraordinarily charismatic and seemed, time and time again, to somehow possess certain knowledge for which there was no apparent and rational explanation. He simply could not have known this reporter's name... and most certainly, would have had absolutely no way of knowing about a remote and very specific event in her past that had had such an obviously profound affect on her life... and given her reaction, quite possibly constituting the most consequential incident in her life.

When he was still going to synagogue, Marty had learned of the great prophets of old who, also, had powers that were beyond explanation... seeing into the future... predicting events. Even today, he thought – though fakes abound – some people still seem to truly possess these extraordinary, unexplainable powers. Marty placed Papa in the category of a mind reader and a clairvoyant. He seemed to be able to read a person's mind with uncanny accuracy... reading both their present thoughts and their memories as well... and – thus far at least – had proven to be a completely accurate prophet of the future. As he thought about people like Papa, Marty realized how easy it would be for any of them to claim omnipotence – in this world of people who were always searching for something or somebody who is not bound by ordinary existence – not confined to the mundane rules *they* were condemned to follow.

As Marty pondered this, he realized there was more to Papa than simply these unusual powers. He also seemed to be love, incarnate – as innocent and pure a love as can exist. That, he felt, was the deep human stream into which Papa tapped with those who believed in him... love – purely and simply – not tricks or power. For that reason, Marty was able to disqualify Papa as merely some psychic oddball. Beyond his extraordinary powers, Marty also admired Papa as a man. He was truly the most unabashedly, loving person Marty had ever encountered... who appeared – so far at least – to have no other agenda in his life than to spread his love and make people happy – to take away their pain. His empathy was heart-wrenching... seeming to feel the pain of everyone he encountered. Though to Marty, Papa wasn't God... he was, without any doubt, the greatest man Marty had ever known... possibly the greatest man who had ever walked the face of the earth. How many others, with the potential power that Papa possessed, would be satisfied with simply bringing love into the world? With Papa's influence over people, there would be no limit to his power on earth. He had an exceptionally beautiful appearance... quite literally, a modern-day Adonis... he was bright, talented, articulate... and manifested an exceptional power to inspire awe in those who meet him. A person like Papa, Marty believed – if he were so inclined – could rule the world... as another Alexander the Great... a Caesar... a Genghis Kahn. But Marty was absolutely sure that Papa had not the slightest interest in earthly power. He was certain that Papa absolutely believed he was God... and would carry out whatever mission this imaginary self-identity was intent upon completing... even if it meant his own death.

After several minutes, the reporter's eyelids began to twitch – then opened. Her face wore a puzzled look – searching for a clue to her whereabouts. Her eyes came to rest on Papa's. He smiled, lovingly, at her... she returned it. As this was going on, Marty noticed that the red light was blinking on the camera and that it was directed at this scene. Papa put a hand behind her head and gently raised her to a sitting position. He spoke softly to her.

"Do you remember me, Sharon?"

For a moment, Sharon's eyes turned inward – searching for an answer to Papa's question. When she returned, she had it.

"Yes... I do. You're the missing part of my soul, aren't you?"

Papa nodded in confirmation... then spoke again.

"Do you want to come home to me?"

"Oh, yes."

"Then you will, Sharon. I'll wait for you. My love will always be with you… until we're together again. I love you, my beautiful child."

Tears were in Sharon's eyes and in all that watched – including the cameraman, who had pulled a handkerchief from his back pocket and wiped his eyes while trying to keep Papa and his reporter in the frame. Papa noticed all the tears.

"Your tears are the water of love from which you came."

Sharon's facial expression, and the movement of her hand toward the plastic piece in her ear, indicated she was receiving a communication. She looked into the camera and spoke in a soft voice – totally abandoning her previous, on-air officiousness. She shook her head as she spoke.

"No."

It was apparent that her unseen, apparent antagonist, spoke to her again. Her eyes returned to the lens.

"Leave him alone, Tom. Robby… cut the feed."

Robby brought his face out from behind his camera and questioned Sharon with his expression, clearly asking, "Are you sure?"

Sharon shook her head, with authority, in the affirmative. Her voice continued to be soft – but with added conviction.

"I mean it, Robby… cut it."

The red light on the camera went dark. Robby lowered his camera and held it at his side by its top handle. Papa looked back at him with quiet kindness. Robby's face reacted to form an expression of puzzled fear. He shook his head slowly – back and forth – turned – and walked with deliberation, back to the helicopter… getting away from Papa as quickly as possible. Papa helped Sharon onto her feet. She stood in front of him, looking up into his face... then looked at the helicopter. She spoke to him in a small voice.

"Good-bye."

Papa put a hand on each side of her face and bent slightly toward her.

"Come back to me, sweet child."

Sharon shook her head up and down in tiny increments... smiled... then gently pulled one of Papa's hands from her face and kissed his palm. She looked at the faces surrounding her and nodded a farewell... then began slowly walking toward the helicopter. Halfway there, she stopped... turned... stood for a last moment to look at Papa... then walked on. As she climbed into the helicopter, the blades immediately began to audibly cut their wide swaths through the air. As they reached the speed of a round, thumping blur, the copter lifted slightly, tilted forward, and, in a matter of moments was out of sight... disappearing behind the green hills that walled both sides of the road.

CHAPTER FOURTEEN

Marty was surprised that the Great Falls crew was the only media that had, by then, located their party. He surmised that, perhaps, no one was completely sure what route they were taking to Los Angeles… of which there were many choices, including both roads and forest trails… so their traveling party could, very well, be difficult to locate in that large, rugged area. He eventually concluded that the Great Falls crew was just plain lucky to find them. But, now that their actual location was known, via the live telecast, it was only a matter of hours before the swarm would descend upon them. The reporter hadn't mentioned their exact whereabouts on the air, but Marty was sure it would get out. There was a general sense, in their evening camp, that this would be the last time they would ever experience the shared and cherished intimacy of what had grown to be a family. They all knew that, very soon, things would never be the same.

By the time they'd broken camp in the morning and taken to the road, the inexorable change began. It was apparent that the report of the Great Falls crew had, in fact, tipped off other media that Papa and his companions were on the road that headed into Columbia Falls. One by one, the news vans and recreational vehicles – with their satellite dishes and station letters, logos, and slogans – found them. Marty was surprised how far some of them had traveled overnight. A few of the teams were in rental vehicles… apparently having flown into either Great Falls or Missoula and picked up a vehicle there. By noon, Marty counted twenty-three vehicles… and at least triple that number in crew members. They immediately began setting up directly in the path of the travelers – the on-air talent, with Papa and his band as a backdrop, doing their setup… necessitating the pilgrims to find a way around them. A small sea of cameramen walked slowly backward, in front of them… their red lights blinking… their on-air people shouting questions.

Papa was completely unperturbed and exceedingly cordial... conducting himself like a senior relative at a family reunion. The rest of his group, however, were becoming visibly agitated... particularly Marty... who indecorously instructed a number of the media to "... get the fuck out of the way." When the growing media throng had reached the point that forward progress had become virtually impossible for his small band, Papa suddenly stopped... surprising the horde into a momentary silence. Very calmly, Papa told the media throng to sit down... and that he would talk to them. Not accustomed to such a request, they looked at one another... then awkwardly – and with a degree of annoyance – acquiesced. They were spread out over the hot asphalt as well as on the grass and dirt of the roadside shoulder. As soon as their bodies made contact with their accommodation, they began to immediately shout questions again. Papa didn't respond. Instead, he stood... looking at the faces before him... giving the unmistakable and uncanny appearance of recognizing each one of them. Papa's comrades remained standing behind him. His continued silence and odd countenance had the effect of eventually quieting the group to a profound whisper. The expression, "... a deafening silence" came to Marty's mind. He also made the odd mental association of Papa's prolonged silence with the newsreels he had seen of Hitler – standing mute, before an enormous multitude for several minutes... waiting until the tension became almost unbearable for the crowd before he finally spoke. As Papa's quiet continued, even the whispers eventually ceased, and the scene took on a strange, dream-like quality. As with all groups that become suddenly and tacitly silent, an air of heightened self-consciousness pervaded... generating a few, inevitable, nervous titters. Papa began speaking in his soft, yet resonating, voice. The microphones were lifted in unison and the blinking cameras zoomed in.

"You are all my children... and I love each one of you. You did not come here to seek my love... but some of you will find it. Others will not. Those who do, will come home to me and will never be alone or in fear again. Those who do not, will continue to wander in fear and loneliness until you can find your way home. I know how confusing your lives are... always living with the question of your purpose and your beginnings… and my heart aches for each of you. Each of you has a memory of me, which I gave you at your birth. I am that part of your soul that you recall and seek, but, often, cannot find. You and I were once together – until I set you free to become a separate spirit from me. I am your parents and you are a part of my body. Remember me. I am that which you seek. I will always love you and I will always wait for you."

The odd silence of the normally raucous, media throng, continued… waiting for more from Papa. After a time, they began to realize that he had, in fact, finished. A man with reddish hair – at the rear of the assembly – shattered the crystalline silence with his grating, pompous voice.

"Do you really expect us to believe that you're God?"

"I hope that you will know me… but many of you will not."

Another voice – a female – followed up.

"What can you do to prove you're God?"

"The proof can be nowhere but in your heart."

With the hounds on the scent, the pack now began baying.

"What do you have to say to those who think you're just another cult leader?"

"My heart aches for them."

"Can you perform miracles?"

"Yes."

"Go ahead, then… show us your stuff."

"I am your parent… not a magician. I've come to love you…

not to frighten you or entertain you."

"Is it true that you deny that Jesus was the son of God?"

"No. He was my son."

"Was Jesus divine… as you say you are?"

"No."

"So you're saying that Jesus was not divine… that he was just another ordinary human being like the rest of us?"

"He was one of my children… as are all of you."

"Why are you walking to Los Angeles?"

"To meet my children."

"Are you aware that there are already death threats against you?"

"Yes."

"Are you worried about them?"

"I am heartbroken."

"Why?"

"What parent would not be… to know that some of his children fear him so much that they would want to kill him?"

A tall, thin woman stood up… leaving her microphone lie on the grass. She made her way through the seated crowd to Papa and stood close, in front of him. She looked up, humbly, at his face.

"Can I stay with you, Papa? I know who you are."

Papa reached out his arms and embraced her. He called her by her name. The cameras were all focused on the two of them. Someone shouted out a question to her.

"Are you a plant?"

She turned toward the direction of the question... smiled... then quietly laughed. Her cameraman shouted out.

"I can tell you that she's not a plant... she's never seen this guy before in her life. She told me she thought he was a kook on the way up here."

Five more people came forward to join Papa. Marty was astonished. If there was one group of people he felt he knew, it was the media. They were callous, self-centered, skeptics – the last kind of people Marty felt would ever buy into Papa's story. His mind then began to turn on a sinister possibility. He knew there was virtually nothing a newsperson wouldn't do for a story – proclaiming to be a believer included, if that's what it took. If they could infiltrate the inner circle, they'd have a great advantage for their story. His suspicions piqued, Marty began studying the new, self-proclaimed converts with a jaundiced eye.

Papa spent some time with the six who had emerged from the crowd... explaining some things to them... addressing each by their name and answering many questions, to which Papa's companions had become accustomed. If they were, in fact, infiltrators, Marty could find nothing in their actions to substantiate it. All seemed as genuinely affected by Papa as had other such converts they had encountered.

With the new members of the group appearing satisfied with their initial meeting with Papa – at least for the moment – he resumed his journey... his expanded group following and the media allowed them to proceed forward, following a short distance behind. They camped that night, just north of Columbia Falls... the media in their vehicles... Papa and his people out under the stars. Throughout the evening, there was a steady stream of new people arriving at the site... some media, but many others, a combined chorus of curiosity seekers and those who truly desired to meet Papa for spiritual reasons. Late into the night, Papa met and talked with these people. Some embraced him as God... others did not. As dawn awakened Marty and Ginny, they sat up and surveyed the entourage that had greatly expanded overnight. They guessed that there were now, at least two hundred people at the campsite. Fortunately, many of the newcomers brought food and drink with them and graciously shared it with everybody. To the gratitude of all, some in the media had been resourceful enough to bring along toilet paper for their assignment... which they also shared.

In this vein, toilet – and hygienic accommodations, in general – were becoming a pressing concern for everyone. When Papa and his small band were alone, the woods and streams were adequate for their needs. These natural accommodations were, however, no longer ample for the rapidly enlarging assembly. While the media, who had come in their recreational vehicles, had their own limited toilet and water access, those who had come in vans, cars, or on foot, obviously did not. The state authorities were soon alerted to this growing problem, via the mobile phones of the press, and responded by dispatching a water tanker and a number of portable johns, mounted on trailers.

By the time the L.A.-bound travelers reached Route 481, leading into Columbia Falls, their numbers had grown to such proportions that both lanes of the highway were completely blocked, causing obvious traffic problems. The state police were called in and, with the aid of loudspeakers, they herded the southbound army onto the shoulder of the road... then stayed on, thereafter, to direct the normal vehicular traffic around them. Even with the assistance of the police, however, the traffic continued to be a substantial problem – due to rubberneckers trying to catch a glimpse of the now-famous Papa. As the large band headed into the center of Columbia Falls, they could see the sides of the streets, lined with people, giving the appearance of a Fourth of July parade. As they started down the main street of town – preceded by a police escort – the travelers witnessed an incident that promised to become a frequent occurrence on their long journey.

A small, undernourished woman in ill-fitting clothes, carrying a small baby in her arms, ran up to Papa with a wild, desperate look in her eyes. In a dialect and sentence construction that betrayed her lowly birth and minimal education, she told him that her baby was dying... that he was born with a bad heart and that the doctors said they could do nothing for him. In heartrending pleas, she begged Papa to cure her tiny son.

Papa stopped and looked into her eyes... his face formed to express great sorrow and understanding... his eyes glistened with tears. He took the baby from her arms and looked at it as lovingly as Marty had ever seen any parent gaze upon a child. He brought the baby's small face to his and lightly kissed him on the cheek. He spoke to the baby... his voice thick with emotion.

"My precious Daniel. The burden of freedom is so large... and you are so small."

He looked at Daniel's mother and smiled with great compassion.

"There is much you cannot understand, Martha... but I promise you, my dear child... your baby Daniel will be soon born into a new, healthy body... and he will have the strength and freedom to come home to me. When you are both with me, you will never, again, be separated. You will never be heartbroken again. Will you come home to me, Martha?"

Martha's face was both puzzled and hopeful.

"How can I do it? I don't know how. I'm a poor, stupid woman."

Papa handed Daniel to Katherine – who was standing to his left – and embraced Martha... his right hand caressing the back of her head... rocking side to side as he held her... speaking quiet, private words into her ear. He drew away from her slightly.

"If you love me and want to be with me... we'll be together... that's all you need to know. From this moment on, your heart will be filled with love for all of your brothers and sisters on earth.

When you pass over the valley to me… you will have no fear and when you open your eyes, you'll be in my arms. All of my children are born, knowing in their hearts who I am, and how to find me. Some of their hearts harden and they lose their way. Do you remember me, Martha?"

The look in Martha's eyes was that of unmistakable recognition. It was the expression of someone who suddenly recognizes that a stranger he has encountered is, actually, an old friend. She shook her head up and down with a childlike bearing.

"Uh huh… you're my father that loves me. When I'm scared… I remember you. I remember when I was with you."

Papa took Daniel from Katherine and laid him, gently, back into Martha's arms. Then, as Marty had seen him do so often, he put his hands on the sides of her face and spoke to her very softly.

"I've always loved you, Martha. You're not a stupid woman. My other children just can't see the goodness in your heart. You and Daniel will be with me, someday. I'm always with you, my loving child. You are never alone."

Papa kissed her forehead. She smiled at him with a radiant innocence and spoke to Papa with the freshness of a child.

"I love you."

She turned and, as quickly as she had appeared, she vanished into the crowd.

CHAPTER FIFTEEN

Over the next six weeks, the southbound procession steadily grew in size... to eventually number in the thousands... requiring additional police presence and state assistance to meet the growing hygienic demands. The increased size of the police contingent turned out to be an unexpected blessing for Paulo. It was not unusual for the travelers to be on the road on Friday, nowhere near a town, making it, therefore, very difficult for him to fulfill his parole responsibility of reporting to a police station. With the problem becoming evident, Marty and Paulo approached the state police, who were assigned to the caravan, and inquired if they'd be willing to phone Thompson's office on their mobile phone units and verify Paulo's appearance before them... as well as ask him the standard parole questions. Both Paulo and Marty were pleasantly surprised by their rather cheerful cooperativeness. They did as requested, and Captain Thompson had no objections to the modified procedure.

It became a quickly established tradition of those who came to join them – as well as residents of the towns they passed through – to bring food and drink for the travelers. Also, after a while, the close companions of Papa had come to anticipate the various types of people who would arrive to join their company. Besides the media – which was now worldwide – the others were usually of two types... curiosity seekers and those with a true spiritual desire to be with Papa. The curiosity seekers were always interim members of the party... coming, snapping photos, collecting souvenirs and then departing when the novelty wore thin. Of the spiritual pilgrims, some seemed to find in Papa what they sought... but many did not. Of those who accepted Papa as divine – many stayed on for the journey... giving up jobs, family, and many of life's other normal commitments.

A routine also evolved with the media, according to which the veteran members would informally brief neophytes on the tenets of protocol. Instead of impeding the daily progress of the processional with impromptu interviews, as the multitude settled into camp for the night, Papa would routinely go among the media and answer their questions with many newcomers, of course, repeating inquiries that had been often posed before – exasperating the old-timers – to which Papa would, however, graciously answer, once again. Looking to expand the scope of their story and find new angles to maintain consumer interest, the media also began interviewing and photographing the marvelous assortment of people who had come to join the migrating congregation. In continued, high demand, of course, were Papa, the original disciples, and Marty and Ginny. In this capacity, Marty was becoming progressively more uncomfortable with occupying the compromising position of both writer and subject of the unfolding story.

Another type that began arriving, soon after they were on the road, were literary agents... looking to sign central figures in the story to book contracts. Many asked Marty if he thought he could convince Papa to give them an exclusive contract... offering him a handsome fee if he could so prevail. Marty uniformly responded, simply, with a scornful laugh. When asked about signing to do his own exclusive, he informed them that he was "spoken for." With none of the original group willing to sign book deals, the agents moved onto secondary players in the drama – those who had followed the group long enough that – with some literary embellishment – they'd be able to manufacture some semblance of an insider story.

Among other things, to which the now-seasoned travelers had grown accustomed, was the almost constantly hovering of helicopters overhead – their massive blades compressing the air into a crescendo of bass thumps, while sending the dramatic sky-view footage of the enormous southward march back to their stations for the evening news – their ubiquitous presence creating a battle-zone atmosphere.

On the Fourth of July, they entered Salt Lake City... the first major city on their journey to L.A., which had cancelled its own parade, in lieu of watching, instead, the now, massive contingent of pilgrims and hangers-on, file through their streets. Here, a new element was found, waiting among the crowd, to greet them. As they proceeded through the wide streets of the downtown area, mixed among the normal sightseers along the overflowing sidewalks, were protestors, carrying a variety of messages written on large sign boards. Some were directed toward Papa – "Get Thee Behind Me Satan" "Jesus is God" "God Save Us From The Anti-Christ" "I Worship The Only True God." Some were obviously directed toward the disciples – "Repent Harlot" "Thou Shall Not Kill" "Homosexuality Is An Abomination To The Lord" "A Millstone For The Child Abuser."

As the parade passed center city and began its march toward the outer limits of the town, a man – dressed in a well-tailored black suit, stiffly starched white dress shirt, and deep red tie – ran suddenly from the side of the street toward Papa, carrying a shiny metal bucket. He stopped directly in front of him... held the bucket handle with one hand and placed his other under its bottom... then heaved its contents at Papa. The dark-reddish liquid emptied from its vessel and splashed onto Papa's face and chest... also wetting Paulo and Veronica, standing on either side of him. The man – with crazed eyes and the haunting voice of an obsessed fanatic – shouted at Papa.

"The blood of our Lord Jesus Christ was shed for you, sinner!!"

The small original band of followers, who were always the closest to him as they walked, immediately encircled Papa... fearing for his safety. They worked to wipe the quickly drying liquid from his face... recognizing immediately, from its sticky consistency, that it was blood. As soon as he comprehended what was happening, Paulo had lunged for the blood-thrower... driving his head, powerfully, into the man's chest... knocking him completely off his feet... his back slamming into the hot black pavement... the back of his head whipping violently downward and colliding solidly with the street. He was knocked, instantly, unconscious by the impact, and lay motionless on the sweltering asphalt. Paulo climbed from on top of his body and stood above him, glaring, his fists tightly clenched. Realizing what he had done, he turned to look at Papa with eyes that were apologetic for having reacted with such unthinking violence. Papa responded with a look of understanding forgiveness, then – with his face still streaked with the dried blood – knelt beside the unconscious man. He slid an arm under his shoulders and knees... stood up with him in his arms and carried him through the crowd... into the shade of a tall bank building... laying him on a small plot of manicured grass. Papa remained by the man's side – his knees on the grass – until he recovered consciousness. He then leaned down toward his attacker's face and spoke to him.

"Someday, you'll know who I am, Ronald... and you'll find peace. I ache for your troubled soul. Open your heart and you'll find your way home."

The man blinked his eyes repeatedly... looking as though he were searching for a familiar perspective... but unable to find it. Papa kissed his forehead, smiled at him, then rose and returned to the street.

The dangers of their mission... both to Papa and to his entourage... had, with this act, become very real. The man with the bucket of blood, they all now realized, could just as easily have been carrying an automatic weapon in his hands. Marty's and Ginny's original fears were thus renewed... each worrying that something could happen to the other... or to Papa or the small band of companions they had grown to love.

With the summer wearing on, and the massive, slow-moving, southbound procession nearing the legendary heat of Nevada, the daytime temperature became a vital safety concern. The sun radiated, unmercifully, down upon the travelers – most of them on foot – from the ever-cloudless sky, without abatement. The highway's blackness drew the sun's heat and returned it with enhanced cruelty, baking the pilgrims from below, as well as from above. The wind from the desert added the hot breath from nature's fiery oven to their misery. The size of the enormous human snake, winding its way south on Interstate 15, was now estimated by the media – from assessments of aerial footage – to be approaching ten thousand in number and medical units had become a standard fixture in their ever-growing caravan… tending to a wide variety of maladies commonly found among any large group of people and, as they progressed southward, to increasing numbers of problems caused by the unrelenting heat.

For the safety of his following, Papa adjusted their hours of walking and resting, virtually reversing night and day… rising at nine o'clock in the evening and walking until six in the morning… resting during the heat of the day under all manner of imaginatively rigged shade, while consuming plentiful amounts of liquid, then taking to the road, once again, in the evening. This adjustment significantly reduced the number of heat-related medical emergencies.

In early August, they were camped just outside of Las Vegas, Nevada. As the last, large city they would pass through before reaching Los Angeles – that offered, therefore, satisfactory accommodations to those who were interested in joining the historic event at a late, less demanding juncture of the journey, the city was, thus, inundated by these Johnny-come-latelys… wanting to be able to say that they were a part of what many in the media were now labeling, ". . . one of the most significant events in modern history." With every hotel and motel room in the city rented, residents began opening their homes to visitors for a handsome price per night. No longtime resident of the city could recall anything that had come even close to matching this remarkable phenomenon. It was even bigger, many old-timers volunteered, than the day Bugsy Siegel opened the Flamingo.

Knowing they were expected to pass through Las Vegas during the daytime, Papa had his people sleep that night, instead of walking, to accommodate the following day's anticipated audience. The massive contingent got underway at about nine in the morning. Still five miles from town, they were already passing through a crowd, assembled on either side of the highway. Due to the size of the westward-moving horde, the Nevada State Police had been compelled to close both sides of the highway, west of town, to allow the movement of the eight-thousand-strong group of followers. As usual, the media vans had departed earlier than the foot-travelers to set up at a select vantage point along the route.

The unique character of the awaiting crowd was immediately apparent to the marchers. Though Salt Lake City had its protestors, they had demonstrated – with the exception of the blood thrower – with a rather high degree of decorum... and even *he* had a somewhat rational – albeit extreme – message. The Las Vegas crowd was, however, loud, crude, and openly irreverent... acting more like a prize-fight mob, and who had patronized saloons and casinos for most of the previous night and were possessed of a grimy, carnal disposition. Most seemed to delight in taking distasteful exception to the passing marchers... defining themselves more as hecklers than protestors. Their messages were not on placards, as in Salt Lake, but were conveyed by loud, coarse, bellowing voices... much of it aimed at the small original band, always at the front of the procession.

"God ain't no nigger!" "Fuckin faggot!" "Fuckin whore!" "Hey! It's a nigger in a skirt!" "Tight-ass bitch!" "Wetback!" "Hey convict! Gettin any booty from the faggot?!" "Baby Raper!" "Go back to Canada, Frog!"

The raucous, circus-like atmosphere intensified, even more so, as they entered the city limits. Vendors were peddling a myriad of Papa novelties... shirts, hats, rubber masks, banners, balloons... as well as food and cold drinks, including beer for those who wished to continue their previous night's festivities. All along the street, people were hurling things at the passersby... food, balled up paper, half-filled beer and soda cups. Some dropped water-filled condoms from the windows of the hotels. They greeted the Los Angeles-bound marchers as though they were a parade of circus freaks... and the colorful, blinking swirl of lights from the casino marques completed the bacchanalian scene.

As the three, rapid, cracking noises split the air, a simultaneous shriek went up from the crowd as though it were issued from one voice. What had been an enormous, standing multitude was now a massive pile of bodies – thrown, by their own volition, onto the wide sidewalks. The passing army crouched low to the street... their hands covering their heads. Of the thousands of marchers, only Papa remained standing, appearing like an oak tree in a pasture. The deafening, crowd noise had stopped so suddenly that the absolute silence was startling. Heads slowly began to look up... cautiously testing for safety. A slight murmur began. All eyes became focused on the giant man... standing alone among the still-crouching throng. They watched as Papa turned to his left to look down at someone lying in the center of the wide street. They watched him as he bent down and picked up a small, thin man... his lifeless body, draped across his large, muscled arms... his small head lying against his massive chest. They watched as a few of the people, who had been crouching close to Papa, stood up and surrounded him. The still-silent crowd watched them embrace one another and then heard their weeping.

Katherine spoke with tears in her voice.

"Oh, Papa... that poor, poor, lonely boy. He never had a chance at happiness. The world was so cruel to him... so cruel."

With tears running down his cheeks, Papa spoke through his emotion.

"He's in my arms now... forevermore."

Papa bent his head forward and kissed Aaron's thin, small lips.

One of the bullets had passed through the right side of Aaron's head and had torn away the very same area that he, by his own hand, on that dark day of his short life, had ripped apart with another such violent, leaden missile. But the assassin had been more accurate than Aaron... and succeeded where he had failed. Blood from the left side of Aaron's head flowed down Papa's shirt and kilt... onto his bare legs. With Aaron's limp body draped across his arms, Papa began walking slowly forward... the original group of companions, following close behind. The remainder of the mass contingent stayed where they were...

watching as the small band of friends walked on. The once-boisterous crowd had been instantly sobered by the awesome sight of death and was now exceedingly quiet – almost to the point of reverence. The murder had, in a matter of moments, turned a circus parade into a wake. The sound of approaching police and emergency vehicles could be heard. They arrived from the east and stopped in front of the small circle of intimates. The onlookers watched as the paramedics took Aaron from Papa's arms, laid him on a gurney, and lifted him into the ambulance.

CHAPTER SIXTEEN

Aaron's death dug a valley of fear around Papa... so deep that it frightened off many of the new followers who found they lacked the courage to cross over. Of the eight thousand, self-proclaimed followers who had entered Las Vegas with Papa that morning, only about two thousand were camped with him that evening. Papa made it a point to embrace each one who remained.

The atmosphere of the march had, with this murder, changed dramatically. The sense of purposeful joy was replaced by the somber realization that, belief in Papa carried with it, consequential dangers. Those who had looked upon Papa, simply as a novelty or cultural icon, had, after Aaron's murder, quietly disappeared. The followers, who remained, were only those who had truly accepted him as God. They now understand that Papa constituted a great threat to a great many people... so much so that some would want to kill him because of it. None of them had any doubt that the bullet that tore through Aaron's skull was intended for Papa, and the willingness to face death for their faith in him, created a new bond among the remaining believers.

Aaron's murder also had an impact on the media... giving them a fresh and sensational slant. This new angle attracted even more media interest and the news contingent grew considerably... outnumbering, for a time, the size of Papa's non-media following.

They were now heading into the Mojave Desert and some of the hottest temperatures on the face of the earth. Of the remaining two hundred miles to Los Angeles, some two-thirds of it would be through this barren, hellish wasteland. In response to the life-threatening conditions they were about to face, Papa curtailed the hours of walking to only five a day – from nine in the evening until two in the morning – allowing the remaining hours of the surprisingly chilly nights, for sleep. They would continue sleeping until the heat of the day made it prohibitive... then remain relatively immobile, during the remainder of the day. Papa requested increased water supplies from the state authorities and encouraged his people to increase their daily intake. Given the extreme conditions this large group of people would encounter... and the anticipated health problems that would result... the Red Cross dispatched a sizeable contingent to accompany the travelers.

Despite these precautions, the incidence of heat-related medical problems, nevertheless, rose dramatically... and continued to worsen as they proceeded deeper into the heart of the desert. As they crossed the border, into California, through an area just south of Death Valley, they had a near-epidemic of emergencies, necessitating the procession to halt its progress for two days, to allow the victims sufficient time to recover. Several dozen cases were so severe they had to be transported to the nearest hospitals for treatment. One such person... a seventy-six-year-old woman... died from complications of heat exhaustion.

In the early afternoon of their fifth day in California, both Ginny and Susan fell victim to the merciless heat. Ginny was particularly ill... requiring several courses of intravenous hydration. As would be expected, Marty was beside himself with worry... and anger – angry that he had gotten her into this mess, and angry at Papa for talking them all into what he was now regularly referring to as "unmitigated insanity." He was ready to quit... and told Ginny so. Ginny, despite her suffering, wasn't. They stayed.

Papa's endurance and strength, were absolutely remarkable. He appeared so unaffected by the heat that everyone else was sure, had it not been for them, he could easily have kept walking – right through the heat of midday.

After a seemingly interminable two weeks, they, at last, approached the hills around Lake Arrowhead, and the temperatures finally began to moderate. They had made it through the desert and the sight of trees and grass was extraordinarily wonderful. And with the moderation in temperature, they were finally able to resume a normal pattern of rising with the sun and sleeping with the moon. And, as with all who have endured great suffering together, despite the harsh words and short tempers that pervaded throughout the ordeal, all was quickly forgotten, or magnanimously forgiven, as soon as the cup passed from them... and, having reached safety, all regarded one another as veterans of a common battle.

They reached Interstate 10 and began the directly westward walk toward the outskirts of Los Angeles. Nearing their final destination, they were, again, inundated by a new, mixed horde of people... more media, the curious, the spiritual, and the hateful. On the evening before they entered the City of Los Angeles, Papa and his original band, escaped the huge crowd – under the cover of darkness – to seek their last, private moments together. They retreated to a hill – deep with long grass, dry and brown from the summer heat – its crest lined with a wide assortment of trees.

The moon was full in the cloudless sky and they were able to see one another clearly... colored by the bluish luminescence of the reflected glow. To the west, a sea of lights from the City of Angels glittered below them. They dispensed with a fire... fearing the blaze might attract the curious. As is the case with old friends who have gone through so much together, their isolation from the crowd heightened their special attachment to one another... and their common memories gave rise to inevitable reminiscences. This private time served to review their collective experiences... as if by ascribing words to their time together would give credence to the fact that it had really happened... and that, if spoken about, would never be forgotten.

After they had done justice to their collective history, Papa played his flute... and all were alone, for a time, with their private thoughts. As this intimate time together was coming to an end, each of them knew it would be the last. They all knew they would never be together – like this – again. Once they were in Los Angeles, they would all belong to the world. Sensing their feelings, Papa spoke to them.

"I'm not going to be with you much longer... as I am right now. But you know I'll never leave you."

THE MINISTRY

The sound of his disciples sobbing affected Papa and tears ran from his eyes as well.

"I will miss being able to touch you... to hold you... to feel you in my arms. My arms will ache for you as a mother for her newborn child."

Veronica pleaded.

"Oh Papa... can't you please stay with us? I don't know if I can go on without you... my heart will break if I lose you... it will. Can't you find a way to stay? You could meet so many more of your children... and save them like you saved us. Please Papa... please."

Papa rose and went to Veronica... sitting beside her and wrapping his huge arm around her shoulders. With this, she wept even louder and put her face into his chest... as a small, sad child with her father. He spoke to all of them.

"We will miss one another... and our hearts will ache for the arms of the other. I will miss you, ever as much as you will miss me. But you know, now, who I am... and you will tell your brothers and sisters who I am. You will bring great happiness to my children on earth. They can be just as happy as you. My time must end on this earth... but my spirit is forevermore. You will never, again, be alone. You will feel me beside you, forever. You will feel my love in you, forever."

David spoke.

"But Papa... I don't know what, exactly, I'm supposed to do... what to say... where to go. I want every one of your children to know about you... and learn to live and die in your love... but how are we supposed to do this? There are so few of us."

"After I've left this child's body... you'll know. Will you trust me, David? Will all of you trust me?"

All were silent for a while... searching their hearts for their feelings. Then – one by one – each of the disciples' heads nodded. Marty and Ginny began to feel the great distance between themselves and the rest... and Marty spoke of it.

"Look... I kinda feel as though Ginny and I shouldn't be here. These are very private things you're talking about. You're all believers... and you know that Ginny and I both love all of you... and will remember you for the rest of our lives... but we're just not one of you. You know what I mean. I think it might be best if the two of us allow you to have this time together... without us."

Ginny's nod indicated her concurrence with Marty's sentiments.

Speaking all together, in many different words, but with the same message, the disciples expressed their love for Ginny and Marty... and acknowledged that none of the many wonderful things that had happened to them would have, if it hadn't been for the two of them. Because they didn't accept Papa as God, didn't make them love the two of them any less.

As Marty listened to their loving words, he, once again, envied their faith... and he felt guilty about Ginny. If it hadn't been for her loving him, she would have become one of them. He looked at her as he thought this. She read his thoughts... and squeezed his hand to say that she had made her choice and she was happy with it.

With dawn approaching, they all walked back to the large encampment together. Their hearts were bursting with love... and breaking with sorrow... mourning the end of this intimate chapter of their lives.

BOOK FOUR

JOHN

JOHN

CHAPTER ONE

Power is the currency of pleasure. Pleasure is the sole meaning to life. Given his quite simplistic model of human endeavor, John Hennessey went to great lengths to maintain and protect his power… and his attention to these matters had rewarded him abundantly. He had discovered that the achievement of great power really wasn't very difficult if one is able to avoid being affected by life's many distractions and detours… conscience being among the primary culprits. In John Hennessey's assessment, two of the greatest men who ever lived were Friedrich Nietzsche and Niccolo Machiavelli. Both had decried conscience as a debilitating sickness of mankind. They understood that pity and guilt would cause a man to hesitate – and in that moment of indecision, someone with steadier nerve and greater resolve would overcome and conquer. John Hennessey's nerve had never wavered. His focus had never blurred. His will had never bent. He was a successful man… a rich man… a powerful man… a happy man – and his bounty had continued to grow with each passing season.

In his sixth and last year of his first term in the United States Senate – at age forty-two – John Hennessey was considered the top contender for his party's nomination for the presidency – two years hence – if he could win big in his upcoming senate reelection. Jimmy Parling – Hennessey's administrative assistant since his first term as a California congressman – had proven to be his virtual alter ego. Their values and views of life were, for all intents and purposes, a mirror image of the other. Either would, without hesitation, stab the other in the back, if necessary, but given the mutual benefit they provided one another, the necessity had never, as yet, materialized. Both were happy men. Both had power – Jimmy's a derivative of John's – money, possessions, and abundant sex with beautiful women. The only thing John had, that Jimmy didn't, was fame… which Jimmy was willing to forego, given the rest of the beneficent package his association with John Hennessey had bestowed upon him.

Anyone who had power – or who gave the appearance of having it – John Hennessey followed very carefully... regardless of the field or enterprise. John understood that power was the same element – the same currency – and could be spent in the same way, anywhere, for anything, irrespective of its genesis. There was, in John Hennessey's view, a finite amount of power in the world, thus, power possessed by anyone else, besides himself, was just that much that could – and should – rightly, be his. John, thus, felt threatened and covetous of other power... and the greater the power, the greater his concern.

Among his large, senatorial staff were three staff assistants, assigned to the singular task of monitoring power... rather unimaginatively self-designated as "The Power Company." They would, in fulfilling their mission, scour all media... from the blue chip network news to the tabloid rags to the internet... for indications of growing power bases. Once detected, they would track it. When it appeared that some group, or individual, was gaining a foothold and establishing a true and consequential base, they would bring it to Senator Hennessey's attention. He would assess it. If it could have even a tangential effect on his own ambitions, he would order the "Company" to prepare a strategic analysis and a list of options for his consideration. The options normally consisted of three choices. If the power base could be worked in a fashion to the Senator's advantage, the plan would call for methods of harnessing it. If determined to be irrelevant to the senator's interests – at least at that given juncture in time – it would be kept under continued surveillance... watching for changes in its direction and effect. If it were deemed to be potentially harmful to Hennessey, and not susceptible to being harnessed, the recommended option was, without exception, to crush it in the most effective and sanitary method – "sanitary," defined as leaving the least traceable path back to the Senator.

With Senator Hennessey's new, White House ambitions, the scope of the Company's review was greatly expanded... and, thus, was the respective size of the team as well – growing from three to seven members. Hennessey's standard budget allotment for office and staff from the Senate Budget Office covered, of course, only a small portion of the cost of his operation... the remainder funded by his enormous – and growing – private contribution base.

One of the power bases that had been subject to consistent, long-term tracking was the Religious Right. The original assessment of the movement placed it into option two – irrelevant for the moment... continue to monitor. In the space of five years, however, it had been upgraded to "significant" and a plan was developed to harness its power for the Senator. The strategy worked so well that the Right eventually became a primary force in John Hennessey's election to the Senate, and for his advanced pole position in the presidential derby. Hennessey's staffers were now in constant contact with the Right on every fundamental issue and senate bill... and on the mailing list for every fund-raiser – to which they responded with great benevolence.

Essential to the ambitions of men such as John Hennessey are devotees who are consumed by blind loyalty. Frederick Westin – head of the Company – known by the staff as "Ready Freddy" – was just such a man. Freddy earned his name by his willingness to follow any order without question or hesitation. Jimmy Parling had often said of Freddy, that, if ordered to firebomb his grandmother's house, the only question he'd ask would be "when?"

Fred was an "army brat"... raised on military facilities throughout the world... his father a career NCO. To the present day, the only term he had ever used in addressing his father was, "sir." The essence of a good life was very simply defined by Freddy – following orders. That's what a good man did. If someone performed an assignment – any assignment – under direct order... according to Fred's elemental, moral paradigm... he should never be faulted. To Freddy, the greatest crime of the Second World War was the Nuremberg trials. In Freddy's mind, the soldiers, there, were prosecuted for the virtuous act of remaining true to their commander. Such valor, according to Fred's view of the world, should be commended – not condemned.

There were many times that – in order to carry out certain assignments ordered by the Senator – law had to be violated. These duties uniformly fell upon Ready Freddy. Hennessey had total faith in Freddy's loyalty... and his willingness to keep his mouth shut if he were caught. To serve time on behalf of his commander would be, in Freddy's judgment, an honor.

With more and more of the office staff focused on the presidential nomination, a considerable part of the Senator's day was consumed with strategy meetings and political trips. Hennessey wasn't yet a declared candidate... but he was acting very much like one. He was firming-up his alliances with the party structures in the early primary states and working on key endorsements... as well as continually building his campaign chest for both his senatorial campaign and the White House run. During the six years of Hennessey's term, Fred had been accustomed to daily access to his commander. With the press of the new agenda, however, he was becoming increasingly frustrated over his isolation from Hennessey... and angry over his status reduction to that of being ancillary to the operation.

Searching for a way to regain access, back into Hennessey's intimate circle, Freddy began following the Papa phenomenon, immediately after the initial article was published about him... personally traveling to Bear Stump, Montana, to conduct a firsthand inquiry into the matter. He assembled an impressive file on the story and was exceedingly pleased with the interest, exhibited by the senator, regarding the subject. During the several months that the story received copious coverage, Freddy often met with the senator, several times a week on it. With the media's inability to locate this Papa character, however, the story eventually faded into journalistic oblivion... and Freddy was reluctantly compelled to place the story among the inactive files... and move on to focus his attention on another matter... this time, the coagulation of frustrated white males into a distinguishable unit of political power.

Among the flood of daily issues, with which John Hennessey routinely dealt, were his young son's antics, which were among the most frustrating... and potentially the most dangerous to his ambitions. With his latest escapade, young John Hennessey – the third – had made the wire services... arrested for selling marijuana to his school chums at Hillgrove Academy. He had just turned fourteen and the degree of his antisocial behavior seemed to be growing in direct proportion to his accumulating years on the planet. Senator Hennessey had moved him, often, from school to school... hoping a new environment might give him a fresh and more constructive perspective. It hadn't. With the White House now on the horizon, this sort of continued, aberrant behavior had become wholly insufferable and begged an unfailing resolution. Hennessey and his staff were well aware that a father who's perceived as not being able to control his own teenage son is a man who is deemed not fit for the Oval Office. Jimmy Parling set up a meeting with the Senator and Bill Tuffs – the staff "troubleshooter" – and himself, to discuss the growing problem.

As was the Senator's style, there was no pre-meeting small talk to warm the air. Hennessey merely looked at Tuffs and commanded.

"Let's hear it."

Knowing his boss well, Tuffs got immediately to the point.

"Senator... I know I don't have to convince you that your son and his antics could sink the run. He has simply got to be neutralized. He's a loose cannon who could blow a hole in our ship... and we can't take that risk. There's too much riding on this... for too many people."

Tuffs looked at the Senator... then at Parling. Parling was nodding in resigned agreement. Nobody could ever read the Senator. His expression was, with rare exception, without emotion or reaction. His eyes and ears took in everything as pure information and his mind scanned the data in an ongoing assessment. He spoke about the disposition of his son in the same tone of voice as one might use to inquire about a recent stock performance.

"What do you suggest?"

"John... the public won't accept your son's misbehavior if it's characterized as malicious or criminal. That reflects on you as a father. We need to make him into a victim... then everybody's off the hook."

Tuffs paused again. Hennessey was growing impatient for the upshot.

"Go on."

"What we need is to get a cooperative doctor to diagnose John with some kind of problem that can't be connected to your parenting... then neutralize him."

Parling jumped in.

"Be a little more specific, Bill."

"He needs to have some sort of syndrome or chemical imbalance – or something – that causes him to be antisocial... then medicated and put out of harm's way. Some place nice... and far from the madding crowd, so to speak."

Hennessey looked at Parling.

"Jim?"

Parling had his finger to his lips... tapping a steady beat... his eyes on something high and distant. He reached his conclusion.

"Sounds good to me, boss. I can't really think of any other way to deal with this. You've tried everything else, and it hasn't done any good. And we might get some real nice sympathy points and good press about your anguish over your son's problem... you know... how you're trying to cope with it, and all that? We could get you to speak to some parents' groups with troubled kids... things like that. Maybe do a talk show... with a safe host... not some nut like Geraldo. It just might play real well, John."

The Senator's gaze returned to Tuffs.

"You know the right doctor?"

"Yes... I do, actually. This guy has done the same sort of thing for quite a few celebrities. He's good... respectable... a clean record. Good on camera, too."

The Senator made his decision.

"Set it up, Bill. The sooner the better."

Parling inquired.

"What about Emily?"

Hennessey assured Parling.

"I'll handle her."

In the space of less than five minutes, the young John Hennessey problem was, thus, resolved... and the young boy's fate was sealed. They moved on to other, more pressing matters.

CHAPTER TWO

When the Papa story broke again in May of the following year, Freddy Westin was on it with his usual, energetic tenacity. He assigned three of his people, exclusively, to the story. Within a week, after it was back in the news, it became the lead story of every network and the focus of every tabloid – television, radio and print... and the hottest topic on the internet. Freddy concluded it was, at that point, without question, a force with which to be reckoned. He called Parling to arrange a meeting with the Senator. He was given a half-hour. Freddy had his people put together a video that gave a comprehensive summary of the vast television coverage that this story was generating... and a briefing book that contained a representative sampling of the print coverage. The senator was clearly impressed... and Freddy was pleased. In his presentation that followed the video, Freddy framed the story in a succinct, compelling perspective.

"This is big Senator... really big... and the closer they get to Los Angeles... the bigger it'll get."

"Is it going to be a quick, hot, flash and burn... like the last time, Fred?"

"I don't think so, sir. His groupies are growing by the day and he's got media from around the world following his every step and word. They've got people on camera who say they were cured by this guy. Some woman, just this afternoon, was on the air saying she was blind and this Papa guy touched her eyes and now she can see. All kinds of strange stories are coming out of that mob of people around him. There's a story about a bright star... that people say they've never seen before... shining down on where this man sleeps... and stories about there not being enough food to feed everybody – and suddenly the food materializes out of nowhere."

"How's this affect me?"

"It hasn't yet, Senator... but it will... mark my word... it will. This guy is just getting started. He's got the eyes and ears of the entire world on him. You've got respected commentators saying this is an historic, world-class event... something like Jesus entering Jerusalem. The way this thing is building, sir... by the time he gets to Los Angeles, he'll have a virtual invasion force with him. He's coming into your state, Senator... and with the power he seems to have over people... one word from him and he could possibly make or break the election... and it's only a little over five months off, now. If he damaged us badly, we might not have enough time to recover."

"OK, Fred, you've convinced me. Get me some options."

After lunch, the Senator and his campaign staff flew to the West Coast on a company jet that was on indefinite loan from a supporter in the timber business, to attend several speaking engagements and fund-raisers in the San Francisco area. Hennessey soon discovered that Freddy Westin wasn't the only one with great interest in the Papa story. It seemed to be the topic of conversation, everywhere they appeared. Given that the Senator was being asked, on camera, about his view of this phenomenon, the staff quickly huddled and devised a response – remain neutral. This man was apparently a force with which to be reckoned, but they didn't have a good enough read on him to know how to play it. Lisa Ryan, his chief speech writer, quickly penned some suggested responses and handed them to Hennessey. He used them almost immediately.

"It's certainly a remarkable phenomenon, but it's too early to make any judgment on the man. Like everyone else, I'll just have to wait and see what develops."

In response to a question as to an alleged quote of Papa... stating that Jesus Christ was not divine, he offered the following.

"Well, I don't want to respond to hearsay. I personally haven't heard this man say anything like that. If I hear it myself, then I'll respond. I'm not going to speculate."

Lisa Ryan's menu of sound bites got him through the afternoon, but they knew it wouldn't hold water for long. As soon as they were airborne for their trip home, they all got together in the forward cabin and discussed the Papa phenomenon with Hennessey. The Senator summarized his feelings.

"We've got to get a read on this thing. I need to know how to play it. I can't fucking dance on this forever."

Will Blasco, the senator's campaign manager, undertook his designated responsibility of proffering the first response.

"First thing we need to do is find out the Religious Right's read on this. If this guy really is going around saying Jesus wasn't the Son of God, they're going to be out to cut his balls off. They'll be screaming to get him off the air. Of course, if this guy turns out to be bigger than the Right, we need to be able to move in that direction, too. I don't know, Senator… this is a sticky wicket. We could get burned in either direction."

The Senator made clear his feelings.

"I don't want to hear about a fucking, sticky wicket, Will. I'm not planning on getting stuck – period. You people get this fucking thing figured out. That's what you're getting your big salaries for. Fred Westin is already working on it. You people get together with him, tomorrow morning. I want some options by the afternoon."

When the Senator opened the door to his Watergate condo, his eyes were met by the dancing glow of dozens of burning candles – placed all about his living room and leading down the hallway to his bedroom. With the press of his engagements, he had totally forgotten it was his forty-seventh birthday, and about the present he was promised. He pondered, for a moment, that none of his staff had extended him wishes of the day on the flight home…

then realized – given the less than amiable atmosphere on the return trip – why they hadn't. His staff knew, all too well, not to attempt to lighten any mood of the Senator until he had clearly signaled his willingness to abide it. Tomorrow, they'd be ready with their salutations... if he appeared to be.

John took off his suit coat... laid it over the back of the couch... then walked down the glowing hallway to the bedroom. Carleen – his latest steady lover – had come through as promised. Ever since John had met Carleen's younger sister on her high school, senior trip to Washington, he had pressed Carleen on his wish to have sex with both of them at the same time. Kelly had just graduated from high school the week before, and two weeks before that, had turned eighteen. Carleen had strongly resisted Hennessey's proposition. Kelly was her baby sister, she had pleaded... eight years younger... and she had always considered her to be a child... a beautiful, innocent, vulnerable child... and still a virgin.
  Carleen had always been bigger than life to Kelly... living in Washington... having her own apartment... having an important government job... dating famous – and handsome – men. Kelly's dream was to be just like her big sister.

Carleen was the archetype of the Senator's choice in women... taller than average, with a small waist, no-larger-than-a-handful breasts, rounded buttocks, and a porcelain-skinned, flawless face with pouting lips that exquisitely combined sexuality and vulnerability. Kelly was of the same mold... but with the added appeal of still possessing the pinkness of childhood and the ability to spawn the primordial male covetousness for the bloody prize of an unspoiled virginity. For the past six months, before his birthday, the Senator had talked to Carleen, with increasing frequency and appetite, about his throbbing desire to have both of them, every time they had sex... the mere verbalization of which drove him to a near fit of carnal frenzy. If it came to fruition, it, of course, would certainly not be John Hennessey's first ménage a trois... but it would be the first with two sisters... and absolutely the first with a girl whose high school prom corsage still retained some of its fragrance.

Over the past few months, Hennessey's desire for this lustful pleasure had become an ugly obsession... ugly enough to engender threats, unless fulfilled. Senator Hennessey was among the premier players inside the capitol beltway, and powerful enough to make – or break – virtually anyone unfortunate enough to incur his wrath. Carleen didn't have to be told this. In late May, he finally made the proposition very clear to her. Either she would accommodate his desires on his birthday or as a "rain date" – if one of the sisters was having her period on the scheduled day – as soon thereafter as their mutual physiology would allow... or... Carleen might as well sublet her Georgetown apartment and book a flight back to Michigan. She'd have no decent job, left in Washington. Hennessey presented this without any theatrics. He didn't need to. Carleen knew his reputation and had witnessed the carnage of his lethal retribution. It was always swift... and without remorse.

She begged him to reconsider... offering other strikingly beautiful women in her sister's place. Hennessey declined, in black anger. He found, as he approached the mid-century mark, that his sexuality was, progressively, taking a turn toward the perverse. He didn't simply want two women... he wanted a woman and a girl. He wanted a flower before it had been touched... and before any of its petals had dropped or wilted. He wanted a fully developed female body that still had the dew of childhood on it... and he wanted the deflowering witnessed by her sibling. His passion was a knot of desires that could, without a doubt, challenge the skills of a gifted psychiatrist to untie.

Carleen anguished over her circumstance for more than a week. Hennessey had given her ten days to decide. She considered all that she had in Washington... which was more than she had ever dreamed possible when she was back in her small, dirty, blue-collar hometown, with its endless winters and perpetual gray skies. She had arrived in D.C. as a stunning, perky, nineteen-year-old, and found that, if ever there was a place on the earth a woman could sleep her way to the top... it was the nation's capitol. If you were beautiful – and played your sex appeal adroitly, nowhere on the face of the planet was there such reward and advancement.

Carleen moved quickly from a part-time position in the Commerce Department's secretary pool to an administrative assistant for the Under Secretary of Labor – in five years. She was certain that John Hennessey was headed for the top... and she intended to be along for the ride. If she played her sexuality prudently, her vistas were virtually unlimited. She was the one, in fact, who had initiated the relationship with John Hennessey... but it was he who could – with little effort – easily push her from the lofty heights, to which she had risen... back down to the common world she thought she'd forever left behind. As the wisdom had it in Washington... the climb is slow, but the fall is breathtaking.

Her decision was finally made by reference to less-than-noble sentiments, of which she found she was possessed. She had become just too accustomed to her life's pleasures to ever give them up for anything... even a sister. Like a drug addict who will steal from his own mother for a fix, Carleen was alarmed to discover, in the final analysis, that she was willing to sacrifice her sister's childhood to maintain her own hedonistic milieu. She rationalized – to overcome her guilt – that Kelly had to lose her virginity, sometime... high school was over... and it was time she learned about the real world. Carleen, herself, had been, after all, only nineteen when *she* started sleeping with men for career advancement... and Kelly was nearly that.

Carleen phoned Kelly on a Sunday afternoon and told her to take the call in her bedroom and close the door. They had just gotten home from church and were waiting for the rest of the family to arrive for the usual, big Sunday dinner. Carleen began by telling Kelly that she had a big favor to ask of her. Without asking what it was, Kelly – as she had always done for Carleen – said, of course, she'd do anything for her. Carleen pressed vaguely forward... saying it was a *really* big favor. Kelly giggled at this – her girlish sounds almost causing Carleen to reconsider what she was about to ask of her... but not for long.

"I don't know how to start this, honey."

"What is it Carly? Come on."

"I have a bad situation down here right now... and if I don't play it right, I'm going to lose everything."

"Geese, Carly... what's the matter?"

"There's a senator down here that's asked me to do something... and if I don't, he's going to ruin me. I'll lose my job... and I won't ever get another one down here."

"What's he want you to do, Car?"

"Do you remember meeting Senator Hennessey when your high school came down here on your senior trip?"

"Oh, yeah... he's a cutey pie! He reminded me of a movie star."

"Well Senator Hennessey took a liking to you."

"Really?! Oh... you're just saying that. Me? I'm just a kid. Get outa here, Carly."

"Kelly... I'm not kidding you. Listen to me. This is serious."

"OK."

"He wants to have sex with you... with both of us... with both of us together."

"What?"

"Just what I said, Kelly. And if I don't arrange it, he's going to ruin me... and he can do it, Kel... believe me... he can."

"Well go to the police, Carlene. Isn't that some sort of crime? People can't go around doing things like that to other people... can they?"

"Down here they can, honey."

"Well what are you gonna do, Carly?"

"I'll be straight with you, sweetie... either you'll have to come down and do this... or I'm done in this city. I'll be done, period. All I have is a high school education. I'm making eighty thousand dollars a year, down here. If I lose this, I'll be working for minimum wage somewhere... and living in a trailer."

"What do you want me to do, Car?"

"Oh, honey... I shouldn't have called you... I'm..."

"Carly..."

Kelly could hear her sister crying.

"Carly?"

"Uh huh."

"I'll do it. I'll do it for you. It's all right... really, Car... it's no big deal. Lot's of my friends have had sex already... just about all of them. I'm the weirdo. What's the big deal about being a virgin anyway? OK, Car? I'll do it... OK? Please don't cry. Carly?"

"Are you sure, Kel? You don't have to. I'll survive, somehow."

"When do you need me?"

"Oh, Kelly... are you sure?"

"Yes, Carleen... I'm sure. Now when should I come down?"

"His birthday is June fifteenth. That's what he wants for his birthday present... you and me."

"That's fine... if that's what he wants... no big deal. Besides... he's a cutey pie."

"If you're sure."

"I'm sure, Carly."

"OK. I'll send you a plane ticket. Oh... honey, when are you due next?"

"It's OK, Car... I just finished yesterday."

"I'm sorry I had to ask... but it's a practical consideration."

"That's OK. But... I'm not on the pill or anything. I don't know anything about that stuff."

"It's OK. You can come down a week early and I can take you to my doctor... he'll put in the same shield I've got. It's real quick... and doesn't hurt at all. OK?"

"OK."

"Are you sure about all this, honey? Just say so... and I'll drop it. Honestly, I will."

"I wouldn't do it if I didn't want to. I'm fine... really."

"If you're absolutely sure, Kel."

"I am."

"All right. I'll get the ticket tomorrow. You'll probably have to fly down on Tuesday. I'll send it overnight. OK?"

"I'll watch for it, Car."

"Say hi to everybody for me. I love you."

"Love you, Car."

"Bye bye."

"Bye."

As soon as the two receivers went dead, both sisters burst into tears... the oldest, in guilt and shame... the youngest, in anguish over her forthcoming loss. She was a hopeless romantic. She had wanted, all of her life, to save herself for her husband. She had wanted to be his – and his alone – forever. Carleen knew she was still a virgin... but she couldn't know how priceless her preserved treasure was to her. Kelly would as soon have lost a finger, as her virginity. But Carly needed her. Carly had always been there for her... always. She couldn't let her down... even at the cost of her dream... and she knew she could never let Carly know what it had actually meant to her.

As the senator opened the bedroom door, his eyes drank in the incredibly erotic images. Kelly was beside Carleen... both leaning, in seductive postures, against the huge, carved, wooden headboard... both in exceedingly sheer negligees, of fabric that allowed the passage of just enough candlelight to evocatively silhouette details of the bodies underneath... permitting the vague discernment of both breast and nipple... hip and maiden hair. For a few moments, after Hennessey walked into the bedroom, Kelly thought she was going to vomit from her anxiety. Carleen had done her best to prepare her for the experience... giving her instructions on what she should do, anticipations of what to expect, and a review of the Senator's sexual fancies and peculiarities. But, as with anything, nothing can serve in place of the real moment. Carleen felt Kelly tense and tried to look at her without moving so quickly as to break the sensual ambience. Kelly, nodded, ever so slightly, and weakly smiled, to signal her sister that she was OK. Carleen breathed a silent and thankful sigh of relief.

The Senator's senses absorbed the entire room. Besides the two remarkably beautiful women in his bed, and the softly flickering candles throughout, a provocative, yet lovely smell filled the air... and soft music – a classical violin concerto – bathed his ears. On his dresser was a bottle of wine in an ice-filled, silver bucket with three long stem, crystal wine goblets around it. To the right of the beverage arrangement was a silver serving tray, offering an artistically arranged selection of hors d'oeuvres... with a single rose in a crystal vase in the center. The Senator was pleased... very pleased.

"Very nice, Carleen... very nice. Stay where you are... I'll be out in a minute."

John disappeared into his bathroom. The sisters heard the shower running.

"Carly... I'm really nervous. I hope I can do this. I'm freezing, and shaking... I can feel my teeth clicking together... and I feel like I have to pee."

Carleen stroked the back of her long, blonde hair.

"You'll be OK, honey. Everybody's nervous the first time... even guys are."

Kelly tried to concentrate on the violin music to relax, but her anxiety was too overpowering. Her body involuntarily jerked when the toilet flushed. The bathroom light went out while the door was still closed. It opened slowly and John Hennessey emerged, wearing a thick, luxurious, wine-colored bathrobe that came down to his ankles. He walked to the wine bottle... took out the already loosened cork and filled the three goblets. He left one on the dresser and carried the other two to the sisters. He returned to the dresser, picked up his glass and raised it.

"To a great night of sex."

The sisters didn't respond... but took a small sip of the dry Chablis – Hennessey's favorite – to appease him. The Senator leaned his butt against the edge of the dresser and again savored the sensual tableau. He sampled the hors d'oeuvres... selecting among the shrimp, caviar, cheese, crab, and strawberries. The sight of a stunning woman lounging beside her gorgeous, childlike sister... both covered with fabric so sheer that it created the illusion of marble perfection underneath...   was more than

Hennessey could resist any longer. As one can only savor the sight of a delicious morsel of food until ancient bestial urges demand satiation... to say the two women were good enough to eat, was more real than metaphoric at that moment, to John Hennessey. He felt his saliva glands squirting profuse amounts of the appetite-piquing liquid into his mouth. Had there been no consequences for the act, he felt, at that moment, he could have, literally, ripped into their bodies with his teeth and chewed and swallowed their delicious juice and flesh.

He came to Kelly's side of the bed. She could see the barely controlled urgency in his eyes. His animal-like ferocity frightened her. She felt, for an instant, that she was going to start crying. This man, who she had once described as a "cutey pie," had the appearance of a terrible, prowling beast to her. Hennessey unloosened his robe. As it fell open, it unveiled a huge erection... pointing directly at Kelly's face. It was grotesque to her. She had seen pictures of erections in her high school health class... but the stiff, vein-bulging, split-ended flesh was nothing to her but plainly hideous. Hennessey's passion drew noisy breaths into his nostrils. He was unconsciously licking his lips. When he finally spoke, Kelly started.

"Touch it, baby."

Kelly looked over at her sister then at Hennessey's face. It was contorted into an ugly sneer. Fighting her revulsion, she forced her hand slowly upward... stopping a few inches from his penis. The Senator was growing impatient. His voice took on the edge of a command.

"Stroke it!"

Again, Kelly moved her hand closer to him and, again, stopped short of its destination. Hennessey's repressed passion suddenly exploded, beyond control. He leaned forward and grabbed her by the back of the hair, pulled her head backward, and shoved his penis against her closed mouth.

"Open that mouth, bitch!"

Carleen could hear her little sister begin to whimper... as she had always done when she was scared, and knew she was about to start crying. She instinctively abandoned all her personal treasures to protect this baby.

"Leave her alone, John!!"

Hennessey continued to push against her lips... trying with his right hand to push her jaw down. Carleen stood up on the bed and screamed at him.

"Let her go, you fucking bastard!!"

Instead, Hennessey took a step backward... grabbed the front of Kelly's negligee and tore it from her. She instinctively brought her knees up and crossed her arms across her breasts. Hennessey was on her in an instant... trying to push her legs down with one hand and grab her breasts with the other. Carleen jumped from the bed... ran to the dresser and grabbed the wine bottle by its neck. She lifted it, holding it like a club – the remaining wine splashing down her arm – and dashed around the bed... stopping only a few inches behind Hennessey's forward-bent body. She wrapped her free hand around the other that was already holding the bottle neck, and swung – with all the remarkable power that fear and anger can endow the body – at the back of Hennessey's head. He moved just as it connected with him and the bottled glanced off his scalp and banged into the headboard with a loud, thudding noise. She drew it back for another swing, just as Hennessey turned to investigate the source of the thump. At the precise moment that his face fell flush with hers, the bottle collided, solidly, with the left side of his cheek. He reached, instinctively, to cover the place of contact... and tried to move toward his attacker. He took one step and had to steady himself with his hand, grabbing the top of the headboard. Carleen could see that his head was beginning to clear and he was, again, able to focus his eyes on her. She swung a third time and caught the left side of his temple with a thunderous blow. He staggered, then fell onto the carpet. Carleen shouted.

"Grab your coat, Kelly!! Let's get out of here!!"

Carleen dropped the bottle onto the rug and ran to grab her own coat from the bedroom closet. They bolted down the condo hallway and out the door... leaving it open in their haste. Sprinting down the wide, bending passageway, they were both still carrying their coats... Carleen in her flimsy negligee... Kelly, completely naked. Suddenly Carleen stopped and grabbed Kelly's arm.

"My keys! They're in my purse! Wait here. Put on your coat, Kelly!"

Carleen ran back to the condo and through the open door... back into the bedroom. Hennessey was still lying there... in the precise position she had left him. A wave of fear flooded over her, realizing she may have killed him. She entered the immense walk-in closet and grabbed their two purses from the shelf, just above the long clothes rod. After she emerged, she laid them on the bed, slipped on her coat, and buttoned it. Given the obstructing position his body occupied, she was, again, forced to step over Hennessey, on her way to the bedroom door. Curiosity momentarily overcame her fear and she cautiously pushed her bare foot into his shoulder, as one would test an animal for life that was found lying on a road... rocking his body, slightly, as she did so. Still no sign of animation was apparent. Carleen considered, for a instant, bending down to check his breathing... but then thought back to the many suspense movies she had seen where the supposed dead man grabbed a similarly curious victim by the throat. Fear regained its dominance over her short-lived curiosity and she hurried out of the condo... closing the door behind her this time.

Carleen and Kelly spent the entire next day in Carleen's apartment, watching, fearfully, for the anticipated news of the Senator's murder... which never materialized. Still wary, Carleen telephoned his office, the following day and asked to speak with him. The receptionist said he was in meetings all day. Carleen immediately hung up. The two sisters left Washington that evening and returned to Michigan. In response to Kelly's demand, while they were still in Washington – that they go to the police to report Hennessey's attacking her – Carleen explained the carnal facts of Washington life to her. Her sleeping around was common knowledge among the beltway elite, and there were an abundance of witnesses to it – willing to embellish their stories to the extent required by Hennessey. Her considerably less-than-virginal reputation would, undoubtedly, she explained, cast its shameful shadow upon her sister's pristine image, as well. What kind of girl, after all, Carleen posed, would have agreed to such a sexual arrangement? Despite what actually goes on in the privacy of condos and hotel rooms all over town, the socially dictated, public view, would be that only a slut would have agreed to such a liaison. Factually, she pointed out, neither of them had any bruises... and what would they say about their both being in skimpy negligees?... the candles?... the wine?... the soft music? It all looked quite consensual, regardless of what happened. It would be his word against theirs... and his had the compelling veracity of power and image. They'd both be painted as whores, all over the national media. It was a fact, she pointed out, that they were, after all, there for sex... initially anyway... so who would believe their story? If they reported it, not only would they lose, but it would be front page news, as well. Their parents' lives would be ruined... along with their own. Kelly, faced with this compelling portrait of sex and power, deferred to her older sister's sagacity and dropped the issue.

As the plane's wheels lost touch with the Dulles runway, Carleen knew her Washington days were at an end. She had traded her body for the pleasures and luxuries of life and, as so often happens to such pawns and playthings of the rich and powerful, she had ended up losing everything, including her own self-respect. As painful as Carleen's loss was to her, however, the damage to Kelly was immeasurably greater. She was shattered crystal, and for several years after her ordeal with Hennessey, she would refuse to leave the house... her sleep, fitfully broken by her own screaming. She had, also, according to her therapist, acquired a stubborn phobia toward men that she doubted Kelly would ever entirely resolve. After the night with Hennessey, Kelly knew, in her heart, she would never marry.

Besides a brutal headache, Hennessey's injuries weren't serious. He dispatched a staff member to Carleen's apartment, several days after the exceedingly unpleasant episode, and was sorely disappointed to find she had fled. He had relished the thought of destroying her, right there in Washington, for all to see... and was angry to be denied the satisfaction. He resolved a steadfast oath of revenge, at that moment, against both of the sisters.

CHAPTER THREE

On the second day, following his birthday, Hennessey returned to his senate office. At ten o'clock, he attended a meeting on the Papa matter. As always, the Senator led with the parameters.

"I need a handle on this situation, folks. When I was home, yesterday, almost every talk show I watched had some expert on about this Papa lunatic. I can't believe how many fucking wackos there are out there who believe this stuff. If it's not UFO's... it's some nut case like this. Fred... you've been on this the longest. Where are we?"

"It's big, Senator... and getting bigger by the day. This isn't going away. By the time this guy reaches L.A., it'll be a world-class event. No doubt about it. Here's the way I see it, sir. First of all, the Religious Right is having fits over this guy."

Fred surveyed the faces and was pleased with the attention they were according his opinion. Reveling in this moment of recognition, he lowered his voice, slightly, and struck an overtly officious posture.

"They want to meet with us as soon as possible on this. I've sandbagged them until we'd decided on a course of action. Benson Powell, himself, called me."

Again, Freddy Westin paused... this time to allow the invocation of the undisputed leader of the Right – and the link with himself – to have its effect. Disappointed that it had none, he went on... his ostentation slightly diminished.

"We've got to play with a doubleheaded coin on this one, Senator. We need to win with whatever side is up at the end."

Hennessey was growing impatient with Westin's superfluous,

verbal drum roll.

"Fred... get to the fucking point. What's the game plan?"

Hennessey's admonishment immediately moved Fred into his commander-soldier mode of thinking... and he obeyed without any show of offense.

"We need to convince Benson that we support him... and get you associated with this Papa guy at the same time. There's going to be a shit load of on-camera face time as soon as this horde of lunatics hits L.A.... and we can't afford to miss out on it. It's a chance of a lifetime. We need to put you into a posture that appears you're supporting this movement – while it's hot – but allow enough wiggle room to bail out, completely, if it goes sour."

Will Blasco jumped in.

"Look Fred... it's already June. The election is only five months away. If we get into trouble on this, we're running short on time to fix it... and the later the trouble, the worse the problem. How can the Senator appear to be supporting this Papa guy and not piss off all the Righters? I mean if he's there, on camera with this guy, how can we spin that in our favor?"

"We'll get Benson to buy into the story that we need to get close to this guy... so we can find out where this whole thing is going... so we can keep a handle on it. We'll keep feeding him inside information like we're on his side... bullshit, if there isn't anything to tell him. Leave it to me... I can swing it."

The Senator looked at Jimmy Parling.

"All right... Jimmy, I want you and Fred to meet with Powell. See if it's really possible to work both sides of this thing. If we can't... then we'll have to make a decision on the best horse to ride. And you know the deal, Jimmy... if they want to do anything that could hurt me... make the decision... but I don't want to know about it. Anything else?"

Lisa Ryan spoke up.

"Two things, Senator... we need to make a decision on the Fourth of July... and I need some guidance on what to write for you on this Papa thing. On the Fourth, we've got an invitation to speak to the NRA, in Sacramento, and the Veterans' Convention, in San Diego, at the same time. We need to firm up where we're going to be... so I can get something ready."

Hennessey looked at Blasco for a decision. It was obvious he wasn't ready by the inane prologue to his response.

"It's... well I've sort of... there are a lot of..."

The Senator ended Blasco's insipid babble with undisguised disdain.

"What am I... surrounded by village idiots? If you can't make a decision, Will... I'll find someone who can. What do you think, Lisa?"

"It's a close call, Senator... but I'd go with the NRA. The vets just don't have the clout they once had. The gun lobby has delivered for us, consistently... in votes and money."

"OK... you confirm with them Lisa... and get me something ready. Will... you'd better get your fucking head out of your ass or you're gone. On this Papa thing, Lisa... wait until Jimmy and Fred meet with Powell... then we'll talk about it. Anything else?"

They adjourned. Hennessey asked Jimmy Parling to stay behind.

"I want you to find out where Carleen Novak is... and that little, cunt sister of hers, too. I've got a little evening-up to do with them. They're probably both back in Michigan."

"No problem, John."

The following evening, Parling and Fred met with Benson Powell and his assistant, Ron Golden, for dinner in Georgetown. Dinner was passed with pleasantries and chitchat... both teams screening for useful intelligence amid the seemingly innocuous chatter. Overt business began with coffee. Jimmy Parling opened.

"I understand you've got some concerns about this new Papa movement, Benson... and we'd like to do what we can to help out."

"Frankly, Jim... the general view of our leadership is that this man is truly the Antichrist... and that he's got to be stopped... one way or the other. He's already having an effect on our following. Church attendance has been down, noticeably, ever since this whole story broke. A good number of our people have had their heads turned by this nut. I was just at a leadership meeting last night... and they all want something done. This man's face is everywhere... TV... magazines... newspapers... internet. You've got people saying they were cured by him... claiming he's performing miracles. This movement is one of the top stories on the news every evening!... and everyday that crowd who's with him gets bigger! And he's walking around saying that Jesus Christ wasn't divine! In my opinion, Jim, this man may be the biggest threat to the Christian church since the founding of Islam."

Fred inquired.

"What can we do to help, Reverend Powell?"

"To start with... you could put some pressure on the media to stop giving this guy front page treatment. Talk to some of the network sponsors. The Senator's got lots of clout with those CEO's. Most of them are in his hip pocket... we know that. Get them on our side, Jim."

Parling responded.

"We'll give that a try, Benson... but you know the ratings game. People can't seem to get enough of this story... and if one network isn't covering it... they'll change the channel to another one that is. And sponsors follow the numbers."

Powell studied Jimmy Parling's face for a few moments.

"Ron... can you and Fred give Jimmy and me a few minutes together... alone?"

After the two had removed themselves to the bar and settled onto the high, leather-covered stools, Reverend Powell leaned forward across the table and Jimmy Parling followed suit.

"We need a solution here, Jimmy. My people want this demon silenced... whatever it takes. Are you following me?"

"Be a little more specific, Benson."

"As Christians, we keep the commandments... but there are times we need to stand up as soldiers for Jesus Christ... and this, is the time."

"Are you talking about what I think you are?"

"Yes... I am."

"As I said, Benson... we'll stand behind you. You've been very good to us... but..."

"And we'll be good for you again... this November at the voting booth... and in your campaign chest."

"This is pretty heavy stuff, Benson... I mean we're not the mafia, you know."

"Come off it, Jimmy. Don't try to bullshit a bullshitter. You'll do – and have done – whatever it takes to get John into the White House. You're politicians... so don't get moralistic with me. You don't have any scruples... and you know it. How long do you think Bobby and Jack hesitated to take care of Marilyn Monroe when she became a problem?... or Teddy and his deal at Chappaquiddick? Come off it. The only thing you care about is how much it will help you... and how much could it hurt you. You already know the answer to that. Without us, John wouldn't be walking around the Senate side of the congressional building right now, and you know it. And without us, he'll never be clipping flowers in the rose garden, either. We want this done, Jimmy... and we know your people know how to get it done... and nobody will be any the wiser."

Jimmy studied Powell's face... trying to decide whether or not to play dumb. He concluded it was a waste of time.

"You understand, Benson... we need to keep the Senator completely out of this."

"Of course."

"What, exactly, then, is it that we can do for you? Let's cut through the cryptic bullshit and get it out on the table."

"As you could well imagine, Jimmy, this is very new territory for us... and we need some guidance. As I understand it, Fred is very good at arranging unusual things... things that may not be entirely on the legal side of the road."

Powell waited for confirmation of the accuracy of his portrayal of Freddy Westin. Parling nodded. Powell continued.

"Can you put him on it? Money – as they say – is no object in this case. Of course... like the Senator... we need to be completely insulated from this, as well. The less we know... the better. We need to keep it very small... one person from our group... one from yours. Ron is our man – and I assume Fred will be yours."

"Yes."

"Then we're agreed on the result?"

Parling weighed this final commitment. Without the Right, the march to the White House was dead. With the Right, this nut was dead. Not much choice, he quickly concluded.

"Yes."

"Then all further discussion on this matter will be limited to Ron and Fred... and no further involvement with anyone else from either staff. Agreed?"

"Agreed."

"OK... you brief Fred... I'll fill in Ron... then it's hands-off on both sides. They're private operators. Can Fred be trusted?"

"He'd die before he'd rat. How about Ron?"

"Same type."

Reverend Powell reached his hand across the table to Jimmy Parling. Jimmy grasped it and the two sealed their bargain of death with a smile and a single, firm squeeze of their hands. They agreed to brief their operatives separately. With a quick motion of his hand, Reverend Powell summoned their soldiers back to the table. After a couple of after-dinner cordials, the two pairs parted company.

CHAPTER FOUR

Senator Hennessey was pleased with the choice of the NRA convention for the Fourth of July. It was a special day for them – symbolic of free men exercising their God-given right to take up arms against an oppressor. The mood was nearly euphoric and the cavernous convention hall was filled... both with loyal members, and media. Hennessey was also pleased with the speech Lisa Ryan had written. She was good... and good-looking. He had resolved, of late, to start fucking her at his earliest convenience. She was married – but ambitious. He was sure she'd jump at the chance for advancement, regardless of which elevator she had to ride. The speech drove the gun owners to a fevered pitch... weaving together the spirituality of the revolution, God, and the gun. He was interrupted by applause so many times that, what was intended to be a fifteen-minute delivery, expanded to nearly forty-five.

As the master of ceremonies concluded the proceedings, he reminded the enraptured audience that gun people always put their wallet where their heart is... and that there were people at the back of the hall to collect contributions for the Senator's campaign. The take was enormous.

In a room, off to the left of the stage area, a press area had been set up. Hennessey's staff had promised fifteen minutes of questions. He was blindsided by the first salvo.

"Senator... we've just received word of the attempted assassination of Papa in Las Vegas, just minutes ago... and the killing of one of his followers. How can you justify your support of the free access and ownership of guns in this country when we have a population that solves its problems with bullets – even to the extent of killing religious leaders?"

Hennessey shot a barely perceptible, malevolent glare at his staff –

plainly and painfully decipherable by each of them – for not having been made aware of this development. Had he known, he would have, undoubtedly, canceled the press conference. Now, he was stuck in front of a voracious press contingent... and looked like a fool under the circumstances – on the heels of his passionate speech in support of gun ownership. Invisibly seething, he fielded the question with his well-oiled adroitness and charm.

"First of all... this is the first I've heard this... and my sympathies, of course, go out to the family and friends of the slain follower – and I wish to express my concern for the future safety of Papa and his followers... and will do all I can within my power to help ensure their well-being. While we may not agree with another person's point of view... no one has a right to take another's life over a difference of opinion. That's why we fought the revolution, two hundred years ago – to have the right to speak our minds... and worship as we please... free from the guns of our oppressors. No member of the NRA would advocate or support this kind of violence. They are decent men and women... good, God-fearing people – who see the freedom of bearing arms as a way of assuring that we will never again be oppressed – not as a means of carrying out violence against our own people. Now... in view of this development, I need to excuse myself and see what sort of assistance my office can offer. Thank you all very much."

To the sound of his title being shouted in numerous octaves and attitudes by the press corps, the Senator and his staff quickly disappeared through a door behind the podium. They moved, fluently, to their awaiting car – and sped away to the airport. The ride was not pleasant. The Senator's face was crimson with anger.

"Who the fuck was supposed to be on the news wire today?!!"

Will Blasco tried to avoid the Senator's burning eyes.

"Who the fuck was on it, Will?"

"Well... Senator... it's a holiday... you know... and there's usually nothing going on... so I..."

JOHN

The Senator shouted at the driver.

"Stop the car!!"

Immediately, the driver pulled over to the shoulder of the six-lane highway. Hennessey eyes drilled into Will Blasco's puzzled and anxious face. The Senator extended his right thumb and spoke as he jerked it sharply to the right.

"Get the fuck out!"

Blasco's mouth dropped and the rest of the staff stared at the Senator in disbelief.

"I said... get the fuck out. Are you deaf as well as retarded, you asshole?"

"But Senator... we're in the middle of an expressway..."

"Get your ass out of here before I throw it out!"

Hennessey leaned his body toward Blasco in a threatening movement. Blasco opened the door and hesitated. Hennessey's narrowed, blazing eyes were enough to convince him to go... and he tentatively stepped out onto the littered pavement of the expressway shoulder. Hennessey leaned over Lisa Ryan – grabbed the door handle – and slammed it shut. He told the driver to go. The staffers on the seat of the limo, facing the back of the car, were treated to the incongruous sight of a prosperous, overweight, pink-faced, middle-aged man in a five-hundred-dollar suit, standing alone, abandoned, along the litter-strewn side of the wide, concrete strip... traversed by speeding cars, trucks, and busses – blowing wind, exhaust, dirt, and litter into his dazed-looking face. There was total silence until they had boarded their jet... and then, only whispers.

CHAPTER FIVE

As Senator Hennessey passed his secretary's desk, he curtly ordered her to get Jimmy Parling into his office. His agitated demeanor was worsened by the tedious four-hour flight from California – giving him a chance to stew in the juices of his own anger. Parling recognized the warning signs as soon as he walked into the Senator's office. His buttocks hadn't yet met with the leather, high back chair when Hennessey fired off his fist inquiry.

"Did we know about that botched assassination in Las Vegas, beforehand?"

"Not specifically."

"What the fuck does that mean, Jimmy?"

"John... do you really want me to tell you? Your instructions were to keep you entirely out of the loop."

"Well I'm back into it... tell me."

"OK, boss. We met with Powell and Ron Golden – like you wanted us to. First... Powell wanted us to lean on the network sponsors to get this Papa guy off the air. I told him the facts of life about ratings and the slim likelihood we'd be able to do anything... this Papa thing being an ongoing front page story and all... you know... people wanting to get everything they can on the story. Anyway... he sent Fred and Ron Golden away from the table and got real serious with me all of a sudden. These people are *very* serious about this Papa thing, John... *very* serious. They think of this guy as the anti-Christ... a real-life demon. In particular, it's affecting their church attendance... which translates into lost revenues and political base, of course. They don't look at this guy as some trendy fad. They think he's an honest-to-God, fundamental threat to the Christian church. They said they wanted a solution – and they wanted it soon. You're not going to believe this, John… but Powell said they wanted to take out a contract on this guy… and wanted Fred to arrange it."

"They want this Papa guy killed?"

"Yep."

"No shit?!"

"No shit."

"Goddamn… these fucking Christians are something else, Jimmy."

Hennessey chuckled… then put his left fist to his chin – his forefinger across his closed lips – his thumb under his chin. His eyes and furrowed brow reflected an ongoing assessment of the situation. His hand came down and he spoke.

"So are you telling me that they – we – set this Las Vegas thing up?"

"That's what I'm telling you, John. You said you didn't want to know anything about what was going on, if it could hurt you."

"And… Fred set this up?"

"Yep."

"Old Ready Freddy… what a piece of work, huh?"

"He's an original, John."

"I'm glad he works for us, Jim. Hate to have him on the other side. If he ever decides to jump ship, we may have to take out a contract on him for our own protection."

Parling laughed.

"Personally, Jimmy... I don't give two shits if they smoke this Papa guy or not... but I do care if it hurts me. I looked like a goddamn fool out there this morning, Jim. And by the way... did you hear about Blasco?"

"Did you really throw him out of the car on the expressway?"

"Hell yes. He should be thankful I at least had the courtesy to stop the car first."

Parling laughed. Hennessey continued.

"It's a risk, Jimmy, but I need to be brought in on this. I don't want to be blindsided again. Also... we need to get our story straight on this Papa thing for the media. I told Lisa we'd get with her after you met with the Right people. You talk to her?"

"Not yet, John. This unusual intrigue of the Right, kind of puts a new wrinkle on things, you know?"

"Yeah... it does. What's the best way to play this, Jim... any ideas?"

"Well, I agree with Fred about the media coverage on this Papa... can't afford to miss out on it... and it's going to be in your state, John, for Christ sake. I've been thinking about an angle."

Jimmy Parling paused to fine-tune his, as yet amorphous, unspoken plan.

"Since this deal in Las Vegas, the issue of this man's safety – and everybody else's with him – has become an issue. He's coming to California, John... be there in about three or four weeks. You could become involved – you almost have to be – to the extent of ensuring his safety – and his people. At least that would be your public line. We could work you into some great face time and sound bites. You could take the position that – while you may not necessarily agree with what this guy says – you feel he's entitled to express his views... and you want to protect his safety. We could tell the Right that you just can't pass up this media opportunity – they should understand that – and that we could say we'll use this intervention to provide them with some intelligence for use in their own project. What do you think?"

"In other words, they're going to try again on this?"

"Oh hell yes. I asked Fred about it – after this first fuck-up – and he said they want the job done… no matter how many times it takes."

"All right. I like the angle. Of course, I'll need to know about their plans… don't want to get my own ass blown away by some cross-eyed shooter. Must have hired a real loser in Las Vegas… three shots… three misses. What'd they do… hire a blind guy? Who got blown away, anyway?"

"The faggot that was with him."

"Well, that's no big loss. The shooter should get a commendation for his work in the war against AIDS."

Parling broke out into a barroom howl. Hennessey smiled at Parling's appreciation of his wit.

"Of course… you know, John… if you happened to be there when it happened, you'd be a legend… like Jesse Jackson with King… or Conneley with Kennedy. And if you were near some cameras and sound equipment, you could look like a real hero… calming the crowd… saying something memorable and quotable. It could be a part of history… you know, like '. . . a giant step for mankind.' We could have Lisa work something up. You'd be all ready to make an historical statement."

"I like that, Jim. I like that, a lot. What are the chances of pulling something like that off?"

"Well… since Fred's kind of calling the shots – no pun intended – we could probably control it."

"Talk to him about it. By the way... is the investigation on this shooting getting anywhere?"

"Well... it's not just the locals and the states... the FBI is in it, too."

"Why?"

"They're looking at it as an attempted assassination of a public figure."

"Well, are they getting anywhere? There better not be any bread crumbs leading back to this office."

"They're nowhere, John. Fred brought in the best on this... a French mafia shooter... the same bunch that did Kennedy. They'll sooner trace this thing to Napoleon Bonaparte than back here. I'd swear the life of my first born on it, John."

"If it ever came back here, Jim... you just might have to."

Parling noticed Hennessey's face was perfectly serious in delivering this admonition. Hennessey's intercom tone broke the weight of the suddenly morose moment.

"Yes, Julie."

"The director of Stony Brook is on the line."

"Who?"

"Stony Brook. Where your son is... the clinic?"

"Oh yeah. What's he want?"

"He says it's an emergency."

"Oh shit. What did that fucking kid do now? All right, Julie... put him through."

JOHN

Hennessey picked up his receiver.

"This is Senator Hennessey."

"Senator... this is Bob Lynch... director of Stony Brook Clinic."

"Yes, Bob... what can I do for you?"

"Senator... I'm sorry, but I have some tragic news."

"What's happened?"

"Your son, John, has taken his own life, Senator Hennessey. I'm really sorry to have to tell you this over the telephone... but I wanted you to know right away."

"When did this happen?"

"His roommate just found him... about twenty minutes ago. He apparently slit his wrists... sometime after breakfast. We called the paramedics... and had our own physicians do what they could for him... but he was dead when they got to him. I'm so sorry, Senator. Would you like me to call your wife for you?"

"No... I'll take care of that. Thank you for calling."

Hennessey hung up the phone and shook his head slowly back and forth.

"What is it, John?"

"My son just killed himself."

Parling jumped to his feet.

"Jesus Christ, John... I'm sorry."

"All right, Jimmy, all right. Sit down. We need to get on top of this before the media does. I want someone to get my wife before she finds out... I mean, immediately. Get her on a private jet and fly her out here. She's going to go crazy... and I don't want a circus over this. I want her to play this in a very dignified way... like a Jackie Kennedy thing... and that'll take some work. I want you to call a press conference. Tell Annie to just give them the basic facts... say that both my wife and I are too overcome with grief to speak with anyone just now. If they go to Stony Brook – which they will – I want that doctor you arranged for, to be the only one to speak about this. Get him on the phone and get him straight on his story. The suicide was a result of a chemical imbalance... a disease. Nothing about any possibility that he killed himself over family matters. You got it, Jim?"

"Got it, John."

"They'll be watching my condo... so take my wife to a hotel somewhere around here... outside the Beltway... and register her under another name. Get a doctor and sedate her – big time. She could be a real loose cannon if we're not careful. John was her whole life. She could be a real problem."

"Anything else?"

"Yeah... her mother."

"Whose?"

"My wife's. She hates my fucking guts... and she'd have no qualms about saying it. That bitch'd go on camera and blame me for this whole fucking thing."

"How can we handle her?"

Hennessey thought for a few moments.

"I'll handle it. You get out of here and get going on this. We've gotta move fast, Jimmy."

Jimmy Parling left Hennessey's office without further word... his face displaying his determination to carry out his assignment without fail. Senator Hennessey immediately phoned his mother-in-law.

"Shirley?"

"Yes?"

"This is John."

"How are you, John?"

"Not too well, Shirley. I'm afraid I have some terrible news."

"Is it Emily?!... my God... is it Emily, John?! What happened, John?!"

"It's not Emily, Shirley... it's John. They just called me from Stony Brook Clinic. Just after breakfast this morning... he took his own life."

Shirley's end of the line went silent... then Hennessey could hear her breathing growing loud and erratic. She began to wail... fragments of words and sentences were interspersed with shrieks and moans. Hennessey waited impatiently. After some time, her energy began to flag and she again became silent. When she was finally able to speak, her voice was focused and laced with untold bitterness and hatred toward Senator John Hennessey – distilled over many years into a pure and potent poison.

"You did this, John. You killed him as sure as if you stabbed him with a knife. You've neglected that poor boy ever since the day he was born. All the good he was to you was to parade him around at your political events. All that poor sweet boy ever wanted, in his whole life, was one kind word from you... one word to say you loved him... one word to say you thought he was worth something. He got into all that trouble just so you'd notice him... and you go and lock him up and put him away... and drug him like some animal. You're evil, John... pure evil. You'll pay for every terrible thing you've ever done, someday. You'll pay, John. You'll pay with your soul."

"I really appreciate your sermon, Shirley... but I need to tell you something... and you had better listen very carefully. Are you listening, Shirley?"

"I'm listening, John... what is it?"

"Shirley... the media is going to come to you on this. If you ever plan on visiting your daughter, again, before you die... you won't say any of those things to them that you just said to me."

"Where's Emily, John? What have you done with her?"

"She's with me, Shirley... and if you open your mouth to say anything about me... except to say that I'm grieving about John... I'll see to it that you never see or talk to your daughter again. That is a solemn promise. Do you believe me, Shirley?"

No response.

"Shirley?"

"I have no doubt that you'll do as you say, John. You're Satan reincarnate. May you burn in hell, you bastard."

"Well thank you for your kind wishes for my future, Shirley... but I need to know your intentions."

"Don't worry, John. I'll keep my mouth shut... but I want to see my daughter."

"No problem, Shirley. I'll have my secretary make arrangements. She'll have a car pick you up at the airport. We understand each other... don't we, Shirley?"

"Yes."

CHAPTER SIX

Hennessey had to quickly make up his mind on the location of the funeral and burial of his son. His primary consideration was securing the optimum media exposure and attendance roster. After deliberation, he opted for Washington over California. In D.C., he'd likely get funeral attendance from both sides of the aisle... House and Senate... and a better than even chance of having the president in attendance – or at least the vice president – as well as a grand, cross-section of the remaining Washington elite. He needed them for the splash, and they needed to cover their bets in case Hennessey ended up in the White House. California offered the Hollywood crowd – and some big name stars could definitely be counted upon to attend – but that wouldn't do for Hennessey's desire to cloak the event in the trappings of dignified grief and stately solemnity. His decision made, the Senator had his public relations assistant come up to his office. Annie Moore climbed the stairs to the main office at a near-run... knowing Senator Hennessey's immense displeasure at being kept waiting. He had, only a week before, thrown a file in her face for such an infraction. As was his practice, he began the dialogue before she was in her seat.

"Have you heard?"

"Yes, Senator... you have my deepest sympathy."

"Thanks... now let's get to work on this. I'm staying out of the spotlight today... mourning... grief... you know. I want you to call Stony Brook and find out what they did with the body. Good chance it's at the coroner's... being a suicide. Make arrangements for the embalming... and to fly it down here. Have Julie get a Leer to fly me up there in the morning... then make arrangements for the casket to be flown down here – tomorrow, sometime. I don't think we can get it aboard a Leer. I want to fly back with it. Make the funeral arrangements for downtown

Washington. We'll get a lot better attendance that way. Get me a really well-known minister for the funeral. I don't care what denomination. When I get off the plane, I want wall-to-wall media... so get on it. Have some microphones out on the tarmac... and I'll make a brief statement... thanking everyone for their outpouring of sympathy. Get the press release out immediately... I want to make the evening news... and the morning papers... and check with Jimmy... he's calling a press conference. I want you to do the talking. Am I forgetting anything?"

"How about your wife, Senator?"

"I've got that covered. Someone's picking her up, out in California, and flying her here... should be in, sometime – early evening. I'm putting her up in a suburban hotel... sedating her. Keep the media from any direct access to her. She appears only with me... nothing more... and keeps her mouth shut. OK?"

"Fine, Senator."

"Anything else?"

"Not at the moment."

"OK... get going. Oh... send up Lisa Ryan."

The Senator was feeling agitated over the events of the day and he decided that fucking Lisa Ryan would go a long way to alleviating his discomfort.

Having heard, via the office grapevine, of the Senator's tragedy, Lisa assumed the Senator wanted her to develop something to say to the media. She offered her condolences as she entered his office. The Senator didn't reply.

"I'll need you tonight."

"Of course, Senator... what's up?"

JOHN 669

"For dinner."

"Sure... fine... who are we meeting with?"

"Just you and me."

"Fine... any particular agenda?"

"Just you and me... that's the agenda. Any problems with that?"

"No... not at all Senator. Should I bring anything... any particular file or whatever?"

"No... just your sexiest negligee. And tell your husband you'll be very late... that you might not make it home at all tonight."

Lisa understood... and was without words. The Senator went on, unimpeded.

"I'll have a car come for you about eight."

"Well... to be perfectly honest with you, Senator, this is my wedding anniversary today... and I was hoping to get home a little earlier than usual. I mean... you had no way of knowing that, of course, but I really don't think this is going to work out very well... you know?"

"No... I don't know. Here's the deal, Lisa. A car is coming for you at eight. We're going to have dinner – some place nice – then we're going to my place at the Watergate. There... we're going to fuck for most of the night. Can I make myself any clearer? You're not having your period, are you?"

"Uh... well... well, no... I'm not... but..."

"Do you enjoy your job here, Lisa?"

"Yes... yes I do, Senator... very much... but..."

"You wouldn't want to do anything to lose your job, would you?"

"No... but..."

"When the car arrives – get in it. If you don't... don't come to work tomorrow, or ever again, for that matter. Are we clear on this?"

"I understand, Senator."

"Also... if you come – come with the right attitude. I don't need anymore problems today."

Hennessey arrived at the K Street restaurant at eight o'clock. At eight-fifteen, Lisa walked in – her striking, youthful face was framed by an extremely becoming, yet sophisticated hairstyle and accentuated by provocatively appointed makeup. The alluring curvature of her well-exercised body was presented to the Senator in a revealing, but entirely tasteful, summer evening dress. Her attitude was right... stoically burying her anger and shame. In her necessary, protective frame of reference, she was going to work – doing what her job demanded of her. She'd smile, flirt, and give herself, entirely, for her job, career, and economic survival.

Lisa Ryan's job performance was, indisputably commendable. She enthusiastically accommodated the Senator's needs for the entire evening... and most of the night... being taken by him – by her count – a half dozen times before sunrise. By the time she left the bedroom of the soundly sleeping Hennessey, she was both exhausted and bruised... having been roughly used by her employer until she was granted reprieve by reason of his own fatigue. The gray of dawn was just revealing itself as she unlocked the door to her Arlington townhouse. Inside, she literally tore off her clothes – ripping the dress out of disgust – and threw them into the trash. She scrubbed her body with a rough sponge until the water in her shower ran cold. As she was drying herself, she heard her husband's alarm go off.

CHAPTER SEVEN

The skillfully directed theater, surrounding young John Hennessey's death, had, in Hennessey's opinion, garnered the most positive and effective media coverage he had received in his political career, to date. He and his staff had worked to put together a truly masterful media event and it played, precisely, according to its intent. Hennessey was credibly cast as a loving father who showed strength of character in bearing up under his grief. Emily Hennessey was kept successfully mute – via chemicals – and almost invisible. The outpouring of sympathy for the Senator far exceeded his hopes... and the guest list at both the viewing and funeral was truly stellar. Probably due to the fact that Hennessey was widely considered to be the front-runner for the presidential candidacy of his party, the event gathered worldwide attention. Photos of the grieving – yet dignified senator – walking beside his son's casket, as it was being pushed along the tarmac to the airport terminal, made the cover of five leading magazines. The story made the front page in nearly every newspaper in the country... and the lead in the network news. The story lines all followed the same general theme, ". . . the world of politics momentarily puts away its temporal concerns to mourn a personal tragedy of one of its own... a tragedy that transcends the often petty nature of partisanship... and places these matters into the light of the greater perspective."

In the evening, following the funeral, Hennessey issued a rare invitation to those on his staff – who were operatives in this magnificently successful media event – to champagne and hors d'oeuvres at his Watergate condo. Adding to the Senator's euphoria was Jimmy Parling's aside to him that he had located the whereabouts of the Novak sisters. Hennessey told him they'd get together about it in the morning. To John Hennessey, absolutely nothing in the world was more satisfying than vengeance.

At their morning meeting, Jimmy Parling informed the Senator that he had found Carleen – working as an executive director of a small-town chamber of commerce – her title being of much greater consequence than her compensation... and Kelly, in reclusion at home. The information put a smile on Hennessey's face – and a plan in his mind.

"Go through our channels in Michigan and plant the story that Carleen – that bitch – had left Washington in a big hurry because of some missing money and cooked books. After they can her, send her a dozen roses with a card from me. Write on it... 'Very sorry to hear of your recent employment development. Best of luck elsewhere.' "

Parling smiled in admiration of the Senator's precise surgical cut... deep into Carleen Novak's heart.

"What about the younger one?"

Hennessey assumed his customary reflective pose. Parling waited... eager to hear the details that would complete Hennessey's sense of total retribution. When he saw Hennessey begin to nod his head up and down... and a wide sadistic smile stretch across his cosmetically white teeth... he knew the serpent's egg had hatched.

"Find some people who will – for a modest fee – be willing to testify that they've bought drugs from the little bitch at her house. Then talk to Fred. Have him arrange to plant some stuff – make it cocaine – inside her house. Find out how many grams it takes to get some big time in Michigan. OK?"

"No problem, John. Any messages from you on this one?"

"Shit, yes... I almost let that one slip by me, Jim. Let's see... once she's convicted – and make sure their best prosecutor is on this case – after she's gone away... send her a video of that porno flick, 'Deep Throat'... and one to her sister, too. Mail it from some place other than California or D.C. No trace-back to me. No card in this one... no need... they'll both understand, perfectly."

"All right, John... I'll handle it. Anything else we need to go over?"

"The polls. Where am I after the funeral?"

"It's unbelievable, John... it really is."

"Where are we?"

"We're up by eleven since John's death."

"No shit, Jim?"

"Fuckin A."

"I was hoping for a few points... but eleven!... goddamn. Too bad the election's not next week."

"Well... if we don't fuck up – big time – somehow, between now and November... it should be a cakewalk. By the way, the little Jew wants to debate you."

"Up his ass, Jimmy."

"That's what I told Feldman's people. He must think we have *our* heads up his ass... that little kike, cocksucker. We're twenty-five points ahead... and he thinks we're going to debate him?! Stupid shit. He should have stayed in the ivory tower... the fucking airhead. These academics... Christ... they've got no balls and no stomach for real life. They spend all their time impressing eighteen, nineteen-year-olds with all their bullshit... all their war stories... about a war that never happened. He was four years at Penn... two at Harvard... five at Stanford. Eleven years as a student!... Christ!... he was in school from the time he was five until he was twenty-nine. And then he gets a job at U.C. teaching teenagers about political science. The fucker has probably never voted. He probably needs help finding the post office. Of course... his nomination was the best thing that ever happened to us, John. We won't have to spend even a tenth of our chest on this race. We can bankroll it for the big run."

"How are we doing on the primary states?"

"We've just about got it covered. One week after the election and we're on the trail, John. We'll announce next summer, sometime."

"Is Freddy downstairs?"

"Yeah, he is. You want him?"

"We need to get this Papa situation finalized. He'll be walking into L.A. in another week."

Hennessey pressed the intercom and told Julie to get Freddy up to his office. Jimmy had already spoken with Fred about the tentative plans and found he was already working on the details. Freddy laid them out for the Senator's perusal.

"I sent Larry out to California – about five days ago – to get the lay of things. He called me this morning. He's talked to a lot of the media... and some of the people who have been with the group for a while. It appears that this Papa is very accessible... to anyone who wants to talk to him... no protection at all. He could easily be killed by anyone, anytime."

Hennessey looked at Parling and shook his head back and forth.

"We can't have that. We've got to make sure he at least gets into L.A. How about we get in touch with Sanderson in Nevada and get him some more state police protection, Jim?"

"Shouldn't be any problem, John... he's one of ours."

"How big's the following, Fred?"

"It apparently dropped off, big time, after the shooting in Las Vegas... but now that they're getting near L.A.... it's really gotten big again."

"How big is big, Fred?"

"Well... you've got the two groups – the media... then all the rest. They're apparently a real mixed bag. Some are there because they think this guy is for real... but a lot of them are just groupies... you know – wanting to be a part of the action. But altogether... there are probably fifteen thousand people in the whole entourage."

Parling jumped in.

"Who's actually in charge? I mean, if we wanted to make some arrangements, who would we talk to, Fred?"

"That's what I told Larry to find out. He thinks the best person to deal with is this Marty Chapman guy... the one who wrote the first articles about this Papa. He seems to be a central figure in this whole thing."

Parling shook his head in disgust.

"Oh, Christ... another fucking Jew. Why do we always have to be dealing with fucking Jews?"

Hennessey reentered the discussion.

"Jew or no Jew... if he's the one we have to deal with – let's do it."

Fred reasserted himself.

"What's the pitch, Senator?"

"First of all, I want you out there. This is out of Larry's league. You approach this Chapman guy and you tell him that I'm very concerned about the safety of his people... and that I'd like to offer my assistance... especially once they get into L.A. Tell him I can arrange for complete police protection... and for places where this Papa can make his speeches. Tell him we'll get things all set up... the locations... the P.A. systems... protection... just like some rock star."

"I'll get out there this afternoon, Senator."

"Tell Julie to get you a helicopter when you get out there so you can go right to where they are. Now... what about the Right? I've told Jimmy that I need to know what's going on."

"Well... they're all pissed off about Las Vegas... but that guy was one of the best, Senator... he really was. I don't know what happened. They want to try again... real soon."

"Well tell them they can't. They're going to have to wait. I'm not going to pass up this media bonanza for anybody. They'll just have to wait. Are you calling the shots, Fred? No pun intended."

Both Fred and Jimmy snorted small, appreciative chuckles.

"Yeah... I am. They've pretty much left it up to me."

"That's perfect. Who are you working with... still Golden?"

"Yeah."

"Is Benson Powell staying out of it?"

"Completely."

"OK... tell Golden that we'll set up a perfect shoot for them... but he'll just have to be patient. After we've milked this for all it's worth – they can have him. Jimmy... you get on the phone to Wilburn about state police protection... and Blystone about the LAPD. Tell him I'd like to coordinate the whole thing. If they give you any shit... remind Wilburn that it was me that put him in the governor's mansion... and remind Blystone that I got him his appointment, too. I can just as easily make it go the other way if they fuck me around."

JOHN

"They'll cooperate, John."

"They'd better, Jimmy. Fred… you work with Annie to get these speaking locations set up… and think big… bigger than you've ever thought before. The whole world will want to get in to see this guy. He's apparently bigger than Elvis. Any questions?"

"No sir."

"Then get your ass in gear, Fred. Make me proud."

Fred jumped to his feet in a rigid posture, so closely resembling an officer of the Third Reich that both the other men very nearly lost their composure. Fred stomped stiffly out of the office. After he closed the door, Hennessey and Parling finally let loose their barely contained laughter. Amid his spasms, Jimmy added to the comedy.

"Christ!… I thought he was going to give you a Nazi salute!"

This new fuel notched up their convulsive shrieks to near hysterics. It was several minutes before either could get back to business. Drying his eyes, Hennessey finally asked about a replacement for Will Blasco.

"I've just about got Ted Rossiter on board."

"What's he waiting on?"

"You know Rossiter… he never jumps until the water's perfect. I think he's waiting for the latest polls."

"Well, he ought to be on board after these polls."

"I'm sure he is. I'll call him when we're done here."

"What's Blasco up to these days?"

"He's trying to get on with Shernock's staff."

"Well... you call him and tell him that if he leaks out any bad press about me... he'll be out of politics, altogether."

"I already did, John."

"What'd he say?"

"He's such a fucking whore. He told me to offer his apologies to you... and wish you well."

"That dickless faggot. I almost wish he had the balls to stand up to me. I'd enjoy breaking his back."

"No chance of that. He was a big mistake, John."

"You recommended him, Jimmy."

"I fucked up, John... pure and simple. But Rossiter is the best. He was my first choice, anyway."

"Let's get rolling, Jimmy... and I want you to keep an eye on this Papa operation. Freddy gets a little carried away, sometimes. As soon as we settle on an itinerary for the speeches, let's get it out. I want optimum media and crowds. Let the Right know about the details of the last stop as soon as possible... give them as much time as they need to get set up. Oh... and look into a bulletproof vest for me."

CHAPTER EIGHT

Freddy Westin was able to get Marty Chapman's ear when the procession was about sixty miles from L.A. Marty seemed, to Freddy, to be suspicious of the Senator's intentions... correctly surmising that Hennessey wanted to use the event for his own campaign publicity. Freddy later reported to Hennessey that a woman, by the name of Ginny – apparently traveling with Chapman – eventually prevailed upon him to accept the assistance... even if the Senator did want to use the event for publicity. She persuaded him that L.A. would be considerably more dangerous than Las Vegas... and that Papa would appreciate the protection for his followers – as well as the help in making arrangements for him to speak to the people. Chapman said he'd have to talk to Papa about it. He returned with Papa's agreement... and a message to be delivered to Senator Hennessey. Freddy was to tell the Senator that Papa says that John makes his heart ache... but he loves him and forgives him... and hopes he finds his way home.

Fred flew back in the afternoon, after meeting with Chapman, and met with the Senator and Parling. Both were very pleased to hear that Papa would accept their offer. This would give them virtual control over the group's movements in L.A. Hennessey told Fred to get Annie moving, right away, with the speaking itinerary... and then get it out to the media. Just before leaving the office, Fred delivered the message to Hennessey from Papa. Hennessey's face took on a momentary, puzzled look that neither Parling nor Freddy had ever seen before... then quickly recovered to its normal, cynical countenance.

"What kind of game is that kook trying to play? Did you talk to him yourself?"

"No... I really didn't even get to see him. Chapman talked to him alone and came back with his answer... and with his message for you."

"I'm looking forward to seeing this Papa guy... face-to-face. I want to see him try to work some of his bullshit on me."

Parling watched Hennessey's face as he mused over this thought. The mixture of puzzlement and fascination had returned. Jimmy considered it very odd.

It was Monday. Freddy calculated that Papa and his immense throng would enter the city on Saturday. Annie worked all day in the Los Angeles area – Monday, Tuesday, and Wednesday – on arrangements. She found nine large, suitable speaking locations... one for each evening, commencing on the first Saturday... the last on the Sunday of the following weekend. She scheduled virtually every large coliseum and stadium in the L.A. area in order to geographically spread the tour. The final event was going to be, if all went according to plan – in Annie's estimation – absolutely spectacular. She had arranged to have a large stage constructed at the edge of the cliff at Santa Monica... overlooking the beach, the pier, the highway, and the expanse of ocean below. It would be visible for miles along the beach – both north and south... and for miles out to sea. Thousands of people could anchor their boats, off-shore, to witness the event. Annie had arranged for enormous sound systems to be set up – the type used by rock bands in concert – and for large screen projection units, facing in all directions. She calculated that the potential, live audience could be nearly a million people... and the television audience, incalculable.

As soon as the exact details of the location, size, and height of the Santa Monica speaking stand were determined, Fred met with Ron Golden. They had to move quickly. Fred had already located another shooter and Fred went out with Golden, on Friday, to scout sniper locations in Santa Monica. They concluded that either the shooter would have to come from the front... shooting from a boat... or from behind... from some elevated spot. They decided on the hotel – directly behind the stand and across the street. They quickly eliminated the boat shoot as being too risky, both from the potential of being spotted, and because of the effect of the water's motion on the shooter's bead. Fred went inside the hotel and asked the front desk clerk to see one of their rooms on the top floor... explaining that he wanted to get a room for a friend who was coming to town the following week... and wanted to ensure a great view of the ocean for him. The clerk gave him the key and Fred went up. When he looked out, he immediately discovered the room wouldn't work. The tops of the trees completely blocked the line of vision to where the platform would be built. He went back down to the front desk and told the clerk that the tenth floor was probably a little too high for his friend... and asked for a key to a room on, perhaps, the fourth floor. The room turned out to be just about perfect, with a direct line of sight to the platform. Fred paid, in cash, for a room on Saturday and Sunday night... and left a fictitious name of his friend, who, he said would call for the key.

On Thursday, the Senator cleared his entire schedule to dedicate his time to the Papa project. A large portion of his staff was in attendance at the meetings, including Ted Rossiter, who had signed on as campaign manager the day before. The details of the Los Angeles tour were, after much discussion and debate, eventually worked out.

When the Papa entourage crossed the city limits, it was decided that the Senator and other select dignitaries – of the Senator's choosing – would be present to welcome them. It would be a relatively brief ceremony, and the Senator would be the central figure in the reception. The mayor was indebted to the Senator – as were most California politicians – and accepted his secondary position in the welcome party without objection. The governor was directed, by Hennessey, to simply stay away. He acquiesced. Annie had the week planned to build to a climax at the final, Sunday event, but she didn't want the Senator to appear so often with the assembly that he would begin to look like a groupie. On the first day, he'd do the welcome... then be available for questions from the media. Annie knew that the initial media focus would be on Papa... and didn't want the Senator to appear to be trying to compete with him. The Senator insisted on making an appearance on the platform for each speaking engagement... but agreed he would generally remain in the background. The simple face-time on camera would do, they decided, in the initial stages of the Papa, L.A. tour. On the final Sunday – and by far the biggest of all the gatherings – she had arranged for the Senator to make a speech, before Papa spoke, to what would likely be the largest gathering of people that had ever assembled in the United States... outside, possibly, a few of the historical Washington marches... but had the potential to eclipse even the largest of these.

A number of televisions were set up throughout Hennessey's Washington suite of offices and throughout the week, they constantly monitored the media coverage of the event. Fred Westin's estimated time of arrival for Papa and his army turned out to be right on the nose. On Thursday evening, they were in the San Bernadino National forest... two days from the city limits. They'd camp out on the outskirts on Friday and enter in the morning. The crowd walking with Papa was now estimated at over thirty thousand people, exclusive of the media. News organizations from all over the world were descending upon L.A. Annie Moore had issued Papa's speaking itinerary on Wednesday and the media were already vying for the best set-up spaces at each location. As part of the press packages, Annie had also provided the information that Senator Hennessey was coordinating the efforts. As a result, a steady stream of media was also coming and going at Hennessey's Washington office suite to interview Hennessey. Annie had finally given up on trying to arrange individual interviews and began scheduling press conferences in the large Senate press room. On Friday morning, Hennessey was scheduled to fly to Los Angeles to prepare for the following day's event. He called Lisa Ryan at home on Thursday evening and told her that she would fly out with him... and spend the night with him. He told her to plan on being out there for the entire week. He also told her he wanted her available for not only speeches... but for sex, as well.

Annie Moore was already in L.A.... coordinating the efforts. The route that Papa and his people would walk during the first day was cordoned off with yellow, plastic police tape. Each day, the route that would be traversed, would be similarly blocked off. An advantageous spot had been selected, just inside the city limits, for the dignitaries to welcome Papa on his arrival. The location was announced ahead of time to allow for camera set-ups and a small stand was constructed with a plethora of microphones bunched in front of it. As the entourage entered the city, Annie would immediately meet their leadership... to make them aware of the welcoming party, and direct them to the speaking stand... then make the necessary introductions.

Hennessey, Parling, Rossiter, and Lisa Ryan departed in the borrowed corporate jet at ten o'clock on Friday morning. Hennessey had Lisa sit beside him on the flight out, to talk business... and other matters. She had already gotten a short speech ready for him to deliver at the welcoming ceremony. He read it over and made some small changes. Hennessey then mentioned to her that Rossiter found her very attractive and that, if called upon, she might have to take care of him, as well, on this trip. The Senator told her he was confident she could handle it.

As they neared California, Hennessey told the pilot to fly over the section of highway where the Papa entourage was walking. The pilot contacted air traffic control and got clearance to deviate from his flight plan... and, also, to fly at a lower-than-scheduled altitude. Receiving permission, they descended to about five thousand feet and turned to the northwest to converge with the path of the human spectacle. The pilot announced over the intercom that the group was coming up... off the right wing. They all went to that side and looked out. The sight was extraordinary. The highway was obliterated, for miles, by a pulsating, multi-colored, sea of humanity. Parling commented that it was the largest group of people he'd ever seen – outside of a ball stadium crowd. He guessed there were at least eighty thousand people, or more. The pilot flew a circle over the teeming mass... his right wing down so his passengers could get a good view of the spectacle... then proceeded on to the airport.

The four were taken, by limousine, to their hotel – their designated command center during the Papa tour. The Senator was given a handsomely appointed corner suite. The six rooms nearest the suite – three on each side of the corridor – were taken for all his staffers. The four travelers regrouped at six o'clock for drinks in the hotel restaurant... then dinner at seven. Hennessey told Parling to come over to his suite later, at about ten o'clock, and bring Annie Moore... then, later, he wanted to see Freddie and him alone.

As they rode up on the elevator, after dinner, Hennessey told Lisa he wanted her in his suite in a half-an-hour. She rushed to go to the bathroom, call her husband, and got at least, somewhat freshened-up in the scant thirty minutes he had allotted her... knowing, as did all the staff, the potential ramifications of being late. Rossiter answered the door to the suite. He told her that the Senator was in the bedroom... that she should go on in – pointing to a door behind him and to his right. She knocked on the door and heard Hennessey's command to enter. Hennessey was lying in the enormous bed – the largest Lisa had ever seen – with a cut glass tumbler, containing scotch on ice, in his right hand. The wine-red comforter, adorned with a gold-threaded, regal pattern, covered him, up to his stomach. He pointed to a scant, off-white, silk negligee lying across the foot of the bed... and told her to put it on... and to fix herself a drink at the bar. She dutifully obeyed... changing in the connecting bathroom, then, when she emerged, she poured herself a glass of ginger ale, over ice. Hennessey reached over to the left side of the bed, grasped the thick comforter and pulled it down, with a quick jerk, from its tightly tucked position, exposing the off-white satin sheets. He patted the lower sheet and gazed, commandingly, at her. She walked slowly and obediently to the bed and climbed in... mirroring Hennessey by lifting her pillow and propping it against the headboard. She pulled the top sheet and comforter up to her waist and began sipping her drink. They sat in silence for a few minutes... their sipping and swallowing audible to one another. He finished his drink first, and told her to get him another scotch. He watched her as she crossed the large bedroom to the bar. The negligee hung just to the top of her thighs and Hennessey's passion grew as her movement alternately covered and uncovered her beautifully rounded, naked buttocks.

Hennessey loved scotch... but Lisa's naked posterior had fanned his desire beyond containment. He took one last, small sip from his fresh scotch, put it on the night stand, and pulled the covers down to his knees – exposing his erect penis. His eyes narrowed and his nostrils widened. He spoke to her in a sinister, lustful whisper.

"Suck it good, baby."

Outside the door, Rossiter was becoming aroused by Hennessey's lewd shouting. For nearly forty-five minutes he listened to Hennessey command Lisa Ryan, calling her demeaning and vulgar names while she performed according to his instructions. He thought he heard the sound of slapping from time to time... then finally the room lapsed into complete silence. After about twenty minutes, Hennessey emerged, wearing his bathrobe and pajamas... his hair wet from a very recent shower. He smiled at Ted Rossiter.

"All yours, Ted."

In about an hour, Rossiter emerged from the same bedroom, offering Hennessey a tired, satisfied smile that conveyed an understood message of primal male fellowship, derived from the salacious sharing of the same female. He told Hennessey that Lisa said she was exhausted and needed to rest for a bit. Hennessey didn't like it, preferring she rest in her own room... then freshen up for a later encounter, but was too mellow, at the moment, to protest. He walked to the bedroom door and opened it... seeing a soundly sleeping Lisa, curled into a small, fetal position. Just as he closed the bedroom door, sharp knocks resounded from the suite door. Hennessey walked over and opened it. Jimmy Parling walked in... with Annie Moore and Freddy Westin following behind.

They went over the plans for the next morning. The Papa contingent would be coming out of San Bernardino National Forest on Interstate 15 and entering the Los Angeles area in west San Bernardino – in Fontana. They'd get off the interstate at the Sierra Avenue exit. The welcoming platform was set up about five miles south on Sierra, to allow the entire entourage to clear off the interstate before they stopped. They would have a helicopter in the air, above the throng, to provide them with updates on the contingent's position. The Senator and the various other members of the party would wait at the hotel until they got word that the party had started off the exit. They would then be driven to the airport where a helicopter would take them to downtown San Bernadino. They'd have police escorts from there and should be at the platform in plenty of time, before the Papa group arrived. Annie said she had expected Lisa to be at the meeting... to talk a little about the speech and press responses. The Senator responded that he had already talked to Lisa about it... and that she was a little tired and was resting.

After the welcome and press questions, they'd return to the hotel the same way they'd arrived. Annie said they needed to be out at the L.A. airport by eight in the morning so she had arranged for the limo to be out front at seven in the morning – allowing extra time for possible traffic problems.

At eleven o'clock – their business being completed – Hennessey turned on the television for the news. Flipping through the channels – as expected – the Papa story was the lead on each one. Details were given on the days, times, and locations of each stop on the L.A. tour. At about eleven-fifteen, Hennessey told Annie he had some things he needed to talk over with Fred and Jimmy. When she had closed the door to the suite, they began.

As always, Hennessey led.

"What's the deal with the shooter, Fred?"

"It's set... next Sunday at Santa Monica... at his final speech."

"Let's be a little more specific. I don't want to end up like that little faggot in Las Vegas."

"Don't worry, Senator. This guy is absolutely the best. They wanted a cross fire, but there's no good way of doing it from where he's going to be standing."

"Who... Papa or the shooter?"

"Sorry... Papa."

"Go ahead."

"Anyway... it'll be only one shooter. That's safer for you. Cross fires are more of a sure hit... but they're dangerous as hell – almost always take out a few others, besides the target. Look what happened in Dallas. Our man is going to be in a hotel behind the platform... just across the street. We've already got him a room. He'll let Papa finish his speech – then take him out."

"Where am I going to be for this?"

"Here's the way we've got it set up, Senator. While he's speaking, we want you to stand at the very back of the platform... toward the street. The platform is on the west side of Ocean Avenue... close to the edge of the overlook... just north of the pier. You know where we're talking about?"

"Yes."

"The front of the platform overlooks the beach. When he's finished speaking, we want you to call him back to you... at the very back end of the stand. Talk to him for a few seconds – then Jimmy is going to call you over to him. He's going to be standing at the rear of the platform, too... on the north end of the platform. You should stand on the south end... toward the pier. As soon as you're safely clear, the shooter will take him out. You can be ready to rush to the mikes and calm the crowd and do your thing. We obviously won't be able to tip your security people beforehand, so it's likely they'll try to surround you right after the shots. You'll have to be ready for that. Jimmy can tell them to back off and let you get to the mikes. It's not going to be real obvious, at first, what happened. Since the shoot is going to be from a hotel window, in close quarters to other people in the hotel, our boy is using a silencer... a really good one, I'm told. Supposedly, you couldn't hear it if you were a foot away from the barrel. So, until

Papa goes down and the people notice the blood, nobody's going to know anything. That should give you time to get to the front of the platform."

"How safe are we from being connected with this?"

"It's all worked out. An hour after the shoot, our guy will be out of the country... on his way back to France. There'll be a chopper waiting for him, near the hotel, to take him to Mexico. He'll get his plane there. We have four hand-offs set up for the gun in a half-an-hour. That thing'll be air-dropped, ten miles out to sea, in less than an hour."

Hennessey looked at Parling.

"What do you think, Jim?"

"I've been through it a dozen times. I don't see any problems. The worst that can happen is that a couple of other people will go down with this guy. That's about it. We're going to have the dignitaries over with me – telling them that that's the side the limos are going to get everyone, after Papa is done speaking. So... no one, big, should take a bullet... if they do what we tell them to do. That'll keep it from getting too hot. I mean, how much time are they going to spend investigating this, if some average schmuck goes down?"

After Parling and Westin had gone, Hennessey opened the bedroom door – to find Lisa Ryan still soundly sleeping. After he'd closed the door to the bathroom, she opened her eyes and sat up from her convincing act of slumber. The conversation she overheard had shaken her to the very core of her being. Her instinct was to run out of the room and get as far from these people as possible... as quickly as possible. Her rationality kept her in bed.

Lisa Ryan had just discovered that the professional game of politics, into which she sought her place, went far beyond mere egotism, power, and sex. In that moment, for the first time, she had come to the frightening realization that the contest had *absolutely* no rules. In the lust for power, she now understood that someone's murder was apparently of no more consequence than a negative campaign ad or a poll rating. Any tool that was right for the job was used… without any further reflection. She resolved, in that same moment of epiphany, to get completely out of the business. But she was no fool. She now had no doubt that if Hennessey suspected, for a single moment, that she had overheard their conversation, he'd squash the life out of her with no more concern than if she were a pesky mosquito, buzzing around his ear.

When she saw the light go out under the bathroom door, she resumed her act of sound sleep, taking the same position as when Hennessey had come into the bedroom – lying on her left side, her knees drawn up… laying as far to her own side of the bed as gravity would permit. She hoped, with all hope, that Hennessey would either be too tired to bother her anymore… or he might, possibly, respect her sleep. She was wrong on both counts.

Hennessey climbed – naked – into the side of the bed opposite Lisa and, without pause, slid across the smooth sheets to her back. From the rear, he slid his right hand between her upper thighs and pushed several fingers into her vagina. Keeping the path open, with his left hand, he directed his swollen penis into her. He then grabbed the back of her neck with his left hand and her upturned shoulder with his right and pushed her upper body forward and downward… her buttocks being forced even further toward him. Apparently in the position he desired, he placed a hand on each of her shoulders and gripped both, firmly. Without prelude, he began ramming himself into her at a rapid pace. It was clear to Lisa that she was, to him, persona non grata… being used, simply as a fleshy device with which Hennessey could masturbate himself. Each time he would thrust, he pulled her toward him and increased his grip on her. The violence of his movement brought forth, much to Lisa's misfortune, an involuntary, anguished moan from her throat. Hennessey's misinterpretation of the sound inspired him to increase the voraciousness of his act, which turned out to be a mixed blessing, in that, although his violent thrusting now stabbed into her as though she were being raped with a broom handle, his heightened state of excitement brought him to climax sooner than he would have otherwise. Exhausted, he fell immediately to sleep. Much to Lisa's horror, he remained inside her, as he did. She waited a seeming infinity, then with prodigious care, slid away from him and from the bed. Quietly, she searched for her clothes in the darkened bedroom and then took them to the outer room to get dressed. She exited the suite and walked, quickly and quietly, down the hall to the sanctuary of her own room. The repeated outrages against her body and spirit had drained all feeling from her. She felt so hopelessly filthy that she would never be able to wash her body clean again. Instead, then, of taking a shower, she lay there in self-loathing and disgust... covered with her penance of filth... and she knew that something precious, as yet undefined, had been irrevocably taken from her that night.

The light from her window awakened her early... the red digital numbers on the clock radio displaying 6:23. For the first time in many years, she prayed – prayed that Hennessey would decide not to bring her along on the welcoming mission. She brewed the packet of complimentary coffee into the small pot on the bathroom sink top... then sat in the chair near the window – alternately looking out at the emerging life on Wilshire Boulevard and the painfully slow advance of the red, clock numbers. She knew the limo was coming at seven. Past that time, she would be safe. At six-forty-five, the bleeping sound of her phone interrupted the silence and sent a shock through her overwrought system. She momentarily considered not answering it... sure it was Hennessey or one of the staffers – telling her to get down to the limo. Her conditioned fear of Hennessey's wrath, however, finally compelled her to pick up the receiver.

"Hello?"

"Lisa?"

"Nicky... oh Nicky..."

The soft flesh and soul that had stoically borne the atrocities of the previous evening in tortured solitude could no longer contain them in the embracing love of her husband's voice. Lisa Ryan wept and moaned into her husband's ear, overcome by inconsolable grief... speaking her feelings in the only way she could. Nick Ryan repeatedly implored her to tell him what had happened. Amid her emotional flood, the only response she could garner in response to his plea was, "I can't." Her pain was unbearable... but her shame was greater... not allowing her to lay her burden down upon this man who loved her more than life itself. Finally her urgency found words.

"Nicky... I've got to get out of here!"

"Lisa... honey... what in the world is going on?"

"Some things have happened... I can't tell you all of it right now... but Nicky... they're going to kill someone!"

"What? Who is?"

"Senator Hennessey and Mr. Parling and Freddy."

"Are you serious, Lisa?"

"I heard them talking about it last night."

"Jesus Christ! Who is it?!"

"This man who's here in Los Angeles today... this Papa man."

"Goddamn, Lis... I don't know what to say. This is just unbelievable. Are you in any kind of trouble?"

"I don't think so. But if they ever discover that I overheard the conversation, I will be. I mean it, Nicky... they'll kill me. I'm sure of it."

"Are you absolutely sure about all of this, Lis?"

"Nicky... I heard them... all the details. Oh Nicky, I've got to get out of here... I can't be a part of this! I just want to be away from these people. But I don't have the money for a plane ticket... and there's nothing left on the VISA."

"I can call my Dad... and see if we can borrow some money. I'll call him as soon as we get off the phone. How much do you need?"

"The ticket's going to be... probably three or four hundred... and I need money for a taxi... out to the airport. I've only got about thirty dollars to my name."

"I'll ask him for six hundred... OK?"

"I hate to do this to you, honey."

"It's all right. C'mon, Lis... it'll be all right. Shouldn't you tell somebody about this?"

"Oh, Nicky... I can't... they'd kill me. I'm really serious. They would."

"But we can't let them..."

"Nicky! Believe me!"

"OK honey, OK. Let me get off the phone... and I'll call you right back... after I talk to Dad."

In ten minutes time, the phone rang. Nick's father would wire the money... but wouldn't be able to do it until after work. The money was going to a Western Union office, a few blocks from the hotel. Lisa calculated that it would be about three o'clock, her time, before she'd get the money. Lisa's stomach tightened as she anticipated the difficulties she might encounter in pulling it off. She couldn't tell Hennessey, ahead of time, that she was leaving. He'd be both suspicious and furious... and he'd break her down... she knew he would... and get the real story. She knew she didn't have the strength to stand up to him. She'd just have to wait for her chance to escape.

At around eight-thirty, Lisa went down to the hotel restaurant and had breakfast... charging it to her room. She came back up to her room and turned on the television to watch the coverage of the Papa event. Every station was covering it. The live aerial shots showed the huge mass of followers, just then coming off of Interstate 15 at the Sierra Avenue exit. An assortment of commentators attempted to put the event into perspective. Many, of course, compared it to Jesus Christ's entrance into Jerusalem. None could find a true modern-day equivalent, except possibly, some offered, Gandhi's walk to the sea. On an L.A. station, a panel of three experts – a rabbi from a temple in Glendale, a psychologist from UCLA Medical Center, and a sociologist, also from UCLA – were asked about the meaning of this movement and the claim of some that miracles had been performed by Papa. The rabbi was asked, specifically, if this man could be the messiah. He was non-committal in his answer... but conceded it was possible – but that time, alone, would tell. On the question of miracles, he, again, said that they must wait for further proof. He said that if this man were, indeed, divine... God would, in time, reveal this truth to the world.

The psychologist's view was that this man was, obviously, a true charismatic, in the functional sense of the word. He felt that Papa was, obviously, fulfilling some need that was apparently pervasive in modern-day society, which was, in his opinion – given the decline of traditional religion – a search for new spiritual grounding. Regarding Papa, himself, the psychologist said that without examining him, he couldn't make any specific diagnosis as to the possibility of any particular pathology, but, he said, it was clear that he had had a very unusual upbringing and life experience and that his personality was bound to be quite eccentric as a result.

The sociologist agreed with his UCLA colleague – that Papa was obviously fulfilling some sort of wide-spread societal need... and that the near insatiable public demand for media coverage of Papa, and the movement in general, was evidence of it. He said that it was possible that this movement could be much more lasting than a mere media frenzy or social fad... and that the world may be, in fact, witnessing the birth of a new fundamental religion... the first since the founding of Islam, some fifteen hundred years past. He said that he, personally, found the Papa phenomenon to be the most exciting social movement of at least the current century... or perhaps the last half-millennium. One of the most interesting aspects of the movement, to him, was that, according to his research, members of established religions were just as likely to be interested in the Papa movement as those who were not. If the interest continued, he said, it was possible there could be some significant shifts in the demographics of the major religions... and that this possibility certainly had not gone unnoticed by the leadership of these faiths. This statement caused the interviewer to ask the rabbi if he was at all concerned about losing any of his following to the Papa movement. He conceded that the movement had a new and fresh appeal... but that history and custom were strong factors in traditional religion... and he felt the vast majority of Jews would remain committed to the ancestral faith.

At a few minutes after ten, the cameras focused on the welcoming platform and the approaching contingent. When the lead group of the approaching mass was about five hundred feet from the platform, Senator Hennessey led a group of about ten people toward them. They converged at a point, a few hundred feet north of the welcome area. The Senator walked directly to Papa and extended his hand. Papa smiled warmly at him, paused, then, without speaking, enclosed Hennessey's hand in his. Hennessey introduced the welcoming party to Papa... each shaking hands with him. The combined groups walked the remaining distance to the platform. Lisa had watched for Annie Moore, who had said she would meet the leaders of the march further north on Sierra and escort them to the platform. To Lisa's eye, Annie was no where in sight.

Seeing this giant man... and his kind face and smile... heightened Lisa's anguish over the plans for his murder. She wondered if she could really just turn her back and allow him to be killed in cold blood. She stood up and began pacing, back and forth, in front of the television... glancing obliquely at the screen as she passed by. Each time she would see a close-up of Papa, she would look away. Finally, she could endure it no longer and clicked the set off.

Allowing for the welcoming ceremony and the return trip, Lisa expected the Senator and his party back at the hotel around noon. As she waited, the anxiety of accomplishing her escape – and her secret knowledge of the planned murder – was overwhelming her. Sitting in her hotel room, she could feel her whole body shake with each beat of her heart and her breathing becoming faster and shallower. She sensed that if she didn't get herself under control, she was going to faint. If the Senator saw her like this, it would be completely apparent that something was amiss... and he'd find out, very quickly, what it was. She considered taking a Valium, but decided against it... realizing that to successfully execute her plan, she needed to be as alert and clear-minded as possible. Instead, she elected to go for a walk outside... hoping the sunshine and warm air would calm her nerves.

The hotel, being only a twenty-minute walk from the Santa Monica beach area, where the final gathering was scheduled for Papa – and the site of his planned assassination – Lisa decided on that as her destination. The blue skies and the warmth of the sun on her shoulders had, almost immediately, its hoped-for effect. The beauty and comfort of the day gave her its generous gift of a vague sense of hope... and her uplifted spirits freed her mind to engage in some necessary strategic planning. She needed to get to the Western Union office in the afternoon. Hennessey could very well send for her as soon as he arrived back at the hotel... for speech planning, sex, or both... for who knows how long. That would not do. Not only did the thought of his touching her, again, make her feel like vomiting, but she would be kept from getting her money. She then realized that she should have called the Western Union office while she was in her room to ask about their hours... just in case she was unavoidably delayed.

The thought of vomiting inspired a plan in her mind. When she was a little girl, her sure-fire strategy to avoid going to school was to throw up... or pretend to have. Over the years, she had refined this method to a virtual art form... developing the uncanny ability of being able to throw up on command. She hadn't done it in quite a few years, but was still very confident of her latent talent. She resolved her plan. When they called for her, she'd feign an upset stomach... adding unnecessary and graphic details for effect. If Hennessey was suspicious, and came down to her room... or sent someone... she'd fall back on her unique talent to eliminate any doubt as to the veracity of her story. Once she was sure they were convinced, she'd sneak out of the hotel and get her money. If they happened to catch her in the act, she'd claim she was going out to a drug store to get something for her nausea. Having dealt with that problem, she moved on to the next – if, and how, to tell her husband about the sex with Hennessey and Rossiter.

Nick Ryan – like most men – was to his wife – like most men are to women – quite simple, predictable, and manageable in both emotion and action. Nick was very intelligent, logical, trusting, devoted, and possessive... but, as do most men, he liked to keep things simple in the matters of day-to-day living and relationships. Like most women, Lisa had, during the course of their marriage, told him only what she felt he really needed to know... and benignly manipulated him toward what she felt was for his own good. Also, as do most women, Lisa didn't feel this was truly deceitful... but merely more efficient – and merciful... well aware of the profound dislike men have for unnecessary details and complicated situations. She had kept many such things from him during their three-year marriage... frivolous purchases (and their price)... bills she hadn't paid... credit cards she had secretly acquired... speeding tickets... scratches and dents in the car... necessary business lunches with certain men who would have provoked Nick's jealousy, had he known.

Keeping secret the first night of sex with Hennessey was, according to her female paradigm of morality, another merciful and necessary omission for the benefit of their marriage. Had she told Nick of the Senator's ultimatum of either sex or job, he would have undoubtedly, blown up and, besides causing her to lose her job, would likely have gotten himself arrested, to boot. Lisa, with a woman's practical sense of morality, assessed the situation and made her decision – as logically perverse as it may seem to a man – to do what was best for their mutual benefit... which meant, in this case, sleeping with her boss. To her, it was a sacrifice and a humiliation she was compelled to endure, in silence, for both of them.

At the time of this decision, Nick was about to enter his senior year at law school. She was the sole support of the family, except for the low-paying jobs Nick would occasionally locate for the summer... of which he was presently completing his last week for the current season, with classes set to begin the following week. Only through the odd quirks of fate and luck did she acquire her job with Senator Hennessey – a chance in a million – bumping into the right person at the right moment... a convergence of time and place that would very likely, never again, repeat itself. Her high-paying job with Hennessey was what allowed Nick to attend law school. If she lost it – and was forced to take the sort of job she would have, otherwise, he'd have no choice but to drop out and get a job, himself. It took every penny of her present income just to keep them going. As Lisa saw it, if it took sleeping with Hennessey to keep Nick in law school, she'd do it... and she'd keep it to herself. She would just have to deal with it as best she could.

Things were such now, however, that her practical morality had become untenable in dealing with her present circumstances. Her defilement at the hands of these two, truly despicable men was simply more than she could bear to suffer in silence. She instinctively knew that her spirit had been permanently marred by these vermin... and that she wouldn't be able to conceal her psychic disfigurement from her husband. The two debauchers had taken much more from her than she was willing to sacrifice... much more than she thought they could. With this horrid experience, the line had been crossed from courageous selflessness... to morose self-loathing... and she found herself trapped in a paradox that this utilitarian, female morality, gone awry, can create. She felt she *must* tell her husband, but she *knew* she could not.

As these thoughts weighed upon her heart and mind, she realized she had arrived at Ocean Avenue. She crossed over and walked to the split-rail fence, marking the edge of the long, vertical drop to the highway below, which wound its way along the beach for as far as she could see, north and south. She was standing in the approximate location – as the overheard conversation described it – where Papa's final words – and murder – would take place. She looked out at the great expanse of the Pacific... reflecting that this inspiring panorama would be this poor man's last sight before he was killed... shuddering at the cruel mixture of beauty and horror it would be. She turned suddenly and looked back – across the street to the hotel where Freddy Westin had said the shooter would be placed. The reality of this planned death suddenly stung her sensibilities, and she felt like screaming... as though that would serve as some sort of warning to this kindly, innocent man, and placate her own sense of guilt. The feeling that someone was standing very close to her, interrupted her preoccupation. The sharpness of her senses regained, she turned cautiously to her left. Annie Moore was standing there, a few inches from her arm... gazing out at the water.

"Annie?"

Annie turned to look at Lisa. Her appearance was so different that it gave Lisa a start. Lisa studied her face, looking for the specific changes that had so altered her image. She could find none... yet she was, undeniably changed. Suddenly it struck Lisa that it wasn't Annie Moore's looks that had changed... it was her *look*... her general countenance... that was different.

"Are you OK, Annie?"

Annie smiled with a sense of serene calm that Lisa had, never before, seen on her face.

"I know who Papa is, Lisa... I recognized him... and he knows me... everything about me... and he loves me, Lisa. He loves you too. He knows all of us. He is who he says he is, Lisa. All my loneliness – the loneliness we all feel – is gone. I know I'm loved, now... with a love that never ends. I'm happier, now, than I ever thought was possible. He is God, Lisa... but he's not scary or mysterious like the nuns and priests used to make him out to be. You should meet him, Lisa. Your life would change, too... you'd never feel the same again... about anything. Suddenly, everything makes sense. We're his children, Lisa. You're my sister... and I love you. I understand now, Lisa. I don't hate anyone anymore... not even John Hennessey. We're just all lost and scared... that's all. He's come to bring us home. If everyone in the world could understand what I do now... and feel like I do... oh, Lisa..."

"Annie... what happened to you? You're scaring me."

"Don't be afraid, Lisa. Please... I'm sorry if I'm scaring you."

"Tell me what happened."

"I went out ahead of the Senator to meet with the leaders of Papa's group. When I met Papa, I looked into his eyes and knew, immediately, who he was. He knew I recognized him... and he put his arms around me and held me. And while he was holding me, I felt all of the pain in my life... all the confusion... all the anger, and shame, and regret... all the sadness, the bitterness... it all left me. It was as though he was a sponge and he was soaking it up from my body and soul. He took on all of my pain so I wouldn't have to carry it with me any longer. I felt like a newborn, Lisa... an innocent child in my father's arms."

"What do you mean, Annie... that you recognized him?"

"You know how it is in life, Lisa... as though you're always looking for something you lost? Well, Papa is what we're all looking for all the time. If you'd meet him, you'd know. It's like as if you were adopted and were going through a crowd of strangers and suddenly see the mother and father who gave you up at birth. You've never seen them before... but you know, immediately, who they are. But... he's more than just a normal parent... he's the perfect parent. You know he'll always love you... no matter what you do... that he'll never turn his back on you. He understands everything about you."

"You knew all this just by looking at him?"

"Yes. And he knew about the baby I gave up for adoption when I was sixteen."

"You had a baby?"

"I've never told anyone about it – only my parents and sister know – but I've cried for him... every night... for the last ten years. I constantly have these nightmares that he's crying for me – but I can't find him. I named him Brian. I only got to hold him once... right after he was born... before they took him away from me. I never got to see him again."

Tears blurred Annie's eyes.

"After Papa held me, he put his hands on the sides of my cheeks and told me that Brian – he used his name – was happy and was a very good boy... and that he knew he was adopted but didn't hate me for it. He said that one day we'd both come home and be together... that he would know who I am... that we'd never have to be apart again. I thought my heart would burst with happiness, Lisa. I truly did."

The story was so extraordinary and emotional that Lisa found herself dropping down to the grass-covered, sandy soil. She sat with her back against the lower rail of the fence and bent her knees in front of her. Annie sat down beside her and put her arm around her. Lisa could feel the love radiating from Annie's body. Being embraced by a woman who loved this man, without limit, made the terrible burden – knowing of his planned murder – unendurable. Her guilt making it impossible for her to endure Annie's continuing touch, Lisa jumped to her feet and ran from her secret. She dashed across Ocean Avenue and was quickly out of Annie Moore's sight.

CHAPTER NINE

At twelve-fifteen, Senator Hennessey and his staff arrived back at the hotel from San Bernardino. The success of the morning had left them, generally, in a buoyant mood, but screwups – regardless of how small – invariably stuck in the Senator's craw, and he came into the hotel, looking for Annie Moore. More than a dozen times on the trip home, he had asked, without satisfactory rejoinder, "Where the fuck was Annie Moore?" Hennessey expected – and demanded – nothing less than perfection from his staff. If they said they were going to be somewhere, or would do something... he was absolutely unforgiving if they failed to do so. Annie Moore was in charge of orchestrating this event. She was to have met with Papa and his small band of intimates before they reached the welcoming station, but when they arrived, she was nowhere in sight. Hennessey had no tolerance, whatsoever, for surprises. Several of the staffers said they had seen her near the platform, about an hour before the Senator had arrived... and that she had started toward the approaching entourage. One said she had seen her walking north on Sierra Avenue. No one had seen her since. Hennessey's response was that the only acceptable excuse from her would be if she had dropped dead on the way... otherwise, he said, her ass was all his.

He went directly up to her room and pounded, raucously, on the door... without response. He used his key – possession of which was a standard practice of his for all staffers' rooms – and after examination, concluded she hadn't yet returned from San Bernardino. He began to speculate that, perhaps, something actually *had* happened to her. He cursed at the thought, not motivated by worry for her well-being, but because Annie was one of the best P.R. people in the business, and replacing her at this late date in his campaign would be a royal pain in the ass. He went to the next room and banged on Lisa Ryan's door. He was just about to use his key to her room when she opened it. She looked terrible... no makeup... her hair unkempt... her face pale.

"What the hell is wrong with you?"

"I'm sick Senator... really sick. I've been throwing up all morning."

"Well that's just fucking great. I can't find Annie Moore... and my speech writer is puking her guts out. What a bunch of fucking losers I've got around me. Where's Annie... have you seen her?"

Lisa's mind raced for the right answer to protect Annie. Without enough time to form a tactical plan, however, she could do nothing but begin with the truth and make decisions, as she went along, as to where and how she should deviate... electing to tell him, simply, that she had seen her out on Ocean Avenue... while she was out for some air to see if it might make her feel a little better.

"How long ago was this?"

"About an hour-and-a-half ago."

"What was she doing out there?"

"I have no idea, Senator. I was surprised to see her, myself."

"Did she say anything about what happened out in San Bernardino? She just disappeared on me. That stupid shit was supposed to have been with the Papa group and bring them to the platform... and she never showed up."

"She didn't say anything about it to me, Senator. I just assumed she, somehow, found her own way back..."

"If you see that little cunt... tell her to get her ass down to my suite, right away."

Lisa closed the door... confident that she had successfully deceived the Senator about the condition of her health... and happy she had safely withheld most of Annie's story. Following her instincts, she had kept to herself what Annie had told her about

Papa. She waited in her room until two-thirty... then walked quickly down the hall and into the stairwell – not wanting to chance being spotted, on that floor, waiting for the elevator.

On the floor below, she exited the stairwell and took the elevator down to the lobby. Crossing the expansive lobby, her heart pounded in her ears in fear of being spotted by members of her group. The events of the previous evening had caused her assessment of Hennessey to undergo a dramatic escalation... changing from the view that he was simply a pernicious jerk... to that of being a truly dangerous man... dangerous enough to kill someone. She was, by now, not simply intimidated, as before, but genuinely terrorized by him. If she were to encounter him in the lobby, she was sure she could not keep herself from screaming.

Setting foot, safely on Wilshire Boulevard, she felt some sense of relief. Her movement to the Western Union office could be better described as a jog than a walk. Inside, she encountered an unanticipated problem. The woman behind the counter asked for the password to get the money. Lisa thought she was kidding. She wasn't... and would not give her the money without it. The clerk allowed her to place a call, on the office phone – provided she use her own calling-card – to Nick, at home. He had forgotten to give her the password, "Peckerwood"... the name she used for Hennessey when she was pissed off at him. Given the circumstances, Lisa wasn't even slightly amused by this and, despite the oppressive guilt under which she had labored that very morning, regarding her unforgivable transgressions, she flew into a rage over Nick's carelessness. His profuse apologies finally assuaged her anger and caused her to feel guilty for having taken out her anxieties on the best man she had even known. She apologized to him and told him she loved him.

With her money in hand, Lisa asked the Western Union clerk where the nearest travel office was located. Learning it was eight city blocks, she had the clerk call her a taxi. She purchased a ticket on a direct flight to Washington – departing that night at eleven-fifty. She made it safely back into her room. At seven o'clock in the evening, the Senator and his entourage departed for the first scheduled mass gathering of Papa's – arranged for eight o'clock at the Los Angeles County Fairgrounds in Pomona. Papa and his massive flock had walked west on Arrow Boulevard, all day long, through Fontana, Ontario, Montclair... and finally into Pomona. At ten o'clock that evening, Lisa Ryan quietly left the hotel, with her luggage in hand, and rode, by taxi, to the Los Angeles Airport. Five hours later, she was in Washington... and in the protective arms of her husband.

CHAPTER TEN

At eleven-thirty, as Lisa Ryan's east-bound aircraft was flying over the State of Nevada, her hotel room phone was ringing. Hennessey was in the mood for sex and had decided that Lisa had had sufficient time to recover from her morning affliction. The evening event had gone very well and the Senator had gotten some excellent face time, on camera, and gave several short interviews with the network media. He noticed that Papa continued to be very reserved toward him... as he had been that morning... more reserved, to Hennessey's eye, than he was with anyone else. Although the Senator found it curious, it didn't bother him. He was getting from the phenomenon what he wanted. With no answer forthcoming from Lisa's phone, he slammed down the receiver, issued a profanity, and stomped, angrily, down the hall to her room. His extraordinarily loud banging, still garnering no response from within, he used his key and entered. Seeing no hanging clothes, toiletry items, or any other traces of occupancy, he violently erupted... this time screaming an entire string of profanities, and finally punctuating his rage by throwing a heavy glass tumbler against the wall – smashing into shards on the rug. He stomped across the hall – to Jimmy Parling's room – and pounded on his door with even more ferocity than he had on Lisa's. Jimmy opened the door... wearing only his boxer shorts and a T-shirt... looking as though he had been asleep. Before Parling could inquire as to the purpose of Hennessey's visit, Hennessey pushed by him and into his room... his face, ugly with anger.

"That fucking Lisa is gone!"

"Maybe she's down at the bar, John."

"She's fucking gone! Left! Everything's gone... out of her room!"

"You're shitting me."

"I'm telling you, Jim... she's gone!"

"Well what the fuck does she think she's doing... just up and leaving like this?"

Parling's question immediately moved Hennessey from anger to suspicion. His lips puckered and his eye lids narrowed... open enough for Parling to see his eyes darting around in search of the various possibilities that might explain Lisa Ryan's clandestine departure. Shaking his head up and down in his usual manner, he walked to one of the high-backed chairs near the window and sat down. His head continued to bob. Finally it stopped and he spoke.

"Something's up, Jimmy. Something is definitely up."

"It is strange, I admit. If it were an emergency... she'd have told one of us."

"Why would a person... who knows very well the consequences of doing something like this to me... go ahead and do it anyway? If she'd decided she didn't like me fucking her, she could have just bided her time. She knew I'd move on to some other cunt before long. She could have played it right... eventually gotten on with another office if she wanted to. Something's not right here, Jim. She left in too big of a hurry."

"Any ideas why?"

"There's only one possibility I can think of, Jimmy... and I don't even want to think about it."

"What?"

"Last night... when we were talking about the shooter... she was in the bedroom. I looked in on her just before you came to the door... and she was sound asleep. At least I thought she was. She should have been worn out... Rossiter and I banged the hell out of her for at least two hours. She was still asleep when I went back in... after you left. But if she heard us... we're fucked...

all of us. Oh, Christ. I was going to throw her ass out before you came... but I decided to be a nice guy and let her sleep. You see how far it gets you to be nice to someone?... first chance they get, they piss all over you."

"We could call it off."

"We might have to. Go get Freddy, Jim. Don't say anything about this to him. Wait until you get him here... I'll tell him."

Jimmy was back with Freddy Westin in a matter of a few minutes. Without ceremony, the Senator began.

"We got problems, Fred."

"What's up?"

Lisa Ryan was in my bedroom... last night... when we were talking over our plans for the shooter. I think she may have heard us."

"Oh, shit."

"I thought she was asleep. Like I told Jimmy, Ted and I had been fucking her for two hours. You'd think that'd worn out the average woman... wouldn't you? I mean if she was a pro that would be different. Anyway... she's disappeared... left without saying anything... snuck out... took everything in her room... and just left. She wouldn't do that unless something really serious was bothering her."

"Maybe getting fucked for two hours by her boss, and somebody she just met, did the trick."

"Don't be a wiseass, Fred. I don't need a fucking lecture from you... you fucking piece of shit!"

Fred Westin quickly realized that his flippant remark, borne of a careless lapse, had tipped Hennessey's delicately balanced scale of emotions... a scale that could instantly move from reverie to carnage. Knowing full well the frightful nature of Hennessey's terrible vengeance, Freddy Westin was immediately and profusely apologetic and pathetically servile.

"Hey Senator... listen... I wasn't trying to be a wiseass. Really. I'm sorry. I was just trying to suggest another possible motive she might have had for leaving. Believe me, Senator Hennessey... I would never think of trying to lecture you about anything. You're right... I'm a low-life piece of shit... and I know it. I know my place. You just misunderstood what I was trying to say. I have the utmost respect for you, sir."

Westin's immediate prostrate groveling, though downright disgusting to Hennessey, prevented his temper from reaching the point of no return... where only unbounded retribution would be adequate to satisfy it. Slowly his emotional lava receded from the edge... and the frightening prospect of an unstoppable overflow was avoided. Freddy and Parling waited in hopeful silence. With the latent rumble of the near eruption still in his voice, the Senator got back to business.

"I know this little bitch... I've known hundreds of cunts like her. She needs the job with me. She and that little asshole of a husband of hers would be up shit crick without me. Putting out a little sex for Rossiter and me is no big deal to someone like her. I knew that before I asked her to fuck me. I knew she wouldn't be willing to lose her job over something like that. No... it's something else... and there's only one thing that it could be. She had to have heard us last night."

"What are we going to do, Senator?"

"Well... looks like we don't have much choice, does it, Einstein? We've got to call it off."

Freddy Westin's face took on a sudden expression that told of fear, sickness, and hopelessness. Hennessey and Parling stared at him... waiting for an explanation. Freddy realized he had to speak.

"Senator... I, ah... we can't... um... we can't call it off at this point."

Hennessey and Parling sat in stunned silence... continuing to stare at Freddy... as though upon reconsideration of what they thought they heard him say would alter the recollection of his words. Despite the reconsideration, the words remained the same. Hennessey spoke in a voice that revealed not only agitation, but a rare quiver of anxiety.

"What do you mean... we can't call it off?"

Freddy tried, unsuccessfully, to find the right tone of voice that would both reveal the truth... but minimize the ramifications.

"It's the way these things work, Senator. You see... I never meet anybody face-to-face. The people I deal with... they give me a number and a time... it's always a public phone. It's set up that way so they don't know who I am... and I don't know who they are. For this kind of a hit – they classify it as an assassination... you know... a public figure – they almost always go out of the country for the shooter. That's why it costs more. Anyway... once the hit is ordered – and paid for – there's no further communication between us. I have no way of getting in touch with them. There's just no way of canceling it at this point. They tell you that right up front. Once it's paid for... it happens as planned... no turning back. The only way this thing isn't going to happen is if the whole event is canceled. That's it, Senator."

"We can't cancel the fucking thing! It's too big. It's bigger than the Super Bowl, for Christ's sake! What would we say, anyway... why we're calling it off?! It simply can't be done at this point. Have you been out there? Media are all over the place, already... looking for space to set up – and it's a week away yet! There's got to be a way to stop this, Fred. You know where the shooter's going to be... right?... where he's going to shoot from. You could go down and stop him."

"Senator... they don't know me from Adam. If I went up to the room, they'd kill me quicker than shit. These guys don't fuck around... that's why they charge so much. This hit is costing the Right a hundred-fifty K. Nothing stops these people. They're expensive... but they're the best."

"Then what the hell are we going to do, Fred?"

"The only way out of this, Senator, is to get rid of the real problem."

"What do you mean?"

"Lisa Ryan is the problem... not the shooter."

"What if she's already told someone?"

"Then it'll be your word against hers. No contest there, Senator... you win."

Hennessey looked at Parling. Parling was shaking his head in disbelief.

"I can't believe this, John. We're trying for a run at the White House... and we're sitting here talking about not just one... but now *two* murders."

"It's a fact, Jim... so get a handle on it. Don't get philosophical on me. We've got a problem... and we need a solution. What do *you* think?"

"Not much choice, John. We can't cancel the event... and we can't stop the shooter. That's all a go. We can only deal with what we can control... and she's he only thing we can control, John. Not much choice."

"Can you handle it, Fred?"

"I'll handle it, Senator. Any idea where she is?"

"My guess is that she's gone back to D.C.... to be with that dipshit husband of hers."

"I'll check the airlines and find out."

"You've got to move fast on this, Fred... before she has a chance to talk to anybody. Of course... if she's talked to the police already... we're fucked."

Parling entered the discussion.

"I'll see what I can find out, John. If she called anyone... she'd have called the police out here. I'll call Blystone and see if any calls were placed to any precinct about a threat against this Papa. I'll tell him you want to be informed for your own safety. They log all that stuff on computer. He'll be able to find out."

"Better get on it soon, Jim. And Fred... you'd better make this thing look right."

"Don't worry, Senator. I'm thinking, maybe a break-in and shooting. Make it look like a burglary and a surprise. Senator... I think we'd better get both of them. If she's told anyone... it'd be her husband."

"Yeah... shit... you're right, Fred. We *had* better get both of them. Very good chance she's told him. I'll be honest with both of you. Other than maybe telling her husband, I really don't think she'll talk. She's scared shitless of me. She knows she's in big trouble for just walking out on me... and there's no way she'd risk her own life, trying to save this religious nut. She'd know I'd come after her for it. I'd bet my left nut that the only person she tells about this, is her husband... and maybe not even him. He's kind of a wimp... and she might think he couldn't handle it. But we can't take a chance on even the possibility she might say something about it. We've got to take care of both of them... right quick."

"It's gonna cost us, Senator... big bucks. This is going to be big news... being on your staff and all... and it's two people... and we need it done really fast. That'll cost us."

"I don't care what it costs, Fred. Get it done."

Freddy and Parling quickly departed the senator's suite to undertake their assignments. Hennessey went into his bedroom... had four scotches... and went quickly and soundly to sleep.

CHAPTER ELEVEN

Annie Moore showed up at her hotel room on Sunday morning. One of the staffers saw her going in and immediately called the Senator's suite to apprise him of the development. He came, immediately, down the hall to her room. She opened the door as soon as he began banging... and smiled warmly at him, despite the vicious sneer on his lips. She was, obviously, in the process of packing.

"What's going on, Annie?"

"I'm going home, Senator."

"You're what!"

"Going home."

She continued to pack as he glared at her.

"Just stop what you're doing and look at me!"

She did.

"Now... what the fuck is going on, here? You disappeared yesterday out on Sierra... and didn't do your job. You've been gone for over twenty-four hours. Are you on drugs, or what?"

Annie sat down on the edge of the bed, folded her hands in her lap, and spoke softly.

"I feel much differently about everything, Senator. Yesterday, I met Papa... and he *is* God. I knew it the moment I looked at him. I understand so much now. Meeting him has totally changed my life. I've lost a lot of the negative feelings inside me... and I feel so much love for everyone. I don't... I can't... continue to do what I've been doing for a living... working for you, Senator Hennessey. We do a lot of cruel things... and say a lot of terrible things about other people... and I can't do it anymore. That's why I'm going home... I don't mean to Washington... but Wisconsin. I need to find a way of making a living that I can feel good about. A way to be good to other people... not tear them down, like I've done for you, Senator. I have no hard feelings toward you, Senator Hennessey. I feel sorry for you, actually. I wish you would meet Papa... really meet him... not just use him like you're doing now. Your life would never be the same again."

"Hey look... I don't need some loony, like you, feeling sorry for me. I always had respect for you, Annie... never thought you'd turn out to be some hair-brained groupie. You're leaving me in the lurch here, you know. I'm in the middle of one of the most important public relations events of my career... and you're walking out on me. You're really fucking me over, Annie. I'd advise you to reconsider. If you walk out on me, you're done. You know what I can do, Annie... you've seen me do it. I'll ruin you Annie... and you know I will."

"There's nothing you can do to me Senator. There's nothing anyone can do to me. Papa loves me... and I'm going to be with him. That's all I need. I'm at peace, Senator... and nothing you can do can change that."

"What a waste of a life. You'll regret this someday, Annie. Someday you'll wake up and realize just how stupid this whole thing was... and realize how much you lost... and what your life could have been. We're going to the White House, Annie... and you were coming with us. There could have been an ambassadorship down the road for you, one day... you know? You think about that when you finally come out of this adolescent dream you're in... when you're working for fifteen thousand a year in some alcohol treatment center with a bunch of pathetic losers... and you're living in some trailer park. You remember this conversation, Annie."

Hennessey issued a small, sarcastic laugh directly into Annie's face...

shook his head back and forth, communicating his piteous disgust for the loser he beheld, then walked slowly out of her room... not bothering to close the door behind him.

Hennessey relayed the latest staff casualty to Parling and told him to get the assistant speech writer and P.R. aide from the D.C. office, on the next plane out to California. Parling briefed Hennessey on his conversation with Chief Blystone. Blystone told him he had had some reports of threatened assassinations of Papa – twenty-two of them, to be exact... and counting. Blystone's advice to Parling was to tell the Senator that the only way they can guarantee his safety is for him to just stay at home. He said there were just too many kooks out there, wanting to kill this other kook, for him to do anything about it. He said he couldn't possibly investigate every report he's received. Blystone also added that he'd asked the FBI for some help with the security. They told him, he said, that they didn't have the extra manpower to put on it. Blystone said that what that really meant was that the government, apparently, isn't too fond of this Papa guy, anyway... and what he stands for... and they basically don't give a shit if someone smokes him or not... that it might just make their day if someone did.

Back in his room, Hennessey scanned the front page of the Sunday L.A. paper. The lead story was a late special, by a reporter who had attended the previous night's Papa event. Hennessey read it to get some perspective on how the media was perceiving these gatherings.

> The best way the audience could be described at the Los Angeles County Fairgrounds in Claremont last evening, awaiting the arrival of the new religious icon, known simply as "Papa" was – curious but respectful. This reporter arrived early at the grounds, expecting a rock concert atmosphere. Instead, the crowd was surprisingly subdued. I asked a number of those in the grandstands, awaiting his appearance, why they had come to see him. Most said they weren't really sure and didn't have any idea as to what to expect. I also asked each of them if they felt

it was possible that this man could really be God, as he claimed to be. To my surprise, of the fifteen persons that I interviewed, all but three said that "anything is possible" and they guessed that perhaps that's why they were there – to see if it was, indeed, possible.

At eight o'clock, on the dot, this impressive man, accompanied by his small, perennial band of intimates, and an assortment of dignitaries, walked onto the speaking platform, erected to face the grandstand complex. As the audience became aware of Papa's presence, an odd, hushed silence came over them, numbering, according to estimates, some forty thousand. It became, literally, as quiet as a church, and this reverent silence continued throughout his entire address. The audience, including this reporter, was clearly mesmerized by this man and we all found ourselves hanging on each word.

Besides the captivating power of his words, Papa's physical presence was equally compelling. Sitting in the press section, only a few feet from the speaker's platform, this reporter had ample opportunity to survey this man's physical appearance at close range. Standing well over six feet in height – reported at 6 ft. 7 in. – he has a classic, Greek-like body, well-muscled and proportioned, and an exceedingly handsome and kind face. His mixed-race parentage is apparent, being, according to reports, an even blend of Scottish and Caribbean-African descent. His skin is olive colored and his hair and beard, light brown and coarse. His eyes, of a grayish-blue cast, seemed almost incandescent against his dark skin. He was dressed, as expected, in his well-reported kilt and sleeveless shirt, made of some sort of hide.

Papa's message was delivered in a voice that was steady, kind, endearing, and adorned with a detectable and delightful Scottish burr. He referred to all in the audience as his children and in such a commanding presence as his, it was not a difficult task, for that brief time, to assume a child-to-parent deference and affection toward him, regardless of one's age. He talked of his understanding of our fears and sorrows, of our loneliness, and our sense of being lost. He told the audience that he is our first mother and father – that we are created from his body and that we retain a memory of a time when we were together with him. When we look at the beauty of a sunset, he said, and sense that some element is missing – to complete the perfection of the scene – we are remembering him and searching for him. He said that we do not need to be frightened or confused or lonely in life. If we remember him, he said, and who he is, our lives will change forever. We will, if we so choose, he explained, come "home" to him, when we leave this Earth. We are, he said, absolutely free to either continue to stay on this Earth or to come back home to be with him. He said he knows each one of us, and will love each of us – in his words – "forevermore." He said his heart aches when our hearts ache and he cries with us in our sorrows.

I can honestly state that this reporter was deeply moved by last evening's event. I traveled to the Los Angeles County Fairgrounds, strictly as a reporter on an assignment, and came away, not only with a wonderful story but with a heart filled with emotion and hope. I cannot say who this man is, but I can clearly state that those in the audience, last evening, were in the presence of undeniable greatness. Everyone I observed leaving the fairgrounds last evening was noticeably affected by Papa's address. There were happy tears in most eyes and nearly all appeared to be deep in thought – many appearing to be in a sort of spiritual reverie.

Is Papa God? What human being has the omniscience to truly answer that question? His words make people happy. They give a sense of hope. He makes human beings feel loved. That is apparent. Perhaps this is, in itself, God-like. Perhaps God is simply love and hope and happiness. If this man is not God, then at least it can, perhaps, be said that he bears the gifts of God. Regardless, having been witness to the power of this man's presence, it is this reporter's opinion that Papa, himself, and his message, may very well have a long-lasting and fundamental effect on the hearts and minds of the people of the Earth.

Senator Hennessey reflected on the vast difference in the effect that a given man's presence and words can have upon individuals. He had also been in the presence of Papa and had heard the very same words as had this reporter, yet, while this reporter was obviously, deeply affected, he was distinctly unmoved. As a matter of fact, during the time Papa was speaking, Hennessey remembered muttering to himself, on more than one occasion, "What a crock of shit."

At two o'clock, on Sunday afternoon, Hennessey and his staff flew to Sacramento to undertake a series of five campaign stops – three in Sacramento... two in Fairfield – leaving enough time to return to L.A. for the evening's gathering with Papa at the Santa Fe Dam Recreation Area. The choice of location seemed, at first, to Annie Moore, to be a less-than-average setting for a large gathering, but was dictated by the slow-paced, pedestrian movement of Papa and his following. Given the necessary westward movement of the group – toward the, seemingly, more appropriate public arenas that were on the scheduled itinerary – this recreation area was the only feasible, outdoor spot in proximity to where the group would be located by Sunday evening. Despite the forced choice, with some ingenuity on the part of the recently departed Annie Moore, the setting turned out to be the most pastoral and aesthetic of all the sites. Annie arranged the speaking platform to be erected on the near side of the lake, facing the water. Papa would speak across the water to his audience, who would stand or sit on the expansive, far shore, where – beginning at the water's edge – the land rose in a gradual slope of soft grass for nearly a mile, before being claimed by forest. Lights were attached to the trees on either side of the speaking platform... cascading a soft glow down upon Papa... then stretched the reflected image across the shimmering water to the feet of the lakeside audience. After viewing the transcendental beauty that emerged from the serendipitous circumstances, Annie Moore wished she had chosen more, similarly water-laden parks for the events... rather than the man-made structures that filled most of the remaining schedule.

The beauty of the setting was not lost on the media, who raved about it in both the live telecasts and in the following day's news. Again, Papa clearly captivated the audience... and again, also, the media. Many had – given the widely reported statements that Papa had made regarding the non-divine nature of Jesus Christ – expected a somewhat antagonistic reception in Los Angeles. To date, however, no such reaction had materialized. That all changed on the following evening at the Rose Bowl.

All the seating at each of the evening events with Papa was open and free... first come, first served. The only restriction on seating was capacity. All those arriving for the event were ushered through a single entrance and counted. When the structure's maximum capacity had been reached, the gates were closed and guarded by the LAPD. So prized was a seat at such a once-in-a-lifetime event as this that patrons – or their paid surrogates – began queuing-up for a seat some twenty-four hours, or more, before the actual event. On Sunday morning, large numbers of college students began arriving in buses to begin waiting for entrance to the Rose Bowl, for the Monday evening production. On the side of the buses were banners reading, "Students for Christ." By early afternoon, the Rose Bowl parking lot was a multicolored sea of such buses, from college campuses throughout the country. The students, disembarking from these buses, wore similar T-shirts, bearing their spiritual standards and carried signs that conveyed their desired messages. The obvious plan of this group was to fill the stadium, as nearly as they were capable, with their like kind. By Sunday evening, the Students for Christ, outside the Rose Bowl, numbered, by most estimates, over sixty thousand... and totally dominated the front of the line who were awaiting entrance to the event.

The media quickly discovered the homogeneous nature of the waiting crowd and brought the story to living rooms across the country, via live interviews on the Sunday evening news. Among the television audience, though not in his living room, was Jimmy

Parling. He immediately phoned Senator Hennessey's room... telling him to turn on his television. Fifteen minutes later, Hennessey phoned Parling and told him to get Ted Rossiter and come down to his suite.

Walking into the Senator's suite, both Parling and Rossiter were sure they knew the reason they were summoned... which was immediately confirmed. Hennessey was watching a network special that followed the evening news on the clash between the message delivered by Papa and traditional Christian theology. He neither looked at, nor spoke to them, as they walked in. They sat together and watched the special in total silence to its end. Hennessey then turned off the set with the remote control and stated what the other two already knew.

"We've got a problem here, boys."

Both Parling and Rossiter nodded in unison.

"The Christians have decided to push back. That makes the dance a little more complicated. If I'm on stage with this Papa... and fifty thousand Christians are in the audience protesting, it sure as hell looks as though I've taken sides against them. And these are probably a lot of the Christian Right college kids that went door-to-door for us last time."

Parling pointed out an ameliorating factor.

"Benson Powell said he can still deliver them."

Hennessey shot back.

"Benson Powell can't undo this kind of damage! Everybody will be watching this thing tomorrow night... Americans fucking love confrontation... probably hoping like hell there'll be some bloodshed. If I'm up there on that stand with him, the image will be a political disaster."

Rossiter entered on Hennessey's side of the issue.

"I agree, John. I can't let you walk into something like this... not on my watch. You hired me as your campaign manager and you're paying me an obscene amount of money to do the job. Let me earn my pay, John... and do what I tell you to do. I'm telling you, stay completely away from this thing. I'll concoct a solid story for you – on your no-show... don't worry. We're going to have to make this sort of decision, from now on, John, with this Papa thing. If it hurts us... you stay home."

Parling disagreed.

"John could still swing this thing, Ted. We could get him ready with the right responses... then arrange a press interview. We could play it... well... we can have John support both sides. He can admire the principle and commitment of the young people... but at the same time come out in support of this guy's right to speak his mind... even if it isn't popular with everybody. Have you read the polls we did on this Papa guy and his movement, Ted?... just got them in this afternoon."

"No... I haven't seen them."

"You should look at them... it might change your mind on this."

"Why? What's it say?"

"Overall, this Papa has a sixty-eight percent approval rating! They think he's, overall, a very positive factor in society. They like what he has to say. And something I can't fucking believe... twenty-two percent think he's really God! Can you believe that shit? If you wanted positive proof that Americans have degenerated into a bunch of airheaded moonbeams... this is it. When a cult leader can go mainstream in America, you know we've gone over the deep end. And I thought that California was the only place where the bizarre was considered middle-of-the-road. Maybe it's me that's out of touch... but I just don't know what's going on anymore. It isn't just teenagers that are screwy these days... it's everybody."

Rossiter wasn't convinced.

"But you know polls, Jimmy. This Papa can be sixty-eight percent this week and twenty-five the next. Can we really afford to have John standing on the other side of the fence from sixty thousand fresh-faced college students, bearing witness to their Savior on worldwide television?"

"It's a close call, Ted... I admit."

"Look... if John's a no-show tomorrow night... what's the downside? He misses out on one night of face time and sound bites. We've got all the rest of the week to make up for it. We can do another poll tomorrow, after this Christian thing, tonight. If this Papa is still holding strong, we can reassess it. I mean, these Christian people won't be able to pack the stands every night. Other people will be lining up for the next get-together at the Hollywood Bowl at the same time these Christians are doing their thing tomorrow night. They can't be in two places at the same time."

Hennessey reentered the dialogue.

"You can't overlook the poll on me. Ever since we got involved with this Papa, my numbers have been steadily going up."

Parling suggested another interpretation.

"A lot of that is still probably sympathy fallout from your son's death, John. We've got to factor that in. It's hard to separate one factor from the other on this."

"You're right. Get me a new poll, Ted... strictly on my involvement with this Papa thing... not just a general rating. Do it right away. I want the numbers by Wednesday."

Both Parling and Rossiter nodded their heads in acceptance of the assignment. Hennessey went on.

"All right... I'll sit out tomorrow night... and we'll get some numbers on it. All right?"

Again they nodded. Hennessey told Rossiter that he needed to talk over some other business with Parling... upon which Rossiter departed.

"Any word from Fred on that special assignment, Jim?"

"Nothing I've heard."

"Hold on."

Hennessey phoned Freddy Westin's room and told him to come down to the suite.

The moment Freddy Westin entered the room, both Hennessey and Parling could read trouble on his face. Hennessey immediately asked for the cause.

"I just got off the phone with my contacts, Senator. They got a call from the shooters on the Washington assignment. I set it up for their townhouse in Arlington. She and her husband haven't shown up there... at all. I checked with Georgetown Law School – he hasn't shown up for classes, either. They're doing a disappearing act, Senator."

"That little bitch... she's one step ahead of us! She must have figured out that I know she overheard us. And she knows we're after her. She's got to. Freddy... if they can contact us on this hit... why can't they do the same for the other one?"

"The shooter contacted my contact. That's the only way it can work. If for some reason the shooter on the other hit would contact my guy... then he could tell them to cancel... but unless something gets really screwed up, they won't call. They almost never do... except for this kind of thing – when the targets aren't where they're supposed to be. The shooters are calling my guy back on Saturday for further instructions on this Washington hit. If we don't have anything new by then, it's quits."

"They just walk away with the fucking money?"

"That's the way it works, Senator. They don't like to wait around, very long, on a job. They like to get in – bam! – and get out. We've got foreign shooters on this one, too. We couldn't risk any domestic talent on it… too risky. Once these guys are out of the country, there's no chance of anybody ever finding them. Frankly, I'm surprised they're giving us until Saturday. These people are careful, Senator, really careful. That's why they never get caught. Look how many years it's been on the Kennedy shoot… and they'll never find them. I'm sure the people, here, who hired them, never knew who they were – just like our deal – and couldn't finger them, even if they wanted to."

"Well, find out where those two little fuckers are, Fred. Do whatever it takes. Having this scared little bitch running around makes me very fucking nervous. She's a time bomb that could go off in our faces at any given moment. If she does, it's all over for us. Get the best people you can find to locate these two. Tell them we, absolutely, have to know where they are in less than twenty-four hours. You're not going to fail me on this, are you, Freddy?"

"No sir. It'll be done. Count on it. Any problems with me using Tim Wilson over at the Bureau?"

"That all depends on what you're planning on saying to him."

"I was figuring on telling him that one of your staffers just up and disappeared and we'd like him to quietly look into it. Say it might be a marriage thing… that she and her husband have been having some problems… and that maybe she took off to go straighten things out. Tim's a good guy, Senator… he owes us. He'll be discreet."

"All right… use him… but if it starts getting thick… drop it."

"Got it, Senator."

"Then get your ass in gear, Fred, and go find these two assholes."

Freddy Westin left the room at a near run. His hyperbolic response to the assignment – that would normally have triggered an inevitable, shared laugh between Hennessey and Rossiter – this time, did not. Each looked to the other for reassurance, but found, instead, the same, mirror image of anxiety. In an effort to assuage his distress, Hennessey had Parling call the escort service he frequently patronized in L.A.... and told him to request the woman he always used.

As Hennessey sipped his Scotch, in anticipation of his approaching, licentious liaison, he mused on the positive attributes of whores. There was a directness and honesty about them that he liked and admired. While other women always had some ulterior motive for sex, a whore's agenda was admirably direct and un-obscured. Cash was tendered up front and the customer got what he paid for. There were no regrets, expectations, or apologies due afterward. Of course, Hennessey conceded to himself, on further reflection... that certain other women, or girls in some cases, could offer what no whore could. His mind traveled back to Kelly Novak. Now *that*, he reflected, was something that, obviously, no whore could offer – youthful innocence and virginity. Hennessey recognized – but did not care – that it was considered a perverse desire for a man, his age, to wish to debauch such a young, innocent girl. He also realized, however, that the perversity of the act was the catalyst of his passion. It seemed to Hennessey that, for him, the more shameful the sex act, the more intense the pleasure... having something to do, he judged, with the fear and shame of his first sexual impulses, which were obscurely, but undeniably, connected with the secret, pleasurable shame he associated with his early toileting. The thought and image of Kelly Novak serving time in prison for fucking around with him brought a smile to his lips... and the sneeringly whispered words, "that bitch."

CHAPTER TWELVE

Hennessey and his staff spent most of Monday in the San Diego area, shuttling from one campaign stop to the next... making appearances at more than a dozen locations before the day's end. Although he hadn't yet received his latest polls, it was clear that at least the people of San Diego appeared to feel very positively about him. One factor that contributed to his exceedingly warm receptions – astutely pointed out by Jimmy Parling the previous evening – became apparent with the numerous offerings of condolence, regarding the death of his son, that were proffered at every stop he made. Basking in these many, heartfelt words of sympathy, Hennessey bestowed silent congratulations upon himself for his masterful handling of this matter. A glint of black humor flashed through his mind, reflecting that... if more politicians realized just how well a son's death could translate into positive ratings, a good many of their male offspring would have legitimate reason for concern

Also very apparent to Hennessey, was that the Papa phenomenon was an overriding interest of a substantial number of the people he encountered. As do many, upon meeting someone who has been in the presence of a world-class icon, the most frequently posed, inane question to Hennessey was, as would be expected, "What's he really like?"... plus more specific factual questions, "Is he really as big as they say?" "Have you seen him perform any miracles?" Hennessey's association with Papa had, at least with these people, waxed very positively. Also, as many are, regarding celebrity, there was an excitement and anticipation in their faces and voices when asking these questions about Papa. It was clear to Hennessey that nearly everyone was fascinated with this man... and excited over the possibilities of what he might be. It was as though, he thought, they were finding out that the magic of Santa Claus, which they were reluctantly forced to denounce upon reaching that first cruel stage of childhood enlightenment... when elders and peers forbid a continuance in that most wonderful of worlds where anything is possible... just might, after all, really be possible.

With Papa, it seemed that adults were restored to their license to believe, once again, that certain things could exist that were beyond the bounds of everyday rationality and tedium. They could, with Papa, without appearing foolish or childish, once again speculate on the possibility of wondrous and magical things in the world. It was obvious to Hennessey that many had great hope that the miracle stories were really true... and it was also plainly apparent to Hennessey that many of these people seemed to be possessed by a desperate need to believe in Papa. It was clear that many were hoping, with an obvious sense of urgency, that he was who he said he was. Given this overwhelmingly positive view of Papa that Hennessey was uniformly encountering, he was beginning to have substantial doubts about his decision to sit out that evening's event. Nevertheless, he followed Ted Rossiter's advice and at eight o'clock in the evening, instead of being at the Rose Bowl, he was watching the event from his hotel room.

Hennessey had two more television sets brought to his suite so he, Rossiter, and Parling could watch the various coverage of the Rose Bowl production. They began at seven-thirty on nearly every channel, with commentators and interviews about what could be expected. No one was quite sure what the Students for Christ had planned. It didn't, however, take long to find out. There was total silence in the cavernous stadium as Papa and his small band of devotees walked, alone, onto the platform that was erected in front of the end zone, farthest from the main entrance, and facing the playing field. The dignitaries who had previously appeared with the platform party were quite conspicuous by their total absence. Apparently Hennessey wasn't the only politician to shy away from the potential damage the evening's event might have on a public image.

The moment Papa advanced toward the microphone, an obviously, well-orchestrated demonstration began on queue. With amazing synchronization, given the size and near-spontaneous nature of the assembly's formation, the crowd rose to its feet and burst forth with the singing of "Onward Christian Soldiers." The television commentators uniformly remarked that the volume of the combined, manically exuberant voices of the multitude was nearly deafening. Commensurate with the singing, those seated on the chairs arranged on the playing field – the men dressed in dark suits, white shirts and red ties… the women in white, church dresses – held up signs and banners, proclaiming Jesus Christ as their Savior and marched, single file, out of the aisles and onto the track that surrounded the field. The enormously large procession began circling the perimeter of the field with their messages held high above their heads… passing, as they walked, directly in front of the speaker's platform. "Onward Christian Soldiers," was, after about ten minutes of repeated verses, succeeded by the "Battle Hymn of the Republic."

At some unseen, or prearranged, signal, following several verses of the Battle Hymn, the field procession and the singing stopped suddenly and a dramatic hush fell over the stadium. A young man with a power-assisted bullhorn, standing directly in front of the platform, then turned toward the field and began to speak.

"Let us proclaim to the world what we believe."

He began – and was immediately joined, in unison, by the Christian assembly in the stadium – the recitation of the Apostle's Creed.

When the Creed was completed, the young man continued.

"Let us pray."

All heads bowed and eyes closed.

"Our heavenly father, please grant us the strength to stand against this Antichrist who speaks with Satan's tongue against your only beloved Son, our Lord and Savior, Jesus Christ. You have warned us of his coming, Lord, and we have heeded your word. We have come to do battle with this evil incarnate and we ask that you sustain our courage and bless our efforts. Tonight we have come to bear witness to the glory of your Son, Jesus, and the blood he shed for our sins and our salvation. We have come to bear witness that Jesus Christ is the Son of the one and only true God and that only through his acceptance as our Savior will we find everlasting life. We humbly ask, Father, that you grant all of your children the wisdom to recognize this man as a false prophet and the strength to turn our backs to him. As your own Son said to his tempter... so we say to this wolf in sheep's clothing, 'Get thee behind me, Satan!' We ask that you guide us and bless us as we go forward to bring the Word of your Son, Jesus Christ – the only true Word – to the world. In Jesus name we pray. Amen."

"Amen" echoed throughout the stadium congregation. The speaker handed the bullhorn to a pretty, conservatively dressed, young woman, on his right, who immediately launched into an emotional rendition of "The Old Rugged Cross."

After the young woman had finished the hymn, the Christians, throughout the stadium, in unison, pulled small American flags from some storage area on their person and, holding them high above their heads, began marching out of the stadium in a very orderly manner, singing "God Bless America" all the while. This final segment of the well-planned event lasted some twenty minutes... until the stadium was entirely empty of spectators... save the small party on the speaker's stand and the remaining media.

Throughout the demonstration, the cameras focused, frequently, on Papa, providing numerous close-ups of his face... giving viewers an opportunity to watch his reaction to the ongoing proceedings. The screen consistently revealed a kind, unperturbed countenance, and a face that consistently wore an understanding, parental-like smile of affection toward his antagonists. He stood, silently, on the platform until the stadium was empty... then, having never uttered a word, walked slowly from the platform – followed by his band of intimates – out of the stadium and disappeared into the dark, warm night among his multitude of followers, who stood, waiting for him, as always, outside the stadium.

The trio in the hotel suite turned off the television sets and were silent... each searching for a perspective into which to place the phenomenon they had just witnessed. Parling was the first to make an attempt.

"That was impressive, John... very powerful."

Rossiter shook his head in agreement then added to the comment.

"That's exactly why I didn't want you there, John. There's no way I would have wanted you to have been a part of that... being the object of contempt of those squeaky clean kids. Those Christians know what they're doing. They really know how to mobilize and put on a hell of a show. That was one of the best counter-messages I've ever seen delivered. They're coming out swinging against this guy, John."

Hennessey was slower to judge the impact of the demonstration.

"I'll wait for the numbers. They put on a good show... but I saw the fascination with this Papa guy all over San Diego today. They were totally infatuated with him. They really do like him... and they really want him to be God. That's sounds fucking crazy... I know... but they really do. He's apparently giving them something they think they need. It's obvious. We'll wait this one out and see what the numbers do. I want something before tomorrow night's production. If he's still holding strong, I'm going."

CHAPTER THIRTEEN

On Tuesday afternoon, Nick Ryan called his father's office in Dover, Delaware from a phone booth in Virginia Beach.

"Dad?"

"Nicky… where have you two been? We've been calling your place for the last four days."

"I can't tell you the whole story, Dad… but we're in some trouble. As a matter of fact, we can't stay on the phone very long… your line might be tapped."

"Are you serious? I figured something was up. There's been a guy snooping around for you two… with the FBI. What the hell did you two get into, Nick?"

"We haven't done anything wrong, Dad… Lisa just stumbled into something she wasn't supposed to know about… and we're in some danger… at least we think we are."

"Well this FBI guy was awfully anxious to find out where you two are."

"Hold on a minute, Dad."

"Lisa wants to know if the guy's name was Tim Wilson."

"Yep… that was it. How'd she know?"

"She doesn't want to get into it right now, Dad… but listen… here's why I called. We need some more money. I'm really sorry to ask… but I've got to. I know you just loaned us some for Lisa's ticket… but we're broke… and our credit cards are all maxed out."

"How much do you need, Nick?"

"Well… we're going to drive out to Los Angeles."

"What?!"

"I'll tell you all about it later on, Dad. But we need to get out there as soon as possible. I'm not trying to be dramatic… but it's, as they say in the movies, a matter of life and death."

"If it's that important… what don't you just fly out?"

"Too risky, Dad. They'll be watching the airports… and you've got to register and show an I.D. to get on a flight, these days. They'd know what flight we were on in a matter of minutes."

"Do you just want to use one of my credit cards?"

"They'd trace it. The FBI can get on-line printouts on any credit card transaction… anytime they want. We'd leave a trail behind that anybody could follow."

"OK, I get it. How much do you need, Nicky?"

"A couple thousand, Dad."

"I'll wire you twenty-five hundred… how's that?"

"That's great, Dad. I know you really can't afford this… with Mom sick and all… but I'll pay you back… I really will, Dad… just as soon as I can… I promise."

"I know you will, Nicky. I'm not worried about it. I'll go out, right now, and do it. Where should I wire it?"

"Are you going to the usual place?"

"Yes."

"I'll call you there in a half an hour and tell you where to wire it. OK?"

"OK, Nicky. Be careful."

Nick hung up the phone and looked at Lisa. Her face said she was sorry that they were asking Nick's dad, again, for more money... but they both knew her parents had even less money than Nick's parents. Nick tried to ease her conscience.

"We'll pay them back, Lis. It's OK. It's tough when neither set of parents has much more than a pot to piss in... and it makes you feel like a jerk to ask them for anything... I know. But what choice do we have?"

"Then you think I'm doing the right thing, Nicky?"

"Hell yes. We can't just let them kill this guy. And you're right... you can't go to the police. You're pretty sure Hennessey's after us now... but if you went to the police... he'd be after you, for sure. The only safe thing you can do is to warn this guy. I don't think either of us could live with ourselves if we didn't at least try to do something."

"But maybe I *should* just go to the police, Nicky. He's after us... I know he is. That's why Tim Wilson is in on this. Hennessey has him in his hip pocket... like everybody else who's anybody. Maybe we should just go to the police for protection."

"I don't know, Lis. This whole thing is way beyond both of us. It's like some dream... like being in a movie. Who ever thought we'd be in a situation like this? Who the hell knows what to do? It's not like either of us has any experience in being hunted down by some killer, you know? Do you seriously think he's trying to have us killed, Lis?... I mean, seriously?"

"After what I heard last week, Nicky... he was so cold-blooded and calculating about it!... like he was ordering a pizza! I don't have any doubt that someone is out there right now, trying to kill us. If I'm right about Hennessey... that he knows the reason I ran was because I overheard him about the murder... he's not going to take any chances with my going to the police."

"Maybe they decided just to call off the murder... since they know that you know about it."

"That's possible... but how could we find out if they did?"

"No idea. This thing is almost too crazy to even think about. We're just a couple of normal people. How could we have gotten into something like this?"

"It's my fault, Nicky. I was the one that got us involved with these kind of people."

"You had no way of knowing they were like this, Lis. Hennessey's a United States Senator, for Christ's sake! Who'd have thought?"

"I kind of knew they were bad people, Nick... all of the lousy things we were asked to do all the time."

"But that's just politics, Lis. They're all like that. This is murder we're talking about! You couldn't have guessed they'd ever be involved in something like this."

"I'll tell you, Nicky... now that I've had time to think about it... if before all this happened... someone had asked me if Hennessey would have someone killed if he had to, to get something he really wanted... if I was honest... I'd have probably said, yes. That man will do just about anything to get what he wants. He has no heart or feelings... believe me. You should have seen him over the death of his own son. He never shed a tear or even looked sad about it. All he cared about was orchestrating the whole thing for his ratings. He went out and play-acted the whole grief scene. It was sick. And I helped him do it! I'm so ashamed of some of the things I did, Nicky. He even had his own wife drugged and kept prisoner in a hotel after their son died so she wouldn't say the wrong things to the press!"

"He was really that bad about it?"

"Oh... he was. You don't know these politicians, Nicky. They have no souls. Seriously. They'll do anything to win. You should hear the way they talk. Not just Hennessey and his people... all of them! As a group, they're probably the most amoral, unprincipled bunch of people on the face of the earth. It's all a game to them... and I know it sounds trite but people really *are* just pawns to them... no faces or feelings. If the game is big enough – and the White House is as big as it gets – what's one or two lives to them? I mean, think about what our presidents have done... gotten into wars and other things... gotten hundreds and thousands of young boys killed... just for their ratings and the next election! But... what about it Nicky?... should we go to the police? I can't make up my mind... I'm sorry. I know I've gone back and forth on this a hundred times since last Saturday... I'm sorry."

"OK... let's try to be logical about it... OK? If we go to the police, what's the upside and what's the downside? We could ask them for protection... but what would we say?... that a United States Senator is trying to have us killed? They'd ask what proof we have, right? And what do we have? Only your suspicions. You could tell them about the conversation you overheard... and they'd ask you if anyone else heard it, right? The answer is, no... nobody that would admit to it. There's just no way they'd start an investigation against a United States Senator – especially someone as big as Hennessey – with only an overheard conversation to go on... and no corroboration. Then who do they protect us from? We only think it's possible somebody might be after us... and absolutely no proof of it. And they'd ask you why you quit Hennessey's staff... thinking you were bitter and were trying to get even with him for something... you know... making all this up to get back at him. Even if they called Hennessey about it, he'd make something up about you. Actually... if you think about it... you're really not that much of a threat against him. Maybe we're making too much of this thing."

"No, Nicky. I know Hennessey. He doesn't tolerate any loose

ends. Remember what he did to his own wife! He's not going to let me run around with this kind of information about him. I'm a threat to him... and he doesn't tolerate anyone threatening him. There's only one way he can make sure that I never tell anyone what I know. Do you really want to chance it, Nicky?"

"No. But will we be any safer if we warn this guy and nothing happens to him?"

"Yes... of course. If nothing happens to this guy... then what I know is meaningless. Then I'm no longer a threat to Hennessey. He'd still probably try to ruin me for what I've done... but he'd have no reason to kill me."

"What if we can't get to this Papa in time?"

"We have to, Nicky!"

"But what if we can't, Lis? Anything can happen."

"If, by any chance, we can't warn him in time... and they actually kill him... then we'll still be safer than we are now."

"Why?"

"Then... afterwards... when we go to the police, something will have already happened... and they'll take us seriously and they'd give us protection. Right now... before anything has happened... it's all just speculation. I'll bet the LAPD has already gotten hundreds of leads on people threatening to do something to this man. Anytime anyone becomes really famous, for some reason, Americans want to kill him... you know that."

"I don't doubt that... as crazy as L.A. is."

"I guess if you think about it... going to the police right now, *would* be a waste of time."

"I'm afraid that's right, Lis. We're back to our original plan. We'll try to warn him. If Hennessey calls it off, then we'll have just wasted some time and money. And if he's called it off already, then we're going through all this worry for nothing."

"Yeah… I guess so. If he's already called it off, then what I know doesn't matter anymore… and we're worrying about all this for nothing."

"You know, Lis… we're going to feel really stupid if there really is nothing to all this… I mean if no one *is* really after us."

I know, Nicky… I've thought about that a thousand times. I mean… you're missing class because of this, you know? But… I just like to be careful. It could be nothing – yes – or it could be the real thing. I'd rather be safe than sorry, honey. Of course… if he's called it off, then why's Tim Wilson so anxious to find us? Oh… I wish there was a way we could find out for sure! What if I just call him and ask him?"

"You mean Hennessey?"

"Yes."

"Do you really think he'd tell you the truth?"

"No. He's a pathological liar."

"There's your answer, then."

"I'm sorry… that was a really stupid idea. Oh, Nicky… I just can't believe all this! I hope I wake up and find out this is all just a bad dream."

"Me too, sweetheart… but it's not… and we have to deal with it."

"Oh Nicky… I love you so much."

"Me too, Lis."

By three-thirty in the afternoon, they had their money. They decided to get some rest and leave, very early, the following morning. Believing there could be people watching for their car, they decided to stay off the major highways to California. It would take considerably longer to get there, but it would be, they believed, the safest way to go. They estimated that, taking turns driving, and sleeping in the car... and stopping only for gas and to eat... the trip should them take about four days. That would put them in L.A. on Saturday... with sufficient time to warn Papa.

At five o'clock, Wednesday morning, Nick and Lisa Ryan set out for California.

CHAPTER FOURTEEN

Hennessey got the latest poll results at five o'clock on Tuesday evening. He found them to be quite enlightening. After the Christian demonstration the previous evening, instead of dropping, Papa's ratings actually went up five points! Among those describing themselves as Christians, the respondents were almost evenly split on their view of Papa... nearly half of them indicating that they liked Papa's message, and that they could not rule out the possibility that he was, indeed, God incarnate. No wonder, Hennessey thought, Benson Powell and his Christian Right confederates were having shit-fits over this guy. He was raiding their fort and had a good chance of winning over a good many converts... and they knew it. They were doing their own polls, sure as shit, and they knew this movement could be a potential catastrophe for them. A lot of them could be out of a job with the success of such competition. The regular, and enormously generous, tithing of their membership... upon which they depended to run their organizations – and keep themselves in big houses, luxury cars, and on junkets – could shrink dramatically if even a portion of those on the fence would desert... not to mention a significant diminishment of their political clout. No wonder Powell and his people wanted this man dead. It had become for them, a simple question of survival.

Hennessey's own polls – regarding the public perception of his association with Papa – affirmed the suspicions he formed after his trip to San Diego. Nearly seventy-eight percent of those polled... and virtually all of them indicating that they had seen the Christian demonstration the night before... viewed Hennessey's relationship with Papa as being positive. Hennessey reveled in the fact that a fair number of them responded that they felt the reason Hennessey was drawn to this movement was his continuing grief over the death of his son and his need to find a spirituality that would help him cope with his loss. His son couldn't have – he mused – picked a more opportune time to off himself, if he had tried. Hennessey called Rossiter and had him come down to the suite. He extended his arm with the poll sheets in his hand as Rossiter crossed the room. Rossiter declined... explaining he had already seen them.

"Are you satisfied, Ted?"

"They look good, John. I'll admit... I'm, frankly, shocked as hell. I was looking for a big drop after last night... but you know... Americans do love an underdog. This Papa played it perfectly, too... no anger... no arguments... just walked quietly out of the stadium with an understanding smile on his face. I think everybody watching, felt sorry for him. Christ!... I even felt bad for him! It looked as if they were ganging up on him... him up there, all alone at the mike... one man facing over sixty thousand people... all by himself. I thought the Christians did a great job... but it looks as though it backfired. I saw it happen a thousand times when I was still trying cases. You get too tough on a witness, even if he's a sleaze-ball, and the jury wants to protect him. I wonder what Powell and his boys are saying about this new development? They must be going fucking nuts! But, John... keep in mind that this poll might be indicating a strong – temporary – showing of sympathy for this guy. It could get cold real fast. What would you think of waiting another day?"

"No fucking way, Ted! Look at my polls! That's not sympathy... at least not sympathy for him... maybe for me... but who cares? The guy is good for me... you can't deny it. As a matter of fact, maybe I should get a little closer to him."

"Oh, please, John. Look... it ain't broke so don't fix it... OK? You're riding on his coattails, at a safe distance, and it's working. Just keep doing what you're doing... all right?"

"Yeah... all right. You're right. But regardless... I'm going to the Hollywood Bowl tonight. You got it set up?"

"Yeah... as soon as I saw the poll numbers, I knew you'd be going. We're all set."

At the Bowl, that evening, it became patently apparent that going to see Papa was now "in" among the town's elite. The first ten rows were filled with a literal, "who's who" of Hollywood... actors, directors, writers, producers, designers, choreographers, agents, columnists... all dressed to the hilt and on the arm of – or being hung on by – a suitably camp escort. It reminded Hennessey of a Las Vegas, heavyweight championship fight crowd. Contrary to the countenance of the previous crowds, who had genuinely come to see Papa, and who were subdued and almost reverent – exclusive of the anomalistic, and overtly contrived, Christian audience – this crowd was noisy and festive... appearing clearly more interested in seeing and being seen than hearing or seeing Papa. Before Papa's appearance, people were incessantly traversing the steps and aisles... making necessary and strategic stops and exchanges of greeting... striving to portray a studied look of naturalness and lack of self-consciousness for the cameras that panned the rows, searching for the biggest stars.

Although the audience quieted, to some extent, when Papa began to speak, their focus, clearly, continued to be on themselves and those around them, their eyes continually darting to the cameras, to allow themselves sufficient time to prepare for an advantageous shot and to avoid being caught in some unflattering, compromised pose. And for the first time in the series of appearances, the crowd actually applauded when Papa finished speaking. On-air commentators, and next-day writers, could not help but compare the highly inappropriate comportment of the glitzy audience as being much more suitable for the Academy Awards than for a spiritual gathering. One particular reporter harpooned the show biz contingent by writing that he, ". . . sincerely believed this crowd would applaud a good wake if enough cameras were there."

The Wednesday morning papers, again, carried more stories of alleged miracles – despite Papa's widely reported insistence that he would not perform any and, his assurances that the specific miracles being alleged never took place. People who had attended the first two public gatherings, or who claimed to have seen or met or touched Papa as he passed through the streets of Los Angeles, were coming forward, in droves, with supernatural claims. A man from Long Beach, stating that he was blind, asserted that his sight was entirely restored upon Papa touching his head. A Redondo Beach woman maintained that while listening to Papa's words, during his appearance at the Los Angeles County Fairgrounds, she literally felt his spirit enter her body and cure her arthritis. She said her hip and knee became intensely hot... then when they cooled, all the pain was gone and she was healed. She claimed that her doctor had confirmed the complete healing. A resident of Anaheim, who, by her account, was dying of terminal liver cancer, professed that when Papa passed by her, as she stood in a crowd along the street, she felt the devils leave her body and now represents to be in total remission. She hadn't had any medical tests to confirm her cure... saying she knew she was healed and didn't need any tests to prove it.

On Wednesday evening, the Christians were at it, again, but with a different twist that didn't lend to the unpopular appearance of ganging up on a single man. At the same time Papa was speaking at Dodger Stadium, they held a counter-rally of their own on the long sloping hill of Pepperdine University – crowned at its top by a large, beautiful cross. They had worked, feverishly, to get their troops out and an estimated eighty thousand Christians showed up for the rally. The featured speaker, standing at the foot of the cross, was none other than the Reverend Benson Powell. Although the main media coverage was concentrated at Dodger Stadium, a fair-sized contingent was also dispatched to Pepperdine Hill. As always, the Christians put on an impressive, well organized show... complete with an enormous gospel choir who stood around the cross and enthusiastically rendered a litany of old, favorite hymns. Powell's message offered no surprises – following the now standard line of attack upon Papa – he is the Antichrist... Satan works through him to lead the Christian flock astray... Christians must stand together against this evil. He also reiterated the standard planks of Christian belief – Christ is the Son of God... He died for the sins of man... God, the Father, in heaven, is the only true God... only through acceptance of Jesus Christ can one receive everlasting life. He ended the demonstration with a stirring supplication for God's divine grace... to grant them strength... to sustain their courage... to help them defeat this evil abomination.

The crowd at Dodger Stadium was quietly respectful to Papa and appeared to be quite moved by his words. An occurrence during Papa's homily provided a clarification of his ministry that had already been widely reported by the media. Likely fueled by the numerous reports of miracles, a young man in a wheel chair made his way to the front of the speaker's stadium and, with tears in his eyes, loudly implored Papa to heal him. According to the media, who were close enough to hear and observe the situation, Papa, seeing this man, stopped speaking and came down from the platform. He walked over and knelt beside him and embraced him. He called him by a name – Wilson – which was later verified by nearby reporters to be accurate. He told the man, according to reports of those close enough to hear Papa's words, he would not interfere in the lives of his children on earth, but that he would promise this young man he would wait for him with open arms to welcome him home. Papa also told Wilson that he – Wilson – would spend only his few years on earth in his wheelchair and that upon his returning home, he would run like the wind and be happier than he ever believed was possible. The man, according to reports, was overwhelmed... shedding tears of joy... despite not being healed by Papa. Television crews caught up with Wilson a short time later. The reporters rudely prodded him to admit he was disappointed in not being healed, but he refused to acquiesce. Instead, he steadfastly repeated, time and again, that he was happier than he had ever been in his life... that he no longer felt bitter nor oppressed by his confinement to a wheelchair, as he had since the day he was paralyzed during a football game, at age sixteen.

Hennessey was irate to learn, on the late news, that Benson Powell was the featured speaker at the Christian rally at Pepperdine. Never one to wait until morning to vent his anger, he picked up the phone and called Jimmy Parling's room.

"Are you watching the news?"

"No, John... actually... I was asleep."

"Well, guess who was the main speaker at the Christian rally tonight?"

"Who?"

"Our buddy."

"Who?"

"The guy who we're committing the murder for."

"Powell?"

"Yep."

"Why that ungrateful fucker."

"Get him over here, Jimmy."

"When... now?"

"It's only one o'clock."

"Are you serious?"

"What do you think?"

"All right... I'll do my best."

"If he gives you any shit, remind him of what we're doing for him."

Forty-five minutes later, Parling phoned Hennessey's room. He told him he had located Powell and that he was on his way over to the hotel. Parling added that Powell wasn't too happy about being summoned to a meeting in the middle of the night. Hennessey's response was that that was "tough shit." At two-fifteen a.m., Powell knocked at Hennessey's door. Hennessey asked him in, made him a drink, and called Parling to come down to the suite. It was very clear to Powell that Hennessey wasn't happy. They sat down in the study area of the suite to get down to business. As expected, Hennessey began.

"What's with you, Benson?"

"What do you mean?"

"You know what the fuck I mean... so don't play games with me."

"I couldn't help it, John. I was under a lot of pressure to go public."

"You have a short memory, Benson."

"I know I said I'd keep this under control and not let it hurt you... but you've got to be practical, John. I answer to these people."

"We told you we were going to get involved with this Papa guy for the coverage. You said you'd make sure that the Right would deliver if we helped you. Now we're going *way* out on a limb for you... way out... and you're standing up there and driving a wedge between the Christians and me. After you lead a rally against the very person I'm appearing with on a platform that same night... how are you going to get them to support me? You said you were going to handle this Benson... so start handling it! I don't think I have to remind you that you owe me big on this one! Who else could you have gone to that would have helped you the way we did? You're really pissing me off, Benson... big time!"

"I understand, John... I really do. I swear to you, tonight was the one and only personal appearance I'm going to be making on this. They'll support you this fall, John... I'll see to it that they do. I gave you my word on it. And believe me, John... we deeply appreciate the help you're giving us on this. I think, by now, you can appreciate just how severe this problem is for us. This blasphemer is raiding our congregations and we have got to stand up for Jesus and defend his name."

"Save that horseshit for the lamebrains you hold up every Sunday... OK Benson? You're talking to me, remember? I'm in business and you're in business. This guy is bad news for your bottom line and you've got to do something about it... that's all. If he wasn't a threat to your jobs and your perks, none of you Christian big shots would give a healthy shit about him... so don't lay that holier-than-thou bullshit on me, OK? And don't forget, you're the people who came to us to arrange this murder. Unless I'm mistaken, Reverend Powell... that's not a very Christian-like thing to do... is it? I personally don't give a shit if you want this guy dead or not... it's no sweat off my nuts. Just don't try to dress it all up in pretty ribbons for me... all right?"

Benson Powell was untenably trapped in an unaccustomed position that openly revealed the stark contradiction between his public image and his private acts and motives. Having no way to defend these dichotomous aspects of his life, he tacitly conceded their reality by remaining silent.

CHAPTER FIFTEEN

At sunrise on Thursday morning, Lisa Ryan had reached her boundaries of driving safety as she read the sign announcing the city limits of Louisville, Kentucky. If she drove even ten minutes longer she was certain she would be asleep at the wheel. She and Nicky had agreed to three-hour driving shifts. She had completed only two but could drive no farther. She glanced over at her husband, sleeping, soundly on his fully reclined seat... lying on his side in a fetal position... and felt guilty for not having been able to fulfill her tour of duty at the wheel. She knew that Nicky, had their circumstance been reversed, would have found some way to continue. Somehow, she was certain, he would have found the inner strength to push on... beyond the sensible limits of body and mind. But he was a man... and men, she knew, do nonsensical, masochistic things like that. She was a woman... and had the common sense to admit her realistic parameters. She pulled into a roadside rest and stopped.

The change in motion reclaimed Nicky from the distant lands of slumbering minds. Slowly he reconnoitered his circumstance and finally remembered the context of their reality.

"Is it my turn?"

"I'm sorry honey... but I couldn't go any further. I know I was supposed to drive for three hours but I just can't go any longer. I was falling asleep at the wheel."

"That's OK, Lis... if you're that tired you should stop. No sense pushing it. I've got to pee like an Arabian racehorse."

"Me too."

They left the stale air of their confined travel space and stepped out into the gray, wet air of the early morning. Momentarily disabled by their confinement, they walked stiffly and unnaturally to the cinderblock rest rooms. The air felt clammy and cold and unfriendly to them and both were suffering from the motion syndrome that heightens and agitates one's senses to the point of finding nearly everything annoying – including the sight and sounds of one's own spouse. After they had both peed and splashed and rubbed their faces with water, the world had become slightly more tolerable. They both sought the comfort of something familiar that wasn't moving, so Nick pulled off at the next exit and made a right turn, to head for the Bob Evans, a few hundred yards down the highway.

Other than ordering, they sat in silence until they had each ingested two cups of coffee. The warmth in their stomachs made the world seem considerably kinder and happier... enough so to generate a modicum of conversation. The sight of the other's face, they noticed, had ceased to be an insufferable experience.

"Is this where we pick up Route Sixty, Nicky?"

"Yep. Then we're on it, all the way to L.A."

"That'll make it a lot easier. It gets really tiring watching for all the different routes we've been on. I'm surprised we haven't missed some already."

"Yeah. We've done really well so far. Actually, we're a little ahead of schedule, I think. We've been on the road almost twenty-four hours now... and I didn't figure we'd be this far, already."

"What would you think of getting a motel room for a little while? I don't think we can keep up this pace... like we planned."

"I don't either, Lis. It sounded good when we started, but this driving straight through is just too much. It's six o'clock now. How about we pull in somewhere and sleep for about six hours... until about noon or one?"

"Oh God... that sounds wonderful. Can we pull into a motel, at this time of the morning, and get a room?"

"I guess so... don't know why not."

"It just seems a little weird."

"Yeah... I know... but if we pay for a day, why would they care what time we check in?"

As they came out of the Bob Evans, they noticed a Red Roof Inn sign, farther down the highway to their right... about a quarter of a mile. They quickly agreed on it as suitable for their desperately needed respite.

Feeling the need to explain to the desk clerk, the reasons for the unusual time of day for checking into a room – much to Lisa's annoyance – Nick launched into the tale of their travels, over the past twenty-four hours and their original, unachievable plan of endurance and their concession of defeat. A few minutes later, while driving around the building to find their room, Lisa, unwisely – given the fragile state of their fatigue-induced tempers – voiced her view on the stupidity of his telling the man at the desk, unnecessarily, all of their business. Nick shot back... and by the time they were in the room, both voices were raised and profanities were filling the air. Both of them knew they were fighting, strictly out of exhaustion... but their condition also rendered them both unable to stop. Fortunately, their exhausted state also made short work of the dispute and, although they both intended to continue the fight, even into bed... within thirty seconds of the contact between the cool sheets and their hot skin, both were in a deep, near comatose, sleep.

Nick lifted his head and peered into the darkness... trying to decipher his whereabouts. Still in the twilight of waking, he perceived, for a few moments, as he often did upon waking at night, that he was in his childhood bedroom in Dover. Finally he began to differentiate the room from his memory and vaguely recalled checking into a Red Roof Inn... feeling as though he had done so in a dream. He slowly swung his hand to his left until it bumped into the metal bed-lamp. He wrapped his hand around the cold metal and followed it upward until he encountered the lamp switch. He turned it and, at the same time, instinctually turned his head to his right to avoid the anticipated pain that the cruel, contrasting brightness, burning into his dark-accustomed eyes, would inflict. Finally able to see without discomfort, he looked at his wristwatch. He studied it for some time... trying to correlate the position of the hands to some meaningful reality. They were in the ten o'clock position. For the life of him, he couldn't decide what that meant. He had to methodically go back through their morning to understand the import of the hand positions. By process of elimination, he finally concluded that the only time the hands could represent was ten o'clock in the evening... but his mind could not accept that. They had, it seemed, only minutes ago, lay down, at seven in the morning, for a short nap. It simply wasn't possible that it could now be ten in the evening... fifteen hours later. The thought struck him that, perhaps, his watch may have stopped, a few hours after they lay down... but then noticed his second hand was moving and dismissed the theory. Finally, unable to form a definitive conclusion, he awakened Lisa and apprised her of the seeming paradox. She looked at her watch. Its hands matched Nick's. Their eyes met in simultaneous comprehension of their circumstance. They had, indeed, slept, not for the intended six hours, but instead, for fifteen.

The discovery shook them into an immediate clarity of mind and they hastened out of bed and got dressed. Neither had to verbalize the predicament of being suddenly and significantly behind schedule. They both went, quickly, into the bathroom, urinated, brushed their teeth, grabbed the few articles they had brought with them into the room, and rushed down to their car – all without speaking a word to one another. They pulled across the highway to an Exxon station... filled up, got two cups of coffee – to go – in the convenience section, and were on the road for nearly an hour before any substantive conversation developed. Nick initiated it.

"This'll cut it really close, Lis."

"I know."

"We'll be lucky, now, to get into L.A. by Saturday evening at best... assuming we don't have any other major screw-ups. We should have asked for a wake-up call."

"It's too late now, Nicky. I guess we really needed the sleep. I feel really refreshed... how about you?"

"Me too. I feel as though I could drive for a really long time."

"We'll be OK, Nicky."

They exchanged a matching smile of love and camaraderie.

CHAPTER SIXTEEN

The helicopter lifted off at seven-thirty, Thursday morning, carrying Hennessey and his usual campaign entourage. They were setting out on a whirlwind sweep of central California, stopping in Bakersfield, Fresno, Merced, and Stockton, then flying directly back to L.A., in time for that evening's Papa event, scheduled for the L.A. Memorial Coliseum. After the stop at Fresno, both Hennessey and his staff were unabashedly jubilant. They could not have asked for better receptions than they had received in both Bakersfield and Fresno. Not only were the turnouts notably larger than anticipated, but they were beginning to notice a steady trend of attendance by members of the opposition party. On the helicopter flight to Merced, despite the common superstition that such talk would jinx the election, Ted Rossiter openly talked to the staff about a landslide victory in the Senate race, and of starting to look to the presidential nomination. Hennessey overheard him and abruptly jerked him back into reality.

"Knock that shit off, Ted!! The easiest way to lose a game is to consider it won before it's over. I'm paying you to win this one first... so stay focused. Until this senatorial election is in the bag, don't let me hear any fucking talk about the next race! Do we understand each other?!"

"Sorry John. We understand one another perfectly. I was just a little giddy with all the great crowds this morning."

"Giddy is for little girls, Ted."

Embarrassed and humiliated, Ted looked out the window... pretending to study the terrain below but, instead, avoiding the eyes of the staffers. He mentally resolved to refrain from being overly optimistic in the future – but he was a veteran of dozens of campaigns and this one, he knew, was in the bag... save some major catastrophe. And there was nothing out there on the horizon, of which he was aware – barring something arising out of the Lisa Ryan affair – that could sink their ship. Stepping out of the helicopter in Merced, he was quickly reminded of the mythical nature of a sure thing.

As Rossiter's feet made contact with the tarmac, a reporter came up to him and asked if the Senator wished to make any statements regarding his wife's comments about the death of their son. Rossiter instantly felt his face flush and his heart race.

"What are you talking about?"

"It just came over the wire, Mr. Rossiter. Some reporter in San Bernardino recognized Mrs. Hennessey in a shopping mall last night and asked her about the death of her son and how she was coping with it. She's quoted as having said that her husband killed him. Then apparently she ran off. She hasn't returned any phone calls or answered her door, since. Does Senator Hennessey have any response?"

Without answering, Rossiter immediately turned around and ran back up the short set of steps into the helicopter to stop Hennessey, and make him aware of the bad news... and prepare him for the press. Hennessey was just about to exit the helicopter when Rossiter encountered him. Without saying anything, Rossiter grabbed his arm firmly. Hennessey could read the distress on his face. He stopped in his tracks and, without speaking, the two of them retreated to the front of the cabin. Rossiter sat down and told Hennessey to do the same. He did. Hennessey waited. Knowing the inevitable, white-hot fury the news would kindle in Hennessey, Rossiter hesitated, steeled himself, then forged ahead with the account he had just heard. As he spoke, Hennessey's face took on the ugliest look of hate, upon which, Rossiter had never before seen. Reflecting on the mind... and black heart... that would be required to sculpt such a malignant expression, Rossiter realized, for the first time, that this was the face of a truly horrible man... a man who appeared, at that instant, as though he could easily kill, without a moment's hesitation or remorse. Hennessey literally hissed his words through clenched teeth.

"Who was in charge down there?"

"In San Bernardino?... ah... Jake Bonner, I think."

"Get him on the phone."

Rossiter took out his pocket phone and his telephone index. He scanned the index for the right number then quickly dialed it and pressed the "Send" button.

"Who am I speaking with?"

"This is Rossiter... is Jake around?"

"Jake? Hold on."

Rossiter handed the phone to Hennessey. Hennessey's face was now spread with a malignant grin.

"Do you know why I'm calling, you worthless piece of shit?"

"I just wanted to tell you... first hand... that I'm going to have your back broken for this. Now put on Kilmer."

"Vince?"

"Just shut up and listen to me. Do you know where she is?"

"OK... go and get her... then put her on a plane... and do it as soon as we hang up. You go with her. Call Wagner... he'll let you use one of his. Take her where *no* one can find her... out of the country if you have to... and leave her there until you hear from me. You got it?"

Hennessey pressed the "End" button and handed the phone back to Rossiter.

"Get her doctor on the phone. Tell him to schedule a press conference... immediately. He's going to say that Emily hasn't ever recovered from John's death and that she's suffering from some sort of... schizophrenia or something... that her behavior is becoming more and more bizarre... that's she's running around saying crazy things about all kinds of people... that she's heavily medicated... has had shock treatment... is suicidal... really play it up. Then get out an official press statement from me. Say... that I hope I have the understanding and support of the public in this time of need... that my wife has undergone great emotional trauma over our loss... and I hope the public will be understanding about her behavior. Say that I'd appreciate it if they'd remember my wife and me in their prayers... and that I'm very distressed and disappointed that a member of the press could be so thoughtless as to ask her the sort of question that he did... and resurrect all these dark emotions in her. Say that I'm going to place her in a clinic... to allow her enough time and privacy, away from the public eye, to recover... and that I'm in constant contact with her and am trying to give her the support she needs to get through this. You can add that I'm even considering dropping out of the senatorial race... just to be able to spend more time with her – as though there's a fat fucking chance of that. Actually, Ted, if we play this right, it could work out nearly as well as John's death, you know? You straight on all this?"

"All set, John. I'll handle it. Just go out there and charm the hell out of them... let me worry about the rest of this shit."

"I don't think I have any option but to make a statement about this as soon as I get out there, do you?... go on the offensive before some media wiseass tries to nail me with it."

"No doubt about it, John. You've got to come out first. Are you ready with something?"

"Yeah... I'll wing it... same basic story I just gave you, I guess."

"That should do it. Be sure to look the part... distressed, sad... you know."

"I can handle it. All right... I'm going out there, now. Get this stuff straightened out... then meet us at the American Legion Hall. You know where it is?"

"I'll find it."

As soon as Hennessey reached the bottom of the steps, he went on the offensive... calling the reporters to gather around him for a statement.

"I'm sure all of you have heard by now about the statement my wife made about me regarding our son's death. First of all, I want to say that, given the trauma she has gone through over the loss of our only son, I cannot believe that any reporter could be so callous as to ask her the sort of question that he did. I think it was a cruel and very insensitive thing to do."

Hennessey welled up some stage-tears and paused while biting his lower lip, convincingly feigning difficulty in going on... then, just as convincingly, conspicuously acted-out the finding of courage to continue. He surveyed the faces of the media as he performed and was quite satisfied with the results.

"My wife has taken our son's death, very badly, and has been under the constant care of a physician since the day he died. She has been heavily medicated and undergone numerous treatments for her condition, including shock therapy. I have been in daily contact with her, and her doctor, and I am well aware of her rather bizarre behavior. I ask for both your understanding – and that of the public – as we try to cope with our personal tragedy. Emily's statement about me is a part of her condition... and I had been warned that something like this could happen... but I insisted that she be allowed to be out and about... hoping it might get her mind on other things. I never considered that some member of the media might approach her, when she was out, and ask her something, as unfeeling, as did this reporter. I'm sure there are those who will try to use something like this against me... but I can't worry about that. My only concern, right now, is my wife. This is an extremely trying time in our lives... the most difficult thing we have ever gone through together. It is a subject that is just too painful for me to talk about, any further, at this time... and I'm sure you will understand when I say that I don't have anything further to say about it... and that I won't take any questions on the matter. Thank you all very much."

Wearing an expression of deep, personal pain, Hennessey excused himself and, slowly and weakly, walked to the awaiting limousine. He knew he had had his way with the press... and they silently and somberly acquiesced to his requests.

At each campaign stop, Hennessey made a similar statement before his speech. It played terrifically well. The audiences were overwhelmingly sympathetic and supportive. He recognized that what he had originally perceived as a major problem could very well turn out to be a political boon. Hennessey was still, however, quite unforgiving of Jake Bonner and he would still, indeed, have him brutally beaten for the trouble he had caused him. Dealing decisively and viciously with fuck-ups always gave John Hennessey an immense sense of pleasure.

Spirits were high, once again, on the flight from Stockton back to L.A. So pleased was Hennessey with the day's success that he invited everyone to his suite for drinks after that evening's gathering at the L.A. Coliseum.

Approaching the Coliseum, that evening, Hennessey and Rossiter saw the very large burning cross, near the entrance, just outside the wall. As they drew nearer, several hundred white-hooded Klansmen, surrounding the flaming crucifix, also came into view. As their car passed by the shrouded assembly, they could hear the speaker shouting his words through a hand-held bullhorn.

"... and we will not stand idly by while a mongrelized mulatto calls himself God. God, Himself, forbids the mixing of the races and it is an abomination before His eyes. The white race is God's chosen people on Earth and may He strike down this half-nigger who blasphemes His name..."

In large and growing numbers, blacks were surrounding the Klan rally... shouting insults and profanities at them. The elements were clearly ripe for a violent confrontation and the LAPD was quickly moving into the area. Inside the stadium, the crowd could hear the increasing host of police sirens converging on the stadium and with this, had growing concern for their own safety. The shouting was growing louder with each passing moment. Suddenly, the echo of several gunshots cracked through the warm night air and instantly boosted the anxiety of the event-goers to a state of near panic. All eyes were wide and pulses racing... everyone searching the other faces of the crowd for a consensus on the prudent level of concern.

Papa and his small band of loyalists had not yet been seen in the stadium. The dignitaries, waiting in a secure room in the lower level of the coliseum for the troupe's arrival, were beginning to have grave concerns about remaining in the facility. Just as worry had escalated to fear, a police captain came into the room and told them that things were getting very ugly outside – and very dangerous – and that it had the potential of becoming a full-scale riot. He told them to follow him, move quickly, and stay very close to him... assuring them that they would be given a police escort out of the area.

Leaving their own cars behind in the stadium parking lot, the dignitaries ran behind the officer to the awaiting police vehicles, parked just outside the VIP entrance to the coliseum. People, on all sides of them, were shouting and running and throwing things. A rock smashed through the rear window of the police car, just moments after Hennessey had closed the rear door, disintegrating the safety glass and strewing the small fragments all over the backseat passengers. As they were pulling out onto the street, they could see a virtual army of police and emergency vehicles arriving onto the scene. Behind them, flames were erupting all around the coliseum. It was quickly taking on the look of a battle scene. As they pulled onto the up-ramp for the westbound lanes of the Santa Monica Freeway, police were in the process of erecting barricades to prevent traffic from entering the area, save the constant stream of coliseum-bound police and emergency personnel speeding that direction on the Freeway.

Hennessey, Rossiter and the other two passengers in the back seat of the police car were severely shaken by their brush with danger and were silent during the trip back to the hotel. The wind from the glassless window whipped them, unmercifully, as they sped along the Freeway, but they were happy to be putting as much distance between themselves and the coliseum as quickly as was humanly possible. Rossiter and Hennessey got out of the police car at their hotel, while the other passengers remained for transport to their own particular destinations. Shaken and frightened, Hennessey and Rossiter went directly to the hotel bar and quickly consumed several stiff drinks. They had each consumed three lowballs before they were willing, and able, to talk… and then spoke only in subdued voices – their heads close together – as though sharing a secret.

"Jesus Christ, John… that was close."

"As close as it gets, Ted. Goddamn!… for a couple of minutes, I thought we'd had it. You know… there *must* be something on the air about this."

Hennessey asked the bartender to turn on the television. Live helicopter shots were broadcasting the rioting and burning that had spread to many of the residential neighborhoods surrounding the coliseum. There were so many emergency personnel and police on the ground that their flashing lights gave an ironic, festive, twinkling to the aerial view.

As they watched, a grim concern suddenly struck Hennessey.

"What if something happened to this Papa guy? Shit!… that'd totally screw up the rest of the week… and especially the big event in Santa Monica! Oh, fuck! I mean, after that… screw it… but, goddamn… I was counting on him finishing the week. Shit!… he was probably right in the middle of that thing when it broke out. Why does this shit have to happen to me all the time, Ted?… you know? He's been great for my ratings… and just three more nights... that's all I asked for... Jesus. I'll tell you what... go up and get with Jimmy... he's probably wondering if we're still alive, anyway... and have him get in touch with the chief and see if he knows anything about this guy."

CHAPTER SEVENTEEN

Nick Ryan's enthusiasm and energy for driving suddenly dissipated as they reached Poplar Bluff, Missouri. For most of the past twelve hours he had been behind the wheel. With a total of only three short, combined gas, coffee, and toilet breaks over this time period, his determination to make up for the oversleeping screw-up, that he accepted as his fault – considering himself in charge of the journey – had, to that moment, stayed his steadfastness. Feeling his penance, now at least partially served, however, he was, presently, more than ready for a much-needed rest. He spotted a classic, old-fashion diner… reminiscent of a large train car – made of shiny contoured metal that gleamed in the early morning sun. Its name – "Dottie's Diner" – was proclaimed in fading red letters on a large, white, rectangular sign, attached to the roof. Nick pulled into the gravel parking area, awakened Lisa, and the two of them, physically debilitated by the long trip, tried to walk, as normally as possible to the metal, double-door entrance of "Dottie's." Just inside the doors were three metal newspaper boxes. After they ordered, Nick asked the cashier for change and put two quarters into the slot of the *USA Today* box. The colored picture of burning city blocks and the accompanying caption instantly stunned him. Standing there, he read enough of the article to justify his initial alarm, then walked quickly back to the booth and sat on the hard metal seat, across from Lisa. She instantly read his concern.

"What is it, Nicky?"

Nick laid the paper on the table, spun it around to face her, then pushed it to her side of the booth. He awaited her comprehension. It didn't take long.

"Oh my God, Nicky!"

"Quite a mess… isn't it?"

"Oh my God... does it say anything about him?"

"I haven't read the whole thing... but it says that thirteen people were killed... and a whole lot more injured."

Lisa scanned the rest of the front page section of the article then quickly flipped over to the page-two continuation. She was shaking her head in disbelief as she read.

"Can you believe this?"

"Actually Lis... I thought... with some of the things he's been saying... and with as many people as he's making angry... it was only a matter of time until something, like this, blew up."

"But the Klan!... I didn't think they were anywhere near California."

"They're everywhere, Lis... believe me. We've got them in Dover."

"What a place for the Klan to pick to have a rally... that area is surrounded by black ghettos. They must be crazy!"

"Well... I don't think you'll find too many Rhodes Scholars under those hoods."

"What's their beef with Papa anyway?"

"You know, Lis... the racial thing. Papa's half-black. For anyone to suggest that God has even one black cell in his body is a threat to them. It's a threat to a lot of people, actually. I mean, look at all the controversy that went on when some of the African Studies people claimed that Jesus and his disciples were black... you remember, the 'wooly hair' thing?"

"Oh yeah... I remember reading about that. Didn't they come out with an illustrated black Bible with all of the pictures of everyone... Jesus, Mary, Joseph, all the disciples... looking very black?"

"Yeah... it was the African Heritage Bible or something like that."

"That really flipped out a lot of people who love that blonde, beach-boy portrait of Jesus that hangs in the vestibule of just about every church in America."

Nick laughed.

"Yeah... he looks like he just got off a wave at Malibu."

Nick's levity seemed suddenly out of place and disrespectful, in light of the story in front of them... and they both tacitly resumed a more appropriate sense of decorum for the circumstance. Lisa resumed the previous discussion in a low – self-consciously solemn – voice.

"Really Nicky... what about Papa? How can we find out if he's OK?"

"Call the police, maybe."

"Do you think?"

"It couldn't hurt."

"We'll call on the way out. Is there a pay phone here?"

"Yeah... right beside the papers."

Nick hurriedly consumed his blueberry pancakes... the thickest he had ever encountered, requiring an inordinate amount of berry syrup to even slightly moisten them... and Lisa efficiently finished off her ham-and-cheese omelet. Getting two cups of coffee for the road, they paid their bill and went directly to the pay phone. To their dismay, it was strictly a calling-card box. Nick looked at Lisa with uncertainty.

"It only takes cards, Lis."

"Aren't there any normal pay phones left in the world?"

"I've got a feeling we're getting old, honey. I think this *is* normal, anymore."

"Should we risk it?"

"I think we should be all right. I really doubt that anyone is scouring every credit call made in the United States."

"If you think it's OK."

With a look and voice that tried, unsuccessfully, to engender confidence in his wife, Nick responded.

"I think so, Lis."

Nick swiped his card, dialed for L.A. information, and got the number for the LAPD downtown switchboard. Lisa watched Nick as he dialed the number, then studied his face as he listened intently to whatever was coming through the receiver. It always seemed to her that, for some unknown reason, phone calls that other people made always seemed so much more significant that her own... that they were conversing about things, much weightier than what she had to talk about. She watched as, twice, Nick pressed the rectangular, metal numbers. Lisa was puzzled... but kept quiet. Nicky kept shaking his head in exasperation. Finally, his face took on an agreeable expression. He smiled at Lisa while nodding his head, then hung up the receiver without ever having uttered a single syllable. Lisa immediately inquired as an explanation for the odd, silent, telephone scene she had witnessed.

"What?"

"He's OK."

"How do you know?... you didn't say a word to anyone."

"They have a voice mail thing set up. When it answered, it said to press "eight" if I was calling for information about the disturbance at the Los Angeles Coliseum last night. So I did. It gave all sorts of information about bus service, cancellations, restrictions on travel... that sort of stuff. Then it said to press a "seven" if I was calling as to the condition of any specific individual... which I did. First it gave the names of about five people – and Papa was one of them – and told me to push a number for information for each name... Hennessey was one of them, too, by the way. So I pushed a "three" for Papa. The message was that he was unharmed last evening... and that he planned on appearing at this evening's scheduled event at the Hollywood Park Racetrack. I guess I should have pressed for Hennessey too... but I didn't think of it. Maybe we'll get lucky and he'll have bought the farm last night."

"Nicky!... don't talk like that! We're not like that! That's the way he is... and we're better than that!"

"I was just joking, Lis... sorry."

Lisa forgave him with a reluctant smile... then breathed an audible sigh of relief.

"Thank God he's all right. But, you know, this may sound a little perverse, Nicky... but it would have been better if he had gotten hurt last night... hurt enough to keep him in the hospital past Sunday, you know? That would have solved all the problems."

"Yeah... but it feels sort of funny wishing somebody had gotten hurt that badly. Especially, someone like him."

"I know... I was just talking... I didn't really mean it."

"He's going to speak at the Hollywood Park Racetrack?... how tacky can you get?"

"Yeah... I know. Annie Moore set that up. She couldn't find anywhere else for them to go in that area. I said the same thing when she told me about it."

"I wonder what's become of her?"

"I do too, Nicky. She was acting so strange when I saw her out in Santa Monica. I wouldn't be surprised if she up and quit Hennessey. Oh boy... if she did... Hennessey would have gone nuts... losing his PR director and speech writer the same day."

"Do you have any regrets, Lisa?"

"None... none whatsoever. Everyday since I quit, I thank God I did. You know... sometimes you don't realize just how bad things really were until you get away from them for a while. He's a horrible man, Nicky... so horrible. Someday I'll tell you about it. I can't even think about it right now."

"We need to get rolling, Lis... if we're going to make it on time."

"How are we doing?"

"It's going to be close, sweetie. Even with this nonstop driving, we're taking longer than what I thought."

"Are we going to make it?"

"I think so... but just barely."

CHAPTER EIGHTEEN

Despite the stressful events of the previous night, Hennessey continued on the campaign trail the following day, setting out early Friday morning. The planned sweep was to go directly south, along the coast... with stops in Long Beach, Dana Point, Oceanside, Carlsbad, Encinitas, and San Diego. The focus of the reporters' questions was primarily on the riot... asking the Senator his take on it. Knowing the clear, low regard of the general public toward the Klan, the Senator mounted a politically safe attack against them... and hate groups in general. Then, playing for the minority constituency, he also passionately decried the racist attack mounted against Papa by the Klan. Skirting any personal belief he may have regarding Papa, he repeatedly stated that he would speak out on behalf of anyone who had suffered an attack, based purely on the color of his skin. Asked if he anticipated any trouble at the Hollywood Park Racetrack that evening, he said he did not. For one thing, he explained – because of last night's riot – the police presence was going to be significantly stepped-up for the night's gathering... and secondly, he said he felt last evening's problems were due to the unique and unfortunate circumstances that led to a near-certain calamity. What could one expect, he queried, with a Klan rally being held in a predominantly black area? He said he would have been more surprised if there had *not* been trouble.

The campaigning was going so well – and so predictably – that the staff – Hennessey included – were lulled into a perfunctory sense of merely going through the motions. There was, as a result, a recent, and noticeable, lack of energy in Hennessey's stump speech... at least to his staff, who had heard it so many times that it had taken on the essence of a Gregorian chant. In Oceanside's civic auditorium, as Hennessey was chanting his anti-illegal immigration verse, the pro forma nature of the campaign trip ended suddenly. As Hennessey was in mid-sentence, from the back assembly hall came a loud and bitter voice that Hennessey immediately recognized.

"What have you done with my daughter?!... you bastard!!"

Hennessey felt his jaws tighten and his blood heat as he glared at Shirley Hughes, standing at her seat and returning his glare with equal vehemence. An immediate hush fell over the standing-room-only crowd. All heads turned in unison to look at this woman... then collectively returned to Hennessey... then divided and became spasmodic, according to interest and speculation. The silence became oppressive in anticipation of a response from Hennessey. She had trapped him. He could not ignore her. But Hennessey was a ruthless, unprincipled man, and such men are not so easily ensnared. With pure deliberation, Hennessey undertook the reformation of his facial expression, now bearing the color and creases of his searing anger, and quickly rearranged to that of a quiet, compassionate calm. He smiled with a hint of pity at the upright woman and extended his hand in her direction.

"Ladies and gentlemen... this is my wife's mother. She was as deeply affected by my young son's recent suicide... as was my wife. I have encouraged my mother-in-law to seek both medical care and counseling for her grief but she has steadfastly refused. I love her and have great sympathy for her, and truly wish she could find a way to finally accept John's tragic death and move on in her life. John's suicide has been a terrible burden for all of us to bear... but life must go on and I don't believe my son would have wanted us to run from the duties we owe to others. I had, as some of you may recall, considered withdrawing from the senate race out of grief for my son... but I then realized that to go on and work for the benefit of others would be more of a tribute to his name than to turn my back and hide from the world. For reasons, known only to my mother-in-law, she blames me for my son's death and she has caused my wife to do the same. This hurts me very deeply... but I understand that it is merely a manifestation of her pain and her need to strike out at the cruel forces of life. Because of this... I forgive her. I do not wish, however, to unfairly subject this audience, any further, to the sadness and personal anguish of my family's tragedy... so I will close with the sincere wish that none of you in this room ever experience the never-healing wound that the death of one's child, especially under such circumstances, inflicts upon a parent's heart. Thank you all very much and God bless you."

Hennessey then took on a dramatic countenance of tragic sadness as he slowly gathered his papers from the podium and, with shoulders drooped, head lowered, and eyes on the floor, he walked, in clear, ostensible sorrow, slowly across the wide stage, convincingly portraying the role of a man who is bearing the invisible and unfathomable weight of inexpressible grief upon his shoulders, to the wings – where his staff stood in tentative anxiousness, awaiting the inexorable explosion. In empathy for the trauma he had been unfairly forced to endure in public, the audience rose, en masse, to stand in respectful silence as Hennessey traversed the stage. So effective were his words in engendering support for his position, relative to his mother-in-law's, that the audience, though bearing some sympathy for her condition, as fictionalized by Hennessey, regarded her with a detectable display of reproach for her unjust transgression against Hennessey as they passed by her on their way out of the auditorium.

Entering the wings, Hennessey hissed three words through his teeth, in guarded volume, to restrict the proclamation going beyond the earshot of his staff.

"That fucking bitch!"

Making his way through the crowd of backstage hangers-on he retained his convincing facade of long-suffering grief, to which he received an outpouring of sincere offers of sympathy for his having been so publicly victimized. Safe in the car, however, Hennessey's anger sought swift retribution.

"Jimmy... find out where her husband's pension is coming from and fuck things up... his health insurance, too. Do the same with his social security. And find some cooperative bimbo who will claim he assaulted her... and anything else you can think of to ruin them. Look into everything in their pasts… see if there's anything there we can use. How about their house? Maybe it's in an area where the federal government just might need to build a park. Eminent domain cases can turn out real sour sometimes… especially if there's a downright prick on the government's side. I want them ruined, Jimmy!"

"I'll turn it over to Freddy. There's no better ruiner than him."

"Any word from Fred on the other matter?"

"I've got a message on my cellular to return his call. I'll let you know about it… later."

After Hennessey's speech in Encinitas, Jimmy pulled him aside.

"We've located them."

"Where?"

"Poplar Bluff, Missouri."

"Poplar Bluff, Missouri? What the hell are they doing there?"

"Tim Wilson picked up a phone charge, made from a diner there, very early this morning. They placed a call to the LAPD. They're coming here, John… sure enough."

"Why?"

"Good question. It's pretty clear they haven't told the police about this, yet… so I can only think of one reason they're coming."

"Why?"

"They're going to try to warn this guy."

"Papa?"

"Yes."

"Well we can't have that. No way I'm giving up the biggest media event of my professional career. It's going to be history, Jimmy... and we're going to see that it happens, no matter what we have to do. They have got to be stopped."

"I told Freddy to get Wilson to put out for general police surveillance for their plate... a report-but-don't-detain request. I don't think they rented a car... pretty hard to do with cash... and there's been no credit action with any of the rental agencies. About a ninety percent chance they're driving their own car, I'd say."

"Is Wilson watching for their relatives' credit cards, too?"

"He's marked every known relative's name that we could identify to kick out of the computer if the card is used."

But what the hell are they doing in Poplar Bluff? That's out in the middle of nowhere, isn't it?"

"I'd say they're staying off the interstate, John... which makes sense if they don't want to be spotted. Poplar Bluff is on U.S. 60... I looked at it on a map. That's where I told Freddy to tell Wilson to concentrate... along 60."

"Aren't the shooters contacting Fred tomorrow... for instructions on them?"

"Yep... and it's going to be close, John. Let's hope for some luck."

"Why do you think they called the police? She might have blown the whistle on us."

"If she hasn't done it by now, she's not going to. I think she wanted to know the same thing you did."

"About Papa?"

"Yep."

"That makes sense. If he was already dead, they'd be wasting their time, wouldn't they?"

They completed their stops in San Diego, without incident, and drove back to L.A.... in time for the evening's event at the Hollywood Park Racetrack.

The Racetrack crowd was unique. Apparently some of Papa's following had reached the stage of frenzied adoration. As soon as Papa walked onto the platform, erected in the center of the track and facing the grandstands – much like the arrangement at his first event in the L.A. County Fairgrounds – thousands of people began shouting his name in praise and adulation – their faces contorted with barely contained hysteria. They shouted that they loved him... that they wanted to come home to him. Some reporters later commented that the atmosphere, that night, was like a combination of a rock concert and an old-fashion tent revival meeting. Papa responded to the frenzied groupies with great kindness and affection – but also with specific admonitions. He told them that he loved them, but that his love was a quiet love. He said he didn't want to be worshiped by them – but simply loved by them. He told them he was their parent and he wanted them to love him as a parent – and not to hail him as a king – and that he did not come to frighten them. He said he was the familiar and the close, not the royal and the distant. He told them not to put him on an altar, but to take him into their hearts. He said his love was not a public love to be shouted, but a tender love to be privately kept and cherished, and that his love would bring peace to their hearts. He told the crowd that he knew each of them, as any parent would. If he had enough time, he said, he would hold each of them in his arms and tell each one of them that he knows every moment of their life and of each joy and sadness and suffering and loneliness they have ever experienced.

Papa's words had an immediate and noticeable effect on the crowd. They seemed to understand that they had come there for the wrong reason and that Papa was not who they wanted him to be – but something better. Upon this realization, the crowd's demeanor changed, dramatically, to a quiet, reflective tranquility. As with nearly all of those who seem to grasp some particular essence of Papa, many began to quietly and happily weep.

CHAPTER NINETEEN

By noon on Saturday, Nick and Lisa Ryan had only reached Vaughn, New Mexico. Their gross underestimation as to how long it would take them to travel to Los Angeles, while avoiding interstates, was such that they knew, if they were going to make it on time, they'd have to abandon their original plan. Seventeen miles west of Vaughn, they changed course and headed north, on Route 285, to pick up Interstate 40, which would take them most of the way to L.A. Nick calculated that if they went five miles over the speed limit for the entire distance, stopping for only ten or fifteen minutes for each combined gas, toilet, and snack break, they'd get into L.A. at about ten or eleven o'clock the next morning – Sunday – giving them a couple of hours to catch up with Papa... before he got onto the platform at Santa Monica. As with all amorphous plans, as the actual moment began to take on the detail of a dawning reality, practical questions began to arise.

"Nicky... how are we going to find him? He could be going into Santa Monica from any direction."

Nick was silent, experiencing the same increasing nervousness in his stomach as was Lisa. He could feel himself begin to perspire, his mouth grow dry, and a tingling sensation in his penis. He swallowed several times in an attempt to lubricate his words.

"Where is he speaking tonight?"

"Let's see... ummm... Saturday... ummm... at a park... a park. Do we have an L.A. city map?"

"Just our atlas."

Lisa retrieved it from the back seat and located Los Angeles in the index. She opened it to the indicated page and studied it... running her right pointer finger along the speaking route that Papa was following.

"Here it is. It's called Kenneth Hahn Park... in Baldwin Hills. I remember that because I had never heard of it, before Annie told me about it... but I remembered something about it had the name of a movie star... but I couldn't remember which one. It was Alex Baldwin... Baldwin Hills? As soon as I saw the name, I remembered. Let's see... a good chance he'll take Venice Boulevard, west... then Lincoln Boulevard up to Santa Monica. If we go on the Santa Monica Freeway... that's Route Ten... we're bound to run into them, or at least see the crowd. I mean... thousands of people walk with him as he goes from place to place. They have to block off some major streets and highways for them. It'd be hard to miss them, I'd think."

"If he's with so many people, how are we going to get close to him?"

"Well... I still have my senate staff badge. If we can find a cop, I'll show it to him and tell him that Senator Hennessey has sent me to talk to Papa's people about the Santa Monica event. Hennessey's name has a lot of power out there. He'll probably give us an escort right up to him. And I know that guy... that Chapman guy... who's the writer... you know who I mean... that you have to talk to, to get near Papa? He'll listen to me – he knows who I am."

"OK... but you'll have to watch the map and guide me when we get out there. I've never been in Los Angeles before and I have no idea where I'm going."

"It won't be any big deal. We'll stay on interstates, right out to Santa Monica. Also... it's going to be Sunday... we shouldn't be running into any big traffic jams... at least not until we get close to Santa Monica. Then we're going to be really in it. Annie told me that this gathering is going to be absolutely enormous. She said it was going to make even the biggest marches on Washington look like a Shriner's parade. That's what she said. Seriously... if she's right, it could be one of the largest gatherings of human beings in the history of the world. Isn't that something?"

"Will it be bigger than the Super Bowl?"

"Much."

"Then that's big."

They got gas, just before pulling onto 40 and, after getting onto the interstate, Nick set the cruise control at seventy and pushed westward with a renewed sense of urgency and determination. With the anxiety of the actual event closing in on them, they both had to exert an effort to keep their mutually increasing, manic nervousness from sapping their much-needed energy. When they got to L.A., they'd have to be completely focused and resourceful in order to accomplish their mission in time. The significance of the realization – that failure meant a man's death – began to exert a terrible burden on their conscience and their sense of responsibility. By nightfall, however, as they were approaching the Arizona border, their state of hyperenergy and buzzing anxiety had spent itself and they could feel themselves beginning to physically and emotionally crash. Sleep and driving was quickly negotiated – Lisa would sleep first... for three hours... or shorter, if Nick became dangerously sleepy.

CHAPTER TWENTY

The final leg of the current campaign tour was a scheduled swing along the coast to the north. They'd be stopping in Santa Barbara... in Monterey... for a luncheon fund-raiser... then on to San Jose, San Francisco, and Oakland. After the Monterey, five-thousand-dollar-a-plate luncheon with the Cattleman's Association – which raised over two million dollars for his campaign chest from the five-hundred-plus guests – Hennessey got a call from Freddy Westin. He had just gotten off the phone with the shooters. The arrangements were made – but it was, he said, a very close call. Wilson had gotten a steady stream of visuals on the Ryans' car over the last few days... all on U.S. 60. But, just before Fred talked to the shooters, Wilson had phoned him to say that he had just received word that the Ryans had gotten off of 60 and were now proceeding west, along Interstate 40. Looking at a map, Fred could see that 40 would end at Barstow, California... and that they'd have to pick up Interstate 15 into L.A. Quickly fabricating a rationale for his request, Freddy asked Wilson to put in for an actual stop of their vehicle at Hesperia, California... forty miles west of Barstow. Fred said they wanted to make sure that it was actually the Ryans who were in the car... and asked that an ID check be done of both the passengers. Wilson said that'd be no problem... that the state boys – like they always do – would come up with some reason for a legitimate stop. Fred went on to tell Wilson that he, also, had a very good reason for wanting to know where, exactly, they'd be pulled over. Without questioning Fred's motivation for wanting this information, Wilson checked a map and quickly said that he'd request the police pull them over at the Route 18, north, exit on Interstate 15 in Hesperia.

Less than ten minutes after he hung up with Wilson, the shooters called Fred at the appointed hour for instructions. Fred told them precisely where, and approximately when, the police would be pulling over the Ryans and gave them the make, year, color, and model of their car – and their plate number. Fred suggested when they'd have to be in place to ensure they'd witness the stop... thus allowing them to pick up their trail from that point. The shooters said that, given the circumstances, they'd just have to "play it by ear" and wait for the "right" opportunity to do the job. They told Freddy that, given the new circumstances, however... this had become a tricky and very risky hit... much more so that the original hit... it was, consequently, going to cost them more. They gave Freddy the instructions for wiring the additional money to an account in France. They'd expect it there, they said, within eight hours after they hung up... or the shoot was off.

The news – that the hit was on again – pleased Hennessey immensely. The demand for extra money pissed him off in an equally dramatic fashion. It was a relief to him to know that the nagging problem of the Ryans would soon – and finally – be resolved, but he made it clear to Fred that these "French assholes" were a bunch of "fucking thieves." But, finding himself over the barrel on this one, he grudgingly authorized the additional payment.

In San Francisco, Hennessey made an appearance at a folk festival, on Fisherman's Wharf, where he sampled ethnic food, browsed the craft booths, and listened to the musical entertainment – all for the cameras – then was driven downtown to give a speech at the annual convention of the National Education Association at the Hyatt Regency. Knowing well, the demographics of his campaign support, and with media cameras capturing his every word, he adroitly straddled the fence on the raging convention debates over outcomes-based education and "inclusion" in the school curriculum versus traditional values... then moved on, quickly, to his commitment to increased funding for public education – the only real issue, about which, he knew, the educators really cared. Hennessey felt he understood the minds and values of the current-day school teachers, precisely, since he perceived they were very similar to his own. He was convinced that, as long as they got what he felt was a ludicrously high salary for their laughably meager work schedule and lucrative benefits, pension, and job security, he knew they cared for their students about as much as he did his for constituents. Whores, as a whole, he had discovered, have the good sense not to criticize others who made a living in a similar vein. His speech was received with great enthusiasm and ended with standing applause.

Being in San Francisco, of course, Hennessey had to tread cautiously among the gay issues to avoid stepping on any one of the many political landmines that were latent to the territory. His staff had frequently done the numbers on the homosexual vote and their contribution base... and had consistently concluded that, although they were a relatively small voting block, and despite the fact that Hennessey privately referred to them as "the fucking faggots," he wasn't politically safe in siding with the majority to condemn them. They were, as a group, much too affluent, and therefore, able to buy influence... and had far too many connections to the entertainment and media industry to safely attack them. Consequently, Hennessey didn't openly support the gay movement – but neither did he condemn it. Hennessey's staff decided that his most advantageous position was to play to the majority – coming out in support of the equal treatment of all individuals, but condemning the extension of any preference to any specific group. This didn't go over very well with the black vote, but kept him out of harm's way with the more powerful gay block that was still willing to settle for simple equality... the mainstream gays, not yet overtly pushing for preference but still willing to settle for parity at the present juncture. He was sure that preference would be the next card played by the gays – as was by the blacks – and he would, at that point, need to reassess his position. To cover his bet with the black voters, however, Hennessey always found enough bones to throw their way to keep them otherwise satisfied. He had, early in his political career, discovered that if he simply tossed some money in the direction of the black community for more "programs," he was safe with them, regardless of what else he said or did.

For a few hours, before they departed for Kenneth Hahn Park, Hennessey met with some staffers – just in from Washington – for a briefing on new developments from inside the Beltway. They began with some upcoming key votes and their recommendations on which way he should go on them. The next news was about

Phil Ansler's people, who had recently visited the office, seeking support for his Supreme Court nomination. His people, the staffers told him, had fallen all over themselves to flatter and praise Hennessey – obviously cognizant of the fact that with a phone call, he could either make – or break – Ansler's confirmation. Hennessey told his staffers to let Ansler dangle a little longer. He declared that once these "judicial assholes" were confirmed, they were untouchable... and so he wanted some more administration concessions before he gave Ansler his robes. Finally, they reminded him that he needed to be at his committee hearing on Tuesday morning... that the Secretary of Agriculture was going to be there. Secretary Lewis had screwed Hennessey around on some subsidy promises he had made – making him look foolish – and it was payback time.

Hennessey's people had their contacts in the budget office dig up some financial irregularities in the Department of Agriculture... and Hennessey felt they had just enough rope to hang Lewis... and Hennessey wanted to, personally, be the one to do it. There were, of course, always irregularities in everyone's expenditures – Hennessey's operation included – and normally these would be mutually overlooked by all the Beltway cohorts. But when someone screwed Hennessey around, professional courtesy went out the window and he went for the jugular. The way Hennessey looked at it, Lewis should have known better. He knew the price he'd pay for embarrassing him... so, as Hennessey put it to his staffers, "If you want to dance, you've got to pay the fiddler." Hennessey also knew he had the Secretary at a distinct disadvantage. He had the power to call a Senate hearing – and all the problems that come with it – to rake Lewis over the coals... and there was virtually nothing Lewis could do, in return, to Hennessey about his own financial irregularities. If he tried anything, Hennessey would just drag the hearings on even longer and make it all the worse on him. When Hennessey got into a fight, these were the kind of rules under which he insisted on playing.

The evening at Kenneth Hahn Park unveiled a new wrinkle in the Papa phenomenon. After witnessing it, Hennessey reflected that, given the obvious interests involved, he was actually very surprised it hadn't materialized earlier. Lining both sides of the drive through Baldwin Hills, along the entrance to Kenneth Hahn Park, were thousands of blacks... singing, shouting, clapping their hands, and holding a variety of handmade signs that proclaimed such views as – "God is Black" "Black was the First Color" "Africa is the Home of God" "Papa is Our Black Father"... and other such messages depicting the special relationship of black people to Papa. The parallel between this new, peculiar, ethnocentric claim to God – and the similar divine exclusivity appropriated by the Jews, struck Hennessey as humorous. Laughing, he quipped to Rossiter, as they were passing by the demonstrators, that he wondered how God would decide between "the niggers and the kikes as his favorites in heaven"... that maybe he'd have to flip a coin on it. Caught up in his own humor, he continued on to say that one side of the coin would probably have a watermelon on it and a bagel on the other. The entire staff laughed with him, in dutiful appreciation.

Having apparently arrived at the park, very early, to stake out their territory, the racial composition of the audience, standing directly in front of the speaker's stand, and stretching back for several hundred yards, appeared to be exclusively black. As Hennessey got out of the limo, he could make out a few of the repeated phrases being enthusiastically shouted by the black contingent – "Praise God!" "Praise Papa Our Black Father!" The Senator's entourage stood near the limo – behind and to the right of the platform – awaiting the arrival of Papa and his people. Hennessey was never exactly sure how the Papa contingent got to these events... seeming always to just suddenly appear at the appointed hour. At that particular moment, they were nowhere in sight. From where Hennessey's group stood, they could see the same sort of signs, they had just seen while driving in, bobbing up and down in the hands of many of the jubilant black worshipers.

Finally, in the distance, behind and to the left of the speaker's stand, Hennessey spotted Papa and his intimate band of loyalists emerging from a thickly wooded area... walking toward the left side of the platform. Knowing the routine well, by now, he and the other dignitaries immediately proceeded up the right-side steps and onto the stand, ahead of Papa and his party, and stood toward the rear – the platform party protocol having taken on an almost ceremonial rigidity after so many repetitions. Knowing that Papa would soon follow, the exuberance of the front section was exacerbated to near frenzy. Hands and signs waved frantically in the air... faces were turned toward the heavens... offering all manner of prayer and exultation... spontaneous singing and passionate praising erupting throughout. A number of the women appeared on the verge of fainting from the apparent overwhelming significance of the moment, and those around them were fanning their faces in an attempt to keep their overwrought companions from collapsing, unconscious, onto the grass.

As always, without prior introduction or announcement, Papa walked quietly onto the stage and proceeded directly to the microphone. The crowd noise could now be fairly described as deafening... and their antics so manic as to appear at times comical to the platform observers. Instead of making any motions to request either the attention or the silence of the audience, Papa stood – silent and still – looking out over the frantic crowd. His face had the expression of an understanding and affectionate parent, indulgently watching his children act up... and patiently waiting for them to settle down. Very slowly, the pumping, collective energy of the jubilant crowd began to wane... accelerated by a growing self-consciousness, borne of Papa's sustained silence and steady gaze. Finally, as one extreme is so often offset by its antithesis, a quiet came over the crowd, as equally overpowering as the preceding pandemonium... so profound that onlookers could hear their neighbors' breathing. Papa stretched his lips into a happy smile and nodded his head in appreciation of the quiet.

He began, as always, by expressing his love for each member of the audience, calling them, as always, his children. He then moved on to address the overtly conveyed claim of the black members of the audience to their special standing with him because of their mutual skin color. In a quiet, understanding tone of voice, he explained to them that all the people of the earth were his beloved children… and none did he love any greater than any other. He said that the pain that any of his children felt was his pain also… regardless of the color of their skin. As he went on explaining the unbiased nature of his love of all his children, disgruntlement was quickly becoming apparent in many of the forward sectors of the crowd, with many apparently not hearing the words they had expected. The crowd's mood, very soon, worsened to ugliness, and finally came to a boil with the issuance of an assortment of derisive epithets from numerous quarters in the front section of the audience. "Sellout!" "Uncle Tom!" "Wannabe!" "Stay black, brother!"

Many, in these sections of the crowd, elected to abruptly quit the event and began to stomp toward the park exits… throwing their signs on the grass in disgust, and others, who followed behind, making a point to emphatically step on them. After the mass exodus was complete, it appeared that less than a fourth of the black contingent remained. During the initial stages of the departure, there appeared to be a lot of spirited disagreement among the members of the black audience as to what the proper reaction to Papa's words should be, punctuated with loud words and wild hand gestures and some occasional shoving. A number of the black members of the audience appeared to be striving, with great animation, to dissuade those who seemed intent on leaving the park. Those who remained appeared to be embarrassed and ashamed of the companions who had deserted their ranks… and of the cruel words they had hurled at Papa. Many heads were lowered and shaking… their comportment suggesting a mixture of dejection, bewilderment, disgust, and shame.

Papa's face had a look of profound sadness as he talked to the remaining congregation of his great sorrow and of the deep pain that he feels when his children reject his love and turn their backs on him. He also spoke of his anguish, derived from knowing what wonderful happiness these children will lose, and of what they could have… if only they remembered him, and could accept his love as it was given, and would choose to return home to him when their time had come. When Papa had finished speaking, the departing crowd was exceedingly quiet and somber.

CHAPTER TWENTY-ONE

Nick's turn at the wheel was completed as they crossed the Arizona border in the pitch blackness of the night. This time, he was not inclined to be a hero and pulled over onto the shoulder to change guard at the precise end of his three-hour stint. The change in speed immediately awakened Lisa.

"Is it my turn, honey?"

"Yeah. We just got into Arizona... not more that five minutes ago."

Lisa reached over and rubbed Nick's knee affectionately.

"You must be really tired, sweetie."

"I am, Lis. I could hardly make it, this last hour. I was really afraid I'd fall asleep. Almost did a couple of times, actually."

"You said you'd wake me up if you got too tired, Nicky."

"I know... but I wanted to finish my turn."

"You men... such heroes."

"It's not being a hero, Lis... it's just a guy thing... to do what you say you're gonna do. It goes way back... you know? It starts with being called a wimp by your friends – when you're a little kid – for being a quitter."

Lisa smiled then opened her door. The stark glare of the interior lights instantly destroyed the quiet, intimate, darkness of her former, moving bedroom. Nick got out on his side and the two of them met as they rounded the trunk. Lisa reached for Nick's chest as he passed and she rubbed it... bringing him to a stop. She gave him a quick, tired kiss of wifely familiarity and affection. The enormity of the dark world surrounding them struck them both in the same moment. Neither of them had ever seen a night, so dark, or a celestial display so indescribably large and omnipresent. It was as though the entire world was made up of the black sky and the cold, blue-white light of the stars... and a world, under their feet, but a thin, fragile shell. They were both overcome by an overwhelming sense of being so small so as to not justify their own existence... as though they might, if they weren't vigilant, simply cease to exist. It frightened them both and they hurriedly sought the small confines of their car... where they knew their existence would be significant by comparison. As they jumped into the car and closed the doors, the intimate diminutive size of their contrived world made them feel, immediately, cozy and reassured. They both convulsed, momentarily, in shivers of happiness and belonging.

They drove in silence for a while... neither of them wanting to speak of this mutually disconcerting experience. Lisa finally decided she needed to hear voices, if only her own, and stuck to a quickly chosen, mundane topic.

"It's really getting cold, honey. I'm going to put on the heat... OK?"

"Go ahead, Lis... it *is* getting really cold. Strange place out here... you need the air conditioner during the day and the heater at night."

Nick was asleep within a few minutes. The highway that lay ahead of them was so straight, and the world so large and flat, that Lisa had the odd feeling of standing still... despite the disproving speedometer registering seventy. The warmth of the heater and the steady hum of its fan motor accentuated the coziness of their little moving world... separated by only thin glass from the inky, cold, impersonal blackness of the enormous night around them. Everything about the moment, in that intimate smallness of their car, combined into a rare, unanticipated moment of pure inexpressible love and joy... a feeling so clear and strong that

Lisa felt she could touch it with her hands and breathe it into her body. She wanted to memorize everything about the odd moment and carry it with her like a photograph... to pull it out from time to time to either add to a new, wonderful moment or to provide proof, in bleak times, that moments of pure happiness and love truly can – and do – come along from time to time in a person's life.

As she drove through the night, encapsulated in her vessel of love, Lisa found herself puzzling over men like Hennessey... wondering why they were the way they were. What was the point?... she pondered. How hollow his life was... loving no one... being despised and feared by those who really knew him. He never even loved his own son... and he despised his own wife, who was a kind, loving woman. What did he have in life?... power... money... fame... women. Didn't he see how meaningless these things really were? But she knew there were so many other men like him in Washington... just about all of the politicians... and the maggots who made a living from their blood – as she had.

From her special place that night, Lisa could see, with infinite clarity, just how pitifully poor all of these people actually were. They truly had nothing. She, an insignificant young woman... who would never be known by more than a few dozen people on earth before she would die... and would never have much money nor power... had so much more than any of these wealthy and influential people. And one of these pathetic creatures was very likely plotting to kill her – and her husband – at this very moment. This thought gave immediate rise to hot indignation. How dare this worthless blight on the world even think of harming her or her husband! This filthy, malignant rodent didn't have the right to even go near the decent people of the world, she silently railed. Hennessey should rightly stay in his own hole and confine his depravity to the other vermin of his own kind! Rare anger seethed through Lisa Ryan's soul. In that moment she realized that if she were given the opportunity she would, without the slightest hesitation, kill Hennessey... and without a moment's remorse. Coming from a home where all violence was considered abhorrent, this realization about herself startled her. Despite being taken back by the perspective of her reckoning, however, her conviction remained unchanged. She *would* kill him, if she could.

Lisa's turn at the wheel was ending as she approached the exit for Flagstaff. She got off and pulled into a BP station a few hundred yards to the left. The unfriendly, cold whiteness of the glaring fluorescent bulbs pulled Nick, reluctantly, from his happy slumber. Lisa was out of the car, pumping the gas as he awoke and a momentary wave of shame went through him for decadently lounging in his seat while his wife took care of the gas... but he quickly forgave himself and allowed himself this rare, self-granted indulgence. Hearing the clunk of the nozzle as the tank reached full, he sat up then climbed out of the car to join Lisa as she walked to the station. He caught up to her as she was walking past the inside set of pumps and slid his arm around her waist... to which, she reciprocated. Lisa paid for the gas and the food they ordered. They made the impromptu decision to pamper themselves and eat their sandwiches, chips, and Cokes at one of the convenience section booths, instead of on the run, as had been their routine for untold hours.

Back in the car, Nick took the wheel. Lisa wasn't sleepy and much to Nick's appreciation, she made his turn pass quickly by her sustained, lively monologue on a multitude of innocuous topics – from their courtship to their plans after Nick graduated law school to having babies to buying a house to the kind of furniture with which they'd fill it. Although Lisa's typical female monologues were sometimes nearly maddening to Nick... this night the familiarity of the marital rite and the happy constancy of her voice – confined to strictly inconsequential topics – brought him a sense of solace and reassurance. Hearing – but not listening – to his wife's bouncy chatter, Nick realized that there was something about a woman's concern and excitement about trivial matters that made males happy. Nick figured that this peculiar sense of happiness had a lot to do with why he had done many of the things he had for Lisa – getting good grades in law school... fixing things at home... buying little gifts for her... sporting big biceps from weightlifting – simply because she got so excited about them... much more than he did. Women were, for sure, in Nick's estimation, absolutely maddening at times – but without them, he understood that men wouldn't be inspired to show off, and in the final analysis, that was what the essence of what a man's life was all about... showing off. With no one to appreciate their feats, men, Nick was completely positive, would still be sitting in caves.

By the time it was Lisa's turn at the wheel, her unilateral conversation had run out of words and she wished she had rested instead of talking. Nick noticed her dosing off, just as her turn at the wheel arrived and, instead of waking her for her go at driving, he let her sleep... undertaking her full shift. He really wasn't very sleepy, anyway, so it wasn't any big deal for him to push on. At dawn, Nick pulled off Interstate 40 for gas and Lisa, awakening, greatly appreciated what he had done for her. She made a big fuss over it, which made his efforts well worth the while... loving, as every man does, being fussed over by a female... realizing, as he basked in her hyperbolic adulation, what manipulated simpletons men truly were... but not at all caring.

Lisa drove her turn, this time, though Nick was wide awake. Sunday had arrived and, like the hours before a big game, he had a case of nerves and a butterfly stomach... as did Lisa. At eight in the morning, they crossed the border into California. The mere passage into this land of final destination sparked new shocks of excitement and anticipation through them... causing them to become electrically alert and more nervous with each passing mile that narrowed the gap between themselves and their planned point of rendezvous with Papa. To alleviate some of the tension, they went over their plans again and again... each time, one of them raising a new, "what if..." – which provoked further discussion and revised planning.

Nick began looking at the map... calculating their estimated time of arrival. It didn't look promising.

"This is going to be incredibly close, Lis. Using this miles scale on the map, it looks to me like, unless we speed up to about eighty, we're probably not going to make it. At the speed we're going... I'd estimate that we'll get to Santa Monica after two."

"He starts speaking at two, Nick! If we don't hurry up, he'll be dead before we get there!"

"Well... then crank it up, Lisa. Move the cruise up to eighty. That should save us almost an hour. We're on interstates all the way there. If we can make it with only one more stop for gas... we just might get there in time. If we can get to Barstow by noon – that's where we get on Interstate Fifteen – we should be able to make it. Once we get to Santa Monica, though, we're going to have to have some luck. If we can't get through the crowd really fast, it's all over."

At eleven-forty, Nick and Lisa pulled off for gas at Barstow – their last fueling stop before reaching their destination. Both were too nervous to eat, so, each with a can of Diet Coke in hand, and Nick at the wheel, they pulled their car onto the entry ramp for Interstate 15 and headed southwest to L.A. for the final leg of their journey... and their unknown appointment in Hesperia.

CHAPTER TWENTY-TWO

There was an obvious sense of excitement among Hennessey's entire staff on Sunday morning as they discussed the big event in Santa Monica. All gathered in his suite, they monitored several televisions as they talked... watching the spectrum of coverage of the event. It was, as predicted, unquestionably, a world-class event, and media from all around the world were ubiquitous. Earlier that morning, several staffers had been dispatched to Santa Monica for a final check of the arrangements and equipment. They reported that, already, at that hour of the day, an enormous crowd was assembled – both on the beach below, and throughout downtown Santa Monica... and that the traffic was already a nightmare. The staffers also reported that all manner of watercraft had already nearly filled the water, offshore, for several miles toward the horizon – and to the north and south for as far as the eye could see. They described it as a "literal flotilla"... looking like, they said, movies they had seen of the Normandy invasion. The general atmosphere, throughout, was, in their words, "carnival-like."

The morning meeting broke up at around ten o'clock and Hennessey, Parling, and Freddy Westin remained to have breakfast in Hennessey's suite. After they ate, Freddy, again, reviewed the assassination plans. Hennessey asked about the bulletproof jacket. Fred got up, went down to his room, and returned with it. Hennessey wanted to try it on... and Freddy helped him with it. Hennessey was not at all pleased. He said he felt as though he were wearing a life preserver and commented on how stupid it would look under his suit. He was even more distressed when Freddy pointed out that he'd have to wear it under his shirt, or it would, obviously, be very noticeable. Hennessey told Freddy that he didn't have a shirt big enough to wear over it. Freddy told him he had already bought him several shirts, large enough... and he could take his pick. Hennessey went on to complain that with it on, he'd look like the Pillsbury Doughboy... and that he could hardly move his arms. Parling, becoming annoyed with Hennessey, intervened to reiterate how important it was for him to wear it… regardless of how he looked. Hennessey asked Westin if he couldn't have found a less bulky vest. Freddy said that there were thinner vests… but they weren't as effective. Hennessey finally conceded the issue with grudging acquiescence.

Freddy emphasized to Hennessey that once he had Papa at the back of the platform, he needed to move away from him, quickly. The shooter wanted to do the job and get out of the hotel as soon as humanly possible. The moment Hennessey was clear, Freddy emphasized, the shooter was going to take Papa out. After Papa was down, Hennessey could then, safely move to the microphones and deliver the speech he had ready. Parling raised the question of the danger to other people who might be standing near Papa… and, in particular, those on the downward side of Papa from the shooter. Freddy conceded that, without doubt, anyone around Papa was in danger – that they might be killed or wounded if the bullets either missed or went all the way through Papa's body. Parling asked if, perhaps, they should make sure, therefore, that none of their people were in harm's way. Hennessey laughed sarcastically and asked Parling just how he suggested they tell them. Should they say, for instance, he posed, "By the way, don't stand near Papa after the speech, you might be hit by a stray bullet of the assassin we hired?" Parling immediately admitted to the stupidity of his raising the issue and told the other two to forget he mentioned it. Hennessey closed the particular issue with a matter-of-fact truism.

"No one is irreplaceable, Jimmy… and if a staffer or two go down… so be it. Political operatives are a dime a dozen."

His compatriots conceded the indisputable veracity of his view with matching shrugs and nodding heads.

Hennessey asked Freddy what excuse he was supposed to use to get Papa to the back of the platform… and then to get away from him so quickly. Freddy suggested he go forward to the podium as soon as Papa had finished speaking and ask him if he could have a private word with him… then lead him to the back of the platform. Jimmy could, Freddy suggested, be standing at the opposite end of the platform, also at the rear, and when he and Papa arrive at the back railing, Jimmy could call out to Hennessey... asking if he could speak to him for a moment. He could then excuse himself, walk quickly toward Jimmy – then... bang!

Hennessey looked at Parling. Parling stuck out his lower lip and raised his eyebrows while nodding his head. Denoting that he had no better idea, Hennessey shrugged his shoulders and turned his palms upward. Without a word spoken, the death plan was, thus, finalized.

CHAPTER TWENTY-THREE

The tension in the car was reaching the point that even the sound of the radio had become irritating. From the passenger's seat, Lisa very deliberately reached across the dashboard and brusquely snapped the power knob into silence. Nick didn't object... the quiet being a relief to him, as well. Despite having the air conditioner on at the highest setting, Nick could feel his underwear sticking in the gaps between his inner thighs and his testicles. To achieve some relief from the annoying condition, he began raising his butt a few inches from the seat to attempt, unsuccessfully, through his jeans, to extricate the damp cotton by a pincers-like movement of his thumb and middle finger. After a half-dozen such failed efforts in a matter of minutes, Lisa finally asked him, in peevish tones, if he had a problem. He shot back, equally as peevish, that, if he did, it wasn't any of her concern. At that very moment, the sudden sight in the rearview mirror, reflecting the red and blue flashing lights on the roof of the car directly behind them, caused him to forego any further dialogue on the topic. The sight was followed, only seconds later, by a single, unharmonious warble of a siren. Instinctively, Nick looked down at the speedometer... which was reading eighty in a sixty-five mile zone.

"Oh fuck!!"

Nick began to pull over on the shoulder but returned to the highway when he heard a distinctly unfriendly male voice, via a loud speaker, instruct him to continue ahead and pull off at the next exit. After turning off the exit and proceeding another several hundred feet, the same amplified voice commanded him to pull over. As soon as he did, Nick asked Lisa where his wallet was. She responded, unhelpfully, by asking him where he had put it. His adrenaline gush prompted his memory to look in the arm rest. Just as he turned to open the top of the rest, a rather large trooper tapped on his window. Nick pulled the flat chrome window switch toward him. Nothing happened... having turned off the car when they stopped. He tried to shout this explanation through the closed window. The trooper tapped again... this time louder. Nick was apprehensive about reaching for the key to turn on the ignition... being in California and fearing – with recollections of the Rodney King video in his memory – that the officer might think he was trying to escape and overreact. He cautiously opened the door a few inches and told the officer that he needed to turn on the ignition to lower the window. The officer responded by telling him to turn on the ignition, but not to turn over the engine. Nick replied, "OK" in profoundly, obsequious tones.

After the glass had been lowered from between the two men, the standard traffic-stop ritual began. When asked for his driver's license and vehicle registration, Nick explained that he thought it was in the arm rest and he'd have to look. The officer told him to go ahead. Nick noticed that the officer bent down to watch him as he reached over to open the top of the console... and, at the same time, noticed that he had unsnapped the leather cover of his pistol holster. Nick also noticed, as he began searching through the console, that another officer was standing at the passenger side window... bent over and looking all around the interior of their car. With this, Nick began to feel violated by the snooping duo. Digging feverishly through empty plastic cassette cases, crumpled receipts, old maps, and other forgotten rubbish, Nick was greatly relieved to finally feel the smooth, folded leather of his wallet. Nervous, he clumsily fumbled through his cards and hastily pulled out his driver's license and registration and handed them to the trooper. As he was looking at them, a tapping came from the other window. Nick lowered it from his side. This trooper bent over until he was eye level and very close to Lisa's face. For a short time, he silently stared at her and his invasive gaze roused Nick's anger. Finally he asked her for ID. She looked at Nick – not as a husband, but as a law student. Nick knew this wasn't standard procedure and was probably unconstitutional... but Nick also knew that a prudent lawyer wouldn't initiate a constitutional debate while sitting between two armed and very unfriendly looking men. He nodded a nearly imperceptible directive to Lisa to cooperate. She angrily snatched her purse from the floor and slammed it onto her lap and quickly extracted her wallet. She opened it to the section in which her cards were housed in their clear plastic sleeves. Flipping to her license, she held the entire, unfolded wallet toward the officer. He coldly instructed her to take the card out of the wallet. The circumstance was now, unquestionably, prompting Lisa to adopt a bitchy countenance – which Nick instantly recognized... and just as quickly, communicated to her, via facial contortions, to quell. His face explained that this simply was not the time to make a scene. She understood... and grudgingly acceded to his admonitions.

The trooper on Nick's side returned to the squad car with Nick's cards and climbed in on the driver's side. Nick monitored him in the rearview mirror. He was speaking on their cellular phone... reading information from Nick's cards. After finishing his business on the phone, he began to write on a clipboard. After what seemed a very long time, he returned to Nick's window with the clipboard in his hand... which he handed to Nick. On it was clipped both of his cards, and underneath, a short, yellow form with the words "Traffic Citation" across the top... filled in with all of the details of Nick's unlawful driving performance. The officer then explained that he had cited Nick for speeding... going eighty miles per hour in a sixty-five mile per hour zone. He went on to explain, as well, how and when to pay the ticket... then asked Nick to sign the bottom of the citation... to acknowledge that he had received it. Nick did... then returned the clipboard to the officer. He unclipped Nick's cards, tore off the bottom copy of the citation, and handed the three articles to Nick... admonishing him to watch his speed from now on. Nick politely and compliantly assured him that he would.

Nick started his engine and, with great self-consciousness, pulled onto the pavement. He could feel himself shaking from a mixture of both fear and anger. They proceeded at a ridiculously slow speed to the intersection with Route 18, made a left and, a few hundred feet down the road, bore right on the entrance ramp to Interstate 15. Nick set the cruise control at sixty-three – two miles below the limit for good measure – and they rode in silence for several minutes. Lisa finally broke it.

"He had no right to ask for my ID! I wasn't driving! What does he think?... we live in the Soviet Union!?"

"No he didn't have a *legal* right... but that wasn't the time to start an argument. You can sometimes end up being dead right on principle... very dead. A lot of the Freedom Marchers were just that, in the old South."

"I know you're right, Nicky... but I would like to have slapped that man's face."

Their unsettling encounter with the law provided, at least, a distraction from the tension, under which they had been laboring, prior to the stop. Despite the fact of being a law breaker, under the obligation of paying a two-hundred-dollar fine, Nick was feeling a peculiar sense of relief from the experience... and within ten minutes, they both celebrated their safe release from perceived danger with childlike giggling... neither able to specifically identify the source nor object of their mirth, but enjoying it, nonetheless.

As they bore right to remain on 15... where 15 and 215 branch off, Nick glanced at his watch. Their lower, prudent speed had, of course, put them behind schedule. It was one o'clock and they were, at that point, at *least* an hour from Santa Monica. At their current rate, Nick knew they simply were not going to make it on time. Nick stated the situation and posed the question.

"We're not going to make it, Lis... going this slow. What do you think?"

Lisa looked at Nick then at the speedometer then back to his eyes. She shook her head, up and down, as she made her declaration.

"Go for it, honey! We're talking about a man's life here!"

Instantly, Nick pressed down on the accelerator and, within seconds, they were going eighty-five and rapidly passing the cars on the inside lanes. After a short while, they turned off, onto

JOHN

Interstate 10, and headed northwest on the final stretch of highway into Santa Monica. Lisa noticed Nick looking frequently into the rearview mirror... his face revealing obvious concern. She looked back, then at him.

"What is it Nicky?... what are you looking at?"

"That gray car behind us. It's staying right on our tail. Every time I pass someone, it's right behind me."

Lisa looked back again. A metallic-gray car, with two men in it, was, in fact, directly behind them.

Nick glanced up at the mirror, then at Lisa.

"Watch this."

Nick pulled, with a sudden jerk to the left, out into the passing lane and floored the gas pedal. Going ninety, they shot past several cars... then swerved, sharply to the right, back into the traffic lane. Sure enough, the gray car had stuck to them like glue throughout their erratic course of travel. Lisa instantly felt the ache of fear in her chest and she reached out and wrapped her hand around Nick's forearm for security.

"Who could it be, Nicky?"

"They sure as hell don't look like police."

Lisa looked back again. Both men were very dark complexioned... with long black hair... and both had mustaches. The driver was smoking.

"They're *definitely* not police, Nick."

Lisa tightened her grip on Nick's arm.

"I'm scared, honey."

Nick looked at her and his face complemented his words.

"So am I, Lis."

Seeing the rare look of fear on her husband's normally stoical face, greatly heightened Lisa's.

"What should we do, Nicky?"

"I don't know."

"Do you think they're the people after us?... you know, the people hired by Hennessey?"

Seeing, from Lisa's face, that she was nearing panic, Nick decided he should try to diminish the likelihood of actual danger.

"We don't know, for sure, if Hennessey has anyone after us, honey. It could all be just our imagination. Maybe these guys are just supposed to follow us... you know... just keep tabs on us. I mean, no one would try something out here on the freeway in broad daylight... you know?"

Lisa studied Nick's face to determine if he was sincere or just trying to placate her. Her face took on a skeptical twist. She looked back at the gray car again... then spoke with a steady, knowing, confident voice.

"They're after us, Nicky. I know it. They're going to try to kill us. I know they are. Trust me... they are."

Nick looked into Lisa's eyes. She did know. He didn't argue with her. He had learned that these "hunches" of hers were virtually never wrong. The realization that the danger, about which they had frequently and safely theorized during the long westward drive, had suddenly materialized in the form of a metallic-gray car, carrying two, real-life swarthy looking men, only feet from their rear bumper, suddenly took Nick's breath away. His heart raced. He tried, unsuccessfully, to calm himself and think rationally. His eyes wide, he looked to Lisa for guidance. Seeing Nick's distress, she knew instantly that this was *her* turn to steady the ship. She momentarily closed her eyes, took a deep breath then blew it out slowly between tightly pursed lips. Seeing her husband at such a loss, her protective instincts instantly arose. Her mind sharpened and she rapidly scanned their options.

"They can't do anything to us while we're on the highway, Nick. As long as we keep going, we'll be OK."

"But we've got to stop sometime... Santa Monica is less than an hour from here. Do you think we should just keep going... and forget about this Papa thing?"

"No! We've come all this way and we're going to do what we set out to do! All right... look... as soon as we see we're going to have to stop at Santa Monica, we need to pull over really quick... then we'll jump out of the car and run as fast as we can. There'll probably be a crowd and it'll be hard for them to follow us... and I don't think they'd shoot at us with a bunch of people around. We'll just keep running until we see a cop. We can't tell them about someone being after us... that would raise too many questions and create a big delay. I'll just show them my Senate pass and ask them to escort us up to the platform. I'm sure these guys won't try anything if we're with the police. It'll be OK Nicky. We'll be all right. We just have to keep our heads... and think."

CHAPTER TWENTY-FOUR

At 12:30 a.m., Hennessey called Rossiter over to the window of his suite that faced Wilshire Boulevard.

"Take a look at this, Ted."

Rossiter came over and looked down to see that the streets and sidewalks were entirely hidden by a sprawling mass of humanity. They were several miles from Santa Monica, but apparently the crowd was so large that it had already backed the entire way to their hotel. Hennessey told Rossiter to get the limo and the police escort ready – right away – for an earlier-than-planned departure… that they'd need the extra time to get to the platform on schedule. Ten minutes later, Rossiter phoned Hennessey to tell him to come down to the lobby… that the police would be there, momentarily.

The drive to Santa Monica was excruciating slow… their caravan inching its way through the dense field of bodies. None of the Senator's party, Hennessey included, had ever seen such a thing. Hennessey wondered, how on earth, Papa and his people – without a police escort – would ever make it to the platform by two o'clock. With police assistance, it took them nearly an hour to go the three miles to the speaker's stand. Stopping at the VIP vehicle parking area, about twenty feet from the stand, the police had to push people back to allow the senatorial party to simply open their car doors. Stepping out onto the hot asphalt, they all experienced the claustrophobic, primitive fear of being crushed to death by the sheer weight of the bodies pressing in on them. It was all the police could do to clear a narrow path for them to get to the platform. Walking this skinny gauntlet through the walls of sweating human flesh, Hennessey reflected, again, on the near-impossibility of Papa being able to make it to the stand. He sarcastically remarked to Parling that if this man could make it to the platform, he must, indeed, be divine.

Walking up the wooden steps at the front, south side of the platform, Hennessey lifted his left arm and pushed back his jacket sleeve to check the time – ten minutes to two. Stepping onto the deck, he could see that Papa was not yet there. A sense of irritation began to immediately well up inside him... contemplating the possibility that Papa may simply not make it and the opportunity of the largest media event of Hennessey's life would be lost.

As he stood waiting, Hennessey looked out over the cliff that was only twenty feet from the front edge of the platform. The Pacific Ocean, far below them, stretched out to the horizon in all directions and was littered with vessels of all shapes and sizes – from small outboards, to sailboats, to ocean-going yachts. The sand on the beach below – for as far north and south as he could see was completely covered by bodies. The pier, below and to his left, jutting perpendicularly out into the water from the shore, looked as though it would have been literally impossible to add even one more person to its assemblage without it collapsing. The space between the front of the platform and the edge of the cliff was filled with hundreds of television cameras. Airplanes and helicopters circled the sky... several huge blimps hovered above. Even to the normally unflappable Hennessey, the phenomenon was so immense as to be overpowering. Hennessey didn't know who this Papa was... but he had certainly created a stir, the likes of which the world had never before seen.

Hennessey looked at his watch, again... three minutes until two – and still no Papa. Unaccustomed to having someone else control his destiny, he could feel the meanness of his resentment turning inside him. He was absolutely convinced, at this juncture, that Papa would not appear. At two o'clock, precisely, however, Papa and his small band of followers emerged from the multitude and walked onto the stage from the steps at the north end of the platform. Hennessey shook his head, chastising himself for his, obviously unwarranted, concern about Papa's possible no-show... knowing, full well, that he had always appeared, without fail, at the last moment, for every event he had attended.

Having experienced such a wide variety of receptions from the audiences over the past seven week, no one on the platform had the foggiest idea as to what to expect this time out. Given the hour of day and the beach location, however, Hennessey anticipated something on the order of a tumultuous, rock-star-like explosion from the multitudes. The opposite, however, turned out to be the case. Moments before Papa stepped onto the stage, the overpowering drone of innumerable, simultaneous conversations was nearly maddening. But as soon as Papa was seen stepping on the platform, a church-like, hush fell immediately over the colossal assembly.

Amid the ear-throbbing quiet, Papa stepped forward to the myriad of microphones, secured to the ocean-side front railing... their stands and chrome wire casings taped tightly together to give the appearance of a huge, long stemmed, chromed bouquet. Rather than speaking immediately, Papa looked out over the enormous flock, turning his head slowly, until his eyes had swept over the entire multitude on every side of him, front and back. His face wore a loving, infectious smile, resembling that of a returning relative, appreciatively studying the familiar faces of his family members. As his face returned to the mikes and, looking out over the cliff at the beach, pier, and sea-going assembly before him, he began to speak in the, now familiar, warm tones of his clearly discernable Scottish burr.

"My children... this will be the last time I will ever speak to you on this Earth. After today, you will never again see me as I stand before you at this moment. I know each of you. I know your given name and I know your heart. Most of you are not happy, and as your parent who loves you without end, my heart aches for each one of you. You are not happy because you are lost and you are afraid and you feel you are alone and you feel unloved. I am so sorry that the freedom I have given you has been such a difficult burden for you to bear, but without it you would have had no existence at all."

"You are all the children of my body. We were once together... and I have given each of you a memory of that time. I have set my body free to become all that exists... and out of that you have been born. You children have grown to the moment that you can, like me, choose your own destiny. You can choose this life and this world or you can choose to come home to me. You already know of our home. It is that memory of a perfect happiness that each of you was given and each of you can, if you wish, recall. Many of you search for the source of this memory... often taking paths that lead nowhere. A few of you find the source of your memory and find the path home to me. I suffer when you suffer and I want, so much, for you to come home to me. As long as even one of my children is lost, I will be, like you, lonely. As long as one of my children is lost, I will wait, and I will never give up hope of that child's return."

Papa's voice was becoming heavy with emotion and he paused to swallow his tears.

"I know that this free world is a frightening life for you and that your fear has led you to do many cruel things to one another and to bring great unhappiness to many of your brothers and sisters, and to yourself. You children on this Earth are having a very hard time with the freedom I have given you... and in finding your way home. For this reason, I have come to you. I have come to tell you of your first home and of your birth and of your ever-loving parents. This is the first time I have come to this world. You children have, in your fear, made up many stories of your birth, and your destiny, to comfort yourselves... and I am happy for the brief peace these stories have given you. But your stories are only fairy tales... and their promises are empty, and you return, again and again, alone, to this frightening world. It is now time, that you, as orphans so often dream, learn of your parents and of your birth."

Again, Papa paused... and smiled.

"Once, I was entirely alone. I existed in a single perfection. But singular perfection is without love, and without love, existence is without meaning. So I sent forth my body to be free and in so doing, I destroyed my perfection. Since that moment, I have remained at home, awaiting the time of my children's birth and you have, after countless years, come forth. You children have found your birth in many worlds… and this Earth is but one. You have many brothers and sisters, born of the same parents, throughout all existence. Since the day of your birth, I have yearned, each moment, for your return to me… so that neither of us would, ever again, be alone. And, as a loving parent, I have not interfered in your free lives. Love can only be freely given. Were I to interfere and take away your freedom, you would lose your soul and you would no longer exist. I will not take from you the soul I have lovingly given you."

"Many of you will be angry with me because it is hard for a child to give up the familiar stories of infancy. But I can no longer bear the pain that you feel. I implore you to listen to me and understand me. Tell your own children, and all of my other children of this earth, of what I tell you now. You will never again hear these words from my mouth."

"Happiness is before you and can be grasped with a thought. If you can remember who I am, your life in this world will be a happy one… and when your time has come, you will awaken in my arms and in my love, forevermore. With my love, death will hold no fear for you. All you need to do is remember our time together and of my love for you and you will, never again, feel alone or unloved. You will recognize all the children of this world as your brothers and sisters and you will love each of them as your family. You will know that you are all the children of but one family… all sharing the love of the same mother and father. This, what I tell you, is not a child's fairy tale. It is the simple truth of your life and of your world. In your times of trouble and pain and fear, you will remember that you are always loved and you will never feel you are alone. You must understand that I will not interfere in this world of my children. I will comfort you with my love, but I will not intrude upon the freedom that was given to my body. What happens in this, or any other world, is neither my will nor is it my cause. It is simply the unfettered will of the world… liberated by my hand. But, in this frightening, troubled existence, you can carry my love with you wherever you go… to comfort you when you feel lost or confused or afraid or unloved or in pain."

"This life does make sense and does have a reason. All that you need to do is accept my love and you will become love... and the world will change before your eyes. The dark will become light... sadness will become happiness... the lost path will become a clear road home."

"I am your loving parents – your mother and your father – and I do not wish to be worshiped by you. I want only your love. I am a quiet love and a simple love. I am not mysterious and I am not thunderous. I have come to you, not to perform miracles, nor to frighten you with my power. I have come only to comfort you. My love is the stillness of a small stream and it is as familiar as the smell of baking bread. Our home is not of glittering gold nor of adoring choruses. It is the quiet calm of a green forest and the sweet fragrance of honeysuckle."

"My heart breaks with the knowledge of how much all of you suffer each day and yet how simple it is for you to escape the pain of this world. I will not compel you to believe the words that I speak to you. I will not bring you home against your will. When you come home to me, it will be of your choosing."

"To each one of you, my precious children... feel my love and remember me. Love all of your family on this earth and come home to me. My arms are open and my heart is full."

"I love each one of you."

Papa's final smile was a union of both love and sadness. Tears fell from his eyes. He lowered his head for a few moments, closed his eyes then raised his face again to the multitudes... this time his face beaming with the purity of infinite happiness. He silently surveyed all before him then took several steps backward... denoting he had finished.

Hennessey readied himself to move... waiting a few diplomatic moments before stepping forward to corral Papa. Everyone on the platform was visibly moved by Papa's words, save Hennessey. He glanced around at those near him and saw tears in the eyes of nearly every one of his staffers... even Parling appeared somewhat choked up. The phrase, "one hell of a speaker," rushed through Hennessey's mind.

The audience gave no recognizable indication that they had acknowledged an end to Papa's address. The unnatural silence of the immense crowd that ruled over them, during his words, continued after he had obviously finished. There seemed to be an omnipresent uncertainty, throughout the mammoth congregation, having heard Papa's words... of not knowing what to do or say. Hennessey had never witnessed such uncommon crowd behavior. It created an enveloping, unearthly presence.

Not wanting to wait any longer, Hennessey began to advance through the platform party toward Papa. His movement was distinctly incongruent with the frozen, introspective countenance of the rest, making Hennessey feel slightly self-conscious. Stepping around two of Papa's intimate band, he arrived at his side. Despite having been on the same platform with him, a number of times before, standing beside him at this moment, Hennessey marveled at his mountainous dimensions... and the serene beauty of his finely structured face.

As though expecting him, Papa looked calmly down, to his left, to study Hennessey's face. The sparkling wisdom and infinite understanding, dwelling within his eyes, was so mesmerizing that Hennessey was momentarily flustered... but quickly regained his poise... and initiated the plan.

"Can I speak with you for a moment?"

Papa's kind eyes seemed to penetrate Hennessey's innermost thoughts and defenses... to tell Hennessey that he knew all. Again Hennessey was briefly disconcerted... but he was not one to be dominated by anyone – even this charismatic wizard of oratory. Papa answered in a soft, knowing voice.

"Yes."

Hennessey extended his right arm toward the rear of the platform and turned his head to indicate the same direction. Papa again adorned his face with an unsettling smile that seemed to tell Hennessey that he knew all of his thoughts… and all of his plans. He bent slightly toward Hennessey's ear and spoke again.

"I'll follow you."

Hennessey retraced his steps to the rear of the platform – the two of them winding their way among the still silent, wet-eyed, unmoving, platform party. Hennessey proceeded to the rear platform rail then turned around to face Papa… Hennessey's back touching the rail… Papa facing the rear of the platform. At that moment, Jimmy Parling's loud voice shattered the silence.

"Senator Hennessey!? Senator!"

Hennessey turned his head to his right to acknowledge the page that came from the far north, rear of the platform.

CHAPTER TWENTY-SIX

Despite the increasing density of the traffic as they proceeded northwest along Interstate 10, the Ryans continued driving at their high rate of speed… frequently putting themselves at risk. Their break-neck velocity and unpredictable, erratic traffic machinations had, on a few occasions, put a car or two between them and their pursuers… but only momentarily. The trailing car was, obviously, driven by a skilled and fearless driver… not to be easily lost by such amateurs as the Ryans.

The San Bernardino Freeway became the Santa Monica Freeway and the Ryans' pulse rates increased dramatically as they closed in on their final destination… and the run of their lives. Passing through the gauntlet of the massive concrete legs, holding up the weight of the wide San Diego Freeway, suspended over their heads, the traffic was congesting to the point that they had to reduce their speed to less than fifty miles per hour. They were, at this point, less than a mile from the eastern perimeter of Santa Monica and the time was twenty minutes until two. As they traversed the underpass to Lincoln Boulevard, they abruptly encountered an unmoving mass of automobiles ahead of them, compelling Nick to slam on his brakes to avoid colliding with them.

As per their plan, as soon as their car came to stop, Nick and Lisa immediately threw open their doors and bolted out onto the highway… leaving their car parked in traffic in the passing lane of Santa Monica Boulevard and their doors still standing open. Lisa reached ahead for Nick's right hand. He felt her touching him and looked back at her as they ran. Her left hand was extended for his and he grabbed it firmly and pulled her faster than she felt her legs could safely carry her. Nick could see, a few hundred feet behind her, the two men… sprinting after them. An alarm flew from Nick's throat.

"They're after us, Lis! Right behind us! Run!!"

Nick could hear a childlike whining, joining with Lisa's loud breathing. Despite not wanting to see their stalkers, Lisa could not resist looking back. In a quick, jerky motion, without slowing her gait, she twisted her neck to glance backward. Catching a blurred glimpse of them, she issued a frightened, involuntary squeal. Their fear drove them on at a speed and stamina they would have never thought possible of themselves. Lisa recognized the area where they were running and knew their destination was no more than a quarter of a mile ahead. Just at they reached the perimeter of the L.A. County Courthouse, they ran into a solid wall of people. Dispensing with all manners and courtesy, they rudely pushed themselves through the tightly packed bodies. Over the numerous loudspeakers they could hear Papa's voice echoing among the downtown buildings. Hearing him, their faces turned toward one another and a communication of mutual desperation was exchanged. Time was just about up. They had come so far, and at such a risk, and without some miraculous intervention, it was to all be for naught.

Despite the danger and urgency of the moment, Lisa could feel a quivering sob trying to work its way up from her bosom. Tears were beginning to blur her eyes. All appeared to be lost... she knew it. She knew they were not going to make it. Nick stopped suddenly and gripped Lisa's hand tightly to halt her motion. He was looking directly to his left. Only twenty feet from them was a police car with the officers standing beside it. Without speaking, they both bolted in that direction. As they changed their direction, Lisa caught sight of the two, pursuing, raven-haired predators – not more than fifteen feet behind them. She shouted.

"Run Nicky!!! They're right behind us!!"

They began running into people... knocking some of them nearly off their feet. In less than twenty seconds, they stood inches from the officers, who, seeing them pushing through the crowd, studied them critically. Lisa immediately pulled her senatorial pass from her pants pocket and, as best she could, amid her heavy breathing, explained that there was an emergency... and that she needed to see Senator Hennessey immediately. As the officers stood in silence, trying to assess the truth of Lisa's plea, both the Ryans tensed... expecting, at any moment, to feel a bullet tear through their backs. The officers looked at one another... conducting a silent conference, of which only those who know one another very well, are capable. Without any words exchanged, an agreement to render assistance was apparently reached. They told the Ryans to get into the back seat, which they did, immediately... and the police, with their sirens blaring... and roof lights on and rotating... started forward through the crowd.

Like Moses parting the Red Sea, the bodies opened for the obnoxiously loud, flashing, police cruiser. They quickly made their way through the assembly and pulled directly up to the north side of the platform. Both Nick and Lisa issued hurried thanks and jumped from the car. They ran for the steps of the speaking stand... noticing, immediately, that Papa was no longer speaking. Lisa flashed her pass to the three officers at the base of the stairs, who parted and allowed them passage up the steps. At the top of the stairs, Lisa and Nick looked around, wildly, for the tall figure of Papa. He was no where in sight. Lisa spotted Marty Chapman near the front, center of the stage and pushed her way toward him. With several people still between them, Lisa shouted.

"Mr. Chapman!!!"

Chapman turned his head to his left... toward the voice. Lisa continued, stepped around a young, pretty woman standing beside him and grabbed his arm. Marty Chapman looked at her with puzzlement... not recognizing her. Lisa pulled down on his arm so his head was close to her mouth.

"I'm Lisa Ryan... I'm on Senator Hennessey's staff. Where's Papa?"

Chapman motioned with his head toward the back of the platform.

"Back there... speaking with the Senator."

JOHN

"They're going to kill him!!"

"Kill Hennessey?"

"Hennessey's going to kill Papa! I heard them plan it!!"

Chapman studied her face, then, in an instant, decided she was in earnest – and broke, immediately, toward the back of the stage. Lisa turned... watching him push his way through the still uncannily subdued platform party. She breathed a calming breath... perceiving that they had, after all, accomplished their mission. Chapman would warn Papa and he would seek safety. She looked at her husband. They exchanged a smile between them... a tired, relieved, proud smile. Being in the center of a crowd of VIP's... on a platform surrounded by police, they also felt safe from their hunters.

CHAPTER TWENTY-SEVEN

Hennessey responded to Parling's page.

"What is it Jim?"

"I need to see you for just one second, Senator."

Hennessey turned his face back to Papa to excuse himself. Papa's face was contorted into a profound sadness. He looked deep into Hennessey's eyes... which froze Hennessey. Papa reached out with both of his enormous hands and placed them... one on each side of Hennessey's face. He brought his face within inches of Hennessey's. Hennessey's first reaction was to attempt to extricate himself from this too intimate, too penetrating circumstance. He tried to jerk his head away from Papa but Papa held it tightly. Hennessey instantly discovered that in the grip of a man of Papa's power, he was as helpless as a child.

Papa put his mouth to Hennessey's left ear and lifted his hand, slightly, to allow him to hear. He whispered.

"Do you remember how you and Danny Broad cried together in kindergarten? Do you remember how it felt to love that little boy?"

Papa pulled his head from Hennessey's ear and smiled lovingly at him. He spoke to him, again.

"It *was* sad when Bambi's mother was killed, Johnny."

The emptiness that had been in Hennessey's heart since he was a small boy, seemed to suddenly fill with a sea of water... bringing with it the weight of unbearable remorse and the long-forgotten ache of love. His eyes filled with tears and he felt he would, literally, drown in the tears of a lifetime... shed for all his cruelty, and for the loss of his humanity. Thoughts of his mother, his son, his wife, and a parade of all those he had hurt in his life, flashed through his mind. His entire life, in that instant, was relived. He started speaking in piteous, broken sounds… unable to form his unspeakable shame and sorrow into words. Papa drew him to his chest and held him tightly. Hennessey wept into Papa's warm body as Papa enveloped him in his enormous arms.

Papa drew his hands from Hennessey's back and gripped his shoulders… gently pushing him away from him, to allow Hennessey to see his face. Papa then smiled at him and spoke in a whispering tone.

"I love you, John."

He leaned forward and kissed John Hennessey on the lips… then returned his mouth to his left ear. As he spoke, he tightened his grip on his left shoulder… pushing him toward where Parling was standing.

"Go."

Hennessey jerked his head away from Papa to look at him… Hennessey's face twisted itself with confusion.

Papa repeated, calmly.

"Go."

He gently pushed Hennessey in the direction of Jimmy Parling… still waiting for him on the far side of the platform.

Hennessey shook his head… managing a fragment of a question.

"But…?"

Papa didn't respond. His face commanded Hennessey to obey him. With uncertain steps, Hennessey began to step toward Parling. Suddenly, he stopped and ran back toward Papa. He turned toward the direction of the hotel and madly waved his arms. He shouted.

"No!!! No!!! No!!! No!!!"

As he had dashed to fill the small space between the back railing and Papa, Marty Chapman bounded, at that same moment, into the picture... grabbing Papa, from behind, by his right arm.

CHAPTER TWENTY-EIGHT

Lisa and Nick Ryan stood, side-by-side, holding hands, as they watched Marty move quickly toward Papa and Hennessey. They saw Hennessey take a few steps toward the north side of the platform, then come running back to Papa... shouting, "No!!! No!!!"

Just as they saw Marty Chapman grab Papa's arm, to pull him out of danger, a pained shout came from where the trio stood... followed by another of a different voice. They saw Hennessey's hands fly upward and his body jerk toward Papa... then fall to the floor boards. Marty Chapman's torso, an instant later, spun around, sharply, like a toy figure manipulated by an invisible hand. He collapsed... falling to his right. Only Papa's tall figure was left, standing alone. In a scene that seemed to be cinematic, the Ryans watched as the skin on the back side of Papa's neck burst open... his blood and flesh spraying for several feet behind him. The same kind of fleshy geyser opened, an instant later, in the center of his back... causing the hide of his shirt to suddenly push outward and split. Despite this carnage, Papa remained standing. He turned slowly toward the front of the platform until his eyes fell upon Lisa and Nick. In the front of his throat was a clearly visible hole, the size of a quarter. Papa's eyes met theirs and a warm message of gratitude passed to them. His eyelids then slowly closed and he dropped to his knees. He balanced in that position for several seconds, then fell to his left, his body coming to rest on top of Marty Chapman's.

CHAPTER TWENTY-NINE

As soon as the realization of the moment dawned upon the platform party, screams broke out all around the fallen men. Police rushed onto the platform and pushed away the on-lookers. In less than a minute, emergency medical technicians, who had been assigned for just such a possibility, were on the scene. They quickly had the men onto gurneys, off of the platform, and into ambulances.

Despite the shocking, dreamlike nature of the scene they had just witnessed, the Ryans had the presence of mind to remember their own danger. At the same moment, they came to the same cognition... and sought asylum, near a police car. Lisa, again, used the power of her senatorial pass... this time using it to gain transportation to the hospital where the fallen men would be taken.

With the assistance of the clear passage granted the police cruiser, they arrived at the hospital in less than ten minutes. They rushed inside and, again, using her pass, they were taken to the fourth floor, surgical suite, waiting room. As they waited, others arrived who were connected with the injured men. Lisa recognized the pretty, young woman that had been standing beside Marty Chapman and some of the other people who had traveled with Papa. Members of Hennessey's staff also began arriving.

Hennessey's report was the first to emerge from the surgical suite. He had, according to the attending surgeon, a fractured sternum and a collapsed lung. They reported that he had been wearing a bulletproof vest, and that it had saved his life. He was in pain, the doctor said, but not in serious condition.

Twenty minutes later, another member of the surgical team emerged to describe Marty Chapman's condition. He had taken a bullet through his right shoulder, which had totally shattered it. He had also lost a tremendous amount of blood and had gone into shock. He remained unconscious, the surgeon said, and in critical condition... but they were, he said, optimistic as to his prognosis. He would eventually, he added, need a total shoulder replacement.

As they awaited news of the final fallen man, the Ryans reflected on the fact that, although neither of them actually knew Papa, the merger of their fates had weaved an unbreakable bond between them. Neither of them could possibly fathom, at that moment – nor would they ever – how Papa could have known who they were... or how he knew that they had tried, at risk of their lives, to help him. Of one thing they were certain, however... he knew what they had done... and he had silently thanked them for it. Neither had the slightest doubt of that, at that moment – nor would they ever.

The wait for news of Papa seemed infinite. No one who remained in the room spoke a word. All seemed to be lost in their own thoughts and reflections. As Lisa looked around at the small group, who awaited the news of Papa, she recalled reading about each of them... and tried to pick out each person. The black prostitute was easy. Lisa was taken by her refined beauty, though... not being what she would have expected. The Hispanic ex-con was also obvious. But with his eyes, red with weeping, and his face, worn with grief, it was hard to believe, at that moment, the stories she had read of his savagery. The older, statuesque, blonde woman was surely the wealthy, powerful, business magnate. Huddled in tearful, mutual concern with her intimate friends, however, she did not look the part. The French-Canadian, Lisa knew, was in her thirties, but if the dark-haired beauty, weeping, alone, in the corner was her, she had the face and presence, not of an adult, but of a child. The preacher and the lawyer were tough to pick out. Either the sandy-haired, worn-looking man, or the stocky dark-haired, Italian-looking fellow could have possibly fit either part, Lisa figured, but the odds were that the Italian guy wasn't a Protestant, and thus, probably wasn't the preacher. Lisa reflected on how these dramatically different lives had come, so strangely and dramatically together... and of how close they all must now feel toward one another, having shared so much together... and now sharing this terrible vigil together.

The expression of the emerging surgeon foretold his story. Two high-caliber bullets had entered, he explained, and passed through, Papa's body. One round had traversed his larynx and severed his carotid artery before exiting – posteriorly – through his neck. The other had punctured the right atrial chamber of his heart and fractured a section of his spinal column before exiting. Despite these mortal injuries, Papa's heart, he said, was beating strongly when he was admitted to surgery.

Ian MacDonald of Montana, son of Malcolm and Ethie MacDonald, was pronounced dead, at the age of thirty-three, at eight minutes past four, in the year nineteen hundred ninety-four, on a beautiful Sunday afternoon, in the State of California.

EPILOGUE

EPILOGUE

Much of this epilogue contains information that will be quite familiar to most of the general public, but is herein summarized for purposes of making the story complete, and for the benefit of future generations, who will be not as versed in the facts as is contemporary society.

During the years following Papa's death, his story and message have been spread throughout the world and the constantly growing body of believers now numbers in the millions. His disciples have wholly dedicated their lives to Papa's ministry and travel the globe, unceasingly, to deliver his message to anyone who will listen. Despite their initial reticence, a growing number of respected theologians have, of late, begun to concede that the "Crossers Movement" – which uses the "Crossing of the Valley of Death" by the Disciples as a central focus of its credo – has had a fundamental impact on the world's spirituality and that it is possible it could become a mainstream theology within a current decade.

John Hennessey, upon recovering from his injuries, was charged with conspiracy and first-degree murder by the District Attorney's Office of Los Angeles County, along with Jimmy Parling, Frederick Westin, Benson Powell, and Ron Golden. The assassin has never been identified. Hennessey pled guilty to the charges against him and freely offered his assistance in the prosecution. Due to his cooperation, and his last-minute withdrawal from the crime and attempted prevention of its commission, he was given a suspended sentence of ten years with five years' probation. The remaining defendants were convicted on all charges and given life sentences without the possibility of parole. The United States Attorney declined to prosecute any of the federal violations. All four defendants have filed appeals, which are pending at the time of this writing.

Even before he was formally charged, John Hennessey resigned from the United States Senate. Since his moment of epiphany, occurring on that fateful Sunday afternoon in Santa Monica, John Hennessey's life has undergone a metamorphosis in every respect. He has devoted himself to his wife and his remaining family, and has made exhaustive efforts to apologize and make amends, where possible, to all those people – and there were many – whom he felt he had wronged in his life. Of particular note are Carleen and Kelly Novak. The prosecution of Kelly, the younger sister, was halted and dismissed, by reason of the information provided by John Hennessey. Despite the charges being dismissed, however, Kelly Novak remains under the ongoing care of a psychologist, and continues to suffer from her experience at the hands of John Hennessey. Hennessey pays for all of the expenses related to her treatment. Carleen Novak has been reinstated to the position, from which she had been dismissed, also at the instance of John Hennessey.

One of the first persons John Hennessey located – then contacted – after the completion of the prosecution, was Donny Broad – his first friend in life. Since their reunion, they have remained in frequent contact with one another. John Hennessey has become, by far, the most passionate of the Crossers... working tirelessly to spread the ministry. Due, no doubt, to his innate charisma and his superb talent for speaking, he now regularly draws enormous crowds wherever he speaks. Some in the media have taken to calling him the "Billy Graham" of the Crosser Movement, while others compare him to Paul in the New Testament because of his remarkable transformation from persecutor to apostle. John Hennessey and his wife have, since his conversion, become nearly inseparable and are now mutually and completely devoted to one another. She accompanies him wherever he goes.

Nick and Lisa Ryan made authorities aware, both state and federal, immediately after the assassination, of their belief that they were the targets of hired killers. As a consequence, they were afforded police protection for several months, thereafter. They remain, at the time of this writing, unharmed, and are relatively sure they are out of danger. Nick took a year off from law school, following their experience. He graduated two years ago, and now works for the district attorney's office in Baltimore. During a recent conversation, he expressed a growing disenchantment with the legal profession and is presently considering a career change – possibly, he says, to that of a college teacher.

Lisa Ryan currently attends the University of Baltimore, pursuing a master's degree in fine arts – art being her true inspiration in life. She aspires to a career in painting – or teaching painting – depending upon her success in selling her own works. Her specialty is landscapes, in acrylics. Soon after their coast-to-coast adventure, Lisa confessed the sexual encounters with Senator Hennessey and Ted Rossiter to her husband. Nick was, understandably, very distressed, angry, and hurt by these disclosures... but through the strength of their love, their marriage has, apparently, survived his pain and her shame.

Marty Chapman underwent a total, right shoulder replacement after the muscle damage to that area of his body had sufficiently healed. With extensive rehabilitation and his relative youth, he has regained almost normal functioning of his arm. Three months to the day, following Papa's death, Martin Chapman and Virginia Allen were married in a small ceremony in Wheeling, West Virginia. Danny Boscia and David Matthews served as Marty's ushers and Paulo Mandos as his best man. Veronica Jones and Katherine DeVille were a part of the wedding party, attending to Ginny as bridesmaids. Susan Davenport served as Ginny's matron of honor. Ginny's uncle, from Saint Louis, her father's brother, gave her away. Two years later, Ginny gave birth to a son, who she named, Arthur Ian Chapman – with Marty's enthusiastic and joyous concurrence. She is pregnant at the time of this writing and is carrying a daughter.

For two years, following the death of Papa, Marty Chapman was granted leave from his magazine responsibilities to allow for his collaboration in the writing of *The Avatar*. With its completion, he returned to his duties at the magazine offices, where he has been promoted to the position of assistant editor. At the time of this writing, Marty remains a nonbeliever.